Mary Eliska Girl Aviatrix

Book 2

Mary Eliska Girl Detective Girl Aviatrix Air Mystery Stories
18 Chapters Girl Detective Girl Aviatrix Air Mystery and Romance
Chapters 1 - 6 © 2022 Case No. 1-11371703511 and Chapters 7 - 18 © 2022 Case No. 1-11376521721

William A. Stricklin

Olympus Story House

CONTENTS

<h1 style="text-align:center">About the Book:</h1>

This is a book about a girl and her marvelous accomplishments in the air. Fictional Mary Eliska Girl Detective Girl Aviatrix is a heroine of modern times. The book concentrates on the efforts of the girls and women who, like their male counterparts, have obtained wonderful results in the air. She wins an airplane by means of her remarkable air feats, and keeps the reader tense with excitement from cover to cover.

<h1 style="text-align:center">About the Writer:</h1>

William A. Stricklin is a Phi Beta Kappa scholar who earned his AB with honors at the University of California, Berkeley. He was Cal student body president and selected as the outstanding cadet of the United States Army ROTC program at UC Berkeley then trained at Fort Lewis, Washington, then Infantry Officer Training School at Fort Benning, Georgia, cloak-and-dagger training at Counterintelligence School, Fort Holabird, Maryland, learning Cold War spy-craft, hence six years active and reserve military service -- followed by his earning a doctor of laws JD degree at Harvard Law School in Class of 1964. He is a member of the Bar Associations of California, Washington and Hawaii. Mary Eliska was his third daughter, whose life was cut short, for whom he has created a longer, fictional life as Mary Eliska Girl Detective Girl Aviatrix.

<h1 style="text-align:center">Writer's Preface Foreshadowing</h1>

Real-life female detectives emerged in the mid-19th century through the young widow Kate Warne, then a Pinkerton Agency detective who helped smuggle Abraham Lincoln away from would-be assassins in Baltimore. In 1856, Kate met with Allan Pinkerton, the founder of the famous Pinkerton Detective Agency, to make an important point: a woman detective could go places that his male detectives could not. The first true girl detective made her debut in The Golden Slipper and Other Problems for Violet Strange (1915). The author, Anna Katharine Green, was an American friend of Conan Doyle's, and had a string of best-sellers featuring female detectives. One of the major selling points of those books was Green's fact-checking every legal detail in her bestselling mysteries. Green created the first famous female sleuth in fiction, the curious spinster Amelia Butterworth, in That Affair Next Door (1897), sketching the original pattern for Agatha Christie's Miss Marple. Our heroine in these two volumes of 18 chapters, Mary Eliska, Girl Detective Girl Aviatrix is a well-off young lady whose grandfather Albert Stricklin is a newspaper publisher in Piedmont, California, who supports her as a reporter for his paper *The Piedmont Star*, aware that she likes to dabble in detective work. Flying in her airplane and driving her jalopy "Calamity Jane", Mary Eliska joins with her three best friends: nieces Jacqueline Gray ("Jax") and Marlow Ray, and nephew news photographer Liam McAdam to solve the occasional case out of curiosity and sometimes to earn money separately from her family. Mary Eliska Girl Detective Girl Aviatrix gives life to my daughter born sixty years ago, March 10, 1963, whose life was cut short in Clifton Springs New York September 12, 1963. She has charming manners, oscillates between tomboyishness and a feminine ideal. She knows law and manifests moral righteousness. Often she wears enviable dresses. Mary Eliska's detective stories and unsolved mysteries I have re-written from the public domain tales by Carolyn Keene (always a pseudonym), Anna Katharine Green, Mildred Augustine Wirt Benson, Frances Crane, and anonymous writers about Penny Parker, Mary Louise, Nancy Drew, and others. Please enjoy reading "Mary Eliska Girl Aviatrix."

Dedication:

Amelia Mary Earhart
Attribution: https://en.wikipedia.org/wiki/Amelia_Earhart

Amelia Mary Earhart beneath the nose of her Lockheed Model 10-E Electra, March 1937 in Oakland, California, before departing on her final round-the-world attempt prior to her disappearance

Born	Amelia Mary Earhart July 24, 1897 Atchison, Kansas, U.S.
Disappeared	July 2, 1937 (aged 39) Pacific Ocean, en route to Howland Island from Lae, New Guinea
Status	Presumed dead[1] January 5, 1939 (aged 41)
Other names	• Lady Lindy (after Charles Lindbergh) • Meeley (childhood)
Alma mater	• Ogontz School • Columbia University (did not graduate from either)
Occupation	• Aviator • author
Known for	Many early aviation records, including first woman to fly solo across the Atlantic Ocean
Spouse	George P. Putnam (m. 1931)
Parent(s)	Samuel Stanton and Amelia Otis Earhart
Awards	• Distinguished Flying Cross • Légion d'honneur • National Aviation Hall of Fame • National Women's Hall of Fame
Website	www.ameliaearhart.com
Signature	

Amelia Mary Earhart (/ˈɛərhɑːrt/ *AIR-hart*, born July 24, 1897; disappeared July 2, 1937; declared dead January 5, 1939) was an American aviation pioneer and writer. Earhart was the first female aviator to fly solo across the Atlantic Ocean. She set many other records, was one of the first aviators to romote commercial air travel, wrote best-selling books about her flying experiences, and was instrumental in the formation of The Ninety-Nines, an organization for female pilots. Born and raised in Atchison, Kansas, and later in Des Moines, Iowa, Earhart developed a passion for adventure at a young age, steadily gaining flying experience from her twenties. In 1928, Earhart became the first female passenger to cross the Atlantic by airplane (accompanying pilot Wilmer Stultz), for which she achieved celebrity status. In 1932, piloting a Lockheed Vega 5B, Earhart made a nonstop solo transatlantic flight, becoming the first woman to achieve such a feat. She received the United States Distinguished Flying Cross for this accomplishment. In 1935, Earhart became a visiting faculty member at Purdue University as an advisor to aeronautical engineering and a career counselor to female students. She was also a member of the National Woman's Party and an early supporter of the Equal Rights Amendment. Known as one of the most inspirational American figures in aviation from the late 1920s throughout the 1930s, Earhart's legacy is often compared to the early aeronautical career of pioneer aviator Charles Lindbergh, as well as to figures like First Lady Eleanor Roosevelt for their close friendship and lasting impact on the issue of women›s causes from that period. During an attempt at becoming the first woman to complete a circumnavigational flight of the globe in 1937 in a Purdue-funded Lockheed Model 10-E Electra, Earhart and navigator Fred Noonan disappeared over the central Pacific Ocean near Howland Island. The two were last seen in Lae, New Guinea, on July 2, 1937, on the last land stop before Howland Island and one of their final legs of the flight. She presumably died in the Pacific during the circumnavigation, just three weeks prior to her fortieth birthday.[10] Nearly one year and six months after she and Noonan disappeared, Earhart was officially declared dead. Investigations and significant public interest in their disappearance still continue over 80 years later. Decades after her presumed death, Earhart was inducted into the National Aviation Hall of Fame in 1968 and the National Women's Hall of Fame in 1973. She now has several commemorative memorials named in her honor around the United States, including an urban park, an airport, a residence hall, a museum, a research foundation, a bridge, a cargo ship, an earth-fill dam, four schools, a hotel, a playhouse, a library, multiple roads, and more. She also has a minor planet, planetary corona, and newly-discovered lunar crater named after her. She is ranked ninth on *Flying*'s list of the 51 Heroes of Aviation.

Acknowledgement of the Original Authors of Chapters 1-18 of this volume; all currently in the Public Domain

- Acknowledgement of the Original Author of Chapter 1: Noel Everingham Sainsbury Jr.
- Acknowledgement of the Original Author of Chapter 2: Noel Everingham Sainsbury Jr.
- Acknowledgement of the Original Author of Chapter 3: Noel Everingham Sainsbury Jr.
- Acknowledgement of the Original Author of Chapter 4: Noel Everingham Sainsbury Jr.
- Acknowledgement of the Original Author of Chapter 5: Edith Harper Lavell
- Acknowledgement of the Original Author of Chapter 6: Edith Harper Lavell
- Acknowledgement of the Original Author of Chapter 7: L. Frank Baum
- Acknowledgement of the Original Author of Chapter 8: L. Frank Baum
- Acknowledgement of the Original Author of Chapter 9: Edith Lavell
- Acknowledgement of the Original Author of Chapter 10: Bess Moyer
- Acknowledgement of the Original Author of Chapter 11: Edith Lavell
- Acknowledgement of the Original Author of Chapter 12: Harrison Bardwell
- Acknowledgement of the Original Author of Chapter 13: Margaret Burnham
- Acknowledgement of the Original Author of Chapter 14: Margaret Burnham
- Acknowledgement of the Original Author of Chapter 15: Margaret Burnham
- Acknowledgement of the Original Author of Chapter 16: Margaret Burnham
- Acknowledgement of the Original Author of Chapter 17: Edith Lavell
- Acknowledgement of the Original Author of Chapter 18: Bess Moyer

CHAPTER 11

The Island Adventure

Chapter 11.1
The "Ladybug"

"There's a young lady here to see you, Mary Eliska," announced Aunt Sally, coming into her niece's room the morning after her niece's return from the St. Louis Ground School. The girl had just graduated, winning both commercial and transport licenses, and, besides that, she was registered as the only feminine airplane mechanic in the country.

"Who is she, Auntie?" inquired Mary Eliska, rubbing her eyes and peering out the window into the lovely June sunshine. What a wonderful day! Too beautiful to spend on the ground! But she sighed as she recalled that at the moment she did not possess a plane.

"A reporter, I believe," replied the older woman. "Miss Hawkins, from the 'News'."

"But I haven't done anything to get into the newspapers," objected Mary Eliska.

"My dear child, you don't have to! Aren't you the only girl who ever flew the Atlantic alone? That's enough to keep you in the spotlight forever."

"But I don't like spot-lights," Mary Eliska insisted, starting to dress. "Couldn't you get rid of her, Auntie?"

Aunt Sally shook her head.

"I tried to, dear. But she wouldn't go. She wants to know your summer plans. I told her you'd probably just spend a quiet vacation with me at Green Falls, where we were last year. But she didn't believe me. She said you weren't the type to take your vacations quietly."

Mary Eliska laughed.

"I guess she's right, Aunt Sally."

Aunt Sally looked troubled. She had been trying for a year—ever since Mary Eliska's father had given her an Arrow Pursuit bi-plane for graduation—to keep the girl out of the air as much as possible, but she had not succeeded. The Stricklins were comfortably well-off, and it was Aunt Sally's wish that Mary Eliska go in for society, and make a good marriage.

But though Mary Eliska enjoyed occasional parties as much as any normal young person, she had a serious purpose in life, to make flying her career just as a young man would.

"You won't go to Green Falls—with all the rest of the crowd?" asked Aunt Sally, anxiously.

"I can't, Aunt Sally. I—I—can't spare the time. I am trying to get a job."

"A job? But you don't need money. Your father's business is dong nicely——"

"Oh, it isn't the money I want," interrupted the girl. "It's the experience."

Mary Eliska finished dressing and came downstairs to meet the young woman who was waiting for her. The reporter insisted that she eat her breakfast while they talked.

"Honestly, I haven't done a thing interesting to the world since my ocean flight!" Mary Eliska said. "Except win my licenses, and all the graduates' names have already been listed in the papers."

The reporter smiled at her as if she were a child.

"My dear girl," she explained, "you are front-page news now, no matter what you do. You are Queen of the Air, and will be until some other woman does something more daring than your flight to Paris alone. So everything you do interests the public. Naturally they want to know what you are planning for the summer. Flying to South America, or Alaska? And what kind of plane do you intend to buy next, since you sold your Bellanca in Paris?"

Mary Eliska yawned, and fingered her mail—a great pile of letters beside her plate. Invitations, mostly from the younger set in Spring City, for she was very popular.

"I'm afraid I don't know yet," she replied, simply.

"Maybe if you read your mail—" suggested the reporter.

"She is to be a bridesmaid at Miss Katherine Clavering's wedding next week," supplied Aunt Sally, entering the dining-room. As usual, social events were all-important to her, especially affairs with the Claverings, the richest people in Spring City. Katherine, or "Kitty," as her friends all called her, was to be married to Lt. Hulbert of the U. S. Flying Corps, and her brother Ralph made no secret of his devotion for Mary Eliska. If he had had his way, they would have been married last Christmas, and aviation jobs would be out of the question for Mary Eliska at the present time.

The girl searched through her mail rapidly, and picked out a letter which interested her above all others. It was from the Pitcairn Autogiro Company in the East.

As she read it, her blue eyes lighted up with enthusiasm, and she examined the enclosed circular with excited interest, completely forgetting her visitor.

The reporter waited patiently for a minute or two.

"Well, what's it all about, Mary Eliska?" she finally inquired.

Mary Eliska looked up at her as if she were startled, and suddenly remembered her caller. She handed her the circular.

"I am going to buy an autogiro," she announced, with decision.

"A what?" demanded her aunt, thinking Mary Eliska referred to some kind of automobile. "A new car?"

The reporter smiled.

"A flying bug?" she demanded.

Aunt Sally gasped in horror. A bug! What would her niece be up to next?

"Mary Eliska!" she exclaimed.

"It's a plane, Aunt Sally," the girl explained. "You ought to like it. It's the very safest kind there is. In the eight or nine years since it was invented, nobody has been killed with one."

Aunt Sally looked doubtful.

"No airplane is safe," she remarked.

"This isn't an airplane. It's an autogiro."

"But it flies?"

"Of course."

Mary Eliska showed her the picture. It was indeed a queer looking object, with its wind-mill-like arrangement on top, and its absence of big wings. As the reporter had observed, its appearance was very like a huge bug.

"They do say it's unusually safe," corroborated the latter. "You'll have to take a ride in it, Aunt Sally."

"Not I!" protested the older woman. "Firm earth is good enough for me.... No, it looks dangerous enough to me."

Mary Eliska smiled; she could never convince her aunt of the joy of flying, or of the minimum risk, if one were a careful pilot. She was glad that her father Albert Stricklin was more broad-minded; if he weren't, she would still be on the ground.

"And where will you go with your Flying Bug, Mary Eliska?" asked the reporter, tapping her pencil on her note-book.

"Not on any long flight," replied the girl, to her aunt's relief. "My aim is to get some sort of aviation job."

"What would you like to do?"

"Anything connected with airplanes. I prefer flying, but I'd be satisfied at the beginning with ground work.... If you will write down your telephone number, Miss Hawkins, I will call you up when I have decided definitely just what my plans will be."

"Thank you very much!" exclaimed the other girl, rising. "I think you are a peach, Mary Eliska. Some celebrities are so mean to us reporters."

"I'm afraid I'm not a real celebrity," laughed Mary Eliska. "I'll be forgotten by the public this time next year. I sincerely hope that more and more girls and women will be doing things in aviation, so that my little stunt will seem trivial. That is progress, you know."

Scarcely had the reporter gone before Aunt Sally was begging Mary Eliska to open her other letters.

"The Junior League picnic is tomorrow," she said. "And Jax Gray is giving a luncheon in honor of Kitty Clavering.... There are probably a lot more things, too...."

Rather listlessly Mary Eliska opened her letters. It was not the same, she thought, without Louise to share everything. Louise Haydock—Louise Mackay now—had been her chum all through school, where they were inseparable. Louise's marriage had meant a sharp break to Mary Eliska, for the Mackays had moved to Wichita, Kansas, where Ted was employed as a flyer.

As if Aunt Sally understood her niece's thoughts, she remarked that Louise was coming for Kitty's wedding.

Mary Eliska's eyes shone with joy.

"Flying?" she inquired, as a matter of course.

"Yes. She and Ted are arriving some time tonight. Mrs. Haydock called up, and asked me to tell you."

Mary Eliska could not read her mail for a few minutes, so intense was her happiness at this splendid news.

"Ted can go with me to see about the autogiro!" she exclaimed. "I do so want his opinion!"

"Go where?"

"To Philadelphia, where the Pitcairn Company is located."

Again Aunt Sally looked annoyed, almost shocked.

"You don't mean to say you'll take time to fly to Philadelphia, with all your engagements?"

Mary Eliska nodded.

"I'll be here for the wedding, Aunt Sally. Don't worry about that. But nothing else is particularly important."

Aunt Sally groaned. What could you do with a girl like Mary Eliska? You might as well have a boy!

The mail was finally opened and sorted, and Mary Eliska dutifully went to a dinner dance at the Country Club that evening with Ralph Clavering. But she was tense all evening, for she was hoping every moment that Louise would arrive.

About midnight the young couple dashed in, radiant in their happiness. To everyone's amusement Louise flew into Mary Eliska's arms in the middle of the dance floor.

"How do you get that way?" demanded Ralph, pretending to be angry. "As if it isn't enough to endure every fellow in the room tapping me when I'm dancing with Mary Eliska, without having girls do it too!"

But the two school friends scarcely heard him. They were so enraptured at seeing each other again.

"I'm going to stay a week!" announced Louise. "Luckily, Ted has some business in Philadelphia and New York, and he'll be flying back and forth."

"Philadelphia!" exclaimed Mary Eliska. "Isn't that great! Can we go with him there?"

"Of course we can, if you don't mind a squeeze. The airplane isn't very big," explained Louise. "But then, we're not fat. Ted'll be tickled to death to have company—he hates flying alone. But why do you want to go to Philadelphia, Mary Eliska?"

"To buy an autogiro!"

"You always were crazy about those things. Remember the time you gave up a dance to fly one?"

"I certainly do. And you wouldn't go with me."

"Well, there was a reason," laughed Louise, making no secret of her admiration for her husband.... "I think Ted'll go day after tomorrow," she continued. "We thought we'd enjoy resting a day, and taking in the Junior League picnic."

"Fine!" agreed Mary Eliska. "That will give everybody a chance to see you. Besides, Aunt Sally would die if I missed that affair. Remember the one last year. Didn't we have fun?"

"We certainly did," smiled Louise, reminiscently. "But it seems like more than a year ago—so much has happened."

"I wasn't even flying then," observed Mary Eliska.

"And I hadn't met Ted!"

"You're a real bride, Lou!" returned Mary Eliska, affectionately. "But you're just the same old dear!"

The following day was just as delightful as it had been the previous year, and the picnic another success. To Mary Eliska it was all the more enjoyable, because of the novelty of seeing her old friends again after the separation caused by a year at the school in St. Louis.

Ted went along with Louise, and entered into all the sports, just as if he had been born and brought up with the crowd in Spring City. Moreover, he was delighted at the prospect of having the two girls go with him the next day, and appeared almost as enthusiastic about the autogiro as Mary Eliska herself.

The weather continued perfect, and the three happy young people took off from Spring City the following morning. An excellent mechanic himself, Ted always kept his plane in tip-top condition, and it was a rare thing indeed for him even to encounter a minor accident. This flight proved no exception; straight and swift through the June skies he flew to the field outside the city of Philadelphia where the autogiros were on display.

"You really expect to buy one today, Mary Eliska?" asked Louise, as she climbed out of the plane.

"Yes—if Ted gives his approval," replied the capable aviatrix. She had always had the greatest confidence in this young red-haired pilot, who had taken her on her first flight, and who had saved her and his wife from disaster upon two occasions.

"Are you sure that it can go fast enough to suit you, Mary Eliska?" asked Ted.

"It can travel a hundred and twenty-five miles an hour, and that ought to satisfy me. If I were entering any air-races, I'd want a special racing plane anyhow, for the occasion. But I'm not going out for races. I want to take a job, and I think an autogiro will be the most convenient plane I can have, to take with me anywhere I want to go. I shan't have to depend on big fields for landing."

"Right-o," agreed the young man.

They walked across the field and were shown a model by an enthusiastic salesman. As the reporter had said, it did look like a flying bug, with its odd windmill-like rotor on top, and its small stub-like wings, which were there mainly to mount the lateral controls or ailerons.

"It isn't so pretty as the Arrow," remarked Louise.

"Handsome is as handsome does," returned Mary Eliska. "If we'd had an autogiro that time in Canada, when our gasoline leaked out, a forced landing wouldn't have been disastrous."

"Why?"

"Because the rotor takes care of that, after the engine is dead," explained Mary Eliska. "An autogiro can come down vertically at a slower rate than we did with our parachutes."

"I'll never forget how scared I was that time we jumped off," remarked her companion. "You know, it's one thing to see other people do it—in the air, or at the movies—and it's something else to step off into space yourself. That all-gone feeling!"

"I don't mind it any more now—it doesn't seem any worse than dropping ten stories in an elevator. But I know what you mean."

"Well, I have never had to jump since," Louise informed her. "But," she continued as they walked around the autogiro, "isn't there really any danger of crashing?"

"You can crash, of course," laughed Mary Eliska. "If you steer straight for another plane, or a tree. But tail-spins are practically impossible; they say no matter what happens the autogiro settles to the ground like a tired hen. It's the principle of centrifugal force—it can't fail."

"Oh, yeah?" remarked Louise, hiding a yawn.

"What I want your opinion on, Ted," added Mary Eliska, turning to the young man, "is the engine. You know more about engines than I do."

"I'm not so sure of that last," he replied, modestly. "Looks O.K. to me—I've been examining it while you girls chattered."

The salesman, who had been listening to the conversation, suddenly burst into a smile. He had been wondering where he had seen that girl before. Now he knew! Her pictures had been in every newspaper in the country. She was Mary Eliska, of course!

"You're Mary Eliska, aren't you?" he demanded, excitedly. "The girl who flew to Paris alone?"

"Yes," answered Mary Eliska, indifferently. She didn't want to talk ancient history now. "This is a P C A—2, isn't it?" she inquired, to bring the man to the subject of autogiros.

"Yes. Fifteen thousand dollars. I suppose it's not necessary to tell *you* what instruments it is equipped with—an experienced flyer like you can recognize them by a glance into the pilot›s cock-pit."

"Yes, I see them. And I had a circular besides.... It's complete, all right. The only thing I don't like about it is the separate passenger's cock-pit. My Arrow Pursuit had a companion cock-pit."

"You can always talk to your passenger through the speaking-tube," the salesman reminded her.

"Yes, of course———"

"And nobody you take along now-a-days will be as talkative as I always was on our trips together," Louise observed, with a smile.

"Talkative!" repeated Mary Eliska, "All you ever wanted to do was sleep! Every time I looked at you on that flight to Canada, you were peacefully dozing!"

"And she still has a bad habit of dropping off," teased Ted.

"So long as that's the only way I 'drop off,' I'm satisfied," concluded Louise.

In spite of their frivolous talk, Mary Eliska had been thinking seriously about the autogiro, and had entirely made up her mind about it.

"I'll take it," she announced. "If you surely approve of it, Ted."

"I do, absolutely."

The salesman looked at her in amazement. Never had he made such an easy sale before. But he did not meet people like Mary Eliska every day!

"Don't you want to try it out?" he suggested. "I can show you how to fly it in a few minutes."

"I have flown one before," she told him. "But I would like to take it up for a few minutes if you don't mind. Am I to have this particular one? I have a certified check in payment."

The salesman blinked his eyes in further consternation. The check right there, the girl ready to take the plane home with her! It was a moment before he could catch his breath.

"Of course," he finally managed to answer. "I'll have her started for you immediately. And—would your friends care to go up with you?"

"Sure!" exclaimed Ted. "We're your best friends, aren't we, Mary Eliska? So oughtn't we to be privileged with the first ride?"

"You certainly are!" replied the famous aviatrix, squeezing Louise's hand in her excitement and delight. "Come on!"

It was the Mackays' first flight in an autogiro, and though they were very much crowded in the passenger's cock-pit, they insisted that that only added to the fun. With a sureness which Ted watched in admiration, Mary Eliska took off and flew around and around the field, putting the new plane through all sorts of tests, proving conclusively that all the claims for it were well-founded.

Fifteen minutes later they came slowly down to earth, landing on the exact spot from which Mary Eliska had taken off.

"Unscramble yourselves!" she cried to her passengers, as she climbed out of the cock-pit. "Let's go pay our bill."

"She's great, Mary Eliska!" approved Louise, as her husband helped her out. "I'm for her, even if she is a funny-looking bug."

"Sh!" cautioned Mary Eliska, solemnly. "You might hurt her feelings. She's—she's—a lady!"

"Ladybug!" exclaimed Louise, with a sudden burst of inspiration.

"Ladybug is right!" agreed her chum enthusiastically. "You've named her for me, Lou!"

Chapter 11.2
The Aviation Job

"It's marvelous!" exclaimed Mary Eliska, as the salesman came to meet her after her test-flight in the autogiro. "Will you have her filled with gasoline and oil, while I sign the contract? I'll take her with me."

The salesman smiled at Ted Mackay.

"In the same way any other woman would buy a hat," he remarked, to Louise's amusement.

"You found it easy to fly, Mary Eliska?" he inquired.

"Wonderful!" she replied. "So simple that a child could almost do it! It certainly is the airplane of the future, or of the present, I should say."

"We'll probably see one perched on everybody's roof within the next five years," teased Louise, although in reality she shared her chum's admiration for it.

While the mechanics gave the autogiro a thorough inspection, the little group strolled to the office to sign the papers and to meet the president of the company.

The salesman introduced Mr. Pitcairn, and added, proudly, "This is *the* Mary Eliska, of world-wide fame! The only woman who ever flew the Atlantic alone! And I have had the honor, to sell Mary Eliska an autogiro!"

Mary Eliska blushed as she shook hands, and her eyelids fluttered in embarrassment. She could never get used to public admiration. Immediately she began to talk about her new possession.

"I want it for every-day flying," she explained. "I think it will be wonderful for that."

"We believe that it is," agreed the older man. "And we are honored indeed, Mary Eliska, that you have chosen it. It will be a feather in our cap."

"Mary Eliska never thinks of things like that," remarked Louise. "But I guess we're glad that she doesn't!"

While Mary Eliska signed the necessary papers, and handed her check to the salesman, the president inquired what her plans included now that she had graduated from the Ground School with such success.

"I don't exactly know," she replied. "I want to get some kind of aviation job—I am more interested in the use of airplanes in every-day life than I am in races and spectacular events, although I understand that these have their place. Of course I haven't found anything to do yet, but I mean to try."

"You expect to give your whole time to flying?" asked the president. He had thought, naturally, that a girl in Mary Eliska's circumstances would just do it for sport.

"Yes—a regular full-time job. I'm not sure what—not selling airplanes, for I don't believe I'd care for that. And not the mail—unless I can't get anything else. You don't happen to know of any openings, do you, Mr. Pitcairn?"

"Let me see," he said. "Things are a little slow now. Of course there are the air-transportation companies, but their routes are about as cut-and-dried as the mail pilot's.... I take it you would rather have a little more excitement.... There's crop dusting, during the summer. You have heard of that, no doubt?"

"Yes, I have read about it."

"You know, then, that one airplane flying over a field can spray as many plants in a day as a hundred of the ordinary spraying machines?"

His listeners gasped in astonishment. What marvelous advances in progress aviation was bringing about!

"I happen to know of a company in the South that is just forming," he continued. "Because of lack of capital, they are in great need of pilots with airplanes of their own. If you are interested, I am sure they would be glad to take you on."

"That sounds very interesting," agreed Mary Eliska, eagerly. "I'm sure I'd like that. And an autogiro ought to be especially adapted for this kind of thing. I could fly so low—and land so easily——"

"Exactly! Incidentally, you'd be doing our company a big favor by showing the public new uses for an autogiro. If Mary Eliska, of international reputation, flies anywhere, the account of it is sure to be in the newspapers!"

"I wouldn't count too much on that, Mr. Pitcairn," protested Mary Eliska, modestly. "I really am not 'news' any more.... But I shall be grateful for the name of this firm, if you will write it down for me. Where is it located?"

"In Georgia—the southern part, Cobb County, near where your father Albert Stricklin's paternal great-grandparents farmed" he informed her. "Here is the address," he added, handing her a card. "And I will write myself today to tell them of their good fortune!"

"Georgia!" repeated Louise. "It's going to be awfully hot there, Mary Eliska. Compared with Green Falls—or even Spring City."

"Why not pick a job in Canada?" suggested Ted. "You'd like Canada, if you didn't choose the coldest part of the year to visit it."

Louise shuddered at the memory of their adventure during the preceding Christmas holidays.

"I never want to see Canada again!" she said. "And I don't believe Mary Eliska does either!"

It was not the memory of that cold night in the Canadian woods, or of the cruelty of the police, however, that made Mary Eliska frown and hesitate now. Nor did the heat of the South trouble her—weather was all in the day's work to her. But the thought of the distance between Georgia and Ohio, and what such a separation might mean to her Aunt Sally, deterred her from accepting the offer immediately. It hardly seemed right to be away all winter and spring, and then to go far off again in the summer.

"Would I have to promise to do this all summer, if I took it on?" she inquired.

"No, certainly not. A month would be enough, for the first time. That would give you August with your family, Mary Eliska, before you accepted a regular aviation job in the fall."

This sounded much better to Mary Eliska, and she promised to write within the next week, if her family agreed.

It was lots of fun riding back to Spring City in her autogiro the following day, although she flew alone, for Louise wanted to return with Ted. Without a mishap of any kind Mary Eliska brought the "Ladybug" down on the field behind her house.

When she entered her home, she found that her father had arrived during her absence. He was waiting for her in the library.

"Daddy!" she cried, joyfully, for Mr. Stricklin's visits were always a pleasant surprise to Mary Eliska. "You came at just the right time! Come out and see my Bug!"

"Must you call it that, Mary Eliska?" asked her Aunt Sally, who, like all good housekeepers detested every sort of insect.

Mary Eliska laughed.

"Take a look at it, Aunt Sally, and see whether you could think of a better name."

Aunt Sally peered through the screen door.

"Where is it?" she asked.

"Come out on the porch, and you can see it," replied Mary Eliska.

Dragging her father and her aunt each by a hand, Mary Eliska gleefully skipped through the door.

"There!" she cried, as one who displays a marvel.

At the top of the hill, on the field behind the lovely Colonial house, they saw the new possession. Or rather, the top of the autogiro, for it was not wholly visible.

"It looks like a clothes-dryer to me," remarked Aunt Sally. "Or a windmill."

"But you agree that I couldn't call it my 'Clothes-dryer,' or my 'Wind-mill,' don't you, Aunt Sally? The words are too long. Besides, Lou thought of the cleverest name—the 'Ladybug.' But you needn't worry, Auntie, she won't ever creep into your spotless house!"

"I should hope not!"

"In a way, Sally," observed Mary Eliska's father, "it's a good name as far as you are concerned. You hate planes—and you hate bugs!"

"Only, Aunt Sally is going to love my autogiro," insisted Mary Eliska, putting her arm affectionately about the older woman, who had been the only mother she had ever known. "One of my biggest reasons for choosing an autogiro was because it is the safest flying machine known." Her tone grew soft, so low that her father could not hear, and she added, with her head turned aside, "I do want you to know that I care about your feelings, Aunt Sally."

Aunt Sally's eyes grew misty; Mary Eliska had always been so sweet, so thoughtful! Her niece couldn't help it, if she had a marvelous brain, and a mechanical mind. No wonder she wanted to use them!

"It's going to be the ambition of my life to convert Aunt Sally to flying," she announced, in a gay tone. "See if I don't, Daddy!"

"I hope so," he said. "How about taking me up for a little fly?"

"A fly?" repeated Mary Eliska, playfully. "You a fly—and my new plane a bug! Oh, think of poor Aunt Sally!"

"Now, Mary Eliska, I do believe you're getting silly!"

But already she was pulling her father down the steps, eager to show off her beloved possession.

Mr. Stricklin proved almost as enthusiastic as his daughter about it. When they returned to the house, he laughingly told Aunt Sally that he was thinking of buying one for himself, to use to fly back and forth from New York, where his business was located.

Aunt Sally groaned.

"Then we'll have two flying maniacs in the house!" she exclaimed.

"No—Mary Eliska and I will usually be up in the air," he corrected, "not often in the house."

Mary Eliska had scarcely time to change from her flyer's suit into an afternoon dress, and no chance at all to talk with her father about Mr. Pitcairn's suggestion about a job, when Ralph Clavering drove over to see her. Mary Eliska was delighted, of course; here was another person to whom she could display her autogiro. Ralph was a licensed pilot, too, although with him flying was only a secondary interest, and he had never had his own plane.

"Come out and see my 'Ladybug'!" she insisted. "And wouldn't you like to try her out? I might let you!"

"No, thanks, Mary Eliska—I'd be sure to do something wrong. Besides, I'd rather talk to you—those things make such an infernal noise. No, just show it to me, and then let's go and have a game of tennis before supper, if you're not too tired."

"I've almost forgotten how to play," replied the girl. "But I'll try. If you will come out and see my 'Ladybug' first."

After they had examined the autogiro, and were driving to the Country Club in Ralph's roadster, the young man turned the conversation to the topic of vacation at Green Falls, the resort at which Mary Eliska's aunt, and most of her friends, had spent the preceding summer. Ralph told Mary Eliska about a new motor boat that he was getting, and spoke of the contests in all sorts of sports that would be repeated this year.

"How soon do you think you can get off, Mary Eliska?" he concluded eagerly.

"Not 'til August, I'm afraid," she replied, to his dismay.

"August!" he repeated, in horror. "You're not going to pull some new stunt on us, are you, Mary Eliska? Fly the Pacific—or the Arctic Ocean?"

The girl laughed, and shook her head.

"I'm through with stunts for a while, Ralph—you needn't worry about that. No; what I am planning now is steady work. I expect to take a job, as soon as Kit's wedding is over."

"A job? Where?"

"In Georgia, probably." She went into details about the proposition.

"You would!" he muttered, sulkily. "And pick out such a hot spot, that nobody would want to go with you.... Mary Eliska, why can't you be sensible like other girls—like my sister Kit, for instance?"

"Kit?"

"Yes. And get married."

He leaned over hopefully, and put his hand on her arm. Now that Mary Eliska had accomplished her ambition in flying the Atlantic, perhaps she would be willing to settle down to marriage and a normal life.

But she drew away, smiling.

"Don't, Ralph!" she warned him. "Remember that you promised me you wouldn't ask me 'til you had finished college."

"All right, all right," he muttered, irritably, resolving that he wouldn't again. Let her wait awhile! She'd probably get tired of working after she'd had a taste of it for a month in that hot climate.

They met Jax Gray and Jim Valier at the tennis courts, and doubled up with them for a couple of sets. But they were badly beaten, for these two were the best team at the Club.

After dinner that evening Mary Eliska had a chance to tell her father and her aunt of her proposed plan for the coming month, and won their consent, when she announced her intention of spending August at Green Falls. To Aunt Sally she put the all-important question of clothes; the older woman promised to get her half a dozen flyer's suits of linen for the trip.

During the next week Mary Eliska accepted enough invitations to satisfy even her Aunt Sally, and she wore one new dress after another, and flitted from tennis match or picnic to tea or dance, as the program happened to be. The grand finale was Kitty's wedding, at the girl's beautiful home just outside of Spring City.

It was a gorgeous affair, and Mary Eliska could not help thinking how Bess Hulbert, the Lieutenant's sister, would have enjoyed it, had she not given her life in the attempt to win the big prize which Mary Eliska herself had captured. Personally, she did not like the affair nearly so much as Louise's simple wedding at Easter.

Mary Eliska was quiet as she drove home beside her Aunt Sally in the limousine. She could not help wondering whether this event did not mark the end of her girlhood, the beginning of her career as a self-supporting woman—out in the world. No longer would she be free to come and go as she liked, to see her old friends at any and all hours of the day and evening. The thought was a little saddening, and she sighed.

Her aunt laid her hand over her niece's.

"Why the sigh, dear?" she inquired. "Tired?"

Mary Eliska nodded.

"Yes—and weddings are so solemn—so sort of sad, aren't they, Auntie? To the other people, I mean—for of course there's nothing sad about Kit and Tom. But it means I won't see them much——"

"It isn't their wedding that causes that, dear," Aunt Sally reminded her. "Kitty and Tom will be back and forth often, I think, for they are not living far away.... But it's you who are leaving the rest, Mary Eliska. Oh, if you only wouldn't go so far away, dear!"

"I guess you're right, Aunt Sally," admitted Mary Eliska. "But I can't have my cake and eat it too. There isn't any flying job in Spring City."

Aunt Sally was silent; there was no use in going over the old argument. Instead, she asked:

"How soon do you go, Mary Eliska?"

"Tomorrow—if the weather is good. I received my map and my instructions several days ago. I'm all ready. The Ladybug's in perfect shape."

"If you only didn't have to go alone!" sighed the older woman.

"Yes. If I only had Lou!"

"Couldn't you take some other girl?"

"As a matter of fact, I did suggest such a thing to Jax Gray. She's competent, you know—has her pilot's license—and she's such a peach of a girl. I know we'd get along beautifully together. But she's all tied up with a tennis match, and can't possibly leave now."

Little did Mary Eliska think, as she took off the following morning in the bright June sunshine, how deeply she was to regret this decision of Jax Gray's, how she was to wish a hundred times within the next week that she had some companion who was a friend.

For the people she fell among proved to be the worst sort of associates.

Chapter 11.3
Kidnapped

As there was no particular hurry about the trip South—it was only June twentieth—the day following the Juneteenth celebration of the emancipation of the enslaved Americans. Mary Eliska decided to go slowly and to stop often. What a marvelous way to see the country, at the most beautiful time of the year! In an autogiro the flight would never become monotonous, for she could fly low enough to watch the landscape.

Ohio—Kentucky—Tennessee—Georgia! Each day she could travel through a different state, putting up each night at a hotel. Fortunately her Aunt Sally had given up worrying about her staying alone in strange cities. For Mary Eliska had already proved herself capable of taking care of herself.

"It is because Mary Eliska is always so dignified," Mr. Stricklin had remarked to his sister. "The girls who make chance acquaintances, and permit familiarities are usually looking for it. Mary Eliska's mind is on her plane—on her navigation—and she is too absorbed to be bothered. I think we are safe, Sally, in trusting her."

"I suppose so," Aunt Sally had agreed. "Though of course she'll always be a little girl to me."

The day after the wedding was warm and the skies were clear; the Ladybug was in perfect condition, and her forty-gallon tank was filled with gasoline, so Mary Eliska decided to carry out her plan. While her Aunt Sally packed her lunch basket and a box with an emergency supply of food, the girl called Miss Hawkins on the telephone as she had promised.

"But don't put it into the paper until after I start," begged Mary Eliska. "I always like to slip off quietly, without any fuss."

"I'll save it for the evening editions," agreed the reporter. "And then you'll be well on your way.... And, thank you again, Mary Eliska."

An hour later she bade her aunt good-by, and was off. Heading her plane south-west, she would avoid the mountains in Kentucky, and pass over the blue-grass region, of which she had so often read. It was an ideal day for a flight, and her heart beat with the same exultation she had always felt when she was in the air; there was no feeling to compare with it on earth. Someone had said it was like being in love—but Mary Eliska had never been in love herself.

For several hours this sense of joy possessed her; then, as noontime came, and she landed to eat her lunch, she suddenly grew lonely. If only Louise were with her! She sighed as she thought that from now on she would probably be traveling alone.

It grew hotter in the afternoon as she progressed farther south, but her engine was functioning so beautifully that she hated to stop. Then the sun went down, and the coolness was so delightful after the heat that she continued on her course longer than she had planned, and did not land until she had crossed the border into Tennessee. There she followed a beacon light that led to an airport, and brought the Ladybug down to earth.

No sooner had she brought the autogiro to a stop than a group of curious people surrounded her.

"What do you-all call this?" drawled a big, good-natured looking man, with the typical Southern accent. "It's a new one on me."

Mary Eliska smiled and explained, asking that the autogiro be housed for the night, and inquired her way to the hotel.

"The hotel ain't so good," replied the man. "But I can direct you to a fine boarding-house."

Everybody that Mary Eliska met in this little town was kindness itself. She found herself in a pleasant home, with a marvelous supper of real old-fashioned Southern cooking, all ready for her. It appeared to be the custom to eat late in the South; no one thought it strange that she should want her supper at nine o'clock.

These good people's hospitality only served to strengthen her confidence in the fact that she was safe in traveling alone. For this reason the shock was all the greater for her when that trust was so rudely shaken later on during the trip.

Mary Eliska liked the town so well that she decided to remain a day, and go over her Ladybug herself. For, she argued sensibly, if no one there had ever heard of an autogiro before, it stood to reason that there would be little chance of a competent inspection by anyone but herself.

Although Miss Hawkins, the reporter, had published the facts concerning her trip that evening, the news had not reached this town in Tennessee immediately. It was not until the next day that the story was reprinted, and someone discovered that this stranger in the autogiro who was visiting them was Mary Eliska of international fame. Then the news spread like wild-fire about the town, and the band was gotten out to give the girl a royal welcome.

It was hardly necessary, with all this celebration, to wire her aunt of her safe arrival in Tennessee; nevertheless Mary Eliska did so, as she had promised when she left home.

Her next day's journey brought her across Tennessee, over the mountains where she had a chance to test her plane's climbing ability, and into Georgia. Here again she was received with hospitality. It seemed almost as if she were making a "good-will" flight, so delighted were the people to greet her and make her at home.

A long flight lay ahead of her—across Georgia, the largest state in the southeast. Over the mountains in the northern part, across cotton and rice and sweet-potato plantations, toward the coast. The weather was hot and dry; she grew tired and thirsty, and the thought of her friends, enjoying the cool breezes at Green Falls made her envious for a while. But she carried plenty of water in her thermos flasks, and she reminded herself that she was having a more thrilling experience than they could possibly have. Tonight she could rest—and sleep.

Her head ached and her body was weary, as she looked at her map and tried to find out just where she was from the land-marks. Dismay took hold of her as she realized that she must have gone off of her course—beyond her destination. The ground below appeared marshy, in many spots entirely covered with water, in which water-lilies and rushes grew in abundance. Where could she possibly be?

Panic seized her as she realized that this was no place to land. Even an autogiro couldn't come down in a swamp. She circled around, and went back. If the light only held out until she reached some sort of level, hard ground!

She thought of her flight over the ocean, when she had been so absolutely alone, and she felt the same desolation, the same fierce terror. Where was she? Where was she going? Wild-eyed, she studied her map.

Then she located herself. This must be the Okefenokee Swamp, in the southeastern part of Georgia. That lonely, forsaken land, some parts of which had never been penetrated by anyone! Treacherous, dangerous ground, which would mean certain death if she attempted to land! Miles and miles of desolation, that only a Native American could safely explore!

There was nothing to do but head the plane towards the west, in hope of passing over the swamp. The sun had set, and darkness was coming on, but Mary Eliska could still see the ground beneath her. The water grew scarcer, and trees—pine and cypress—here and there covered the land. But still the earth looked marshy, too treacherous for a landing.

A terrifying thought seized her when she remembered that she had not filled her gasoline tank that morning. Glancing at the indicator, she saw that she had only three gallons left. Would that be enough to take her out of this "trembling land," which was the meaning of the Native American word, "Okefenokee"? Just after her father Albert Stricklin completed infantry training at Fort Benning, Georgia, three classmates had drowned in this swamp.

It was like a horrible night-mare, watching the decreasing gasoline supply, the fading light, and the trees and the swamp beneath her. Her breath came in gasps; the idea of death in a swamp was more horrible than that of drowning in the middle of the Atlantic, for the former would be a lingering torture.

But at last to her delight she saw the trees widen, and a level stretch of dry sand below. This must be an island, she concluded, for she had read that there were half a dozen or so of these in the swamp, and that they were several miles in length. If this were true, she could land, and be safe for the night at least.

She brought her autogiro lower, and with her flash-light and her glasses examined the ground. Yes, there was space enough for a landing, with a plane like hers. She uttered a gasp of relief.

But she had rejoiced too soon, for when she lifted her eyes from the ground to the level of her plane she was startled breathless by the sight of another airplane, which had come out of nowhere, apparently, and was rushing madly at her. As if it were actually aiming to crash into her! As if this were warfare, and the oncoming plane an enemy, intent upon her destruction!

In that instant she realized that this was an old plane—possibly one of those abandoned by the Army at Fort Benning—one that would not now pass inspection. No wonder it was tipping so strangely; it must be out of the pilot's control.

Mary Eliska did the only thing possible, for she was too low to turn. She dropped gracefully to the ground, avoiding a tree by a few inches. Thank goodness, it was solid beneath her!

The other airplane was landing too, she observed, landing with a speed that was ten times that of the autogiro, in a space that was far too small. The inevitable occurred; Mary Eliska closed her eyes as she saw it about to crash. A terrifying thud followed; then a scream of fright—and Mary Eliska opened her eyes to see the plane on its side, nosed into a bank of bushes. Had it not been for that undergrowth, the wreck would have been far worse than it was.

Mary Eliska had turned off her engine, and she jumped out of the autogiro immediately and rushed to the scene of the disaster. What a smash it was! No one would ever fly that airplane again!

Two people were lying tangled up in the wreckage, whether dead or alive Mary Eliska could not immediately tell.

At her approach the man in the rear cock-pit opened his eyes and began to move his hands and legs.

"Got a good knife, Mary Eliska?" he yelled, to the girl's profound astonishment.

"I'll get one," she replied, wondering how he could possibly know her name. Or was he delirious, and thought he was talking to some other Mary Eliska?

Hurrying back to her own plane she took out her thermos flasks and her tool-kit, and returned to the spot of the wreck. It was too dark now to see the men distinctly, until she turned on her flash-light. As she came closer, she saw that the man who had spoken was wriggling himself free. His face was scratched, blood was running down his hands, but he apparently was not seriously hurt.

"Lucky this is an open plane," he muttered. "Now give me a hand, me girl!"

Mary Eliska did not like his tone, but she could not refuse to help a human being in distress. Gradually he crawled out.

"Now for Susie!" he announced, as he raised himself unsteadily on his legs. Mary Eliska gasped. Was the other occupant a woman? A thrill of relief passed over her, for she had been terrified at the idea of being alone with such a hard-looking man in this desolate spot.

"A girl?" she stammered, pressing close to the plane.

"Yeah. Me wife. Her name's Susie."

Mary Eliska flashed the light under the wreckage of the plane, and distinguished a young woman in a flyer's suit. She was unconscious.

Without another word they both set silently to work to disentangle her. At last they dragged her out—still unconscious. But she evidently was still alive, though the man remarked that her arm must be broken—and maybe an ankle or two. He seemed very matter-of-fact about it all.

"What's in that flask?" he demanded abruptly, of Mary Eliska.

"Water," she replied.

"Water!" he snarled angrily. "Water!"

He looked as if he meant to hit her, and Mary Eliska recoiled in terror.

He looked as if he meant to hit her, and Mary Eliska recoiled in terror.

"Go hunt my flask in that wreck!" he commanded.

"Do it yourself!" returned Mary Eliska, with sudden spirit. "How do I know that that plane won't burst into flames any minute?"

She was surprised at her sudden display of independence; she had always depended upon Louise to stick up for their rights. But she had risen to the occasion, now that she was alone.

The man started to swear, when suddenly the girl on the ground opened her eyes.

"Take care, Slats!" she begged, to Mary Eliska's astonishment. "We'll need this girl and her plane—for I can't fly now!"

The man called "Slats" subsided, and went over to the wreckage. Mary Eliska bent over the injured "Susie," and put the flask of water to her lips.

Like the man's, the girl's face was scratched and bleeding, and she began to moan of the pain in her wrist. Her helmet had been pushed off, and her blond hair hung about her face. Her lips were painted a brighter red than even blood could have colored them.

"Where are you hurt?" asked Mary Eliska, wiping the girl's face with her handkerchief, and pushing the hair out of her eyes.

"My wrist, worst. And this ankle. And my back."

"If I have enough gasoline, we'll take you to a hospital in my plane."

"No! No!" cried the girl, in terror.

"Why not?" questioned Mary Eliska.

"You'll find out," replied the other, mysteriously, closing her eyes in pain.

Mary Eliska had no way of guessing what she meant, so she sat waiting in silence until the man returned. Five minutes later he appeared with a tank of gasoline, and a flask of brandy, which he gave to his wife to drink.

"We're ready to go now, Mary Eliska," he announced. "You can help me carry Susie over to your Bug."

Again Mary Eliska started violently at the mention of her own name.

"Do you really know me?" she asked.

"Sure we do! You're Mary Eliska. Think you're about the smartest thing there is in the air today. Bought one of them new-fangled bugs. Ain't that right?"

"Partly," admitted Mary Eliska, wincing at the slur in his remark. "But how could you possibly know?"

"Because we are out to get you. Wasn't your story in all the newspapers, tellin' all about this trip of your'n? And ain't your Bug the easiest thing to spot in the air?"

"Out to get me!" repeated Mary Eliska. "Do you mean that you wanted to kill me?"

"No, lady. You're more use to us alive than dead—for a while, anyway. No. Our gang decided we could pick up a hundred grand easier by kidnapping you than by swiping jewelry. It was my idea!" He swelled with pride, believing himself exceedingly clever. "And that's what you get for wanting to have your picture and glories in the papers all the time!"

Mary Eliska listened wild-eyed to this information, and edged closer to Susie, as if her only protection would be found in the girl.

"So now these is your orders: You fly us to our camp tonight, and we'll keep you there. You can sleep with Susie. We won't hurt you, if you do what we tell you, and don't get fresh, or try to get away. Once you do that, we shoot. And believe me, I can aim—O.K. I've had a sight of practice in my business! I'm a mighty successful man—in my line."

"And what is your line, outside of kidnapping?" asked Mary Eliska.

"High-class robbery. Banks. Big jewels. We don't never hold up nobody on the street, for a few dollars. Too petty for us! Nope! We're big men. Slick! Clever! Ask Susie!"

"Does Susie like all this?"

"Sure she does. We winter in Europe, and South America, and she struts around with all the big dames, flashing diamonds and duds that make 'em all look pale.... Now come along!"

It was useless to argue or talk anymore, so Mary Eliska did as she was told, and together they got Susie into the passenger's cock-pit of the autogiro. Her husband sat with her, holding his pistol up threateningly at the back of Mary Eliska's head.

"Go where I tell you!" he ordered.

"I haven't much gasoline," she protested.

"I've got an extra flask here. But I'm not pouring it in 'til we need it, which I don't think we will. The camp ain't far—on Black Jack Island."

"Black Jack Island," Mary Eliska repeated to herself. "What an appropriate name!"

She was terrified, of course, but there was nothing to do except follow directions, and in a few minutes she brought the airplane down on the island that the man had specified.

"Leave the Bug here, Mary Eliska," he commanded, as he lifted Susie out of the plane. "And go ahead of me, as I tell you."

For several minutes the little procession made their way to the center of the island, over the white sand towards the cypress and pine trees that grew in greater profusion. Mary Eliska did not look back, but she knew that while "Slats" carried Susie with one arm, he kept his pistol at her back with his other hand. At last, by the aid of her flash-light, Mary Eliska spied several tents set up near together, and a welcome smell of food cooking greeted her as she advanced.

"Stop here!" came the order. "This is where you spend the night!"

Chapter 11.4
Captive

Mary Eliska and her companions stopped in front of a large tent that was dimly lighted within by a lantern. Two men were standing inside—one bending over an oil cook-stove, the other at the door.

"We got Mary Eliska!" announced "Slats" triumphantly. "Without even smashing her plane!"

He pushed through the doorway, past the other man, and deposited Susie on a cot by the wall of the tent.

The man at the stove, a big, fat, repulsive looking brute, turned around and uttered an ugly, "Hah!"

"Susie hurt?" inquired the tall, thin man who had been standing at the edge of the tent.

"Yeah. Crashed her plane. I've got some scratches meself, but I ain't whinin'!"

"My ankle's broken!" sobbed Susie, unable to suffer any longer in silence. "Hurry up and get some bandages, Doc!"

Mary Eliska, who had been standing perfectly still during this conversation, was startled by the use of the name "Doc." Was it possible that this man was a physician? If so, wouldn't he perhaps be above the level of the others—and might she not expect, if not sympathy, at least fair play from him? But "Slats" instantly shattered her hopes with his explanation.

"This is the 'Doc,' Mary Eliska," he said. "We call him that because he fixes up all our aches and cuts for us. In a profession like our'n, it ain't safe to meddle with 'saw-bones' and hospitals. They keep records."

Mary Eliska smiled at the idea of calling robbery a "profession," but she made no comment.

"So long as you'll be with us fer a while," continued her captor, "I'll interduce you to everybody. That there cook is 'Beefy.' Ain't he a good ad for his own cookin'?"

Mary Eliska nodded; she could hardly be expected to laugh at such a poor joke under the circumstances.

"You can go over and wash—there's water in Susie's tent—if you want to, while the 'Doc' fixes Susie up. Then we'll eat."

Glad to be alone for a moment, Mary Eliska stepped across to the tent which the man had indicated, hidden behind some pine trees a few yards away. Guiding herself by her flash-light, she found the entrance, and dropped down on a cot inside.

Letting the light go off, she sat, dry-eyed and utterly hopeless, staring into the darkness. What terrible fate was hanging over her, she dared not imagine. Would they torture her, perhaps, if her father refused to raise the ransom, and called the police to his aid?

In these last few hours she had learned to realize how infinitely crueler human-beings were than the elements of nature. The ice and snow, the cold winds of Canada, or the vast, trackless depths of the Atlantic could never bring about such untold agony as these fiends in human form. She almost wished that she had gone down, like Bess Hulbert, in the ocean, before she had lived to learn how evil men could be.

A call from the mess-tent, as she supposed the larger one to be, aroused her from her unhappy meditations, and she hastily turned on the light and washed from a pitcher of water on a soap-box in Susie's tent.

When she returned to the group, she found them already seated about a board table, plunging into the food like hungry animals. Susie, who sat with her bandaged ankle propped up on a box, was the only one who ate with any manners at all. But it had been a long time since Mary Eliska had tasted food, and she was too hungry to be deterred by the sight of "Beefy" putting his fingers into his plate. So she sat down next to Susie, and silently started to eat.

She found the meal exceedingly good, and was surprised at her own appetite, for she hardly expected to be able to enjoy anything under the circumstances.

The lantern threw a weird, ghastly light over the strange, ugly faces about her, and the silence was unbroken, except by the noise and clatter of eating. A tenseness took possession of her; she wished desperately that somebody would say something. It was exactly like a horrible dream, whose spell could not be destroyed. And still no one uttered a word until the meal was concluded.

"You girls can go to bed now," Slats announced, finally. "I'll carry you over, Susie, and give you a gun, in case Mary Eliska tries to sneak off in the night." He smiled with vicious triumph.

"I'm afraid that wouldn't do me any good," replied Mary Eliska, trying to make her voice sound normal. "I haven't an idea where I am."

"On Black Jack Island, in the Okefenokee Swamp," he again told her. "With water all around you. Get that! You can't get away, without a boat or a plane. And I'm tellin' you now, I seen to it that your Bug's bone-dry!"

With a conceited grin, he leaned over and picked up his wife so roughly that she cried out in pain.

When they were alone, the girls took off some of their outer garments, and lay down on their cots. Mary Eliska longed to talk, but she was afraid to begin, for fear it would only lead to some sort of punishment. So she lay still, trying to forget her troubles, to believe everything would come out right in the end, when her father paid the ransom.

She was just dozing off, when she was abruptly aroused by agonized sobs from her tent-mate. She sat up and asked her companion whether there was anything she could get her. But Susie did not answer; she continued to cry wildly like a child of six.

"Oh, my ankle! My ankle!" she moaned. And then she used worse language than any Mary Eliska had ever heard—from man or woman.

Mary Eliska was sorry for her, but she could not help contrasting this girl's cowardice in the face of physical pain with Jax Gray's, when the latter had met with a similar accident, and had smiled bravely at the hurt. She thought, too, of Ted Mackay's courage in the hospital, and Susie suffered by the comparisons.

"Is there anything I can do?" she asked, again.

"No. Only take me to a *real* doctor—or a hospital."

"I'd be glad to, if your husband would let me fly my plane!"

"Well, he won't!" There followed more oaths. "What does he care—so long as he ain't the one that's hurt?" She continued to cry hysterically, until a snarling order came from without the tent.

"Shut up your noise!" bawled her husband, and Susie softened her sobbing.

Mary Eliska lay very still, thinking. Dared she suggest that the other girl deceive her husband—or would she only be punished for such an idea? She decided to give it a try.

"You must know where the men keep the gasoline," she whispered. "Wouldn't you rather have your ankle fixed right, and not run the chance of being a cripple for life?"

"What do you mean?" demanded Susie, raising her head from her pillow.

"I mean—wait 'til the men are asleep, and then you tell me where the gasoline is, and we'll sneak off. I'd take you to a hospital, and I'd promise never to tell on you."

"And lose all that ransom money? Slats'd never forgive me!"

"But what good's money, if you're a cripple?" countered Mary Eliska.

"Yeah—I see what you mean," agreed Susie. "Only we'd never get away with it. They'd hear us gettin' out—remember I can't walk by myself.... No, Mary Eliska—it's no go."

Disappointed, Mary Eliska dropped back on the cot, seeing that further argument was no use, and, fortunately, fell quickly asleep. Had she not been so tired, she would probably have been disturbed during the night, for Susie tossed and moaned without any regard for her companion. But Mary Eliska slept the sleep of exhaustion.

Just as dawn was beginning to show a faint light through the door of the tent, Mary Eliska was rudely awakened by a gruff voice. Startled, she looked into the unpleasant face of Susie's husband, and she shuddered as she recalled where she was. The thought flashed into her mind that soldiers and criminals were usually shot at sunrise, and her hands shook with fear. What was the man going to do to her?

"Get up, Mary Eliska!" he commanded. "You're working today."

"Working?"

"Yeah. Flying."

"Where?" she demanded, with a trace of hope. If she were allowed to fly, there might be some hope of escape.

"Across the swamp. To an island out in the ocean."

"Oh!"

An island! It sounded like imprisonment. She thought of Napoleon on St. Helena, and she remembered the stories of the cruelties to the French convicts, sentenced to die on an island. Terrible climate, probably, reeking with disease. A slow death that would be far greater torture than being shot—hours of lingering agony, when she would think of her father and her aunt, and of the suffering that she was causing them! And, worst of all, no one to rescue her, as Ted had twice saved her from disasters that were not half so dreadful!

But she did not cry; she was disgusted with tears after the way that Susie had carried on the night before, over her sprained ankle. After all, it was no one else's fault that she had selected this job; she had taken it on, and she must see it through, no matter what the outcome.

When she had washed and dressed, she walked over to the big tent, where she found breakfast ready. Bacon and eggs and coffee—and even oranges! Evidently they meant to feed her well—for this much she could be thankful.

She ate in silence with the three men, for Slats did not carry Susie to the table. When they had finished, and the men were lighting their pipes, Slats pushed back his tin plate and began to talk.

"Our idea in running you down was to get a neat little ransom, Mary Eliska," he repeated, with the same triumphant grin which she had grown to loathe. She winced, too, at each repetition of her first name, though there was no way that she could stop him from using it.

"We figgered your old man could come across with a couple hundred thousand to get you back. When we get ready, we'll let him know. But in the meantime, we ain't ready."

He winked knowingly at Beefy, and a cold shiver of fear crept over Mary Eliska. If they would only get the thing over quickly! Anything would be better than the awful suspense.

The speaker laughed at her expression of terror.

"Don't be scared, Mary Eliska. We ain't a goin' a hurt you…. It just happens we need you for a couple days in our business."

"Your business?" she faltered.

"Yeah. We got some jewelry right here in this tent worth about a hundred grand. We fly across to an island with it, where a steamer picks it up and gets it to our agent in South America."

"But what has that to do with me?" asked Mary Eliska. Did they mean to leave her on the island, or send her to South America?

"Just this: we're usin' your Bug and you as pilot fer the job. Susie's the only one of our gang can fly, and now she and the Jenny are busted, we'll use you. Get me?"

Mary Eliska nodded, sadly. So she was to be made to play a criminal part in their ugly game! How she wished they would be caught!

"And you needn't scheme to get away," Slats added. "Because I'll be right behind you, with me gun loaded!"

Mary Eliska made no reply; after all there was nothing to be said. She must take his orders, or be instantly killed.

"Ready now?" he inquired, satisfied with her silence. "We always work early in the day. Maybe you better come over with me and take a look at your plane, and I'll give you some gasoline. See if she's O.K."

Dutifully Mary Eliska accompanied the man to the edge of the island, and there was the autogiro, safe and sound as ever—her only friend in the world, it seemed!

She looked about her at the marshy water, the trees and vegetation of the swamp, and then up into the sky, which she searched vainly for an airplane. But except for the birds, there was no sign of life in that desolate, vast expanse of land and sky. Not a human habitation in sight!

Desperately, she wished that she could think of some plan to outwit this lawless gang, but everything seemed hopeless, as long as Slats carried that pistol aimed at her head. So she meekly inspected the autogiro and climbed into the cock-pit.

Her companion was in a good humor; he was enjoying the whole situation immensely, pleased at his own cleverness. He liked to fly, and he admired the autogiro; he even went so far as to say he believed he'd keep this one for Susie.

Mary Eliska said nothing, but she was thinking what a mistake that would be for him to make. Much as she would hate to lose her autogiro, she realized that its possession would give the gang away to the police. It was one thing to steal jewelry and money, and another to take a plane, of a make of which there were only perhaps a hundred in existence.

They flew over the trees, eastward to the prairie land, and then on through the coastal plain to the Atlantic Ocean. Whether they were crossing Florida or Georgia, Mary Eliska did not know, and for once she was not interested in the country. The sun rose as they came to the water, but that beautiful sight, too, made no impression upon the unhappy girl. Nothing but the sight of a plane or a boat—the promise of rescue—could have any meaning for her.

On and on she went, leaving the land behind them, until finally they sighted an island possibly five miles out. The man behind her shouted to her to land, and she circled about, finally coming down on the beach.

As she brought her autogiro to earth, she was once more impressed by the loneliness, the barrenness of it all. No habitation of any kind, not even a tent! Motionless she sat in the cock-pit, wondering whether she couldn't get away while this thief was unloading his treasure.

Slats, however, was too wise for any such trick; he commanded Mary Eliska to get out of the plane, and help him carry a heavy box across the island where a growth of bushes concealed a hole in the ground, which was evidently the pre-arranged hiding-place. In silence they buried the treasure and returned to the autogiro.

Retracing their course under his direction, Mary Eliska flew back to the encampment. Here they found the others finishing their lunch, and Susie was sitting with them, apparently much brighter and better, for she was laughing and talking to her companions.

As Mary Eliska and her captor finished their meal, a stranger put in his stealthy appearance at the door of the tent. He was well-dressed, in riding-breeches, and clean-shaven. Mary Eliska's heart gave a wild bound of hope. Was it possible that this man was an officer of the law, and the criminals were caught?

But Beefy's greeting to the visitor instantly dispelled her hopes.

"Hello, Jake!" he exclaimed. "What's new?"

"Everything ripe for tonight," announced the new-comer, briefly. "Ready to start now?"

Slats stood up. "O.K. with me," he said. "Want some grub first, Jake?"

"No—I just ate." The stranger turned smilingly to Mary Eliska. "And how's the most famous girl-pilot in the world?"

Mary Eliska recoiled in horror. So he too knew all about the plot to catch her! Another member of this terrible gang!

As she did not answer, he shrugged his shoulders.

"Got the lines out about her yet?" he inquired, of the other men.

"No," replied Slats. "We had a smash-up—wrecked Susie and the Jenny, so we'll need Mary Eliska to fly her plane for us 'til this job's over tonight. I'll give you the high sign when I'm ready to let her old man know."

The four men stood together at the door of the tent.

"We're leaving for a day—maybe two," Slats informed Mary Eliska. "But Susie's watching you, with a gun. And your plane's dry, so I wouldn't advise to try any get-away. There's swamps everywhere....

"So long...."A moment later the girls heard the men tramp away to the boat that the newcomer had brought to the edge of the island.

Chapter 11.5
Escape

It was with a sigh of relief that Mary Eliska watched her captors disappear. Not that she had any hope of getting free—without gasoline—but at least she would not see those dreadful men for a few hours. Susie was not nearly so bad.

"I hope you can cook," remarked Susie, surveying her bandaged ankle.

"Oh, yes," replied Mary Eliska. "I've often camped out before."

"Then we can enjoy ourselves for a while. I'm glad to get rid of that gang.... And, Mary Eliska—how 'bout if we be friends? No use making things worse by getting mad at *me*."

"True," admitted Mary Eliska, though she wondered what she could possibly find in common with the other girl that might inspire friendship.

Seeing a kettle of water steaming on the oilstove, she set herself to the task of washing the dishes.

"Wish I could help," remarked Susie, in a friendly tone. "But after this there won't be so many dishes—for just the two of us."

"When do you expect them back?" inquired her prisoner.

"Tomorrow morning, probably. If they get their loot."

"Suppose they get caught?" suggested Mary Eliska.

"They won't. Don't worry! They've been planning this crack for months, and you can bet everything's all set just right. They never get caught."

Mary Eliska sighed. It wasn't very promising.

"Tell me how you got into a gang like this?" she asked, suddenly.

"I fell for Slats," replied the other girl. "Thought he was a rich guy—he spent so much money on me. I was working as a clerk at an airport, and learning to fly. We ran off and got married."

"But when you discovered that he wasn't straight, why didn't you leave him?"

"Couldn't. He said he'd hunt me down, and 'bump me off,' if I did. And he meant it, too. Slats isn't afraid of anything.... I saw right away that he didn't want a wife, but a pilot, who'd do what he said.... The only fun I get out of it is in the winter, when we go to Europe or South America, and live like swells. Then he lets me spend all the money I want."

"But doesn't it make you feel dreadful—at night, sometimes, or when you're alone—to think of leading such a wicked life?"

"Now, Mary Eliska, be yourself!" answered Susie, flippantly. "No preaching! From you, or anybody else!"

Mary Eliska turned away and completed her task in silence. What was the use of talking to a person like that? She knew now what was meant by the term "hard-boiled." If ever a word described anyone, that word described Susie.

She wondered, as she worked, whether it would be worth-while to repeat her suggestion of the night before. Susie's ankle was so much better today that she would not be so eager to get to a real doctor. Still, there could be no harm in trying.

"Wouldn't you like to go off in my autogiro today?" she inquired, without turning around.

Her companion laughed bitterly.

"Not a chance!" she replied. "Didn't you see Beefy take that big can to the boat with him? That was *gasoline*."

"Oh!" exclaimed Mary Eliska, her hopes dashed to the ground. "You mean they don't trust you?"

"They don't trust anybody!" announced Susie, emphatically. "It don't pay—in a game like theirs."

"Would you have gone with me?" inquired Mary Eliska. "If they hadn't taken it?"

"I don't know. My ankle's better. But I'm sick and tired of Slats, though I guess I'd miss the cash and the excitement. And I guess I'd be too scared he'd get me in the end if I double-crossed him."

Mary Eliska was silent. Now that this hope was frustrated, she must think of something else. Surely this was her chance of escape—with the men away, and her only companion a cripple.

But the swamp—the dreadful swamp was all about her. How far into the depth of the Okefenokee she was, she did not know. It was all a vast unexplored wilderness to her.

"Alive with snakes and wild animals, and alligators, I suppose," she mused. Yet nothing savage could be worse than those three fiends in human flesh who were holding her captive. She determined to face anything rather than them. Yes; she would run away, if it meant swimming the swamp!

There was no use loading herself down with food, she concluded, for most of her trip would be through the water. She would stop at her plane and take out some chocolate, and her knife; thus lightly equipped, she would face the wilderness alone.

"Mary Eliska," said Susie, interrupting these thoughts, "will you go to my tent and get me a magazine I have there? I think it's under the cot."

Mary Eliska nodded, repressing a smile. She would go, but she would not come back!

Stepping into the smaller tent, she dropped the flap, and picked up her flash-light. Then, raising the wall on the other side, she crept out through the trees to the edge of the island and circled about until she reached the autogiro. This would give her a few minutes extra before Susie should realize that she had gone.

As she stood there beside her plane for a moment, wondering whether she would ever see it again, she had her first real sight of the Okefenokee Swamp from the ground. Cypress and slash pine trees grew in abundance, and heavy moss hung about. In the water all around her, she noticed rushes and water-lilies, and ferns grew everywhere in profusion. Beneath the surface, she could see thick vegetation; would this, she wondered, support her weight if she were to attempt to walk in it?

In the afternoon sunlight the water, the trees, were perfectly still; except for the birds, the silence was profound. How desolate it was! Her wrist-watch informed her that it was already four o'clock. Five hours more, and darkness would come on, enveloping everything in a blackness such as a city-dweller never sees. Even the sky might be hidden by the trees, and the wild animals would be prowling stealthily about in search of food. She shuddered and hesitated.

"But I have an even chance with the animals," she thought. "And with those thieves, I am sure to lose!" So valiantly, she stepped out into the water.

The depth was not great at this point, and she discovered that, though the soft muck sunk beneath her feet, she could still make progress. The hard rains of July and August had not yet set in, and the "bays," as the stretches of shallow water were called, had not risen to any great height.

Laboriously she waded onward, choosing a thick growth of trees in the distance as her goal. Surely, she thought, where the trees could grow there must be some dry land. If she could make that spot by nightfall, she could hide in their depths and sleep. Then tomorrow she could press on to the westward, and perhaps reach the end of the swamp.

It was a slow, weary progress that she accomplished, and she had to pick her way carefully, measuring the depth of the water with a stick which she had cut from a pine on Black Jack Island, but she kept resolutely on until her watch registered seven o'clock. Then, all of a sudden, the stick sunk so deeply into the muck that she knew she would have to swim, and she hastily ate the chocolate which was to be her evening meal, and plunged forward to swim.

As the time slowly passed, she watched Black Jack Island fading in the distance, and hope swelled in her heart. She was nearing land at last—perhaps only an island—but even if she were not out of the swamp, at least she would be away from her enemies. She smiled when she pictured the consternation and anger of the men at finding her gone.

She swam on for some distance, now and then pausing to cut the grasses that became entangled about her legs. Her shoes were heavy, but she hated to take them off, for they were a help in the shallow water.

After an hour of this exercise, she was utterly exhausted, and she looked about her in dismay. What if she should drown now, in the midst of her own country—after she had conquered the Atlantic Ocean successfully? The thought was absurd; she steeled herself to press forward, for she was coming nearer to that bank of trees. Surely, there lay safety!

Had she but known it, she was now entering one of the so-called "Gator Roads" of the swamp—channels of water which the alligators followed. But it looked promising to the tired, hungry girl.

The foliage was growing thicker now, and the water-way narrowing. Some distance on, the trees met overhead, and beautiful moss hung from their branches, shutting out the setting sunlight, and forming a lovely green bower. But Mary Eliska was scarcely conscious of this beauty, for she was breathing with difficulty, panting with fatigue. If she could only make that bank—where the land seemed firm!

A big tree had fallen across the water, and she managed to reach it, and to cling to it for support while she rested. Her feet hung down in the muck, and she realized that the water was comparatively shallow. She wanted to laugh aloud in her relief.

Pulling herself up by her hands, she decided to walk the log to the bank, and had just poised herself upon its rather perilous round surface, when she encountered the greatest shock in her life thus far. Not ten yards away, in the very water where she would have been now, had she not mounted the log—was an alligator, at least eight feet long! Brave as she was usually in the face of dangers, she let out a piercing scream of terror at the sight of this horrible monster. Alligators had eaten her father Albert Stricklin's three classmates following their shared Fort Benning infantry training.

"Now I've got to walk the log!" she thought. "It's death if I fall off!"

She watched the alligator a minute or two while she regained her self-control, and made sure that he was not moving. Then, with eyes straight ahead, she started to walk the log.

Once, toward the middle, she swayed, but it was only for a second. She straightened herself staunchly and marched on—to dry land.

Oh, the joy of feeling her feet on firm ground again! To know that whatever misfortune might come on the morrow, she was safe for that night at least! She could not drown, or be tortured by enemies; her only danger would come from snakes. She would take the precaution to explore her sleeping-place thoroughly before she lay down.

Weary as she was, she did not stop until she had gone farther into the island. The trees were denser here than they had been at Black Jack; it would be more difficult to land an autogiro, if by chance Susie should follow her. Nevertheless, she resolved to stay hidden as much as possible.

Away from the shore, she finally dropped to the ground and took off her wet shoes and stockings.

"Not that it will do me much good in the morning to start off dry," she thought bitterly. "But anyhow, I don't want to sleep in them." And then she removed her outer garments.

"Wouldn't supper taste good!" she said aloud, envying Susie that well-filled larder at the camp. But Mary Eliska knew that there was no danger of her starving so soon, after that big noon-day meal, and she put the thought of food from her mind. Water she could not forget so easily. After half an hour's thirst, she decided to risk a drink from the swamp. Had she but known that the water of the Okefenokee is not poisonous, she would have enjoyed her drink more. The "peat" gives it a queer taste, but it is harmless.

She was relieved, in her return to the water, to see that the alligator had gone—which way, she could not tell. Though she was desolately lonely in that vast abandoned wilderness, she did not care for the companionship of so ugly a beast!

When she returned to the spot which she had selected for her camp, she took her knife from its wet case and cut a few stout sticks from a tree. With these she would explore the ground before she lay down, and keep them at her side while she slept, as some sort of protection from snakes.

As with the water, however, Mary Eliska's fears regarding snakes proved unnecessary, for the report of a large number of these in the Okefenokee Swamp had been proved by hunters to have been exaggerated. As a matter of fact, Mary Eliska did not see one during her entire visit to the swamp.

She waited until the daylight had faded, and darkness completely enveloped the landscape before she lay down to rest. The stars were still visible here and there through the trees, and, as upon the occasion of her lonely flight to Paris, they somehow seemed friendly. After an hour or so, she slipped off to sleep.

Only once during that strange, desolate night did she awaken, and that was when something cold and wet suddenly touched her face. She started up fearfully, seizing a stick with one hand and her knife with the other, squinting her eyes for snakes. Her flash-light had of course been thrown away during her swim, so she could not immediately identify the enemy that had awakened her.

She laughed out loud when she finally saw what it was. She had rolled over against her shoes, which were still cold and clammy with water!

She went back to sleep again, and did not awaken until the sun was well up in the sky. She had no way of telling the exact time, for her watch refused to go after its bath in the swamp, but Mary Eliska judged from the sun that it must be nine o'clock at least. Her clothing was dry, at any rate, and her shoes only a little damp. But what a sight she was, she thought, after that long swim!

She went down to the water's edge to wash, and to drink the water that must serve as her breakfast, and looked carefully about her—into the sky, and on the water—for the sight of her enemies. For she had no doubt that as soon as the thieves returned, they would go in search of her, believing that she could not have gotten far away.

She was relieved to see nothing, no sign of human beings anywhere, and she paused to watch some wild birds fly past overhead. Everything was peaceful and quiet—like a Sunday morning in the country. It was hard to believe that wickedness existed in such a beautiful world.

Then, abruptly, she noticed the soft swish of water not far away from her, and she looked up quickly, expecting to see the alligator again. In that awful second, her worst fears were realized. A canoe, with two men aboard, was coming straight towards her. The thieves! They had sighted her—they were wildly waving their arms.

It was too late to hide!

Chapter 11.6
The Enemy in the Autogiro

Defeated, miserable, hopeless, Mary Eliska sank to the ground and buried her face in her hands, waiting for the dreaded approach of her enemies. Oh, the cruelty of fate, to deliver her to them again, after her superhuman effort to escape! Bitter tears rushed to her eyes, scalding her face, and she sat as one expecting death, listening to the rhythmic dip of the paddles, as the canoe came closer and closer.

She kept her face hidden until the sound ceased, informing her thereby that the craft had stopped at her side. Tensely she waited for the harsh snarl of her captor's voice. But to her incredulous amazement, she heard instead the soft, deep, well-bred tones of a Southerner!

"Can we be of any help to you, Miss?" inquired the speaker.

Mary Eliska looked up instantly into the kind eyes of two exceedingly attractive young men.

"Oh! Please!" she gasped, the tears still running from her eyes. "Yes, please!"

And then, for the first time in her life, Mary Eliska fainted.

When she came to, she was lying on the ground, with two strangers bending over her, one offering her water, and the other hot coffee from a thermos bottle. A warm glow of happiness surged over her as she realized that she was among real human beings—not animals, or criminals. Though not naturally impulsive, she longed to throw her arms about these boys and weep with gratitude. If they had been girls, she would not have hesitated a moment.

Instead, she sat up and smiled her sweetest smile, so that, bedraggled as she was, she was still beautiful. The boys, man-like, each urged his particular offering upon her.

"Put that coffee down, Hal!" commanded the tall, fair youth at her right. "A lady who has just fainted doesn't want coffee."

"I do, though," Mary Eliska assured him. "I want water, and coffee—and anything else you have to eat. I fainted from hunger as much as from anything else."

The boy called "Hal" looked pleased at her acceptance of his gift, and he hurried back to the canoe for some food.

"Are you alone?" asked the other, who remained at Mary Eliska's side. "And how do you happen to be here?"

"It's a long story," replied the girl, wondering just how much of it she had better tell. It was all so incredulous, that perhaps they wouldn't believe her if she did tell them.

"First have some food," suggested the boy who had gone to the canoe. "How long has it been since you ate?"

"Only yesterday noon—and I even had some chocolate about six o'clock. But after that I waded and swam from Black Jack Island to this place—whatever it is."

"This is 'Billy's Island,'" the boys informed her. "Named after 'Billy Bowlegs,' the Indian who once lived here.... But, Great Guns!" exclaimed Hal, "that's five miles at least! Nobody ever tried to swim the Okefenokee Swamp before!"

"Well, it seemed like twenty-five," remarked Mary Eliska. "And I hope nobody ever has to try it again."

She did not go on with her story immediately, for she was too busy eating bananas—one right after another. Nothing had ever tasted so good! Meanwhile, the boys introduced themselves as Hal—short for Harold—Perry, and Jackson Carter, both Juniors at the University of Florida.

"We're both on the archery team at college," Jackson explained. "And we take a little trip into the Okefenokee each summer, to try out our bows and arrows on the wild game here. We camp each night on one of the islands."

"Then you know the Swamp pretty well," remarked Mary Eliska, with relief. They would be able to take her back to civilization.

"The southern end of it—yes," replied Hal.

"Now tell us who you are," urged Jackson Carter, regarding Mary Eliska with silent admiration. There was no doubt about it, she certainly was an attractive girl.

Mary Eliska hesitated a moment, and determined not to mention her first name. She was tired of all the publicity and disaster which her ocean flight had brought her. Besides, these boys might think she was just posing as Mary Eliska, the famous aviatrix, in order to impress them. She would tell them only her middle name, instead.

"I am Ann Stricklin, from Ohio," she replied. "I was flying my new plane when I got lost over the swamp, and had to come down on the first dry land I saw, because my gasoline was running low, and I didn't know how far the water extended."

"Smashed your plane?" inquired Hal, evidently satisfied with the explanation.

"No. But unfortunately I fell among a gang of thieves, and they stole it, and tried to hold me prisoner on Black Jack Island. But yesterday I got away, as I told you."

Both boys gazed at Mary Eliska in admiration and wonder. What a plucky girl she must be!

"Thieves in the swamp!" repeated Hal. "Not Indians?—a lot of Indians used to live here, and they might have come back."

"No. White men—and one girl. Regular thieves, the kind that rob banks and jewelry stores."

"But what were they doing? Hiding from justice?"

"I don't think so," answered Mary Eliska. "Because I don't think anybody suspects them in particular. They have a regular camp on Black Jack Island, and they bring whatever they steal there, and transfer it by airplane to an island in the Atlantic Ocean, where it's picked up by another partner in a boat."

Jackson let out a whistle.

"Pretty slick, aren't they? But they'll get caught sometime."

"I sincerely hope so. Unfortunately, though, nobody could identify them as thieves, because they haven't been caught before."

"You could," remarked Hal.

"Yes, if I ever see them again. Do we have to pass Black Jack Island to get out of the swamp?"

"I'm afraid so—but we needn't go very close to it—it's some distance from the regular 'Gator Road' we always follow."

"'Gator Road'?" repeated Mary Eliska. "There aren't any roads in the swamp, are there?"

"They're water channels," Hal explained. "Short for alligator-roads."

Mary Eliska shuddered.

"I saw an alligator last night," she told them. "I hope we don't meet any more."

"You poor girl!" exclaimed Jackson. "It seems to me you've had most every dreadful experience anybody could have in the last twenty-four hours!"

"But they're over now," laughed Mary Eliska, wondering what the boys would say if she told them the real account of the kidnapping.

Even now Jackson Carter was looking at her strangely. She seemed like such a nice girl—but what sort of family could she have come from, that would allow her to roam around the country unchaperoned and alone? He himself was of an old-fashioned Southern family, who regarded such independence in young women as mere boldness. Yet Mary Eliska seemed anything but ill-bred, or bold.

"Aren't your family worried about you, Aunt Sally?" he inquired. "So far away—in an airplane?"

"They must be by now," she replied with a pang of distress. "I had promised to wire them every day—and it's been three nights now since I could. My aunt probably is afraid I have been killed."

"Your aunt?"

"Yes. My mother is dead, and my aunt has always taken care of me."

"But she lets you do pretty much as you please I take it. You northern girls certainly are different."

"Well, not exactly." Mary Eliska could not explain without telling the whole story of her life, so she decided to let the matter pass. "Hadn't we better be pushing on, if we expect to get out of the swamp before dark?"

"Yes," replied Hal. "But don't set your heart on that, Aunt Sally. I don't know whether we can or not. But we'll get past Black Jack Island, and at least as far as Soldiers' Camp Island."

"Soldiers' Camp Island?" repeated Mary Eliska.

"Yes. The story goes that some Civil War soldiers deserted, and hid there. I don't know how true it is, but it certainly is a good place to hide."

"Don't I know!" sighed Mary Eliska.

They climbed into the canoe, putting Mary Eliska on some blankets in the center, and started upon their journey. For the first time since her visit to the swamp, Mary Eliska was at last able to enjoy its beauty. The thick ferns, the cypress trees growing in abundance, the pines and the water-lilies! What a difference a boat could make! Yesterday she hated the rushes and the moss; today she found everything lovely.

Avoiding the island where the thieves were camped, the boys made a wide circle, and did not pass even in sight of it. With each mile of progress, Mary Eliska's spirits rose higher and higher, until finally she suggested that they sing. She just had to find some outlet for her joy and thanksgiving.

"It must be long after noon," remarked Jackson, as they finished a familiar college song. "Hadn't we better eat?"

"I see an island ahead—I think it's Soldiers' Camp," replied Hal. "Wouldn't it be nice to stop and make some coffee?"

"I'm hot enough without any fire or hot coffee," returned Jackson, wiping the perspiration from his face. "But I would like to stretch my legs."

"Let me do the cooking!" urged Mary Eliska, eagerly. "I'd love to prove some use to you, after all the trouble I've made."

"You haven't been any trouble!" protested Jackson, whose admiration for Mary Eliska had been growing by leaps and bounds, in spite of the fact that he could not wholly approve of her. For the past three hours he had been sitting in the stern of the canoe, gazing at her lovely profile, listening to the charm of her soft voice. Yet he knew he had better not allow himself to care for this girl; she was just the type his mother disapproved of, and with Jackson Carter, his mother's wishes were supreme.

They pulled up to the island and unloaded the canoe. There were all sorts of supplies— bacon, canned beans, fruit, and biscuits, as well as tea, coffee, sugar and canned milk. Even a little folding stove to set over a fire, and a coffee-pot.

"What a perfectly delightful spot!" exclaimed Mary Eliska, as she walked some distance inland. "Look at these lovely little houses! Why, I could almost live in them myself!"

What she referred to were the clumps, here and there, of cypress trees and overgrowing vines and evergreens, which, as a matter of fact, the hunters often used to camp in during their visits to the swamp. They were very attractive indeed, and would afford complete privacy, Mary Eliska thought, if she were obliged to spend another night in the Okefenokee.

The boys made a fire on the edge of the water, and Mary Eliska insisted that they go off for half an hour while she prepared the meal. She laughed and sang as she toasted the dry biscuits and the bacon, and boiled the coffee. What fun it was to picnic when you were among friends—even if they were very new ones!

When the boys came back, they each proudly displayed a wild goose, as proof of their ability with the bow and arrow. Then, like three happy, carefree school-children, they sat down to their meal, having forgotten all about the thieves for the time being.

The shock was all the more terrible, therefore, when they suddenly looked up into the sky and saw the autogiro overhead. Mary Eliska was the first to identify the plane, to guess what danger they were in. She stumbled to her feet, pulling Jackson with her, and just as she opened her mouth to tell them to flee with her into the depths of the island, a shot rang out from the autogiro, and a bullet whizzed past the little group, so innocently enjoying their picnic!

Chapter 11.7
The Smash-Up

The robbery which was so carefully planned by the gang of thieves who had kidnapped Mary Eliska, was highly successful. One of the largest banks in Jacksonville was entered just before closing time on the afternoon of June 23rd by four masked robbers, who calmly took thousands of dollars in cash and securities, and escaped to a waiting car, without being identified or caught. By a secret route these men suddenly disappeared—whither, no one but Mary Eliska and Susie knew. By midnight they were back again in the swamp, and by dawn they had reached Black Jack Island.

Exhausted from their journey, three of the men dropped down on their cots and fell instantly asleep. The fourth—Susie's husband—stopped to look into his wife's tent. Flashing the light inside, he peered through the doorway. There was Susie, sleeping peacefully on her cot. But the other bed was empty!

"Susie!" he yelled at her. "Where's Mary Eliska?"

The girl awakened abruptly, and sat up, blinking her eyes at the unexpected light. For a moment she could not think what he meant. Then she remembered her prisoner.

"She's gone," she replied. "Beat it this afternoon."

"How?" he demanded roughly, coming over and shaking her by the arm. Susie winced, and pulled herself free.

"You leave me alone!" she warned him. "How do I know how Mary Eliska got away? Could I run after her?"

"No, but you might 'ave watched her!" snarled Slats. "Didn't I tell you to?"

"Watching wouldn't keep her here," retorted Susie.

"Is her Bug still there?" he inquired.

"Yeah. I hobbled over and took a look myself."

"Oh, you did, did you?" Then, worn out and disappointed, Slats started to swear.

Susie sat still, regarding him with contempt. How vulgar such language sounded, when you actually stopped and listened to it! She did not realize it at the time, but just the few hours which she had spent with Mary Eliska had given her a new view-point. Or rather, had brought back her training as a child, before she had "gone bad."

When the man's anger had spent itself in violent words, he began to wonder how on earth Mary Eliska could have escaped.

"No human being could get far in this here bog, without a boat or a plane!" he exclaimed. "She must be around here somewhere."

"Why don't you go look for her!" demanded Susie, with a sneer. She was beginning to be glad that Mary Eliska had gotten away.

Her husband turned on her savagely.

"Look a here, Susie, if you helped that kid to get away—!" He held up his fist threateningly. "I'll make you sorry! Give you a dose of the medicine I was saving for Mary Eliska!"

"What do you mean?" she demanded, trembling.

"This gun!" he replied.

"Well, I didn't," she hastened to assure him. "Mary Eliska slipped off when I wasn't watching.... But do you mean you were going to shoot Mary Eliska?"

"Sure, you fool! That's what kidnappers always do. Bait the big fish 'til they get the cash, then kill the victim, and ship the corpse. If we sent Mary Eliska back alive, she'd have us in the Pen in no time. Our game'd be up."

Susie shivered; she had not realized that the men had any intention of going to that end. True, Slats had once killed a bank messenger, but Susie always excused him on the ground of self-defense. "Hard-boiled" as she was, the idea of shooting an innocent girl like Mary Eliska was too much for her to approve. She felt suddenly sick with the horror of it all.

Slats sat down for a moment on the empty cot, while he thought things over. Mary Eliska must not escape to tell the world of her experience and to give such accurate descriptions of the gang that they would have to be caught. Aside from the matter of the ransom which the kidnapping ought to bring them, they dared not let her go. The case called for immediate action.

"Can you fly that Bug, Susie?" he demanded, abruptly breaking the silence.

"I guess so," replied the girl. "They say they're easier than airplanes."

"O.K. Then we're off. Get dressed as quick as you can."

"But Slats," protested Susie, rubbing her injured ankle, "don't forget I've been hurt!"

"Rats!" was his unsympathetic reply. "Get busy. I'll be getting the gasoline, and some grub. We'll need coffee—and a lot of it."

Distasteful as the plan was, Susie could do nothing but obey. But she was feeling very miserable as she ate her breakfast, very sorry for the "poor, brave kid," as she called Mary Eliska, very resentful against her husband.

The latter helped her down to the autogiro and put her into the pilot's cock-pit, where she sat for some minutes examining the controls. The dawn had changed into daylight, and the swamp was beautiful in the early morning sunrise. But, like Mary Eliska, Susie did not even notice it.

Impatient at the delay, her husband demanded, "Got the idea how to run her?"

"Sure," she replied, listlessly. "Start her up and climb in…. Where do you want to go!"

"Circle all around—flying low, so that we can spot the kid if she's here. If we don't see her in the water, we'll stop at some of the islands, and look there. She can't 'ave got out of this swamp."

"O.K.," agreed Susie.

Without much difficulty the girl ran the autogiro along the edge of the island until it rose into the air. It was easy enough to keep it flying; the test would come when she had to make a landing. But Susie decided never to worry about anything until the time came. Luck was usually with her; her only serious crash had been the one of two days previous, and, after all, there was a reason for that.

Slats, who spurned learning how to fly, because he considered his a master-mind, above such practical work, was, nevertheless, enjoying the ride. He congratulated himself upon his own cleverness in securing this new plane for the gang.

"Like her, Susie?" he shouted, through the speaking-tube.

The girl nodded, indifferently.

"You can have her!" he announced, proudly, as if he were giving her a costly present of his own purchasing.

Susie drew down the corners of her lips in scorn, but made no reply. Didn't he realize that she would never dare fly this autogiro where anyone could see her? That the police all over the country would be on the look-out for this very plane? She was understanding for the first time that money was not much use without freedom.

As she sat in the cock-pit, silently thinking things over, she made up her mind not to try to help Slats in his search. She would have to continue to guide the plane, of course, for she never for one moment forgot the pistol that her husband kept ready to enforce his orders with. But she would not attempt to spot Mary Eliska, nor would she inform him if she did happen by chance to see the girl. No; it would be better to let "the poor kid" die by natural causes in the swamp than for her to be killed by Slats in cold-blooded murder.

Over the trees and tropical plants of the swamp they continued to fly, until the sun rose directly overhead, and they knew that it was noon. All the while Slats kept his eyes glued to the ground, without any success. Not a sign of human life did he see. Movements in the swamp—yes—snakes and birds, and even an alligator—but no girl! Yet he felt sure that even if Mary Eliska were hiding, she would come out at the sound of the plane, for by this time she would realize that escape was impossible. Driven by the pangs of hunger, she would have to surrender to her fate. But noon passed, and they found no trace of her.

Perhaps she was dead by this time, the man thought bitterly—killed by a snake, or drowned in the treacherous water! He would not mind that, if he could only find her dead body. Without it, without the assurance that she was not still at large, he dared not seek a reward. What a lot of money he would be losing!

"We'll land on an island, and have some grub," he shouted to his companion. "Fly south to 'Soldiers' Camp.'"

"O.K.," replied the girl, beginning to doubt her ability to make a landing. But she was afraid to disobey—and besides, they had to come down sometime.

After that things happened with a rapidity that must have startled the peaceful bird-life in the Okefenokee Swamp. Approaching the island, Susie and her husband spotted the carefree picnic at the same moment, and the former made a sudden, sharp turn in the hope of hiding the sight from Slats. At the same instant, he took out his pistol and fired at the group—at Mary Eliska in particular—missing her only because of Susie's rapid change of the position of the plane.

The sharp angle had its effect upon the pilot; she lurched over, striking her injured ankle against the rudder, swerving the plane violently to the other side. Panic-stricken, she tried to right the plane, but she had not even throttled the engine down to a landing speed. The inevitable crash followed. With an impact that was frightful, the autogiro headed for a tree with relentless speed, struck it and bounced thirty feet into the air.

By some miracle Susie, crouched as she was in the cock-pit, was not thrown out, but her husband, who had not taken the precaution to wear a safety-belt, was bounced wildly into the air, and landed, face-downward, on a rock.

During all this excitement, Mary Eliska and her companions stood tensely rooted to the spot, the girl gripping Jackson Carter's hand as if he were her one support. As the crash came, she dropped her head on his shoulder and moaned aloud, totally unconscious of the fact that the young man was still little more than a stranger to her.

A cry from Susie aroused her to the fact that the girl was still alive. Ignoring the man who had brought about the catastrophe by his hasty shot, all three young people rushed to Susie's aid.

The plane was only partially turned over; the rotor and the wheels were injured, and the nose smashed, but it did not look to Mary Eliska as if there had been any serious harm to the engine. Susie's head was cut, and two teeth were knocked out, but apparently no bones had been broken. Very carefully the boys lifted her from the cock-pit and laid her on the ground.

"I have a first-aid kit in the canoe," said Hal, immediately. "I'll get it and fix up this cut. It doesn't seem awfully deep."

"Does it hurt very much, Susie?" asked Mary Eliska, offering her a drink of water.

"Not as much as my ankle. And my poor mouth! Without these teeth! My looks are ruined!"

"No, they're not," answered Mary Eliska, comfortingly. "Any good dentist can fix you up so nobody will ever know the difference."

Still no one said anything about the man who was lying so silently on the rock a dozen yards away. It was Hal Perry, returning from the canoe, who made the announcement which they had all been secretly expecting.

"The man with the gun is dead," he said, quietly, not knowing how Susie would take the news.

"So he got his at last," muttered the latter, with a certain grim satisfaction. "Nobody—not even his widow—is goin' to shed a single tear!"

Chapter 11.8
The Chief of Police

Half an hour after the accident, Susie expressed a desire to eat, and Mary Eliska hastened to supply her with food. While the girl ate her lunch, the little group discussed their plans.

"Is my bag still in the autogiro?" asked Mary Eliska, surveying the disreputable suit which she had worn for three days. What a relief it would be to get into clean clothing!

"It was when we left," replied Susie. "If it didn't bounce out when we crashed.... Mary Eliska," she added apologetically, "I'm awful sorry about your plane. I—I—didn't mean to crack it up."

"I know you didn't, Susie. I think it can be repaired, if we can get the new parts to this forsaken place. Probably we can—by airplane."

Jackson Carter, who had been only half listening to this conversation, interrupted by telling the girls that he and Hal would take care of the burying of the criminal. "Unless," he added, turning to Susie, "you would want to take the body back to your home?"

"We haven't any home," Susie admitted sadly. "And no friends, outside the gang.... No, it's better for him to lie here in this swamp—where he meant to plant Mary Eliska."

The implication was lost to the boys, who did not know the story of the kidnapping, and who thought of Mary Eliska as "Ann."

"Then first we'll help you get your bag out of the autogiro, Mary Eliska," offered Jackson. "You can go back into one of those little 'houses,' and change into clean clothing, if you want to, while we attend to the burying."

"Wait a minute," urged Mary Eliska. "I think we ought to decide what we'll do about tonight. We can't all four get into that canoe, so Susie and I had better stay here, hadn't we? You could wire my aunt for me, couldn't you?"

To Mary Eliska's amazement, before either of the boys had a chance to reply, Susie put in a protest.

"It ain't safe for you to be here an hour more than you have to," she said. "Don't forget there's still three rough guys hot on your trail.... No, I'll stay alone, if you leave me some grub, and a blanket. You can come back for me when you bring somebody to fix your plane." This generous offer came as a complete surprise to Mary Eliska; she had not realized before that this girl had swung over to her side. What a splendid sign it was! Susie must have decided to cut free from these criminals, now that her husband was dead.

"That's great of you, Susie," replied Mary Eliska. "And you needn't worry that I'll ever tell the authorities anything bad about you! I was afraid I oughtn't to leave you alone—but if you really don't mind——"

The other girl shrugged her shoulders.

"I'll get along O.K. I'm used to being left by myself. But don't stay away too long."

The arrangements suited the boys perfectly, for they were anxious to be out of the swamp as soon as possible. With fast paddling, they ought to be able to reach a little town in Florida by dark, where they believed that they could hire an automobile to take them home.

Fifteen minutes later Mary Eliska stepped out from the enclosure, dressed in a pale blue voile—the only dress she carried in her bag, for she had shipped her trunk to Atlanta, where she had expected to report for work. The wearing of clean clothing was a pleasure second only to that of using a comb and a tooth-brush. She felt like a different girl.

If she had seemed pretty to Jackson Carter before, in that disheveled green linen suit, she was radiantly beautiful now. Returning from his gruesome task, he stood still, lost in admiration.

Mary Eliska laughed at his amazement.

"Do I look like another girl?" she inquired.

"The same girl—glorified," he answered, with awe.

Having unloaded the canoe of its food and blankets, and assured themselves that Susie was able to hobble around with the aid of a stick, the three young people pushed off. It was only three o'clock; all these occurrences—the crash, the death of the criminal, his burial—had taken place in less than two hours!

For some time the boys paddled forward in silence, each of the three occupants of the canoe lost in his or her own thoughts. Hal was going over the exciting events of the last two hours; Jackson was thinking of Mary Eliska—or "Ann"—Stricklin, and wondering whether her hiding her head on his shoulder had meant that she cared for him. Mary Eliska's mind, however, was occupied with the immediate future—with the part she might play in assisting the police to catch those arch criminals who were still at large.

It was she who first broke the silence.

"What would be the nearest large city to this southern end of the swamp?" she inquired.

"Jacksonville, Florida," replied Hal, immediately. "That's where we both live."

"Then that's where I want to go," announced Mary Eliska. "Have they a good police department?"

"Best in the country," boasted Jackson.... "Mary Eliska," he added, "would you stay at our home while you are in the city?"

"I'd love to," agreed the girl immediately. All through the South, until she had lost her way in the Okefenokee, she had met with this same southern hospitality, and had found it charming.

Jackson Carter was overjoyed at her acceptance, yet he was a little fearful of the reception his mother would give to a girl who was so different from all his other friends. Surely, however, the older woman must see how fine Mary Eliska was, and accept her for her own lovely charm.

The hours passed swiftly and the daylight was fast fading when the boys finally informed Mary Eliska that she was out of the swamp. With a prayer of thanksgiving, she gave it one last look, hardly able to believe her good fortune. Less than twenty-four hours ago, she had been miserably lost in its depths. Now she was free to live again in civilization, untortured by the fears that had held her in such terror for the last three days.

Leaving the canoe in a boat-house on the bank of the small stream which they had been following out of the swamp, they walked to the nearest village and asked for the Post Office. Here Mary Eliska made arrangements to send a wire to her aunt, in which, however, she did not mention the fact that she had been kidnapped.

"Have been lost in Okefenokee Swamp," she wrote. "But not hurt. Wire me at Jacksonville, Fla. Love—Mary Eliska."

Her next move was to send for her trunk from Atlanta, and to wire for new parts for the autogiro, and while the boys looked up a place to eat supper, she bought a Jacksonville newspaper. She hoped there would be nothing in it about her, for she hated so much publicity.

The first item that struck her eye was the announcement of the Jacksonville Bank robbery. More than a hundred thousand dollars had been stolen—in cash and securities—by four masked bandits on the afternoon of June twenty-third, and still no trace of them had been found.

"That money must be at Black Jack Island," she thought, resolving to get this information to the police early the following day.

She had to go through the paper twice before she found her own name. It was only a tiny notice, among the aviation briefs, and copied from an Ohio paper—stating the fact that Mary Eliska, world-famous aviatrix, had not been heard from for three days, and asking that the airports of Georgia report any sight of her autogiro.

Mary Eliska breathed a sigh of relief, as she saw how inconspicuous this notice was. For some reason she did not want Jackson Carter or Hal Perry to connect her with the famous flyer, and she longed above everything to keep the story of the kidnapping from her aunt's ears.

The boys came back with the information that they had found a place to eat, and took Mary Eliska to a little frame house where a widow ran a sort of restaurant. The cottage was run-down and out-of-repair, but everything inside was neat and clean, and the food, though plain, was excellent.

"How long will it take us to get to Jacksonville?" inquired Mary Eliska, as they finished the meal.

"Two or three hours," replied Hal. "Providing we have no mishaps. Why?"

Mary Eliska repressed a sigh. She was very tired, and longed intensely for sleep in a real bed. These last two nights in the swamp had taken their toll of her vitality.

"If only we had a plane!" she said.

"It wouldn't do me any good," remarked Jackson. "I've never been in one—and I've promised my grandmother I won't fly until I'm twenty-one."

"Oh, I'm so sorry," offered Mary Eliska, with genuine sympathy. Life without flying seemed a dreary thing to her.

The only car which the boys had been able to hire was a dilapidated Ford that looked as if it would hardly last the trip. But it proved to be better than its appearance; over the lovely hard roads of Florida it traveled comparatively smoothly. To Mary Eliska's amazement, she found when they reached Jacksonville that she had slept most of the way.

The short rest had freshened her considerably, and she suddenly decided to go to the Police Headquarters that night. It was her duty to report the crash of her plane, and the death of that criminal. She wished that she had thought to ask Susie his real name—she was going to feel rather silly calling him "Slats."

With this purpose in mind, she asked Jackson what time it was.

"Half-past nine," was his reply. "Why?"

"Because I think I ought to report to the Police tonight about those thieves. I understand that it was a bank in Jacksonville that they robbed."

"Which bank?" demanded the boy, excitedly.

"'The First National,' the paper says."

At this information, Jackson Carter dropped back in his seat and groaned. His mother's bank —where all of her money was kept! The bank of which his uncle was president! This was going to mean trouble to the whole Carter family.

"Will you please take my bag to your house, and leave the address with me?" asked Mary Eliska, not knowing what Jackson was suffering. "I'll take a taxi out to your home, after I see the Chief of Police."

"Yes, yes, of course," agreed the young man, still absorbed in his own thoughts.

It was a late hour to visit the Chief of Police, but when Mary Eliska explained her reason to an officer at the City Hall, the latter sent for the chief immediately.

When Captain Magee came in a few minutes later, Mary Eliska was impressed with his appearance and delighted with his dignified and courteous manner. She smiled at him confidently; how different he was from those officers of the law with whom she had come in contact in Canada!

"I am going to tell you my whole story, if you will promise not to repeat the part about the kidnapping to the newspapers," she began. "I don't want my people at home to hear of that—for, after all, it is over now, and I am safe."

"Kidnapping!" repeated the officer. "You don't mean to say that you have been kidnapped?"

"Yes. My name is Mary Eliska —I am the girl who flew the Atlantic in May." She blushed, for she hated to talk about herself, or to appear to boast about her own exploits, but this time it was necessary. "Here in Jacksonville, among friends, I am going to be known as Ann Stricklin, because I want to avoid publicity." Her blue eyes became pleading, and she asked, in an almost child-like tone, "You won't tell on me, will you, Captain Magee?"

He smiled. "No, I won't tell. Unless it becomes necessary."

"Thank you so much! Well, to continue: I bought a new autogiro and flew down here to report to a company in Atlanta about a job spraying crops, and the newspapers printed the route of my flight. Early in the evening of June 22nd I lost my way over the Okefenokee Swamp, and finally landed on an island. A plane had been chasing me, as I later learned after it landed—or rather crashed—beside mine. The man in it held me at the point of a gun and compelled me to fly my autogiro to their camp on Black Jack Island, where I was to be held for a ransom. *That man was the chief of the gang of bandits that robbed the Jacksonville bank.*"

She paused a moment for breath, and the Captain leaned forward eagerly. The story, which might have seemed incredulous to an ordinary person, was perfectly believable to him. He was used to the ways of criminals.

"But how did you get away?" he demanded.

"I never should have, if it hadn't been for this bank robbery," she explained. "While the men went off, I escaped, and was picked up by a couple of Jacksonville boys in a canoe."

Mary Eliska went on to relate the happenings of the afternoon, concluding with the death of the ring-leader of the gang, whom she knew only as "Slats." She spoke lightly of Susie, showing her merely as a weak pawn in her husband's hands.

The criminals' method of disposing of their stolen valuables was another interesting point in her story, and she told Captain Magee about the barren island in the ocean.

"Now whether this stuff is still on the island or at the camp," she concluded, "I don't know. But I am ready to go and help you find out."

"You mean you are actually willing to go back into that swamp?" the officer asked. "To show us the way?"

"Of course! That's why I came to you tonight. So that we can make arrangements for tomorrow."

"But it may be very dangerous, Mary Eliska! These men will be armed, and will shoot at sight."

"I'll take a chance. Can we go tomorrow morning? By plane?"

"By airplane?"

"Yes. Any other way would be too slow. They may have escaped already."

"But an airplane will be so much noisier than a boat. They'll hear you coming."

"We'll have to take that chance." She stood up. "If you will get a plane, Captain Magee—a large one—I will fly it, to save space. Then we can take two or three armed guards."

"How do you know that you can fly any plane I happen to get, Mary Eliska?" he inquired, incredulously.

"You see, I'm a transport pilot," she explained. "We have to be able to manage most anything.... Can you send a car out for me to the Carters' home, early in the morning?" She handed the Captain the address.

"Yes. I'll telephone as soon as I can make all the arrangements," he agreed, seeing that he could not change her from her purpose.

Mary Eliska thanked him and hurried out to the waiting taxi. It was growing late, long after ten o'clock, and she was anxious to be in bed.

Jackson Carter himself came to the door when she rang the bell.

"Where is your mother?" she asked, immediately, for there was no sign of a hostess inside.

"She is ill," replied the young man. "The bad news about the bank—a great deal of our money was lost—knocked her terribly. She hasn't told grandmother, or it might kill her. So I had the maid get the guest room ready, and hope that you will excuse them both."

Mary Eliska nodded; she had no way of knowing that Mrs. Carter had protested about entertaining this girl whom Jackson had "picked up" on his canoe trip, and had stubbornly refused to see her. The woman had worked herself into such a state of nerves over her losses and over this incident that she had actually made herself ill.

"I'm so sorry," said Mary Eliska, sympathetically. "If I weren't so tired, I'd go to a hotel, for this is no time for your mother to be bothered with a guest. But I'll just stay tonight, and leave early tomorrow. I'm flying to the swamp again with the police officers."

"Ann!" cried Jackson aghast, using her name unconsciously. "Don't, please! It's dangerous— you may be killed.... And, and, besides——"

"Besides, what?"

"Besides, it isn't done. You shouldn't go off to lonely places like that, without an older woman along."

Mary Eliska smiled.

"I can't be bothered with social codes at a time like this," she said. "I have to do all I can to get that money back. Think of the hundreds of people hurt by that bank robbery—if the bank is forced to close its doors! Including your own mother and grandmother! No, I just have to go."

"Let me go instead," he suggested.

"You wouldn't know just where the camp is. It's pretty well hidden, and I know the only spot where a landing is possible. Besides, you can't fly a plane."

"You mean you will pilot the plane yourself? Your autogiro's broken."

"Oh, it'll be another plane—a hired one. Now please don't argue any more, Mr. Carter— you sound like my aunt—and let me go to bed. And will you ask one of the servants to waken me at seven o'clock?"

"Good night, then, Mary Eliska," he said, almost sorrowfully, for it seemed like the end of what might have been a wonderful friendship for Jackson Carter.

Chapter 11.9
Two Prisoners

Mary Eliska's telephone call came early the following morning, and after a simple breakfast served by the cook, she left in the car which Captain Magee sent. Not one of the Carter family appeared at the meal, and there was no message of any kind. Mary Eliska, however, attributed this to Mrs. Carter's illness, and wrote a polite note of thanks to her hostess.

She found three plain-clothes men waiting for her at the police station, and they joined her in the car which then took them to the airport. A large cabin plane, capable of accommodating six persons, had been wheeled out on the runway, awaiting their arrival and two service men were standing beside it.

"You are sure you can pilot her, Miss?" inquired one of these men, skeptically.

Mary Eliska opened her bag and took out her two licenses—mechanic's and transport pilot's—and handed them to him.

"A mechanic!" he exclaimed, in amazement. "Gee whiz! Will wonders never cease? It's the first time I ever laid eyes on a lady-mechanic!"

Mary Eliska laughed.

"May I look the plane over before we start?" she asked. "And will you map out the quickest course to Okefenokee Swamp! I want to get into the southern part of it—Black Jack Island, if you know where that is."

With a grin the man disappeared to consult someone in the hangar, and Mary Eliska went ahead with the examination.

"There ought to be plenty of room in here to bring back any prisoners we may get," she said, cheerfully. "I think too, that you had better send for some food and water, Sergeant— for we can't tell how long we may be gone."

When she announced herself satisfied with the inspection, she and her three companions climbed into the cabin while the mechanic fired the engine. The plane taxied along the runway and rose gracefully into the air, to the admiration of the three officers, none of whom could fly.

"You're there with the goods, Mary Eliska!" shouted the one named "Worth," who apparently was in charge of the expedition.

"Don't praise me too soon," returned Mary Eliska. "That was child's play. But wait 'til it comes to landing on that island in the swamp. There is only one spot big enough, in a plane like this."

"Well, we got plenty of gasoline," remarked Worth, cheerfully. "I'm not afraid. I'm enjoying the flight. It isn't every day that we go up in the skies on our job."

Mary Eliska was enjoying it, too. She flew carefully, watching her map, her instruments, and the landscape below. They flew over the island where they had left Susie, and Mary Eliska made a mental note of the location, in case she should be able to pick the girl up on the return trip.

It was difficult to keep her direction, for the swamp, covered as it was with grasses and trees, seemed like an unbroken, monotonous expanse from the air, but Mary Eliska had succeeded in spotting the little stream down which the boys had paddled the canoe, and she resolved to follow that to the place where they had picked her up. After that it ought to be easy to locate Black Jack Island and the camp of the thieves.

But it was not as simple as she had hoped, even after she had located the island. Again and again she circled about, looking for a space large enough to make a landing. Finally she found what must be the edge of the island, for the water came up unevenly, but this beach appeared very small. It was one thing to bring the autogiro safely to earth in a place like this, and another to land a big plane.

When she had selected her spot, she determined to try "fish-tailing." She glided with considerable speed toward her field; as she approached it, she swung her airplane from side to side, exposing the flat side of the plane's body to the air so as to kill the speed.

Her companions, who had no idea what she was doing, looked at Mary Eliska in alarm. Had she lost control of the plane, and were they about to be dashed to pieces?

But a glance at their pilot's calm, confident expression allayed their fears. This girl knew what she was doing! They need not be afraid.

Often at the ground school she had been compelled to land on a given spot—such as a square of canvas; it was no wonder that she now felt sure of herself. A moment later she came down on the very mark that she had selected.

"Pretty neat!" exclaimed Worth, in admiration.

Mary Eliska turned off the engine and prepared to get out of the plane. But the Sergeant stopped her.

"You stay in here, Mary Eliska!" he ordered. "This is no place for a girl."

"But I have to show you where the camp is," she protested.

"Then show us from here! And remember, too, that you are our pilot. If anything happened to you, we couldn't get out of this swamp."

Mary Eliska saw the reasoning in this last argument, and agreed to remain inside of the cabin until she should be summoned. She sat there tensely, while the three men advanced cautiously towards the trees at the center of the island.

They had not gone more than a dozen yards when a shot rang out from behind a tree, and a bullet whizzed past over their heads. A cry burst from Mary Eliska's lips, then an exclamation of relief at the assurance that her companions were unhurt.

"So they're still here!" she thought, excitedly, clasping her hands so tightly together that they grew numb with the pressure. "Oh, if the men only get them without being shot!"

The officers' pistols replied rapidly to the shot from the thieves, in such quick succession that Mary Eliska could almost imagine that she was in an actual war zone. But the volley lasted only a moment, for the thieves were short of bullets since "Slats'" disappearance, and before anyone was hurt, "Beefy" and "Jake" surrendered to Sergeant Worth.

Watching the whole proceeding from the window of the plane, Mary Eliska drew a deep sigh of relief. Then suddenly she remembered the third member of the gang—the man nicknamed "Doc." Where was he? Hiding in the background, waiting to shoot them all down when they were off guard?

Cautiously, therefore, Mary Eliska leaned out of the side of the plane and called to Sergeant Worth to come back to her. Leaving the two thieves in charge of the other men, who instantly handcuffed them, Worth returned to the airplane, smiling over his easy victory.

With his assistance Mary Eliska jumped out of the cabin and whispered her warning into his ear. The man scowled in disappointment.

"This fellow may be waiting for you, Mary Eliska," he said. "You stay right here—behind the plane, while I go find out where he is."

Mary Eliska did as she was told, expecting every moment to hear renewed shooting.

"Where's your other man?" she heard Worth shout, as he approached the prisoners.

"Gone!" snarled Jake. "Two of 'em sneaked off. Double-crossed us, and took the kale!"

"Money? What money?" demanded Worth, instantly, hoping to surprise the man into a confession.

"Nothin'. None of your business," muttered Jake, seeing that he had made a mistake by saying too much.

"You needn't try to hide anything," remarked the officer, contemptuously. "We know all about the bank robbery—and other jobs, too—that you fellows can account for. You'll serve plenty of time!"

Impatient at the delay, Mary Eliska felt that she had to be at the scene of action, to hear what had happened to the "Doc," who evidently was not on the island. She ran forward, just in time to hear Jake's explanation.

"One fellow made off with the girl in the plane yesterday morning," he said. "The other guy must have beat it later on in the day—while us two was still asleep. Took the boat and the cash. We ain't got nothin' here of any value—outside of food.... Huh! Why, if there ain't Mary Eliska herself!"

Angry as she was at this insolent manner of addressing her, Mary Eliska could not help smiling at the man's consternation. But she was terribly disappointed to learn that the money was gone. That meant that they had failed to accomplish the main purpose with which she had set out—to restore to the innocent bank depositors the savings which they had lost through no fault of their own.

"Perhaps the money's over on the island in the ocean," she suggested hopefully. "I had to help bury some boxes of jewels there while I was a prisoner—and those may still be there, too. Shall we fly over immediately, Sergeant Worth?"

"You know the way?" the latter inquired, in surprise. His admiration for this plucky girl was growing every minute.

"Oh, yes, I think so. We can make these men direct us if I forget. They are sure to know."

After a hasty search of Black Jack Island was completed—to make sure that the third man was not still in hiding—the party returned to the airplane, and Mary Eliska made ready to take off once more. This was an exceedingly difficult feat, with a large plane, but the experienced aviatrix calculated everything before she made the attempt, and the airplane left the ground at the exact time that she had planned. She directed it eastward now, out over the Georgia coast, on to the Atlantic. She remembered the course perfectly, spotting the identical island without any help from the prisoners, and landed on the wide barren beach without any difficulty.

Once they were out of the plane she recalled even the hiding-place, where "Slats" had placed the jewels, and she led the way through the underbrush. Unrolling the stone, and pushing the sand aside at her direction, the detectives brought out the three tin boxes which Mary Eliska herself had been forced to help conceal.

Opening them up right there by twisting the locks, the officers gazed at their contents in speechless amazement. Two diamond necklaces, a string of real pearls, innumerable rings and pins and watches. And a bracelet of priceless emeralds!

"Whew!" exclaimed Sergeant Worth, the perspiration running down his face.

"The Van Tyn diamonds!" declared one of the detectives. "And these pearls solve the mystery of that robbery at the Kenworthy estate!"

"Yeah. And that big jewelry store in Atlanta!" added another, breathlessly. "Say, does this uncover a lot of money? I'll tell the world!"

"It'll mean a nice little reward for Mary Eliska," remarked Sergeant Worth, with a smile.

Mary Eliska shook her head.

"No, I don't want it," she said. "If there is any reward, it can be divided among you men. You faced the guns!"

"But Mary Eliska ———"

Mary Eliska held up her hand. "I mean it," she said. "If you can't use it yourselves, perhaps your wives—or your children can."

"It would mean heaven to me," murmured one of the detectives—a quiet man, who had scarcely spoken during the entire flight. "My child needs an operation———"

"Then it's settled," concluded Mary Eliska. Suddenly she glanced timidly at Sergeant Worth, almost as if she were about to ask a favor. "Could we eat, Sergeant?" she asked. "I'm so hungry."

"Why of course!" replied the latter. "I'm sorry, I'd forgotten all about lunch—but it must be way past noon. Griggs," he added to one of his men, "you go and unload that basket."

It was an oddly assorted group that sat down to that picnic lunch on the beach—the two thieves, the three police officers, and the slender, fair-haired girl in her linen flying suit. Mary Eliska could not help smiling to herself as she thought of what Jackson Carter's horror would be at her association with people like these. Yet how foolish he was! One look at Sergeant Worth's face, kindly as it was, assured her that she was well protected with him at her side.

She wished that she might stop at Soldiers' Camp Island on the return trip, but it was out of her way, and already the plane was loaded to its capacity. So she mapped her return trip in a straight line back to the city of Jacksonville. Late that afternoon she landed at the airport, where the group separated, the detectives and the prisoners taking one taxi to the police station, Mary Eliska taking another to a hotel.

It was only when she was quietly in her own room, with her bag unpacked, that she realized how tired she was. What a strain she had been through! How she longed for relaxation of some kind! If only she had Louise with her—or somebody else from Spring City!

She rested for an hour before dinner, but the thought of eating alone was not pleasant, with only a newspaper for her companion. She brightened, however, when the idea came to her to call her Aunt Sally on the long-distance wire. It would mean a great deal to hear that dear, familiar voice.

She did not have time after dinner to put in the call immediately, for just as she was leaving the dining-room, she was herself summoned to the telephone. Who could it be, she wondered. Nothing interesting, probably, for none of her friends knew where to get her. No doubt it was Captain Magee, congratulating her on the success of the afternoon.

To her surprise, it was Jackson Carter who said, "Hello!

"Can I drive in to the hotel to see you, Ann?" he asked.

"How is your mother, Mr. Carter?" she inquired, instead of answering his question.

"She's all right." "Am I to meet her?"

The young man coughed in embarrassment. He would have liked to have kept the truth from her, but he could not lie to a girl like Mary Eliska, any more than he could lie to his mother.

"I guess I better tell you, Ann—mother's old-fashioned—and—she doesn't approve of you. She says I may not invite you out here again. I'm awfully sorry—I've tried to make her understand———-"

"Please don't bother," interrupted Mary Eliska, coolly. "Perhaps it is better that an acquaintance like ours end as casually as it started.... Good-by, Mr. Carter. And thank you again for rescuing me."

"Ann! Ann! I can't let you go out of my life———" But she had quietly replaced the receiver.

The tears came to her eyes, but she told herself that she was foolish. She would probably have to get used to things like this, if she meant to do a man's work in the world. It was worth it. Oh, the glorious feeling of power which she had experienced that morning when she stepped into that huge plane, and knew that she could control its flight! The satisfaction of conquering difficulties, solving problems, being of use to others as she had been today! Yes, it was worth all the snubs of every society woman in the United States!

For a moment she sat beside the telephone, waiting to get control of herself, when she suddenly heard a beloved voice behind her. Two voices—three voices—then two pairs of arms around her neck! Jax Gray's and Louise Mackay's—and Ted was standing behind them!

"Oh!" she gasped, squeezing both girls at once. "Am I dreaming? It's too good to be true!"

"Are you O.K., darling?" demanded Louise, kissing her chum again and again. "When we read about your long flight south, and then heard nothing of you for three days, we got worried. So we managed to hop off."

"You angels!" cried Mary Eliska. "Oh, I might have known you would! When everything looked blackest———"

"You mean about being lost in the Okefenokee Swamp?"

"Worse than that.... Let me call Aunt Sally, while you get a room, and I'll tell you the whole story after that.... But first tell me how long you can stay."

"Ted and I can only stay 'til tomorrow morning," replied Louise, "so long as you are all right. But Jax Gray'll keep you company—she thought you might be lonely——"

"That isn't half of it!" interrupted Mary Eliska. "I was so lonely tonight that I couldn't eat. I just felt sick. Worse, far worse than my flight to France, because that was over quickly, and this just seemed to stretch out interminably."

"Now do call your Aunt," urged Jax Gray. "She must be dying to hear from you—and we'll have you all evening. By the way, I'm rooming with you?"

"Nowhere else in the world!" exclaimed Mary Eliska, giving the girl an extra hug in her joy. "Room 420—and I'll be there in a minute!"

Chapter 11.10
Susie Disappears

When Mary Eliska entered her hotel bed-room after the conversation with her Aunt Sally over the long-distance wire, she found two pleasant surprises awaiting her. The first of these that she saw was her trunk, sent on from Atlanta. The second was a telegram from the Pitcairn Autogiro Company.

Her new roommate, who was bending over her own suit-case, looked up expectantly.

"Good news, Mary Eliska?" she inquired.

"Splendid!" replied the other girl. "The parts for my 'Ladybug' have been shipped from Miami, where the company has some autogiros on exhibition. They'll be at the Jacksonville Airport tomorrow."

"Then your Ladybug is damaged?" asked Jax Gray, who had heard nothing of the story as yet, beyond the bare facts that had been in the newspapers. All that she had read was that Mary Eliska, famous aviatrix, who had been lost in the Okefenokee Swamp for several days, had turned up in Jacksonville, Florida.

"Yes, quite a smash-up," answered Mary Eliska. "But I wasn't in it. Another girl was flying——" She stopped abruptly. "Wait 'til Lou and Ted are with us, Jax Gray, so I can tell the story all at once. I'm rather fed up with it myself. I'd loads rather hear what you've been doing at Spring City."

"O.K.," agreed her companion, cheerfully, and proceeded to report to Mary Eliska all the news that she could remember.

"What I can't understand," remarked Mary Eliska, a few minutes later, as she unpacked her trunk and took a flowered chiffon which she decided to wear, "is how everyone finds me at this hotel. I didn't know where I'd be staying when I sent those telegrams yesterday."

"I can answer that," replied Jax Gray, immediately. "It's your friends at the City Hall. The Chief of Police there directed us. It was Ted's idea to go to him, for I never would have thought of it."

"Ted knows that Lou and I have a failing for police stations and Court Houses," laughed Mary Eliska, recalling their experience in Canada the previous winter.

Five minutes later the girls joined the young Mackays on a cool upper porch of the hotel, where they were able to be by themselves. It was then that Mary Eliska told her story, first extracting a promise from the group never to mention the kidnapping episode to anyone else, lest the news get back to her Aunt Sally. The other girls listened in amazement, now and then interrupting with exclamations of horror at the outrage of it all. Ted sat grimly silent, more angry than anyone.

"And if you hadn't escaped, we probably shouldn't have gotten there in time," observed Louise. "To rescue you, I mean. Because of course they meant to kill you in the end."

"Did you realize that at the time?" asked Jax Gray.

"Not exactly," replied Mary Eliska. "Though I really feared something much worse. I thought they would imprison me on that island in the ocean, and let me die of starvation. And I was horribly afraid of those men. I tried to keep with Susie until they went away."

"It was that bank robbery that saved your life," remarked Louise. "And spelled ruin for them. If they hadn't been so greedy——"

"Exactly!" exclaimed Mary Eliska. "That's one reason why I feel it's my solemn duty to try to catch the fourth man, and get that money back. I'm really the only person who could identify him—except Susie."

"Do you honestly think she'll reform?" asked Jax Gray.

"I hope so. If those new parts for the autogiro really come tomorrow, we'll fly over and get her, Jax Gray."

"I'm crazy to see her," returned the latter. "And I'd enjoy going to the jail to see those two prisoners, and gloat over their punishment!"

"Jax Gray's as vindictive as I am!" joked Louise. "Remember all the dark futures I used to wish for Bess Hulbert?"

"Poor Bess!" sighed Mary Eliska. "She certainly got hers——"

Thinking that the girls had heard enough of Mary Eliska's unpleasant experiences, Ted interrupted them by suggesting that they all go somewhere and have something to eat.

"If it's cool, I'm for it," agreed Louise, jumping up and putting her hand through her husband's arm.

"You're not too tired, are you, Mary Eliska?" she inquired.

"Not a bit!" protested the girl. "I feel like a new person since you three arrived.... There's a lovely screened tea-garden across the street that looks awfully attractive. Shall we go there?"

Mary Eliska was right in her impression; the place was charming. Instead of the customary artificial flowers or tiny bouquets so often seen in restaurants, real rose-bushes showered their profusion of fragrance all about the edges of the screen garden. Surprisingly, everyone was hungry; the three visitors because they had eaten only a light picnic supper, Mary Eliska because she had been too homesick to eat much alone. The food proved as delightful as the surroundings, and they all enjoyed it immensely.

While Jax Gray was, eating her ice, she noticed some people that she seemed to remember—sitting at a table in back of Mary Eliska. But she could not place them.

"Mary Eliska," she said softly, "see that young man over there at that table back of you—to the right—with an older woman? Don't turn around now, he's staring at us.... He looks sort of familiar to me, and I'm positive I've seen that woman before. Do you know them, or are they people I have met at Palm Beach sometime, one of those winters when we went to Florida?"

Mary Eliska waited a moment, and then casually turned her head in the direction which Jax Gray had indicated. The boy was Jackson Carter!

In relating her story of the rescue by the two boys in the canoe, Mary Eliska had not even mentioned their names, and had omitted entirely her visit to the Carter home. After her telephone conversation with Jackson this evening, she had decided to forget all about him.

She noticed that Jax Gray was smiling and nodding.

"I remember her now," she explained. "A Mrs. Carter—she chummed a lot with mother at Palm Beach. And that's her son—he wasn't more than fourteen the last time I saw him.... I think I'll go over and speak to them." Mary Eliska flushed and tried to hide her embarrassment by talking to Louise and Ted about their flight. But Jax Gray came back in a moment.

"I've got an invitation for us, Mary Eliska!" she announced. "Finish your lemon ice, and come over and meet the Carters. All of you!"

Mary Eliska hesitated. She did not know what to say. Evidently Jackson had not recognized her, or else was deliberately concealing the fact that he knew her.

"All right," agreed Louise, rising and pulling Ted by the hand, for her youthful husband was s'til shy about meeting the people whom he termed the "four hundred." But his manners were as good as anyone's, and Louise was always proud of him.

They stepped over to the table, Mary Eliska reluctantly following them.

"Mrs. Carter, I want you to meet Mrs. Mackay—our chaperon." Jax Gray winked slyly at Louise. "And Mary Eliska, the famous aviatrix! And Mr. Mackay.... And this is Mr. Carter."

The young people bowed in recognition of the introduction, but Jackson gave no sign that he had ever seen Mary Eliska before.

"Mrs. Carter says that so long as our chaperon is leaving tomorrow, we must come over and stay at her house, Mary Eliska," Jax Gray said. "You see, Mrs. Carter," she continued, turning to the older woman, "we're not so strict in the North about chaperons as you are here—but Mary Eliska's aunt would like to be. It really worries her to have her niece batting around alone in an airplane."

Horribly embarrassed, her eyelids fluttering so that she could not see anybody distinctly, Mary Eliska tried to summon words to decline the invitation. It would be impossible for her to accept.

"We'd love to have you, girls," Mrs. Carter assured them. "For as long as you can stay.... How I would enjoy seeing your mother, Dorothy! You must tell me all about her."

"I'm awfully sorry," stammered Mary Eliska, still avoiding Jackson's eyes, "but I'm afraid we can't possibly make it. The fact is, I am expecting to get my autogiro tomorrow, and that will take us away from Jacksonville."

"Bring it out to our place!" urged the young man, with the deepest pleading in his tone. It was the first time that he had spoken, and everybody was surprised at his eagerness. That is, everybody except Mary Eliska—who had heard the same pleading over the telephone a few hours before.

His mother smiled approvingly. She was glad to see that her son was interested in Jax Gray, for her father John and mother Deanna were wealthy people, of unquestionable social position.

But, had she known it, Jackson did not even see Jax Gray. He was lost in admiration of Mary Eliska—The Aviatrix, as he thought of her. In her pale chiffon dress she looked absolutely ravishing. How could he ever have doubted that she was of good family?

"No, thank you ever so much, but we can't possibly," Mary Eliska repeated. "We—or rather I—have work to do. Of course if Jax Gray wants to go———"

She looked at the other girl fearfully. How she would hate to lose her!

Jax Gray's reply, however, was reassuring.

"No, Mrs. Carter, I must stick with Mary Eliska. It isn't often that my mother gives in and lets me go off like this, and I mean to take advantage of it Besides, there's adventure ahead!"

Mrs. Carter sighed; these modern girls were beyond her comprehension. She was thankful that her only child was a boy.

While Jax Gray was saying good-by, explaining that the Mackays had to be up early in the morning, Jackson managed a whisper to Mary Eliska.

"When can I see you, Ann? I just *must*!"

Mary Eliska smiled; she was in command of herself again. She had won in a difficult situation.

"Some time when we both winter at Palm Beach or Miami," she replied, lightly, as she nodded good-by to his mother.

The young man's interest in Mary Eliska had not escaped Jax Gray's notice. When they had left the restaurant, she remarked, teasingly:

"You certainly made a hit, my dear. But I'm just as glad you turned down their invitation. The Carters have a marvelous home, I believe, but they're about 1890 vintage. They don't know that there was a War."

"Well, we really haven't any time to lose," was her companion's reply. "I'm almost afraid now that Susie will be gone when we get to that island. And I'm in a hurry to help the police trace that other thief with the money."

"Adventure is right!" laughed Jax Gray, as the girls said good-by to Ted and Louise, and went to their room.

The Mackays left soon after dawn the following morning, but Mary Eliska and Jax Gray had decided to have a good sleep. They did not waken until after ten o'clock, when they heard the telephone ringing in their ears.

It was Jax Gray who answered it.

"Oh, hello, Jackson!" she said, with a wink at Mary Eliska. "I used to call you by your first name, so I suppose I might as well now. How's everything?"

"Just fine," replied the young man. "And Jax Gray—may I speak to Mary Eliska?"

"O.K.," answered the girl, holding the telephone towards Mary Eliska.

"Not awake yet!" yawned Mary Eliska, burying her head in the pillow.

"She says she's not awake yet," explained Jax Gray, laughingly. "Better call later, Jackson—after we get some breakfast."

Replacing the telephone, she turned to her roommate.

"That big boy certainly fell for you, Mary Eliska!" she exclaimed, still unaware of the fact that Jackson had not met her for just the first time.

"Well, I didn't fall for him," the other stated, firmly. "And Jax Gray, please, from now on I'm not at home when he calls."

Jax Gray was surprised at this announcement; it was unlike Mary Eliska not to be friendly to everybody. Why had she taken such a dislike to a young man as handsome as Jackson Carter?

"May I ask you a personal question, Mary Eliska?" she inquired.

"Why certainly, Jax Gray!"

"Are you engaged to Ralph Clavering—and is that why you're turning other men away?"

Mary Eliska laughed at the idea.

"No, Jax Gray—I'm not engaged to anybody. And I don't want to be. I want to be free for a while. But not from my girl-friends!" she added hastily, reaching over and giving Jax Gray a hug. "Oh, Jax Gray, if I could ever tell you what it meant to me to have you three breeze in last night! Honestly, I was awfully low."

"It was Lou's idea," explained Jax Gray. "I guess she thought you would be—so far away from everybody—even if you hadn't been in any difficulty."

"Lou's a peach," observed Mary Eliska.

They ordered a tray sent up to their room, and lingered lazily over their breakfast. Before they had finished the telephone rang again. This time it was the Jacksonville Airport, informing Mary Eliska that the new parts for her autogiro had arrived.

"I'll have to hurry!" she said to Jax Gray. "I don't want to lose a minute now."

"Just what are your plans, Mary Eliska?" asked the other girl, as she, too, started to dress.

"Go to the airport and have the parts for the Ladybug put into a plane. Then fly to Soldiers' Camp Island, taking another mechanic along. I'll help this man fix the autogiro—collect Susie—and fly back here."

"You really believe you can fix it in one day?"

"Yes, of course. Why not!"

"Well," said Jax Gray slowly, "I think if you don't mind, I'll stay here. You'll need all the space you can get in your plane to carry those parts to the wreck. And I'd be fearfully bored standing around while you work."

"I guess you're right," agreed Mary Eliska. "It would be better for me to take two men—a pilot and a mechanic. Because I can't fly this hired plane back again—I'll have to pilot the Ladybug."

"And you have to bring Susie too," Jax Gray reminded her.

Mary Eliska lost no time in getting ready, and she was pleased to have left the hotel before Jackson Carter had a chance to telephone again. She found a "repair" plane waiting for her at the airport, and she made note of the new parts for the autogiro that were already packed into it. Two men were prepared to go with her—one a pilot, the other a mechanic. For once in her life Mary Eliska was to ride as a passenger.

The day was hot and dry, but over the swamp the air seemed cooler and fresher. The rainy season was late, everybody said; by this time of year the swamp was usually flooded.

As the plane flew over the desolate expanse, Mary Eliska smiled to herself at the familiarity of the landscape. She was getting to be an authority on the Okefenokee Swamp; she never need fear again being lost in its southern part, at least. Although the pilot had a reliable map, he found Mary Eliska's directions helpful, and before noon they came down on Soldiers' Camp Island.

The first thing that struck their notice was the autogiro, still leaning over on its side, looking pathetically helpless in its plight. But Susie was not in sight.

While the men unloaded their tools and the new parts for the damaged plane, Mary Eliska went in search of the girl she had left there two days before. It was queer, she thought, that Susie had not come out to meet them at the sound of their motor. Was it possible that she was sick—or only asleep?

The island was a comparatively large one, several miles in length, and Mary Eliska decided immediately to explore it. Susie might be waiting somewhere within its depths, helpless or hurt, if she had fallen on her injured ankle. It would be necessary to make a thorough search.

Mary Eliska ran back to the autogiro to inquire whether the men needed her help, and explained what she was about to do.

"We don't need you yet, Miss," replied the mechanic. "Later on, when she's almost finished, you can help me look her over, and take her up for a test."

"By the way, Mary Eliska," put in the pilot, "did you think to bring any food for lunch? I only brought water."

Mary Eliska shook her head regretfully. How could she have been so stupid? Had her excitement over regaining her autogiro destroyed all her common sense?

"I'm awfully sorry," she said. "I just plain forgot! And I usually have some in the autogiro, but those thieves took it out.... Wait, though! There may be some on the island. We left a half a dozen cans with this girl."

A search of the little "houses" farther in on the island revealed what she had been hoping for—the remainder of the supplies the boys had left with Susie, consisting of two cans of baked beans, tea, coffee, sugar and canned milk. This ought to be enough for their lunch, and she ran back immediately to the men with the good news.

For the next two hours Mary Eliska searched the island diligently, calling Susie by name at frequent intervals. But no answer came in reply, and she found no trace of the girl. Susie had completely vanished.

Weary and hungry she returned to the shore of the island where the men were working, and was delighted at the progress they had made. The job was almost finished.

"I can't find the girl," she told them. "But I've collected enough fire-wood to cook our coffee and beans. We'll have our lunch in a little while."

Two hours later the autogiro was finished, ready for its flight back to Jacksonville. The engine was running smoothly; Mary Eliska climbed into the cock-pit and took it up in the air for a test flight. She found everything satisfactory; dipping low, she gave the others the signal to leave. With her Ladybug in the lead, the two planes made record time back to Jacksonville.

"She's as good as new," she told the mechanic joyfully, after both planes had landed, and she was paying her bill. "I wish I could fly her right over to my hotel."

"I believe you almost could," remarked the man, admiringly. "Land her at the front entrance, like a taxi-cab!"

"I'm afraid I'll have to take an ordinary cab," sighed Mary Eliska, spotting one out near the gate. "Thanks a lot—and good-by! I'm in a hurry to be back."

It was after six when Mary Eliska ascended the steps of her hotel, and found Jax Gray waiting for her on the porch, trying in vain to keep cool.

"Where's Susie?" she demanded, immediately.

"Gone!" replied Mary Eliska. "I searched the whole island carefully—but not a sign of her!"

"Where could she go?" demanded Jax Gray. "Do you 'spose some canoe picked her up—maybe those same boys that rescued you?"

Mary Eliska shook her head. Not those boys, any way! "What I'm afraid of is that the fourth man of the gang—the only one who escaped, you know—picked her up in his boat."

"Not so good—not so good," muttered her companion.

"No, it isn't. Just when I thought Susie had reformed, too—and cut free from those criminals!" Mary Eliska uttered a deep sigh.

"Well, let's forget her," suggested the other girl, cheerfully. "I've been waiting all afternoon to take you for a swim—so let's go, and have our dinner later. I understand there's a marvelous pool a couple of blocks away."

Mary Eliska's face brightened. What could possibly be better on such a hot day!

"Let's go!" she exclaimed. "Lead me to it."

After her disappointment at losing Susie, and her strenuous day in the heat, the relaxation of swimming in the lovely out-door pool was exactly what Mary Eliska needed. The water was cool and refreshing, and the surroundings charming.

For half an hour Mary Eliska swam lazily about, resting now and then on her back, occasionally mounting the board for a dive. At last she felt that she had had enough, and seated herself on the edge of the pool, dangling her feet in the water, and watching Jax Gray perform all sorts of fancy dives, for the other girl was a real champion.

"What a marvelous girl Jax Gray is," Mary Eliska was thinking, when she was suddenly startled by the sound of a masculine voice, almost in her very ear.

"Ann! Think of finding you here!"

Mary Eliska squirmed a little, thinking that the man must have made a mistake in thinking she was some other girl. For the time being, she forgot all about her middle name.

"Mary Eliska," insisted the voice.

Turning about, she saw Jackson behind her,

"How do you do?" she said, coolly.

The young man became embarrassed at her manner. He did not know what to say.

"Jax Gray is a marvelous diver," he muttered, though it wasn't that that he wanted to talk about.

"Yes, I think so," agreed Mary Eliska.

There was a silence. The girl made no effort to be entertaining.

"You really are the girl who flew across the ocean alone, and won that big prize?" he persisted.

"Yes." Mary Eliska made a half-hearted gesture to repress a yawn. Jackson Carter needn't think he could buy her favor by flattery!

"But why didn't you tell Hal and me that, when we found you in the swamp?"

"It had no particular bearing on the subject, that I could see."

"If my mother had known that——"

"If your mother didn't wish to receive me at her home," interrupted Mary Eliska, "there was no reason in the world why she should. Everyone has a right to her own opinion!"

"But now that we've been formally introduced, it's different," he urged. "Please tell me how long you'll be in Jacksonville."

"We're leaving tomorrow," she said, rising. "And will you please excuse me—as I see Jax Gray going to the dressing-room?"

Chapter 11.11
The Island in the Ocean

"I certainly am sorry we don't have Susie with us," remarked Jax Gray, as the girls sat down to their late dinner that evening, after their refreshing swim. "I thought she'd be better than a 'talkie' for amusement."

"Yes, you would have enjoyed her, Jax Gray," agreed Mary Eliska, picking up the menu and studying it with a great deal of interest. "I'm going to order everything here, Jax Gray. I'm simply starved."

"So am I, though I ought to be ashamed to admit it. You should have seen the lunch I ate!"

"And you should have seen my lunch!" returned Mary Eliska. "We forgot to carry anything, but fortunately Susie had left beans and coffee on the island."

"Is that all you had?"

Mary Eliska nodded, and gave her order to the waiter.

"I'd certainly like to know where Susie is now," she remarked, after she had satisfied the sharpest pangs of hunger with an iced fruit-cup.

"Yes, so would I," agreed Jax Gray. "Her disappearance will make it a lot harder to trace that other thief.... Do you really expect to do anything about hunting him, Mary Eliska?"

"Indeed I do! Tomorrow's only the twenty-seventh, and I don't have to report to Atlanta until July first. I'm going to use those four days."

"But what could you possibly do?" inquired Jax Gray. "How would you know where to go—without even a suggestion from Susie?"

"I have a theory," explained the other girl. "Wait 'til I eat some of this beef-steak, and I'll tell you about it."

"I'm crazy to hear it, because I'll be with you all the time. Mother said I must start back home the first of July—the day you go to Atlanta. I have my ticket bought."

For a few moments Mary Eliska ate her dinner in silence, enjoying every mouthful as only a hungry person can. Then, lowering her voice so that there was no danger of being overheard, she told her chum her plan.

"I've thought it all out," she began. "This is what must have happened: That thief—the 'Doc,' as the gang called him—took the boat and the money the day after the bank robbery, when he woke up and found that Susie and her husband had flown away in the autogiro, and the other two were still asleep. His idea was to get out of the swamp to the St. Mary's or some other river, that would take him to the ocean."

"And get on a steamer?" demanded Jax Gray. "But Mary Eliska, if he did that, he's out of the country by now."

"I'm not so sure of that. A canoe trip like that would take a good while—the Okefenokee is fifty miles at least from the coast. And he'd be afraid to take a train—or an automobile, for fear of being seen. Besides, I don't think he'd take a steamer right away. He'd want to go to that island first."

"In his canoe?" inquired the other, skeptically.

"No, of course not. He'd hire a motor-boat—or steal one."

"I still don't understand why he'd want to get to that island," remarked Jax Gray.

"For two reasons," explained Mary Eliska. "One because he expected to pick up those jewels—which we have already taken away—and the other reason is that the gang has arrangements with some party that owns a steamer, to stop at the island on certain specified dates. That would be his way of getting out of the country."

"It does sound plausible," admitted Jax Gray. "What a brain you have, Mary Eliska!"

"Not a bit of that, Jax Gray! It's only that I've been so closely associated with these criminals that I'm beginning to see their motives."

"And where does Susie come into all this?"

"The man must have seen her on Soldiers' Camp Island, from his canoe. Or rather, he saw the wrecked autogiro, and knew she must be there."

"And forced her to go with him?"

"Probably. He didn't want to take any chances, leaving her free to help the police."

Mary Eliska paused for a moment to eat the salad with which she had been served, and glanced about the dining-room. No one seemed to know her, or notice her—for that she was sincerely thankful.

It was not until they had finished their dinner and found a cool, secluded spot on the veranda, that she went on with her plan.

"What I mean to do," she said quietly, "is to fly back to the camp on Black Jack Island early tomorrow. Not that I expect to find anyone there—but merely to get my direction—to go on to that island in the ocean. I don't know its name, so I couldn't look it up on the map."

"You really expect to catch those two on that island?" asked Jax Gray, excitedly. "Will you take the police along?"

"No! I don't want to tell them a word about all this, except to say that I am going scouting about the country, and to ask for a couple of revolvers.... And, in answer to your first question, I don't really expect to find Susie and the 'Doc' there yet. But I believe they'll be along soon."

"And we wait for them there?"

"Yes. Take them unawares. Susie will probably be on our side, and we can plan something with her.... Of course this is all only theory. Maybe there isn't a thing in it. That gang was slick; they seemed to know how to drop right off the face of the earth. And I believe this man may be the cleverest of them all. He was quiet; it's the boasting kind, like Susie's husband, who usually get caught first.... So you can see why I don't want any of the police along."

"We better take plenty of food, though," remarked Jax Gray.

"We will take some—but don't forget that we can easily fly back to the coast each night. The island is only a few miles out—it's nothing in a plane."

"True," admitted the other.

"And we'll keep our room here at the hotel, for we want some place as headquarters. We'll put a few over-night necessities into my bag."

"O.K. I'll order a roast chicken and a chocolate cake from the dining-room tonight."

"Oranges, too," added Mary Eliska. "They always taste so good. I mustn't forget to fill my thermos-bottles, either."

They went to bed early that night, in order to get a good start on the following morning. Jax Gray, who was particularly enthusiastic about the chocolate cake, carried the basket of food, while Mary Eliska took the handbag. They arrived at the City Hall immediately after breakfast, and were ushered right into Captain Magee's office.

"No news of the fourth man yet," he said, after he had greeted Mary Eliska and been introduced to Jax Gray. "But I've sent out a call for him by radio, so that all ships are to be warned to be on the look-out for a fellow of his description."

"There's something else I want to tell you," added Mary Eliska, "that may help to spot him. There is probably a girl with him." Then, rather reluctantly, she told what she knew of Susie, begging the Captain not to punish her too severely if she were found.

"And now," she concluded, "Jax Gray and I want to do a little scouting ourselves—in the autogiro—and I want to know whether you will lend us a couple of .38s for the undertaking."

The Captain smiled whimsically. What an unusual girl Mary Eliska was! No wonder she had done things no other girl had even tried.

"Of course I will," he said. "Though such a request is rather out of the ordinary———"

"This is an extraordinary occasion," remarked Mary Eliska.

"Don't you want a detective to go with you?" he asked.

"No, thank you, we haven't room in the autogiro. Besides, we don't want to waste his time—for it may be only a wild goose chase. But if you will lend us a couple of revolvers, I think we shall be safe."

"Can you shoot?"

"If it is necessary. But I don't think it will be. The girl got to be very friendly with me, after her husband was killed. If I had only gotten to her in time, I think I could have saved her. As it is, she may not have joined the man of her own free will. You see she had been hurt, and was partially helpless. So he could do most anything he liked with her, if he had her alone."

"Well, good luck to you!" said the Captain. "I certainly take off my hat to a plucky pair of girls."

When Mary Eliska and Jax Gray arrived at the airport they found the Ladybug in readiness for its second flight into the swamp. Mary Eliska inspected her, and piled in the equipment.

"I feel as if the Okefenokee Swamp were my home," she remarked, as she headed the autogiro in that direction. "I could almost fly it blind!"

"Don't!" warned Jax Gray. "Your friend the Doc is still at large, and he may be watching for us with a gun."

This was Jax Gray's first view of the swamp, and as they approached it, she was amazed at the vast expanse of it, stretching out in every direction.

"It's huge, isn't it?" she shouted to Mary Eliska, through the speaking-tube.

"Forty miles long and thirty wide," was the reply. "But we see only the southern end of it."

Conversation was difficult, so the girls gave it up until they came to Black Jack Island, where Mary Eliska had been held a prisoner.

"Shall we get out?" she asked her companion. "Or go straight on to the ocean?"

"Let's get out," replied Jax Gray. "They might possibly be here, you know. Besides, I'm crazy to see their camp."

Mary Eliska brought the autogiro to earth and the girls climbed out cautiously, their revolvers in readiness, lest the enemy appear. But there was no human sound—nothing but the birds and the insects.

"Watch out for snakes, Jax Gray!" warned Mary Eliska. "I'd almost rather meet the Doc than a snake, I believe."

They walked carefully towards the camp only to find it absolutely deserted.

"Let's look all around," suggested Mary Eliska, who remembered everything only too well. "We'll begin with the mess-tent."

Quietly at first, they snooped around, peering into boxes of provisions, looking under the cots, behind the tents, and, when they were quite sure that they were alone, they began to act more natural, to laugh and joke with each other.

Mary Eliska showed Jax Gray the tent which she had shared with Susie that one night of her captivity, and they both smiled over the sight of the magazine which had led to Mary Eliska's escape.

"We could even stay here all night if we had to," Jax Gray remarked. "Seems comfortable enough."

Mary Eliska shuddered.

"Never again!" she protested. "But we may as well eat some lunch before we fly to that island. I'm hungry."

"And thirsty. But it isn't so hot here as it was in Jacksonville."

"No. And the island out in the ocean ought to be cooler yet. You may like it so well that you'll want to spend the summer there. Only it has no tents or cots, like this camp."

"Thank you, I'd rather not play Robinson Crusoe," replied Jax Gray.

"Poor man!" sighed Mary Eliska. "If he'd only had an airplane, how simple it would have been for him."

They ate their lunch, and then, for the third time, Mary Eliska flew across the Okefenokee and over the coastal plain of Georgia—out to the barren island in the ocean where the treasure had been hidden. The desolate loneliness of the spot impressed her companion.

"You suggested this as a summer resort!" she remarked, when they had landed. "Why, I don't even see a fishing-boat!"

"That's just the trouble," replied Mary Eliska. "The first time I flew here—with Susie's husband—I looked about desperately for somebody to shout to for help. And there wasn't a soul! Nothing but ocean and sky.... Do you have your revolver handy, Jax Gray?"

"Yes. Right here. But I don't know much about shooting."

"I'm sure we shan't have to. I just want to explore. But 'be prepared' is our motto."

"I will be. I won't shoot you, either, Mary Eliska—you can count on me for that."

Climbing out of the autogiro they walked towards the center of the island where the sand was soft and the underbrush thick. Perhaps, thought Mary Eliska, there might be more hiding places than the one hole which she knew; it would be worthwhile to make a thorough search. On and on they plodded, the sand sinking into their shoes, the sun beating down upon them with full blast, for what trees there were, were not high enough to afford much shade. It was difficult to find the hiding place in such monotonous desolation, but at last she came to the spot.

"Somebody's been here since I came with the police!" she said to Jax Gray, "because we left the stones as we found them. But it looks as if the hole is empty."

She was correct in her surmise. After five minutes of pushing the sand away, Mary Eliska had assured herself that nothing was there.

"Let's go down to the opposite shore from the one we came in on," suggested Jax Gray. "And explore that."

"All right," agreed Mary Eliska. "If you can stand walking through this sand again...." She stopped abruptly, peering towards the shore. An instant later she dragged the other girl to the ground. "The Doc!" she whispered, hoarsely. "I saw him down by the water—maybe there's a boat coming!"

"What shall we do?" demanded Jax Gray, clutching her revolver tightly.

"Wait 'til he gets on—and follow in the autogiro. I've got plenty of gasoline.... Let's be creeping back to the Ladybug."

The girls kept well hidden behind the underbrush, crawling along on their hands and knees. Suddenly Jax Gray stopped; she had struck something solid. A canvas bag—two bags, stuffed full with something. Could it be the money?

Breathless, they both stopped while Mary Eliska untwisted with her pen-knife the coarse pieces of wire around the tops of the bags, and dumped out the contents. Money in an amount they had never seen before! Hundred-dollar bills in rolls that they had no time to count, bonds in thousand-dollar denominations!

"Hide it quickly, Jax Gray!" whispered Mary Eliska. "In your pockets, your riding-breeches—stuff some of it in my clothes—while I re-fill these bags with sand.... And have your revolver ready."

Chapter 11.12
The Money-Bags

Mary Eliska's theories regarding the fourth member of the gang of thieves had been only partially correct. As she had surmised, the "Doc" slipped off in the canoe from Black Jack Island while his companions slept, and he did stop at Soldiers' Camp. But it was not he who compelled Susie to go with him, but the girl herself who insisted upon accompanying him.

Susie's desire to reform had been sincere while Mary Eliska was with her. She had actually meant to cut free from the gang and go back to a normal mode of life—earning her living as she had done when she met her husband. No more sneaking about in fear of the law, no more hiding in that desolate camp in the Okefenokee Swamp! She would get a job at an airport, and take up flying again. She might even become famous—like Mary Eliska!

But unfortunately, after the famous aviatrix left her alone, her enthusiasm faded, and her faith in her ability to make a "come-back" died as suddenly as it was born. How could she ever hope to be free from the stain of her last two years of living—since her marriage to "Slats"? If Mary Eliska did not turn her over to the police authorities, someone else would. She might have to serve five or ten years in prison.

As the afternoon passed, she grew more and more miserable, more anxious to get away. If only she had a boat! If her ankle were not so painful, and her bandaged head not so conspicuous! If there were only some way for her to escape!

Having no appetite, she made no pretense at preparing any supper for herself. There was still some cold tea left from lunch; she decided to make that her meal, and an hour later she fell asleep where she was, right on the shore of the island.

The sun was rising over the swamp when she awakened the following morning, and she sat up with difficulty, cramped by her uncomfortable position in sleep.

"I might as well be dead—with Slats," she thought, morbidly, as she viewed the desolation around her. Again she tried to rise, when the soft sound of a paddle, dipping into the quiet water attracted her attention. She waited breathlessly. Were the boys coming back so soon?

Not long afterward a canoe came into sight. Susie's heart leaped with joy when she recognized who was guiding it. The Doc!

"Doc!" she cried. "Bill Rickers!" she added, using the man's real name. "It's Susie!"

The man pulled up to the island, amazed at finding her there. In the dawning light he saw the autogiro, lying half on its side.

"Where's Slats?" he demanded.

"Dead," answered the girl, immediately. "We had a wreck.... Will you take me with you?" she begged. "I'm almost crazy here all by myself."

"I wanted to make a get-away alone," he muttered.

"You have the money!" she cried, jumping at once to the correct conclusion. "Where are the other two men?"

"Asleep at Black Jack Island."

"And where are you going?"

"Out of the swamp—across the state, and then over to our island. The yacht's due there tomorrow—I want to be ready to go with it."

"O.K. with me," agreed Susie, as if she had been invited to go. "Let's push off now—or wait—we'll eat some breakfast. There's beans and cold tea."

"Maybe you could be some use," remarked the man, as he ate the meager breakfast. "If we could get a plane. And I am sorry for you, Kid—all alone here with Slats dead."

Susie gave him no chance to change his mind. Hobbling out to the little "house" where the boys had put the blanket and the extra food, she picked up the former, smoothed her dress and her hair, and returned to announce herself ready. They pushed off again, following the little stream out of the swamp.

"How do you expect to get across the state?" asked the girl, wearily, when late that afternoon, they brought their canoe to a landing. She had slept a little in the boat, but she was still very tired.

"Hitch-hike, I reckon," was the reply. "If we go hirin' any cars, somebody might get suspicious. Once at the coast, I count on rentin' a little fishing-boat from some fellow—one big enough to take us to the island."

"I can't hitch-hike," objected Susie.

"Don't then,—stay here," answered the man, indifferently.

"You know I can't do that, either. Let's go to that house over there, and see if we can't get some supper. Maybe they have an old Ford or a team of horses."

"You foot the bill?" he asked, shrewdly. With all that money in his possession, this man had no intention of spending any of it on anyone but himself.

Susie considered a moment. She hadn't any money at all—she always got what she wanted from her husband. But she owned some costly jewelry.

"I'll give you this diamond," she offered, "if you get me safe out of the country. And no walkin'!"

"O.K.," he muttered, his greedy eyes gleaming at the sight of the beautiful jewel. "You win. Go ask the woman yourself."

It was thus, by strange coincidence, that Susie and the Doc rode across Georgia that evening in the same Ford that had driven Mary Eliska and the boys to Jacksonville the night before. They reached a seaport town a little after midnight, and Susie succeeded in finding a house to stay in, though her companion preferred to remain out-doors, for he said he "didn't trust nobody." In the morning, when she joined him, he had rented an old motor-boat from a fisherman. "Rent" was the word he used, but he had not the slightest intention of returning it.

"You can run her, Susie," he said. "You're better at engines than I am, and she'll need coaxing. I'll steer."

It was a difficult cruise, for at times the engine coughed and died, and Susie had to try all sorts of methods to start her up again. When they finally came within sight of the island, the motor sputtered its last and refused to function any longer. The man managed to get the boat inshore by riding the waves, and using the oars kept at the bottom of the boat for just such an emergency.

About the time Mary Eliska and Jax Gray were eating their lunch on Black Jack Island, Susie and the Doc were making their landing. They pulled in at the opposite shore from the one which the girls later used in the autogiro. The man's first concern was with the hiding-place where he expected to find the boxes of jewels. His disappointment was keen when he discovered that they had been taken away.

"The cops has found us out!" he snarled angrily at Susie, as if it were her fault. "They'll be back again—I'll bet you! We gotta get out of here!"

"How?" demanded Susie. "Not in that boat?"

"Nope. Maybe the yacht will be along early, but it ain't likely. It usually runs after dark."

Dumping his bags in the sand not far from the hole, he tried to think what would be best to do.

"We gotta act quick, Susie—if the cops come. No use tryin' to put up a fight—with only one gun, and them two bags to guard.... You watch on that other shore, and I'll go back to the one we came in on. Whatever they come in—airplane or boat—we gotta swipe. Hide if you see anything comin', give 'em a chance to get into the island—and grab their boat. Give me a signal——"

"How?" she interrupted.

"You take the gun, and shoot when you're ready to push off.... If I see anybody on my side, I'll whistle, as near like a bird as I can." He grinned to himself; if the police came in anything but an airplane, he wouldn't bother with Susie. Let her face the music!

"O.K. But I couldn't run, Doc. Don't forget that."

"I ain't forgettin'," he returned.

They separated, and for two hours waited tensely, keeping a sharp look-out for the rescuing yacht, hoping against hope that it would arrive before the police. But at three o'clock their worst fears were realized. Susie saw the autogiro coming towards them, and hobbled off into the depths of the island to conceal herself. Lying flat on the sand, she was not able to identify the people who got out of the plane, but she could see that they both wore riding-breeches, and she believed they were men. So she kept still until they had disappeared into the underbrush. Then she began to creep laboriously, in a round-about fashion, to the autogiro.

Susie's progress was slow; she did not reach the plane until after Mary Eliska and Jax Gray had succeeded in emptying the bags of the money, and refilled them with sand. The girls had just recognized the man on the shore, and were creeping farther into the island, out of sight of him, when the shot of the pistol rang out above the roar of the ocean. They had no way of knowing that Susie had fired it.

A moment later they heard the rustle and crackle of underbrush, as the man came towards them. From her hiding place, now some distance from the bags, Mary Eliska raised her head cautiously, and saw the thief retrieve the bags with a grab. Then he dashed back to the shore, circled the island on the harder sand, and reached the opposite shore, where the autogiro was standing.

"Why doesn't he come after us?" whispered Mary Eliska, in amazement.

"He will soon, I'm afraid," replied Jax Gray hoarsely, clutching her revolver tightly. "But I'm going to shoot if he does!"

"So am I," answered Mary Eliska, calmly. "We've got the advantage—we're hidden."

Tensely they waited for five minutes—possibly ten; then something they had not thought of happened. The engine of the autogiro began to roar!

"They're stealing the Ladybug!" cried Mary Eliska, aghast at such a calamity. "Susie must be with him! Jax Gray, we can't let them do that!"

Regardless of the danger, Mary Eliska jumped up excitedly, and rushed to a clearing, where she had a view of the shore. She was just in time to see her beloved autogiro taxi along the beach and rise into the air.

Jax Gray dashed to her side, and the two girls stood together in helpless agony of spirit.

"Prisoners!" cried Jax Gray, at last, dropping her useless revolver into the sand.

"Robinson Crusoes!" added Mary Eliska, bitterly. "No better off! No plane!"

"With thousands of dollars!" groaned her companion, ironically. "Where money is no good at all!"

Chapter 11.13
The Broken Motor-Boat

The two girls continued to stand perfectly still on the sand, gazing at the retreating autogiro, which apparently was flying out farther over the ocean, and circling about in a strange manner.

"Why don't they fly towards the coast—towards Georgia?" demanded Jax Gray, in bewilderment.

Mary Eliska took her spyglasses out of her pocket, and squinted through them at the plane.

"I see a boat!" she exclaimed. "It must be that yacht the gang had arrangements with—to pick up the stuff they steal.... Yes, and that's another island.... Look, Jax Gray—see if I'm right."

The other girl took the glasses, and confirmed Mary Eliska's statement.

"Yes, it is.... And the Ladybug's landing on it.... Two people getting out—must be Susie and the Doc—and boarding the boat.... Mary Eliska! They're leaving the plane on the island!"

It was true indeed; taking turns at the glasses, the girls watched the yacht push off into the ocean.

"And here we are—and there's the Ladybug!" remarked Mary Eliska, grimly. "Just out of reach! The question is—how to get to her."

"Swim," suggested Jax Gray.

"Maybe you could, Jax Gray. But I'd be afraid of sharks."

"No, I don't think I'll try it either. Besides, the currents probably awfully strong."

"Oh, if Jackson and Hal would only rescue us now!" lamented Mary Eliska. "I wouldn't treat them a bit coolly."

The truth of that situation flashed upon Jax Gray.

"Was it Jackson Carter who rescued you before, Mary Eliska?" she asked.

Mary Eliska blushed. "Yes—it was," she admitted.

"Then why did you treat him so cruelly? I should think you would have been everlastingly grateful."

"I was. 'til his mother snubbed me—and he even doubted that I was a nice girl, just because I was traveling about alone. Then, when you introduced me, he wanted to be friends. Naturally I was hurt."

"I don't blame you! But Mrs. Carter is terribly old-fashioned."

While they were talking they had been slowly advancing towards the beach. Suddenly Mary Eliska spied a pile of articles near the spot where the autogiro had taken off.

"Look, Jax Gray!" she cried. "There's our stuff on the shore! The basket! My over-night bag—and I guess that other box is my tool kit, that I always keep in the plane! Come on!"

Breathlessly they dashed down to the shore and found that their belongings had indeed been tossed out of the autogiro.

"This proves that Susie's our friend!" cried Mary Eliska, hopefully. "She must have done this."

"Fine friend—to steal the plane!" returned Jax Gray. "She didn't have to go with that man!"

"Maybe not.... I'm afraid I can't understand her," mourned Mary Eliska. "Half good, and half bad——"

"Don't worry about Susie," urged her companion. "We have enough to think about for ourselves.... Still, it is nice that we eat tonight. Aren't we lucky to have that food?"

Jax Gray's forced cheerfulness brought their wretched plight back to Mary Eliska. How selfish she had been, to drag this other girl into this wretched business, when she came South to enjoy a holiday!

"Oh, Jax Gray!" she wailed, "I can't tell you how sorry I am—about bringing you in on this! I had no right to let you come. Your mother will never forgive me. It was different with Lou. When she set out on those wild adventures with me, her parents knew what to expect."

"Cheer up, we're not dead yet," was the reassuring reply. "Things aren't so black. Our enemy is safely out of the country, I take it, and Captain Magee is sure to look us up soon, when he doesn't hear from us. Besides, a friendly boat may come along at any minute."

"Jax Gray, you're one girl in a thousand!" cried Mary Eliska, giving her chum a hug. "You're just an old peach, not to be complaining. And for my own sake, I'm so thankful you're with me! Just imagine how I'd feel all alone!"

"Well, let's enjoy ourselves while the food lasts. Let's carry it inshore farther, and find a camping place. You have matches in your pocket?"

"Always!" replied Mary Eliska, thinking of her experience in Canada, when she had lost her matches with her plane. "I keep my pockets as full as a man's now, so if I am separated from my plane, I'm not helpless."

"Wise girl! You're learning, Mary Eliska. In a year or two you can do exploring, like Byrd—if there are any places left to explore."

"I guess Aunt Sally will make me sit home with folded hands after this," remarked Mary Eliska, soberly. "If we aren't rescued soon, it will be bound to get into the newspapers."

She stooped over and opened her tool-box, in which she carried all sorts of things besides actual tools. A flash-light, a knife, wire and string, even nails and nuts. And down in the corner she found several cans of food, which she thought the bandits had taken out when they emptied the plane of its gasoline that first day in the swamp.

"This is going to be a big help," she said. "We might even build a boat——"

"Out of underbrush?" asked Jax Gray, sarcastically. "Why, there isn't a decent tree on the whole island."

"I'm afraid you're right," sighed Mary Eliska. "Well, come on—let's get farther in, and take this money out of our clothing. Money can be a nuisance sometimes," she added, jokingly.

They picked up their possessions, Mary Eliska taking the tool-box, and Jax Gray the bag and basket of food, and hunted the shadiest spot they could find for their camp. Then they set about diligently unloading the money, and stuffing it into the over-night bag, which they first emptied of its contents.

"Let's see what we have to keep us alive," suggested Jax Gray, peering into the basket. "Three quarters of a chicken, ten oranges, almost a whole cake, four bananas, and eight rolls, besides that stuff you found. And one thermos bottle full of water—and another half full."

"It's the lack of water that's going to make it hardest," observed Mary Eliska. "If only the ocean weren't salty."

"Well, maybe we shan't even need all this! If we rig up some kind of signal of distress———"

"What shall we use? Clothing?"

"We might take hundred-dollar bills," laughed Jax Gray. "They're the most worthless things we have now."

"True. Only think how glad the people will be to get them back. Mrs. Carter, for instance.... I have it!" exclaimed Mary Eliska, brightly. "Our pajamas! Lucky we put them into the bag! We won't need them in the day-time, and no boat could see a signal at night anyway."

"Good idea!" approved her chum. "Now let's leave all this stuff here, and explore the island. We might find something—and anyhow, it will give us something to do."

Arm in arm they returned to the beach, where the sand was harder, and began to circle the island. They had gone half way around—to the opposite shore—when they both spied the old motor boat at the same moment. So great was their joy that they jumped up and down, hugging each other wildly.

"Of course that's what the man came in!" cried Mary Eliska. "We might have known he and Susie couldn't swim the ocean!"

They started to race to the boat, and arrived together. Jax Gray immediately set about examining it for leaks, while Mary Eliska gave her attention to the engine.

"It's broken," she said. "But I'm sure I can fix it. You know how I love to take motors apart. Just give me a day———"

"Darling, you can have a week if you want!" agreed Jax Gray, wild with happiness and relief. "We can make our food last."

"A day or maybe two ought to be enough. Then we can get to that other island and retrieve the Ladybug, before anybody even misses us!"

"It seems to be pretty sound," said Jax Gray. "No leaks, or anything. And there are even a couple of oars in the bottom, if the engine won't go."

"Oars wouldn't take us far, with such a heavy boat. But I'm sure I can fix the motor, and there's a can of gasoline here, besides what's in the tank.... But I don't believe I better start now—I'd just get it apart, and the daylight would be gone. I'll get up early tomorrow...."

"Suits me," agreed the other. "Now let's go back to our camp and fix some supper."

Both girls felt exceedingly cheerful as they collected sticks and lighted a fire. From one of Mary Eliska's cans they took out tea, but the rest they left unopened. The beans and jam and biscuits would keep until after the picnic food was gone.

"I have a bright idea," remarked Jax Gray, as she ate a leg of chicken. "Why couldn't we make chicken soup, out of the bones and sea-water? You have to put salt in it anyway, don't you?"

"Yes, but I'm afraid it would be too salty. It would make us so thirsty we'd want to drink all our water at once.... Still, we might try. We wouldn't be wasting anything."

"Too bad we haven't sore throats," said Jax Gray, still in a mood for joking.

"Sore throats!" repeated Mary Eliska, in amazement. "What's the connection between chicken soup and sore throats?"

"Nothing—I was only trying to think up ways to use salt water. We always have to gargle with salt water, at home, when we have sore throats. Doesn't your Aunt Sally make you do that?"

Her companion laughed. "No, we always use Listerine. But it's an idea. Think up some more, Jax Gray—we'll get some uses for it yet!"

They drank very sparingly of the water in the thermos bottle—one cup apiece—and decided to limit themselves to that at each meal. Sometimes they would substitute oranges—how thankful they were that they had brought so many!

Their light-hardheartedness diminished as the sun went down and darkness settled over the island. The loneliness of the night, the solemn roar of the ocean, the isolation of the island, appalled them. Not a human being except themselves—not a human sound!

But they had each other, and this comfort was so overwhelming to Mary Eliska, that it shut out all her other troubles. She could not help exulting every few minutes over the joy of having a companion, and Jax Gray was thankful that she was there, so long as Mary Eliska had to meet with such a fate. Yes, surely, they would make the best of things.

They slept well that night, for the sand, covered with leaves the girls had plucked, made a soft bed. A breeze from the ocean was so cooling that Mary Eliska had to pull their slickers over them as a covering. The stars shone in a friendly sky; hand in hand, as Mary Eliska and Lou had so often slept, the two girls dropped off into unconsciousness.

Their first thought upon awakening, after remembering where they were, was the autogiro. Their second was the motor-boat. They could not eat any breakfast until they had made sure that both of these were still safe.

"That island doesn't look very far away, does it?" Jax Gray remarked, after they had satisfied themselves upon these two questions.

"No, it doesn't," agreed Mary Eliska, taking out her spyglasses. "Only, you can't tell by appearances—they're so deceiving on the ocean."

They went back to their camp and breakfasted on oranges and rolls, finishing off with chocolate cake.

"Because we might as well enjoy it while it is fresh," Jax Gray said laughingly. Neither girl ever had to worry about indigestion.

All day long Mary Eliska worked on the engine, with her companion at her side, watching her in admiration. All that day and the next. On the evening of the twenty-ninth of June she announced that she was finished. The engine was condescending to run!

"Tomorrow we get the Ladybug!" Mary Eliska announced, exultantly. "And get back to Jacksonville in time to keep our engagements for July first!"

They were very happy as they sat beside their camp fire that night, eating their supper of baked beans and crackers and oranges. Happy and light-hearted, never thinking to glance at the sky, and to guess the meaning of the dark clouds that were gathering. Had they only done so, they might have gone to the autogiro that night in their repaired motor-boat—and saved their relatives and friends all the anguish and anxiety that they were to experience during the coming days.

But neither Mary Eliska nor Jax Gray gave the weather a thought; they went to sleep that night in the joyful expectation of returning to Jacksonville the following day.

At dawn the storm came, pouring down upon them in torrents, arousing the ocean to terrifying waves, shutting out the sight of the island where the autogiro was waiting—imprisoning the girls once more in their desolate loneliness. And now practically all of their food was gone!

Chapter 11.14
Searching Parties

When Mary Eliska and Jax Gray left Jacksonville Airport on the morning of June twenty-seventh in the Ladybug, and flew into the Okefenokee Swamp, they fully expected to telephone to their families that night, or at least to send a wire to them, as they had promised. So when Aunt Sally heard nothing from her niece she became anxious, and directed her chauffeur to drive her to Mrs. Gray's cottage.

Both women were established at Green Falls for the summer, which was the favorite resort of all Mary Eliska's friends from Spring City. It was there that the girl had called her aunt from Jacksonville, the night that Jax Gray and the Mackays had arrived. Only one telegram had she received since that time.

Mrs. Gray, who was less inclined to be nervous than Aunt Sally, tried to reassure the latter, saying that she realized how busy the girls would be. But when June twenty-eighth passed without any word from them, she too became alarmed, and together the two women put in a long-distance call to Captain Magee at Jacksonville.

Briefly he told them what he knew—of Mary Eliska's decision to go "scouting," as she called it. And of her request for the revolvers.

The shock of that piece of news was almost too much for Aunt Sally. She jumped to the conclusion that the girls were dead.

"Aren't you doing a thing to find them, Captain?" she demanded, harshly.

"I was thinking about it," he replied. "But after all, they've only been gone two days——"

"You don't know my niece!" interrupted the unhappy woman. "Mary Eliska always wires or telephones me every day, when she goes on these flying trips. She doesn't forget. It's because she can't—she has been injured or killed!"

"I hope not," he replied. "But I will send a plane over the Okefenokee Swamp tomorrow, Aunt Sally," he promised.

The two women gazed at each other in helpless dismay at the conclusion of this conversation. What could they possibly do, aside from informing the newspapers—a decision which they carried out immediately.

Accordingly, on June twenty-ninth, every newspaper in the country stated the fact that Mary Eliska, the famous aviatrix who had flown to Paris alone, was missing again—somewhere in Georgia—probably in the Okefenokee Swamp, with a chum, Miss Jax Gray of Spring City, who was also a pilot.

The unhappy news instantly produced the effect which Aunt Sally hoped it would accomplish. It aroused no fewer than five searching parties, all bent upon locating these two popular girls.

Captain Magee's men were the first to go. Summoning Sergeant Worth, he commandeered a plane from the airport, and directed the pilot to fly over the swamp, searching from the air by means of spyglasses.

The second party was composed of the girls' fathers, both of whom were in New York City at the time. Mr. Gray telephoned Mr. Stricklin, and after sending a wire to their families, they boarded a Florida train together.

The third volunteers were two young men at Green Falls, two college boys who considered Mary Eliska and Jax Gray their special girl-friends, though neither of them was engaged, Jim Valier and Ralph Clavering heard the sad news at the out-door pool at Green Falls, just as they were about to join a group of young people for a swim. Kitty Hulbert, Ralph's married sister, read the head-lines aloud.

"Jim," muttered Ralph, when Kitty finished, "let's do something! We can take a plane to Florida—and go on a search from there."

"O.K.," agreed the other boy, and quietly and quickly the two young men disappeared from the group.

The story came to the Mackays in Washington, where Ted had business on his return from Georgia. The instant that Louise read it, she jumped up in excitement.

"We must go, Ted!" she cried. "You can get your vacation now."

"I'll wire immediately," he agreed, without an instant's hesitation, and he went out to make the necessary arrangements and to order his plane in readiness.

The fifth and last party was none other than Mary Eliska's two latest admirers, the two young men she had mentioned to Jax Gray in the hope of a rescue—Jackson Carter and Hal Perry.

All in all, it ought to have been enough to satisfy Aunt Sally that every effort was being made to find the girls and to bring them back to safety.

The airplane from the police department was the first of these groups to get into action, the first to enter the swamp. Yet it did not actually enter it, but merely flew above it, for the pilot, less experienced than Mary Eliska herself, did not believe it possible to come down on one of those islands. For hours, however, he circled about, over the bog, and the cypress-trees, while Sergeant Worth in the rear cock-pit scanned the landscape with his spyglasses. But neither man saw any trace of the autogiro or the girls, and late that afternoon they had to return in discouragement to Captain Magee.

"I couldn't even locate that camp on the island," Worth said. "The one where we got the prisoners, you know. Unless you have the exact directions, it's hard to find anything in that swamp.... And—I don't see much use in trying again."

Captain Magee looked exceedingly grave; he was genuinely worried. He blamed himself for letting the girls go alone. But there had been nothing official about the project—he had not really expected that they would run into the criminal. Besides, Mary Eliska had seemed so capable, and both girls were so eager to go.

"We mustn't give up, Worth," he said quietly. "It's more important to find these girls than a dozen criminals. We owe it to them, to their families—to the whole country. Everybody has admiration and affection for Mary Eliska, after all she has done.... You'll have to go back tomorrow—or get another man, if you feel too discouraged."

"No, I'm only too glad to help," the other assured him. "I would do anything in the world for Mary Eliska. But I don't see how it can do any good. A scouting party in boats would be much more likely to be successful."

"We'll try that, too, as soon as I can get some men together. But tomorrow you fly out over the ocean to that island where the thieves had the jewels. The girls might be stranded there. Take another pilot, and a bigger plane."

Worth looked doubtful.

"We haven't any way of locating that island, either," he said. "It was Mary Eliska who took us there before, and I have no idea where it is."

"Just do your best, Worth," urged the Captain. "Fly around all the islands near the Georgia coast, keeping a sharp look-out for the autogiro."

"Rain or shine? It looks like a storm tomorrow."

"Yes, whatever the weather, you must go—or get someone else."

So, in spite of the terrible downpour and the high winds of June thirtieth, a cabin monoplane flew across Georgia and out over the ocean to a group of islands just off the coast.

Three men were aboard—two experienced pilots, one of whom was also a mechanic—besides the police officer.

Leaving the coast behind, they flew out into the grayness that was ocean and sky. The waves were high, the sea rough and angry, and the rain was coming down in sheets, blinding their vision, but they pressed on, two of the men keeping their spyglasses on the water, watching for islands. They passed over several, but they were small, with little or no place to land. Eagerly the men watched for some sign of human life, some signal, some glimpse of the autogiro.

"They'd never be alive if we did find them," remarked Worth, gloomily. "And if they did run into that gangster, he'd surely have made away with them."

"If only it would clear up," grumbled the pilot. "So we could see something!"

They were flying much lower now, for it was comparatively safe over the water, and despite the weather, they were able to spot the islands. All of a sudden the mechanic uttered a sharp cry.

"There she is! Look! Over there!"

"Mary Eliska?" demanded Worth, excitedly. "Where?"

"Not the girl! The plane—the autogiro! See—that island to the west! See the wind-mill on top?"

"By George! You're right!" agreed Worth, a thrill running up and down his spine. Thank Heaven, he hadn't given up!

The pilot directed the plane over the island and circled about, landing finally some distance from the autogiro. A glance at the latter assured them that it had not been wrecked. Why, then, hadn't the girls come back? Was it possible that all this scare had risen to alarm the world for the simple reason that Mary Eliska had run out of gasoline?

The three men climbed out of the cabin and shouted as loud as they could, since the girls had evidently failed to hear their plane, above the noise of the storm and the roar of the ocean. Eagerly they waited for a reply. But when none came, fear crept over them all.

Had the girls died of starvation, or was there foul play of some kind? With gloomy forebodings, they walked about the beach, seeking evidence of some kind to tell the story of what had happened.

Finding nothing, the mechanic began to examine the autogiro. She was undamaged, unhurt—everything in order, gasoline in the tank. The engine started easily in answer to his test, and ran smoothly until he turned it off. No, the gallant little Ladybug could not be blamed for whatever disaster had taken place!

Then, forgetful of the weather, the three men set out to search the island thoroughly. Buckled in oil-skin coats, they felt protected themselves, but Worth shuddered as he thought of these girls alone in such desolation, with no roof to cover them, no food to satisfy their hunger, or water for their thirst. Gloomy and discouraged they plowed through the wet sand, calling the girls' names. Finally, abandoning the hope of finding them alive, they set themselves to the gruesome task of looking among the underbrush for their bodies. At last they gave up.

"We'll fasten a canvas sheet over these bushes, so that we can locate the island, and we'll pin a note on it to say that we'll be back," decided Worth, "in case they are alive. One of you men take the autogiro, and the other the plane, and we'll go back now."

The rain was abating somewhat, and the two planes made the return trip without any mishaps, arriving at the Jacksonville Airport before dark that evening.

A wildly enthusiastic crowd, which had collected in spite of the weather, greeted them with resounding cheers. The Ladybug was back again—safe and sound! Women cried with joy, men threw their hats into the air, children clapped their hands and whistled. In a miniature way it was a demonstration like the one given Lindbergh upon his arrival at the French Flying Field. But it was a false rejoicing, and the gayety was quickly changed into despair when the pilot reported that the girls themselves had not been found.

Weary and disappointed, the crowd turned away, and Sergeant Worth told the sad story to the newspaper reporters who waited to interview him, before he returned to the police headquarters.

Captain Magee was terribly affected by the news. Mary Eliska might have been his own daughter, from the grief which he could not conceal.

Two well-dressed young men were waiting in his office when Worth arrived, and they listened to the grim account. They were the first of the rescue parties to arrive from the North—Jim Valier and Ralph Clavering.

"These two young men are friends of Mary Eliska and Jax Gray," explained the Captain. "They want to go into the swamp tomorrow in a boat.... Perhaps the girls have reached the main-land, or perhaps that autogiro was stolen, and they never were on the island at all.... Anyhow, we'll search the swamp again. Will you go with them, Worth?"

"Certainly," agreed the sergeant, though he felt as if it would be fruitless. Those girls were at the bottom of the ocean, he was sure!

"A light motor-boat ought to be able to go up that little stream," continued the Captain. "I will have one ready at the edge of the swamp tomorrow morning at ten o'clock. If you young men will come here at nine, I'll send you over there in a car."

Jim and Ralph expressed their thanks to the officer, and promised to be on hand at the arranged time in the morning. But, like Sergeant Worth, they were exceedingly discouraged; they had little hope of success.

When they awakened the following morning, which was the first day of July—the day that Mary Eliska should have reported to Atlanta—they found that it was still raining, although the storm had ceased, giving way to a dismal drizzle. What an unpleasant day to start off on an excursion like theirs, that was gloomy at best! Yet the weather did not deter them from their purpose, nor did it stop Hal Perry and Jackson who started earlier that morning in their canoe.

But it was difficult with a motor-boat, and all three of the men were unfamiliar with the swamp and its little streams. No one knew where to turn off, as Jackson and Hal had learned from many vacations, and after pushing ahead for two or three hours, they found themselves off their course—grounded.

"It's no use," muttered Worth. "We can't make it in a motor-boat. Magee's never been in the swamp, or he would have known. We'll have to turn back and get a canoe!"

"A whole day wasted!" growled Ralph angrily, as if it were the sergeants fault. "A day! When every minute is precious!"

"Well, it's nobody's fault," remarked Worth. "The sooner we get back the better."

"Nobody's fault!" repeated Ralph. "No—ignorance is O.K.—if it pertains to the police! They shouldn't know a thing about the country around them!"

"No use getting mad at policemen, Ralph," drawled good-natured Jim Valier. "Haven't you learned from driving a car that it doesn't pay? Besides, they're always right."

"No, we're often very wrong," said Worth, humbly and seriously. "And maybe you don't think I care, Mr. Clavering, about finding those girls. But I do! I haven't thought about a thing but that for the last three days."

Ralph made no answer, but applied his attention to searching the landscape with his glasses. But, like everybody else thus far, he found nothing.

Discouraged and silent, they managed to push the boat into the deeper water and to turn it around. All that afternoon they spent in retracing the progress they had made, and returned to the Captain's office just before supper.

"You want to try it again in canoes?" asked Captain Magee.

"Yes," replied Ralph. "Without any of your police this time. No use taking an extra man— it only means more provisions to carry."

"True. But you must be careful of snakes and alligators."

The boys looked none too pleased at the idea, but when they remembered that Mary Eliska and Jax Gray, if still alive, would be subjected to the same perils, they were all the more eager to go.

This time, they decided, they would do it scientifically; they would go prepared with a map of the swamp, equipment, food, and rifles. And above all, a compass! And they would not give up until they had searched every part of that dismal Okefenokee Swamp!

So, cheered by the optimism of youth and the promise of another day, the boys slept well that night.

Chapter 11.15
The Empty Island

The same morning upon which Ralph Clavering and Jim Valier went into the Okefenokee Swamp in a canoe, the fourth searching party arrived. Delayed by a stop-over in Norfolk, Virginia, where Ted had some business for the company, he and Louise did not reach the

Jacksonville Airport until the morning of July second. Leaving the plane at the field, they taxied immediately to the City Hall, arriving there a little after ten.

They did not expect any good news about the missing girls, for they had read the papers and had inquired the latest word at the airport. They had gazed at the Ladybug, so forlorn and desolate in the hangar, and their fears were dark. Even Louise, who was usually optimistic, believed this time it was the end. Yet how dreadful it was! That Mary Eliska, so young, with such a glorious future before her, should perish like this before she was twenty! When she had the whole world at her feet—a world she had won not through mere beauty and charm— although she was both beautiful and charming, but through her courage, her ability, her modesty! Louise made no attempt to hide the tears that rolled down her cheeks; even her husband's strong arm about her shoulders could not stop her sobs.

"Don't give up yet, dear!" he urged. "Why, you and I haven't even had our try."

The girl smiled bravely through her tears.

"I know, Ted dear. I'll try to remember." Her eyes brightened with genuine hope. "It always has been *you* who have rescued her! Maybe you will this time."

"We're going to make a bigger effort than ever before," he reassured her. "Because this time I have you to help me."

The minute they entered the City Hall they saw that something had happened. Louise's heart gave a wild leap of excitement. Were Mary Eliska and Jax Gray safe?

But no. If they were, somebody would be shouting the news from the house-tops—and no one was looking particularity jubilant. There was a crowd outside, but it was not an exulting one. Was it possible that they had found the girls—dead? In spite of the heat of the day, a cold shiver of horror crept over Louise, and she clung tightly to her husband's arm.

They had little difficulty in passing through the crowd to the captain's office, for the latter had given orders to his men that Mary Eliska's and Jax Gray's friends and relatives were to be admitted immediately, whenever they appeared.

As they entered the room, they saw half a dozen officials standing around, several in plain clothes, with only badges to identify them. And on a chair by the desk, opposite Captain Magee, a strange young woman was sitting.

The girl was flashily dressed—or over-dressed—in the latest style. A long green gown trailed almost to the floor, not quite concealing a bandaged ankle. Her little, off-the-face hat of the same bright color was decorated with a diamond bar-pin. Her lips and her cheeks were painted, and there was a gap in her mouth where two front teeth had been knocked out.

The Captain nodded to the Mackays to sit down, and he continued the questions he was putting to this young woman.

"You might as well confess if you know where that man is—with all the bank's money!" he was saying. "I know your scheme. Pretending you don't know where he escaped, so that you won't be locked up, and can get back to him!" His eyes narrowed, and he lowered his voice to an uncanny whisper. "But we'll keep you here 'til you tell where that thief is!"

"I can't tell you—when I don't know!" she persisted. "He ran off from me—he never wanted me with him anyway. I'll swear to it, Sir, if you think I'm lyin'.... Besides, he hasn't got that money."

"Then where is it?"

"Mary Eliska—and the cops she had with her—tricked us, double-crossed us, by swiping the money and fillin' the bags with sand. The Doc was in such a Hurry to get away from those cops, he never found it out 'til we were on that yacht. He was afraid to go back."

Captain Magee leaned forward eagerly at the mention of Mary Eliska's name. She was far more important than the money that had been stolen.

"Mary Eliska?" he demanded. "With the police? Where did you see her?"

Susie shook her head.

"No, I didn't actually see her. But I saw her Bug, with her stuff in it—a bag and a basket of food. I tossed them out of the plane, too, so she wouldn't starve when we swiped the plane. You can put that down to my credit."

"You stole the autogiro?"

"No. Only borrowed it. Left it on an island—you can get it when you want it."

"We have it.... Now, suppose instead of my asking you questions, you tell us the whole story, Miss——?"

"*Mrs.* Slider, if you please," she said. «I am a widow." She lowered her eyes dramatically, enjoying the sensation of holding the center of the stage.

"Well," she began, "after my husband got killed in the plane accident that Mary Eliska probably told you about, she and I got to be quite good friends. I even promised to leave the gang and go straight, for I never really took part in any of their stealing myself—believe it or not! Mary Eliska left me on that island in the swamp, and promised to come back for me when she came for the Bug."

"But you weren't there when Mary Eliska returned!" Captain Magee reminded her.

"No. I got terrible lonesome. If you ever spend a night in the swamp with only a dead man for company—oh, he was buried all right, but it was spooky just the same—you'd excuse me for takin' the first way out, Sir. The Doc come along, in his canoe, and I promised him my diamond ring if he'd take me away.... Well, we got out of the swamp in his boat, and hired a Ford across Georgia. Then we took a motor-boat out to that island in the ocean."

Everyone waited breathlessly; at last the girl was coming to the part they all longed to hear about—the part of the story in which Mary Eliska figured. Pausing dramatically, Susie asked for a glass of water.

"Go on!" urged the captain, as soon as she had drained it.

"It was a terrible boat," she finally continued. "An awful old one. You can imagine going ten miles out to sea in a thing like that! The engine gave out——"

"Never mind all that!" commanded the officer, impatiently. "Come to the point."

"Yes, Sir.... Well, we got to the island finally, and waited for the yacht that was to pick us up and take us to Panama, but before she come along, the autogiro arrived. Mary Eliska—and the police, of course."

"Did you see them—the police, I mean?" was the next question.

"No, we didn't. We were too scared, so we hid 'til they got out of the plane and searched the island. Then we grabbed the bags and ran for the plane. I flew the Bug out to sea, and in a few minutes we spotted our yacht, and signaled it to stop on another island. That's where we left Mary Eliska's plane.... When we got to Panama, the Doc slipped off, and I got caught.... So you see there's nothing to punish *me* for—you got the autogiro back, and the cops, or Mary Eliska, took the money——"

"There were no policemen with Mary Eliska," Captain Magee informed Susie. "Only another girl. But they are lost."

"They must be still on that island, waiting for you to come for them. Nothing could hurt them, and they had some food...."

This was enough for Ted Mackay. Jumping to his feet, he announced his intention of flying there immediately.

"Give me the latitude and longitude of that island!" he demanded. "There isn't a moment to lose!"

"The what?" asked Susie, wrinkling her nose.

"Show me where it is on a map," explained Ted.

"Yeah," agreed Susie, pointing out the island on a map of the Georgia coast, which the Captain took from his desk. "But what's the grand rush?"

"You've forgotten the storm we just had!" said the young man. "The girls may be sick or dead by this time."

"Girls," repeated Susie, significantly. "It beats everything the way they fooled us—in their riding-breeches! If the Doc ever finds out he ran away from a pair of girls——"

"Never mind all that, Mrs. Slider," interrupted Captain Magee, signaling to the prison matron to take the girl away.... "Now, Mr. Mackay, is there anything I can do for you, before you go?"

"You might get me a taxi," replied Ted. "To take my wife and myself to the airport."

"Take my private car," offered the Captain, rising to say good-by. "And good luck to you!"

Louise was so excited at the whole occurrence that she could scarcely sit still in the limousine, as it sped over to the airport.

"If we only aren't too late! Ted, do you suppose they're starved? What does it feel like to starve to death? Or to die of thirst?"

"I wouldn't worry too much about thirst," he reassured her. "Because of that big rain we had. They could get water from it, you know."

"I never thought of that!"

"The worst is over now, I'm sure," continued Ted. "Five days isn't so long, and the girl said they had food. Besides, it wasn't cold. Think of that time you girls were lost in Canada!"

Louise shuddered; she could still remember that long, hopeless night very vividly, when she and Mary Eliska had jumped from parachutes down into the snow of the Canadian Woods, and how they had been forced to keep walking to avoid freezing to death.

"Still, we found a shack to sleep in. And Mary Eliska and Jax Gray haven't even a blanket to cover them in all that storm!"

"Well, they were together, that's one thing to be thankful for."

"Yes—and I'm glad Mary Eliska's companion is Jax Gray. Of all our crowd at Spring City, Jax Gray is the nicest girl—after Mary Eliska, of course. Most of the girls, like Kitty Clavering—Kitty Hulbert, I mean—or Sue Emery, would be pitying themselves so that they'd make Mary Eliska miserable. But not Jax Gray. She always sees the bright side of everything."

"And wasn't it clever the way they got hold of that money, and fooled that bandit!" exulted Ted. "My, but that was slick. And think what it's going to mean to that bank and its depositors! Because if that fellow hadn't been fooled, he'd have made off with it. I don't believe they'll ever find him now."

"I guess nobody will care if he never comes back to the United States!" agreed Louise.

They arrived at the airport and found the plane in readiness, wheeled out on the runway, and Ted took time to give it an inspection himself, while Louise ran off to get the necessary supplies—some food and water, and a first-aid kit, as a necessary precaution. She borrowed sweaters and knickers from the supply at the airport, for she reasoned that Mary Eliska and Jax Gray would be chilled and drenched from the rain. Dry clothing ought to be a god-send, even if they used it only on the short trip back in the plane.

Inside of an hour they took off. It was still drizzling, but Ted was such an experienced navigator that he had no difficulty at all in flying in any kind of weather, and he found the island from Susie's directions. Shortly after noon, he brought it down on the beach.

A feeling of apprehension stole over Louise, when she saw neither of the girls on the shore to greet them. In spite of the noise of ocean, surely they would have heard the plane! Why weren't they there? Ted turned off the motor, and looked about expectantly.

"Do you suppose they're both sick—or injured?" faltered Louise. She did not add, "or dead," but she could not help thinking it.

"Maybe they didn't hear us. Let's shout together—'Mary Eliska and Jax Gray!' If they hear their first names, they'll know we're friends, maybe recognize our voices. You see they may be hiding—for fear it's that gangster returning."

"I never thought of that," replied Louise, more hopefully. "All right—both together when I count three.

"One—two—three!"

"MARY ELISKA AND JAX GRAY!"

Their voices rose clearly over the splashing of the waves, and they waited tensely.

But there was no reply! They waited, and tried again.... Still silence.... Louise put out her hand, and grasped her husband's, in fear.

"What does it mean?" she cried, in anguish. "Is this surely the right island? There seemed to be a lot of them."

"Maybe it isn't" he answered, optimistically. "That girl seemed to be telling the truth—but she was a queer one. Besides, she might not be sure which island it was.... Anyway, we'll search. If Mary Eliska and Jax Gray were here, we'll see some evidences of their camp—burnt out fires, or worn paths, or something. Come on, let's start!"

Arm in arm they began their search, stepping carefully through the underbrush, now and then stopping to call, "Mary Eliska" or "Jax Gray," in the hope that the girls might only have been asleep. They did not have to go far before they saw that at least someone had been here recently, for there was a path worn through the underbrush.

Farther and farther in they went, until they came to a small cluster of pine trees. And here, sure enough, they found the remains, or rather the ashes, for the place had been left neat, of a camp fire.

The sight of this forsaken spot brought sudden tears to Louise's eyes.

"They've been dragged off and killed! I just know it!" she moaned.

"Don't cry, please, dear," begged Ted. "We're not sure yet. This may not be their island—their fire. Somebody else may have camped here. Let's look about a bit."

Slowly they walked around the place, examining the ground for some forgotten belonging that would identify the former campers. Noticing a pile of leaves where someone had evidently made a bed, Louise kicked them aside with her foot, and she saw an empty matchbox. It wasn't much, but it was something, and she leaned over and picked it up.

The letters on the lid leaped out at her like living tongues. Marked with a purple rubber-stamp over the trade-mark, were the words: "J. Vetter, Spring City, Ohio."

The explanation was only too plain. No one but Jax Gray and Mary Eliska could have used that box. Louise dropped to the ground in an agony of wretchedness, and buried her face in her hands.

Even the optimistic Ted found all his hopes blasted by this little box. Gloom spread over his features, and he sat down beside his wife, comforting her as best he could.

For fifteen minutes, perhaps, they remained motionless, overcome by the thought of their friends' awful death. The food which they had brought with the idea of sharing a gay picnic lunch with Jax Gray and Mary Eliska was forgotten. Though they had not eaten since breakfast, neither Ted nor Louise could have swallowed a mouthful.

At last Ted got up, gently raising Louise to her feet. Each silently decided to make one more search—a gruesome one this time—for the girls' bodies.

Round and round the island they walked, looking carefully, among the underbrush, near to the beach, even scanning the water with their spyglasses. But they saw nothing. That one matchbox had been their only evidence. Like good campers to the end, Mary Eliska and Jax Gray had burned every trace of rubbish.

It was mid-afternoon when Ted realized that Louise was faint from hunger and thirst, and he made her sit down while he brought some supplies from the plane. She drank the water eagerly, but she could not eat. For Louise Mackay was going through the deepest tragedy of her young life: her first experience with the loss of a loved one.

During the entire flight homeward she kept her hand on Ted's knee, but she did not utter a word.

Chapter 11.16
Searching the Ocean

Louise and Ted Mackay did not go to the police headquarters that night. They were too miserable, too discouraged by the outcome of their excursion to the island. After leaving the plane at the airport, Ted called Captain Magee on the telephone, and briefly related the results of their flight.

Supper was a dreary affair for them both. It was only by putting forth a tremendous effort that they ate at all—in an attempt to stave off exhaustion. The ice cream, at least, tasted good to Louise, for she was still very hot.

The worst ordeal of all came after the meal, just as the saddened young couple were passing through the hotel lobby to take the elevator to their room. Louise suddenly recognized two familiar figures at the desk, two men who had just arrived with their luggage. Mr. Gray and Mr. Stricklin—the fathers of the two unfortunate girls!

The tears which Louise had bravely forced back ever since her collapse at the discovery of the matchbox on the island, rushed to her eyes again. How could they ever tell these two men the terrible news?

For an instant she hoped they would not see her or her husband, that she could at least put off the evil tidings until the morning. But it was not to be. Mary Eliska's father recognized her instantly, and came quickly towards her.

"Louise!" he exclaimed, holding out his hand. "And Ted! Any news?"

Louise could not answer for the sob that was choking her, and Ted, shy as he always was, knew it was his duty to explain.

"Bad news, Sir," he said. "We had information this morning that the girls were stranded on an island in the ocean, and that their autogiro had been stolen from them. As you probably read in the newspaper, it was found yesterday.... We—Lou and I—flew to the island where the girls were supposed to be, this afternoon, and found evidences of their camp—burnt out fires—but no trace of the girls."

Mr. Stricklin looked grave.

"But they may have been rescued," suggested Mr. Gray, who had the same optimistic disposition as his daughter.

"Possibly," admitted Ted. "But if they had, wouldn't we have heard? The whole country is waiting for news of those two brave girls."

"I'm afraid you're right," agreed Mr. Stricklin, darkly. "Yes, you must be right. Foul play———"

"Or the ocean!" put in Louise. "Oh, the cruel, dreadful ocean! If it couldn't swallow Mary Eliska up on her flight to Paris, it had to have its revenge now!"

"Have you had your dinner, Sir?" asked Ted of Mr. Stricklin.

"Yes. On the train. Suppose we get our rooms—I'll ask for a private sitting-room—and then we can all go up and discuss the matter together from every angle, and decide upon what is the best thing for us to do."

Louise brightened at this ray of hope.

"Then you're not going to give up yet, Mr. Stricklin?" she inquired.

"Never, 'til we find them—dead or alive. We're going to think of no news as good news."

Mr. Gray nodded his approval.

"I have a week's vacation," added Ted, "and I shall be at your service."

"Thank you, my boy," answered Mr. Stricklin, gratefully. He was a great admirer of Ted Mackay, ever since he had recovered from his prejudice against him because he was the son of a ne'er-do-well.

The new-comers made their arrangements at the desk, and were fortunate enough to secure a very pleasant suite. Louise and Ted went up in the elevator with them, and Mr. Stricklin ordered coffee to be sent to the room.

They settled down into the easy chairs and Louise poured the iced-coffee. The evening was hot, but there were large windows on three sides of the sitting-room, and a lovely breeze was blowing. Mr. Stricklin brought out cigars and offered one to Ted.

"But I suppose you'd rather have a cigarette," he said, when Ted refused.

"No thank you, Sir. I never smoke. A great many of us pilots don't. We want to keep as fit as possible."

Mr. Stricklin nodded. Mary Eliska had never expressed any desire to smoke, and he supposed it was for the same reason.

"There are two places where the girls might be," he said slowly, as he puffed on his cigar. "On another of those small islands, off the coast, or in some boat—on the ocean. If they had reached the coast, we should have heard of it."

"A boat!" repeated Louise, with sudden inspiration. "There was that broken down motor-boat, that the girl and the gangster used to get to the island! Could Jax Gray and Mary Eliska have gone off in that?"

"What boat?" demanded Mr. Stricklin and Mr. Gray, both at once.

Louise explained by repeating most of the story which they had heard from Susie that morning.

"Funny we didn't think of that before," observed Ted. "Come to remember, I didn't see any boat this afternoon. Did you, Lou?"

"No, I didn't. And we searched the whole island," she explained to the older men. "We'd surely have seen it if there had been one."

"This sounds hopeful!" exclaimed Mr. Gray, joyfully. "If it didn't have a leak——"

"But didn't you say that it was broken?" asked Mr. Stricklin.

"The girl said the engine was broken, but as far as I know, the boat itself was sound," replied Ted.

"Mary Eliska could fix the engine!" cried Louise, almost hysterical in her relief. For the first time since the finding of the matchbox, she actually believed that Mary Eliska and Jax Gray were still alive.

"We'll work on that theory, anyway," decided Mr. Stricklin. "And go out on the ocean tomorrow."

Before they could discuss their plans any further, the telephone on the desk interrupted them, and Mr. Stricklin was informed that there were two young men who wanted to see him—Ralph Clavering and James Valier.

"Well, of all things!" exclaimed Mr. Stricklin, who had not even known that the boys had started South. "Yes," he added to the clerk on the phone, "ask them to come up right away, by all means."

"Who? What?" demanded Louise, eagerly. "Any news?"

"I don't know yet. Ralph and Jim are here."

"They would be," smiled Louise. Mary Eliska could never get away from Ralph Clavering, no matter how far she went.

A minute later the boys appeared, dressed in camping clothes, looking very unlike the neat, immaculate young men they always appeared to be at Spring City, or at Green Falls. Even if they took part in athletics at home, their white flannels were always spotless. But now, except for the fact that their faces were clean and shaved, they looked like tramps.

Ralph and Jim were just as much surprised to see Ted and Louise as the latter were at their visit.

"Where in the world have you been?" demanded Louise, in amazement at their appearance. "You both look as if you had been ship-wrecked and lost besides."

"We have," muttered Jim, sinking wearily into a seat, and extending his long legs in front of him. "Please pardon our slouching, Lou—but we're dead."

"But where have you been?" repeated Mr. Stricklin.

"In the Okefenokee Swamp!" answered Ralph. "And if Lou weren't here, I'd tell you what it's like, in no uncertain language!"

Mr. Stricklin smiled, and yet he was horror stricken. If these boys found it so dreadful, what must it have seemed like to Mary Eliska?

"Tell us about it!" he urged. "But wait, have you had your supper?"

"Yes. We had food along with us. We left the canoe at the edge of the stream, and taxied back here, because we have rooms in this hotel. They told us at the desk that 'Mary Eliska's father had arrived,' so we didn't wait even to change our clothing. We had to get the news of the girls immediately."

"I'm afraid there isn't much to tell," sighed Louise. "At least nothing hopeful." Briefly she repeated what she and Ted had been doing all afternoon, as a result of Susie's capture and story, and she displayed the matchbox, with the name of Spring City stamped on its lid.

"I recall Mary Eliska's getting that from her aunt," remarked Ralph, dolefully. "She asked for half a dozen boxes, and Aunt Sally got them right away, so she wouldn't forget."

"Now tell us what you boys have been doing," urged Mr. Gray. "And Louise, why don't you pour them some of this iced-coffee? It really is very refreshing.

Briefly Ralph told his story, aided now and then by Jim. Their second expedition into the swamp had been as useless as their first, though they admitted the superiority of a canoe over a motor-boat, if one knew where to go. But they had become hopelessly lost in a couple of hours, in spite of their maps, and, as time passed, they became all the more certain that the girls were not in the swamp. They decided to turn back, in order to concentrate their efforts on the islands near where the autogiro had been found.

Susie's story naturally confirmed their suspicions, and they instantly agreed with Mr. Stricklin to abandon all further search of the Okefenokee.

"I believe the thing to do," announced the latter, after serious contemplation, "is to hire a yacht, and cruise all along the Georgia and Florida coast. The most reasonable explanation to me is that Mary Eliska and Jax Gray are adrift somewhere in that motor-boat. Either the engine is broken beyond repair, or the gasoline has given out."

"Or that terrible storm has wrecked them," faltered Louise, who could not silence her fear of the ocean. "Upset that little boat, and——"

"Don't, Lou!" cried Jim. "Don't even think of things like that, unless we find an empty boat!"

"I'll try not to," she promised.

"Well, whatever has happened, the ocean is the place for us to be, if we hope to rescue the girls," concluded Mr. Stricklin, "You all agree on that point?"

Everyone assented, and Ralph and Jim expressed their desire to get into action immediately.

"We ought to be able to get a yacht tomorrow," continued Mr. Stricklin. "Because of the publicity of this affair someone who has one ready will probably be glad to rent it to us on the spot. I think I'll go to the newspaper office tonight, and have the request broadcast by radio."

"Great!" exclaimed Louise, jumping up excitedly. "And can we all go with you tomorrow, on the cruise, I mean, Mr. Stricklin?"

"You can do just as you prefer—go with me, or use your own plane to fly around over the islands."

"I think that would be the better plan for us, Sir," put in Ted. "And we can keep in touch with you by signals."

The group separated at last, the older men to call their families by long-distance, the young people to get a good night's sleep after their strenuous day. In the morning they re-assembled at breakfast, when Mr. Stricklin announced the good news that he had been offered a yacht by a wealthy man in Jacksonville.

"He even refused to take any rent for it, much as I urged him to," he added. "And he's lending us the crew besides. It seems too good to be true."

"All of which goes to show just how popular Mary Eliska is—with everybody!" explained Louise. "Oh, we simply must find her!"

There were no preparations to be made for the cruise, because the owner of the yacht assured Mr. Stricklin that everything was in readiness, so by ten o'clock on the morning of July third, the little party, composed of the two fathers and the two boy-friends of the lost girls stepped aboard the boat. It was a beautiful little yacht, complete in every detail. Under any other circumstances the men would have been overjoyed at the prospect of such a pleasant trip. As it was, they were too worried to think of anything but Mary Eliska and Jax Gray.

"What a marvelous time we could be having if the girls were aboard!" lamented Ralph. "Dance and play bridge all day, every day, with no other fellows to cut in on us, and take them away! I say, Jim, we might even come back engaged if we had a chance like that!"

"Much more likely they'd be so sick of us they'd never want to see us again!" returned the other, shrewdly. "No—cruising's all right. But I'd rather be in Green Falls if Mary Eliska and Jax Gray were with us."

"Maybe this will teach Mary Eliska a lesson," grumbled Ralph. Then he suddenly remembered her job, with the Spraying Company in Atlanta. He couldn't pretend to be sorry if she lost it. The speedy little yacht cruised all day along the coast, while the men played bridge, and smoked, and ate the most excellent meals, cooked and served by an efficient staff. But underneath all this comfort ran an under-current of anxiety, especially towards evening, when darkness came on, and no sign of the girls had been seen.

Several airplanes had flown over their heads during the day, and once they saw Ted's plane. Dropping low, Louise waved her handkerchief, which was the pre-arranged signal to tell them that the flyers had found nothing, and Ralph waved his in return, conveying the same information. Should they have anything to report, Ted announced that he would put his plane through a series of stunts, and, in the case of the yacht's making a discovery, Jim Valier promised to climb up on the rail. But the airplane and the yacht passed each other with only a dismal fluttering of handkerchiefs.

"Something's bound to happen tomorrow," said Jim, as he crawled into his bunk that night. "It'll be the fourth of July!"

"By Jove! It will!" exclaimed Ralph. "We ought to get some bang-up excitement!"

But the thing that happened was what they had all been silently dreading—the fate which only Louise had mentioned, that night in the hotel sitting-room.

About noon—off the coast of Florida—Jim Valier spotted an overturned old motor-boat, bouncing helplessly about on the ocean!

Chapter 11.17
On to Cuba

When the storm came at dawn on the thirtieth of June, it awakened Mary Eliska first. As the rain descended upon the slickers that covered the girls, and upon their faces, Jax Gray merely buried her head sleepily under the raincoat, but Mary Eliska sat bolt upright on the bed of leaves.

The wind was howling about the lonely island, and the rain was pouring down in sheets. The blackness of it all was terrifying, yet she knew that she must get up.

"Jax Gray!" she whispered, hoarsely. "Wake up!"

Her companion opened her eyes sleepily as she pushed the slicker aside.

"Yes.... Why Mary Eliska, it's—pouring!"

"It certainly is." Mary Eliska was slipping on her shoes and her knickers over her pajamas. "We've got to rescue the boat."

"Why?"

"Because water mustn't get into the gasoline. And because the tide might come up high enough to wash the boat out to sea."

"O.K.," replied Jax Gray, now quite wide awake. "I'm with you, Mary Eliska—in just a second."

Holding on to each other's hands, they made their way with difficulty down to the beach where the boat had been left, and together they dragged it back and covered it with one of the slickers.

Panting from the effort, they dropped back on the sand and sat down, not bothering about the rain that was descending relentlessly upon them, soaking them to the skin.

"We might as well use the other slicker as a roof for ourselves," suggested Jax Gray, as she got to her feet again. "We can hang it over some bushes, and crawl under it."

"That's an idea!" approved Mary Eliska. "I was wondering how one raincoat could keep us both dry."

"It won't keep us dry—we're wet now. But it will protect us from the worst force of this cloud-burst."

They went back to their camping site and arranged the slicker as best they could—carefully putting the bag of money and the box of tools under it, before they crawled in themselves. The bushes were wet, and so was the ground, but the girls were saved the discomfort of having the rain actually pour in their faces.

They watched the storm for some time, hoping that it would soon abate, and finally, becoming drowsy, they fell asleep again, with their feet sticking out under the covering.

Cramped by the awkward position, they awakened in a couple of hours. Daylight had arrived—but not sunlight. It was still raining steadily and dismally.

"Don't you suppose we can go today?" asked Jax Gray.

"Maybe later on," replied Mary Eliska, cheerfully. "There's one thing good about this, Jax Gray. We can get a drink."

"How heavenly!" exclaimed the other, sitting up. "But how do we manage it? We won't get much by just opening our mouths!"

"Get up carefully. I'm sure there's a lot of water lodging on the top of this slicker. Wait—get the thermos bottles out of the tool-box first. We'll use the cups, and then stand them up to catch the rain as it falls."

Mary Eliska's surmise was correct; there was so much water on the slicker that it was in danger of collapsing any moment. They dipped their cups into the pool and drank eagerly. How good it tasted to their parched throats!

"There must be more down on the boat's cover," suggested Jax Gray. "Let's get it, and pour it into our thermos bottles."

When they had carried out this idea, they set the bottles firmly in the sand, and crept back under cover.

"Shall we eat?" asked Jax Gray, after watching the rain for some minutes in silence.

"Let's wait a while—'til noon, if we can. We have only those two oranges and a half a dozen crackers. It'll be something to look forward to."

"There's still some tea and sugar—and one can of milk," the other reminded her. "You know we didn't use them, because we couldn't afford the water. Now it'll be different."

"I'd forgotten all about that!" exclaimed Mary Eliska, smiling. "Let's have tea and one cracker for lunch, and save the oranges for supper."

"But how can we ever hope to build a fire in this rain? We'd never find any dry sticks—and if we made one under here, we'd be smoked out."

"I hadn't thought of that. But we can make cold tea. If we leave the leaves in the water long enough, they'll flavor it—anyway, that's what I read in an ad one time."

"You think of everything, Mary Eliska! It's no wonder you've gotten out of a dozen disasters that would have killed an ordinary girl!"

"Now Jax Gray!" protested the other girl, modestly. "Just so long as we get out of this one, I'll be satisfied."

To help pass the tediousness of the long gloomy day, the girls took a brisk walk encircling the entire island. Soaked as they were before they started, they decided it would be foolish to stop because of the rain. The sight of the ocean, wild and angry as it was because of the storm, aroused their wonder and admiration, and rewarded them for their wet excursion. In vain they squinted through the spyglasses for a glimpse of the autogiro, but even the island on which it had been left by Susie was obliterated from their vision.

It was no wonder, therefore, that they did not see the plane which brought Sergeant Worth and the two pilots to that other island. All unaware that Ladybug had flown home that afternoon, the girls finally settled down after dark to try to sleep under their improvised roof.

When they awakened the following morning, they were disappointed not to see the sun. It was still raining, but no longer in torrents; the storm had slackened to a monotonous drizzle.

"We better go," said Mary Eliska, as they breakfasted on tea and two crackers apiece. "I can keep the engine pretty well covered up. And this rain may keep up for days."

"I shouldn't care to keep up this reducing diet for days," observed Jax Gray. "If we were only too fat, Mary Eliska, how we would welcome such a chance to starve ourselves!"

"Yes.... If—Oh, Jax Gray, don't you wish we had a thick steak now—smothered in mushrooms——"

"With creamed potatoes and fresh peas——"

"Fruit salad and cheese wafers——"

"Meringues, salted nuts, and coffee!"

Both girls suddenly laughed out loud.

"Anyway, we can both have our drinks of water," concluded Jax Gray. "And they say thirst is worse than hunger."

"We'll fill both thermos bottles before we push off," said Mary Eliska. "But I'm counting on reaching the Ladybug before noon, and then we ought to get to the Georgia coast by two o'clock."

"Where we eat that dinner!" added Jax Gray.

Carrying their belongings, they walked down to the beach in their rain-soaked clothing, and pushed the boat out towards the water. The ocean was still so high and so rough that Mary Eliska hesitated a moment.

"Do you think we can make it?" asked Jax Gray, noticing the expression of doubt on her companion's face.

"Yes, I think so. That island didn't look far, yesterday."

"That's true. But I can't see it now, Mary Eliska. Suppose the storm had washed the Ladybug away—or even the whole island?"

Mary Eliska shuddered, realizing that there was that possibility. She took the glasses from her pocket, and peered through them in the direction she remembered the island to be.

"I can't see a thing but ocean," she stated. "The waves are so high. But let's go in that direction anyway. It must be there."

She turned to the motor-boat and attempted to start the engine, but for some minutes she labored in vain, for the engine refused to catch. Was everything in the world against them, Jax Gray silently wondered, as she watched Mary Eliska repeat her efforts with infinite patience.

At last, however, there was a sputter, and the motor started. The girls pushed the boat into the water and climbed into it.

It would have been great sport riding the waves, had it not been for the grave danger attached. This was no sporting contest, with a life-guard in readiness to rescue them if anything went wrong! It was a race between life and death.

The wind had died down, however, and the sea was gradually growing calmer. Up and down the little boat bobbed, now in the trough of a wave, seemingly under a mountain of water—now rising again to a height that made the girls think of a scenic-railway at a pleasure park. Jax Gray screamed with excitement, but Mary Eliska's lips were set in a firm line of determination, her attention riveted on the engine

By some miracle, it seemed to the girls, the little boat forged triumphantly ahead, with its motor running smoothly. A feeling of confidence was gradually taking the place of fear, and Jax Gray strained her eyes for the island that was their goal. Half an hour later she spotted it, and almost upset the boat in her joy.

"There it is, Mary Eliska!" she cried, excitedly. "Oh, Mary Eliska, we're saved! We're———" She stopped suddenly, hardly able to believe her eyes. The autogiro was gone!

"What's the matter, Jax Gray?" asked Mary Eliska, unable to understand the abrupt end of her chum's rejoicing. "Anything wrong!"

"Yes.... The Ladybug's gone!"

"What? Oh, it can't be!" Mary Eliska's voice was hoarse with terror. "Look again, Jax Gray—you have the glasses."

Jax Gray squinted her eyes, but was rewarded by no trace of the plane.

"You take a look, Mary Eliska," she suggested. "Maybe you can see better."

The other girl eagerly caught the glasses which her companion tossed, and with trembling fingers held them to her eyes. The island was in plain sight now, but it was a ghastly fact that the autogiro had completely disappeared.

Mary Eliska continued to gaze at the barren spot, her eyes fixed and staring, as if she were looking at death itself. Then, dropping the glasses into her lap, she seemed to be thinking intently.

"It's true, Jax Gray," she said, in an expressionless tone. "Yet that must be the right island.... Something has happened.... I don't know whether the wind could have lifted the Ladybug— or whether that gangster came back for it.... In any case, there's only one thing for us to do."

"Yes?" faltered Jax Gray, biting her lips to keep back the tears. She must not fail Mary Eliska now, in her darkest hour.

"Turn the boat around, and make for the shore. We mustn't waste another drop of gasoline. It—won't last forever."

"Shall we go back to our island—if we can find it?" asked Jax Gray, as she turned the wheel.

"No, we'll go straight west.... Or is that the west? Oh, if we only had a compass, or the sun to guide us.... But that must be the right direction."

Mary Eliska was speaking bravely, trying to keep her voice normal, and her companion took heart from her manner. The boat went forward in the opposite direction, presumably towards the coast.

Half an hour passed in silence, each girl intent upon her task. Mary Eliska took out her extra can of gasoline and filled the tank. Once Jax Gray drank some water from the thermos bottle and reminded Mary Eliska of hers. All the while they continued to keep a sharp look-out for the coast.

Another hour passed, and the girls' hunger began to assault them. The rain continued to fall, and weariness stole over them both. They were too weak and too tired to talk.

At last Mary Eliska broke the silence by asking Jax Gray to take another good look for the coast through the glasses. She did not add that it was vital this time, that the gasoline was running very low. On a rough sea like this, oars would be out of the question, even if the girls had been as strong as boys.

"I can't see anything but water," was the reply.

But just at that moment Mary Eliska saw something that held her speechless with terror. The boat was springing a leak! Water appeared to be pouring in by the bucket-full!

As the significance of this catastrophe dawned upon Mary Eliska, her throat grew dry and parched; the words with which she meant to tell Jax Gray choked her so that she could not speak. How, oh how could she possibly inform her brave chum of what was literally their death sentence!

It was Jax Gray, however, who spoke instead. Rather, she cried out hysterically,

"Mary Eliska, I see a boat! A steam-boat! Coming towards us!"

"Where?" gasped the other girl, her heart beating wildly between hope and fear.

"Right ahead! Look! You can see her without the glasses now!"

Mary Eliska shot a swift glance at the approaching boat, then looked again at the floor, where the water was fast deepening. Would the rescue come in time? And would the boat stop at their signal of distress?

Wild with excitement, both girls raised their arms and waved desperately at the approaching craft, until it was only fifty yards away. Then they both shouted with a power and volume that they would not have believed they possessed.

The oncoming boat decreased its speed until it was almost beside the girls' sinking craft. To their overwhelming joy and relief, they saw that it was stopping. A man appeared on the deck, and called to them in a pleasant voice.

"In trouble, girls?"

"Our boat's sinking!" shouted Mary Eliska to Jax Gray's amazement, for the latter was s'til unaware of the immediate tragedy that was threatening them. "Can you take us aboard?"

"Sure!" he replied. "Wait 'til I get a rope ladder."

While he was gone, Mary Eliska pointed to the water in the boat, which by this time Jax Gray had seen, and signaled to the other girl to say nothing of their experiences to this man, until they learned more about him. Mary Eliska's recent association with criminals had made her exceedingly wary.

"Pull up closer," instructed the man, as he returned with the ladder. "Now, can you climb?"

"Easily!" Jax Gray assured him. "We're in knickers, anyhow."

"May we throw our stuff on board first?" inquired Mary Eliska, picking up the bag which contained, besides their few possessions, all the bank's money.

"Sure! Anything breakable in it?"

"Only a couple of mirrors," returned Jax Gray, who had regained her cheerfulness with amazing speed. "And we're not afraid of bad luck," she added.

A moment later the girls climbed to safety, and pressed their rescuer's hand in gratitude. It seemed like a miracle to them both, and the old seaman was like an angel from heaven.

"How soon will we get to the coast?" asked Mary Eliska eagerly. The man shook his head. "We can't go to the coast," he replied. "We're headed for Cuba."

"But we must get back as soon as possible," pleaded Mary Eliska, beginning to wonder whether she was about to be kidnapped again.

"You were headed for the open ocean," the seaman informed her, to both girls' consternation. "And that's where we have to go. I can't stop at the United States.... I'm awfully sorry...."

Chapter 11.18
Luck for Ted and Louise

Mary Eliska and Jax Gray stood still on the deck of the old boat, grasping the rail with their hands, and looking intently at their rescuer. He was a typical old seaman, with tanned, roughened face, a gray beard, and kindly blue eyes.

"That was a narrow escape," he remarked. "What do you girls mean by going out on a rough sea like this, in a shell like you had?"

"We couldn't help it," Mary Eliska replied. "And we thought the boat was safe. We didn't know it was going to spring a leak.... Would it take very long to run us to the coast, Mr.—Captain——?"

"Smallweed," supplied the man. "And everybody calls me 'Cap'n'."

"Well, would it, Captain Smallweed?" repeated Mary Eliska, amused at the name. He ought to be at home on the island they had just come from, she thought—there were so many "small weeds" growing there!

"Too long fer me to stop," he replied, to the girls' dismay. "I got to get back to my family, in Havana." His blue eyes twinkled. "Why? What have you girls got in that bag, that's so important to deliver in a hurry?"

"You think we're boot-leggers!" laughed Jax Gray. "Don't you, Captain?"

"I wouldn't be surprised at anything," he answered, smiling. "I've seen just as nice-lookin' girls as you——"

"I'm afraid we're not very nice looking," sighed Mary Eliska, surveying their drenched, bedraggled clothing. "But we're really not boot-leggers.... We want to get back so that we can telephone to our families. They probably think that storm was the end of us."

"Well, I'm sorry, but I can't go off my course. Like to, if I had the time——"

"Well, if you can't, you can't—that's all there is to it," said Mary Eliska, philosophically. "We're glad to be alive at all, and I don't suppose a couple of days will make any difference."

"How long do you think it will take you to get to Cuba?" put in Jax Gray anxiously. There was no use fussing, of course, but she could not forget that her mother and father would be frantic by this time.

"I'm reckonin' on dockin' at Havana the fourth of July. This is only the first, but these are stormy seas, and we have to expect delays.... Now come on inside, out o' this drizzle. You girls are drenched—I'll have to give you the only cabin I got. To get yourselves dry in."

Stooping over, he picked up Mary Eliska's tool-box, and finding it heavy, eyed it suspiciously.

"You girls gangsters?" he asked, unexpectedly. "Got any guns on you?"

Both girls felt themselves growing red at this accusation, yet they could not deny it wholly.

"That box has the tools in it which I used to fix up the engine of the motor-boat," Mary Eliska finally explained. "And you can take our word that we're not gangsters."

But they were exceedingly nervous as they followed the Captain to the cabin where there were two bunks, one on top of the other. Suppose he should decide to search them—and find not only the two revolvers, but all that money besides! He would never believe their story!

"When you get dry, I'll take you over the whole boat," he said. "I carry tobacco up the coast every couple of months. Used to have a sail-boat—that was the real thing! But this little lady's speedy—and better in a storm like we just had."

"How can we ever thank you enough, Captain Smallweed?" cried Jax Gray, suddenly overwhelmed by a sense of gratitude for their safety. "Our fathers will send you a handsome reward when we get back home."

"Never mind that," smiled the man. "I've got a girl of my own—she's married now—but she's still a kid to me, and I know how I'd want her treated.... Now, you can bolt this door if you want to, so there won't be any danger of either of the two other fellows aboard coming in accidentally—and you can get yourselves dry."

"There's—there's just one thing, Captain," stammered Mary Eliska. "We're dreadfully hungry. Could we have a piece of bread, or anything to eat?"

"You poor kids!" he exclaimed, in a fatherly tone. "Come on down to the kitchen, and you can help yourselves."

Though the food he provided was not the steak dinner they had been dreaming about on the island, it tasted good to those two starved girls. Captain Smallweed made tea for them, and brought out bread and smoked sausages, and Mary Eliska and Jax Gray ate every crumb of the repast.

"We were marooned on an island during that storm," Mary Eliska explained. "And we have had nothing but a couple of oranges and a few crackers for two days."

"Well, you'll get a good supper," the Captain promised them. "That's why I'm not givin' you more now. I'll knock on your door about eight o'clock, if you ain't awake before then. That's when we usually eat."

When the girls were finally alone in their cabin, they gazed first at their bag of money, then at each other, and suddenly started to laugh. It was such a ridiculous situation. During those lonely days of exile on the island they had pictured their return so differently. It would be a grand occasion, with exciting telephone calls to their families, a marvelous dinner at a hotel, perhaps a radio broadcast of their safe landing! Instead of all that, here they were, stowed away in a shabby boat, suspected of crime, and feasting on stale bread and hot dogs for their banquet! Worst of all there would be three weary days of waiting before informing the world of their safety! Yet they were thankful indeed that they had been rescued at all, and by a man as kind-hearted as the old sea captain.

"I don't really think he'll bother any more about that bag," said Mary Eliska, as she took off her wet shoes. "If only we can get it back to Jacksonville safely, from Cuba! If we only had the Ladybug!"

"It's a mystery where she could have vanished to," observed Jax Gray. "But I suppose that is a small thing, compared to saving our lives."

"You'll never go anywhere with me again," sighed Mary Eliska. "Jax Gray!" she exclaimed abruptly, "I'd forgotten all about my job!"

"I hadn't forgotten I was to start back North today," remarked the other girl. "Jim Valier was going to motor over and meet me at the station when my train came in."

"Poor Jim!" sighed Mary Eliska, little thinking that the young man had no intention of doing that. "He'll have a good wait. But Jim can always sleep, on any occasion."

"I guess he won't expect me.... We must be reported as missing by now—in all the newspapers."

"Of course. I'd forgotten...."

The girls wrapped themselves in blankets and slept the rest of the afternoon, to waken in time to see the sun, which had appeared at last, just setting over the sea. Their clothing was still damp and disheveled, but they put it on and went up on deck to hunt their benefactor.

"We want you to let us cook," announced Jax Gray, as she spied him. "We insist on making ourselves useful."

The man smiled pleasantly.

"All right," he agreed. "You can—tomorrow. But supper's ready now. Come on down."

They followed the Captain into the kitchen, where another man was placing a dish of potatoes on the wooden table, which did not boast of a cover.

"Meet Steve, ladies," her said—"my friend the pilot."

The girls nodded, and Jax Gray asked, with anxiety, "But who's guiding the boat now, while Mr. Steve eats his supper?"

Both men laughed at her concern.

"There's another one besides us. He takes his turn, and so do I. We never all three eat or sleep at the same time."

It was a merry meal, though an exceedingly greasy one of fried potatoes and underdone bacon. The coffee, too, was none too good—for it was weak and muddy-looking. Nevertheless, both girls praised the supper extravagantly, for it tasted good to them, but they inwardly resolved to show the men the next day how food ought to be cooked.

The next two days passed pleasantly enough, for the girls were able to busy themselves with the meals, and the men's appreciation was plenty of reward for their efforts. In their off hours they relaxed by watching the ocean and scanning the sky for airplanes, the make of which Mary Eliska could often guess. Sometimes they played checkers with each other, or with Captain Smallweed, to the latter's delight. But never again was the suspicious-looking tool-box mentioned, until Mary Eliska herself handed it over to Steve, saying that she did not want to bother to take it to Havana.

By the time July third arrived, their boat was well out of the range of the yacht that was cruising in search of them, and on July fourth—the day that Jim Valier spotted the overturned motor-boat early in the morning—Captain Smallweed docked safely at Cuba.

"Where do you girls want to go now?" asked the Captain, as the party stepped ashore. "Want to come along home with me, and meet the wife? She can rig you up in some decent clothes."

"Thank you very much," replied Mary Eliska, "but we want to get to a telephone as soon as possible, so that we can get in touch with our families. So if you would just get us a taxi, and send us to the best hotel in Havana——"

"In those rigs?" inquired the other, in amazement. "Everybody will stare at you! They dress well in Cuba, you know."

"Oh, we're past caring about appearances," laughed Mary Eliska. "So stop that taxi for us, will you please, Captain?... And thank you a thousand times for all you have done for us."

"You'll hear from our fathers soon," added Jax Gray, as she too shook hands with the old man.

Cautiously protecting the bag, into which Mary Eliska had stuffed the revolvers under the money, the girls taxied to the best hotel in the city. The driver eyed them suspiciously, and the clerk at the desk stared at them as if they were hoboes. But he condescended to assign them a room when they showed evidence of paying in advance.

"We want a long-distance wire first of all," announced Mary Eliska. "We'd like to telephone from our rooms——"

She stopped abruptly, for two slender arms were suddenly thrust about her neck, and kisses were being pressed violently upon her lips and cheeks. Louise Mackay stood behind them! Louise, with her husband, both in flyers' suits.

Try as she could, the girl could not utter a word. The tears ran down her cheeks, and she continued to kiss first Mary Eliska and then Jax Gray in the wildest ecstasy.

"I can't believe it!" she said at last. "Is it really, truly you, Mary Eliska darling?"

"What's left of us," replied Mary Eliska, laughing. "Did you ever see two such sights as we are?"

"I never saw anyone or anything in my life that looked half so good to me!" returned Louise, fervently. She stepped back and laid her hand on her husband's arm, for so far Ted had not had a chance to say anything, or be included in the welcome. "Tell me it's true, Ted—that I'm not dreaming!" she urged. "I simply can't believe it."

"It's the best, the truest thing in the world," the young man assured her.

"We were positive you were dead," Louise explained. "We had so much evidence to prove it—the empty island where you were marooned, the overturned motor-boat that Jim Valier spotted early this morning——"

"Jim Valier!" repeated Jax Gray, in amazement. "Where would Jim see our old boat?"

"Jim and Ralph and your two fathers are on a yacht, searching for you. They broadcast by radio any news they get. And Ted and I have flown to every island anywhere near the coast. We finished searching them all, so we landed here this morning, just for a rest."

"Then you have a plane!" cried Mary Eliska, in delight. "You can take us back to Florida! I'd so hate to get into another boat—I simply loathe the sight of them."

"Do tell us what happened to you," urged Ted. "I don't understand how we missed you everywhere."

"It's a pretty long story," replied Jax Gray. "I think we better phone our families first. They must be almost crazy."

"They are," agreed Ted. "You go up in your room and phone them while I go to a radio station and broadcast the news."

"And I'll tell you what I'll do in the meanwhile," offered Louise. "I'll go out and buy you some decent clothing!"

Chapter 11.19
The Return

Until the second of July, Mary Eliska's aunt, Aunt Sally, had managed, with Mrs. Gray's help, to keep hoping that the girls were still alive. Then her brother's long-distance call from Jacksonville, informing her that he was going to sea in a yacht in search of Mary Eliska and Jax Gray confirmed all the fears she was secretly cherishing. That night she collapsed and went to bed a nervous wreck.

After once mentioning the fact that Mary Eliska was still reported missing in the newspapers, Aunt Sally's housekeeper learned not to speak of the girl again. It seemed as if the older woman could not bear to talk about her niece; in the few days since her disappearance she had aged rapidly. She lay listlessly on her bed, not seeing anyone, not even her dear friend Mrs. Gray.

It was about noon on the fourth of July that the telephone operator informed the housekeeper that Havana was calling Aunt Sally. The good woman replied that her mistress was sick in bed, and that she would take the message for her. Her hands trembled as she awaited what she believed would be the announcement of Mary Eliska's death.

Faint and far off came the astounding words: "Aunt Sally, this is Mary Eliska."

"Wait!" cried the woman, shaking as if she had heard a ghost. "I'll get your aunt, Miss Mary Eliska."

Rushing to the bed-room, she handed Aunt Sally the bed-side telephone.

"It's Miss Mary Eliska," she whispered.

Doubting her senses, the patient sat up and took the instrument.

"Hello," she said, doubtfully.

"Darling Aunt Sally! It's Mary Eliska!" was the almost unbelievable reply at the other end of the wire.

Aunt Sally sobbed; she could not say a word.

"Aunt Sally? Are you there?" demanded the girl.

"Yes, yes—dear! Oh, are you all right? Not hurt?"

"Not a bit. Jax Gray and I are both fine—she's talking to her mother now. We're—in Cuba."

"Cuba!" repeated the startled woman. "I thought it was the Okefenokee Swamp, or the Atlantic Ocean! Your father and Mr. Gray are looking for you."

"Yes, I know. Ted and Louise are here, and Ted's broadcasting the news of our safe arrival now…. Probably Daddy has heard by this time."

"When will you be home, dear?" inquired Aunt Sally.

"Soon, I hope…. But we have to stop in Jacksonville first…. Aunt Sally, couldn't you come to Jacksonville? We're just dying to see you!"

Aunt Sally considered; she hated to tell Mary Eliska that she was sick in bed. But wait—was she? Wasn't it only nerves after all? Why, this good news made her feel like a different person!

"All right, dear," she agreed. "If Mrs. Gray will, I'll try to arrange it. Shall I send a wire?"

"Yes," replied Mary Eliska. "To Captain Magee, at the City Hall, Jacksonville. I'll be there in a day or so…. Now good-by, dear Auntie!"

While Mary Eliska waited for Jax Gray to come back from her call, which the latter had put in from another instrument, she opened the bag and took out their few possessions that were covering the money. They must be very careful not to let anything happen to all that wealth, she thought—they must never go out of the room and leave it, if only for a minute.

How dreadful it would be if it were stolen now, after they had successfully brought it through all their dangerous adventures!

Jax Gray returned in a couple of minutes, and the girls got ready to enjoy the luxury of a real bath, in a real tub. How good the warm water felt, how wonderful the big, soft bath towels! They spent an hour bathing and washing their hair, and trying to make their nails presentable with Louise's manicure set.

They had scarcely finished when the latter returned, followed by a porter carrying innumerable boxes and packages in his arms.

"I've bought everything for you from the skin out," she announced gayly, as she put the load on the floor. "Even hats and shoes, though I knew I was taking a chance at them. But I remembered that you and I often wore each other's things at school, Mary Eliska, and I judged that Jax Gray would wear a size smaller. I do hope you can wear them, just 'til you get to your trunks at Jacksonville."

"You're an angel, Lou!" cried Mary Eliska, excited at the prospect of looking clean and respectable again.

"See if you like them," urged Louise. "I got a blue dress for you, Mary Eliska, to match your eyes—and a pink one for Jax Gray."

"To match my eyes?" teased the latter.

All three girls began immediately to untie the packages, and drew out the purchases one after another with exclamations of admiration. Jax Gray said that she was so used to seeing dirty knickers that she had positively forgotten what dainty clothing looked like.

"Well, hurry up and dress!" urged Louise. "We want to eat lunch in about ten minutes. Ted means to take off at two o'clock, if you girls think you can be ready by then."

"We surely can!" cried Mary Eliska, joyfully. She couldn't wait to get back.

"You'll burn your old stuff, won't you?" asked Louise. "This bag's a sight, too—why not stuff your old clothing into it, and ask the porter to take it away!"

Mary Eliska and Jax Gray let out a wild cry of protest at the same moment, and the other girl frowned.

"Why not?" she inquired.

"Sh!" whispered Mary Eliska. "That bag has thousands of dollars in it. Belonging to the Jacksonville bank."

"Oh! You really have that money? And kept it all this time?"

"Yes. But don't say a word about it out loud. We'll take it with us into the dining-room, and wear our new hats, so nobody will think it queer."

They found Ted in the lobby of the hotel as they got out of the elevator, and they went into the dining-room to order the meal that Mary Eliska and Jax Gray had been longing for on the island. It tasted good to them, but not so good, they had to admit, as the sausages and stale bread and hot tea which Captain Smallweed provided, when they were almost starved.

It was during the meal that they pieced the story together. Mary Eliska began by telling of the finding of the money in the bags and the discovery of the last member of the gang on the island.

"But why he ran away without shooting us is a mystery to us," put in Jax Gray.

"He thought that you had armed policemen with you," explained Louise. "We learned that later from Susie. She was captured a couple of days ago—in Panama."

"Where is she now?" demanded Mary Eliska, excitedly.

"In jail, of course."

"And the man they called the 'Doc'?"

"No," replied Ted. "Unfortunately he got away—fled the country. Lucky you girls got hold of the money, or the bank would never have seen it again.... And by the way, there's a big reward—ten thousand dollars, I believe."

"Ten thousand dollars!" repeated Jax Gray, in amazement. "What do you think of that, Mary Eliska?"

"Wonderful!" cried the latter, joyously. "Five thousand apiece. Well, I'm glad you're going to get something out of this dreadful experience, Jax Gray—that I selfishly dragged you into. And my part will go towards a new autogiro."

"A new autogiro!" exclaimed Louise, in surprise. "You don't need one, Mary Eliska. The Ladybug's safe and sound—at the Jacksonville airport."

"What? You mean that?" Mary Eliska seized the other girl's hand in almost incredulous rapture. "How did it get there?"

"The police found it that day it stormed so. And a pilot flew it back to Jacksonville."

Mary Eliska and Jax Gray gazed at each other in full realization at last of the mysterious disappearance of the plane which they had mourned as lost forever.

If Mary Eliska was eager to get back to Jacksonville before, she was doubly so now. She could hardly contain her excitement during that flight across the Gulf of Mexico and over the state of Florida to the northern part. She kept urging Ted to put on more speed, to let the motor out to its limit, but the young man, realizing the load he was carrying, was not to be tempted beyond his better judgment.

They arrived at Jacksonville just as it was growing dusk, and flew over the city, now so familiar to them all, to the airport on its outskirts. Gracefully the skillful pilot swooped down the field to his landing.

The usual number of employees came out to greet them, but hardly had the girls climbed out of the plane when a resounding shout went up over the field. Mary Eliska and Jax Gray had been recognized!

A crowd collected immediately, a crowd that had been prepared by Ted's radio message that afternoon, to welcome the two popular girls back to civilization. It was all that Mary Eliska and Jax Gray could do to wave and shout greetings in return.

"I just want one look at my Ladybug," said Mary Eliska. "If you good people will let me get through———"

At this request, an accommodating official picked her right up on his shoulder, and carried her, amid the laughter of the crowd, triumphantly to the hangar where the autogiro was housed.

"Oh, you dear Ladybug!" whispered Mary Eliska, not wanting anyone to think she was silly, but so overcome with joy that she had to say something. No one but a pilot could understand the genuine affection which she felt for her autogiro.

"I'll be over to fly you tomorrow," she added, under her breath. Then, turning to the man who had conducted her across the field, she asked him whether he could as easily take her to the waiting taxi-cab.

They were off at last, waving and smiling to the enthusiastic crowd.

"Be sure to stay in Jacksonville 'til Saturday," the people begged them. "We're going to celebrate for you then!"

The girls nodded, and the taxi driver sped away with orders to go straight to the City Hall.

Captain Magee, who had received a call from the airport, was ready and waiting for them. Ted carried the shabby, worn bag into his office, and Mary Eliska put it into the Captain's hands herself.

"The bank's money," she explained. "And the two revolvers. We never had to use them at all."

"But we'd have died without them," added Jax Gray. "Of fright—if nothing else."

In vain Captain Magee tried to tell the girls how wonderfully brave he thought they had been, but he was so overcome by feeling that he groped for words and stammered—ending by pressing both Mary Eliska's and Jax Gray's hands in silence.

"Two young girls like you—" he finally managed to say—"succeeding where the police and everybody else failed! Capturing a hundred thousand dollars by a clever trick———"

"Is there really that much?" inquired Jax Gray. "Of course we never counted it."

The officer smiled at their unconcern. In spite of all their ability, they still seemed like children to him.

"By the way, Mary Eliska," he said, "I had a wire from your aunt this afternoon. She will arrive in Jacksonville Saturday morning—accompanied by Mrs. Gray."

This final piece of good news was just what the girls needed to complete their perfect day. Their eyes lighted up with happiness, and they squeezed each other's hands in joy.

"And your fathers ought to be back tomorrow. I'll send them straight to the hotel," he added. "So don't go away."

"Wild horses couldn't drag us!" returned Mary Eliska. "We're just dying to see them.... Now, good-by, Captain Magee.... We must go and get some dinner."

So, back in the hotel in Jacksonville, Jax Gray and Mary Eliska spent their first enjoyable evening for a week—celebrating their safe return with their dear friends, the Mackays.

Chapter 11.20
Conclusion

The girls' first visitor the following day was not, as they had hoped, the party from the yacht, but a woman. "Who can it be?" demanded Jax Gray, for the clerk at the desk had not sent up a name with the message.

"A reporter, probably," yawned Mary Eliska. "They'll be hot on our trail now, Jax Gray. That was one good thing about the island—we didn't have to read newspapers or give interviews."

"You're not wishing you were back again?"

"Never!" affirmed Mary Eliska, surveying the breakfast tray which she and Jax Gray had been luxuriously enjoying. "I don't care for cold tea and crackers as a steady diet."

"But what shall we do about this visitor?" persisted her companion. "The clerk's still waiting for our reply."

"Oh, tell him to send her up, I suppose. After all, the poor girls have to earn a living."

As Jax Gray gave the message over the telephone, Mary Eliska surveyed the room with a frown of distaste.

"It's not so neat, Jax Gray—to receive a caller," she remarked. "Maybe we ought to have gone downstairs. "Think I better try to call him back?"

"No, I guess it's too late now—the girl's probably on the elevator by this time. Anyhow, it really doesn't matter. Newspaper women are usually awfully good sports."

To their amazement and chagrin, it was not a reporter to whom, a moment later, Jax Gray opened the door. A beautifully dressed woman stood before them, smiling nervously. It was Mrs. Carter—Jackson Carter's mother! "How do you do, Mrs. Carter!" exclaimed Jax Gray. "Do come in—if you can pardon the appearance of this room."

The older woman seemed scarcely to notice the unmade beds or the open trunks. She nodded to Mary Eliska as she entered, but she appeared like a person with something serious on her mind.

"How did you know where to find us?" inquired Jax Gray, after she had cleared a chair for their visitor.

"It's in all the papers," the latter replied. "Haven't you read about yourselves? Why, everybody in town thinks you two girls are simply marvelous! Rescuing that money was a miracle in itself—an act of courage that Jacksonville will always be grateful to you for."

"It's awfully nice of you to say so," murmured Jax Gray, for Mary Eliska remained silent. Somehow the latter could never feel at home with this woman.

"Our city is planning a parade and celebration in your honor," she continued. "And the Daughters of the Confederacy would like to invite you to a dinner and reception afterwards. That is one of the reasons why I came to see you—to extend the invitation in person."

"It's extremely kind of you," assented Jax Gray. "We'll be delighted to accept, won't we, Mary Eliska?"

"Why, yes—of course—only—" Mary Eliska paused, hoping that she was not appearing rude.

"Except what, my dear!" asked Mrs. Carter.

"Well, it's marvelous of you to do it for us, but you see our fathers are coming—and Jax Gray's mother—and my Aunt Sally——"

"But they are included, of course! There will be both men and women at the banquet, and my brother-in-law, the president of the bank that was robbed, hopes to present you girls with the reward."

"Oh, it's going to be great fun, Mary Eliska!" exclaimed Jax Gray, excitedly. "We've just got to be there!"

"Yes, it will be charming," agreed the other girl. "We'll be delighted to come—if we may bring our friends."

There seemed nothing more to say, yet Mrs. Carter made no move towards going. To fill an awkward pause, Jax Gray inquired how Jackson was.

"Jackson has been away since the first of July," replied the older woman. "I haven't heard anything from him, and I am quite anxious, though he warned me he couldn't write. He and his chum, Hal Perry, went into the Okefenokee Swamp to search for you girls."

"The Okefenokee Swamp!" repeated Mary Eliska. It seemed ages since she had been lost in that desolate expanse.

"Yes. And I wondered, Mary Eliska, whether you would be willing to fly up to the northern end, up towards Camp Cordelia, and look for them. Oh, I don't mean go into the swamp again—that would be too dreadful—but just fly around it."

"Yes, of course," agreed Mary Eliska, not knowing what else to say. "If you will let me wait until my Daddy comes, so I can take him with me."

"Naturally!"

Mrs. Carter rose at last, but she still appeared to be embarrassed.

"There is something else I want to say to you, Mary Eliska. An apology, this time. I know now that you are the same girl my son rescued in the swamp and brought home to our house. The girl to whom I was so rude.... I—I want to beg your pardon."

It was a great deal from a woman of Mrs. Carter's dignity and importance, and Mary Eliska was deeply touched.

"This is very sweet of you, Mrs. Carter," she said. "And of course I understand how you felt at the time. I'm only too glad to forget all about it.... And," she added, holding out her hand, "I'll go to your son's rescue, as he has twice gone to mine—as soon as my Daddy comes."

Still the visitor hesitated, even after she had shaken hands with both the girls, and had reached the doorway.

"Would you girls consider bringing your families out to our home, to spend the weekend with us?" she asked, more as one seeking than as one bestowing a favor.

Jax Gray did not answer this time; she looked inquiringly at Mary Eliska.

"It would be lovely," replied the latter, with genuine enthusiasm. "But I am afraid there are too many of us. You see there are two friends with us now—Mr. and Mrs. Mackay, who picked us up in Havana—and there are two more with our fathers on the yacht. With my aunt and Jax Gray's mother, it will make ten in all. And that is too big a crowd for any place but a hotel!"

"Not at all!" protested Mrs. Carter. "I should love it. We have plenty of room, and plenty of servants—and we enjoy house-parties. How I shall look forward to seeing your mother, Dorothy!... You will come, won't you, girls—as soon as the whole party is together?"

With such a pressing invitation as this, they could not do otherwise than graciously accept, and, satisfied at last, Mrs. Carter bade them good-by.

There was no opportunity to discuss this unexpected visit, for no sooner had this caller departed than others began to arrive. Louise dashed into the room on her return from breakfasting with Ted in the dining-room, and before Jax Gray and Mary Eliska could repeat the invitation to her, news came that the yachting party had arrived.

The reunion of the two girls with their fathers was touching to see. For some minutes they clung to one another in the lobby of the hotel, regardless of the strangers about. Ralph Clavering and Jim Valier stood in the background, unnoticed.

About three o'clock that afternoon Mary Eliska suddenly remembered her promise to Mrs. Carter in regard to flying over the Okefenokee Swamp in search of Jackson, and she suggested to her father that they go to the airport immediately.

Mr. Stricklin shook his head decidedly. "No, daughter," he said. "You will never have my consent again to fly within fifty miles of that dismal swamp!"

"But we must be within fifty miles of it now," returned Mary Eliska. "Shall we leave Jacksonville?"

"Now, Mary Eliska! You know what I mean." "But how shall I tell Mrs. Carter? I promised, you know."

"You can leave that to me," he replied. "I'll explain."

But it was not necessary to do this, for the woman telephoned herself almost immediately to say that the boys had arrived by automobile half an hour ago. She concluded by reminding Mary Eliska that she was expecting the whole party the following day for luncheon.

Saturday dawned clear and bright, and the parade was scheduled for the early morning, before the sun's rays became blistering. Mary Eliska and Jax Gray occupied seats of honor on the canopied grandstand, beside the Mayor, and they bowed and smiled to everyone that passed by.

Aunt Sally and Mrs. Gray arrived just in time to witness the demonstration, in honor of their two brave girls.

CHAPTER 12

The Mystery of Seal Islands

CHAPTER 12.1
A BITTER BLOW

"I say, Mary Eliska, thought you were going to do some work for that Mr. Howe of the Federal Service. Did it fall through?"

"Haven't heard much more about it, John," Mary Eliska answered her brother, as she poured maple syrup over a serving of piping hot pancakes. Her mother came in at that moment with a replenished bowl of oatmeal, and she paused with an anxious glance at her young daughter.

"Hope you do not hear anything more about it, dear. I feel that your activities in helping clear up the mystery at Lurtiss Field placed you in any number of very dangerous situations. Being a pilot is hazardous enough without adding to the difficulties by running down air-gangsters of any kind," she said soberly.

"Perhaps Mr. Howe has discovered that he does not require your services. In work of that nature very often, when men on the job think they have struck a hard snag, something comes up suddenly which clears the matter so they do not require outside assistance," remarked Albert Stricklin, then smiled at his wife. "As a maker of pancakes, my dear, you draw first prize. The only drawback to such a breakfast is a man's limited capacity."

"You aren't announcing that you have been limiting yourself!" Mary Eliska laughed.

"No, that isn't my claim, but I have to confess that my limit is in sight," he told her.

"Tough luck, Dad. Now, I am only getting well started," Mary Eliska said, then added to her mother, "If you drew prizes for all the good things you cook you would have to have a museum for them as large as Colonel Lindbergh's in St. Louis."

"Second the motion," John put in, then went on to his young sister, "Who's the lady you have been piloting along the coast the last couple of weeks? Larry Kingsley told me she's got loads of money and has taken to taxiing about in the air with no particular objective."

"Oh, that is Lyudmila Shkrebneva. Her husband used to be in the fur business and when he died she sold her interest to a big syndicate, she told me, because she knew there wasn't much chance of her making a success against such competition. She is keen on aviation, and bought herself a plane but has never been able to get a license. I asked Mr. Trowbridge and he said he thought it was because she showed very little judgment in an emergency; she cracked-up three times, and they forbade her to fly alone."

"I should think they would," Mrs. Stricklin exclaimed indignantly.

"That's all I know about her, except that she is madder than a dozen wet hens at the government for depriving her of the right to fly; and she seems to be interested in fishes."

"Fishes?"

"Yes. She always carries a wonderful pair of glasses, and when we are over the water orders that I fly low and as slowly as possible while she examines the deep. I have to keep my eyes on the board, so I haven't been able to look at what attracts her attention especially, but a couple of times she has seemed very pleased over what she examined, and appears to admire the schools of fish we have followed a couple of times. Guess it's a hobby of hers, and she hasn't anything special to do, so she rides it—"

"Or rides the air," John laughed.

"Are you children riding in with me?" Albert Stricklin asked. "The time is getting short."

"I am, Dad, thanks. If you will take me as far as the subway in Jamaica, I'll land just in time for class," John answered.

"Phil will be here to pick me up, thank you," Mary Eliska replied, so, as the meal was finished, and the last pancake had disappeared, they left the table to start on the day's occupations. John raced up the stairs, three at a jump, while his sister gave her mother a hand straightening the dining room as she waited for Phil Fisher to take her to the flying field.

"I hear the motor, my dear," Mrs. Stricklin interrupted. "You'd better hurry."

"He's early this morning, but probably he has something to do before schedule." The girl hastened with her own preparations so that when the young man appeared at the door she was properly helmeted and all ready to take the air.

"Top of the morning to you," Phil called cheerily. "Your esteemed passenger wants to make an early start, so the boys will have Skybird warmed up for you and you can start as soon as you get to the field."

"It's mighty good of you to come and fetch me," Mary Eliska smiled at the president's son, who had not so many weeks before gone through a series of exciting, dangerous air-adventures with her. But those things were all in the day's work and belonged to the past; the new day awaited them.

"It isn't much of a hop, and as Lyudmila Shkrebneva has all the earmarks of being a good customer, she must be humored," Phil grinned. "Just the same, I'm glad they wished her on you and Skybird instead of the Moth and yours truly."

"Well, it's no particular fun piloting her. I wish she'd decide she wants variety, and give you all a chance at the job," Mary Eliska told him. They were making their way to where the Moth, Phil's own imported machine, waited to leap in the air with them. "I say, when is Mr. Howe going to start that investigation he spoke of a few weeks ago. Heard anything about it?"

"You are not so fed up on Lyudmila Shkrebneva that you want to get away from us all, are you?" he demanded.

"No, of course not, but I was wondering what his plan was and what happened to it, if anything," Mary Eliska answered.

"Glad to hear you do not want to leave. Gosh, to lose our only girl aviatrix would be—unthinkable; but, come to think of it, Howe came to the house to see Dad one day last week, perhaps they are getting it fixed up for you to take on the job. I heard the Old Man say the Federal representative would be at the office today, so perhaps you'll get some information. Here we are." They reached the airplane and Mary Eliska climbed into the seat beside the pilot's, adjusted straps and parachute, while the young man gave his machine a thorough looking-over then took his own place.

"Any idea what it's all about?"

"A small one. Several governments—ours and a couple of others, are trying to trace down illegal seal fishing; catch the lads who don't follow the rules. Contact." They were off, and Mary Eliska inquired no more about the government work because Phil's account of it sounded quite as tame as piloting Lyudmila Shkrebneva. Presently the Moth dropped out of the sky, landed near the office of the Lurtiss Airplane Company and a bit later the girl aviatrix presented herself at the private office of Mr. Trowbridge for whom she worked when she first joined the organization as a secretary. Mr. Wallace, one of the special instructors, was already there, and when Mary Eliska entered, they both rose to their feet to wish her good morning.

"Anything special?" she asked when greetings were exchanged.

"Only Lyudmila Shkrebneva. She ought to be here any minute," Mr. Trowbridge replied.

"Howe is coming in this morning," Mr. Wallace added.

"Phil told me—"

"Yes, and here I am," Mr. Howe announced himself as he entered. "They told me you were all in here, so I took the liberty of coming in without knocking; I can go out the same way if you like."

"You can stay here, without knocking," Mr. Trowbridge hastened to assure him. "I'm thinking Mary Eliska is glad to see you."

"She has been handling a job that is dull as ditch-water," Wallace put in quickly.

"She will not find my work dull, but it will be cold, for it may take her to the Bering Sea," Mr. Howe informed them. "I expect to be ready for her soon."

"It sounds no end exciting," Mary Eliska said and her blue eyes sparkled. A job that would take her to the Bering Sea appeared to have endless possibilities and she was keenly interested. Just then the phone rang and Mr. Trowbridge answered it.

"Your passenger has arrived," he told Mary Eliska.

"I'll go right down."

"See you later," Mr. Howe called after her as she hurried away. Ten minutes later Skybird, her own prize plane, was taxied to the edge of the field, where Mary Eliska and her passenger, a tall, slender woman, whose flying costume, however, gave her huge proportions, waited. The machine came up just as Mr. Wallace and Mr. Howe, in the company's carrying automobile started for the further end of the field.

"There is to be a test for the racing machines this evening, Mary Eliska," the instructor called as he brought the car to a stop close to where the two were standing. Mary Eliska noticed that the Federal man gave her companion a swift, all-inclusive glance, but since that was the way with Mr. Howe, and he always looked everybody up and down, she did not think anything about it.

"Hope I can watch it," she replied.

"All set, Mary Eliska." Skybird came to a stop a few yards away, so, forgetting everything else, Mary Eliska turned her whole attention to the task at hand. Presently all was ready, and in another moment, Skybird was leaping into the air, carrying her pilot and passenger up a steep climb until they were well in the air, then her nose was leveled and she shot east and south, as Lyudmila Shkrebneva designated the direction she wished to take.

Having taken the woman every day for over two weeks, Mary Eliska knew pretty well how high and fast she preferred to travel, so they did not waste any time on discussions, but shot ahead swiftly. Almost as soon as she was seated, Lyudmila Shkrebneva got the powerful field glasses out of their case, and as soon as they were over the water, trained them on its smooth surface. The day was clear, the sky blue, and the sea calm, so the task of piloting was not arduous, and Mary Eliska let her mind wander on speculations about her companion. That the woman was wealthy was obvious, but for the first time the girl began to wonder about her interest in things in the ocean. It occurred to her that the woman might be looking for sunken vessels, or something of that nature, but she had never let a word drop regarding what she sought. Then it struck Mary Eliska that she was a bit mysterious. Although it wasn't necessary for passengers to explain their businesses or hobbies, still when anyone traveled day after day with the same pilot it was only natural that they should establish more or less friendly relations and exchange odds and ends about each other. Thinking it over carefully, the girl realized that except for the facts that Lyudmila Shkrebneva's husband had come to the United States from Russia when he was a lad, that he had gone into the fur business, and had been dead two years, she knew nothing more than the bit of information gleaned in the office regarding the failure to pass the flying tests to fly her own machine.

"Follow the coast south and keep outside the Government limit," Lyudmila Shkrebneva directed after they had been in the air about an hour. "Have you plenty of gasoline? I want to remain up several hours."

"Plenty," Mary Eliska assured her but she was becoming really puzzled about her passenger. It could not be possible that Lyudmila Shkrebneva was in search of vessels carrying liquor, for she never showed the slightest interest in ships of any description when they were sighted, but this was the first time she expressed a desire to keep beyond the jurisdiction of the United States. The request was strange and the girl pilot felt oddly disturbed by it.

But if Lyudmila Shkrebneva was doing anything forbidden by the laws of the United States, she gave no sign of it during the hours which followed. Her glasses swept the water as they had every other day, and if she noticed the ships, large or small, plowing through them, she was remarkably successful in keeping the fact to herself. Except for her usual directions regarding the course they were to follow, she said nothing more; and at noon she signified her desire to return to land. She requested that they come down on the southern part of New Jersey, but here she merely led the way to a restaurant where she ordered lunch for both of them.

Seated across from her, Mary Eliska noted that she might be about thirty-five years old, and her mouth, which was rather large, was set firmly, like a mask. Without consulting her companion, she ordered an excellent meal, and after the first course was set before them, her face relaxed somewhat, as if she suddenly realized her duties as a hostess.

"You are an excellent pilot, Mary Eliska," she remarked. There was a musical quality to her voice, as if she might sing a good contralto, and when her eyes softened it gave her features an expression of real charm.

"Thank you," Mary Eliska replied, a bit at a loss. Since she had started to wonder about her passenger a feeling of awkwardness came over her, and she flushed with embarrassment.

"There is little money these days in commercial piloting, I am informed," Lyudmila Shkrebneva went on in a chatty sort of fashion as if she were filling in the gap with small talk.

"I like the work," the girl answered.

"You doubtless have many passengers and various experiences?"

"I guess we all do," Mary Eliska replied. Something inside her warned her that perhaps it would be just as well if she did not become too confidential over her work. Since she had won her own license she had learned much about human nature, and every day she was adding to that store of knowledge, either through her own experiences or those of her co-pilots, so her bump of caution was developing rapidly.

"Ah, the waiter." The man appeared and the meal was eaten almost in silence. Twice Mary Eliska tried to break the awkwardness of the situation, but the replies from her companion were the briefest possible, so she gave up the attempt after the second failure. She was glad when the meal was over and they returned to Skybird. They took their places and several times during the return trip, the pilot saw her companion give her short quick glances.

There was something about Lyudmila Shkrebneva which made Mary Eliska recall the time Phil had been employed to take an old man on regular trips to Philadelphia. Young Fisher had described his passenger as "falling to pieces," but after a number of trips, Mary Eliska had chanced to see the pair in the air; the ancient man pressing a pistol to the back of his pilot's head. It wasn't a pleasant memory, in fact it added greatly to the girl's uneasiness, but, if her companion's intention was evil, she gave no evidence of it. They reached the field in good time without mishap, and as soon as they were out of the cockpit, the passenger turned for an instant.

"Tomorrow I shall come at the same time."

"Let them know at the office," Mary Eliska replied mechanically. Just at that moment Phil's Moth came roaring over the field and lighted close by. He waved to Mary Eliska, who waited for him.

"Have a wild time?"

"Wild as a plate of soup." Mary Eliska told him how she had spent the hours and what had been passing through her mind. They walked slowly toward the office and Phil listened thoughtfully.

"Wonder what her game is anyway? I'm going to tell Trowbridge to have some—"

"I say, Kingsley." Someone called the president's son, and with a nod to his companion, he strode off to see what was wanted.

Mary Eliska proceeded, but as she went she wished she had not spoken to Phil of her nervousness. Probably it was just silly and she certainly didn't want to be relieved of the responsibility because she was afraid. After all, there wasn't a thing in the world to be afraid of, nothing but a collection of wild guesses. It was unlike the time the "old man" had tried to appropriate the Moth, for then the country was filled with horrible stories of "Blue Air-pirates," but now everything was as it should be. In fact, life was a bit dull except for the unending joy of racing into the sky. By that time she reached Mr. Trowbridge's office, but as she opened the door she heard Mr. Wallace saying angrily, "Well, I'll be darned if I see it. Oh, oh, hello Mary Eliska." With that he rushed out of the room and banged the door so hard that it jarred the place.

"Oh, er, oh," Mr. Trowbridge glanced at her, then began to fumble with some papers on his desk. "Wallace is a bit upset, you'll have to excuse him."

"Sorry if I interrupted—""Er, no, you didn't. That is, well, you have to be told—"

"Is something wrong, Mr. Trowbridge?" she asked quietly. "Well, er, yes there is—""Anything happened to Mother or—"

"Oh, no, what a blundering ass I am; but, you know, it's this way, the stock market—well, you've heard how it broke a lot of people. We have to—er, reduce expenses, er, you see—there was a meeting, and some of the pilots have to go—I'm sorry, hate to lose you, hate it like fury, and so does Wallace."

"Oh, I say, Mary Eliska—" he paused, then walked briskly to his desk, cleared his throat, opened and closed a drawer, and without looking at her again, spoke with an effort. "I'm sorry about this—" he got up again, "but, don't take it so hard. You've got one of the best records of any pilot in the country, you own Skybird, and you are sure to pick up something quickly."

"I, I wasn't thinking of that," she managed to answer. It was her first position since she had been graduated from business school, so of course it was the first time she had lost one, and now it swept over her, like an on-rushing tide, that she was outside of the organization; she was no longer a part of the Lurtiss Airplane Company. She swallowed, bravely endeavoring to buck up or snap out of her depression, but it wasn't easy.

"No, surely you weren't. Sit down a moment and collect yourself. This financial mess is likely to adjust itself overnight, then the whole works will be booming again. It can't be anything more than temporary, and in a few weeks you'll be back again. You'll be the first one recalled, for your service has been excellent, excellent."

"Thank you so much, Mr. Trowbridge—"

"There's a lot of pick-up work. Odds and ends; people hiring planes for trips and business purposes. With Skybird you can find plenty to do. If I may make a suggestion, I'd say do some of that sort of thing temporarily—but—then," he glanced at her and frowned. "You probably won't want to see one of us again, ever—"

"I'll be glad to come back whenever you have a place for me," she told him hastily. Mr. Trowbridge was feeling so miserable that Mary Eliska was sorry for him and tried to cheer him up.

"That's great. Knew you were not the sore-head kind. You can understand how things *will* happen—"

"I guess I don't very well, but I am sure you have all been most kind to me. I'd rather be dismissed because of reducing expenses than because I didn't do my job well. Mr. Howe was in this morning. Did he say anything about the work he wanted done?"

"Well, er, he did mention it, but I believe he left for Washington and I don't know when he'll be back. He can get your address from us any time he wants it, or you could send him a note—"

"Guess I won't do that, but I will leave the address, thank you." She wrote it down for him and was glad to be able to do something for a moment. "If he wants me he can find me easily enough. You have been mighty kind—I'm wondering if—if it will seem—that is, I wish you would tell the others that I appreciate—I—somehow I don't feel exactly like saying goodbye to them—"

"I'll be glad to. They will understand." Mr. Trowbridge answered so quickly that she was a little startled at his readiness, but that, too, passed out of her mind immediately.

"I'll get Skybird—"

"One of the boys will fix her up for you, and any time you want her given an overhauling, drop down here. She'll be taken care of the same as usual; we'd feel neglected if you did not permit us to do that for you." He tried to smile, but the effort was not much of a success.

"Thank you—" Quickly she faced about and hurried out of the office, closing the door after her much more softly than Mr. Wallace had done a few minutes before. She did not notice as she made her way to the big entrance, but before she got half way to the hangar, she met Phil.

"Oh, here you are, say" he stopped short. "What's the matter, Mary Eliska, you look as if you'd seen a ghost!"

"I'm all right," she answered and blinked furiously.

"Where you going?" demanded Phil.

"Home."

"Let me take you." He swung in beside her.

"Thank you, I'm going alone—Oh, it's all right, I mean I'm all right, but, well, Mr. Trowbridge just told me about the—"

"About the what?"

"He told me the firm has to let some of its pilots go, and I am one of them." Phil stopped short, caught her arm and swung her around so that she faced him.

"What the heck are you talking about?" he demanded.

"I just lost my job and I guess I am making an awful boob of myself." She forced her lips into a good imitation of a smile.

"I say, you are full of—quit kidding—"

"I am not kidding, Phil."

"You mean to say Trowbridge just told you that you can't work here anymore," he persisted.

"Yes I do," she answered. "So long, Phil."

"I say, wait a minute, while I look into this," he called, but a plane was roaring onto the field and the noise of the motor drowned his voice so the girl did not hear. Her throat choked as she hurried to get away, and after staring at her a few minutes, young Fisher, his forehead puckered in a deep frown, strode toward the office, and met Trowbridge just coming out. "What's the big idea?" he demanded.

"You mean about Mary Eliska?"

"Of course," Phil snapped.

"Howe has some sort of idea that he wants to put into operation. He believes that it will help him capture a choice collection of bandits and he thinks some of them will make use of Mary Eliska, so she's in the Government employ really, but she doesn't know it."

"It sounds blamed putrid to me," Phil declared, and he started down the steps.

"Give it a trial, Phil, for it's a whale of a thing," the man urged. "We don't any of us think much of the plan, but she promised to help him and probably his way is best."

"Well—" Just then the familiar roar of Skybird's engine announced that their Girl Sky Pilot was on her way home, and if Mary Eliska could have had an inkling of that conversation, it would have brightened the outlook of everything for weeks to come. But she was blissfully unconscious that she was playing a part, and life seemed to be of the deepest indigo.

It took Skybird only a short time to get her young owner home and to her own new hangar. The Stricklins lived on the outskirts of one of Long Island's many small towns, east of the flying field on a part of an ancient farm. There were several acres in the property and since they had become interested in aviation, John and his sister had built a house for their planes out of an old barn. They had smoothed off a fair runway, not as good, of course, as those on the regulation fields, but it was fairly smooth and perfectly safe for landing and taking-off. Skybird was brought down in a perfect three-point and mechanically the girl glanced at the wind-sock fluttering under the old weather-cock.

There was a catch in the girl's throat when she unlocked the long sliding doors and assured herself that her brother's plane, the Falcon, which that young man rarely used since he was back at college, was properly placed so her own machine could be run in easily. While she was attending to the task she heard the house door open, and realized that her mother was probably coming out to learn why she was home so early. With a determined effort she shook off the gloom, or at least its outward appearance, so when Mrs. Stricklin appeared she was greeted by a smiling young daughter.

"'Lo, Mummy," she called.

"All right, my dear?"

"Top hole. As soon as I lock the door I'll be in with you," she answered with a disarming cheeriness.

"May I help?"

"Sure, tell me if I'm getting too close to the Falcon's wings."

"You have plenty of space." Presently the two machines were locked in to exchange confidences if they felt so disposed, while Mary Eliska and her mother walked arm in arm to the house. "I suppose you have to take someone in the morning and that is why you have brought Skybird home for a visit."

"No, that's a wrong guess, Mummy." They went into the house and Mrs. Stricklin glanced anxiously at the girl.

"Sure you are all right, dear?"

"Fine as silk. Fact is, Mummy, the stock-market slump has hit some of our directors, hard, and the company has to reduce expenses. Mr. Trowbridge told me when I came back with my passenger this afternoon."

"The stock-market slump; why, that was months ago!"

"I don't know much about it except what I heard you and Dad saying last fall. Is it possible that it still affects business?" Mary Eliska didn't ask because she was at all interested in the "Bulls and Bears of Wall Street," but just for the sake of talking. She removed her flying coat and hat and hung them, with a sigh, in the hall closet, wondering a bit sadly how soon she would use them again. She knew that she simply couldn't leave the beloved Skybird idle in the hangar; she would certainly take it out for pleasure, but that was different from being really a part of the great force of men and women aiding in the world's grand and almost brand-new industry.

"Probably," her mother answered. "Your father was saying only a few nights ago that a good many big business men have gone on with their projects confident that the financial situation would improve, but while it is getting better, the growth is slow and any number of them have had to drop out."

"Dad didn't get hit, did he?"

"No dear, he has some stock in various concerns but it is not the kind that fluctuates with an erratic market."

"Mr. Trowbridge suggested that I pick up some odds and ends for a while and probably in a few weeks things will be better with the company and I can go back. He was sort of shot up when he told me," Mary Eliska explained.

"I'll be mighty glad to have my girl home with me for a while," Mrs. Stricklin smiled.

"And it will not be hard on my own feelings, to stay," she laughed. "I've been thinking I may go in for some record-breaking flights—"

"My dear—" her mother protested.

"I don't mean stunts; just long-distance hops."

"But will Skybird carry gasoline enough for trips?"

"She'll go a lot, Mummy. You know Skybird has been a sort of pet of Mr. Wallace's and he's put all sorts of improvements into her. She's a top-notch bird and no one except us and a few men in the company really know how capable she is, and we're not telling."

"Suppose you stay home for a day or two anyway before you fly off from the nest, Honey," her mother pleaded.

"All right. Tell you what, I'll take you joy-riding around the skies," she promised and although Mrs. Stricklin made no objection and fully appreciated that flying was a splendid means of travel, she just could not think of herself as a successful joy-rider.

That evening when Mr. Stricklin reached home he heard the news with some surprise and questioned Mary Eliska closely. However, he did not make any guesses and did his best to cheer her up.

"You have been most fortunate, my dear, as a young business woman, and this is the first time you have lost a position, so it seems more tragic than anything else in the world, but as you gain experience you will understand that almost any enterprise has its ups and downs, the downs often being in the majority. Sudden changes are frequently necessary. Just figure up your assets; you have Skybird, an A-One license, know how to be a good secretary in case you cannot get a pilot's berth, some money in the savings bank—"

"And health," her mother added.

"And the best family in the world," Mary Eliska laughed. "My goodness, when I come to count my blessings they mount up to the skies, almost."

"That's the way to look at it," her father encouraged. "Life is not all a path of roses, and sometimes even the roses have thorns. When things run along too smoothly one gets careless and unprepared to face the rough places."

"Guess it is like flying," Mary Eliska answered. "You have to keep alert for the pockets, bumps, and cliffs, besides watching the machinery, if you don't want a smash."

"That's the idea. I know your mother will be happy if you remain grounded for a while, and I am sure that if I try hard, I can bear up under it," he grinned mischievously.

"Dad, you are a fraud," the girl laughed heartily.

"As long as my efforts are not flat tires I'll survive that," he retorted, and after that the fact that she had lost her position was dismissed, the three spent a thoroughly enjoyable evening. Before she hopped into bed that night, Mary Eliska glanced at the converted hangar and couldn't suppress a little sigh.

"As a good sport, I am something of a flat tire myself," she said softly and was about to turn away from the window when she thought she caught sight of something moving slowly along the door. Instantly forgetting sleepiness she stared hard for fully a minute until she convinced herself that there was something there. "It may be a dog," she told herself, for although the Stricklins didn't have one, most of the neighbors did, and at night the beasts were given to prowling about the community.

Watching a bit longer the girl came to the conclusion that if it was a dog the beast was behaving oddly. She didn't recall ever seeing one move so stealthily. She reasoned that it might be getting ready to pounce on something, but in the darkness she couldn't see a thing it could be after. If it was a man, a prowler, what was he doing near the hangar? Her heart leaped to her throat as she thought of Skybird poised inside beside the Falcon, but certainly no one would dream of trying to steal the ancient plane belonging to her brother, for its days of usefulness were practically over. Yet, she was sure that no one knew that her own prize machine rested behind that door. The huddled bunch of blackness moved forward, gave a little leap, and she leaned over the sill.

"Sure, it's a dog. Probably one of the big ones on a neighborly tour of investigation." She watched a bit longer, and was just about to get into bed when she spied a thin streak of light, like a carefully shaded flash, that cast a faint glow on the ground. Then it began to travel swiftly up toward the lock and to her straining ears came the faintest sound of scraping. Quick as a thought Mary Eliska threw on a robe, jammed her feet into her slippers as she hurried across the room, then raced to her Father's door, where she knocked.

"Dad, dad," she called softly.

"My dear, what is the matter?" Mrs. Stricklin had heard and leaped out of bed in fright before her husband was fully awake. Her hand moved along the wall for the electric switch, but Mary Eliska placed her own over it quickly.

"Don't, Mummy," she whispered.

"What is the matter, Mary Eliska?" her father asked. He was wide awake now and up beside her. "Are you sick?"

"No, Dad, but someone is trying to get into the hangar!"

"To get into the hangar?"

"Yes, I saw someone moving by the door and watched it. Thought it was a dog, then whoever it is turned on a little light by the opening," she explained excitedly.

"No one would try to steal the airplanes, either of them, dear, it would make too much noise," he protested.

"If they get the door open they could muffle the machine a bit, roll it out and get away," she insisted.

"That is so," he admitted.

"They would not have to take it far before they start the engine, then they can get off in it. Skybird doesn't need any warming up—"

"That's so. Come into your room." The adults' own sleeping quarters did not face the rear, so the old barn could not be seen or watched from their windows.

"You must be careful, both of you," Mrs. Stricklin urged anxiously.

"We will." Albert Stricklin had already gotten into his own shoes, which he did not stop to tie, while his wife handed him his bath robe, which was dark colored and warm.

"Come along." The pair, with Mrs. Stricklin following in the distance, proceeded quickly. In a moment they were at the window, and there was no doubting the fact that prowlers of some kind were working to open the door. The light shone in a faint round circle over the lock, and a figure, which looked tall and grotesque, was busy with a tool. So far as they could see, only one person was at the hangar but they were reasonably sure that at least one guard was on duty to warn the robber if necessary.

"I'm going out—." Mr. Stricklin caught her quickly. "Do nothing of the kind," he ordered firmly.

"Get me that old shotgun out of the closet. Be careful of it."

"All right." She flew swiftly to the place where her father stored all sorts of odds and ends, including an ancient double-barreled shotgun which had been one of his treasures when he was a young man. Since the children had grown up it had been kept loaded and both of them had been taught how to handle it without danger. Quickly Mary Eliska took it from its hooks and hurried back to her father.

"Thank you. Stand back." He rested the long barrel on the sill, the sight trained on the barn, then, without an unnecessary sound, he pulled the trigger, first one, then the other. There was a loud report, followed instantly by a hail of lead which crackled as it spattered over a wide surface.

CHAPTER 12.3
A STRANGE PROPOSAL

Simultaneously with the sound of peppering bullets came a furious string of oaths. A second figure leaped from the corner of the old building and then the gun spoke again. This time, amid the hail of small bullets came a muffled cry of pain, subdued curses, and a swift scrambling of two pairs of feet taking their owners helter-skelter from the vicinity. From a distance came the roar of a motor thrown open quickly somewhere down the road, a clutch released as if by frantic hands, then an automobile in motion, but moving slowly.

"Nipped them," Dad declared with satisfaction.

"Wish you could have done more than that," Mary Eliska said without any compunction.

"At any rate, they are frightened away. Turn on the lights, Mother, please, and we'll do some investigating." Mrs. Stricklin pressed the switches which immediately illuminated the whole house, and the sounds of shouts came from the home of the nearest neighbors. This was taken up by other persons, while someone on a motorcycle seemed to turn as if giving chase after the robbers.

"Don't go out," Mrs. Stricklin urged as her husband began to don his trousers hastily under his robe.

"It's quite safe," he assured her. Before he was ready there came a pounding at the door—alarmed voices shouted, "You people all right, Stricklin?"

"That's Mr. Howard. He's the sheriff of the county and must have been in the neighborhood."

"I'll be right down," Mrs. Stricklin called. Presently the officer of the law was standing in the hall, while she explained what had happened.

"Glad nobody's hurt, least-wise, none of you folks. I'll go out and have a look around." There was a business-like gun in his hand and his chin was set firmly.

"I'm coming with you," Mr. Stricklin called from the top of the stairs as he hurried to join the sheriff.

"I'm coming too, Dad."

"Stay with your mother, please," he answered, so Mary Eliska obeyed.

"There isn't a thing you can do out there, Honey," Mrs. Stricklin assured her. "And you might get in the way."

So the girl had to be content to remain inside, while sounds of people running, sharp questions, brief answers, and the noise of automobiles stopping while the occupants demanded to know what was the difficulty came to them from outside. Half an hour later Mr. Stricklin came back with the sheriff and their nearest neighbor, and although they were greatly excited, they had discovered nothing more than some footprints of the robbers, and the place where a large car had been parked by the side of the road, obviously waiting to assist the thieves in their enterprise, or get them away from the scene of their mischief.

"That's a good lock you have on the building," the sheriff announced. "Kept them from opening the door right away."

"Mighty good thing your daughter happened to look out of her window before she turned in to bed," remarked the neighbor.

"Yes, indeed it is."

"I call the best part that you had a pop-gun to pepper them with. I heard one cry out, and from my window I saw that the fellow hiding nearest the barn grabbed toward his face."

"From that window of yours you must have had a pretty good look at them, even if it was dark," said the sheriff.

"Did, for an instant. The lad that got nipped seemed like a big boy; tall, stout chap I should say, but the way he sprinted after the gun went off, he sure is agile."

"Did you hear them at the hangar?" Mary Eliska asked.

"No. Fact is, we were in bed and my wife asked me to open our window a bit wider. These spring nights are warming considerable. I just got the window up when the shot came. The lad at the door surely had a vocabulary! Then the second shot ripped about and the fat fellow squealed."

"It was fortunate that you happened to be in the neighborhood, Mr. Howard," said Mrs. Stricklin.

"I was cutting across lots for home when I heard the shots. I'd been at the town hall where we had a hot session over some concessions and taxes. Just got through and I was so tired I was for getting home by the shortest route, even if it took me through other people's property," explained the sheriff.

"We are very much—" Just then a motorcycle sputtered up to the house and its rider flung himself off vigorously. Before he could knock, Mr. Stricklin was at the door and threw it open.

"Hello, I say, I happened to be riding near here, sort of meandering along not making much noise and I passed a big car parked back of those elm trees. Thought it was a spooning party, so came along minding my own business, then I heard shots and almost at the same time the motor of the limousine was started. I put on the brakes just in time to keep from hitting a man who was running toward the road, and he hopped into the car, another fellow right after him."

"Did you turn around and chase them?" Mary Eliska asked eagerly.

"Yes, Miss, I did, but they opened her up and went 'hell bent for election,' I beg your pardon. And pretty soon I couldn't see anything but the dust they made, and there was plenty of that." He fumbled in the pocket of his jacket.

"Get the number?" the sheriff snapped.

"Bet your socks," the boy grinned. "Here she is."

"Good piece of work." Mr. Howard took the scrap of paper upon which the license number had been hastily scrawled.

"Wrote it down quick so I wouldn't forget it. Anybody hurt?"

"Thank you, we are all right," Mrs. Stricklin assured him. "Won't you have a cup of coffee, or something to eat?" The chap was about John's age.

"Thanks just the same. I'll ooze along. You people will want to get back to bed. If you care to bump-the-bumps with me, sheriff, I'll give you a lift on this cycle."

"Thanks. I'll get home as fast as I can and start things humming on the telephone. Spread this number over the country through the broadcasting stations and find out who owns that car."

"Ought not to be hard finding the would-be thieves," the boy grinned.

"Looks as if it might be easy, thanks to your good sense."

"Say it with flowers," the lad chuckled. "Come along. As long as I live I may never get another chance to have a sheriff in the saddle behind me. How I wish a cop would try to stop me on this trip."

The pair went off amid the reports of the motorcycle, and then the neighbors, assured that the Stricklins were unhurt and in no further danger, departed. Before she went to bed Mary Eliska took another look at the old barn-hangar where Skybird and the Falcon were still resting securely. With a sigh of relief she glanced toward the sky, which was mighty dark, but she caught the faint outline of the moon shining through as if she had decided to lighten things up a bit in the vicinity of the beloved airplane and its owner. In spite of the excitement and terror, the girl was so weary that she dropped off to sleep at once and it was late when she awakened. To her amazement she heard voices in the vicinity of the hangar, but when she hopped out of bed, she saw it was her Dad there with the village electrician.

"Good morning, dear, I thought I heard you moving about."

"Morning, Mummy. What are they doing out there?"

"Your father decided to have a good alarm put on the door so that the next unwelcome hand that tries to tamper with it will wake up the neighborhood," she explained.

"Dad's a dear," the girl answered.

"I've always thought so," her mother admitted.

"And you have known him a lot longer than I have," Mary Eliska chuckled.

"How would you like some breakfast here—"

"Top hole, but I'm going to get into some clothes and come down and get it before you spoil me entirely," she laughed and gave her mother a resounding kiss. "Oh, isn't it great that there was no damage really done!"

"Simply great."

"Did Mr. Howard get any news of the robbers?"

"We haven't heard anything from him this morning, but your father plans to stop at his office on the way in to town."

While Mary Eliska was eating her belated breakfast any number of neighbors came in to congratulate the family because its property was safe, and, those who did not know the facts, to get details of the attempted theft. Once the conversation was interrupted by the sudden and sharp clanging of a bell which made them all jump. But Mrs. Stricklin glanced out of the window and saw the electrician waving his hand so she knew he was merely testing the alarm, and reassured the callers.

"Sounds louder than the fire bell," Mary Eliska remarked, and they agreed that she was right and it would certainly wake everybody in the neighborhood if it went off at night.

After the guests had taken their departure the girl helped her mother and when the bell was finally installed, they went out to inspect the job. The alarm was set low on the wall, the wiring ran back through the thick planks, which had been bored so they were not exposed, and could not be either ripped out or cut without difficulty.

"Keep them set all of the time," the man explained, "and remember whenever you want to open the door to switch them off. I'm to put some more on the windows, so your plane will certainly be well protected and ought to be safe."

"That's what we want," Mrs. Stricklin told him, then turned to her daughter. "That is our telephone, dear."

"I'll go and answer it," Mary Eliska replied, and ran to the house as fast as she could. The bell was still ringing so she knew that the party had not been discouraged over the delay and given up getting in touch with the family. "Hello," she spoke into the phone.

"I wish to speak with Mary Eliska," came the reply, and although the voice sounded familiar, Mary Eliska could not recognize it immediately.

"This is Mary Eliska," she said.

"Mary Eliska?"

"Yes."

"How do you do! This is Lyudmila Shkrebneva."

"Oh!" Mary Eliska wasn't at all delighted at the announcement.

"Today I went early to the field; waited for you an unreasonable length of time, then found, upon inquiry, that you are no longer with the Lurtiss Airplane Company."

"Yes."

"I was sorry, of course. Well, I took the liberty of asking them for your address and communicating with you. I prefer you to one of the men for my pilot; also your little plane rides very comfortably. This morning is wasted, but the afternoon is still young. I should like to engage you to take me along the coast as usual. Can you meet me in, say, half an hour?"

"Well—" Mary Eliska hesitated.

"You will be well paid. You have not connected, as yet, with another firm, or taken on a passenger?"

"No," Mary Eliska had to admit. Just then her mother came hurrying in lest the call be from her husband. She glanced at her daughter and saw the look of doubt on the young face.

"What is it, dear?" she asked softly. Mary Eliska put the instrument low and spoke softly.

"Lyudmila Shkrebneva wants me to take her up this afternoon."

"Perhaps you will feel more comfortable if you are flying," her mother suggested.

"You will meet me?" came the demand in her ear.

"All right," she agreed.

"In half an hour."

"Yes." She hung up the receiver and explained the call to her mother, but she said nothing about her uneasiness of the day before. The idea of getting an immediate assignment did make her feel less dispirited, and when she thought of the previous afternoon, she dismissed it promptly. "Probably all poppy-cock," she told herself.

"It will not be difficult flying and if you have been taking her up every day, she may want to engage you regularly," Mrs. Stricklin remarked. "I know you will feel better satisfied, although I was beginning to hope I should have you to myself for a few days."

"Ever get tired of me, Mummy?"

"Of all the idiotic questions ever asked, that takes the grand prize!" Mrs. Stricklin answered. "Can I help you?"

"Of course you can."

The getting ready did not take long, and exactly half an hour later, Skybird lighted about a mile from the Flying Field where the girl Aviatrix found her passenger had just arrived. The woman came in a taxicab, nodded a greeting, paid the driver, then came briskly to the waiting plane. Her throat was wrapped in a scarf.

"I am glad that you could come," she said, but the words were stilted, not especially cordial, and again that inexplicable feeling of uneasiness swept over Mary Eliska.

"It was good of you to think of me," she responded, although she very much wanted to open the throttle and go sailing off, leaving her passenger to seek another pilot to take her on her mysterious mission. However, she suppressed the desire and opened the door of the cockpit instead. Lyudmila Shkrebneva took her place and quickly adjusted herself, but it wasn't until Skybird had them high in the air a few moments later that Mary Eliska noticed the woman had a bit of gauze and a long strip of courtplaster on her lower jaw. They were sailing over the eastern corner of the Lurtiss Field and a pang of sadness made Mary Eliska blink hard as she glanced down at the familiar scene.

There near the end was the long hangar with the pilots' quarters close by. The middle of the ground was marked off for landing, runways, lights and signals. Further along, to one side were the special houses for special planes; Skybird used to occupy one of them, and beyond them was the huge factory building, nearly all glass, with the executive and other offices facing the road. If she closed her eyes for a moment, Mary Eliska could picture every inch of the whole plant. Here and there were animated-looking objects which she knew were men or women workers; the bus and one of the company's cars were racing along like a couple of toys. Resolutely she turned her face away and applied herself with determination to the task at hand. Once she noticed that Lyudmila Shkrebneva was looking at her in the mirror, but she smiled behind her goggles. She wasn't going to let her passenger know how she felt about being separated from her former work, its varied interests, and happy companionships.

"Straight west," Lyudmila Shkrebneva directed with apparent indifference. They had been flying but a short time when Mary Eliska became conscious that a second plane had risen from the take-off grounds she knew so well, and although she longed to look back, or give her wings the three-waggle-signal, she held Skybird at a respectful angle. The machine came racing swiftly and once she caught a glimpse of it as it flashed into her mirror. The pilot was zooming higher than Skybird and although the distance was too great for her to tell who was flying it did look like Larry's plane. The sight of it gave her another pang of loneliness, then, for companionship's sake, she glanced at the woman beside her and again noticed the bit of white adhesive which protruded above the chinstrap of her helmet.

"Wonder what happened to her face," was her mental question, but the answer was doubtless any one of a dozen possibilities and she didn't waste time in surmises. Lyudmila Shkrebneva took up the speaking tube and Mary Eliska attached the end so she could hear what was to be said. "You have an exceptionally fine airplane," Lyudmila Shkrebneva remarked.

"I think so," Mary Eliska answered with a smile.

"Care to sell it?" The girl was so astonished that she gasped.

"No, indeed, I do not," she answered emphatically.

"I am anxious to purchase a good one, and am willing to pay well for this," the woman persisted.

"Not for sale at any price. I wouldn't part with Skybird," was the positive answer, and Lyudmila Shkrebneva smiled.

"I should have known that you would rather part with an eye. Let us turn back—I am a little tired today."

"All right." Skybird climbed and curved widely, and then Mary Eliska noticed two airplanes in the air, one coming up from the south, and the other rushing north. They were both going at a swift speed and it struck the girl pilot that this was the first time she had been out with Lyudmila Shkrebneva that airplanes had come anywhere near them. It also flashed through her mind that perhaps the presence of the flyers was the reason for her passenger's sudden weariness, but as far as she could tell the woman was not conscious of their presence in the air. Once or twice she glanced indifferently at the water, then, when they were soaring in fine style over Long Island, the field glasses were put in their case.

"Where shall I take you?" Mary Eliska asked.

"To the Huntington depot, or as near as you can."

"It's some distance from the railroad."

"I can get a lift."

Presently they were gliding to earth, but before she alighted Lyudmila Shkrebneva turned again to her pilot. "You do not care to change your mind about selling your airplane?"

"Skybird isn't for sale!"

"Very well. I have some work, observation work which will take me greater distances. It is something in which my husband was interested, a theory of his; he left copious notes, but they are unfinished and I am occupying myself in trying to complete his work." Her voice sounded weary and Mary Eliska suddenly felt sorry for her.

"It is fine that you can carry on for him," she said.

"I suppose so. The question is, can you accompany me on a more or less erratic course for about ten days or two weeks? Your airplane is especially adapted for my purpose; it is comfortable and durable. I have no license, so could not fly it even if I purchased it, so, if I can hire you both, that will answer nicely."

"Well, I—"

"You will be well paid—"

"I wasn't thinking of the money," Mary Eliska said hastily. "I'll have to talk it over with Dad and Mother. What shall I tell them I am expected to do?"

"Nothing more than you have been doing," she answered with a smile. "I'll call your home tomorrow evening and you can give me your answer."

CHAPTER 12.4
A STARTLING DISCOVERY

Flying home at a good speed Mary Eliska considered the offer she had just received and tried to decide whether or not she cared to accept it. Today was the first time since they had started the trips together that her passenger had showed any signs of being especially companionable and her sadness had instantly aroused the young pilot's sympathy, but she was still not attracted by the woman; in fact she found an indefinable something which she positively disliked. The girl realized that Lyudmila Shkrebneva's attention was entirely absorbed with her own project and efforts to carry on her husband's work; also that while flying her own mind must be fully occupied with her job; but the taciturnity of the woman seemed more than concentration on her affairs, whatever they were. There was something hard in her expression and her jaw set more like an over-bearing man's than a woman's.

Thinking of the jaw the girl wondered about the strip of plaster which evidently protected some wound, and she tried to figure what it might be. This persistence of her mind in going back to the injured feature made Mary Eliska impatient with herself; it seemed to her that she was trying to find out something which was both unimportant and none of her business. Anyone might get a bump, a bruise, a cut, or an insect bite on her face, and keeping it covered was nothing more than ordinary common sense, especially when her face might be exposed to the force of the wind while they were flying.

Glancing at her watch she calculated that she would reach home about the same time her father did and they could talk the matter over, but when she thought of her uneasiness regarding her prospective employer she realized that she really had nothing tangible to tell him. There wasn't a thing that Lyudmila Shkrebneva had said or done which could be used as an excuse for refusing the offer. By that time Skybird was near their village, so Mary Eliska throttled the engine and glided down close to the hangar entrance, which was open to admit her, for Mrs. Stricklin had heard the familiar roar in the heavens, shut off the alarm and shoved the entrance wide.

"Thanks, Mummy," Mary Eliska called as she rode past. Presently she was out of the cockpit, but before the two reached the veranda, Mr. Stricklin's car came rolling up the drive.

"Hello, children," he shouted cheerfully. The auto was quickly put in its own section of the old barn and he joined them.

"Hear anything from the sheriff?" Mary Eliska inquired first thing.

"Not much. The license of the car is registered under the name of Shkrebneva, a woman, but that is as much as I got—"

"Shkrebneva?" Mary Eliska exclaimed in amazement, then again into her mind leaped the memory of that scar on her cheek.

"Yes. Howard said he'd drop in this evening and give us further details, if there are any."

"Why, Dad, that's the name of the woman I was taking along the coast. I took her again this afternoon."

"You did!"

"And today she had a piece of tape on her chin, as if it had been hurt in some way."

"Humph. Well, my dear, it seems hardly possible that the woman would come herself and try to take your plane."

"Do you think Dad hit her with some of that shot?" Mrs. Stricklin asked quickly.

"I don't know, Mummy. That piece of tape has been on my mind all afternoon; I couldn't keep from wondering about it," Mary Eliska answered, then went on, "She wants me to take her on a trip."

"Well, we'll certainly look into the lady's reputation before you do anything of that kind," Dad declared positively. "Suppose we take a run down to Howard's office and talk it over with him—"

"Suppose you come in and eat your dinner before it is spoiled," Mrs. Stricklin interrupted. "You can go later, or telephone him."

"Guess you're right," Dad grinned. "I'm hollow as a bass drum and there is no such desperate rush about the matter." The startling discovery formed the chief topic of conversation during the meal.

"The name is an unusual one but there may be others in the country," Mrs. Stricklin remarked. "But it does seem odd that it should be her car and that she should have a wound of some kind on her face this morning."

"It's all circumstantial," Mr. Stricklin added. "Did she usually come to the flying field in a taxi?"

"No, she came in her own car. I didn't think anything about the taxi today, but she might have used that because she was uncertain where we would land. We've come down in a different place every time I have taken her," Mary Eliska explained.

"Still, I can't think that she herself would try to appropriate your plane. She has, as I understand it, limitless money," Dad said.

"That's what I heard at the office," Mary Eliska admitted.

"How did the woman impress you?" Mrs. Stricklin asked.

"Not very favorably," the girl admitted. "But when I tried to reason it out, I had nothing really to dislike her for."

"That sounds to me like Howard's car," said Dad as a machine came up the drive. He raised himself in his chair and looked out of the window. "It's the sheriff. We'll have a talk with him." Presently the officer was admitted but his expression was one of disappointment.

"We haven't accomplished a thing in discovering those thieves, Mr. Stricklin," he began. "The machine belongs to a Lyudmila Shkrebneva, all right, and it was found in Delaware on a side road late this afternoon. Probably been abandoned."

"Oh."

"The owner isn't a bit of help, for she reported her car missing late yesterday afternoon. She said she had been doing some flying, then drove into town to keep an appointment in a beauty parlor. When she was fixed up and came out to go home, the limousine was gone. She reported it right away, and as I said before, it was discovered today."

"Oh. Did you see her?"

"No. There wasn't any use in doing that. Whoever had been driving was mighty careless for it was covered with mud from stem to stern. You hit one of the fellows, and I figure they went as fast and as far as they could, then stopped to get the wound dressed. The police are making inquiries among the doctors hereabout trying to find one who had a late call to attend to a split-open jaw. I'll meander along, I promised the wife I'd take her to the movies tonight. Sorry there isn't anything better to report."

"Thank you for coming in and telling us. After all, no one was hurt and the planes are safe," said Mrs. Stricklin.

"That's right," Dad added. "And I've had a fine alarm system put on the hangar, so if anyone comes prowling around again, he will wake the world."

"Good thing. Well, good-bye." The sheriff drove off and the family returned to the unfinished meal. All of them were mighty sober.

"Just goes to show how perfectly damning circumstantial evidence can be, doesn't it? Here's a woman, one who knows flying, whose face has been injured in some way unknown, and whose car is seen parked near here for the robber's getaway. You know, if she hadn't reported the limousine missing things might have been very unpleasant for her," Dad remarked thoughtfully.

"And she is probably doing exactly what she says—just trying to carry on her husband's unfinished work. Don't you think it will be all right for me to tell her I'll take her on the trip, Dad? I feel sort of ashamed of myself for being so suspicious of everything."

"Guess it would, dear. Suppose I make a few judicial inquiries to be on the safe side. She isn't to call up before tomorrow evening, and by that time I can know a little about her," he replied.

"That's a good idea," Mrs. Stricklin agreed, so it was left that way.

"How about taking my family to the movies?" Dad proposed, and they accepted without a dissenting vote.

The evening was spent delightfully, and the next afternoon Mr. Stricklin called up from the city to inform his daughter that as far as it was possible to learn, Lyudmila Shkrebneva was above reproach. She had a great deal of money, a part of which she had made herself by first class business investments, and the rest she had secured when she sold her husband's fur business. She had a reputation for being quiet and conservative, considerate of her employees and active on several very worth-while philanthropic boards. So Mary Eliska packed a bag for the trip and during the remainder of the time, attended to giving Skybird a good inspection.

"Wish I could drop down on the field and give her to one of the mechanics to fix up," she said regretfully. She meant that there was not time to do it, not that she felt she couldn't ask for the accommodation, for she was positive that the courtesy would be extended to her cordially. She had nearly finished the task when her mother called, and when she went to answer the telephone, found it was Lyudmila Shkrebneva.

"I have called for your answer, Mary Eliska," came the rich voice.

"If you could see my suitcase and the way I have been working on the plane, you would know it," Mary Eliska said as pleasantly as she possibly could.

"Then you will go."

"Very glad to," she replied.

"Meet me tomorrow at Elizabeth. I shall be there at eleven o'clock. Is that too early?"

"Not at all," Mary Eliska replied. They talked a few moments longer about the meeting place.

"I presume you will fetch a warm coat."

"Oh, yes, I have it all ready. Thank you." She hung up the receiver and although she was trying hard to feel glad about the prospect before her, she wished heartily that she had said no, or that she could have said she had other work to do. "I'm a little idiot," she told herself, and then went back to the plane to finish getting it ready.

The next morning at a few minutes before eleven, Skybird brought her out of a lower-sky near the New Jersey town and a few minutes later, Lyudmila Shkrebneva drove up in her own car. Mary Eliska noticed that its fender had been bent, and when the woman alighted, she stopped a moment to speak to the chauffeur about having repairs made. He listened respectfully, then transferred her luggage to the waiting Skybird, where he assisted in storing it safely.

While these final preparations were going on, Mary Eliska heard a plane flying so low that she glanced up to see if the machine was coming down with its engine running, but she decided that the pilot must have had some difficulty in the take-off. He was climbing rather slowly, and she wondered if he was an inexperienced amateur in trouble or showing off to admiring friends who might be watching him.

"Is that all, Madame?" the chauffeur asked.

"Yes, thank you, that is all. We are quite properly packed, I think, Mary Eliska, but you had better make sure." Mary Eliska glanced at the tiny baggage compartment, which was certainly well filled, and nodded. "Then we can start as soon as you are ready."

"I am ready now," Mary Eliska told her. Lyudmila Shkrebneva took her place, adjusted straps and chute, nodded to the chauffeur, who was already back in the battered limousine, then glanced at the sky.

"Go south, toward Florida, about twelve miles out. The weather looks a little doubtful, we may as well have the cover over our heads," she said.

"All right." Mary Eliska slid the top into place and made it secure, then assuring herself that she could start without cutting anyone in two with the propeller, she opened the throttle. The engine roared, Skybird moved forward swiftly, lifted thirty feet further along, then rose majestically into the air. They zoomed, circled in wide loops, ascending in spirals, and at five thousand feet, leveled off. Mary Eliska set the plane's nose toward the Atlantic, for she knew that her passenger preferred to travel above the water rather than the land. Ten minutes later the shore line was almost completely hidden by the haze which was lowering over the coast. Straight east they flew, only once seeing another plane. It was a small one which came alongside in a friendly fashion, but the distance was too great for the girl to see who was at the controls. Skybird was twenty miles out when Lyudmila Shkrebneva indicated that she wanted to turn south, and in a moment that was accomplished. The sky did not look as threatening as it had from the shore and Mary Eliska hoped that if a storm was brewing, she was going to get away from it.

They had been traveling about an hour when Lyudmila Shkrebneva got a book out and opened it, preparing to read. Mary Eliska switched the light on so she could see better, and the woman glanced at the control board, seemed to make a mental calculation of the figures and dials, nodded, and then bent again over her reading. It wasn't anything more suspicious than a mystery story and for the next half hour the woman did not lift her head again. She seemed perfectly indifferent to everything but the story. The little plane that had followed them out had fallen behind and lower, and the girl Aviatrix judged that its speed was not very great. She wished it would come alongside because it is always rather jolly riding with another machine in the air. In less than an hour it had been left far behind.

Early in the evening Skybird glided down at Charleston, W. Virginia, where Lyudmila Shkrebneva had arranged for refueling and accommodations for the night at a small hostelry near the flying field. They took a cab to the hotel, which was an interesting old place, with a long low-ceilinged dining room. The apartment was a comfortable one with three rooms and bath and while they were refreshing themselves the woman broke the silence.

"As a companionable person I am not a great success, Mary Eliska. Tonight I am a bit fatigued and I think I shall have dinner sent up, but if you have never been in this place and are not too tired, I am sure that you will enjoy the atmosphere of downstairs. This house used to be patronized by members of Virginia's old families, and a few still cling to it; you may find it interesting."

"Thank you, I believe I shall, but I will be up early. Are you planning to leave in the morning?" Mary Eliska asked.

"I do not know. It depends upon how I feel and what the weather looks like. I shall retire as soon as I have finished dinner," Lyudmila Shkrebneva answered. With her helmet off the gauze and tape completely covered the wound on her chin, and when she thought of her former suspicions, the girl Aviatrix wanted to apologize for her stupid idea that her employer could possibly have been in any way connected with the attempted theft of Skybird. She hurried with her dressing, and before she was ready, the waiter appeared with the tray.

"Anything I can do?" Mary Eliska asked.

"Not a thing, thank you. Take your key, for I shall probably be asleep by the time you return."

"I have it. Good night."

"Good night."

Mary Eliska made her way along the winding hall of the old house and decided that the house was one of those which had been built a good many years ago with later wings and additions. Twice she had to step down a couple of steps, and once around a sharp corner she had to go up three. However, she had no difficulty in getting to the main floor, which was cheery with old fashioned chandeliers that had yards of long crystals dangling so that the light sparkled through them, and the slightest breeze, or current of air passing set them tinkling merrily. Presently she was in the dining room and a very courteous old colored man, who looked as if he had stepped out of a picture of an ancient plantation home before the Civil war, showed her to a table from which she got an excellent view of the whole room. Most of the tables were occupied, for it was late, but a few others came in when she was eating her first course. She noticed a party of young people, three men and two girls, who looked as if they were bound for a party of some kind, and when they were seated they made the place ring with their fun. They were rather a contrast from the other diners, but they were not boisterous nor ill-bred with their jollification.

"Pardon me, isn't this Mary Eliska!" It was a delightful Southern drawl and Mary Eliska looked up into the eyes of Mr. Powell, a young man who had taken the flying course under Mr. Wallace at Lurtiss Field, and whom she had helped pass his exams.

"Mr. Powell, how do you do?"

"Fine, Mary Eliska, and I am mighty glad to see you in our midst. I told my friends that I am going to ask you to join us; you look as if you are alone," Mr. Powell announced cheerfully. "Don't turn me down, for you can see we are desperately in need of another girl; especially since the two you see are my sisters." Mary Eliska glanced at the other table and saw one of the girls coming toward her.

"How do you do, Mary Eliska," she greeted. "How delightful meeting you here. My brother has spoken of you often; I believe you taught him colors when he was taking his course in aviation. Please join us; we will be very pleased to have you."

"This is Helen, Mary Eliska. I am sure you cannot refuse her; no one ever does," the young man insisted, so Mary Eliska accepted the cordial invitation and soon was one of the party. She was also introduced to Evelyn Powell and their cousins, Alton Manwell and Edward Crawford. There was no lack of sincerity and cordiality in their acceptance of the stranger, and as they were every one of them interested in aviation, they had no end of things to talk about.

"We are going to an amateur show and you must come along," Miss Powell informed the guest. "We were to have another girl with us, but she had to break her engagement, so her ticket will not be wasted, and we shall have the pleasure of your company," Mr. Crawford added.

"It's rather a queer performance. You may be bored to death. Confirmed bachelor, Mark Anthony by name, but no relation to the ancient Cleo. He has a wonderful house, full of everything from every place in the world, and every once in a while he gives parties," Evelyn chatted.

"I didn't bring anything very party-like to wear," Mary Eliska started to object, but they paid no attention to that."You look stunning and Helen has an extra scarf in the car. It will make you look more like a million dollars than you do," insisted Evelyn, so the matter was settled.

Mary Eliska had been penned up in a cock-pit the greater part of the day, and a bit of fun was more than welcome. When the dinner was finished, the six of them were driven to the home of the confirmed bachelor and before his house they saw dozens of other cars lined up on both sides of the drive. They were led up the wide marble stairway, into a huge reception hall, where Mary Eliska caught a glimpse of a very tall man who looked marvelously well in his evening clothes and was evidently the host. He was greeting the new arrivals pleasantly, and near him, facing the door they were entering, was an elegantly dressed woman, who glanced their way but was immediately shut off from Mary Eliska's vision. But the one glance startled Mary Eliska. It was Lyudmila Shkrebneva.

"She must have felt better after she finished dinner," Mary Eliska remarked to herself, but when she reached her host's side, there was no sign of her employer, but she did not think anything of that, for the rooms were crowded.

CHAPTER 12.5
A QUEER MYSTERY

When the performance was over and the guests were exclaiming about the charming entertainment they had seen, thanking Mr. Anthony for giving them such a delightful evening, and later taking their departure, Mary Eliska glanced about for Lyudmila Shkrebneva, but did not see her. During the entertainment the rooms had been darkened except about the stage, so the girl Aviatrix thought nothing of missing her employer then, but when the whole place was brilliantly lighted and the assembly moving somewhat like a narrow reception line, it seemed odd that the woman was nowhere in sight. With Miss Powell and her party, Mary Eliska also thanked her host.

"I am very happy if my efforts have given such a charming stranger in our city an hour's pleasure," Mr. Anthony told her, speaking as if she were the only person in the room and had his undivided attention. Just then others came up, so she passed on with an impression that the gentleman, being a true Southerner, could make himself very agreeable.

"Anthony should be in the Diplomatic service," young Powell remarked when they were all in the car again.

"He always gives one a feeling that his only interest in life is to serve one," Helen added. "I am so glad that you could come with us, Mary Eliska. If you are going to be in Charleston tomorrow, I shall be delighted to take you about a bit."

"That is something I will not know until tomorrow," Mary Eliska told her. "You have been most kind. I should have had rather a dull evening had I not met you."

"Here we are at your hotel. Hope you can stay over," Powell said as he helped her out. She bade the others good night, thanked them again, then the young aviator saw her safely to the elevator. "I'll be on hand to help entertain you if you do not fly away."

Up in her own room, when Mary Eliska switched on the light she noticed that the door between the two bedrooms was closed. She listened for a sound of anyone moving about, but the place was as still as if it was deserted. Before retiring, there was a note to be written to the family at home, and in it she told of the lovely old hotel with its aristocratic guests, the meeting with Powell and his sisters, the trip to Mr. Anthony's, and the fact that Lyudmila Shkrebneva was also there. Finally, adding no end of love for them all, she sealed the envelope, then went down the hall to the mail chute. When she returned there was still no sound from the other room and as she undressed, she tried to figure out why the woman had not nodded to her, and why she had disappeared like the foam on a ginger ale.

"Here I am imagining things about her again," she scolded mentally. "She probably knows Mr. Anthony and he persuaded her to come for a little while, then she went home and is now in bed asleep."

With this very logical conclusion she got into her own bed, switched off the light and immediately fell asleep, but she spent the night dreaming of vain efforts to fly away from Lyudmila Shkrebneva and the charming Mr. Anthony, who kept bobbing up, like a Jack-in-the-box, just when she was sure that she had left him behind, nor did she manage to evade the bachelor until she flew off over the North Pole. It was snowing, she thought, and she shivered as she brought the plane down, but instead of stopping, Skybird dropped, and dropped and dropped until at last she struggled so hard to right it that she woke herself up. Morning had not put in an appearance, but the night had turned cooler and she had kicked off the covers, so with a sigh of relief that it was only a dream, she turned over and enjoyed a more restful sleep.

When she awakened she heard someone moving in the other room and guessed that Lyudmila Shkrebneva was already stirring. As the time had not been set for their departure, Mary Eliska lost no time in dressing, and when she was finished, sure that her employer was up, she knocked at the door, but to her surprise received no answer. She tried again, without success, then someone tapped at her own door. It proved to be the maid who told her that word had been left that the woman was not to be disturbed, that she wished to sleep late. This was certainly puzzling, for the girl was positive that she had heard movements in the other room.

"Well, if she wants to take another snooze it's her own business. I wonder why in the dickens everything she does makes me uneasy?" she said to herself, and then prepared to go to breakfast. She took her key with her, and when she stepped out into the hall she was startled to see Mr. Anthony coming down the hall to Lyudmila Shkrebneva's door. If the man recognized her, he gave no sign of it, but glancing at the number, turned and went in the opposite direction as if he had made a mistake in the room. Again the feeling of uneasiness came over Mary Eliska and she simply could not shake it off. At the desk downstairs she asked if her employer had left any word regarding when she intended to check out, and the clerk answered in the negative.

"Lyudmila Shkrebneva did not say when she is leaving, but she leases that apartment by the year," he explained obligingly.

Mary Eliska went in to breakfast and when she had finished she was called to the telephone. It proved to be young Powell who wanted to know if she was staying in town but she couldn't give him any information. "I do not expect to leave right away," she said, and then explained the situation.

"Suppose Helen and I come up and in case you are not leaving soon we can bat around together?"

"That's mighty nice of you. I should be very glad to see you." It did not take the two Powells long to get there, and the three sought a quiet corner in the rambling old lobby.

"By the way, you have not said why you are here," Powell remarked.

"Why, Brother, what an impudent question," Helen protested.

"That's all right between aviators," he laughed.

"Of course it is," Mary Eliska defended him quickly. "I really cannot tell you why I came nor whither I go. I might say I came hither from thither and I am going hence; why do I not know."

"Sounds mysterious. What sort of bird is this Lyudmila Shkrebneva?" Powell inquired.

"She seems perfectly all right," was the answer.

"Why the *seems*—"

"Robert," Helen objected.

"I have a queer sort of feeling about her; I can't explain it. Last night she was at Mr. Anthony's but I only caught a glimpse of her, and this morning—" She broke off and flushed. "I have to admit that I am making a whole mountain range out of less than an ant hill, but the truth is, every simple thing she does seems mysterious. Guess I have been developing nerves."

"Tell me about it," Robert urged quietly. "If it's nerves, going over the facts will show them up in their true light and you'll feel better. We all get to a point where things do not seem right."

"Perhaps it would be a good idea," she admitted, then told him of her relations with Lyudmila Shkrebneva, leaving out nothing, not even the attempted theft of Skybird.

"Humph," Powell grunted. "There really isn't a thing alarming in what you have told me, Mary Eliska, but just the same, even though our reasons insist that everything is hunky— when you get a hunch as strong as the one you have, don't disregard it, that's my motto. I believe aviators have a sort of sixth sense that warns them, or tries to, and it's always a safe bet to pay strict attention. I've heard other flyers say the same thing, so, if I were you, I'd watch my step mighty carefully."

"Don't make her feel worse than she does," Helen urged.

"I'm not trying to; just want her to take every advantage of the faculty she has and not disregard a warning, even if it seems a foolish one. Here's our number and address; keep in touch with us and if anything comes up, get into communication with us right away." He took out his card and wrote the telephone number on it.

"We will all be happy to assist you in any way," Helen added.

"Thank you so much."

"Mary Eliska, Mary Eliska," called a page.

"I am Mary Eliska," Mary Eliska told him.

"Lyudmila Shkrebneva would like you to go up," he told her.

"All right. I'll say so-long for now, and thank you so much."

"Hope we can see you again before you leave," Helen said, and just then they saw Mark Anthony strolling leisurely through the lobby.

"Humph," grunted Powell, "I never saw him here before."

"Isn't he an Old Family?" Mary Eliska asked mischievously.

"No, he's a New Family; rotten with money, so he gets and does anything he wants to. Glad to have seen you, even for a little while."

Mary Eliska took the card, then hurried to the elevator and presently came to her own room. The connecting door was open, so she went in immediately and found Lyudmila Shkrebneva in negligee, the wound on her chin covered with adhesive tape. A waiter had left a tray a few moments before and the woman was preparing to eat her breakfast.

"Did you have a good night?" she asked politely.

"Very pleasant," Mary Eliska answered. "I met an old friend, Robert Powell, and his sisters at dinner and they took me to a theatrical at Mr. Anthony's home."

"Then you were not bored with Charleston. I do not care for the place and rarely go out. The people seem to me excessively stupid, and the city, most of it, antiquated. Did you have breakfast?"

"Yes, thank you."

"The maid said you had gone down, so I ordered only one. I had a wretched night, thought I should never get to sleep, but when I did I made up for it by not waking until fifteen minutes ago," Lyudmila Shkrebneva said and her statements startled the girl.

Mary Eliska wondered if the woman was claiming that she had not left the room since they parted the evening before, but she refrained from saying anything more about the theatricals. She was absolutely convinced that it could have been no one else who was standing beside Mr. Anthony as he received his guests, and she was also convinced that her employer had been up that morning before she herself was awake. Why the woman should deliberately lie over anything so trivial made Mary Eliska recall Powell's warning to watch her step, and, casting logic aside, she determined to pay heed to what he had said.

"I am sorry you did not have a more comfortable night," she replied, then added, "The page said you wanted me."

"Yes. I wanted to be sure that you had breakfasted and to tell you that we will leave here about one o'clock, so have your lunch before you go, and if you want to do any errands, you can," Lyudmila Shkrebneva said.

"Guess I haven't much in the way of errands but I'll tell them to have—"

"I have already notified them to have the plane in readiness."

"Then I shall not need to bother. I see there is a store near the hotel; I'll run up there and get some handkerchiefs. I came away without a good supply," Mary Eliska told her, then, as the woman seemed to have nothing more to say, she returned to the lobby very uneasy in mind.

For less than two pins Mary Eliska would have told her employer that she was returning home at once, but such an act appeared more foolhardy than cautious. It took only a few minutes to get the handkerchiefs she required, then she saw attractive cards of the city, and stationery. On the impulse of the moment she bought paper and envelope and wrote a hasty note to Robert Powell, telling him that she was leaving in a couple of hours, the place where Skybird had been left, and expressing a wish that if he had his own plane and could come waggling his wings to her as they had in the days when they were both learning to fly she would feel easier. She added a word of thanks to his sister, then signed her name, but after that she put in the fact that Lyudmila Shkrebneva had said she was in her room all night—as if she had not been to Mr. Anthony's.

"*I know I'm awfully silly, but at the next landing I am going to resign from the job.*

"*Sincerely yours, Mary Eliska.*"

"Can I get a messenger to deliver this?" she asked the woman who had been serving her.

"I'll take it, lady," a small boy offered, so at a nod from the woman she gave him a coin and made sure that he knew where to go. "Aw, that isn't far away," he said scornfully, and tucking it into his pocket, he raced off with the letter. As soon as he had gone, Mary Eliska wished she had not been so silly as to tell Robert Powell such a trivial matter. After paying for her purchases she returned to the lobby where she sat at one of the desks, wrote a note and sent cards to the family. That finished, she ate her lunch in the dining room, but felt so uncomfortable that she didn't enjoy it at all.

Promptly at one o'clock they left the hotel in one of its own buses and drove quickly to the small flying field where they found Skybird already wheeled out of the hangar. Although a mechanic was beside the plane, the girl Aviatrix took time to assure herself that everything was as it should be, while Lyudmila Shkrebneva took her place in the cock-pit.

"I went over everything, Miss," the mechanic told her.

"Thank you, I know you did, but where I learned to fly one of the things they stressed was to be positive yourself that things were all right. You certainly did a good job and you put in a full supply of gasoline."

"Those were orders," he told her. She climbed to her own place, and when at last all was as it should be, she nodded to him, and he gave them a start, not that he needed to, for Skybird was a self-starter in every way; perfectly capable of taking off without assistance. The chap stood watching the plane with keen admiration, and when she lifted, Mary Eliska waved him a farewell.

Quickly they climbed to three thousand feet, then Lyudmila Shkrebneva signaled that it was high enough. She picked up the speaking tube and Mary Eliska listened, for the woman never gave her directions until they were started.

"Turn in a half circle, then go straight northwest until I tell you to change the course or come down," she said. Skybird promptly did the turn and then leveled off, her nose pointing the route indicated. Mary Eliska was surprised, for they were going inland instead of over the water as usual. Glancing at her chart she reckoned that the course would take her across the United States into the southwestern part of Canada, provided they continued long enough. Lyudmila Shkrebneva sat watching the control board for a few minutes, then proceeded to produce another book and buried herself in its pages.

"I believe that her saying she is carrying on some work started by her husband is just so much bologna. We haven't done a blooming thing since we started—except fly—and she certainly isn't accomplishing anything while she's reading a mystery story. That's that. And I'm dropping out of the business at the next stop—that is more of that," was the girl's mental resolve, and she set her lips in a firm line to emphasize her resolution.

They had been in the air less than ten minutes, when suddenly, out of the sky to the right, and higher than Skybird was flying, swept a shining new plane, its wings waggling furiously. Mary Eliska's heart gave a great leap, and she responded, but not quite so vigorously as Powell. His plane swooped down across her path and as it flashed by she could see that he was not alone. Whoever was in the cock-pit with him waved a gloved hand, and Mary Eliska replied to that also. Not changing her course by a hair, Skybird roared steadily on, the other plane circled about her once, then with a final waggle, zoomed up, spiraled, and then turned back. The girl Aviatrix smiled as her friends disappeared, then she happened to look into the mirror and saw that Lyudmila Shkrebneva had been watching the performance with an interest which was none too kindly.

"Who are they?" she snapped.

"Robert Powell and his sister," Mary Eliska told her. "The people I met last night." They were using the telephone.

"How do they happen to be here when we start?" For an instant Mary Eliska was going to tell her the truth, that she had sent word she was leaving and Powell had come to see her off, but his warning to "watch her step" flashed through her mind.

"I do not know how they happen to be around," she answered, which was true enough. "Guess he saw the plane go up and came over to say goodbye in case it was Skybird." There was a peculiarly hard look in Lyudmila Shkrebneva's eyes during the explanation, and she looked steadily at her pilot for several seconds, then dropped her eyes back to her book.

CHAPTER 12.6
KIDNAPPED

As Mary Eliska attended strictly to her business she became thoroughly convinced that her "hunch" regarding her employer was well worth heeding; that the woman's mission was not only mysterious and confusing, but that it was an enterprise with which she did not care to be associated a minute longer than that she could possibly help. Following the course set, going higher when the country beneath them demanded it, or lower as permitted, she thought things out carefully. Skybird did not carry gasoline enough to take her back to Long Island, but she had money enough with her to drop down onto a landing field and purchase more; also she knew that even if she hadn't the cash she could give them a draft on her bank in New York if they were not willing to accept a check.

Carefully studying the chart, which she knew almost by heart anyway, she realized that the route they were following was, for the most part, well out of the usual air lines, but there were several places where she would fly parallel or across those laid out. Mary Eliska thought of the towns and cities over which they would pass, calculated their location and which ones she would be near early in the evening, when the woman beside her would probably order a landing. They had been flying nearly three hours when Lyudmila Shkrebneva glanced up at the speedometer.

"I wish that you would go a little faster," she directed, so the Girl Aviatrix nodded and opened up a bit wider, but she did not put on full speed. They had been averaging eighty miles an hour, so she increased it to ninety-five, which meant that when conditions permitted she was doing more, and less when the air and country were not so favorable. Another hour passed and Mary Eliska began to wonder when they were to come down, but Lyudmila Shkrebneva still seemed absorbed in her book, although Mary Eliska was positive that she was not so intent as she was trying to pretend.

Glancing at the sky, Mary Eliska saw, far ahead, a dark cloud rising in the west which looked as if it might cause them trouble in the course of a few hours, but she paid little attention to it for she figured they would have landed before the storm reached them, or they reached it. To get a better view of the world, she gradually increased her height a thousand feet. Roaring swiftly along she saw, far ahead of them, a large plane which looked like one which carried passengers, and another time, when her eyes rested a moment on the mirror, she saw a small plane behind them. This looked like an ordinary machine with one passenger—or perhaps no one but its pilot, and while she watched the tiny speck, it dropped lower and out of her range of vision.

Studying the chart again, without seeming to do more than observe the various controls the girl Aviatrix looked for the nearest flying field. In another hour they would be over Wisconsin, for the end of Lake Michigan was tossing beneath them, and on its rough surface raced a huge speed boat across the great body in exactly the same direction that Skybird was flying a mile above. The water was thickly dotted with numerous boats, large and small, but this little one, which looked no bigger than a dark dot with a long foamy tail, attracted the girl's attention because of its speed. Skybird soon left it behind, however. Glancing about the horizon, she saw that they were well away from the storm, but she anticipated bad weather for the following day. A bit later, listening to the radio reports, this calculation of hers was confirmed by the Bureau from Washington.

From time-to-time Lyudmila Shkrebneva glanced up, studied the dials, chart and the whole array, for even if she hadn't qualified for a license, and could not pilot a plane, it was not because she did not thoroughly understand every bit of flying. She just happened to be one of the persons whose knowledge on the subject was not sufficient to make her act wisely at all times in any emergency. Even though she never asked to carry a passenger, wanted nothing more than to fly herself, a plane in the air piloted by a man or woman who might behave erratically, was a menace to the world below. She might suddenly crash into a building, come down with a blazing machine in a dry forest and start a fire which would do countless dollars-worth of damage, or she might drop on a gasoline tank and blow the whole vicinity to tooth-picks.

Suddenly, as Mary Eliska visualized the chart she realized that it would not be very long, according to the course they were following and the speed they were going, before Skybird crossed the border into Canada. She would be on foreign soil without the usual curtsy to the Dominion, also they were getting further and further away from Long Island and her own home. If she was not going to continue the trip, why not stop now? As a matter of fact, why had she come so far at all; why hadn't she dropped down a couple of hours ago and informed Lyudmila Shkrebneva that she was not going on, land that lady wherever she wanted to be landed, then go on east? Silently scolding herself for her stupidity, the girl decided that if Lyudmila Shkrebneva did not order a descent within the next few minutes, Skybird would make a landing without it. As if she rather suspected something of what was going on in her companion's mind, Lyudmila Shkrebneva closed her book, looked about at the sun, which had almost set, then taking a package from under the seat, proceeded to open it. To Mary Eliska's surprise it contained food; it seemed enough for several generous meals, including thermos bottles with hot and cold drinks.

"We will have something to eat in the air," the woman announced quite casually, but there was something deadly in her tone. However, Mary Eliska had herself well in hand and she answered firmly.

"I am sorry, Lyudmila Shkrebneva, but I am going down," she answered.

"Why?" the woman asked quietly.

"We need gasoline for one thing—"

"Not yet," Lyudmila Shkrebneva interrupted.

"I have been at the controls steadily and I do not believe that it would be safe for me to continue much longer without a rest and a proper meal."

"You will find everything that you can possibly get in a proper meal anywhere," Lyudmila Shkrebneva told her coolly, and added, "And as for a rest, I'll relieve you."

"I cannot permit that," Mary Eliska answered. "Without a license you could not fly and my plane is different from the usual ones; I would rather not have anyone who is not accustomed to it try to operate it."

"Well, have something to eat," Lyudmila Shkrebneva said wearily. "It is still quite light. When I was learning to fly I once saw three sunsets. I'd very much like to get at least one more view of the sun tonight. Zoom Skybird up high so that we will have a magnificent view to remember when we go to sleep tonight."

"All right," Mary Eliska agreed with great relief. She was glad there was no argument and she resolved that she would not tell her employer she could not go on until they were safely landed. So that there was no danger of getting over into Canada, she spiraled as she climbed and decreased the plane's speed.

"Should you like milk, tea or coffee to drink?" Lyudmila Shkrebneva asked as she arranged the food, which certainly looked appetizing, especially since Mary Eliska had eaten almost no lunch.

"Tea, if it has plenty of milk and not too strong."

"Sugar, how many lumps?"

"A small one, thank you." The drinks were poured into deep paper cups which were half-filled carefully to prevent spilling. Skybird was leveled, her dials and controls set so that her pilot could relax a bit and enjoy the meal. It was not long before they saw the sun again in all its splendor, and watched a second setting, which was certainly well worth waiting for because the air was clear and the countless brilliant rays, were flung fan-like from the rim of the horizon.

"Cake or pie, or will you have another sandwich?" Lyudmila Shkrebneva asked a bit later.

"Cake, it sounds simpler to consume," Mary Eliska laughed. One simply couldn't help feeling secure, riding like a part of the gorgeous spectacle, and the girl wondered if she hadn't been premature in her decision to abandon her employer.

"I'll fill your cup again."

"Only half," Mary Eliska said hastily.

"Cannot measure it," Lyudmila Shkrebneva smiled and her pilot thought if she were only as pleasant all of the time they might go on forever.

"Thank you. I do feel better. Guess I did not realize how hungry I was," Mary Eliska told her.

"Didn't you have anything to eat before you left the hotel?"

"Just a salad, but I wasn't hungry then. This has tasted very good, every bit of it."

"Sure you have had enough?"

"Yes, thank you."

"You still have a tank of gasoline, haven't you?" Lyudmila Shkrebneva consulted the indicator to see how much was in the plane.

"Yes, but I believe we had better get down soon because we are getting away from towns and even farms. We do not want to be stranded in the open all night," Mary Eliska consulted the chart.

"Very true. Have you done any night flying?"

"Oh yes, but not any oftener than I could help. Of course there are a great many guides and riding under the stars is mighty attractive but one never can tell what might happen; storms come up suddenly, and mountains have a disconcerting habit of bobbing in front of a plane when it is least desirable." They talked through the telephone and finally Mary Eliska decided upon the best place for their landing, turned sharply off the course toward the southeast.

"Why do you go back?" Lyudmila Shkrebneva asked her.

"We will get better landing accommodations; at least, I know the field and I am sure of it," the girl answered.

"All right, one should never interfere with the pilot, but if we go forward we will have less distance to travel tomorrow."

"We have put half the continent behind us since we started," Mary Eliska reminded her and the woman made no further objections.

They flew on for a quarter of an hour, then suddenly Mary Eliska had a sharp pain between her eyes and she blinked in bewilderment, but it went away again quickly so she decided that it wasn't anything to worry about. However, she increased her speed, for if she was going to be sick, she wanted to get on the ground as quickly as possible. But now there was no sign of the sun, all of its brilliant colors had faded to dull grey, which was rapidly growing darker, and although the girl searched the heavens, she did not see a single star blinking back at her. Far in the distance she caught the faint flicker of a light which she was sure was the landing field she sought and a glance at the chart verified her calculation. Setting her course, she headed Skybird in as straight a line as possible and decreased the speed, banked in preparation for the glide when she was near enough. Then again came that stabbing pain, but this time it was in her head.

Brushing her hand over her forehead and opening the strap of her helmet she felt better again and she hoped hard that her companion would not notice that anything was wrong. Lyudmila Shkrebneva might go into a panic if she discovered her pilot was ill and perhaps do something in her excitement which would bring them all down in a smash. On they flew, the lights getting nearer and nearer; and bigger and bigger, then, suddenly, they began to dance into a long line which Mary Eliska knew was an optical illusion. Glancing forward she decided that she could begin the descent, but when she reached toward the control-board, it seemed to get further and further away from her. Finally she managed to close the switch and forcing herself with every ounce of strength and courage she possessed, she struggled to make the field without a smash-up.

But, to the girl's amazement, she felt rather than saw, that Skybird instead of starting toward the earth, began to climb steadily, moving in a wide circle; she could tell that by the wind in her face, then the plane rose more swiftly, thundering upward at top speed. Frantically the pilot endeavored to find the proper switches, but it was so dark that even in the lighted cock-pit she could not see the board nor its indicators, except in a blurred sort of way.

"Are you all right, Mary Eliska?" It was Lyudmila Shkrebneva's voice speaking through the tube.

"I am trying to go down, to make a landing—I'm—"

"You are trying to, but you are climbing and you are going to keep on climbing—"

"W-what—what do you m-mean—" Mary Eliska tried desperately to gather her wandering faculties.

"Simply that you are obeying orders!"

"We can't f-fly at night," Mary Eliska protested, then a feeling of horror swept over her, for suddenly she understood. Something she had eaten was paralyzing her faculties, making her helpless there in Skybird, flying swiftly a mile above the ground and far from the landing field where she knew she had friends.

"Whether we can or not, we are going to." The woman forced her back in her seat and took over the management of the controls. "You will learn before you are much older not to have your aviator friends watching us when we take-off—"

"I didn't h-h—" But her voice trailed off, her head wobbled forward on her chest, and if Skybird had started a nose dive that moment, her pilot could have done nothing to prevent her tearing straight to the ground and digging a ten-foot hole for herself in the ground. The girl, for a couple of moments was partly conscious, but that too left her quickly and she was completely out of the picture, at the mercy of the mysterious Lyudmila Shkrebneva, if she had any mercy, which was very doubtful.

Lyudmila Shkrebneva glanced with eyes that blazed hatefully at her unconscious companion, then, as she had to attend to several things immediately she first reset the course of the plane and when it was back in the route it had been pursuing when Mary Eliska announced her determination to land for the night, then, as managing the machine from any other seat than the pilot's was an awkward one she loosened the girl's safety-strap and her own. Keeping an alert eye on the indicators she quickly made the transfer, and over her features came a look of keen satisfaction.

"You will taunt me that I could not get a license, and that only you can operate your precious Skybird! Well, I'm going to operate it now and if it flies us both to death, you have it coming to you; you little fool." She laughed harshly, and into the dark eyes, which had worn nothing but boredom and indifference for so long, flashed insane fury. "For next to nothing, I'd dump you out of the cock-pit, you silly girl!"

For a moment she looked at Mary Eliska as if determined to do just that, but finally she curbed herself, drew her companion's safety-belt tighter, and ran her fingers around it mechanically, for she had been thoroughly drilled in every phase of the work she longed with her whole soul to follow the rest of her life. Finding that as it should be, she saw to the chute and its rip-ring; assuring herself that in changing their places she had put nothing out of adjustment. Again she gave her attention to the plane, which was behaving perfectly, and as her fingers touched the controls her whole body tingled, as if the digits were lingering over some current which instantly filled her with life and animation.

Assured that all was as it should be she took a short strap from the food container and wrapping that twice about her victim's feet, buckled it on the side where she could see that it was not worked open; nor that it could be without the aid of fingers. Mary Eliska had taken off her long gauntlet gloves while she ate and drank, so Lyudmila Shkrebneva slipped them back onto her hands. Then with a second strap she secured the girl's arms to her sides, but again the air-mindedness in her forced her to place the left one, which was nearest to her, close to the life-saving rip-ring.

"Now, now," she laughed shrilly, and if Skybird had been making less noise the sound might have startled the people beneath them, for it was so harsh and bitter that it was uncanny.

By that time the gasoline indicator showed that the plane required replenishing, so she poured in the reserve tank, calculated how long it would last her, did some mental figuring, then increased the speed until it was going at a dangerous rate. She had not done enough flying so that she was any too familiar with the surface of the country, so she zoomed high to avoid mountains. Her next act was to shut off the engine to listen for other planes whose pilots might be following her. As Skybird glided to earth the woman heard two of them. One seemed to be far behind her; it might have come up when Mary Eliska failed to land on the flying field. The other was directly south, apparently coming straight across her course.

CHAPTER 12.7
A PRISONER

Having ascertained that there were two airplanes in the air, Lyudmila Shkrebneva opened her throttle again, turned the machine as if she were returning to the field and glanced at the indicator to be sure that her nose and tail lights were on. Looking toward the other machines she mentally calculated their course and watched the one which was coming to the south of her. She noted with a scowl that when she came around it swerved off its route considerably, but the second pilot exhibited his lack of interest in her movements by rushing steadily forward, zooming to be well out of her way, and passing on toward the Canadian border.

"If you are following me I shall give you a good run for your money," the woman snapped furiously.

She lifted Skybird's nose, climbed gradually to seven thousand feet, leveled off, then proceeded at an even keel, racing at the machine's top speed; then she started to descend, going more and more slowly, until the altimeter registered two thousand feet. At that level she shut off her engine a moment to listen, glanced at the chart, and then convinced that the larger plane was determined to keep tabs on her, she shut off the lights, and risked a smash-up by gliding to a thousand feet. She could see the larger plane high and in back of her, the roar of its engine sufficient to drown that of Skybird; then she opened the throttle, keeping the head and tail lights out, throwing a cover over the dim light in the cock-pit, and began to climb slowly.

Skybird rushed swiftly forward at its highest speed, lifting gradually and Lyudmila Shkrebneva kept her eyes on the covered control-board, shielding it so that the glow could not be seen by anyone in the air. Twice she glanced over her shoulder and through the blackness of the starless heavens could see the other plane moving more swiftly now toward the spot where its pilot must have calculated that she had made her landing. It was descending gradually and with a chuckle of satisfaction over the scheme she had planned to shake off possible pursuers, she lifted Skybird's nose again and climbed more steeply. At ten thousand feet she came around in a wide sweep then reset her course for the northwest which they had been following since the take-off.

Occasionally she looked at the unconscious girl beside her, and once, when she saw by the clock how long it had been since Mary Eliska passed beyond the realm of consciousness, she pressed her finger over the girl's wrist. In a moment she ascertained that the pulse was beating, although very slowly, then she drew up the gauntlet and unhooked the throat band of the coat.

"If you die, I don't give a care, but I'd rather you wouldn't, for I'm going to take a lot of the conceit out of you and your friends before I get through with you. But die if you want to, for I'll drop you overboard into one of the lakes. This part of the world is full of them and you'll go down so far they will never be able to tell that you didn't do it naturally. I'll see to that." She spoke as if she expected to be heard and understood, but Skybird had hit a mighty rough place in the air and for the next five minutes demanded every bit of her attention.

Making a careful survey of the heavens and the world beneath her, she bared her teeth and grinned maliciously, because there wasn't a sign of another plane. She calculated that by the time the second pilot had shut off his engine to descend, if he did, Skybird was too far on its way for them to hear its engine, so would be lost to them for good.

"And they won't pick me up again," she declared with satisfaction, but although she felt confident that she was safe from pursuit, she made it her business to be alert every moment. The fact that the night was dark and there were no stars, helped her, for the instant a plane's light flashed into the sky she would be able to see it easily. By that time a stiff wind was blowing. It shrieked dismally through the struts and braces, and Skybird plugged on and on with a wail of protest. One thing she watched with the greatest care was the engine, for she did not know how it would stand up on an endurance flight. But it was hitting steadily, behaving quite as if it had not traveled for hours and seemed perfectly capable of going on indefinitely.

They had crossed the border and were well into Canada when a slight movement on the part of her prisoner warned her that the girl was regaining consciousness. She glanced at the white face, saw the head move slightly, the lips part, but the movement ceased after a minute, and Mary Eliska sank back into a state of unconsciousness. With so many things to observe, Lyudmila Shkrebneva grew less cautious and folded the cover she had spread over the cock-pit lights, but she dimmed everything except those she actually needed to read the dials in front of her. The wind was shrieking now, so she tried to set a course which would keep her out of the storm which she knew as surely rising, and continued the flight without showing a light.

According to the chart they were rushing over a mountainous section and here she zoomed high, lest they meet an obstruction. Her experience with altimeters had not included the latest model on Skybird so she was fearful lest the instrument fail to warn her in time to avoid collision with the immovable face of a rocky cliff. Then examining the chart, she swerved sharply out of her course and suddenly, from far ahead she saw another plane circling in wide sweeps. It carried four lights, two blue, one red and the other green.

The sight of this airman gave Lyudmila Shkrebneva no terrors, for she blinked one of her lights for a moment, then switched it out again. This she repeated twice and flew steadily on until five minutes later the two machines were flying side by side, the other plane, which was larger, slightly above Skybird.

In the meantime Mary Eliska had returned to consciousness and was fully aware of what was going on about her. The drug she had been given had caused a sort of paralysis but her mind had cleared several minutes before she stirred. The first thing she knew was the fact that Lyudmila Shkrebneva's fingers were pressed against her wrist but at that time she was utterly unable to move so much as an eyelash, so she remained as if still completely under the influence of the dope which had been given to her in something she ate. Her head ached furiously, and it seemed as if pins and needles were pricking her whole body.

Slowly the sensation, except the headache, faded, and she was able to think. She tried to remember of what Lyudmila Shkrebneva had accused her when the drug began to take effect, but she couldn't remember. By the feel of the plane, the girl Aviatrix was able to tell something of how they were flying and she tried to form a plan of escape. As her body recovered she had ventured to move, and in this way had ascertained that she was strapped tightly and was helpless in the passenger seat. The effort to move had been excruciating and when she relaxed again it was as much exhaustion as design.

By the shrill whistle through the struts Mary Eliska knew that they were flying against a high wind, and as Skybird bucked forward, her engine roaring, and every part of her wailing a protest, she was sure that Lyudmila Shkrebneva must be fully occupied with the task of keeping the plane balanced. There were times when it fairly jumped, others when it half twisted, and more when the wings dipped under the force of the on-rushing storm, and creaked as if they were being ripped off the fuselage.

Cautiously the girl lifted one eyelid and verified her calculations for Lyudmila Shkrebneva was leaning far forward in the seat, battling with every ounce of strength and knowledge she possessed. There was almost no light in the cock-pit and Mary Eliska wondered if they were flying without head and tail lights. She wished she could get a glimpse of the control board. What she wanted to see most was the clock, which would tell her how long she had been unconscious. She reasoned that it was not likely they had landed anywhere; for a trussed girl would certainly arouse suspicion and immediate demands for an explanation. If the fact that she was bound went unobserved, still it would be noticed that she was either asleep or ill; someone would be sure to investigate.

If they had not landed, and had traveled any length of time at the speed they were going, the gasoline supply must be nearly exhausted. Venturing to open her eyes wide and look at the sky all she could see was pitch darkness so that did not help her discover how long she had been unconscious, but she had a positive hunch that it had been some hours. If this was right they would be compelled to land soon to replenish the fuel supply.

Lyudmila Shkrebneva had drawn on her gauntlets, but she hadn't made a very smooth job of it. There was a rip in the lining of the right one and Mary Eliska's finger had gone in the wrong way. It was the hand nearest the outside of the cock-pit, so she risked moving it slightly, then she wondered if she couldn't do something after all to leave a clue as to which way she went. All of her flying clothes were marked with a stamp in indelible ink with her full name. This included the inside of her gauntlet cuffs.

Mary Eliska's heart hammered hopefully as she stealthily wriggled her fingers, pressing them tightly to her side and moving her arm back. She couldn't do this more than half an inch, but repeating the performance patiently and with the utmost caution she finally succeeded in getting her hand well out. Then, waiting a moment, the next time *Skybird* gave a bump, she flipped the glove as high as she could, and with one half-opened eye, she rejoiced to see that the plane dropped sharply, the wind caught the thing as if it were a leaf and bore it off into the darkness. The girl knew that it would probably land miles from where it left her and she prayed that it would be found soon. She knew, also, that it would probably be some time before her absence or disappearance was noticed. Mrs. Stricklin would have the letters from Charleston, and when no more arrived she would start an inquiry. Her dad would get in touch with Mr. Trowbridge or Mr. Wallace.

Even though she was no longer an employee of the Lurtiss Airplane Company, Mary Eliska hadn't the slightest doubt that the firm, its entire force if necessary, would be put out to search for her. She could hear Phil Fisher's wrathful explosions, and see Larry marching out after the best machine, climbing grimly into its cock-pit and roaring furiously off in pursuit. Thinking of the loyalty of every one of them she wondered if Lyudmila Shkrebneva realized it and hoped hard that the woman didn't. Of course everyone knew perfectly well that any pilot, man or woman, who was lost immediately became the focus of the world's attention until the plane appeared or the wreck was discovered; but everyone could not appreciate the perfect camaraderie which existed in the firm's organization; especially among the flyers. If it was rumored that Mary Eliska was missing nothing would be left undone to locate her.

Mary Eliska had no doubt that Lyudmila Shkrebneva would take every possible precaution, and now the girl thought of the possibility of escaping when they came down for fuel. She tried again to catch a glimpse of the control board but that was hopeless, so she gave it up. It was a strain to remain in the same position but she forced herself to do it for she was positive that the instant her captor realized that she had come to her senses, she would take further precautions to see that there was no opportunity for her to get away.

Suddenly, on the wind which came to her, she smelled a strong tang of salt water; enough so that she decided they were nearing one of the coasts and that the storm was coming from there. The air was only intermittently salty so she guessed they were still some distance away from the ocean, whichever one it was. Then through the darkness and to her right, she saw a plane flying high and carrying four lights. Almost at once the lights on Skybird were flashed, then Mary Eliska was sure that they had been traveling without them. Evidently the woman had been afraid of someone's following after her. Now the course was changed sharply and presently Skybird was racing to the left of a plane about twice as large as her own.

Although Mary Eliska wanted to see what this was all about she dared not move, for she was sure that the other machine carried no friend of hers. Peeping cautiously she saw the machine zoom up sharply, they seemed to be going through some sort of maneuver. Lyudmila Shkrebneva had raised herself in the pilot's seat as far as the safety strap would permit, then in a moment the larger plane came around to the right. The girl Aviatrix promptly closed her eyes lest its pilot warn the woman that she was awake.

Twice the two planes circled, then the larger one rose sharply on Mary Eliska's side, and a moment later she could see the underside of a monoplane; its huge floats looking like the bottoms of small flat boats. In another second something like a weight dropped into Mary Eliska's lap and instantly Lyudmila Shkrebneva caught it up, so the girl decided that her captor must be receiving a message, or sending one by the other pilot, but the next instant something dragged across her knees and unable to contain herself any longer, she raised her lids, only to close them again quickly, for the woman was standing over her. At the moment her face was raised, but then she looked down.

What the girl Aviatrix saw made her gasp in astonishment and fear, for Lyudmila Shkrebneva was hauling in a long tube, which must mean that she was going to refuel from the air and not come down at all, at least until the supply was depleted. She might take on a full supply, as much as they had had when they left Charleston, and unless the woman went to sleep over the stick, she could keep going until the following day.

Sick with horror, Mary Eliska tried to make her brain function properly, but it was filled with the wildest terrors and in spite of warm clothing, she felt as cold as if she were wearing summer clothing. In the day time, under the best of conditions, what the two planes were trying to do could be accomplished with skilled pilots at both controls, but in the middle of the night, with a woman at the receiving end of the tube who had been disqualified as a flyer, it was a desperately risky undertaking. Skybird's nose might be jammed up into the other plane's underpinning or drop so low that the tube would be broken and the machine sprayed with the highly inflammable mixture. A dozen things could happen so quickly to make a smash-up inevitable. She wondered dully why Lyudmila Shkrebneva didn't take in new containers, which would be less dangerous, and when the girl recalled that the woman had been considered incompetent as a pilot, she was no longer surprised. Probably her examiners had realized that she was too foolhardy to trust with a license.

There were a number of slips, disconnections and reconnections during the performance, and it seemed to Mary Eliska as if hours passed before the work was finally achieved and she felt the long tube with its heavy weight being dragged across her knees again and at last heard them thump and bump against the side of Skybird while the other pilot hauled them up to his own machine. Then Lyudmila Shkrebneva resumed her seat and her appropriated task, but the girl felt her slip down as if weary from the strain. She opened her eyes a bit to see if the woman was able to do anything more and found that she was busy with the controls, and circling in a wide sweep, the second plane was soaring out of her way, the end of the tube extending behind. Then it disappeared from sight.

Again Mary Eliska's nostrils were filled with that strong odor from the sea and Skybird zoomed courageously forward, carrying with her every vestige of hope that she might help herself or get help when they were forced to land. There was not a chance in the world that they could come down for hours, unless the engine gave them trouble, and no one knew better than the girl Aviatrix that every inch of her plane's machinery was the best possible and that it would stand long hours of the hardest grilling without showing a sign of weakness. She wondered over and over why Lyudmila Shkrebneva had kidnaped her and tried to remember what the woman had said as she was losing consciousness, but her head ached with the effort. Then she thought of the glove she had dropped and resolved to get the other one off and send it after the first if possible.

Removing the right gauntlet, which was furthest from Lyudmila Shkrebneva's side had been comparatively easy, but slipping out of the other which was placed close to the rip-ring of her parachute and almost under the woman's nose, was a more dangerous undertaking, but Mary Eliska wasn't built of the stuff that quits; she knew that a quitter never wins and a winner never quits, so she watched until her companion was leaning far enough forward so that the motion of the arm would not attract her attention. Fortunately for Mary Eliska, the woman decided to dim the lights in the cock-pit, so she herself could not see so easily and must keep close to the control-board to watch the dials.

Slowly and cautiously, the girl wriggled her fingers until finally they were partly out of the gauntlet, then she managed to slip it along toward her right hand, hoping to draw it across her lap and throw it as she had the other. Just then, Lyudmila Shkrebneva tipped Skybird's nose at a sharp angle and climbed swiftly for several minutes, then leveled and shut off her motor. By that time the smell of salt water permeated the air and Mary Eliska was desperately anxious to get the glove over before they reached the shore line where it might be lost in the ocean. In this project Lyudmila Shkrebneva helped her by leaning far over her own side of the plane, searching beneath her, and Mary Eliska clearly heard the pounding of the breakers. With a slight twist of her body she transferred the gauntlet to her right hand, and with a second flip of her fingers, sent it over the side.

Lyudmila Shkrebneva settled quickly back into her seat while the heavens were split with a million tongues of forked lightning, and after a breathless instant, a terrific crack of thunder boomed and crashed as if bent on the destruction of the whole universe.

CHAPTER 12.8
THROUGH THE STORM

If Mary Eliska had really been unconscious when the fury of the storm burst upon them, with the repeated cutting flashes of light and the thunder booming like a terrific bombardment all about the gallant little Skybird, she would have come to if there was any life in her at all. She started up with a wild cry, then remembered instantly that she was supposed to be just coming out of a prolonged period of sleep, and so, strained forward on her straps, stared around as if she had no knowledge of anything which had transpired, and struggled to free herself from the belts that held her secure.

At first Lyudmila Shkrebneva was too fully occupied to pay any attention to the plane's real pilot, and the girl managed to take in the whole situation. The lightning revealed an endless surge of white rollers stretched row after row and piling themselves on top of one another as the gale lashed them like an escaped demon. Her first sensation was one of dismayed certainty that her second glove had gone into the raging water beneath them, so that its chances of being picked up were ruined; the tiny thing would never be recovered and the name printed indelibly on the stiff cuff would never be deciphered.

Twisting and wriggling to get free of her bonds, Mary Eliska verified what she already suspected, that they were secured well out of her reach. The rain began to pour down on them in great sheets as if the heavens had suddenly opened and dumped the accumulation of years on the struggling machine. She managed to catch a glimpse of the indicators and saw that the tanks were well filled; the altimeter registered eight thousand feet but it was going lower with each jerk of the pointer. Whether the engine was functioning or not she couldn't tell, because the howling wind deadened every other sound as Skybird tipped and spun like a helpless leaf.

"Let me loose," Mary Eliska shrieked, but if Lyudmila Shkrebneva heard, she paid no attention, but battled with grim determination with the controls, endeavoring to climb above the tempest which was pressing down on them with such power that it seemed impossible for the plane to lift an inch.

"Let me fly her," the girl pleaded frantically, for she realized above everything else, that Lyudmila Shkrebneva was losing her head, and that their chances of getting out of the dilemma were growing more and more remote. She strained so far forward that her shoulder touched that of the woman, who whirled about angrily, her teeth bared like those of a snarling animal at bay.

"Get out of the way!" She shoved her back into the drenched seat and shook her fist in her face. "Stay where you are or I'll throw you out!" Mary Eliska couldn't hear a word, but there was no mistaking the command. "If *I* can't get us out, the three of us will go down together. I won't have it said that you saved me." Again the clenched fist shot close to the girl's face, and probably if there had been a moment to waste, she would have been struck.

With a furious snarl, Lyudmila Shkrebneva turned her attention back to her job, and after a grilling ten minutes, Skybird's nose began to lift slowly. The brave little plane climbed sturdily into the gale, which continued to fight every fraction of an inch gained. Ten minutes more and they struggled above the worst of the storm, then Lyudmila Shkrebneva took time to put the cover over the top of the machine. Before it was closed she scanned the heavens and waters as best she could, but there was no sign of another plane in the air or ship on the ocean. When the cover was finally in place, the cock-pit no longer acted as a space to fill and help drag them to destruction, but the rain beat on the top, and in spite of the lights Lyudmila Shkrebneva turned on both inside and outside, the lightning filled the whole atmosphere with its weird glow, changing the cheerful illumination to a ghastly, sulphurous hue.

Consulting the altimeter again, Lyudmila Shkrebneva forced the plane to climb higher, but there seemed to be no ceiling to the storm, and they could not get above its rage. The wind veered around until it was on Skybird's tail, and its force drove her ahead at a terrific speed. Here the woman showed a bit more sense than before, by letting the tempest carry them forward instead of struggling against it. She also kept climbing, but at a gradual ascent. The tiny clock on the control-board ticked away two hours, but they seemed more like one hundred and twenty years than that many minutes to the imprisoned young girl. It was nearly morning and if they succeeded in coming through the storm, the first streaks of dawn would be flashing across the heavens in another hour. But that hour too went by bringing no hopeful rays of day to relieve the blackness. On and on they went, once the tank had to be replenished, and once the engine crackled alarmingly for a moment, but that was adjusted. Two hours later they had traveled nearly two hundred miles. It was still raining, but a bit of light was beginning to force its way through the darkness.

Lyudmila Shkrebneva stubbornly refused to release her prisoner or ask advice, although her hands trembled and her body quivered with terror and weariness under the continuous strain, but she did not say another word to the girl beside her, nor did Mary Eliska waste her own strength to plead that she might be given the management of Skybird. She could not help admire the indomitable grit of the woman even while she deplored the fact that such courage was misdirected.

Another hour dragged on before there was the faintest sign that they might win through if Skybird could hang together through the awful beating she was getting. The rain pounded against her, the gale pressed her down spasmodically, tossed her up again like a plaything, but all the time shoved her forward. It seemed to the girl as if every section in her construction must surely be ripped apart any moment, and Mary Eliska's heart was grateful for the skill and careful workmanship which had been put into her little craft.

The girl Aviatrix's head no longer ached from the effects of the drug, and her mind was clearer as she tried to figure how she might get free of her bonds, but whenever she wiggled too strenuously, Lyudmila Shkrebneva would look at her maliciously and glance at the buckles to be sure that they were where she had put them. Thinking of the construction of the plane brought back to Mary Eliska's mind the fact that Mr. Wallace had installed an alarm button; one which was in some way tuned with the broadcasting band, and her heart leaped. Months before when the Blue Pirate Terror had been making a determined effort to force her out of the sky she had pressed her foot over one of the narrow boards in the flooring and by this means had released a spring carefully hidden. If she wasn't too far away from any broadcasting or radio station she might be heard again, but she knew that the other time she had used this emergency, dozens of men were listening for it and had instantly sprung into action.

Leaning over, as if weary, Mary Eliska studied the floor for the tiny knot which marked the secret section, but the cloak Lyudmila Shkrebneva had used to dim the lights on the control board was over it. However, she knew well exactly where it was located, and although she had never released it from the passenger's seat, she repeated in her mind the directions. She must reach it with her heel and press hard with the side of it until she felt it give, then she was to hold it so a second, after which it was to be again released.

Mary Eliska hadn't the faintest idea where they were, nor could she tell from the charts, for the compass was on the further side of the control-board and as Lyudmila Shkrebneva managed the machine her body obstructed the view. She feared they were so far away that it would do no good at all to use Mr. Wallace's clever little invention, but just because she was uncertain of the result she wasn't passing up even an uncertain effort which might help the searchers locate her. She moved her bound feet forward experimentally under the cloak, but although she tried pressing with her heel she found no spot which responded to the force. However, she might get a chance later, so she watched for an opportunity.

Another hour went by slowly, then Lyudmila Shkrebneva got out the container of food; poured herself a drink of strong coffee which she drank black, then took another. That steadied her nerves somewhat and she filled a cup for Mary Eliska, but to this she added a quantity of milk and held it to the girl's lips. It had been in the thermos bottle and was a sickish warm, a nasty mixture, but she drank it gratefully, for her throat was dry as parchment, and her tongue swollen.

"Thank you," she said when the last drop was gone, but she didn't expect to be heard.

After that the woman got out more food, and between operations necessary to keep Skybird balanced, she managed to feed the girl beside her some bread-and-butter sandwiches, topping them off with a little water poured from a tin container. The amount of food, water and the fact that arrangements had been made for the refueling in the air was convincing proof that the woman had carefully planned this scheme, but there was no fathoming the reason for it. When the meal was finished, what was left was stored away again, the cloak was folded, put out of the way, and Mary Eliska's heart leaped hopefully.

It took the girl Aviatrix only a few moments to locate the tiny knot in the floor, which was still wet from the drenching it had received while the cover was open. The little square with its outline so dim it could barely be seen was inches away from her feet, and thanking her lucky star that Lyudmila Shkrebneva had not been able to secure her feet to the seat, she calculated its position. It was still raining, the wind was still blowing them forward and Mary Eliska yawned wearily as she glanced at the shelter above them. Stretching her back, which was strained and aching in every muscle, she managed slowly to give her body a luxuriant treat by moving every part of it, including her feet. They went in the direction of the knot, but when she leaned forward a trifle she saw that it was not far enough.

At that moment Lyudmila Shkrebneva drew herself up in her own seat, leaned back to relax her pain-racked limbs, and then Mary Eliska took advantage of the opportunity offered. She slid low, her feet extended as far as she could get them, and when she guessed that they were in the right spot, she pressed hard. But there was no yield, not the slightest movement, and she grew faint with discouragement. Then she reasoned that the water might have swollen the board, so she pressed again, throwing every ounce of her strength into that heel. Still it did not sink. Moving her foot a trifle she tried again, harder than ever and kept it up. At last the wee board gave slightly, so, with a heart beating furiously, she continued to push on it with all her strength. Anxiously she held the position for fully a minute, dreading every second that her companion might suspect some sort of trick, but apparently Lyudmila Shkrebneva was confident that her prisoner was helpless. Just then Skybird began to buck, as if it was riding steep rollers, and the attention of his pilot was demanded.

"Get back, out of the way," she ordered harshly and gave the girl a shove.

Thankful that the command had been delayed so long, Mary Eliska sat up quickly in her seat, her eyes swept the little square, and she saw it slip slowly into place. At least the signal was set and if only some government wireless man or anybody at all would pick it up and start inquiries as to its cause, they could tell at Lurtiss Field where Skybird was and possibly trace her to her destination.

It was getting extremely cold, more so than the altitude would warrant unless they had been coming steadily north. To occupy her mind, Mary Eliska tried to calculate how far they had come if they had followed the course the woman had set when they left Charleston, but there were so many "ifs" to the reasoning, that she couldn't get even an idea, so she gave it up. As soon as she could read the indicators she would be able to tell. Now she was tired, hopelessly so, and her heavy lids dropped over her eyes, but she forced herself to keep them open. Lyudmila Shkrebneva too, must be greatly fatigued; she couldn't stand such a strain indefinitely, and besides, unless they were refueled again, they would be compelled to make a landing very shortly.

In order to keep herself awake, Mary Eliska went over carefully in her mind every detail of the days since that first morning when she and Skybird had been engaged to take Lyudmila Shkrebneva on her mysterious mission. At first she had given her passenger little thought, but the seeming aimlessness of their flights, together with the woman's taciturnity had made her uneasy. She tried hard to recall anything she had done to offend the woman or arouse her animosity, but could recall nothing. Again she tried to remember the words she had heard vaguely when she was sinking into unconsciousness, but they continued to elude her. She wondered if by any possible chance Lyudmila Shkrebneva had objected to young Powell's seeing them off, but promptly dismissed the idea as too absurd for consideration. Who could mind the appearance of the fun-loving chap and his sister? No, Mary Eliska was sure that it was something that went back further, and again she racked her brain for the answer.

"At any rate, I guess she isn't interested in killing me or she would have done it long ago; she has had opportunity enough. She might have given me a second dose of drug, bigger than the other, and finished the job. If she had wanted to do anything of that kind, I certainly gave her a good chance when I ate and drank. Wonder why I wasn't afraid to take the food! I might have been afraid not to, I don't know. Heavens, I'd like to go to sleep, but I can't desert Skybird—I won't," she resolved, but it was a resolution mighty difficult to keep.

No matter how long the engine stood up, the plane held together, and the fuel lasted; the woman was bound to reach a point when her body refused to act. Even now she was moving in jerks, staring three and four times at the different indicators before she was positive of the readings. Her breath came in painful gasps; Mary Eliska could tell that by the way her shoulders heaved; she moved her feet as if they felt weighted, and twice her head nodded, but it was brought up always with a quick jerk. As soon as the woman's will power weakened, as it surely must, then Mary Eliska was sure that she could manage to get free of her bonds. She could wriggle and twist until she could reach the buckle, and with one arm loose, the rest would be but the work of a moment; then she could take charge, and would see to it that Lyudmila Shkrebneva did not get the upper hand again.

As she glanced at the woman, whose fatigue was obvious, she determined to make a try for her freedom at once for it was probable that if Lyudmila Shkrebneva fainted from strain and exhaustion, she would get herself so tangled with the controls of the plane that before Mary Eliska could get loose, Skybird would have her nose buried in the bottom of the ocean, if it was still under them, or in the ground if they were traveling over land. After fifteen minutes, during which she moved her elbow not more than an inch at a time, the girl finally got her left hand back to the buckle, but maintaining the same position for so long a period had made her fingers so cold and numb that contact with the hard metal sent thousands of pins and needles stinging through her body. It took considerable time before the digits could feel with any accuracy, but at last they did. She could not risk a glance at what she was trying to do, but she felt the end of the strap, placed her fingers well over it, and slowly drew them back until there was a hump in the leather. Under this lee-way she pushed with her thumb, then working breathlessly she got the strap through the end of the buckle.

At that moment Lyudmila Shkrebneva leaned back as if she suspected something amiss and glanced at her companion, but her eyes were so heavy, and Mary Eliska looked so much as if she were nearly asleep, that she devoted her energy to the job at hand, which was demanding enough. It was still raining, but not so violently, the wind blew with an angry roar as if furious with Skybird for not being brought down in splinters, while intermittent flashes of lightning and a far-off bombing of thunder kept them reminded that they were in the greatest danger, so the robber-pilot bent forward again. Three minutes later Mary Eliska pushed the tongue of the buckle out of the hole.

Never had Mary Eliska's heart hammered so furiously as it did while her fingers gradually got the strap through, but at last it was accomplished. She wriggled just enough to draw it under her back, which loosened her right arm. It had been tight so long that there was almost no sensation left, and as the blood began to circulate more normally the pain was excruciating. The belt had been wound about her arm in three twists, and being mighty careful that the strap across her body remained, to all appearances, as usual, she finally got it free. What should she do next was the question which immediately confronted her. She made up her mind that the best thing to do was to allow her body to relax as much as possible so that if she had to make a quick move, she would be able to manage. In the meantime, she might get an opportunity to free her feet.

With this project in mind, Mary Eliska drew her feet back carefully, at the same time lowering her right hand. She was glad that the gauntlets had been removed, and wondered a little why Lyudmila Shkrebneva had not missed them. But she evidently didn't and that was something to be thankful for. It was half an hour before she finally brought her fingers into contact with the strap, the buckle of which was in the back, then drooping forward as if she were asleep, she gave a great sigh, and closed her lids, but her hand worked quickly and presently the strap was off. She couldn't prevent its dropping down, but she was banking on the fact that Lyudmila Shkrebneva had been paying no attention to her. Cautiously moving her toes and ankles, the girl slowly began to feel more normal. Although she was horribly weary, she determined that in a few minutes she would take charge of the situation. But a moment later, Lyudmila Shkrebneva shut off the engine and Skybird began to glide down; whether it was to the earth or water, there was no telling, but she was coming down, and the pilot was evidently preparing to make a landing.

"If she does," Mary Eliska thought, "she'll surely discover that I got loose."

CHAPTER 12.9
MAROONED

What was to happen when they finally landed, Mary Eliska could not even guess, but she determined to be on the alert. She judged they had maintained a high altitude, and this fact was promptly verified as she watched Lyudmila Shkrebneva attend to the plane. Soon she took time to slide the cover from over the cock-pit and all that could be seen was a thick fog which enveloped them. The woman scanned the earth beneath her and as she did that Mary Eliska managed to catch a glimpse of the fuel indicator, the needle of which showed that they could go very little further.

The fact promptly banished a sudden idea of pushing the woman out and racing back into the heavens, for such a scheme would be foolhardy, inasmuch as Skybird could carry her only a short distance. Her second plan depended greatly upon what happened when the plane's wheels touched the ground, if they did, but Mary Eliska made ready to snatch any opportunity which offered itself. She hated to abandon the machine; that would have to be her last resort, for she realized that the woman wasn't coming down any place where she did not expect to find friends and accommodations. Carefully drawing up her right hand, she found the latch to the door at her side, and at the same time got loose her safety strap so that it could not hold her back. The chute would also hamper any quick movement, but before she could manage to rid herself of the awkward bulky thing, Skybird touched ground.

A few feet away was a huge fire, which looked as if it had been built as a beacon for the woman, but even its blaze was veiled by the swirling fog which surrounded it. As the plane curved, its wheels bumped first one side, then the other; once they struck something so large that they jumped, so Lyudmila Shkrebneva was fully occupied in bringing the machine to a stop. Blurred figures of men moved between them and the fire, and at last when Skybird stopped, they came forward. There was a confused murmur of voices.

"Hurry and help me," Lyudmila Shkrebneva snapped, but her voice cracked shrilly.

"We're here—"

"Been waitin' fer hours," snapped one who seemed in charge of the party. "Keeping this fire going. What kept you?"

"Think I could do any better through that storm—"

"Aw, that's it, eh? Flew yourself. The boss said you'd probably try that fool trick."

"What was the matter with the girl doing it—she'd have—"

"Shut your fool mouth. Get her out and be quick about it, you think she's so wonderful—" Lyudmila Shkrebneva swore roundly.

"She'd have done it quicker. It's only fool's luck that you didn't have a smash-up."

"Get her out—" Lyudmila Shkrebneva stamped her feet furiously.

"Did you kill her?" One of the men came close to the woman, and his tone was threatening. "You'll get yours from the boss if she's hurt; he needs her in this business and you had your orders."

"I tell you she's all right, only asleep. Get her out. We're both nearly dead."

But Mary Eliska didn't wait to hear anything more. She threw her weight against the door, jumped out under the shelter of Skybird's wing, and leaped into the dense fog. Instantly three men who had been coming around the plane, sprang toward her. There followed a wild scramble of feet as the girl ran desperately from the scene, but the chute interfered, although she tried hard to get out of it as she fled.

"Bring up some of those torches," one of the men bellowed. "She can't get far."

Immediately a dozen firebrands were being brandished through the fog, in a moment her footprints were discovered and panting men rushed in pursuit. The rough ground, the unwieldy chute, and her own weariness were almost too much for the fleeing girl, but she pushed on as fast as she could, hoping to find some place into which she could dodge, and trying to plant her feet on rocks which would leave no tell-tale trail. It was amazing that she managed to keep going so long, but suddenly the leader of the men caught sight of her.

"You ain't going to be hurt, Miss, and you're headin' out to sea," he called, and although his voice was rough, there was nothing in it to fear. Just at that moment a wave splashed over Mary Eliska's ankles, verifying the last part of his statement; but a wave of discouragement even larger and more formidable than the water piled over her, completely dispelling every hope of escape.

"Oh, please," she cried—but that was all she could say, for her head seemed ready to burst open with pain, sharp daggers stung her eyes, and just as the man reached her, her body grew limp.

"That wildcat gave you a hard time," he remarked as he picked her up in his arms, but what he said or did was lost to the girl, for she had fainted dead away. It was lucky he was there, because she would have slumped into the water, been tossed helplessly on the incoming tide, and no one could have saved her from being crushed among the rocks.

Being a healthy girl the state of unconsciousness did not last long and a bit later she opened her eyes again. A dark woman, who looked like an Native American had her in charge; while one of the men stood ready with a flask, some of the contents of which was still stinging her throat. Her flying suit had been opened and she was stretched out on a rough bed of boughs, and another Native American, a younger one, unfastened her shoes. It wasn't a comforting sight, but it was evident that every one of them was bent on bringing her to and making her as comfortable as possible.

"Here, that's the girl! Take a bit more of this and it will knock the kinks out of you," the man urged. He was the man who had picked her up, and there was a smoldering light in his eyes as if, regardless of what the situation might really be, his sympathies were with Mary Eliska.

"I'm lots better," she managed to gasp. "Thank you so much."

"Sure, but you'll be better still. Come along, this won't hurt you, and you surely do need it. The natives will do the little things to help you." He went over with the flask and Mary Eliska obeyed without further protest. Her good sense told her that she must do everything possible to regain her strength if she expected to get away from the place. She wanted to ask where she was, but decided it might be better to wait until she was more sure of herself and those around her.

"I ain't never been in favor of this kidnaping business, Wat," said one of the men who was standing by. "It always sets the crowd against you."

"Well, keep your shirt on, Slim," Wat answered under his breath. "Better yell fer some of that soup," he added.

"Come along with the soup," Slim shouted.

"Think I'm at the Pole." A third man appeared with a tin of steaming soup, which the woman took from him.

"That's good. Let Nomie feed you a little at a time, and if they don't treat you right, yell for Wat and I'll come running." He grinned down at her, then spoke to Nomie, who nodded that she understood, but Mary Eliska didn't catch the words.

"Good," said Nomie, as she sniffed the contents of the bowl. Then she took a crust of hard bread, dipped it into the liquid. "Too hot," she told Mary Eliska. "Eat little from crust."

It was an odd way of taking nourishment, but Mary Eliska was glad that she wasn't required to sit up and eat, for although the brandy she had swallowed was tingling warmly, she was woefully tired and making any sort of physical effort seemed impossible. The "soup" tasted of clams and milk, and she thought she had never eaten anything better. Conscientiously Nomie fed her, a little at a time, until finally it was cooler and she used a spoon instead of the bread, but she did not hasten the performance. The men had withdrawn tactfully to the other side of the huge bon-fire which was being raked into a smaller space as it was no longer needed as a beacon. Mary Eliska wondered dully how it had helped Lyudmila Shkrebneva to know where to come down, but just then she saw Slim passing with a bundle of rockets and understood that the gang must have been shooting them intermittently while they waited, and more frequently when they heard the plane roaring toward them out of the fog.

"More bye and bye," Nomie said at last, and she handed the dish to the young girl. "Fix bed, Natell," she added. The Native American girl hurried away, and presently Wat returned.

"Feel able to walk?" he asked gruffly.

"Guess so," Mary Eliska answered. She managed to get to her feet, and although she felt better, she was still wobbly.

"Give her a hand there," Wat ordered.

"Good," agreed Nomie and she slipped her strong arm about Mary Eliska's waist. "This way." They proceeded slowly away from the fire, and presently, a few yards ahead, she saw a small blaze through the fog.

"Here you are!" Natell was standing in a low doorway.

"Now, get some sleep. Nobody's going to hurt you," Wat said quietly, and the two native women helped her stumble inside.

Mary Eliska was too weary to pay much attention to anything, except that the room she entered appeared to be a long, low one with many bright colored draperies hanging on the wall. In a moment she was led to a rude bed, the top of which was piled high with pillows, and as she seated herself on the edge, she saw another one a few feet away. Across the top of it lay Lyudmila Shkrebneva, already sound asleep. Nomie and her young daughter made short work of helping their charge out of a part of her clothes, but they hadn't finished, when her weary lids closed over her eyes as she fell asleep.

Although she had no idea what time it was when she opened her eyes again, the girl Aviatrix had slept around the clock. The Native Americans had certainly made her very comfortable among the huge pillows, and now she yawned and stretched luxuriously. Turning over she saw that close to the bed the girl, Natell, was seated, her small brown hands busily darting back and forth over a piece of weaving. Her keen ears must have been alert for a sound from her charge, for she immediately called shrilly. "No-mee, No-mee!" Nomie came at once and glanced at the blinking young pilot.

"Good," she greeted soberly.

"She is awake," announced Natell.

"Of course I am awake, but—" A bit of the recollection of the horrors through which she had gone, returned to her mind, and instinctively she glanced toward the second bed where she had seen Lyudmila Shkrebneva recovering from her own exhaustion, but the woman wasn't there and the bed had been smoothed. As far as she could tell there was no one in the room but the natives and herself. "Where am I? I mean, what is this place?" she asked curiously.

"Island," Nomie answered. She was getting the white girl's clothes out of a queer sort of chest that looked as if it had been made of pieces of driftwood. As the woman showed no inclination of imparting more information, Mary Eliska decided that it might be the better part of wisdom to be content with what she had learned.

"Fine!" Natell spread the garments before their owner with true feminine interest, and in another moment, Nomie produced the traveling bag from behind one of the curtains, as well as the wrist watch they had taken off to add to her comfort while she slept. The time-piece was going but Mary Eliska stared at it in amazement, for it showed less than two hours later than the hour they had landed.

"How long did I sleep?" she asked quickly.

"One sun," Nomie smiled at her.

"Good sleep," Natell added, with a wide grin.

"I should say so," Mary Eliska replied laughing. She had a hunch that it might be greatly to her advantage to be as friendly as possible with the people of the island, because recalling the dialogue which had passed between Wat and Slim after the arrival of Skybird, their attitude toward her abduction, or kidnaping was one of strong disapproval. The native women, too, were kindly disposed and Mary Eliska wondered to what tribe they belonged. She had seen any number of Native Americans in the United States and in Canada also, when she was touring with the Wallaces, but while the two who were caring for her had high cheek bones, dark eyes, and skin, they looked as if they belonged to another race entirely. While she put on her clothes, Nomie was fussing about a small oil stove, and presently the odor of coffee permeated the dwelling. Ready at last she noticed that Natell's eyes were attracted by a string of red beads among the articles in the tray of her bag.

"Eat," invited Nomie.

"You may have these," Mary Eliska picked up the beads and fastened the strand about the younger girl's neck.

"No, no, no," she said quickly, and glanced with evident anxiety around the room as if she expected someone to step out.

"What?" demanded Nomie coming to the girl.

"See." Natell looked wistfully at her mother, who also took a hasty glance over her shoulder.

"Please let her keep them!" Mary Eliska pleaded. "If you do not want anyone to know I gave them to her, slip them out of sight. I have more. See!" She pointed to other ornaments in her bag, and after a few words exchanged in their own tongue, Nomie nodded her head.

"Good," she agreed, and immediately Natell fixed the neck of her homespun dress so that the treasure could not be seen. Her mother drew a chair, cut from the stump of a tree, before an equally primitive table and spread out a meal of cornbread, fish and coffee. To this she added, surreptitiously, as if as a special treat, a tablespoonful of honey.

"Thank you very much," Mary Eliska said, for she had an idea that the settlement did not boast of very much of the sweet.

"Good," the woman replied, but she kept her eyes on the door while Natell stood just outside of it until the girl Aviatrix had consumed the delicacy.

Mary Eliska wondered why the great secrecy and reached the conclusion that Nomie's general orders had been that she was to do nothing more than absolutely necessary for the prisoner. When the meal was finished, she rose to go outside partly because the place was stuffy, and partly because she wanted to know if she were to be kept within certain limits. Neither of the natives made any move to detain her and once beyond the low entrance her first thought was for Skybird, but the plane was nowhere in sight.

The day was clear and in front of the dwelling the rocky land sloped toward the water. Here and there were stretches of white sand, washed up by the high tides, and a bit further back the girl could see a few clusters of shrubs and trees whose sturdy trunks were bent and twisted as if they had maintained their place despite the gales which had beaten them without mercy. Walking slowly toward the edge of the Island, she paused to look back and then discovered that there was really no house; that the entrance was cut or dug from the face of a low cliff, nor was there a sign of another habitation.

Mary Eliska's next thought was to find tracks of her machine, but she didn't, nor did she come across any blackened spot which the bon-fire had left. Trying to reconstruct the place from when she landed on it she discovered that the highwater mark came to within a few yards of the cliff, and calculating quickly she figured that there had been at least two changes in the tide while she slept, so all marks would be completely obliterated.

As there appeared to be no one to object to her walking about wherever she chose, the girl proceeded slowly along the edge of the beach, which was rugged and irregular. Locating the position of the sun did not help her reach any solution to the question of where she was marooned, but a bit later when she climbed to the top of a hill she knew without doubt that she was on an island; and because of the coldness in the air and the course Lyudmila Shkrebneva had set when they left Charleston, she was positive that she was pretty far north. How far, she had no way of telling. Every few minutes she scanned the sky for a glimpse of Skybird or a rescuing plane, but the heavens were as empty as the vast expanse of sea that surrounded her.

Figuring the time since anyone she knew had heard of or from her the girl Aviatrix felt positive that a search of some kind must be already started. She had no hope of the second glove's having been found, but if the first one was picked up and passed on to any authority, at least they would have something upon which to work. Then, if Mr. Wallace's invention had not failed, and had been heeded, the men of Lurtiss field would certainly have further assistance in finding her. Again she looked about for a trace of the gallant little plane, but found nothing.

"Wonder if anyone has gone up in her," she remarked to herself. Then she wondered where Lyudmila Shkrebneva had gone. She guessed that the woman was not on this particular island, anyway, then suddenly she sat down and chuckled. "I'll bet she's gone off in Skybird, and if she has, that little buzzer will be her Waterloo, for with the spring down, it will start again whenever the plane is taken into the air. Wouldn't it be topping if Lyudmila Shkrebneva gets herself caught!" But, although the idea was certainly amusing, Mary Eliska sighed. "She's got too much sense, anyway, to go flying over the country in Skybird—she'll know everyone will be on the lookout for the machine."

CHAPTER 12.10
TREACHERY

The realization that Lyudmila Shkrebneva was too clever a woman to permit herself to be so easily caught ruined the tiny bit of fun Mary Eliska had found in days. For minutes she stood, staring out at the sea and trying desperately to convince herself that she would soon find a way to escape. At first the fact that she were allowed to go about without guards and not kept under cover appeared to be a good thing, but as she thought that over, she made up her mind that this particular island was so far away from any line of travel or settlement that her captors had no fear of her being found by plane or boat; and she couldn't get away, so they were safe in letting her roam at will.

"No one would take Skybird up," she said aloud because it was pleasant to hear something beside the ceaseless splash of the water on the shore. "Then," she added a bit later, "perhaps it's still here." The abode of Nomie was built in a rock so that anyone passing would not notice that it was a habitation; so perhaps a similar hiding place had been found for her plane.

Hopefully she set out again, and this time she investigated every high rock, shrub, clump of trees, and low cliff. For an hour she continued the search, and although she half skirted the island, there was little difference in the scene from one point to another. The sameness of it all was appallingly dreary. She tried hard to keep thoughts of her mother and father out of her mind, for she knew just how anxious and worried they must be. She could picture them listening for the familiar roar of the machine which would announce her return; running to the telephone every time it rang, eager for news that didn't come; hurrying to the door when the mail-man whistled, only to be disappointed when he brought no card or letter. Dad was doubtlessly making brave efforts to assure his wife that their daughter was quite safe— perhaps even fibbing a bit in an effort to make it easier. He had probably already got in touch with Mr. Trowbridge and her former flying-mates had been urged to keep an eye out for their girl Aviatrix, as they had dubbed her.

All those things made her heart sick and she wandered on and on hardly noticing where she went and twice she had to scramble up over rocks to get out of water into which her stumbling feet had taken her. At last, utterly weary and discouraged, she sank down on a hard wide stretch of sand and buried her head on her arm. Although she was nearly overcome with discouragement she did not give way to tears, for she knew they wouldn't help any. There was nothing she could do but wait, no matter how long it was. She sat quietly for a quarter of an hour and felt more rested, then a sort of plan formed itself in her mind. She must find out just where she was! With that information she might discover a way to escape. But with that encouraging idea, into her brain popped a hopeful thought that she would probably be watched to some extent and any move she made would be immediately reported. As she sat there feeling desperately lonely, she heard a gruff voice a short distance further on and recognized the man Wat, but could not see him.

"Well, I've fixed her up, just as you want, but whether you like it or not, I'm telling you it's no good. My advice—"

"I'm not asking you for your advice." That harsh voice was none other than Lyudmila Shkrebneva's.

"You're gettin' it gratis, see! When the Boss finds out how you balled up the works you're going to get plenty, I don't care how much of a drag you have with him. He told you what to do and you didn't do as he ordered—"

"Will you shut up!" The woman screamed.

"No, I won't. You haven't got a leg to stand on—"

"I tell you the girl was having us spied on—"

"You can tell me all you like, but I don't believe it, see? Now, this stunt you want to pull is a fizzle—and you'll get thrown as sure as you're born. You were told to stay here and look after the girl—"

"How do you know so much about what I was told?"

"That's an easy one. I was told that when the pair of you got here you'd stay, see, so I know those were your orders. If you found you were spied on, you had your orders to go on to Miami and keep away from here, and you were to keep out of the pilot seat. Instead of that you signaled that you were coming along O.K. and it wasn't until the re-fill that anyone knew you were at the controls—"

"I brought the plane through, didn't I? And I gave the fellows that were spying on us the slip, didn't I?" There was proud defiance in her tone.

"I'm not so sure that you did. You got here, yes, with the girl almost dead, and you flew the plane to satisfy your own conceit—"

"This airplane belongs to me, understand, I'm doing what I please with it and you are obeying my orders regarding it! Bear that in mind. I made up my mind I was going to have it the first time I rode in it, if I had to steal it."

"Yes!" Wat remarked without much interest.

"Yes. Now I've got it, it's mine, I'm keeping it in payment for the buckshot that girl's father peppered on my chin. As long as there is the faintest sign of a scar, I'll feel they are still in my debt." She spoke with such passion that Mary Eliska gasped in amazement and horror.

"Yes. Well, all I've got to say is that it's a pity her father had such darned poor aim—." Just then an engine roared and cut off further remarks, and Mary Eliska leaped to her feet, for she recognized Skybird's thunder. A moment later it rounded a curve and came rushing swiftly along the hard stretch of beach.

"Oh, they have painted her white," the girl gasped. Sure enough, Skybird, all her own beautiful trimming concealed under the color which would make her hardest to pick out in the sky, was rushing forward swiftly, gaining speed at every turn of her whirling propeller. With an exclamation of dismay, Mary Eliska started to run across the beach to her beloved machine and at that moment, Lyudmila Shkrebneva saw her. The woman's expression grew uglier than anything the girl had ever seen in her life and with a lurch Skybird was spun around sharply; it was tearing after her and in another minute she would be cut to pieces in that cruel wheel. The plane's nose was pointed directly at the girl, rushing like some maddened demon to destroy her. There was no time to think or act. The only thing she could do was drop flat on her face and pray.

"God help me," formed on her lips, but before the words were out of her mouth, she felt something brush the full length of her body and knew that the machine had lifted before it touched her and was already two feet in the air. "Thank you," she sighed gratefully then raised her head lest Lyudmila Shkrebneva discover that by a miracle her fiendish plan had failed, and turn back to finish it, but Skybird was climbing at top speed and was half way across the island.

"Hurt, Miss?" Wat came running.

"Thank you, no," she told him.

"You're mighty lucky." His rough face was white through its tan and to relieve his feelings, he shook his fist after the racing plane and its pilot.

"I hope you fly to perdition," he shouted.

"Second the motion," Mary Eliska added, then she began to laugh hysterically and Wat stared down at her.

"Sure you're all right?" he asked again.

"Positive," she told him.

"You sure got a good guardian angel!"

"You don't seem overly fond of Lyudmila Shkrebneva."

"I don't know anyone who is," he replied.

"Did you paint Skybird—the plane?" she ventured to ask.

"Yes," he admitted. "She's got money in these works so I had to, because she told me to, but it was a hurry-up job just on the outside. It's hardly dry yet, but that flying fool couldn't wait."

"She did appear to be in a hurry," the girl remarked.

Mary Eliska didn't say so, but he had given her the information she wanted. They had not taken time to go over the inside of the machine and it was possible that the signal buzzer would be heard by someone. The girl wanted awfully to ask Wat where they were, but decided against being too inquisitive.

"I see the kid, Natell, over on the hill. Guess it's time you got something more to eat," he told her.

"That would be welcome," Mary Eliska replied with a smile. She started toward the young Native American girl, but Wat called.

"I say, Mary Eliska!"

"Yes." She turned about.

"Thought I'd tell you it's about three hundred miles, airline, to the nearest coast."

"Three hundred miles!" she exclaimed in dismay.

"Yah, kind of a long stretch when you figure doing it on a raft fer instance, or a canoe," he added.

"I hadn't been thinking of a raft," she grinned.

"Reckon not, but you might. Building one would be a real good way to fill in your time, if you're a good hand with a hammer, but don't set no store by it."

"As a hammerer I'm bad, but I might have tried it. Thanks so much for the tip."

"Keep it for what it's worth," he replied and strode off in the opposite direction.

Hurrying toward the waiting Natell, the girl Aviatrix's step was light for she felt that after all its seeming hopelessness, the hours had not been devoid of results. She had learned that Wat and his companions were located on the opposite side of the island, that Lyudmila Shkrebneva had gone off in the repainted Skybird, whose nose pointed east when she disappeared on the horizon, which meant that the nearest point of land was probably that way, three hundred miles. Recalling her maps and large bodies of water in the north, she wondered if the island was in the Bering Sea. If it was, the mainland must be Alaska, United States territory.

If she wasn't west of Alaska the island might be in one of the large bodies to the north of Canada, but that wouldn't make a bit of difference, for every pilot, worthy of the name, was a citizen of the world, and the sudden disappearance of one in any part of the globe immediately aroused the interest of every land. It was a mighty comforting thought and Mary Eliska was humming a little tune when she joined Natell, who looked at her with wide eyes.

"That wooden bird could not destroy you," she said as if she could hardly believe the evidence of her own optics.

"No." Mary Eliska was about to explain that while she might have been cut to shreds, the plane hadn't really touched her, but then she recalled reading that Native Americans have many superstitions and if they believed that she was favored by the Gods or had a charmed life, they might be inveigled into helping her escape. She had also read that the natives succeeded in traveling with their frail crafts over waters a white man, unless driven by desperation, would refuse to attempt; and safely reach ports unbelievably distant. The pair reached the dug-out and the young girl immediately started to speak swiftly to her mother in their own tongue and the girl Aviatrix guessed that the older woman was getting the details of the miraculous escape of their white charge. Nomie's own eyes widened during the recital and at its close, she crossed herself piously.

"Eat," she invited.

"Thank you."

The evening meal consisted of reindeer meat, dried potatoes baked in a sort of pancake form, cornbread which was whiter than that she had eaten earlier in the day, coffee sweetened with canned milk, and a paste of dried fruits. The girl was mighty hungry and she ate her full share, but she watched that she did not overstep the bounds of good breeding. She realized that probably every mouthful had to be brought at regular intervals, not too close together, from the distant mainland and that the rations of Nomie and Natell were necessarily doled out with care so the supplies would not be depleted before they could be replenished. The food tasted good and Nomie seemed to appreciate the fact that her guest or prisoner was not too finical.

Glancing about the primitive living quarters, Mary Eliska thought of her mother and recalled long ago days when she was a little girl, with a little girl's likes and dislikes for different foods. Then, Mrs. Stricklin had told her if she would learn to eat anything put before her, when she grew up she would save herself all sorts of unpleasant experiences and keep from being classified by her friends as too much of a nuisance to have around when they were inviting guests.

"It's a mighty good thing Mom taught me that," she said to herself, "for I certainly have landed in all sorts of places, been given all sorts of things to eat, and it has always been jolly." She thought of "Pa and Ma Perkins," into whose treacherous "backyard" she had brought the Wallace's when she was flying blind through a bad fog.

But it wasn't possible, in the face of her present dilemma to keep her mind on experiences of the past and as she thought of what she had seen of the island Mary Eliska wondered if there was any sort of wireless station on it. She hadn't seen anything like an antenna, but it seemed hardly possible that the men stationed here had no means of communicating with the outside world. Immediately she began to think seriously of the radio. One of the men had said that Lyudmila Shkrebneva had signaled that all was O.K. when she was flying toward them. She must have carried some sort of instrument which she had used, but, rack her brain as hard as she could, Mary Eliska couldn't recall a moment when a communication had been sent out. To be sure it might have been done when she was unconscious; also it might have been done on Skybird's radio, but that was not equipped to send. If a station picked her up there were certain signals she could send, a sort of code; also, if Mr. Wallace's special apparatus was sprung, she could reply to questions, but in order to do that she had to press a switch, which looked like one of the screws on the dial-board. This fact was known to only a few officials inside and outside of the Lurtiss organization; Lyudmila Shkrebneva was ignorant of their existence, so she could not very well avail herself of them.

The girl Aviatrix resolved that on the following day she would search for a radio. Ever since she could remember, John had built them, so she grew up with more than an average understanding of their construction and operation; also, she had learned more during her period of training at Lurtiss Field for Mr. Wallace considered that a pilot who did not understand sending and receiving, as well as rig-up, was only half trained. Now, if she could locate a set here she would watch for an opportunity to send out an S.O.S. But she would have to find out first where she was located; just saying that she was on an island which she thought was in the Bering Sea would not be much help. Not only the Bering Sea but every large body of water had numberless uncharted islands and this particular one was probably chosen by the Boss, whoever he was, because of its location and apparent barrenness.

When the meal was finished Mary Eliska offered to help Nomie, but she was brushed aside, although not unkindly, so she went out again. The sun was still high and the girl realized that because she was a good way north there would be a great difference in the length of the days and nights, and she wondered if she would see any of the marvelous coloring and brilliant spectacles of which she had read, but the heavens were clouding over, and far in the horizon she discovered a mist which looked very much like a gathering fog.

"Hope it isn't going to be as thick as it was the other day when we landed," she remarked, and as she knew a great deal about the density and speed of the all-enveloping mists, she kept her eye on it to be sure that she did not wander too far away. Recalling the treachery of the shore line she had no doubt that she could very quickly lose herself. Observation was also a branch of an aviator's training, besides it was a part of Mary Eliska's nature, so as she walked slowly in the opposite direction from that she had taken earlier in the day, she carefully noted every rock, counted her steps when she crossed smooth stretches, and turned about frequently so that she would be familiar with the appearance of the landscape when she returned.

She had been walking nearly an hour by her watch, which she had kept running although she knew the time must be different on the Island than it was at home, when she noticed a hill which rose gradually a short distance in front of her. The fog was coming in, but she was sure she could manage to get back safely, so she proceeded until she was standing on the top. There she discovered that it extended in a long, narrow plateau which seemed almost straight, but as she went along she saw that it curved slightly toward the water. The wind was blowing so cold that she wrapped her coat around her tightly and decided to go on and see what it was like on the other side. The surface was not entirely flat; in places it dipped slightly, as if worn down by storms, and in a couple of sections were wide cracks, such as those made by ice in the crevices of rocks.

The whole flat was deadly monotonous and Mary Eliska was about to return before she was caught in the fog, when suddenly, as if from beneath her feet, she heard a confusion of strange sounds. Breaking the island's solitude as it did, it made her jump, and then, controlling her nerves, she paused to listen. It seemed to her as if it was some kind of an animal, then after a moment she wondered if it could be a baby, but she instantly dismissed that idea. Walking back carefully to the widest crack she had crossed, she bent over to hear better, then got down on her stomach to see what might be there. It occurred to her that some young animal might have fallen through and was unable to climb out; it might be hurt and she could help it. But the crevice was dark and then she heard the noises again and distinguished voices. Quickly she pressed her ear close, then jumped, for a hand was laid on her shoulder.

CHAPTER 12.11
A FIGHT IN THE NIGHT

That hand gripping her shoulder made Mary Eliska's heart skip a beat, but after a moment when it didn't yank her to her feet she gathered courage to look around. To her great relief she saw that it was Nomie.

"Fog coming," the Native American said, scarcely above a whisper.

"I'll come," Mary Eliska answered quickly and rose to her feet. Her companion put her fingers over her lips, which the girl understood to mean that they must keep very quiet, then the pair hurried stealthily across the plateau. When they were well below the hill, Nomie paused, her face very sober.

"Keep way from cracks," she said briefly.

"I thought it was a baby animal of some kind. I was going to help it up if I could," she explained and Nomie looked at her searchingly. "That is true," Mary Eliska added emphatically.

"Good," Nomie appeared relieved and willing to believe the story, but she went on. "Noises you hear, things you know not, pay no heed to. I give you leave to walk; you will make me trouble—"

"I'll be mighty careful," Mary Eliska put in hastily. "You have been very good to me and I appreciate it."

"Speak not of the noise or the crack," the woman urged.

"Not a word to anyone."

"Busy yourself with watching the sky," was the woman's advice.

"All right," she promised, but her mind was endeavoring to solve the mystery of the plateau.

Mary Eliska thought it might be the living quarters of Wat and the men, but if that was all, why had Nomie been so fearful? There was certainly something going on under those rocks which was a secret that was guarded with extreme care and if it had been one of the men who had discovered her trying to fathom it, things might go very hard with her. From what the Native American woman said, the white girl gathered that she was expected to keep a close watch on her prisoner, and an exhibition of too much inquisitiveness would surely cost her what liberty she enjoyed. Presently they reached the dug-out, and after watching the woman gather some bits of driftwood from the beach, they went inside.

"Go to bed," Nomie said quietly. "Sleep very sound," she added "You be sick if get no rest."

"I'm not tired," Mary Eliska answered, but there was something in the woman's eyes which seemed to plead with her to obey, so greatly puzzled, she added, "Not very tired, but I believe I'll feel better if I lie down for a while."

"Good," the woman answered. "Just like you are, lie down," She tugged at the pillows piled on the corner bed, and guessing that she was to be hidden, Mary Eliska stretched herself among them. A moment later anyone coming into the room, unless they knew that she was there, would not have noticed her.

For minutes Mary Eliska lay still as a mouse, every nerve tense to know what was going to happen, but as the time went on and she did not hear anything more than the splashing of the waves against the rocks outside, the drip of heavy fog, which had rolled in thickly, and the Native American woman moving about the dug-out, her mind leaped back to the discovery of the crack on the plateau, and to wondering what the mystery could be. Then, suddenly she heard a whining noise, something like the sounds beneath the rocks, followed by a gruff barking and snorting, which could not belong to a dog. It kept up for an hour, then seemed to die down, and, because effects of the strain she had been through had not entirely worn off, her eyelids closed and she drifted off to sleep, but not quite soundly enough to make her absolutely oblivious of her surroundings. Into her lulled brain leaped a train of thoughts, half dream and half reality. The past and the present, the possible and the impossible in a conglomeration of fancies, but suddenly her eyes popped wide open and every faculty was alert.

The first thing she saw was Nomie standing near the bed, but her head was turned toward the door and her body was stiff, as if she anticipated some great danger. Not daring to move, Mary Eliska listened, then she heard the unmistakable scraping of a boat on the rocks as if it were being shoved high to prevent its being taken out by the tide. This was followed by men's gruff voices, and finally the sound of stamping feet making their way to the Native American's house. Just then a distant voice hailed the newcomers, and Nomie said something scarcely above a whisper to Natell, who jumped up from the other side of the room, hurried across to her mother and then quickly parting the nearest heavy draperies, the young girl disappeared.

From out on the darkening beach there came the sound of an exchange of calls, then it seemed to Mary Eliska as if the man who had greeted the boatmen must have joined them, for his voice was mingled with the others. All that she could make out of the conversation was its punctuation of oaths, and while this was going on, Nomie stepped stealthily to the door, got back of it and started to close it, but it was made of heavy timbers and did not move easily. Just as she was about to give it the last shove, a great boot was stuck over the sill, and a drunken voice brawled.

"Gwan, No-mee, none of that. Give me something to drink!"

"Got none," she answered.

"Sure you have. Come across with it quick."

"Got none," she repeated. "Go Wat for some. He keeps," she answered. "Go way, you get killed the Boss find you here."

"Sure I will, but he's too far away to find me," the man laughed wickedly, then shouted to the others, "Come on! Nomie's trying to hold out on us! Give me a hand!"

"Say, don't do that! The Boss will be mad as anything and you know the last time you smashed things he told you that after the next spree he'd kill you! You were on your knees with the barrel of gun in your mouth." The man who was speaking was the one who had called, so Mary Eliska judged that he must be a member of the group on the island.

"Well, tell her to open the door. I'm not going to smash anything. I want some coffee; the woman can make me some." The voice was considerably less belligerent, but the fellow was just intoxicated enough to be stubborn.

"Go back to the boat and get your own cook to make you a barrel of coffee. Let the woman alone, I tell you, or I'll send for Wat."

"Yes, you'll send fer Wat—well, who'll you send, Brick Top, one of my crew? I'll shoot the first man that stirs a leg."

"Now, look here, Cap, you get back in the boat and go about your business, and I won't say a word about seeing you here. If you don't beat it, you're going to make trouble for your whole crew. Go on back and sleep it off, then come over and get the cargo," Brick Top urged.

"Come along, Cap, he's givin' you good talk. If you don't, we'll take the boat and pull back without you, see?" That was one of the crew, and others of its members, evidently not caring to share in the captain's punishment if he persisted in disobeying, backed him up quickly. In a moment by the sounds, Cap was being led meekly away, but suddenly his voice rose again.

"I'm not going to my ship 'til I say how-de-do to Nomie. I ain't landing on her shore an' goin' off 'sif I ain't a gentleman." Then followed a scuffle and soon the Cap, leering broadly, had forced his way into the house. "Ain't goin' 'way—"

"Get him away," Nomie shrieked.

"Aw, shut up, woman. Bible says women should keep still. You're makin' too much noise—"

"Come out of there," Brick Top snapped angrily.

"Blowed if I do," retorted the Cap, and with a powerful swing of his arm, the back of his hand struck Brick Top such a resounding blow that he reeled across the room. "You're like Nomie, you say too much with your mouth." But the younger man recovered himself quickly and sprang at the drunken captain.

"You fool," he roared furiously, "will you get out?"

"No," Cap bellowed, mightily encouraged by the success of his first attack. "And no blasted redhead's going to make me."

"No? Well, you'll change your tune," Red snapped.

"Come on, Cap," one of the crew urged. They were crowding in the door, and one of them tried to catch the captain's collar, but he lolled aside, then, with head down like a charging bull, he rushed at the smaller man, caught him about the waist, lifted him in the air and would have broken his back in another moment if Nomie hadn't thrown a kettle which struck him in the head. This dazed him for an instant so that his hold was broken and Red wriggled out of his grasp, but his tight-fitting fur cap saved the captain from more serious damage.

"Oh, you'll hit me from behind," he howled, believing Red responsible for the blow. He leaped at the young fellow and immediately the pair were in the throes of such a violent conflict that it did not seem possible that either of them could come out alive. They crashed in first one corner then the other with lightning speed, and as Mary Eliska heard and caught glimpses of the horrible spectacle she was nearly overcome with nausea. She thought that any moment the built-in bed would be ripped from the wall to which it was fastened and she wondered dully why none of the crew interfered. Then she found herself trying to calculate just how long it would be before the courageous little Red would be reduced to an unrecognizable mass of flesh.

It occurred to the girl Aviatrix that it was because of her presence that Red had so strenuously objected to the captain's entering the dugout, and thinking back, she believed that Nomie must have sighted the boat on the water. That would explain her reason for wanting the white girl out of sight when the small boat came ashore with the men whose rough temper was well known to her. By that time the two bodies crashed against the foot of the bed and a huge hand clutched the pillows to keep him from falling, but Cap's foot slipped on the wet floor. He flung himself up with all his strength, clutched at the upright support, but under his weight the sapling gave way, the corner of the bed came down with its pile of protecting pillows cascading into the room. Quick as a flash, Mary Eliska rolled to the further side, but the tumbling piece of furniture prevented her from keeping out of sight, so she was forced to get to her feet close to the wall, what was left of the bed—rolling in front of her. Just as Cap raised his ugly head and caught sight of her terrified white face, the huge form of Wat rushed in and hurled forward, the man's legs whipped about the captain's body like a powerful vise, one hand snatched back the fur hat while the other brought the butt end of a gun down on the man's head so hard that he was immediately knocked unconscious. During the last part of the fight, the curious crew had crowded into the room, and now Wat turned on them. Beyond the door, Mary Eliska caught a glimpse of Slim and other familiar faces, set grimly, while the barrel of more than one gun was in evidence.

"What are you fellows doing here?" he demanded sharply.

"Cap ordered us to bring him over," the nearest boatman replied.

"We gotta obey the captain's orders on a boat or it's mutiny," another took up defiantly.

"Yes?"

"Yes." This came from several voices.

"Well, let me tell you something. There isn't a man jack of you who does not know perfectly well that the captain's jurisdiction is a very limited one. Your boat was posted with orders every one of you could read, and you were told to remain aboard until I sent for you, or gave you sailing orders. Isn't that so?"

"Yes," one of the men at the back admitted reluctantly.

"Slim!" called Wat.

"Right here." Slim answered.

"Have some of the boys put these fellows in irons, and you'd better leave two or three to swab deck and mend the furniture."

"Right-O. Want them aboard the ship or here?"

"On the island," Wat answered after a moment's hesitation. Then he heaved the unconscious body of the captain through the door to be dragged out by some of Slim's company. Slim gave sharp orders.

"Round em up an' rope em, then, forward march," the young fellow ordered with a mixture of soldier and cowboy.

"We can't march the captain, Slim."

"Leave somebody to guard him while you get a stretcher," Slim replied as if he was getting a great deal of satisfaction out of his job at that particular moment.

"Are you hurt, Mary Eliska?" Wat asked and his voice still sounded as if he was in command of a company.

"No, I'm not, thank you," she said with a sob, which she promptly smothered. "Oh, oh, I'm so glad you came—I never saw anything so ghastly—"

"I hope you never do again," he told her quietly. "But, I want the truth. You are really not hurt, the fighters didn't touch you, or that bunk injure you? Don't be afraid, let Nomie take care of you if you are not perfectly O.K."

"I am perfectly all right," she assured him.

"Good," he gave a little sigh of relief then snapped again: "Slim."

"Coming," shouted Slim.

"Take Mary Eliska out and walk with her along the beach. The fog isn't so bad now and the fresh air will help her recover quickly. Are the rest of the men on the job?"

"Yes, sir, everyone."

"Let me walk with Mr. Slim too," Natell begged as she bobbed up from somewhere.

"If your mother doesn't need you," Wat smiled at the little girl. "You've been a great kid tonight, and the next boat that comes in is going to bring something mighty nice for you."

"You bet," Slim added with a grin. "That boat will have two nice things for you. I'll get my sister to buy you something dandy."

"Good," Nomie nodded, so Natell joined the pair as they made their way out onto the beach. A bucket brigade was already marching toward the door with brimming pails of water to "swab deck."

"Did Natell go for you?" Mary Eliska asked. She was thinking of how the little girl had disappeared among the draperies just before the arrival of the boatmen.

"Sure she did, and how!" Slim answered unsuspectingly, then his companion knew that there was at least two ways of getting in and out of the Native American woman's home, and she resolved that sometime she would explore it if she were ever left alone.

"In my luggage I have some strings of colored beads," the white girl went on. "They are not much, just sort of attractive. You must let me give her some of them right away because it will be a long time before you and Wat can get your presents here, won't it?"

"Be a few weeks," Slim admitted cautiously. "Sure, give her some of yours if you like. Can't be any objection to that."

"All right, Natell, tomorrow you shall have a nice long string of red beads, the prettiest ones I have."

"Good," the girl replied softly, apparently understanding that Mary Eliska had overcome the necessity for secrecy regarding the string she already had.

"If you like one of the others, you may have two strings," Mary Eliska added, no end relieved that the matter of the gift was so simply settled.

"Better walk carefully here," Slim warned, as he changed places with her so that she was on the inside of the beach. "Sort of treacherous at night; beastly in the fog."

"It feels good to be out," Mary Eliska told him as they went on. For half an hour they walked, saying little, until the density of the mist began to chill the white girl, then they returned to the dugout, which except for the wetness of the recent "swabbing," and strips of new boards nailed over the broken furniture, looked exactly as it had before the invasion of the belligerent captain. They found Wat smoking thoughtfully before the door, and after bidding the women good-night, the two men strode off into the darkness. The walk had tired her, so Mary Eliska was really glad to go to bed and in spite of the horrors of the night, she soon dropped off into a sound sleep. When she awakened in the morning, the two Native Americans were already busy with some task, and Nomie lost no time in preparing food for her charge.

"Go fishing," she informed Mary Eliska when the meal was finished, so, after adding a string of blue beads to the red ones Natell was proudly showing that morning, and adding a storm coat to her costume, the girl Aviatrix followed the women out into the sunlight, for every bit of fog had been dispelled. They cut across the island toward the northwest and on a smooth little cove, tugged a deep canoe, which certainly had not been there the day before when the white girl did her exploring.

"The island must be full of hiding places," she remarked to herself, and wondered how much it concealed. By that time Mary Eliska was so full of the mystery of the place that being marooned or imprisoned there was receding further back in her brain; although nothing could make her forget the anxiety she knew must weigh down her own home in far away Long Island, but she determined that if she ever succeeded in getting away, she would be able to give some real information as to what enterprise was conducted there. She thought of Mr. Howe, and then it occurred to her that she was to have had a mission with him. "It couldn't have been more exciting than this thing I've stumbled, or been piloted into."

"Sit here." Nomie designated with a nod a thin cushion in the middle of the boat, which reminded the white girl of pictures she had seen of native-made crafts. She took her place cautiously, for it looked as if it would take very little to turn the thing over, but Natell hopped in one end, then with a short paddle held the boat steady until her mother was safely in the other. Without a word the pair dipped their paddles and the canoe shot speedily over the water, going toward the northwest.

"Little island, much fish," Nomie remarked and Mary Eliska didn't know whether she was speaking of the land they were leaving behind, or another one.

"Is that so," she replied, and Nomie, who was facing her, nodded.

They sped along over the blue water, occasionally pausing to drop a line, and once the Native American woman set a trawler which glistened as it dragged yards behind them. Natell seemed to keep an eye on this, but nothing was caught, and after an hour they reached another island, almost as barren as the one they had left. They sent the boat slowly in and out among jagged rocks and the white girl marveled that they were not dashed against the sharp edges which protruded dangerously all about them.

"Like go shore?" Nomie asked. "Nice shells. Tide going down."

"That will be fine," Mary Eliska agreed readily, so the canoe's nose was shot into an opening between two great wall-like cliffs which looked as if at one time it had been a solid mass. The woman steadied the boat while the girl climbed ashore, and Natell pointed to a series of shelves.

"Climb to top easy," she smiled.

"Shout if tired. We call when ready," Nomie added to the directions, when at last they were ready to pull off. "Take care."

"Thank you," Mary Eliska answered. She wasn't particularly interested in the island, but she was mighty grateful at the opportunity to be alone for a while. She hoped that in the solitude some practical plan would present itself, and she also wondered if this fishing expedition had been gotten up in order to get her out of the way. She recalled that something had been said the night before about a "load" for the captain's boat, so perhaps Wat did not want an audience while this was going on. Then she remembered that she had not caught sight of the vessel, but she hadn't thought of it that morning, so she had not looked. It was doubtless lying-to out beyond the shallow water.

Accepting Natell's suggestion, Mary Eliska climbed to the top of the cliff, which was not very high, then wandered about aimlessly until she came to a long point of wide flat rock which was scarcely above the water. Here she saw quite a collection of brightly colored shells, and as the tide was going out, she started to gather a few of them. Paying little attention to how many steps she took, she went on and on until her hands were full, then glancing up, she saw a short distance ahead was another island, smaller than the one she was on, and the great ledge appeared to join on it. The second island was dense with timber, whose dark green was a great relief after the monotony of sea, sky and white sands, so, watching her step she proceeded and presently was standing under the wide spreading branches of a grove of scrub evergreen.

"Now I appreciate trees more than I ever did before." Glancing back at the ledge, which the dropping tide revealed more and more, she felt it safe to proceed and thoroughly enjoy the wonderful treat. Some places she couldn't get through at all, but for several minutes she proceeded inland, then, suddenly she stopped, stared, rubbed her eyes and looked again, for well concealed in the underbrush, but unmistakable, was a tip of an airplane wing. Her first thought was that some pilot had been brought down and she parted the brush to investigate.

"Reach for the sky, you, and don't turn around!" The command was snapped out sharply and Mary Eliska's hands went over her head without delay.

CHAPTER 12.12
A SECOND CAPTIVE

"Keep 'em up."

Mary Eliska's heart hammered, but she misunderstood the last part of the order, and faced about quickly.

"Say, what are you doing; I told you not to turn around!"

"I'm not," Mary Eliska retorted.

"You're—say, you're a girl!" A decidedly unkempt looking young man, with nothing more deadly in his hands than a knotted stick, came toward her quickly. "You look like Mary Eliska, the kid pilot."

"I am Mary Eliska and I'm not a kid," she replied indignantly as she dropped her hands.

"Sure, I saw you when you were touring with the Wallaces. What the— that is, I mean, what are you doing up here?" His hand went to his collar as if to adjust his tie, but there was none there, and a look of dismay spread over his bewhiskered features. "My name's Arnold, but I'm no relation to the guy who tried to betray his country."

"I am a prisoner, Mr. Arnold," she told him.

"You look it. Tell me another," he answered.

"Just the same, that's the truth," she replied, and then, as there was a stump handy, she sat down. "Please don't let me keep you standing. Are we in the Bering Sea?" Arnold sat down with a chuckle.

"The island is," he told her.

"What islands are they, I mean, what are their names?"

"Don't believe these have any because they are not very large, but they belong to the Pribilof group. I believe this is the farthest north and it's a bit over three hundred miles to Alaska."

"Thanks," she said with a sigh. "It's mighty nice to know where one is at. I was piloting for a woman called Shkrebneva; and she fed me some kind of dope that knocked me out, then tied me up like a chicken ready to roast, and brought me to an island below here."

"Shkrebneva?"

"Yes."

"Go on and tell me the rest." There was no doubt in his tone or manner now.

"Guess I'm what is called kidnaped," Mary Eliska began, then told him quickly all that had happened to her right up to that moment.

"You certainly have been having a terrible time," he remarked soberly. "What was that spring thing in your plane?"

"It's an invention of Mr. Wallace's and I really cannot tell much about it except that it's tuned with the radio stations' broadcasting band and when it is open, if the signal is investigated, Skybird can be located."

"That's rich! And Shkrebneva went off in your plane; flying right into the arms of the police looking for you. Wish I could see the performance."

"I don't believe she will do anything so stupid as fly into anyone's arms, but just the same, they can find out where Skybird goes, that is, if the thing works. Now, tell me, what are you doing here?"

"Sort of a prisoner myself," he answered.

"Oh, did somebody catch you?"

"In a way, yes. I was one of the war air-kids, and after that didn't want to do anything but fly, but the woods were full of fellows trying to do the same thing and the jobs were almost as few and far apart as hen's teeth. Well, I grubbed around like a ground-hog at a desk I finally landed until I saved enough money to buy a plane."

"Yes," Mary Eliska was intensely interested.

"That was before Col. Lindbergh made the air a place for Americans to fly in and while I hopped about, here, there and several other places I wasn't exactly a bright and shining success. Then one day I answered an advertisement I read in a middle west paper and took off on a job that seemed too good to be true. As they told me I would be working for a chain of business firms, I swallowed it hook, line and sinker, with the pole and reel thrown in, and didn't think anything of it when I carried males and females all over the map. I figured they were members of boards, big business stuff with headquarters scattered." He paused again and frowned.

"I see," the girl encouraged.

"I'd been with them a year, and had a real roll in the bank before I made my first trip to Alaska with any of them. It was six months after that before I went over to the Pribilof Islands—"

"Is that where we are?"

"Yes, but not the main ones. They are a bit further south, but these little fellows I guess are all on the same range, like an underseas chain of mountains," he answered, then went on. "I carried mail, supplies and stuff back and forth between them and the mainland, sometimes down to the Aleutian Islands. The Native American woman you call Nomie is an Aleut."

"I wondered."

"That's what she is. Her husband was a seal fisher and got killed when the kid was little. They had the dugout and lived where you're being held so she stayed and worked for the gang, she nurses them when they get sick, and all that sort of thing."

"She's been mighty nice to me," Mary Eliska said quickly.

"She's a darned good Native American and she had to make her living somehow, same as a lot of the rest of us."

"Of course," Mary Eliska agreed.

"At first I hopped on Nomie's island and hopped off again within an hour. Sometimes I took a bale of furs that I thought the other Native Americans had left there to be sold in the States or Canada. Gee—this story is stretching out and we gotta remember that tide."

"It was going down," Mary Eliska told him.

"Yes, I know it. Well then I began to make longer stops and carry bigger loads, and after a while I happened to pick up a magazine with an article and pictures of the Pribilofs. It told about the seal fishing, how there used to be thousands of the beasts killed every year even at mating time. The United States bought the islands from Russia along with Alaska in and made laws to prevent the seals being exterminated. Before the war, I think it was, the United States, Japan, Great Britain and Russia made a treaty agreeing that the white men were not to do any more seal slaughtering. The Native Americans, because they don't do it in such wholesale lots and because it means the only means of living to a great many of them, are the only people who can kill the migrating seals. They have to do it in canoes with spears or harpoons, can't use guns or motor boats. It was a mighty interesting article, told how the seals start up in pairs from all over the country to raise their young ones."

"Why sure, there's a wonderful story Rudyard Kipling wrote called The White Seal. My mother read it to me when I was a kid, and I always loved it. The White Seal went to an Island called St. Paul's."

"That's it. I liked that story too. Well, I knew radio as well as flying, so by and by I had to relieve the regular chap at that."

"I've wondered if they have a radio."

"They have, but it isn't much of one. It's just used for signals. While I was doing that I discovered that when the seals came up in April and all through the summer, a bunch of them were run through a sort of pen and killed. There aren't as many of them coming up now as there used to be but the gang goes after them any old way and slaughters two hundred times more than the Native Americans bring in every season. It was while I was there that Wat was put in charge. I figured he was in the same boat with me; that he had been working for them for a long time before they let him get hep to what was going on, then they'd sunk him so deep he couldn't do anything but hang on; besides he's got a kid sister in Saranac trying to get a permanent T. B. cure and that costs a lot of money. I know because he asked me to drop down there one time and pay the bill—it was some bill, and I saw the kid, she's only about thirteen years old."

"That's too bad," Mary Eliska said.

"Sure. Well, I'm free, white, and twenty-one, and when I figured I was signed up with a bunch of crooks I made up my mind to quit. I got a full-sized fondness for my Uncle Sam, been batting about other countries a lot, so while I don't think the United States hasn't room for improvement, it suits me right down to the ground, and I haven't any hankering to end my brilliant career in a Federal prison while the guy I work for stays hidden and lets me hold the bag. First I thought Shkrebneva was the head of the thing, then I heard Wat tell her where to get off at a couple of times for not obeying orders, but she's got some money invested in the business so does somewhat as she pleases."

"I wish she hadn't picked on me," Mary Eliska said ruefully.

"She got everlastingly sore when she could not get a license, and I figure, from what you say, that while she was flying around with you, she got jealous because you landed what she couldn't. When a woman of her type gets jealous, she's deadlier than a whole herd of males. Probably they planned to get you to work for them as a sort of blind, but she couldn't wait, and shoved the works hard. Anyway, when I made up my mind to quit, I knew I had to do it mighty carefully. I wasn't leaving Nomie's very often then and it wasn't easy, but finally one day I started off in the plane, that was about six weeks ago, but they must have been wise. Wat wasn't there that day and the fellow in charge had the machine gun turned on me before I could get very high. The shot ripped off my tail but I gave the bus the gasoline and went on just the same. Couldn't do a very good job of steering, and it was foggy, so this is as far as I got. Now, you know all about me." He stared ahead with a scowl.

"My goodness, how have you managed to live? Were you hurt when you came down?"

"Hurt some, sure, but not bad. Got a crack on my head that seems to have affected my eyes. Then I discovered a vessel wrecked off the other side and managed to salvage her stores. Hunted for some of the crew but none of them got as far as the island, I guess. Been trying to fix up the bird again, but it's been slow work and I've been wondering if I can fly her when she is finally fixed."

"Well, if you can't," Mary Eliska said eagerly, "I can."

"By Jove, that's so. Tell you what, you go back with Nomie and come here again. Know how to paddle a canoe?"

"A little, but I could never manage one of the native boats."

"Get Natell to teach you. Take advantage of everything you can while you're stranded. The whole country will be looking for you by this time, and they won't stop. Nobody knows I disappeared, but maybe when they get you out, someone will help me."

"Of course they will. Do you think I'll go off without you?" Mary Eliska demanded indignantly. Wasn't he a fellow pilot in distress? "And, when we get to the United States you can have your eyes attended to and they'll be all right again."

"Say, funny thing. I've heard about you in a lot of different places and from different people, and the same phrase popped into my head that I've heard about you. They all say, you're a great kid, but," he added hastily, "They don't mean that you're a baby, or anything like that; and I don't either, you know what I mean."

"Sure," she agreed heartily.

"Now, while we've been talking, I've got a sort of plan."

"What is it?"

"You go back with Nomie. Don't say a word about seeing me, and come with her again as often as she'll fetch you. Perhaps they'll let you have a little boat. I can't put up any kind of signal for I don't want them to spot me before I'm ready to take off. You don't do any more snooping around because I know the whole works and you might get into further difficulties. Just keep your eyes open ordinarily and wait. I'll look around for you every day and see you when you are coming this way, then if you have any news you can tell me, and if I think of anything more, I can tell you. I'll go on, finishing the plane, and if we don't get away before that's ready, we can make a plan to give them the slip. There was a small boat on that vessel and I've got it hauled up under some weeds; haven't thought of using it, but we may be glad to have it," he proposed eagerly and Mary Eliska was intensely interested.

"That's a corking plan."

"I don't suppose you have any of your instruments."

"They are all in Skybird."

"I have a pocket compass off the ship, a real good one. You take it back with you and keep it out of sight. If you should come alone, it will help you." He gave her the highly sensitive instrument and after examining it carefully, she dropped it into the pocket of her blouse.

"May I see the plane?"

"Sure." He swept an armful of boughs and sand off the machine showing that he had not only been working on the plane, but had cleared a take-off space which he covered again. "Nomie and Natell come up around the other end of these twin islands for fish and wood a couple of times a week, but neither have been over here yet. You're my first caller and I guess I didn't give you a very polite reception." He noticed that the girl, although she made a hasty examination of the plane, seemed to see every detail.

"Your reception was all right and the bus looks great. It's a wonder to me that you didn't have more of a crack-up than you did when you came down."

"I tried my darndest to save the pieces," he grinned.

"And you've got these parts fixed evenly. Why you're doing a bang-up job. Did you find tools on the vessel?"

"Sure, a whole load of them in the carpenter's outfit. Don't know where the tub came from, her name was scraped off, but I surely thanked Providence for depositing the boat right here. There is still some of her left. Perhaps, next time you come you can go around and see what's left of her if the sea doesn't bang her up."

"I should like to very much," Mary Eliska answered, then went on a bit anxiously. "Guess I'd better not linger too long now or Nomie might take it into her head to come looking for me. Now that we've talked over the plan I won't try to do any investigating. I suppose that crack I saw and the noise I heard is the place where the seals are driven and killed."

"That's right, it is, although the seals do not come up in any great numbers any more. Be mighty careful to let them all think over there that you haven't any interest in what they are doing. Wat's pretty decent, as decent as he can be, but he's only one. He and Slim are in a bad crowd of rough-necks. You had a sample of that last night, so be careful," he urged.

"I will," she promised. "It's much easier now that I know where I am located and something about the place. Wonder who the big Boss of the whole thing is?"

"So do I, but the information we have may help in catching the Chief Mogul himself."

"We'll hope so."

"You know, that stranded vessel sounds mighty mysterious to me."

"She is mysterious, but I've been so busy with my own troubles I haven't given her very much thought. I'll see what I can learn from what is left of her. Perhaps we can solve that mystery too, since we've gone into the business," he laughed.

"I'll trot along. If Nomie brings me this way again, or I can come alone, how will I find you, by coming around here?" she asked.

"If I see that you are alone I'll come down to the beach or one of the coves and meet you," he replied. "I'll come with you now to the ledge and see that you get over all right. You don't want to slide off into the Bering. It's cold and wet all the way to the bottom, and that's a good mile."

Presently the two had reached the ledge, found the water a foot lower than when she crossed earlier, so she hurried forward while he watched closely, ready to spring at the first sign of danger, but she reached the other side safely.

"I hear Natell," she called back to him. "So long!"

"S'long, Aviatrix," he answered.

Mary Eliska ran as fast as she could to the nearest point and saw the canoe moving swiftly toward the end of the island, but when the Native Americans sighted her, they paddled more slowly. The white girl, in her trim aviation suit stood an instant outlined against the blue sky as she paused to glance back toward the wooded island where she saw Arnold outlined dimly against the dark green of the forest behind him, then she hurried toward the bit of beach where Nomie and Natell waited.

Riding back from the twin-islands to Nomie's in the bottom of the native canoe, Mary Eliska's heart beat confidently and she felt that her guardian angel had certainly been more than careful of her welfare, but it was mighty difficult to hold her face straight, her lips from smiling complacently or joyously. She managed to control herself, to keep her mouth from betraying her, and it was not difficult to either drop her lids or gaze out over the dancing waters of Bering Sea. It was great to know where she was and she resolved to follow Arnold's instructions to the letter and make no move which would arouse the suspicions of the men on the island. She would avoid being more than ordinarily interested in her surroundings, and at least appear not to be too observant of what went on around her.

The white girl sighed with relief when she saw the desolate island loom up suddenly, looking for all the world as if not a living soul ever went within miles of it.

Presently the canoe shot into a cove and Nomie nodded for her to land, so, while they steadied the boat, she stepped ashore. Immediately the women bent to the oars again and in a few minutes disappeared from sight around a long point of land. Mary Eliska sat down, making the best picture of disconsolation that she could, but with her face hidden between her knees, she could indulge herself in a first-class relaxation of her features, and she smiled broadly. Why shouldn't she! Arnold would get the plane ready in record time, she would go over to twin-islands another day, and they would fly away. It was merely a matter of a short wait and in the meantime she would have a rather jolly experience living with the Native American woman and her daughter; furthermore, the seals promised no end of entertainment.

"I am going to have a real good time," she told herself. "This isn't a half bad place, and I wager I am the first white girl to visit it, which will be something to tell the newspaper reporters when I get home." Just then Natell appeared and beckoned with her finger and Mary Eliska followed to see what was wanted.

Natell lead the way around the opposite end of the island to a huge flat section. Here she paused and motioned Mary Eliska to remain perfectly still. For about two minutes she did, then, a little way out, she saw a pair of dark eyes staring at her, and a moment later, a young seal hauled himself to the land and started in her direction. He came quite close, within four feet, then stopped again, but just then someone of his family called him, and he returned to the water. When he was gone, Natell crept cautiously forward among the rocks, then, with a movement like lightning, she reached down and came up again with a tiny seal in her arms. He whined pitifully, but his curiosity was greater than his fear, so he gave her a sniff.

"Oh, the cunning little fellow," Mary Eliska exclaimed. She petted the baby, but about ten minutes later there was another bark from the water and the young seal flapped comically in front of her. He was so funny that she threw back her head and laughed heartily, she couldn't help it, but it scared the little fellow and he scrambled away. "Next time I must be more polite when I have company," she told herself.

CHAPTER 13

The Phantom Airship

CHAPTER 13.1.
THE GOLDEN BUTTERFLY.

"**B**ill! Bill! where are you?"

Mary Eliska came flying down the red-brick path, a rustling newspaper clutched in her hand.

"Here I am, sis,—what's up?"

The door of a long, low shed at the farther end of the old-fashioned garden opened as a clattering sound of hammering abruptly ceased. Bill Stricklin, a wavy-haired lad of seventeen, or thereabouts, stood in the portal. Except for an unusual feature on his trousers Bill looked very business-like in his white trousers, blue shirt and rolled up sleeves. In his hand was a shiny hammer.

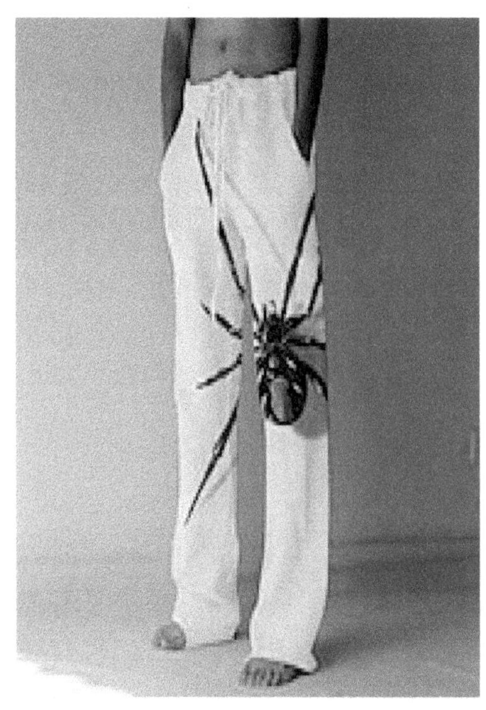

Mary Eliska, quite regardless of a big, black widow spider prominently designed on the left leg of her brother Bill's white trousers, threw her arms around his neck in one of her "bear hugs," while Bill, boy-like, wriggled in her clasp as best he could.

"Now, just look here," cried Mary Eliska, quite out of breath with her own vehemence. She flourished the paper under Bill's nose and, imitating the traditional voice of a town crier, announced: "Hear ye! Hear ye! Hear ye! Bill Stricklin or any of the ambitious aviators—now is your chance! Great news from the front! Third and last call!"

"You've got auctioneering, the Supreme Court and war times, mixed up a bit, haven't you?" asked Bill with masculine condescension, but gazing fondly at his vivacious sister nevertheless.

Mary Eliska made a little face and then thrust forth the paper for Bill's examination.

"Read that, you unenthusiastic person," she demanded, "and then tell me if you don't think that Mary Eliska has good reason to feel somewhat more enthusiastic than comports with her usual dignity and well-known icy reserve—ahem!"

"Good gracious, sis!" exclaimed Bill, as he scanned the news-sheet, "why this is just what we were wishing for, isn't it? It's our chance if we can only grasp it and make good."

"We can! We will!" exclaimed Mary Eliska, striking an attitude and holding one hand above her glossy head. "Read it out, Bill, so that Monsieur Bleriot can hear it."

M. Bleriot, a French bull-dog, who had dignifiedly followed Mary Eliska's mad career down the path, gazed up appreciatively, as Bill read out:

"Big Chance for Sky Boys!
"Ironmaster Higgins of Acatonick Offers Ten
Thousand Dollars In Prizes for Flights and Planes."

"Ten thousand dollars, just think!" cried Mary Eliska, clasping her hands one minute and the next stooping to caress M. Bleriot. "Oh, Bill! Do you think we could?"

"Could what? you indefinite person?" parried Bill, although his eyes were dancing and he knew well enough what his vivacious sister was driving at.

"Could win that ten thousand dollars, of course, you goose."

Bill laughed.

"It's not all offered in a lump sum," he rejoined. "Listen; there is a first prize of five thousand dollars for the boy under eighteen who makes the longest sustained flight in an airplane of his own construction—with the exception of the engine, that is; and here's another of two thousand five hundred dollars to the glider making the best and longest sustained flight, and another of one thousand five hundred to the boy flying the most carefully constructed machine and the one bearing the most ingenious devices for perfecting the art of flying and—and—oh listen, Mary Eliska!"

"I am—oh, I am!" breathed Mary Eliska with half assumed breathlessness.

"There's a prize offered for girls!"

"No!"

"Yes. Now don't say any more that girls are downtrodden and neglected by the bright minds of the day. Here it is, all in black and white, a prize of a whole thousand to the young lady who makes a successful flight. There, what do you think of that?"

"That Mr. Higgins is a mean old thing," pouted Mary Eliska, "five thousand dollars to the successful boy and only one thousand to the successful girl. It's discrimination, that's what it is. Don't you read every day in the papers about girls and women making almost as good flights as the men? Didn't a—a Mademoiselle somebody-or-other make a flight around the bell tower at Bruges the other day, and hasn't Col. Roosevelt's daughter been up in one, and isn't there a regular school for women fliers at Washington, and—and—?"

"Didn't the suffragettes promise to drop 'Votes for Women' placards from the air upon the devoted heads of the British Parliament, you up to date young person?" finished Bill, teasingly.

Mary Eliska made a dash for him but the boy dodged into the shed, closely followed by his sister.

But as she crossed the threshold Mary Eliska's wild swoop became a decorous stroll, so to speak. She paused, all out of breath, beneath a spreading expanse of yellow balloon silk, braced and strengthened with brightly gleaming wires and stays,—one wing of the big monoplane upon which her brother had spent all his spare time for the past year. The flying thing was almost completed now. It stood in its shed, with its scarab-like wings outspread like a newly alighted yellow butterfly, which, by a stroke of ill luck, had found itself installed in a gloomy cage instead of the bright, open spaces of its native element.

In one corner of the shed was a large crate surrounded by some smaller ones. The large one had been partially opened and Mary Eliska gave a little squeal of delight as her eyes fell on it.

"Oh, Bill, that's it?"

"That's it," rejoined the boy proudly, lifting a bit of sacking from the contents of the opened crate, "isn't it a beauty?"

The lifted covering had exposed a gleam of bright, scarlet enamel, and the glint of polished brass. To Bill the contents of that crate was the splendid new motor for his airplane. But to Mary Eliska, just then, it was something far different. A bit of a mist dimmed her shining eyes for an instant. Her voice grew very sober.

"Three thousand dollars—oh, Bill, it scares me!"

Bill crossed the shed and threw an arm about his sister's neck.

"Don't be frightened, sis," he breathed in an assuring tone, "it's going to be all right. Why, can't you see that the very first thing that happens is a chance to win $5,000?"

"I know that. But that contest is not to come off for more than a month and—and supposing someone should have a better machine than yours?"

For an instant that air of absolute assurance, which truth to tell, had made Bill some enemies, and which was his greatest fault, left him. His face clouded and he looked troubled. But it was as momentary as the cloud-shadow that passes over a summer wheat field.

"It'll be all right, sis," he rejoined, confidently, "and if it isn't, I can always sell out to Thatcher Allen. You know he said that his offer held good at any time."

"I know that, Bill," rejoined Mary Eliska, seriously, "but we could never do that. We could neither of us go against father's wishes like that. He—well, Bill, it's not to be thought of. Poor dad—"

Her bright eyes filled with tears as her mind travelled back to a scene of a year before when Albert Stricklin had ceased from troubling with the affairs of this world, and commended his children to the care of their maiden aunt— their Aunt Sally, with whom, since their mother's death some years before, the little family had made their home.

Poor Albert Stricklin had been that hopelessly impracticable creature—an inventor. Fortunately for himself, however, Albert Stricklin had a small fortune of his own so that he had been enabled to carry on his dreaming and planning without embarrassing his family. Bill and Mary Eliska had both been sent to good boarding schools, Punahou and La Pietra, and had known, in fact, very little of home life after their mother's death which had occurred several years before, as already said.

Albert Stricklin, in his dreamy, abstract way, had cared dearly for his children. But those other children of his—the off-springs of his brain—that surrounded him in his workshop, had, somehow, seemed always to mean more to him. And so the young Stricklins had grown up without the benefit of home influences.

On Mary Eliska's naturally sweet, vivacious character, this had not made so much difference. But Bill had developed, in spite of his real sterling worth and ability, into a headstrong, rather self-opinionated lad. His success at school in athletics and the studies which he cared about "mugging" at had not tended to decrease these qualities.

It had come as a shock to both of them a year before when two telegrams were dispatched— one to Mary Eliska's school near Diamond Head, and the other to Bill in Manoa Valley, telling them to return to the Long Island village of Sandy Bay at once. Their father—that half-shadowy being—was very ill.

The messages had not exaggerated the seriousness of the situation. Three days after his children reached his side Albert Stricklin gently breathed his last, dying, as he had lived, so quietly, that the end had come before they realized it. But in those last brief moments Bill came to know his father better than ever before. He learned that the dream of his parent had been to produce an airplane free from the defects of its forerunners,—a safe vehicle for passengers or freight. How far he had progressed in this there was no time for him to tell before the end came. But Bill, interested already in aeronautics at school, where he had been president of "The Honolulu High Fliers"—a model airplane association,—eagerly took up his father's desire that he would try to carry on his work, and began to take lessons in flying.

In the shed which had been Albert Stricklin's workshop the framework of an airplane already stood. And with the aid of what money his father had left him, Bill had carried on the work 'til now it was almost completed. But the three thousand dollars which had gone for the motor had completely exhausted the lad's legacy. As Mary Eliska put it, all their eggs were in an "aerial basket."

But how much Mary Eliska had aided him, in what had, in the last few months possessed all his thoughts, Bill did not guess. To what extent her encouragement had spurred him on to surmount seemingly unconquerable difficulties, and how she had actually aided him in constructing the machine, his ambition never realized. Not innately selfish, Bill was yet too used to having his own way to attribute his success to anyone but himself.

Sometimes, brave, loyal little Mary Eliska, try as she might, could not disguise this from herself, and it pained her a good deal. But she had uncomplainingly, ungrudgingly, aided her brother Bill, without hoping for, or expecting, the appreciation she sometimes felt she was really entitled to. But her great love for her brother Bill kept Mary Eliska from ever betraying to him or anyone else an iota of her inner feelings.

So intent had the brother and sister been on their talk that neither of them had noticed, while they conversed, that a big four-door touring car, aglitter with gleaming maroon paint, and with a long, low hood concealing a powerful engine, had glided up to the white gate in the picket fence surrounding Aunt Sally's old- fashioned cottage. From it a frank, pleasant-faced lad and an unusually striking girl, tall, slender and with a glossy mass of bond hair attractively on her shapely head, had alighted.

Hearing the sound of voices from the open door of the shed in which The Golden Butterfly, as Mary Eliska had christened it, was nearing completion, they, without ceremony, at once made their way toward it. Mary Eliska, glancing up from her sad reverie at the sound of footsteps, gave a glad little cry as she beheld the visitors standing framed in the sunlight of the open door. While she and the tall, girl mingled their contrasting tresses in an exuberant school-girl caress, the lad and Bill Stricklin, were, boy fashion, slapping one another on the back and shaking hands with just as much enthusiasm.

"Why, if this isn't simply delightful, Jax Gray, you dear old thing," cried the delighted Mary Eliska, as, with both hands on her chum's shoulders, she held Jax Gray off at arm's length, the better to scrutinize her handsome face, "and Liam McAdams, too," as she turned to the lad with a bright smile of welcome; "wherever did you two come from?"

"From the clouds?" demanded Bill.

"No, hardly, although I don't wonder at your asking such a question," laughed Jax Gray, merrily, exchanging greetings with Bill. "Bill Stricklin, positively I can see your wings sprouting."

They all laughed heartily at this, while Jax Gray ran on to explain that she and her brother were stopping for the summer at Seaview Towers, a summer estate which their father, a Wall Street power, had leased for the season. Of course, explained the merry girl, who had been Mary Eliska's closest chum at school, her first thought had been to take a spin over in her new motor car and look up her friends, for Bill and Liam McAdams had been almost as close chums as the girls. "And so this is the wonderful Golden Butterfly that you wrote to me about?" exclaimed Jax Gray enthusiastically after the first buzz of conversation subsided.

"Yes, this is it," said Bill with great satisfaction in his tones, "and I'm proud of it, I can tell you. I think I've made a success of it."

Jax Gray and Liam McAdams exchanged glances. And then Jax Gray stole a look at Mary Eliska, but no cloud had crossed the face of Bill's sister. "Oh, you darling," thought Jax Gray, "you're too sweet for anything. I just know how much you contributed to the Golden Butterfly's existence, and yet you won't detract a bit from Bill's self-satisfaction."

As for Liam McAdams, he said nothing. He glanced rather oddly at Bill for an instant. Then his eyes turned to Mary Eliska's face. Perhaps they dwelt there fo

r rather a long period of time. At any rate, they were still fixed on her brave beauty when a sudden shadow fell across the stream of sunlight that poured into the open portal of the workshop.

"Ah! So this is the place in which young genius finds its habitation;" grated out a rather harsh, unpleasant voice.

They all looked up. Perhaps none of them—Liam McAdams least of all—was pleased at the interruption. The newcomer was a tall, angular man, with a withered, clean-shaven face,—what Mary Eliska called a "money making face"; and surely that described Thatcher Allen, as he stood there in his black, none-too-new garments, and his square-toed shoes. One could fairly catch the avaricious glint in his eyes as he squinted rapidly over the new airplane's outlines.

By his side stood a youth who was, so far as dress went at any rate, the exact opposite of the elder man. Weenie Allen—or just Weenie as he was usually called—was dressed in elaborate motoring costume. His goggles, of the latest and most exaggerated design, were shoved up off his countenance now, exposing to view a good-looking browned face. It was marred, however, by the same restless, strained look that could be seen on his father's visage.

"We're not intruding, I hope," he hastened to say, coming forward with a cordiality that seemed somewhat forced.

"Not in the least," said Mary Eliska, hastily, realizing that none of them had perhaps looked very cordial, "won't you come in?"

Weenie Allen, bestowing an admiring glance on her, seemed to be about to accept. His father, however, struck in:

"I'll leave you with the young folks, my boy, while I go up to the house. I have some business with your Aunt Sally."

As he shuffled off, Mary Eliska and Bill exchanged somewhat uneasy glances. What business could this old man—in some respects a power financially and otherwise in Sandy Beach—have with their aunt?

"Say, Mary Eliska," spoke up Weenie Allen, suddenly, "ain't you going to introduce me to your friends? And how about inviting us all to have some of those strawberries Pop and I noticed as we came down the path?"

"Well, he isn't a bit backward about coming forward!" thought Jax Gray as the young people, with due formality, went through the ceremony of introductions.

CHAPTER 13.2.
SUSPENSE AND ACHIEVEMENT.

It was a week after Weenie Allen's visit to the Stricklin home, on one windless, steamy morning, when the pearl-gray mist still lay in the smooth hollows running back from the coast, that The Golden Butterfly was wheeled out of her cocoon—so to speak—and dragged up the hillside at the back of the white, green-shuttered cottage. Aunt Sally, a sweet-faced old lady, whose cheek was still blooming despite the passage of the years, stood on the back porch of the house watching the process.

If Aunt Sally's face had been somewhat less cheerful than usual since her talk with Thatcher Allen, all the clouds had been chased from it now. She watched as eagerly as a girl while Bill and Mary Eliska, aided by Jax Gray and Liam McAdams and two other lads, friends of Bill's from the village, dragged the brand-new airplane up the hillside.

The excited chatter and laughter of the young folks rang out merrily as they worked—for it was work to get the 'plane, light as it was, up the grade. Fortunately—for Bill had no desire of a crowd to witness his initial ascent in the new 'plane—the Stricklin house was some distance out of the village, and there were no near neighbors. The place had, in fact, once been a farm house, and although the acreage still was in the possession of Aunt Sally it was not worked.

A more ideal place for flying could not be imagined. Smooth slopes—unwooded, except in clumps—were all about. To the north glimmered the sparkling waters of Long Island Sound, while to the south stretched fertile farming land, devoted to crop-raising and pasturage.

Very business-like the young people looked as they hauled the monoplane up the hill. Bill and Liam McAdams wore leather puttees, trousers fashioned somewhat like riding breeches, and leather coats. On their heads were caps of the latter material, well- padded within and provided with visors pierced with goggles.

The girls wore shirt waists, outing skirts and "sensible" walking boots. Jax Gray had on her "Shaker" motoring bonnet, in which she looked very captivating indeed. Mary Eliska's glossy hair, unadorned, but tightly confined in a net, formed her hair covering. Both girls were all a-tiptoe with excitement, for although Bill had had experience with airplanes, and so, in a limited way, had Liam McAdams, this feature of the sport was new to them.

At last the summit was reached, and Bill, after calling a halt, took a brief but comprehensive survey of the Golden Butterfly. This done, he climbed into the chassis—or body—of the thing, and leaning over the machinery he rapidly tested all the adjustments and examined the lubricating devices to see that all was in order. Everything appeared to be.

"Well," said Bill, with some self-complacency, stepping out of the machine, "everything seems to be ready for the initial flight of the Golden Butterfly, my lords and gentlemen."

"And ladies, if you please," put in Jax Gray, in a voice that was vibrant with excitement, despite her endeavor to keep calm.

"And ladies," added Bill, with a gallant bow in her direction.

Mary Eliska in the meantime, like an anxious little mother fussing over dolls, had been examining the airplane once more. Suddenly she gave a little cry. The exclamation interrupted Bill who was explaining, with great satisfaction, that everything was all right.

"I've looked it over and if there had been anything wrong it couldn't have escaped my notice," he observed rather pompously.

"Oh, Bill! Just look here! The spring of this landing wheel is all slack!"

This was the exclamation from Mary Eliska that brought up Bill somewhat shortly in the midst of his self-confident harangue.

"By George, so it is, sis!" exclaimed Bill, reddening a little, while Lem Sidney, one of his chums, observed with a chuckle to Jeff Stokes, that Mary Eliska appeared to know as much, if not more, about the machine than did Bill.

The spring was soon tightened by means of a monkey wrench. But that did not prevent them all realizing that had it not been for Mary Eliska's acute observation a serious accident might have occurred. This done, even Mary Eliska's anxious glances could not detect any other flaw in the machine. "What time did that aviator fellow say he would show up?" then demanded Liam McAdams, abruptly.

"He should be here now," rejoined Bill. "I've half a mind to start anyhow. I can manage the machine I am very certain."

"Oh, Bill!" cried Mary Eliska, reprovingly, "you know you promised aunty that you wouldn't do anything 'til Mr. Hal Homer got here."

"All right, sis," put in Bill, hastily, "don't be scared. I'll stick to my word."

"Hullo!" cried Liam McAdams, suddenly, "there comes an auto now."

"So it is," exclaimed the others, as a black touring car came whizzing down the road below them. It soon halted, and a figure in leather garments with gaitered legs alighted and hastened across the fields toward the party clustered about the airplane. The car was left in charge of the chauffeur.

As Liam McAdams had guessed, the new arrival proved to be Hal Homer, the well-known cross-country flier, from whom Bill had taken some vacation time aviation lessons.

"He's awfully good looking," whispered Jax Gray to Mary Eliska, after introductions to the dapper young aviator had been extended by Bill.

"Oh, so—so," rejoined Mary Eliska, with a toss of her head.

"Maybe you know someone who is handsomer?" questioned Jax Gray with a mischievous side glance of her fine eyes.

Mary Eliska flushed under her fair skin. But Jax Gray laughed with good-humored raillery.

"Liam McAdams surely is a good-looking boy," she said, "if he hadn't a pug nose."

"A pug nose!" flared up Mary Eliska. "Oh, Jax Gray, how can—"

Then she stopped short in confusion while Jax Gray laughed the more at her discomfiture.

Young Mr. Homer lost no time in starting operations. He ordered his helpers to secure the machine to a small tree growing nearby by means of a stout rope Bill had brought with him. This done, and the monoplane thus secured from flying away when her engine was started, he set the sparking and gasoline levers and threw in the switch. Bill and Liam McAdams, the latter acting under Bill's instructions, flew to the propeller.

The Golden Butterfly being a monoplane, this was in front of the machine.

"Be careful when you feel it start, to leap aside," warned Bill, "or you might be beheaded."

"I never lose my head in an emergency," joked Liam McAdams.

But just the same his heart beat, as did those of all of them but Hal Homer's, as he and Bill started to swing the great shiny wooden driving appliance.

Once, twice, three times they swung it around, exerting all their force. The fourth time they were rewarded by a feeble sigh from the engine—a sixty horse power motor.

All at once—Bang!

"Let go!" yelled Bill, jumping backward.

Liam McAdams in his hurry to obey stumbled and fell backward in a heap. He rolled some distance down the hill unnoticed, before he succeeded in stopping his motion. In the meantime the others—even Mary Eliska—were too absorbed in the sight before them to watch Liam McAdams.

Simultaneously with the sharp report the propeller had whirled around swiftly. The next instant it was a mere gray blur, while a furious wind from its revolving blades swept the onlookers. Blue smoke spurted from the exhausts, mingled with flame, and the uproar was terrific.

The Golden Butterfly, like a thing of life, struggled at her moorings. The rope stretched and strained, taut as a violin string, under the pull. But it held fast, and after a while Aviator Homer slowed down the engine and finally stopped it, after adjusting a mis-fire in one of the cylinders. As the propeller became once more visible and then came to a stop, the boys broke into cheers, while the girls, too, voiced their enthusiasm.

"Oh, Mary Eliska, isn't it a darling!" cried Jax Gray.

"Airplanes are not usually called 'darlings,'" responded Mary Eliska with assumed severity, "but—oh, Jax Gray, it's—it's—a jewel and—"

"I'm dying for a ride in it!" burst in Jax Gray.

"Then if you will consent to live a little longer I hope to have the pleasure of saving your life," put in Bill, gallantly.

"Oh, Bill! I can ride in it now!" gasped Jax Gray, while Mary Eliska clasped her hands and snuggled up close to her chum.

"Well, no, hardly just yet," laughed Bill, "but after Homer has tested her thoroughly out I guess you girls can take a spin."

"You know I'm going to learn to handle one," declared Mary Eliska, as Bill made off once more. "I know a good deal about the theoretical part of it already."

"Well, theory wouldn't do you much good in a mile-long tumble," quoth Jax Gray, sagely.

"Nonsense," rejoined Mary Eliska. "Mr. Homer says one is as safe in an airplane, if one is careful, as in an auto."

"Safer I guess, the way that brother of mine drives sometimes," replied Jax Gray. "He calls it 'burning up the road.' But—oh, look, they're casting off, or whatever it is you do to an airship when you turn her loose. Oh!"

Snatching off her motoring bonnet Jax Gray began waving it furiously. While they had been talking the rope had been cast loose, and now, with Mr. Homer himself at the driving wheel, in cap and goggles, the engine was being started once more.

In wrapt excitement both girls stood breathless. So intent were they on the scene transpiring before them that they had not noticed the approach of a second auto on the road below. From it Weenie Allen had alighted and hastened up the hill, after "parking" his machine, as if in fear that he would be too late to view the proceedings.

A sneering look was on his rather handsome face as he rapidly climbed the hill. He reached a position behind the two girls just as the aviator gave the signal to let go of the machine—to the rear structure of which Lem Sidney and Jeff Stokes were perspiringly clinging, their heels digging into the soft turf to steady themselves.

As Mr. Homer's hand swung backward and downward they let go. Instantly, like an arrow from a bow, the monoplane—the work of Mary Eliska and Bill—was off. How it scudded across the hill top! Blue smoke and flame shot from its exhaust. Its operator sat hunched over his machinery looking, with his goggles, like some creature of the lower regions. Mary Eliska clasped her hands and stood a-tiptoe breathlessly as it scudded along.

"Oh, will it rise?" she breathed, her color coming and going in her excitement.

"I'll bet ten dollars it won't fly any more than an earthworm."

Mary Eliska turned swiftly, indignantly. Her color flamed and her eyes blazed angrily. Jax Gray, hardly less indignant at the sneering tone and words, also faced about.

"Good morning, girls," said Weenie Allen, easily, raising his motoring cap nonchalantly, "I came to see the ascension, but I'm afraid that it's going to be a descension."

"I think you're hateful, Weenie Allen, to talk like that," cried Mary Eliska, angrily, stamping her foot with her hands on her hips. "Our airplane will rise. It just will, I tell you—oh, gracious!"

She broke off in confusion and stood aghast for a moment. The swiftly scudding airplane had stopped its skittering over the grass and had come to an abrupt stop at a distance of about five hundred yards.

Already the boys were running across the turf toward it at top speed. The girls could see Mr. Homer clambering out of the chassis as the machine came to a standstill.

"Ha! Ha! just as I thought," chuckled Weenie Allen, viciously, "that thing is a dead failure."

Poor Mary Eliska, tears in her eyes at this seeming disaster, was stung fairly out of herself. She switched around on Weenie Allen with a suddenness that made her skirt fly out and that young gentleman step precipitately backward.

"It isn't a failure, Weenie Allen," she cried, with blazing eyes. "How dare you come here to sneer at us. We didn't invite you. Oh, I could—"

But Jax Gray had seized her arm and succeeded in checking Mary Eliska just in time. She whispered something to the indignant girl, who, with a scornful look at Weenie Allen, turned and, with her friend, ran lightly off toward the stranded airplane.

"By Jove, I really thought for a minute she was going to slap my face," chuckled Weenie Allen to himself. "How pretty she is when she is angry. But I guess if she knew what I do about certain affairs she wouldn't be quite so fresh with me."

He cast a glance at the airplane around which the anxious young people were now clustering thickly.

"If that thing is a success," he mused, as he strode off to join them, "so much the better for me. I think I could use an airplane. I don't see why I should let Bill Stricklin beat me out at anything. Ah! They've started the engine again and—by ginger, she's rising! She's going up! She's flying!"

The small irregularity in the working of the engine, which had brought the plane to a stop, had been quickly remedied. Even Weenie Allen, little as he liked Bill, could not help but join in the cheers as the Golden Butterfly, swinging in an easy circle, began to climb—higher and higher toward the fleecy clouds that flecked the blue dome above.

As for Mary Eliska, she jumped up and down in her enthusiasm 'til her golden hair was tumbling in a tangle about her pink shells of ears.

"Oh, goody! goody! goody!" she squealed in the intensity of her joy.

CHAPTER 13.3.
THE CLOUDS GATHER.

"And so unless we can raise that money somehow within a short time we shall have to leave dear old Shadyside!"

It was Bill who spoke, in troubled tones, some days after the successful flight of the Golden Butterfly. They were seated in the cool-looking living room of Aunt Sally's home. The sun filtering in through the Venetian blinds, fell in patches on the polished floors—Mary Eliska's work, for Aunt Sally's circumstances had been for some time too straitened to afford the servants she formerly had. But she had kept all knowledge of her struggle from her nephew and niece, until now the time had arrived when she felt that she could conceal no longer the object of old Thatcher Allen's visit to her.

The old man, Thatcher Allen, among other things, was President of the Sandy Bay Bank. This bank, although the children did not know it, had long held a mortgage on Aunt Sally's property. The kindly, sweet-souled lady had incurred the debt to forward her brother's dreams. For poor Albert Stricklin had always been "just on the verge of making a fortune." Thatcher Allen's errand was to state that the interest being long overdue and there being no immediate prospect of settlement the bank would have to foreclose. The real reason for this anxiety, which of course Aunt Sally, simple-minded lady, could not know, was, that a real estate concern wanted to purchase the property to erect a summer colony.

"But what of my securities in—and—and—?" inquired poor Aunt Sally, who really knew no more of business than Mary Eliska's French bull-dog.

"In the depressed state of the market that class of securities is worth nothing, madam," was the response, "in addition, though I have refrained from telling you so 'til now, your account at the bank is much overdrawn. However," he had continued, "to show you that we mean to be fair with you we will say nothing about that, but unless the bank gets its interest we must have the land."

It was Aunt Sally's relation of the true state of affairs to Bill and Mary Eliska that sunny afternoon that had brought forth Bill's exclamation recorded at the beginning of this chapter.

"But, auntie," burst out Mary Eliska, blankly, "does the man mean to say that there is nothing, absolutely nothing, on which we can realize anything?"

Aunt Sally shook her head slowly.

"There is nothing we can do," she rejoined, sadly. "We shall have to leave dear old Shadyside and the land will be cut up and sold to strangers. Land which the first Stricklin settled on and which has been in the family ever since. Oh, dear!" and Aunt Sally, never the most strong-minded of women, drew out her handkerchief and began to sniff ominously. Mary Eliska, looking bewitchingly pretty in a simple muslin frock, wrinkled her forehead seriously.

"It can't—it simply can't be as bad as all that," she persisted. "We can raise the money somehow."

"Five thousand dollars!" cried Aunt Sally.

"Phew! That is a lot of money," from Bill. But Mary Eliska had jumped up from her chair.

"The contest, Bill! The contest!" she was exclaiming. "We must write this very day for particulars. If the Golden Butterfly can win that prize—"

"By Jove, sis, it's five thousand dollars, isn't it?" burst out Bill, almost equally excited. "I'd forgotten all about it up 'til now. What an idiot I am. If only—"

He stopped short suddenly, struck by a depressing thought. Probably there were plenty of machines, most of them far better than the Golden Butterfly, entered in the contest which they had read about. His enthusiasm died away—as was the way with Bill—almost as quickly as it had flamed up.

But Mary Eliska would not hear of hesitation. She made Bill sit down that very night and write to the committee in charge of the Higgins' prize. Under her brave, independent urgings things began to look brighter. It was a fairly cheerful party that sat down to a simple supper that evening.

"Oh, dear," sighed Mary Eliska, in the course of the meal, "if only I knew someone who needed a bright young woman to run an airplane, how I'd jump at the job."

"You ought to get a high salary at it anyhow," rather dolefully joked Bill.

"And make a high jump, too," laughed Mary Eliska; "but seriously, auntie, I can run the Butterfly almost as well as Bill. Mr. Homer said so before he left. He said: 'Well, Aunt Sally, I've taught you all I know about an airplane. The rest lies with you, of course.'" Mary Eliska went on modestly: "I could run an auto before. I learned on the one that Jax Gray had at school, so it really wasn't hard to get to understand the engine. Don't you think I'm almost as good a—" Mary Eliska paused for a word—"a—sky pilot!" she cried triumphantly, "as good a sky pilot as you are, Bill?"

"Almost," modestly admitted Bill, his mouth full of strawberry shortcake, "but never mind about that now, sis. There are more important things to be thought of than that. I'm going into town tomorrow for two things. One is to see Thatcher Allen myself. It takes a man to tackle these things—"

"Oh, dear!" sniffed Mary Eliska.

"The other bit of business I have to attend to," went on Bill, "is to get a position. It's time I was a breadwinner." Bill thought that sounded rather well and went on—"a breadwinner."

"Oh, Bill!" cried his aunt, admiringly, "do you think you'll be able to get a position?"

"Without a doubt, aunt," rejoined Bill, confidently; "no doubt several business houses would be glad—to have me with them," Bill was going to say but he thought better of it and concluded, "to give me a chance."

Mary Eliska said nothing, which rather irritated the boy. He concluded, however, that being a girl, she could hardly be expected to appreciate the responsibilities of the man of the household. For since that afternoon and its disclosures, Bill had, in his own mind, assumed that important position.

Somewhat to Bill's surprise he found no difficulty in obtaining access to Thatcher Allen at the bank. On the contrary, had he been expected he could not have been ushered into the old man's presence with greater promptness. He stated his business briefly and straightforwardly.

"Now, Thatcher Allen," he concluded, "is there no way in which this matter can be straightened out?"

The old man, in the rusty black suit, picked up a pen and began drawing scrawly diagrams on the blotter in front of him. Apparently he was in deep thought. But had Bill been able to penetrate that mask-like face he would have been startled at what was passing in Thatcher Allen's mind. At last he spoke:

"I understand that you have built an airplane which is a success?" he questioned.

"That's right, sir," said Bill, flushing proudly; "but the ideas we put into it were my father's—Albert Stricklin's -- every one of them. He practically made it his life work, you see, and—"

"And you beggared yourself carrying those ideas out, eh?" snarled the old man. "Oh, you need not look astonished. I know all about your affairs. More than you think for. And now having expended a wicked sum for the engine of this flying thing where do you expect to reap your profit?"

Bill was rather taken aback. In the past days—since the first wonderful flight of the Golden Butterfly—he had not given much thought to that part of it. He realized this now with a rather embarrassed feeling. Old Thatcher Allen eyed him keenly.

"Why—father, before he died, spoke of the government, sir. He wanted the United States to have the benefit of the machine if it proved successful."

"Bah!" sneered old Thatcher Allen, scornfully, "a mere visionary dream of an inventor. Now I have a business proposition to make to you. I myself am interested in airplanes—or rather in their manufacture."

"You, Thatcher Allen!" Bill looked his astonishment. The last vehicle in the world one would have thought of in connection with "Old Money Grubber," as he was sometimes called behind his back, was an airplane. If he had been given to such things Bill would have concluded the old man was joking.

"Yes, sir," snapped Thatcher Allen, "I am. But not directly. It's on Weenie Allen's account. He tells me that he has a chance to organize a company to give airplane exhibitions and also to manufacture them. But he has not been able to find a suitable machine, or one that was not fully covered by patents 'til he saw yours in flight the other day."

Suddenly he raised his voice: "Weenie! Come here a minute."

Almost immediately, through a door which Bill had not hitherto noticed, but which evidently led into an adjoining office, the figure of Thatcher Allen's son Weenie appeared. To his chagrin, Bill realized that almost every word he had said to the father must have been overheard by the son.

Weenie Allen, who was dressed in a flashy gray suit, with trousers rolled up very high to exhibit electric blue socks of the same hue as his necktie, greeted Bill, who felt suddenly very shabby and insignificant, with a patronizing nod.

"Sorry you're in difficulties, Bill," he said, "but you never were a business chap even at school."

The memory of certain monetary transactions in which Weenie Allen had been concerned occurred to Bill. Weenie's patronizing air angered him. He would have liked to make some sharp, meaning retort. But the thought of Mary Eliska and his Aunt Sally restrained him. Bill was beginning to learn fast.

"You needn't bother to tell me anything about the case," went on Weenie Allen. "I accidentally overheard all that you said. Now, Bill, my father has stated the case to you correctly. I've got a chance to make money with airplanes if I can only get hold of a new model. You've got just what I want."

"Come to the point, my boy, come to the point," urged his father.

"I'm getting there, ain't I?" snarled the dutiful son. "Well, Bill, you're in pretty tight straits. We can foreclose on that mortgage any day we want to. But we won't do it if you give us a square deal. Forget the government. Make a deal with us consigning to me the right to manufacture and exhibit those airplanes and I'll set aside that mortgage and give you a thousand dollars to boot."

"And suppose I won't accept that offer?" asked Bill, slowly. "Then we shall have to go ahead and foreclose. We want that land anyhow, but I am even more anxious to set up my son in a paying business," exclaimed old Thatcher Allen. "Our offer is a fair one. It amounts to giving you six thousand dollars for a thing of canvas, wire and clockwork."

"Rather more than that, sir," said Bill, in a steady voice, although he was inwardly blazing.

"Well, what do you say?" asked Weenie Allen, eagerly. "We'll draw up the papers right now if you say so."

But Bill was learning fast. He knew that the offer just made him had been an inadequate one.

"I'd like to have time to think it over," he said, hesitatingly.

"Take all the time you want," said old Thatcher Allen, with a wave of his shriveled, claw-like hand.

But Weenie Allen did not seem so pleased. It flashed across his mind that Bill wanted to consult with Mary Eliska, and somehow Weenie Allen felt that in that case his offer would meet with refusal. He therefore resolved to put in a heavy blow.

"But I want to start at once," he said. "I can't wait any length of time. When you think that if you don't accept my offer you'll all be without a roof over your heads I should think that for the sake of your sister and your aunt you'd accept."

"They'll never be in that position while I can work," rejoined Bill, with a flushed face. He rose and picked up his hat. Somehow he felt that he could not stand Weenie Allen very many minutes more. "Yes, very fine talk, but what can you do?" snarled Thatcher Allen.

CHAPTER 13.4.
JAX GRAY AND BILL.

Bill flung back some sort of answer and hastened out of the office. As he made his way up the sunny street outside, however, he could not get out of his mind the words of Thatcher Allen. After all, they were true; "what could he do?" Mentally, as he walked along, Bill ran over the list of his accomplishments. He came to the conclusion that airplane building and flying was where his greatest strength lay. But how was he to proceed to make money with his knowledge?

At this point in his meditations, when, unnoticed, he had almost reached the end of the elm-shaded village street, a loud "Honk! Honk!" suddenly startled him.

He looked up, and his gloom vanished like a summer cloud as he saw smiling down on him from the driver's seat of the big auto which had just rolled up beside him, the sunny countenance of Jax Gray. She was in automobile attire and looked unusually attractive.

"Oh, I am so glad I've run across you," she exclaimed.

"You almost did," laughed Bill.

"Did what?"

"Run across me, of course," was the response. "But what are you doing in town? And driving your own car, too. Where is Liam?"

"Oh, he had to do an errand for father."

"And so you are acting as chauffeur?"

"Yes, don't I make a nice one?"

"You certainly do," rejoined the lad with a great deal of emphasis.

"Well, that being the case, you are commanded to jump in by me at once. I've got an errand or two to do and then I'm driving home. We'll go by your place and I can drop you there."

"That's very good of you—" began Bill, but Jax Gray cut him short. "It's really selfish," she exclaimed. "I was looking for an escort. I really need one. You haven't got a revolver with you, have you?"

"Good gracious," exclaimed the astonished boy as he climbed into the big car; "no, of course not. Whatever do you want one for?"

"Why," confided Jax Gray, as they sped along, "I'm on my way to the bank. Mother is going to a big dinner party tonight and I volunteered to fetch out her jewels for her from the safe deposit vault where she keeps them."

"And you were afraid of robbers holding you up?"

"Of course not," laughed the girl, skillfully dodging a vagrant dog that sped across the road in front of the big car; "but just the same, I'm glad to have a nice big boy like you with me. You see, some of the jewels are very valuable, and one never knows what might happen."

"No," agreed Bill; "but in broad daylight, on the road between Sandy Bay and your home, there could hardly be any risk. For instance, who would know that you had valuables in the car?"

"Nobody, except some of the servants at home probably," responded Jax Gray. "But here's the bank."

As she spoke she skillfully manipulated her levers and pedals and brought the car to a stop against the curb as neatly as any driver could have accomplished it.

The car had hardly come to a stop before the bank door flew open and Weenie Allen emerged, his features drawn up into what he meant to be a pleasing smile, but which more resembled a smirk.

Jax Gray, ignoring his proffered hand, leaped lightly to the sidewalk and, responding somewhat frigidly to his pleasantries, made her way into the bank. A cold nod was all that had passed between Weenie Allen and Bill, though Weenie Allen had looked astonished at beholding Bill in Jax Gray's car. Before long the girl tripped out of the building once more. But this time she carried with her a black leather case. Weenie Allen was once more at her side and insisted on helping her into the car, holding her arm rather tightly as he did so.

"I wish I could accompany you," he said. "Ten thousand dollars' worth of jewels is a rather risky thing to carry about."

"Oh, I have a splendid escort, thank you," spoke up Jax Gray, frigidly. She drew on her gauntlets and began fumbling with the levers. Bill was already out of the car and cranking up.

"It would be the pleasure of the ride," said Weenie Allen, in a low voice. "If I were with you I could almost wish somebody would try to hold us up so that I could show you what I could do in your defense."

"Just as you did that day at school when poor little Henry Willis was being beaten by that big bully Hank Jones?" asked Jax Gray, quietly. Weenie Allen's glances, and the emphasis he threw into what he said, were very distasteful to her, and she took what proved an effectual means of squelching him.

"You know I had a sore wrist that day and couldn't get into a fight with Hank," said Weenie Allen, but his eyes were downcast and he had not much more to say. Presently the auto chugged off, leaving the disgruntled youth standing on the sidewalk following the car with his eyes.

"So you're trying to win out Jax Gray, are you?" the over-dressed lad thought to himself. "Well, Bill Stricklin, I guess that settles you. I've never liked you, and now that I've a chance to get the upper hand of you I'm going to use it. You'll regret this auto ride today in days to come, or I'm very much mistaken."

He turned and reëntered the bank, but presently emerged again in a leather coat of black material, black leggings and black cap and goggles. Hauling out his motor-cycle from a rack in front of the bank he wheeled it into the street, and with an admiring crowd of small boys looking on, started the swift, four-cylindered machine. In a cloud of dust he vanished in the same direction as had Jax Gray's car.

Jax Gray, once the confines of the village were past, "let the car out." They sped along, chatting merrily. The roads about Sandy Bay were ideal for automobiling, and perhaps neither of the young occupants of the car noticed how fast they were going when the vehicle topped a small rise and began descending a long steep grade at the bottom of which the railroad, which approached on a curve, was visible in two shining parallel streaks of metal.

Suddenly there came a shrill, long drawn whistle.

"Hullo, a train!" exclaimed Bill. "Must be a freight; there's no regular passenger scheduled to run at this time of day."

"That's right," agreed Jax Gray. "I guess I'll slow down a bit 'til we see how close it is to the crossing."

She pressed her foot on the brake pedal and shoved hard.

But to her astonishment there was no diminution in the speed of the car. It plunged forward down the hill, gaining impetus every second.

"Better slow up, Jax Gray," warned Bill, who had not noticed the girl grow white and faint, as the possibility of what might occur if she could not control the car flashed before her.

"I—I can't!" she gasped.

"The emergency brake!" almost shouted Bill. Below them he had seen a swiftly moving column of white smoke. It was the approaching train. Now it whistled once more. That meant it was close upon the crossing toward which the car was racing at terrific speed.

"I've—I've tried it. It's jammed or something! Oh, Bill! the train!"

Before she could say any more Bill had risen from his seat, and gently, but firmly, removed the girl's trembling hands from the steering wheel. With might and main he tried to check the car. But all he did was in vain. Drops of perspiration stood out upon his forehead. Jax Gray, utterly unnerved, sank back in her seat and hid her face with her gloved hands.

Above the roar of the on-dashing car could be heard the sharp puffing of the approaching locomotive. Bill tugged as if he would tear his muscle out at the brake lever, but it refused to budge. A sort of desperate coolness came over him. But Jax Gray, who had uncovered her eyes for an instant, gave a sudden shrill scream.

"Oh, we'll be killed! Look,—the train! We'll crash into it!"

"Sit down, Jax Gray," ordered Bill, sternly, for the excited girl had seemed to be on the point of jumping from the car as it swayed and bumped toward what seemed certain annihilation, at a terrific rate.

Bill glanced desperately about him. The hill was enclosed by steepish banks with hedgerows at the top. But at one point he thought he saw a chance of escape.

As he despairingly changed the direction of the car two figures sprang from behind the hedge and gazed in amazement at the runaway auto.

"They'll be killed to a certainty!" cried one.

Indeed it seemed so. With Jax Gray in a dead faint and Bill looking straight into the dark face of danger the uncontrolled car tore onward toward the train. The engineer saw it now and blew his whistle shrilly.

CHAPTER 13.5.
A NARROW ESCAPE.

But Bill's quick eye had noted one loophole of escape,—a gap in the bank.

Truly it was taking a terrible risk to dash the car through it. The boy did not know what lay beyond, and in taking the chance he was running almost as great a risk of annihilation as if he kept straight on. But to have done the latter would have been to crash into a solid wall of moving freight cars as they bumped across the grade crossing.

It was almost certain that they would be thrown out and maybe injured. But Bill did not hesitate. With a quick twist of his steering wheel he sent the car spinning on two wheels for the gap. For an instant it seemed as if the vehicle would capsize under the sudden change of direction. But it did not, although it tilted over at a dangerous angle.

Whiz-z-z-z-z!

In a flash they were through the gap, the landscape blurring, so terrific was the speed.

The next instant there was a sickening shock. Instinctively Bill threw out an arm to protect his fair companion. Hardly had he done so before he felt himself impelled through the air as if from a catapult, and all grew blank.

When Bill came to himself his head ached as if it would burst. It was some few seconds, in fact, before he realized what had occurred. When he did he looked about him. A few paces away lay the still form of Jax Gray. She was stretched out on a cushion upon which she must have fallen. For an instant, as he gazed at her features as pale as marble, and her closed eyes, a dreadful thought flashed across Bill's mind. What if she were dead?

But to his great relief he speedily ascertained that the girl was breathing. An ugly bruise on her forehead may have accounted for her continued swoon although she had fainted with terror the instant the train appeared beneath them on the crossing.

The car, its hood crumpled up as if it had been made of paper instead of metal, stood at the foot of a tree not far off.

"No wonder we were thrown out," thought Bill, as he gazed at the wreck and considered the speed at which they had encountered the obstruction. "The wonder is we escaped with our lives."

After a brief and ineffectual attempt to arouse the girl the boy looked about him for some means of assistance. The cowardly train crew had not stopped when they saw the accident. Visions of damage suits and summary discharges may have drifted through their minds, for extra freights were supposed to send flagmen to the crossing to warn all traffic of the train's approach.

Suddenly Bill recollected the two men he had seen spring from behind the hedge as the runaway auto approached the gap. What had become of them? Apparently they had taken to their heels also, for not a sign was to be seen of them.

"Odd," thought the boy to himself; "one would think the first instinct of a human being at seeing an accident like this would be to stay and help. But, hold on, maybe they've gone for a doctor. A retired physician, Dr. Mays, lives not far from here. In the meantime if I could only get some cold water."

Suddenly he spied a small brook at the foot of the hill. Ill and dazed as he felt Bill sprinted toward it, and wetting his handkerchief hastened back to Jax Gray. Kneeling by her side he bathed her forehead. He was rewarded in a few moments by beholding her eyelids flutter and open. In a few seconds more she was fully conscious, but weak and shaken. Bill collected the scattered cushions from the wreck, and placing them like a mattress laid the girl upon them.

She thanked him with a wan smile and then lay still once more. Bill wisely did not speak. He judged that perfect quiet was what she wanted at that moment.

While he sat by her side meditating what to do a sudden noise caused him to look upward.

It was a noise like the drone of a giant bumble bee. It came from directly above his head.

"The Golden Butterfly!" shouted Bill, springing to his feet.

Above him, at an elevation of some thousand feet, the yellow wings of the Stricklin airplane were outlined against the blue, like the form of one of her namesakes.

Bill shouted and waved frantically. Presently he was rewarded by the flutter of a handkerchief from the chassis of the 'plane. At the same instant it was swung about, and revolving in graceful circles began to spiral down to the earth.

"Hooray! It's Mary Eliska and Liam McAdams!" cried Bill. "I recollect now Jax Gray told me that Liam McAdams was to have a lesson today."

Ten minutes later the airplane lighted in the field not a hundred yards from the wreck. As it reached the ground Mary Eliska started the engine at reduced speed. The aerial marvel began to scoot across the field toward Bill as obediently as if it had been an automobile under perfect control.

Agitated as he was Bill could not help feeling enthusiastic as the huge, glittering, flying thing came closer, its engine roaring and its propeller whirring angrily, and yet, the dainty girl in the motor bonnet who was driving it had it under perfect control every second. Throwing back a lever and cutting off the spark and the gasoline, Mary Eliska brought the airplane to a stop with a jerk.

Liam McAdams, with alarmed questions on his lips, sprang out, while Bill helped his sister to alight.

"Good gracious, whatever has happened?" gasped the girl, as she stood on the ground and viewed the still form of her chum Jax Gray, over which Liam McAdams was bending in genuine alarm.

"It's all right, sis," Bill assured her, "Jax Gray is not badly hurt. See—she is looking up at you."

Mary Eliska sped lightly over the turf to her chum's side.

"Oh, Mary Eliska, dear, I'm so glad you've come. It was dreadful. But Bill was so brave. I'm sure I owe my life to him, for the last thing I recollect we were heading direct for the train."

She would have said more, but Mary Eliska held up an admonitory finger. Turning to Bill she sought an explanation of all that occurred. It was soon told, and then the question of summoning a physician came up.

In the midst of the discussion Mary Eliska gave a glad little cry.

"The airplane! I can fly over to Doctor Mays' house. There's a dandy big pasture in the rear in which to alight."

"By George, that's so," agreed Bill, "and I guess, although it sounds a bit startling, it's the only thing to do. We can't run the car and nobody will be along here for hours perhaps. This road isn't travelled much."

But Mary Eliska, with that quick decision which was characteristic of her, was already half way to the airplane. A moment more and she was in the chassis, and slipping into the driver's seat began adjusting the motor.

"I'll leave you to look after Jax Gray," said Bill to Liam McAdams, "while I go along with Mary Eliska. I'm not sure that she is as expert in managing an airplane as she thinks she is."

"Well, she brought me over here at a great rate, anyhow," put in Liam McAdams, loyally.

"And in the nick of time, too," said Bill, warmly pressing the other's hand.

"Oh, do be back as quickly as possible, my foot hurts dreadfully," moaned poor Jax Gray, "and my head feels as if a thousand dwarfs were hammering away inside it."

"We'll be back before you expect us," Bill said, cheerily. Liam McAdams shouted something, but his words were drowned in the roar of the motor as Bill clambered into the Golden Butterfly and Mary Eliska started the engine.

The airplane dashed forward over the smooth turf and then seemed to take the air as lightly and easily as a bit of gossamer. Straight up it soared, high above the tree tops, and was speedily reduced to a fast-diminishing speck in the northwest in which direction lay Doctor Mays' home. Looking downward from the speeding flyer the boy and girl aviators could see, spread out below them like a checkerboard, the fertile Long Island landscape.

Through it ran the railroad, looking like a glittering ribbon of steel. Off to the north the sea sparkled, a few white sails dotting its surface. The Black Rock lighthouse, painted in bands of red and white, formed a conspicuous object.

All at once, on the road beneath them, Bill spied a solitary motor-cyclist whom, even at the height to which they had now risen, he recognized as Weenie Allen. He called his sister's attention to the rider.

"He must have passed right by where the accident happened," he remarked; "that road has no outlet for some distance. Funny that he didn't come to help us."

"You must remember that the banks and hedge hid the place from the road," Mary Eliska reminded him. "Even Weenie Allen wouldn't have willfully passed by you when you were in such straits."

"I don't think so, either," agreed Bill, "and come to think of it, bending over his handlebars as he is, he would not be likely to have noticed the gap we ploughed through."

"Look," cried Mary Eliska suddenly, "he's stopping."

The girl was right. The motor-cycling boy, whose pace had hitherto been as fast as that of the airplane, could now be seen to slacken his machine and finally stop it. Leaning it against a fence he clambered into an adjoining field, and with every evidence of extreme caution he crept toward a patch of woods at no great distance.

"What can he be doing?" exclaimed Mary Eliska.

As she spoke they saw the boy below them take something from his hip pocket.

"A pistol!" cried Bill.

The next instant Weenie Allen had vanished into the patch of woods without having noticed the aerial observers, or, at least, so it appeared.

CHAPTER 13.6.
A ROADSIDE MYSTERY.

"Now, what could he be up to?" Bill wondered as they sped on.

"Give it up," laughed Mary Eliska, "unless he was going rabbit shooting."

"Rabbit shooting with a pistol—and in June—oh, Mary Eliska, I thought you were more of a sport than that."

"Well, can you suggest any solution?"

"Frankly—no. But I've been forgetting something which the sight of Weenie Allen reminded me of," and Bill at once plunged into an account of his interview with the banker and his son.

To his great relief Mary Eliska agreed with him that on no account must the airplane be turned over to Thatcher Allen, but her mind was sadly troubled, nevertheless, by what her brother told her concerning Thatcher Allen's attitude.

"It looks as if he was bent on hounding us," she sighed.

"It surely does," agreed Bill, "but look, sis—there's Doctor Mays' house off there. You'll have to make a landing in that field back of the barn."

Mary Eliska nodded and deftly touched a lever or two. The airplane began to descend.

"Want me to take the helm?" inquired Bill.

If Mary Eliska had dared to turn her head she would have flashed an indignant glance at her brother. As it was she had to content herself with a very haughty, "No, indeed."

Bill laughed.

"You surely are the original Girl Aviatrix," he exclaimed.

"Huh!" cried Mary Eliska, "by no means the original one, my dear. There are lots of them in Europe and there soon will be in this country, too."

"I hope so," responded Bill, "riding with a pretty girl in an airplane just suits me."

But Mary Eliska did not reply, and for a good reason. They were now just above the pasture lot in which she meant to descend, and below them, as they dropped, an amusing scene was transpiring.

The Doctor's horse, old Dobbin, was dashing madly around in circles, faster than he had gone in twenty years of solid respectability; the two cows, and an old mother pig with her family, joined him as the strange whirring thing from the sky dropped lowering above them. As for the chickens, they flew wildly in every direction, clucking as if they had gone mad.

In the midst of the turmoil a rear door opened and a kindly-faced old man with white whiskers and a pair of big spectacles perched on his nose, emerged, to see what could be causing all the disturbance. He fairly dropped the big book he was holding, in his astonishment as he beheld a glistening object, like a huge yellow and spangled bird, dropping in his very back yard, so to speak. But the next instant he recovered himself.

"Bless my soul," exclaimed Dr. Mays, for it was the retired physician himself, "I thought for a moment that the fabled days of the gigantic Roc, with which Sinbad the sailor had his adventures, had returned.

"It must be those Stricklin children. Ah!" he exclaimed, as the airplane alighted and came to a standstill, "it is! Dear me, what a century we are living in! Boys and girls flying about like—like—my chickens!"

He "clucked" reassuringly to the terrified birds as he hastened toward the now stationary machine. Bill and his sister came forward to greet the venerable old doctor as he approached.

Bill hastily explained their errand, being interrupted constantly by the physician's exclamations of astonishment.

"Go back with you? Of course, I will, my children. Will one of you help me catch old Dobbin and harness him? My man Jake is in town today."

"Oh, doctor," cried Mary Eliska, entreatingly, "can't we persuade you to go back with us in the Golden Butterfly?"

"To fly! Good heavens!"

The aged physician threw up his hands at the idea.

"It is perfectly safe, sir," put in Bill. "Safer than old Dobbin in his present frame of mind, I should imagine."

They all had to laugh as they looked at the hitherto staid and sober equine careening about the pasture with his tail held high, and from time to time emitting shrill whinnies of terror at the sight of the strange thing which had landed in his domain.

"I don't know, I really don't," hesitated Dr. Mays. "The very idea of an old man like me riding in an airplane. It's—it's—"

"Just splendid," laughed Mary Eliska, merrily, "and, doctor, I've often heard you say to father that it was a physician's duty to keep pace with modern invention."

"Quite right! Quite right! I often told your poor father so," cried Dr. Mays. "Well, my dear, it may be revolutionary and unbecoming to a man of my years, but I actually believe I will brave a new element in that flying machine of yours. More especially as we can reach my young patient much quicker in that way."

While Dr. Mays, who was a widower and childless, went to hunt up an old cap, as headgear for his novel journey, Bill obtained permission to use the doctor's telephone. He called up Jax Gray's home and related briefly to Deanna Hoffinger what had occurred, and asked that an automobile be sent to the scene of the accident.

Deanna Hoffinger, who at first had been seriously alarmed, was reassured by Bill's quiet manner of breaking the news to her, and promised to come over herself at once. By this time Doctor Mays was ready, and the young people noted, not without amusement, that under his assumed air of confidence the benevolent old gentleman was not a little worried at the idea of braving what was to him a new element.

The Golden Butterfly was equipped with a small extension seat at the stern of her chassis, and into this Bill dropped after it had been pulled out. Dr. Mays was seated in the center, as being the heaviest of the party, while Mary Eliska resumed her place at the steering and driving apparatus.

"All ready behind?" she called out, laughingly, as they settled down.

"All right here, my dear," responded the doctor with an inward conviction that all was wrong.

"Go ahead, sis," cried Bill. "Hold tight, doctor, to those straps on the side."

With a roar and a whirring thunder of its exhausts the motor was started up. Dr. Mays paled, but, as Bill afterward expressed it, "he was dead game." Forward shot the airplane across the hitherto peaceful pasture lot which was now turned into a crazy circus of terrified animals.

"Wh-wh-when are we going up?"

The doctor asked the question rather jerkily as the airplane sped over the uneven ground, jolting, and jouncing tremendously despite its chilled-steel spiral springs.

"In a moment," explained Bill; "the extra weight makes her slower in rising than usual."

"Look out, child!" yelled the doctor, suddenly, "you'll crash into the fence."

He half rose, but Bill pulled him back.

"It's all right, doctor," he said reassuringly.

But to the physician it seemed far otherwise. The fence he had alluded to, a tall, five-barred, white-washed affair, loomed right up in front of them. It seemed as if the airplane, scudding over the ground like a scared jackrabbit, must crash into it.

But no such thing happened.

As the 'plane neared the obstruction something seemed to impel it upward. Mary Eliska pulled a lever and twisted a valve, and the motor, beating like a fevered pulse, answered with an angry roar.

The Golden Butterfly rose gracefully, just grazing the fence top, like a jumping horse. But, unlike the latter, it did not come down upon the other side. Instead, it soared upward in a steady gradient.

The doctor, his first alarm over, gazed about him with wonder, and perhaps a bit of awe. Many times had he and his dead friend, Mr. Stricklin, talked over aerial possibilities, and he had always listened with interest to what the inventor had to say. But that he should actually be riding in such a marvelous craft seemed like a dream to this venerable man of science.

After his first feeling of alarm had worn off the physician found that riding in an airplane after the preliminary run with its bumps and jouncings is over, is very like drifting gently over the fleeciest of clouds in a gossamer car, if such a thing can be imagined. In other words, the Golden Butterfly seemed not to be moving fast, but to be floating in the crystal-clear atmosphere. But a glance over the edge of the high-sided chassis soon showed the physician that she was tearing along at a great rate at a height of about five hundred feet. Fields, woods, streams and small farmhouses swam by beneath their keel.

"Well, doctor, how do you like it?" Bill ventured, after a few moments.

"Like it!" repeated the physician; "my lad, it's—it's—it's bully!"

And thus did his dignity fall like a mantle from Doctor Mays after a few moments in Mary Eliska's, the girl aviator's, Golden Butterfly.

A few moments later they came in sight of the field in which they had left poor Jax Gray lying by the side of the wrecked automobile.

Hardly had they alighted before Liam McAdams, a rather worried look on his face, was at the side of the airplane.

"Say, Bill," he exclaimed, "you didn't happen to put that jewel case in your pocket for safe keeping after the accident, did you?"

"Why, no. Jax Gray had it and slipped it under the seat while she was driving," cried Bill. "Why?"

"Because it's gone!" exclaimed Liam McAdams, somewhat blankly.

"Gone! Impossible!" protested Bill.

"But it is. I've searched the field thoroughly in the vicinity of the car, and I can't find a single trace of it."

"It couldn't have been stolen."

It was Mary Eliska who spoke.

Bill thought a moment. All at once the recollection of Weenie Allen's queer actions when they had seen him on the road below them flashed into his mind. The road, as he had observed, led past the scene of the accident.

Would it have been possible for Weenie Allen to enter the field while they lay unconscious there? After an instant's figuring Bill had to dismiss the idea. Had such been the case, the son of the banker would have been much further off when they observed him from the airplane than he had been. The speed he was making would have carried him far from the wrecked auto had he been near it at the time the accident occurred.

What, then, could have become of the jewel case?

"It must be here," exclaimed Bill, positively; "nobody could have taken it."

While Dr. Mays bent over Jax Gray and examined her injured ankle the others searched the field in every reasonable direction. But not a trace of the jewel case could they find.

All at once, the noise of a horse's hoofs coming at a rapid trot was heard from the road. Bill, thinking it might be some one of whom he might make inquiries, hastened to the hedge and peered over. He saw, coming toward him, a disreputable-looking old ramshackle rig, driven by a red-haired man of big frame who was slouchily dressed. His chin had once been shaven, but now the hair stood out on it like bristles on an old tooth brush. By the side of this individual was seated none other than the immaculate Weenie Allen, in his motor-cycling clothes.

"Why, that's Gid Gibbons, the most disreputable character about here," exclaimed Bill, in amazement. "What can Weenie Allen be doing with him?"

He now noted, to his further astonishment and perplexity, that there was a third person in the rig—Gid Gibbon's daughter, a pretty girl in a coarse way, and given to loud dressing. She had plenty of black hair and a pair of dark eyes that might have been beautiful if they had not had a certain hard, defiant look in them.

As they drew near Weenie Allen turned and seemed to whisper something to the girl, whose name was Hester, at which they both laughed heartily.

CHAPTER 13.7.
MARY ELISKA IS PUZZLED.

"Hello, Gid," hailed Bill, thinking that perhaps the ne'er-do-well, who conducted a small blacksmith shop some distance off, might be able to throw some light on the mystery. "Hello, yourself," was the response in a harsh, gutteral voice as Gid drew in his reins and the conveyance came to a stop. Bill raised his hat to Hester Gibbons and nodded coldly to Weenie. "Good gracious, what's been happening?" shrilled out the girl. "An accident," said Bill, and went on rapidly to explain what had occurred.

"And the worst of it is," the boy went on, "that besides the accident Deanna Hoffinger has suffered a serious loss. A wallet containing valuable jewelry has vanished entirely." Bill watched Weenie Allen closely as he spoke and thought that he saw him change color. It might have likewise been Weenie, but he could have sworn that the girl, too, looked confused. Gid puckered up his lips and emitted a whistle.

"Lost a wallet with jewelry in it, eh?" he repeated.

"Have you looked everywhere for it?" asked Weenie Allen, with an appearance of great solicitude.

"Everywhere we can think of," rejoined Bill. He turned to Liam McAdams, who had just joined him. Liam McAdams looked despondent and worried. A glance at his countenance convinced Bill that the jewel case was still missing.

"I'll get out and help you look for it myself," said Weenie Allen suddenly. "It's awfully queer. Deanna Hoffinger remarked when she left the bank that she would take particular care of the jewels."

"I wonder if anyone passed on this road while we were unconscious?" queried Bill, looking narrowly at Weenie Allen. To his surprise, Weenie answered with a great show of frankness.

"It's very odd," he exclaimed, "but I myself must have gone by this place not more than a few moments after the smash-up. I was on my way to Gid Gibbons' blacksmith shop to get a part of my motor-cycle fixed up. I guess if I hadn't been bending over my brakes as I rode downhill I'd have seen the place myself."

"Guess so," struck in Gid, with a grin; "no one never accused you of being blind."

"My motor-cycle was in worse repair than I thought," went on Weenie Allen, "and so I left it at Gid's place and accepted his offer to ride into town with him."

This all sounded plausible enough. Yet Bill noted that Weenie Allen had not mentioned his little excursion into the wood with the pistol. What was he trying to conceal? What had been his mission there?

While these thoughts flashed through Bill's mind Gid and his daughter had followed Weenie Allen's example and now joined the searchers. By this time, Jax Gray, under the doctor's ministrations, was able to sit up. Her face was pale as marble, partly from suffering, for her ankle still gave her considerable pain, and partly from agitation at the loss of the jewels.

There was a sudden puffing of an auto, and presently Deanna Hoffinger herself, in a smaller car than the wrecked one, was driven into the group by one of the employees of her husband's estate. As gently as possible, after first explanations had been made, Jax Gray broke the news to her. Deanna Hoffinger, a tall, stately woman, went white as she heard.

"One of those jewels, a ruby, was an heirloom that has been in the family for years," she exclaimed. "I would not have lost it for all the others. Has every place been searched thoroughly?" "Everywhere, mamma," responded Jax Gray.

"Bin over ther ground with a fine-tooth comb, mum," said the uncouth Gid. Deanna Hoffinger raised her lorgnette and regarded the unabashed Gid with a look tinged with some disgust. But Gid merely showed his yellow fangs, in what he intended to be a pleasant smile, in reply, and lifted his hat with clumsy gallantry.

"What was the last you saw of the jewels?" asked Deanna Hoffinger of her daughter, after Jax Gray had been tenderly carried to the other auto and made comfortable.

"It was just before we started down the hill," was the reply. "I felt to see if it was safe under the seat just before the car got away from me."

"Then they were there just before the accident, of course," put in Deanna Hoffinger. "And now they are missing in this mysterious way."

"Well, they couldn't have walked off," said Weenie; "somebody may have taken them while you were unconscious. Unless—"

He stopped and glanced at Bill, who felt his face flushing angrily. There had been a queer intonation in Weenie Allen's tones.

"Unless what?" put in Jax Gray, looking at Weenie directly in the eyes. His dropped under the scrutiny of the straightforward girl.

"I suppose you mean unless I took them," struck in Bill, angrily. There was a hard note of defiance in his tones which sounded strange there.

Weenie Allen glanced at him quickly and then said in a low voice:

"Well, it does look odd, you know, and—" "Don't dare to say another word like that!"

Mary Eliska, her soft eyes blazing, stepped forward before Deanna Hoffinger could stop her. Gid Gibbon's daughter watched the angry girl with a contemptuous smile. But Weenie Allen went white and shrank back. "I—I didn't mean anything," he stammered.

"Children! Children!" exclaimed Deanna Hoffinger "no more of this. It seems that there is a mystery here, and perhaps someday it will be solved. But in the meantime I wish no suspicion, or doubt even, cast on anyone." If they had been watching Weenie Allen they would have seen his face brighten up at this. Muttering something in an undertone to Gid, he slunk off, accompanied by his disreputable blacksmith companion and the latter's daughter.

Gid's daughter, Hester, flung back a glance of contempt at the others, of which
they took not the slightest notice.

Dr. Mays elected to return home by means of Deanna Hoffinger's auto. He declared, laughingly, that he had had quite enough excitement that morning for a man of his years. A few moments after the departure of Weenie Allen and his strange companions therefore, Deanna Hoffinger's auto, towing the injured car by means of a rope brought along for that purpose, set out on its return journey. Liam McAdams rode beside his sister, who made a brave effort to bid a cheery good-bye to the young aviators.

But, somehow, all of them felt that a constraint had been suddenly born among them, arising out of the mystery of the missing jewels. The next day posters, announcing a reward for the recovery of the jewels, were hurriedly struck off at Sandy Bay printing office, and distributed throughout the town and the surrounding country. In due course the Stricklin household, of course, received one, and the perusal of it did not add to their cheerfulness.

The bills gave a description of the accident and the circumstances, and Bill could not but feel that any logical person reading the things would come to the conclusion that Bill Stricklin probably knew more about the facts of the case, at least, than anyone else.

In addition to the disconcerting bills the regular police officials of Sandy Bay visited the Stricklin home and interrogated Bill, to Mary Eliska's huge indignation. But worse was to come; private detectives also came and questioned and cross-questioned him at great length.

Bill could not but feel with all this that he was an object of suspicion, but he bravely went about as before and tried to hide his inner thoughts as closely as possible.

Jax Gray soon recovered and was up and about once more. The four young folks interchanged visits and motored and "aeroed" together as freely as before, but they somehow all felt that the air was charged with some influence that made things quite different to what they had been before the accident and the subsequent mysterious vanishing of the jewels.

Mary Eliska privately made up her mind, with a truly feminine intuition, that Weenie Allen had something to do with the affair. Recalling his strange visit to the wood, she even visited the place by herself one day to see if she could light upon any clue that might serve to clear things up. But, as might have been expected, she found nothing.

Her trip over had been made in the Golden Butterfly. Disappointed at her lack of success, for she had almost allowed herself to believe that she would, in some queer fashion, happen upon a clue, the girl was preparing to return, when something happened.

A rod, connecting a warping lever with the right wing of the monoplane, snapped with a sharp crack.

"Oh, dear!" exclaimed Mary Eliska to herself, "what shall I do?"

She looked about her as if seeking for information from her surroundings. All at once she became aware that two men had emerged from the wood behind her and were watching her closely.

Plucky as the girl was, she felt her heart beat a little quicker as she gazed. There was something so very piercing in their scrutiny.

Suddenly one of them stepped forward, and Mary Eliska saw, to her astonishment, that she knew him. More astonishing still, the man was trembling and white-faced as if in alarm at something.

It was Morgan, the butler at Deanna Hoffinger's.

"Why, Morgan, whatever are you doing here?" exclaimed Mary Eliska as she breathed more freely.

The man hesitated. His companion, whom Mary Eliska could now see was an employee about the Hoffinger stables, came to his rescue.

"Why, miss, we've been doin' a bit of trapping in the woods there."

"Yes, miss, that's hit," struck in Morgan, a stout, puffy-faced Englishman with "side burns."

"A bit o' poaching, as you might say, miss. I 'opes you won't tell on hus."

"Good gracious, no," laughed Mary Eliska, immensely relieved to find that the two men were not strangers. "I thought you looked scared when you saw me, Morgan."

"Yes, miss. You see, I haint used in hold England ter see young ledies a flyin' round like bloomin'—bloomin' pertater bugs, hif you'll pardon the comparison, miss. But 'as yer 'ad han h'accident?"

"I have," rejoined Mary Eliska, restraining an impulse to say "I 'ave." "It's not much. If there was a blacksmith shop round here I could get it fixed in a jiffy. It's just this rod that's snapped."

"Why, miss," puffed Morgan, "Gid Gibbon's place isn't more than a few paces, as you might say, from 'ere. Why don't you take that rod there? Hi'll h'escort yer."

"Why, that's so," agreed Mary Eliska, "how stupid of me not to have thought of it. Gid can fix it in a few minutes."

Selecting a small wrench from the tool box Mary Eliska deftly unbolted the broken rod, and then, with Morgan and his companion as guides, she set off across the fields for Gid's shop, which she now recalled was a short distance up the road, but hidden from the spot where the Butterfly had dropped by a patch of woods.

"By the way, Morgan," the girl asked, suddenly, "has anything more been heard of the missing jewels?" To Mary Eliska's astonishment the man started and stammered. "Yes, miss— that is—no, miss. I means, miss, that there ain't been no news, miss, hof hany kind, miss."

Mary Eliska nodded without appearing to note the man's confusion.

"It's a queer affair, miss," put in Morgan's companion, whose name was Giles.

"It is, indeed," rejoined Mary Eliska. "I do wish it could all be cleared up."

"Same 'ere, miss, hi'm sure," struck in Morgan, mopping his puffy face. He seemed to have, in great part, recovered his composure.

"Well, there is the blacksmith shop," said the other man presently, as they emerged from the fields upon the road through a sliding gate. He pointed to a long, low, ramshackle structure at the cross-roads. Beside it stood a fairly neat cottage and beyond this again a brand-new shed, from which proceeded a great sound of hammering.

As Morgan and Giles left her, to make a shortcut home across lots, Mary Eliska set off at a brisk pace, holding the broken rod in her hands. She almost dropped the bits of metal an instant later in a great surprise that she encountered.

The door of the brand-new building opened and out stepped Weenie Allen, in overalls and jumper. Suddenly he became aware of Mary Eliska's advancing figure and halted, staring at her.

CHAPTER 13.8.
HESTER'S RUBY.

The door of the shed had been opened wide, but Weenie Allen closed it swiftly as if in great anxiety to conceal what was within. Then it was that Mary Eliska first became aware of something she had not noticed before. Above the portal was a signboard upon which was painted in staring red letters:

"Office and Works of the Weenie Allen Airplane Co."

Hardly had Mary Eliska digested this astonishing sign before Weenie Allen, his look of startled surprise replaced by a smile, advanced, cap in hand, to meet her.

"Why, whatever brings you here?" he asked, with the air of easy familiarity which Mary Eliska disliked so much. "I guess that that sign gave you a kind of a start, eh?"

"It certainly did," agreed Mary Eliska, "and it gives me even more of a start to see you working, Weenie Allen."

"Huh," grunted the youth, beneath whose blue overalls were visible a pair of gaudy socks of the kind he affected, "I guess you think that I can't make good as well as anyone else when I try. Bill wouldn't go into a deal with me on that airplane of his, so I just got busy and started a concern of my own."

"Do you mean you are actually building an airplane?"

"Yes. Got orders for several of them," rejoined the swaggering youth. "So far I've only had Gid to help me, but I guess I'll have to enlarge the plant pretty soon. You see that Bill would have been wiser to sell me that 'plane of his at the start-off. As things are now, the Thatcher Allen Airplane Company is going to discount anything in its line."

"Well, I am glad of that," said Mary Eliska, briskly, and with some trace of asperity. Weenie Allen's conceited, confident air jarred upon her sadly. "But I came over here to find Mr. Gibbons. I want him to repair this rod for me."

"Why, that's off an airplane!" exclaimed Weenie Allen, eagerly; "you must have come to earth in the Golden Butterfly quite close to here."

"Why, yes. In that field yonder," rejoined Mary Eliska, some instinct telling her not to disclose the true object of her visit there; "my motor went wrong and I had to descend."

"What field did you come down in? That one by the clump of woods round the bend in the road?" asked Weenie Allen, with just a trace of anxiety in his tone.

"Yes. It was lucky I was so close. Morgan and Giles—"

"What, Morgan and Giles were there?"

Weenie Allen seemed tremendously excited all of a sudden.

"Why, yes. What of it?"

But Weenie Allen had pulled himself together.

"Oh, nothing," he said, in a matter-of-fact tone. "I only thought they were a long way from home, that's all. But here comes Gid now. Hey, Gid! Mary Eliska wants a rod welded. Can you do it for her right away?"

"Sure," responded the ill-favored blacksmith, shuffling up. His chin was more bristly than ever, and his shifty blue eyes blinked like a rat's beady orbs as he took the bits of metal.

"A flaw," he declared, examining them; "wonder it didn't break sooner. Come on to the forge, miss, and I'll fix it for you in a brace-of-shakes." Off he shuffled toward the ramshackle forge, Mary Eliska following. Behind her came Weenie Allen. As they passed the cottage Hester Gibbons came flying down the path, but stopped at a sign from Weenie Allen. The youth dropped farther behind, and as Mary Eliska followed Gid into the forge and the bellows began roaring, they began to talk in low tones.

"Do you think she can suspect anything?" asked Hester at one point. "Not a thing," was the confident response. "That pale-faced old gopher, Morgan, was in the wood this afternoon, though. She told me that. The existence of the Thatcher Allen Airplane Company has become known rather before I wanted it to, also. However, they may as well know now as any other time that they aren't the only fliers in the air. I guess the Thatcher Allen airplane will beat anything in its line ever seen."

"I guess it will," laughed Hester, and then, for some unknown reason, they both burst into fits of immoderate laughter. Evidently something connected with Weenie Allen's new enterprise was deemed highly amusing by both of them.

Mary Eliska left without seeing Hester, although from behind a blind in the cottage, the girl watched her closely enough. Gid, whatever his other shortcomings might have been, was a good blacksmith, and the rod was well repaired. Mary Eliska soon had it adjusted, and was about to clamber into the chassis and start home when a shout from the road made her look up. An automobile stood there, and in it were Jax Gray and Liam McAdams. They hailed her excitedly, and Mary Eliska hastily threw out the switch which she had just adjusted and hastened across the field to them.

She soon saw that Jax Gray was waving a leather pocket case above her head and that her face was flushed and excited.

"My dear Jax Gray, whatever has happened?" she cried, as she came up to the side of the auto.

"Happened!" echoed Jax Gray. "Why, my dear, the most extraordinary, inexplicable thing you ever heard of."

"In other words, 'we are up in the air,'" quoth the slangy Liam McAdams, "even if we don't own an airplane."

"You see this case," cried Jax Gray, extending the leather wallet for Mary Eliska's inspection. "Well, that's the case that held mamma's jewels. It was returned most strangely to us this afternoon. We found it on the porch after lunch.

"Oh, Jax Gray! the jewels were in it. I'm so glad."

"No, girlie, it was empty."

"Empty!" echoed Mary Eliska, "and nobody knows how it came there?"

"No, we must have been at lunch at the time. None of the servants know anything about the matter, either. It's a real, dark and deep mystery."

"It's all of that, my dear Watson," proclaimed Liam McAdams, folding his arms and scowling in imitation of a famous detective of fiction. "Why on earth should the thief want to return the wallet? You'd think he'd dodge such a risk of being arrested."

But Mary Eliska had been looking at the wallet which had so amazingly reappeared.

"Why, Jax Gray," she cried, "it's all mud-stained. It looks as if it had been buried somewhere."

"It certainly does," agreed Liam McAdams, "but even that doesn't give us any more to go on than the theory that the jewels have been buried some place."

"And been dug up again," put in Mary Eliska, quickly.

After some more conversation the group was about to break up, when Jax Gray exclaimed suddenly:

"Oh, by the way, did you hear about Jeff Stokes? No, I see you haven't. Well, he's been appointed wireless operator at Rocky Point."

"Oh, I'm so glad," cried Mary Eliska, impulsively; "that's been his ambition for a long time."

Rocky Point was a projecting neck of land about two miles east of Sandy Bay. It was quite an important signalling station for ships passing up and down the Sound. The position which Jeff Stokes had secured was a lucrative one in a way, and, at any rate, was in direct line of promotion.

The two waited to watch Mary Eliska take the air in her now staunch airplane. It was not until she had vanished with a whirr and a whiz that Liam McAdams thought of starting his own car.

"Gracious," cried Jax Gray, as they sped along, "how I wish that the mystery of those jewels could be cleared up."

As she spoke they were passing by the cottage occupied by Gid Gibbons.

"Oh, look, there's that horrid Weenie Allen and Gid Gibbons' daughter at the gate," cried Jax Gray.

At the same instant as she uttered the exclamation, Hester Gibbons looked up in time to see Jax Gray's gaze concentrated upon her. She whisked about, her skirts swinging as she did so. But she did not turn quickly enough for Jax Gray's sharp eyes not to see that she snatched at something she had been wearing at her throat. The millionaire's daughter was almost certain that the object Hester snatched at in such a hurry was a ruby brooch, or at least an imitation of one. She had distinctly caught a ruddy flash as Hester's hand moved to her throat.

Liam McAdams, too, had noticed it, it seemed, for he suddenly observed: "Seems queer for Hester to be wearing jewelry. Her father must be making money fast nowadays."

"Yes," said Jax Gray, but her voice was distant and preoccupied. She was certain that her eyes had not deceived her. It had been a ruby that Hester Gibbons had pulled off and hastened to conceal. Obeying an impulse, she turned and gazed back over the top of the tonneau.

Through the dust cloud behind the car she could see that Hester and Weenie Allen were once more in deep conversation at the gate. She wondered what they could find so engrossing to talk about, and also speculated on several other things. She, however, avoided mentioning her suddenly aroused suspicions to Liam McAdams. He was so hasty. Inwardly she made a resolve to seek out Mary Eliska the first thing the next day and compare notes with her. She could not help feeling that matters were assuming a very complicated aspect.

CHAPTER 13.9.
A RACE AGAINST TIME.

One evening, a week later, Mary Eliska and her brother were tightening up some braces on the Golden Butterfly after an afternoon's flight along the coast, when the sharp "honk! honk!" of an automobile from the road attracted their attention. Running to the door, Mary Eliska saw Liam McAdams and his sister in the "Gee Whizz," as their red auto had been christened.

But that there was something the matter with the Gee Whizz was evident. The motor, ungeared, was coughing and gasping in a painful manner. Liam McAdams shouted as he saw the two.

"Say, you aviators, come here and see what you can do to doctor a poor creeping earthworm of an auto."

Laughing at his tone and words, Mary Eliska and her brother hastened down the path and through the gate.

"Something's wrong with the transmission," explained Liam McAdams.

"What's the trouble?" asked Bill.

"What a question, you goose?" cried Jax Gray; "if we knew we'd have fixed it long ago."

"It's doubly annoying," said Liam McAdams, in an impatient voice, "because we got a wire from father tonight, saying that he would take us on a trip to Washington with him if we arrived in New York by eight-thirty."

"Oh, you poor dears," exclaimed Mary Eliska, "and if you don't get there at that time?"

"We can't go, that's all," said Jax Gray, tragically clasping her gloved hands.

"Bother the luck," muttered Liam McAdams, with masculine grumpiness. "Found out what's the trouble, Bill?"

"Yes," was the response; "one of your gears is stripped. I'm afraid that there'll be no Washington trip for you folksies."

The tears rose in Jax Gray's fine eyes. Liam McAdams looked cross, and an abrupt silence fell.

It was Mary Eliska who broke it with a suggestion.

"There's a train leaves Central Riverview junction at six, isn't there?"

"I believe so," rejoined Jax Gray, in a doleful voice; "we took it one night, I remember, when we missed the through cars from Sandy Bay."

"It's five now," nodded Mary Eliska, examining the dial of a tiny watch, one of the last presents her father Albert Stricklin had given her.

"Fat chance of getting this old hurdy-gurdy fixed up in time to make it," grumbled Liam McAdams.

"You don't have to," cried Mary Eliska, with a note of triumph.

"Don't have to!"

It was Jax Gray who echoed the remark.

"No, indeed. Our aerial express will start for the junction in a few minutes, and—"

But the rest was drowned in an enthusiastic shout. Jax Gray threw her arms about her chum and fairly hugged her.

"You darling. We can make it?"

"We must," was the business-like rejoinder. "Bill, you get the Butterfly out and fill the lubricator tank. We've got enough gasoline."

Bill and Liam McAdams, arm in arm, hastened off to the shed. The two girls followed more leisurely. It was not long before everything was in readiness, but fast as they worked it was nearly half an hour before preparations were all complete.

Then they climbed in and Mary Eliska started the engine. But the next instant she shut it off again.

"The second cylinder is missing fire," she pronounced.

Bill bent over the refractory part of the motor and soon had it adjusted. Then the motor settled down to a steady tune, the regular humming throb that delights the heart of the aviator.

"All ready?" inquired Mary Eliska, adjusting her hood and goggles and turning about.

"Right Oh!" hailed Liam McAdams.

"Now, boys and girls, prepare for a long run," warned Mary Eliska; "with this load it will take a long time to rise."

The airplane was speeded up and soon traversed the slope leading from the back of the shed to the summit of the little hill at the rear of the Stricklin place. As it topped the rise Mary Eliska turned on full power. The Golden Butterfly dashed forward and then, after what seemed a long interval, began to rise. Up it soared, its motor laboring bravely under its heavy burden. In the dusk blue flames could be seen occasionally spurting from the exhausts. It would have been a weird, perhaps a terrifying sight to anyone unused to it—the flight of this roaring, flaming, sky monster, through the evening gloom.

"We've got half an hour to make the twenty miles," shouted Bill, from his seat beside his sister. Mary Eliska set her little white even teeth and nodded.

"I'm going to make for the tracks and follow them. That's the quickest way," she said.

It seemed only a few seconds later that the red and green lights of a semaphore signal flashed up below them.

"Bradley's Crossing," announced Bill.

Swinging the airplane about, Mary Eliska began flying directly above the tracks.

"No sign of the train yet—we may make it," said Liam McAdams, pulling out his watch. It showed a quarter to six, and they had fifteen miles to travel, or so Bill estimated the distance.

"Let her out for a mile-a-minute," he exclaimed.

Mary Eliska only nodded. She was far too busy getting all the work she could out of the motor. An extra passenger makes a lot of difference to an airplane, and the Butterfly was only built to accommodate three. But she was answering gallantly to the strain.

On she flew above the tracks, every now and then roaring above some astonished crossing keeper or track-walker.

Suddenly, from somewhere behind them, they heard a long, moaning whistle.

"The train!" shouted Jax Gray.

In her excitement she gripped Bill's arm tightly and peered back.

All at once, around a curve, the locomotive came into view—black smoke spouting from its funnel and a column of white steam pouring from its safety valves.

"She'll beat us," cried Liam McAdams, despairingly, as the thunder of the speeding train grew louder. The setting sun flashed on the varnished sides of the cars.

The engineer thrust his head out of the cab window and gazed upward. His attention had been attracted by the roaring of the motor overhead.

He broke into a yell and waved his hand as he saw the flying airplane dashing along above him. The next instant his hand sought the whistle cord.

"Toot! toot! toot!"

The occupants of the airplane waved their hands. To their chagrin, however, they saw that, overloaded as the airplane was, the train was gaining on them in leaps and bounds. Its windows were black with heads now as passengers, regardless of the danger of encountering some trackside obstacle, leaned out and gazed up at the Golden Butterfly roaring along like some great Thunder Lizard of the dark ages.

"Don't they stop anywhere between here and the junction?" gasped Liam McAdams.

Bill shook his head.

"It's a through train from Montauk," he said; "they make all the speed they can."

"Two minutes," cried Jax Gray, suddenly; "we won't do it."

But Mary Eliska had suddenly swung off the tracks and was cutting across country. She had seen that the track took a long curve just before it entered the junction. By taking a direct "crow flight" across country she might beat it after all.

And she did. As the train came thundering into the station and stopped with a mighty screaming of brakes and hiss of escaping steam, the airplane came to earth in the flat park-like space in front of the depot.

"Tumble out quick!" shouted Bill, "she only stops a jiffy."

Jax Gray and Liam McAdams lost no time in obeying.

"Good-bye, you darlings!" cried Jax Gray, as she sped after her brother toward the station. "We'll get our tickets on the train!" shouted Liam McAdams, as they vanished.

"All ab-o-a-r-d!" The conductor's voice ran peremptorily out. He had seen the race between the airplane and the train, but even that could not disturb a conductor's desire to start on time.

As the wheels began to revolve, Liam McAdams and Jax Gray swung on to the steps of the rear parlor car. As they did so the passengers broke into an involuntary cheer. The shouts of approval at the up-to-date manner in which the young folks had "made their train," mingled with the puffing of the locomotive as it sped off.

Among the spectators of the sensational feat had been a broad-shouldered, bronzed man in a big sombrero hat, who sat in the same parlor car which Liam McAdams and Jax Gray had entered. He looked like a Westerner. As the train gathered headway he suddenly, after an interval of deep thought, struck one big brawny hand upon his knee and exclaimed to himself:

"It's the very thing—the very thing. With a fleet of those I could develop the Jupiter and astonish the mining world."

He rose, with the slowness of a powerful man, and made his way back to where Liam McAdams and Jax Gray were sitting. Raising his broad-brimmed hat with old-fashioned courtesy, he addressed himself to Liam McAdams and was soon deep in conversation with him.

CHAPTER 13.10.
THE RIVAL AIRPLANE.

In the meanwhile, the exciting race against time had resulted in overheating the Golden Butterfly's cylinders, and a stop of an hour or more at the junction was necessary. Thus it was quite dark when the young Stricklins were ready to make for home. A small crowd had gathered to see them start, for there was a little community of houses scattered about the junction.

They decided to go the way they had come, namely, to follow the tracks to the crossing and then turn off for home. It was their first experience in night piloting, and when they were ready Mary Eliska switched on the tiny shaded bulb that illuminated the compass. This done, she started the engine, and the Golden Butterfly shot into the air under its reduced load with an almost buoyant sense of freedom.

The crossing was reached in several minutes less than it had taken them to reach the junction on the going trip. Mary Eliska turned off as she marked the glowing lights beneath her, and presently the Golden Butterfly was skimming along above dark woodlands and gloom-enshrouded meadows. There was something awe inspiring about this night flying. Above them the canopy of the stars stretched like a mantle spangled with silver sequins. Below, the earth showed as a black void.

They were flying slowly to avoid overheating the cylinders again. Suddenly a bright glare shot up against the night from below, and a little ahead of them. It died down almost instantly, only to flash up once more.

"Gid Gibbons's forge!" exclaimed Bill. "Let's fly over by there and see what he's doing."

"All right," agreed Mary Eliska; "ever since my visit there I have felt a great interest in Mr. Gibbons. But we'll have to make haste, there's some wind coming before long."

The girl was right. A filmy mist, like a veil, had spread over the stars, dimming their bright lamps, and a wind was beginning to sigh in the trees under them.

But they had not reached Gid Gibbons's place, or rather a location above it, when an astonishing thing happened. From the ground a red light and a green light set at some distance apart began to rise. Up and up they climbed through the night in long, swinging circles. Between them was dimly visible the dark outlines of some fabric.

"An airplane!" cried the boy and girl, simultaneously.

"Weenie Allen's airplane!" cried Mary Eliska, an instant later.

"And—oh, Bill—it can fly!" she added, admiringly.

"No doubt of that," was the rather grudging reply, as the red and green lights soared up and up.

"Keep clear of it, sis, we don't want a collision," warned Bill.

"Oh, I'd like to get close and see it," breathed Mary Eliska. "I never would have credited Weenie Allen with being able to do it."

"Nor I," exclaimed Bill, his dislike of Weenie Allen giving place to admiration—genuine admiration—of the other's ingenuity.

"Well, he's beaten me out at my own particular specialty," he exclaimed presently, after an interval in which the lights had climbed far above the Golden Butterfly. "That's a better machine than ours, Mary Eliska."

"I guess we'll have to admit that," rejoined the girl, with a sigh. "I wonder if he'll enter for the prize?"

"Of course. With a craft like that he'd be foolish if he didn't. Odd that he's trying it out at night, though."

"I suppose he wants to keep secret what it can do and then spring it on an astonished world," rejoined Mary Eliska. "Good gracious!" she broke off hurriedly.

The airplane had given a sudden lurch, and at the same instant a sharp puff of wind struck them both in the face. Mary Eliska's hands fairly flashed among her levers, and she averted what might have been a bad predicament.

Involuntarily, at the same instant, Bill had glanced up at the other airplane to see how it was faring. To his astonishment the lights did not seem to waver.

"Wow, Mary Eliska!" he cried, "that puff didn't even bother Weenie Allen's craft. It was uncanny to see her weather it."

"There's something uncanny about it altogether," sniffed Mary Eliska; "it's a regular phantom airship."

"That's just what it is," agreed Bill, "but I'm afraid it is a substantial enough phantom to carry off that $5,000.00 prize."

Another puff prevented Mary Eliska from replying just then. Once more the Golden Butterfly careened violently, and then, under Mary Eliska's skillful handling, righted herself. But this time the puff was followed by a steady rush of wind.

"Better turn, Mary Eliska, before it gets any worse," advised Bill; "we're off our course now."

"I—I tried to," exclaimed Mary Eliska, desperately, "but the wind won't let me. I don't dare to."

"We must," exclaimed Bill, with a serious note in his voice; "if this wind freshens much more we won't be able to turn at all."

He leaned forward and took the wheel from his sister. But the instant he tried to steer the airplane round, the wind, rising under one wing tip, careened her to a perilous angle.

"No go," he said; "we've got to keep on going."

"But where can we land?" asked Mary Eliska, a little catch in her voice.

"We'll have to take chances on that," decided Bill. "It would be suicidal to try to buck this wind."

The breeze had now freshened 'til it was singing an Aeolian song in every wire and brace of the Golden Butterfly. Brother and sister could feel the stout fabric vibrate under the strain of the blast.

The airplane was moving swiftly now. But it was the toy of the wind, which grew stronger every minute. The dark landscape beneath fairly flew by under them. Neither of them thought to look back at the red and green lights in the sky behind them.

All at once, Bill, who had leaned over his sister's shoulder and glanced at the compass, gave a sharp cry.

"We've got to turn, sis," he said, in a tense, sharp voice.

"What do you mean, Bill? Are we in any very serious danger?"

The girl's voice shook nervously in response to the anxiety expressed in her brother's tone.

"Danger!" echoed Bill. "Girlie, we are being blown out to sea!"

Blown out to sea! The words held a real poignant terror for Mary Eliska.

"Oh, Bill, we must do something!" she cried, helplessly.

"Yes, but what? We can't, we daren't turn about. The machine would tip like a bucket. No, we must keep on and trust to luck."

Mary Eliska shuddered. Hurtled along in the wind-driven darkness, brother and sister sat in silence, waiting for the first warning that they were approaching the sea.

In the blackness it was impossible to see anything ahead, and the starlight, which, dim as it was, might have helped, had been overcast by a filmy covering of light clouds.

Once or twice as they were hurried helplessly along, the propeller beating desperately against the wind, they saw, far below them, the cheerful lights of some farmhouse. Farther off a glare against the sky indicated the lights of Sandy Bay.

How they wished that they were safe and sound at home, as they were blown onward by the wind, going faster and faster every minute.

Bill, his pulses beating hard, and every nerve at tension, had taken the wheel from his sister, even at the risk of careening the airplane when they shifted their positions. Every now and then he tried to turn ever so little, but each time a tip at a dangerous angle warned him not to attempt such a thing.

All at once Mary Eliska uttered a shrill cry.

"Oh, Bill! The sea!"

Above the screeching of the wind and the hum of the motor they could now hear another sound, the thunder of the surf on the beach.

Straining his eyes ahead Bill could see now the white gleam of the breakers as they broke in showers of spray on the seashore. A real sense of terror, such as he had never felt before, clutched at his heart as he heard and saw.

But controlling his voice, he turned to Mary Eliska.

"Be brave, little sister," he said; "we'll pull through all right."

Mary Eliska said nothing in response. She dared not trust her voice to speak just at that moment. White faced and with staring, fixed eyes, she sat motionless and silent, as the

Golden Butterfly was driven out above the roaring surf and the tossing waves. To her alarmed imagination the sea seemed to be reaching up hungry arms for the two daring young aviators.

Suddenly she was half blinded by a brilliant flash of light which bathed the airplane in a flood of radiance. The next instant it was gone, but they could see the great shaft of radiance sweeping around the compass.

"It's the light!" cried Bill. "The Rocky Point light!"

CHAPTER 13.11.
IN DIREST PERIL.

"Oh, if we could only work around and land on the point," exclaimed Mary Eliska. "There's a fine, smooth field there; in fact, it's all bare ground, without rocks or trees."

"Yes, and Jeff Stokes is wireless operator there, too," rejoined her brother. "Hullo," he exclaimed an instant later, "the wind is shifting a bit. I almost got her head round that time."

"Then there is a chance, Bill!"

"Yes, sis, but don't count too much on it."

Like a skillful jockey handling a restive horse, Bill worked the Golden Butterfly about on the shifting air currents. If once he could turn her nose toward the land he was sure that he would be able to make the ground by driving the airplane down on a slanting angle.

Once or twice, while he strove with hand and brain against the elements, he caught his breath with a gasping intake—so near had they come to overturning. But, thanks to the wind eddies of the point, it was possible, after a deal of breathless maneuvering, to get the airplane headed for the land.

The instant he found himself in this position Bill threw on all his power and then, "bucking" the wind, like a ship beating up to windward, he rushed down through the night upon the point. As he did so the rays of the slowly revolving light flashed brightly upon the laboring airplane. In the radiance it looked like some struggling night bird beating its way against the storm and darkness.

As Mary Eliska had said, the point was clear of rocks or brush, and a landing was made without much difficulty once the airplane had been turned. Just as a ship can face the waves with comparative security, so an airplane, being driven into the teeth of a gale, is secure so long as she does not "broach to"; in other words, get sidewise to the blast. It was touch and go with the Golden Butterfly for several minutes, though, during that struggle with the elements, and two more thankful young hearts rarely beat than Mary Eliska's and Bill's as they stepped from the machine and made it fast by pointed braces provided for the purpose.

Hardly had she touched the ground before a door in the lower part of the lighthouse opened and the form of Jeff Stokes emerged. He told them that the struggle with the wind had been seen by the light-keeper and himself, and he was warm in his congratulations of the daring young aviators. The light-keeper, a grizzled man named Zeb. Beasley, followed close on Jeff's heels.

"Come right into the house and hev some supper," he said warmly. "It's only rough fare, but you're welcome. My misses will be glad to have you."

Truth to tell, both Mary Eliska and her brother were almost famished and worn out after the tension of the struggle with the wind. This being so, they were glad enough to accept the light-keeper's kind invitation.

Mary Eliska's first action, however, was to hasten to the 'phone in the lighthouse and call up their aunt. Aunt Sally, who had been badly worried over their prolonged absence, was much relieved to learn that they were safe and sound.

Mrs. Beasley, a motherly woman of middle age, took charge of Mary Eliska while Jeff Stokes entertained Bill. Jeff said that he liked the life at the light, lonesome as it grew sometimes. When he felt blue he used to relieve the monotony by talking, by means of invisible waves, with other operators. He wiled many a weary hour away in this manner, he said.

Suddenly, in the midst of their talk, he excused himself and hastened to the small room in which his instruments were. The place, filled with shiny, mysterious apparatus and networked above with wires, was as neat as a pin.

"Someone's calling," Jeff explained.

His quick ear had caught the faint "tick-tick" hardly audible to the untrained ears, which told him that a message was vibrating through the night. Slipping over his head a metallic apparatus, not unlike the telephone receivers worn by "Central," Jeff began listening intently. Drawing a pad toward him, he was soon writing down the message as it was ticked off. Presently it was completed, by which time Mary Eliska was one of his audience.

"'Steamer Valiant, Captain Briggs, of London, wishes to be reported as passing Rocky Point, bound for Boston,'" read off Jeff. "Hum—nothing very exciting there."

"What are you going to do now?" asked Mary Eliska, as Jeff, the message in his hand, turned to another table, one on which were arranged some ordinary telegraph instruments.

"Send it by ordinary wire telegraphy into the head office in New York," he said.

"Why not send it by wireless?" asked Mary Eliska.

"Too much chance of delay and getting cross currents," explained Jeff. "We found that for quick transmission of ordinary business, that the wire is best, unless the atmospheric conditions are just right."

Suddenly, one of the telegraph instruments began to crackle and click loudly.

"Phew!" said Jeff, listening intently; "here's something that will interest you folks."

"What is it?" asked Mary Eliska, eagerly.

"It's—wait a minute 'til I catch the last—" Jeff listened a few seconds more and then faced about. "Why, that message was a dispatch from the Sandy Bay correspondent of the New York Planet to his paper," he said. "It was an article telling that Weenie Allen has completed a successful airplane which made a wonderful flight tonight in a stiff wind. He says that Thatcher Allen has formed a company and means to manufacture similar craft. Then there was a lot of taffy about what a fine young fellow Weenie Allen is, and how bright, and so on. Wonder if it's true?"

"I can vouch for that," said Mary Eliska. "I've seen his factory. It's out by Gid Gibbons' shop."

"So that's where Gid is getting all his money," exclaimed Jeff. "I saw him spending it like water in Sandy Bay the other day. Hester's got a lot of new dresses and hats, too."

Mary Eliska's heart beat a little faster. This sounded like a corroboration of her suspicions. Where could such a man as Gid Gibbons be getting such large amounts of money as he seemed to have recently? But before she could ask any more questions Mrs. Beasley announced supper. Speculation was rife in Mary Eliska's mind as they sat down to the broiled sea bass, freshly caught, home-grown potatoes and string beans and other good things which the light-keeper had designated as "rough fare." Mary Eliska was fain to admit afterward, and so was Bill, that never had she enjoyed anything so much as that meal in the old lighthouse with the wind roaring about it and the rough, kindly faces of their entertainers smiling on them.

Good-natured Mrs. Beasley soon after arranged sleeping accommodations for her young guests, and that night the young aviators slumbered peacefully, while above them the great revolving light swept steadily in slow circles, warning vessels passing up and down the Sound of the dangerous proximity of Rocky Point.

The next day dawned bright and fair. The sea lay like a sheet of blue glass, with scarcely a ripple to mar its polished surface. The last trace of the wind had died down.

"We'll have no more breeze 'til sundown," announced Mr. Beasley at breakfast. Like most men of his profession, he was an earnest and accurate student of the weather. After breakfast Jeff Stokes, who had been on duty all night, was relieved by his assistant, a young man who boarded in the village and rode over to his duty on a motor-cycle.

"Well," said Bill, after they had thanked their good-hearted entertainers warmly, "I guess it's time for us to be getting home."

But Mary Eliska had noted a wistful look in Jeff Stokes' eyes as he stood by the side of the airplane, which an examination had already shown to be none the worse for its buffeting of the night before.

"Would you like to try a little flight, Jeff?" she asked.

"Would I?" echoed the youth; "will a duck swim?"

"Yes, I believe so," laughed Bill, "and so can a certain young wireless operator fly."

"Gee, Bill, you mean it?"

"Of course, if you're not scared."

There was a mischievous twinkle in Bill's eye as he bent over the engine.

"How would you like a ride, Mr. Beasley?" asked Mary Eliska presently, while Bill adjusted the engine.

The weather-beaten old fellow fairly threw up his hands.

"Land of Goshen, miss!" he exclaimed, "I've lived on the earth and sea, man and boy, for fifty years, and I ain't agoin' ter tempt Providence by embarking in a sky clipper at this late day."

"You bet you ain't," put in Mrs. Beasley with deep conviction. "Why, if you ever done such a thing we'd be like to be read out of church—not but what it's all right for young folks if they know how to manage the contraptions."

"Now, then, Jeff, if you are ready will you get in?" said Bill presently.

The slender young wireless operator hopped into the chassis with alacrity. But his face was a bit pallid from excitement at the idea of the new method of locomotion he was about to test.

Last good-byes were said, and the motor began to whirr like a gigantic locust. There was a grinding and buzzing as the gears meshed and the airplane began to scud off.

"Fer all ther world like some big, pesky grasshopper," declared Mrs. Beasley, as it scudded off across the smooth turf.

But if the good lady was astonished, then it was nothing to her amazement when a moment later the Butterfly soared up into the air, lifting as gently on the windless atmosphere as a bit of drifting gossamer.

Up and up it swept in graceful hawk-like circles.

"Dear Suz!" shrieked Mrs. Beasley presently, "if they ain't agoin' out ter sea!"

"Just what they air," shouted her husband, shading his eyes with a wrinkled hand. "I never thought ter have lived ter have seen such a thing!"

Bill had been unable to resist the temptation to take a little spin out above the glassy, scarcely heaving water. The gulls, soaring above it, viewed with amazement the invasion of their realm by this buzzing, angry looking monster. They flew about it shrieking.

"Goodness, I hope they don't attack us," exclaimed Mary Eliska.

"Not likely," was Bill's response. "They think we are some kind of big bird, I guess, and want to have a game with us."

As they swept on, all agreed that never had they felt such a feeling of exhilaration as came to them as they swooped and swung above the glistening blue water, for all the world like some huge bird. Once or twice motor boats went by beneath them, and the occupants looked up at first in wonderment and then in enthusiasm at the sight the Golden Butterfly and her three young occupants presented.

But all at once the steady song of the engine began to grow different. It "skipped" and sputtered and coughed. Blue smoke rolled from the exhausts. The airplane began to waver and sag.

Jeff Stokes turned rather pale.

"What is the matter?" he gasped, steadying his voice as much as he could as the airplane began to drop steadily down toward the water beneath them.

"The gasoline's given out," rejoined Bill in a voice which was full of anxiety.

"Oh, Bill, what shall we do?"

Mary Eliska gasped as the airplane, its propeller beating the air more and more feebly, began to descend with greater rapidity.

"We'll have to volplane to some land if we can, and if we can't we must take our chances for it in the water," was Bill's grim reply.

CHAPTER 13.12.
WHAT HAPPENED ON THE ISLAND.

"Look," cried Mary Eliska suddenly, "isn't that a small island below there? Maybe we can make that?"

"I'll try to," was the answer, as Bill gripped the steering wheel more firmly.

At the same instant the motor, with a gasp and a sputter, gave out altogether. But Bill knew how to volplane; that is, to reach the earth by swinging the airplane in circles so that her stability was maintained even with the power cut off.

He began to execute this maneuver now. The island which Mary Eliska had indicated was a small spot of land some five miles off the shore. It was sandy and barren looking on one side, though at the farther end from them there grew some trees and scrubby looking bushes.

If he could only keep the airplane from sagging down into the sea Bill was confident he could land at the place in safety. But it was still some distance off and the airplane was still dropping with much greater rapidity than seemed comfortable. Both Bill and his sister were expert swimmers, and the boy knew that Jeff was at home in the water. But at the same time, if they struck the surface of the sea, there was the chance that they might become entangled in the airplane and drowned before they had an opportunity to save themselves. So it was with a keen sense of apprehension that the boy exercised all the air craft of which he was master in bringing his sky cruiser downward.

"Oh!" cried Mary Eliska suddenly as the Golden Butterfly gave a sickening downward drop like a stone plunging to vacancy.

But the empty "air pocket" which the craft had struck was a small one, and the next instant the atmosphere caught the broad wings and buoyed the airplane up from what seemed to be destined to be a disastrous fall.

The drop had, however, had one good effect. It had thrown the airplane almost on end, and in that manner drained a few last driblets of gasoline from the depleted tank into the feed pipes.

It was only a little fuel, but it was enough to cause the engine to resume operations for a couple of minutes. Taking advantage of this lucky accident, Bill drove forward, and as the propeller came once more to a standstill the Golden Butterfly sank down into a bed of sand which made her almost at once stationary.

"Well, we are—aerial Robinson Crusoes," exclaimed Mary Eliska as, having clambered out of the chassis, she stood surveying the little island which they had so fortunately landed upon.

"Yes, and if we don't get some gasoline pretty quick we'll be Crusoes in a mighty uncomfortable sense," commented Bill, moodily gazing about at the surrounding sea, smooth as a sheet of glass and without the sign of a boat upon it. Far off on the horizon there hung a three-masted schooner, all her sails set, in the flat calm. But she was too far off to aid them even had she been able to.

"Tell you what we'll do, let's explore the island," said Jeff Stokes suddenly.

"Of course," cried Mary Eliska, clapping her hands, "that's what everybody does in story books when they are stranded on a desert island, and right after that they always find just what they want, even down to a silver-mounted manicure set."

"I'd like to see a tin-mounted can of gasoline," grunted Bill. Nevertheless after seeing to the engine of the airplane he was willing enough to set out with the others to explore this little spot of land in the Sound.

It was so small that it did not take them long to reach the summit of the low peak into which it rose in the center.

"Oh, there's a little hut!" cried Mary Eliska, suddenly.

Sure enough, below them, and half overgrown with tall weeds and scrub growth, was a half-ruined hut. It was doubtless the relic of some fisherman who had once used the island as headquarters. But it had, apparently, long lapsed into disuse.

Hardly had they spied it before Bill made another discovery. Drawn up in a miniature cove not far from the hut was a trim and trig white motor boat, seemingly, from her long narrow shape and powerful engines, capable of great speed.

Here was a discovery! A motor boat meant gasoline and companionship.

With a soft cry of joy Mary Eliska was dashing forward toward the hut, from which they could now hear proceeding the hum of human voices, when Bill suddenly checked her. From the doorway there had suddenly issued the figure of Morgan, the Hoffingers' butler. He gazed about him with a look of half alarmed suspicion on his flabby face. The young aviators instinctively crouched back behind a screen of green brush. They felt a suddenly aroused premonition that everything was not as it should be.

"H'its nothink," said Morgan, addressing someone within the hut, after he had gazed about a little more without seeing anything to further alarm his suspicions.

"All right, if that's the case come back in here," came another voice from inside the hut.

"Giles!" recognized the astonished Mary Eliska. But another and a greater surprise was yet in store for them when they heard another voice strike into the conversation. There was no mistaking the tones for any others than Weenie Allen's.

"You chaps are nervous as kittens," he was saying, "who on earth would come to this island? We are as private here as if we were in the South Seas. Now go ahead, Morgan, with what you were saying."

"Well, what h'I says is this," spoke up the English butler, "a fair diwision and no favoritism. You say you want a third? You ain't h'entitled to h'it. H'it was h'only by h'accident that you found h'out h'our secret h'and h'I thinks you ought to be content with what you can get."

"Very well," was the rejoinder, "but as you fellows know, I've got you in my power. You daren't make a move without consulting me. If you try any monkey tricks I'll crush you so quick you won't know what struck you. The police are still carrying on their investigation, and—"

But here the voices sank so low that the eager young listeners could hear no more. But their eyes shone as they exchanged glances. Somehow both Mary Eliska and Bill felt that the conversation had related to the mysterious vanishing of the jewels. This at least appeared clear from Weenie Allen's reference to the police.

"We'd better get back to the other side of the island before they come out and see us," counseled Mary Eliska. "If they were to find out we had been spying on them they might get frightened and spirit the jewels away from wherever they have them concealed, for I'm just as sure now that they are all three mixed up in it as I am that—that—"

"We have no gasoline," put in Bill.

"But you have no proof and nothing to go upon," objected Jeff Stokes who was, like most folks around Sandy Bay, familiar with the details of the strange occurrence.

"That's just the trouble," said Mary Eliska, "and it is just as impossible to go ahead in the case as it is for us to fly without fuel."

"Mary Eliska!" cried Bill, suddenly, "look at that!"

"That" was a ten gallon can of gasoline standing on the beach by the side of the motor boat. Evidently, to drag her bow up on the beach, they had lightened the craft so as to make the task easier, for several ropes, water jars and other bits of marine tackle lay about.

"If we could only get it," sighed Mary Eliska.

"Yes, if," was the rejoinder from Bill, "but we can't steal it, and, as you say, it might spoil everything if Weenie Allen thought that we had overheard any of his talk."

"Look out!" warned Jeff Stokes in a whisper the next instant. The warning did not come a bit too soon. The door of the hut opened and the party which had been in conference inside emerged. They made straight for the motor boat, which Jeff Stokes had, in the meantime, recognized as one that was for hire at Sandy Bay.

"Come on, boys, we've got to be getting back," urged Weenie Allen moving quickly and preparing to shove the craft off.

"Wait 'til I chuck some of this truck in," grumbled Giles.

He stooped and rapidly threw in the ropes and other gear scattered about. Then as Weenie Allen and the flabby-faced butler shoved the craft off he made a hasty scramble for the boat's bow, leaping in as she floated free of the beach.

"H'I soy," shouted Morgan, "you forgot the bloomin' gasoline."

"Better put back and get it," growled Giles; "if you fellows had helped me a bit instead of givin' advice it wouldn't have bin forgotten."

"Oh, we can't bother with it now," struck in Weenie Allen, impatiently, "we've plenty in the tank to take us back. I'm not going to delay any longer."

He spun over the fly wheel as he spoke and the motor boat began to cut rapidly through the water headed for Sandy Bay. As soon as it had gone a safe distance the three stranded young adventurers joined hands and executed a wild war dance of joy. By a means almost miraculous they had fallen across the very thing they needed.

"It's just like the story books!" cried Mary Eliska, delightedly.

They raced down toward the coveted can, which was half full of the precious fuel. Enough to get them ashore at any rate. Before returning to the stranded airplane they examined the hut, but found nothing in it but a few broken-down bits of furniture.

"Queer," commented Jeff, "I half expected to find something."

"Not likely," laughed Bill, "they're too foxy for that."

"What do you suppose they came to the island for?" asked Mary Eliska.

"To get a quiet place to talk where they would not be observed by anyone who knew them, I guess," rejoined her brother. "Oh, if only we could solve the mystery. It's tantalizing to be so close to it and yet with so many tangled ends left raveled."

"Be patient," advised Mary Eliska, "it will all come out in time. And now I'm as famished for lunch as the Golden Butterfly is, so let's fill up the tank and then head for home."

"Second the motion," laughed Jeff Stokes.

Half an hour later the Golden Butterfly once more rose, and without incident or mishap winged her way back to Rocky Point.

CHAPTER 13.13.
JUKES DADE APPEARS.

The aviation field at Acatonick a few days before the big contests for juvenile aviators was alive with action and color. The spot selected was a flat, smooth field of some fifty acres on the outskirts of the town.

The grass spread a green carpet, thickly sprinkled with wild flowers, while at one side of the place was a row of green-painted sheds known as the "hangars."

"Hangar is French for shed," Mary Eliska had explained to a group of friends from Sandy Bay whom she was showing over the grounds, "and I think that *shed* is a whole lot better word than 'Ongar,' which is the way you are supposed to pronounce it."

One of the sheds—as in deference to Mary Eliska we shall call them—was of a different color, and stood somewhat apart from the rest. It was also much larger and bore in consequential-looking letters over its door the words:

"Thatcher Allen Airplane Company. Keep Out."

And to see that this notice was enforced to the letter, Weenie Allen had installed a red-nosed watchman with a formidable club at the portal. Considerable secrecy, in fact, had been observed concerning his airplane. Several large boxes had arrived one night and been hustled as quickly as possible into the shed.

The shed assigned to Bill Stricklin, happened, by an odd coincidence, to be immediately next door to the Thatcher Allen shed. The second day of their stay at Acatonick, Bill, on coming down to the field from the hotel at which he and Mary Eliska and Aunt Sally were stopping, was much surprised to be greeted by Weenie Allen, with some effusiveness.

After a lot of preliminary hemming and hawing, Weenie Allen broached to Bill once more the proposition of selling the Golden Butterfly.

"But I thought you had a fine type of airplane of your own," said Bill, wondering at this renewal of Weenie Allen's offer.

"So I have," was the rejoinder, "but now that I have established my business on a paying business basis I can handle another type. You know mine is a biplane model."

Bill nodded. He had no liking for Weenie Allen, but the other was so effusive that he felt it was incumbent on him to meet the other lad half way, as the saying is.

"I'd like to have a look at your craft sometime," he said.

"Not much you won't," rejoined Weenie Allen, quickly, "you'll see her on the day she wins the big prize and not before."

"You seem to have it won already," rejoined Bill, rather contemptuously.

"Oh, yes," was the confident reply, "I'm going to simply fly rings around you and the rest, so you'd better take up my offer now, for after the race your Golden Butterfly stock won't be worth a penny."

"I'm not so certain about that," was the answer.

"Then you won't take up my offer. I'll raise it another two hundred."

Bill smiled and shook his head. Something in his refusal angered the other lad.

"Well as you wish," he said, strolling off, "but dad has been pretty lenient with you up to date. As you won't meet us half way, though I'm going to advise him to force you to sell the Golden Butterfly."

"How?" "By foreclosing that mortgage without further delay."

Weenie Allen whipped the words out with a vicious intonation. All his mean nature surged up into his face as he spoke. Bill breathed a little quicker. But outwardly he was calm and cold as ice.

"That's your privilege," he said shortly, turning away, but that night he and Mary Eliska had a troubled discussion about ways and means, and it became more than ever evident to them how much depended on winning the five thousand dollar prize.

There were several aspirants in the juvenile class on the grounds as well as fliers of more mature years, for Mr. Higgins had interested some other capitalists, and it had been decided to make quite an event out of the aerial meet.

On the day before the race, which meant so much to them, Mary Eliska and Bill decided to take a practice spin across country in their 'plane. The capable looking machine excited much favorable comment when it was wheeled out of its shed. Several of the other competitors gathered about it while the engine was being tuned up. Among them was a surly looking chap with a dark, roughly-shaven chin and a pair of shifty eyes. He stood beside Weenie Allen, who was also in the crowd about the Golden Butterfly.

The Sandy Bay boy gazed on with a sneering look while our two young aviators got everything in readiness. This took some time for everybody was anxious to take a hand in the work, and it was quite a task to kindly, but steadfastly, reject these offers, well meant as they were.

At last everything appeared to be in good shape and with a buzz and a whirr the engine was tried out. It worked perfectly, and before the crowd had had time to cheer, the airplane shot up from the ground in front of its shed with hardly any preliminary run. Then came a belated cheer.

"That's the craft that wins the big prize," said a stout, good-natured looking man.

"Don't you be so certain," snapped out Weenie Allen, who stood close by, and to whom the words were gall.

"Why, what's the matter with you, my young friend," asked the jovial man; "you must be meaning to get it yourself."

"That's right," was the confident reply.

"Well, don't count your aerial chicks before they're hatched," was the merry rejoinder. A laugh at Weenie Allen's expense went up from the crowd. The boy flushed angrily and strode off in the direction of his hangar.

"Confound that young Jackanapes of a Bill Stricklin," he muttered, as he went; "he gets ahead of me every time. But I'll fix him. Pop needs that land, and if Bill wins this race the Stricklins can pay off that mortgage and be on the road to riches. Well, I guess I'll settle all that. But I'll have to act quickly."

"You seem to be sore on that Stricklin boy," came a voice at his shoulder suddenly.

Weenie Allen turned quickly to find himself confronted by the unprepossessing individual who had stood at his side during the start of the Golden Butterfly, which was by this time almost out of sight in the eastward.

"Why, what do you know about it?" he asked, sharply.

"Well," was the rejoinder, "being an observing sort of an individual I figured out that you were not best pleased at seeing what a fine airplane that kid has. Right, ain't I?"

He coolly took from his pocket a disgusting-looking cigar stump and proceeded to light it, leering impudently into Weenie Allen's face the while.

"Well, maybe you are and then again you may not be," was the Sandy Bay youngster's cautious reply; "but how does it interest you?"

"Because I haven't any more use for him than you have, and if you make it worth my while I'll give you a bit of information that will be of value to you."

"What do you mean?" inquired Weenie Allen, beginning to listen with more attention than he had hitherto shown.

"Just this, that I'm Jukes Dade, who used to work for Mr. Stricklin years ago, but he discharged me for—for—well for a little fault of drinking I had. Come now, don't you recognize me?"

"By George, I do," exclaimed Weenie Allen; "but it was so many years ago you were with Mr. Stricklin that I hardly knew you. You have changed greatly."

"I may have," was the reply in bitter tones. "I've been through enough. But there's one thing I ain't never forgotten in all these years, and that is my resolve to get even on old man Stricklin."

"But he is dead," put in Weenie Allen, wondering at the baleful expression of hatred that had come into the man's face.

"All true enough. I heard that some time ago. But if I can injure the son in any way, I'd like to do it. I've got a wrong to avenge, and if you want to pay well to have Bill Stricklin put out of the race tomorrow I'm your man." "Hush, don't talk so loudly. Some folks over there are looking at us."

"Oh, well, if you're afraid to—" "No, no, that isn't it. I must prevent Bill winning that race tomorrow at all hazards. Come into my hangar and we can talk quietly."

"Ah, that's the talk," was the rejoinder, and Jukes Dade chuckled with grim delight. "You want a little job of work done to settle our friend's hash. Well, you've come to the right shop when you meet up with old Jukes Dade who has an axe of his own to grind."

CHAPTER 13.14.
A GIRL AVIATOR'S ADVENTURE.

In the meantime, Mary Eliska and Bill, the former at the steering wheel and controls, were skimming through the air above the charming country surrounding Acatonick. The exhilaration of flying, the thrill and zest of it, were strong upon them as they glided along, and they made an extended flight.

"She is working like a three-hundred-dollar watch," cried Bill joyously as the speedy monoplane flew onward.

"She's a darling," was Mary Eliska's enthusiastic response. "I'm sure that if nothing happens you'll win that race tomorrow, Bill."

"I hope so, little sister," was the response, "for there's a whole lot depending on it."

"But just think. If you only do we shall be at the end of our troubles."

"Not quite, sis," Bill reminded her, "that affair of the missing jewels is still a mystery, and as long as it stays so some folks will always be suspicious of me."

"Oh, Bill, don't say such things. Nobody but the horridest of the horrid would—"

"Unluckily," struck in the boy, "there are a lot of the horridest of the horrid in this world, and some of them are in Sandy Bay."

He laughed and then went on more seriously:

"It's a pretty nasty feeling, I can tell you, to know that you are unjustly suspected by several folks of—of—er—knowing more about an affair of that kind than you tell."

"What can have become of the jewels?"

"Ah, that's just it. Of course we have our suspicion, based really on nothing, that Weenie Allen knows something about them. But if he did why would he place that wallet on the porch of Jax Gray's home?"

"It's beyond me."

"And beyond me, too. I'm quite sure that nobody was about the place when the accident happened, and I could not have been unconscious more than a few seconds. Now who could have stolen the wallet in that time?"

"It will all come out in time. I'm sure of it, Bill, dear," said Mary Eliska, earnestly. "Perhaps it will turn out to be not such a mystery after all."

"I don't know," was Bill's rejoinder. "Deanna Hoffinger has had some of the cleverest detectives in the country on the case, and a description of the jewels, some of which were heirlooms, has been wired everywhere broadcast. But up to date none of them have turned up at any pawnshops or other likely places."

For some moments more they talked in this strain, when Mary Eliska suddenly gave a cry and pointed below. They were passing over a tiny lake surrounded by steeply sloping banks, wooded with beautiful trees. It was an isolated spot, no human habitation being near at hand apparently.

"Oh, isn't that pretty?" cried Mary Eliska delightedly. "It looks as if it might have come out of a picture book."

"And the sight of that water reminds me that I'm terribly thirsty," said Bill. "I bet there are some springs by that lake, or if there are not maybe the water is good to drink from the lake itself."

"Let's go down and see," said Mary Eliska, with a bright smile, and setting over a lever and twisting a couple of valves she began to depress the airplane.

"There's a good landing place off there to the right of the end of the lake," cried Bill, indicating a bare spot where some land seemed to have been cleared at one time.

"All right, my brilliant brother," laughed Mary Eliska merrily. "I saw it at least five minutes ago. Hold tight, I'm going to drop fast."

To anyone less accustomed to aerial navigation than our two young friends, the downward plunge would have been alarming in its velocity. But to them it was merely exciting. Within a few feet of the ground, just when it seemed they must dash against the surface of the earth with crushing force, Mary Eliska set the planes on a rising angle and the Golden Eagle settled to earth as gracefully as a tired bird.

"Well, here we are," exclaimed Bill, looking about him at the sylvan scene as they alighted; "and now what comes next?"

"A hunt for the spring, of course," cried Mary Eliska, placing one hand on her brother's shoulder and nimbly leaping from the chassis to the soft, springy ground. And off they set toward the margin of the little lake below them.

"Reminds me of Ponce de Leon's hunt for a spring," laughed Bill, who felt in high spirits over the fine way the Golden Butterfly had conducted herself.

"But he was looking for the Fountain of Eternal Youth," said Mary Eliska, quickly.

"Wonder if he'd have been any happier if he'd found it," murmured Bill, philosophically.

"If he'd been a woman he would," said Mary Eliska.

"Would what? Have found it?"

"No, you goose, but have been perfectly happy if he had attained perpetual youth. Why, I think—Why, whatever was that?"

The girl broke off short in her laughing remarks and an expression of startled astonishment crept over her features.

"Why, it's someone groaning," cried Bill, after a brief period of listening.

"Yes. Someone in pain, too. It's off this way. Come on, Bill, let us find out what is the matter."

Without a thought of personal danger, but with all her warm girlish sympathy aroused, plucky Mary Eliska plunged off on to a path, from a spot along which it appeared the injured person must be groaning. But Bill caught her arm and pulled her back while he stepped in front of her.

"Let me go first, sis," he said; "we don't know what may be the matter."

Mary Eliska dutifully tiptoed along behind, as with hearts that beat somewhat faster than usual they made their way down the narrow path which led them into the deep gloom of the deeper woods. All at once Bill halted. They had arrived on the edge of a little clearing in the midst of which stood a tiny and roughly built hut with a big stone chimney at one end. Although the place was primitive it was scrupulously neat.

Painted white with green shutters, with a bright flower garden in front, it was a veritable picture of rural thrift.

The boy hesitated for an instant as they stood on the opposite edge of the cleared ground. There was no question but that they had reached the place whence the groans had proceeded. As they stood there the grim sounds began once more, after being hushed for an instant. Now, however, they took coherent form.

"Oh, help me! Help me!"

Bill was undetermined no longer. Directing Mary Eliska to remain outside 'til he summoned her, he walked rapidly, and with a firm step, up the path leading to the hut, and entered. It was so dark inside that at first he could see nothing. But pretty soon he spied a huddled form in one corner.

"Oh, don't hurt me! I'm only a harmless old man! I have no money," cried the cringing figure, as Bill entered.

"I don't want to hurt you," said the boy kindly; "I want to help you."

He now saw that the form in the corner was that of an old man with a silvery beard and long white hair. From a gash on his forehead blood was flowing, and the wound seemed to have been recently inflicted.

"What is the matter? What has happened?" asked Bill, gently, as he raised the old man to a chair into which he fell limply.

"Water! water!" he cried, feebly.

Bill hastened outside saying to himself as he went:

"This is a case for Mary Eliska."

Summoning her he hastily related what had occurred and the warm-hearted girl, with many exclamations of pity, hastened to the wounded man's side.

"Get me some water quick, Bill," she exclaimed, tearing a long strip from her linen petticoat to serve as a bandage. Outside the hut, Bill soon found a spring, back of a rickety stable in which the old man had a horse and a ramshackle buggy.

When he returned with the water the poor old fellow took a long draught from a cup Mary Eliska held to his lips and the girl then deftly washed and bandaged his wound. This done the venerable old man seemed to rally, and sitting up in his chair thanked his young friends warmly. Bill, in the meantime, had been looking about the hut and saw that it was furnished in plain, but tidy style. Over the great open fireplace, at one end, hung a big picture. Evidently the canvas was many years old. It was the portrait of a fine, self-reliant looking young man in early manhood. His blue eyes gazed confidently out from the picture and a smile of seeming satisfaction quivered about his lips.

"I'll bet that's a fellow who has got on in the world," thought Bill to himself as he scanned the capable, strong features.

"Ah," said the old man, observing the lad's interest in the painting, "that picture is a relic of old, old days. It is a portrait of my brother James. He—But I must tell you how I came to be in the sad condition in which you found me. Have you a comfortable chair, miss? Yes, very well, then I will tell you what happened this afternoon in this hut, and will then relate to you something of my own story for I was not always a hermit and an outcast."

CHAPTER 13.15.
THE HERMIT OF THE WOODS.

"My name is Peter Bell," began the old man, "and many years ago I was like any other happy, care-free young man, who is the son of well-to-do parents. I had a brother named James Bell, who was much younger than me. We were very fond of each other and inseparable.

"Our home was on the Long Island coast and we often went boating. One day when we were out in my boat a storm came up and she capsized. I tried to save my brother who was a poor swimmer. But in the midst of my efforts the bulwark of the wave-tossed boat struck my head and rendered me insensible. It seems, however, I must have clung to the boat, for when I came to myself I had almost been blown ashore, and, striking out, I soon reached it.

"But to my horror I soon saw that people shunned me. In some way the story got about that I had saved myself at the expense of my brother's life. Such stories are always readily credited among the majority of people in a small town and the tale spread like wildfire with exaggerations. Driven half wild by the general contempt which I met on every side I left home one night, and having a sum of money in my own right I decided to live the life of a recluse.

"I recollected this spot to which I had come on hunting expeditions in brighter days. Not long after, grief over my brother's death resulted in my mother's life coming to a close, and shortly afterward my father's demise occurred.

"They left but little, but I managed to secure that portrait of my brother you see hanging up there and a few bits of favorite furniture associated with happier times.

"I have lived here ever since and have become reconciled to my fate. From time to time I used to advertise for news of my brother, offering rewards, but long ago I stopped that, and have no doubt that he perished in the storm, although for a time I comforted myself by thinking that he might, by some strange chance, have been saved.

"In some way a rumor has spread through the countryside that I have much wealth hidden here, and this afternoon four masked men entered the hut and when I protested, in reply to their demands, that I had no money, they struck me down and searched the house. Then cursing me for a fraud and an impostor because they found no gold they left, leaving me to my fate."

"You have no idea who the men were?" asked Bill who, like Mary Eliska, had listened with close attention to the old man's story.

"Yes, I think they were young men of bad reputation from a neighboring village; however, I am not sure. I am certain that I recollected hearing the voice of one of them when I was in the market in that village some time ago."

"Oh, then, you do go into town sometimes?" asked Bill.

"Oh, yes," rejoined the hermit, "but no more than I can help. I have long since departed from the ways of the world and the habitations of men. But I gather herbs in the woods for miles about and sell them to folks in the villages."

"I suppose that is why you have the horse and cart?" put in Mary Eliska, who had been gazing out of the window and had noticed the tumbledown barn.

"Yes," rejoined the old man. "I am not as active as I was once and my old bones will not carry me as far as they used to. So I drive old Dobbin when I have a journey of any length to make."

The hermit would not hear of any help being summoned for him. He said that he was in no danger of a second attack, as the search of his little property had been thorough and had resulted in the rascals, who had invaded his haunts, getting nothing for their pains. Refusing some refreshment the old man offered, the young aviators soon after left the hut, promising to call in again in a few days and give the hermit an opportunity to see the airplane in which he was much interested. The old man asked them many questions about the races of the next day and seemed interested in hearing the details.

The Golden Butterfly they found just as they had left her, and clambering on board they were soon winging their way back to Acatonick where, as you may imagine, they had an interesting story of the incidents of the afternoon to relate to Aunt Sally that evening.

"I never saw such children for adventures in all my born days," she declared, "but I have a letter here which I must show you. I am afraid it means that we shall have to leave the old home."

She drew an envelope from her handbag which lay on a table of the hotel room and handed it to Bill. On opening it, he found that it contained a formal notice from the Sandy

Bay Bank, that unless the accumulated interest and other moneys owing them were paid up within a week that foreclosure proceedings would be taken. The boy gave a disconsolate whistle as he finished reading the letter aloud and handed it back.

He had hardly done so when there came a rap on the door of the room. "I wonder who that can be so late?" thought Bill, getting up and going to the door.

A bellboy stood there with a note.

"A messenger just brought this from the aviation grounds," he said. "Any answer?"

"Wait a minute," said Bill, skimming hastily through the note. It was typewritten and signed:—James Jarvis, Superintendent of Arrangements.

"Dear sir: You are requested to report at the executive tent at once. An important meeting will take place affecting the competitors in the races tomorrow."

This was what Bill read. Then he turned to the bellboy and told the lad to inform the messenger that he would be there as soon as possible.

"Queer though," he said to Mary Eliska and his aunt. "I didn't know of any meeting that was scheduled to take place tonight. I guess it's one that's been called at the eleventh hour to make some arrangements."

"That must be it," agreed Mary Eliska. "Shall I come with you?"

"No, thanks, sis," rejoined the boy; "you'd better get to bed. It's going to be an exciting day tomorrow for us all."

The boy snatched up his cap and with a hasty good-bye, was off.

Downstairs in the lobby of the hotel he found the messenger awaiting him,—a shifty-eyed man with a blue chin. It was, in fact, Jukes Dade, who, in a different suit of clothes and with a clean shave and haircut, looked a trifle more presentable than he had earlier in the day when he made himself known to Weenie Allen.

"This way, sir," he said, with a fawning sort of bow.

"Out of this door is the quickest," said Bill quickly, with a feeling that he would rather walk to the grounds alone than with such a companion.

"But we're not going to walk, sir. The committee has sent an auto for you."

"A car, eh?" said Bill; "well, that's considerate of them. I'll tell my sister. She might like to come along, too."

The messenger shook his head.

"Sorry, sir; but we've got to pick up some other aviators on our way and every bit of room in the car will be taken."

"Oh, very well, then," said Bill, "lead on."

The blue-chinned Dade shuffled across the lobby with a furtive air.

"Funny," thought Bill. "I've seen that chap some place before, but to save my life I can't place him."

Cudgeling his brains to try to recall where he had met the man, Bill passed through the hotel lobby and out into the street. In the lamplight he saw a big car standing at the curb, shaking as its ungeared engine puffed and chugged. A chauffeur, with an auto mask and goggles on, sat on the front seat. Bill got in behind in the tonneau while the messenger took his seat by the chauffeur.

He said something in a low whisper to the driver and the next instant there was a grinding whirr as the gears were connected and the car rolled forward.

"Well, they've got a good fast car here," thought Bill, as the machine sped along over the roads. "At this rate we ought to be at the grounds in—"

But what was this? Surely the road they were on was not the right one. Leaning forward he touched the chauffeur on the shoulder.

"This isn't the road to the grounds," he said.

"Oh, yes it is," put in the messenger; "it's a short cut, though. Isn't it, Fred?"

The chauffeur did not speak but merely nodded his head.

Although by no means satisfied with the explanation, Bill made no immediate comment. In the meantime they had passed the outskirts of the little town and were now whizzing along an unlighted road bordered with big trees. On and on they went, and Bill, every minute, grew more uneasy. Where could they be taking him?

"Where are you going?" he demanded suddenly, his suspicion showing in his tone as he rose in the tonneau and leaned forward. "I want you to know that—"

But before he could utter another word the blue-chinned messenger did an astonishing thing. With a quick, imperceptible movement he produced a revolver and thrust its gleaming barrel up under Bill's nose.

"Sit back and keep quiet," he warned, "and you'll be all right. If you make a holler you'll get what's in this barker."

As he spoke the auto began to slow down, and presently a dark form stepped from the shadows of the trees ahead and stood awaiting its coming.

CHAPTER 13.16.
THE ENEMY'S MOVE.

Bill's first feeling was one of indignation at the fellow's impudence.

"What do you mean by such conduct," he blurted out angrily. "Take me to the aviation grounds at once, or—"

"That's just where we are taking you away from, young fellow," sneered the man behind the pistol. "Ah! Don't move. I'm very nervous and if I get excited this pistol might go off. It's very light on the trigger."

As he spoke the auto slowed down almost to a standstill, and the man who had evidently been waiting for it, swung himself on the running board and joined the others on the front seat. Like the driver, he wore a motoring mask and goggles which effectively concealed his features, and yet to Bill there was something familiar even about the muffled-up figure. Once the third man was aboard, the auto plunged forward once more at breakneck speed. It rocked from side to side on the rough road as it flew along. But the man with the pistol kept his weapon levelled at Bill throughout all its jouncings and joltings.

Like a wise boy, Bill had concluded that it would be worse than foolish to attempt any resistance to his abductors. So he sat motionless and silent as the car tore onward through the night. He had not the least idea where they were, nor for what place they could be bound. Nor had he yet had time to think over the reason for this bold kidnapping.

Now, however, it was plain that the object of the trip was to take him to some place and hold him prisoner 'til the aero race was over. It struck him with cruel force that, unless he could manage to escape, the object of the expedition seemed very likely to prove successful.

All at once the car struck a bump in the road with a violent wrenching thud. It leaped into the air like a live thing while a frightened shout burst from the throats of the men on the front seat. Mechanically Bill gripped the sides of the tonneau to avoid being thrown out like a missile.

The next instant, with a rasping grind and a sickening swaying and jouncing the car tore full tilt down the side of the road, which, at this point, was banked, and fetched up motionless and hub-deep in a pool of dark water.

"Don't let the kid escape," came a shout from the man who had boarded the car on the roadside, as the auto ceased to move.

But before the words had left his lips Bill had perceived that the water in the pond was not much more than knee high. Quick as a cat he was out of the tonneau before any of the others had time to collect their wits. As the man shouted his warning the lad struck out through the oozy ground, seeking, with every ounce of his strength, to shroud himself in the darkness at the pond edge before the pistol wielder could locate him.

But he had not gone more than a few steps when—

Bang!

A red flash cut the night behind him and a bullet whistled by his ear.

"Look out, you fool, you don't want to kill him," came a voice behind him.

"Gid Gibbons," flashed through Bill's mind. He was almost at a thick clump of alders now. As he heard the splashing of the bodies of the abductors, as they took to the water after him, he plunged into the coppice and pushed rapidly on into its intricacies.

Shouts and cries came from behind him, and suddenly a blinding shaft of white radiance cut through the blackness. They had turned on the searchlight of the car in a determined effort to locate their escaped prisoner.

As the light penetrated among the maze of alder trunks, Bill threw himself flat. While his pursuers hunted about, muttering and angrily discussing the situation, he crouched in his shelter, hardly daring to breathe. After what seemed an eternity of suspense he heard one of the men, whose voice he seemed to recognize as that of the pistol carrier, angrily declaiming.

"Aw, what's ther use, ther kid is a mile off by this time, worse luck."

"Hush, don't talk so loud," came another voice. "You don't know who may be about."

"Well, we'd better be getting that car out of the mud and making ourselves scarce," came in the tones which Bill was certain were those of Gid Gibbons. "If there's a hue and cry raised about this and they find that car stranded here they can easy trace us."

"That's so," was the response in the voice of Jukes Dade. "Come on, boys, we'll get her out of this confounded slough if we can, and get back to town."

The voices died away as they retreated, splashing like water animals through the mud and ooze.

As silence fell once more Bill straightened up from his unpleasant situation and looked about him. The night was starry, and above his head he could see The Dipper. He knew that the outside stars of this constellation pointed to the North Star and he soon had the latter located. This gave him the points of the compass, and figuring that Acatonick must lie to the east of his present position, he struck out in that direction as nearly as he could.

He had no idea of the time, to his great chagrin, for in his haste to obey the forged summons to the flying track he had forgotten to bring his watch. In fact, in his hurry, he had slipped into an old coat, the pockets of which contained nothing more useful to him than a packet of chewing gum. He slipped a wad of this into his mouth to "keep him company" as he expressed it to himself, and grittily went forward.

The wood ended presently, and he found himself in a field with woods on all three sides, except that on which the swamp impinged. Little as he liked the idea of plunging into pathless woods, with nothing to guide him but the stars, as he glimpsed them through the trees, there was no help for it. Go on he must. Crossing the field rapidly he soon reached the border of the tangle and entered its black shadows. Keeping as straight a line as he could he hastened forward, and to his great delight, soon saw that the trees were beginning to thin out, and that beyond lay, apparently, open country.

"Hooray, I'm bound to strike a road before long now," thought Bill gleefully and quickened his pace.

He had not gone more than a few paces, however, when through the trees he heard a strange sound. It was a clinking sound like the rattling of a chain.

The boy was bold enough, but the mysterious sound on the edge of that dark wood caused his pulses to beat a bit quicker. What could it be?

Gradually, as he stood still among the trees, the sound drew closer.

"Ghosts in story books always clank chains," thought Bill, to himself. "Now if I believed in such things, I—"

He stopped short abruptly, as, from behind a clump of brush in the direction from whence the clanking had proceeded, there suddenly emerged a tall form all in white.

"Good gracious!" cried Bill, considerably startled by the sight of this sudden apparition. "I do believe—"

But at the sight of the white form he had involuntarily given a backward step. Without the slightest warning he felt the ground suddenly give way under his feet, and his body shot down through space.

Down, down he shot, a hundred mad thoughts twisting dizzily in his head.

All at once his progress was arrested. Before he could realize what had happened he felt a flood of icy cold water close over his head and a mighty ringing and roaring in his ears.

But Bill was used to diving, and he automatically, almost, held his breath 'til he shot to the surface again. Then he extended his hands and found that his fingers encountered a rough stone wall of some kind.

"I'm in an old well," gasped the boy as the truth suddenly flashed across him. He looked upward. Far above him, as if seen through a telescope, he could see the glittering stars. They were reflected, also, in the agitated water about him.

Somewhat to his astonishment, for the thought of death itself had been in his mind as he hurtled downward, Bill found that he was unhurt. But his present position was by no means one to invite congratulations. At the bottom of an old well in the midst of lonely fields he might stay a long time before rescue would arrive.

And in the meantime,—but Bill bravely put such thoughts resolutely out of his head, and began to feel about him to see if it was not possible to find some rough places in the sides of the excavation by which he might clamber to the surface. But his fingers only encountered stonework set far too smoothly to be of any service to him.

Then he suddenly noticed what he had not observed before, and that was that a rope depended from above, trailing its end down into the water. It was too thin to bear his weight, but the boy thought he could utilize it to keep himself above the surface without effort.

Tying a loop knot in it he thrust an arm through the noose and found that he could sustain himself very comfortably. Then he began to shout. Loudly at first—and then more feebly as his voice grew tired. But no answering sound came back to him.

For the first time since he had found himself in his predicament cold fear clutched at the young aviator's heart.

What if nobody heard him and he was compelled to remain at the bottom of the old well?

As this thought shot through his mind Bill noticed, too, that a deadly chill was beginning to creep up his limbs. He shivered waist deep in the chilly water as if he had an ague.

CHAPTER 13.17.
A COWARD AND HIS WAYS.

Mary Eliska awoke the next day with a feeling of distinct uneasiness. She and her aunt had sat up 'til after midnight awaiting Bill's return, but, as we know, the lad was in a position from which he could not extricate himself. An attempt had been made to communicate with the aviation grounds, but an unlucky airplane had blundered against the telephone wire during an afternoon flight, snapping the thread of communication.

In spite of the late hour at which they had retired, however, Aunt Sally and her niece were up betimes. But early as it was they found the little town all astir. Excursion trains were already pouring their crowds into the place and the streets were fairly alive with humanity.

Mary Eliska's first act on awaking was to gaze out of the window, beneath which some fine trees grew. Not a breath of wind stirred their leaves. The air was as clear and undisturbed as it was possible for it to be.

Donning a white duck skirt and a plain shirt waist, and dressing her hair in a becomingly simple style, Mary Eliska hastened to the office of the hotel, and going to the telephone switchboard asked the operator to put her in communication with Bill's room. But after several minutes spent in a vain attempt to obtain an answer Central had to inform the anxious girl that there was no reply.

Thinking that after his late absence of the night before Bill might have overslept, Mary Eliska despatched a bellboy to his room. But the report came back that the room was empty and that Bill's bed had not been slept in.

"See if you can get the executive office on the aviation grounds," said Mary Eliska to the 'phone girl. But although the wire had been repaired and communication was easily established, there was no news of Bill. Worse still for Mary Eliska's peace of mind, she learned now, for the first time, that there had been no meeting at the aviation field the night before.

"If your brother got a note to that effect it was a forgery," said the official who answered the call.

Mary Eliska fairly flew upstairs to her aunt's room. Rapidly she informed Aunt Sally of what had happened.

"Oh, I'm certain now that that hateful Weenie Allen has something to do with it," she almost sobbed.

"Hush, dear," said her aunt, although in the gentle lady's breast a great fear had arisen, "everything may be all right. At any rate, I do not believe that anyone, no matter how anxious they were that you should not compete in the race, would dare to resort to such methods to keep Bill out of the contest."

"I don't know so much about that, auntie," rejoined the girl. "I was in our hangar yesterday afternoon and I noticed a horrid looking man prowling about with Weenie Allen. If it had not been too improbable I should say that I knew the man's face."

"My dear!" exclaimed the good lady in astonishment.

"Well," rejoined Mary Eliska with conviction, "I'm almost sure that the man was Jukes Dade, a workman who once was employed in his laboratory and workshop by my father. He was a skillful mechanic, but dad had to discharge him because he drank fearfully. He swore at the time that he would get even with us in some way. But we never heard any more of him. Yet if that really was him with Weenie Allen yesterday I'm awfully afraid that there is some mischief stirring."

"What you say, my dear, makes me also very anxious," responded Aunt Sally. "Perhaps we had better communicate with the police at once."

"Not yet, aunt," breathed Mary Eliska; "you see, Bill may turn up in time for the race, and if he does, everything will be all right."

"But, Mary Eliska—"

"On the other hand, if we spread an alarm that he is missing we shall be declared out of the contest."

"I see what you mean, my dear," was the response, "and I suppose that what you say is best. I feel positive, somehow, that we shall have news of Bill before long, and that no harm has come to him."

But the morning wore on, and no word came. In the meantime, every available source of information had been canvassed thoroughly without result. Bill Stricklin had totally vanished; or so it seemed.

Mary Eliska, as in duty bound, spent all she could spare of the morning at the aviation field, putting the finishing touches on the Golden Butterfly. The big contest was not to be held 'til the afternoon, and in the meantime, some of the smaller events were flown off. But Mary Eliska was too heartsick to watch the airplanes thunder around the course, which was marked out by red and white "pylons" or signal towers.

Instead, she remained in the hangar and kept a watchful eye on Weenie Allen, who, with some mechanics and the same man she had noticed about the hangar the day before, was very busy over his machine, apparently. But no one obtained even a glimpse of Weenie Allen's air craft, for it was not wheeled out, and, except when one or the other of his party dodged in or out, the doors of his hangar were closed.

In the course of the morning Weenie Allen's father arrived, and not long after, to Mary Eliska's unbounded delight, Jax Gray and Liam McAdams and a party of friends drove up to the Stricklin hangar.

"Why, Mary Eliska, what is the matter with you? You look positively—er—er—dowdy!" exclaimed Jax Gray, gazing at her friend after first greetings were over.

"And Bill, where is Bill?" demanded Liam McAdams.

"Yes, where is he? We want him to explain the points of this gasoline turkey-buzzard to us," cried Ed. Taylor, one of the gay party.

"I expect him here any minute," rejoined Mary Eliska, and then drawing Jax Gray and Liam McAdams aside she related to them, in a voice that shook in spite of herself, the mysterious occurrences of the night, and Bill's total disappearance.

"I'm going right over now and ask Weenie Allen if he knows anything about it," announced Liam McAdams indignantly as soon as the girl had concluded.

"Oh, don't, please don't," begged his sister.

"I don't think it would be wise to, now," put in Mary Eliska.

But Liam McAdams was not to be shaken in his purpose. Weenie Allen was outside his hangar smoking a cigarette and swaggering about when Liam McAdams approached him. Perhaps the self-assertive youth felt a bit alarmed at the look in Liam McAdams's eye as he stepped up, but he assumed an impudent expression and blew out a puff of smoke which he did not try to avert from Liam McAdams's face.

"Good morning, Weenie Allen," said Liam McAdams, bottling up his temper at the other's insulting manners, "can you give me a few minutes of private conversation?"

"Hum, well I don't know. What's it about?" inquired Thatcher Allen more impudently than ever.

"It's about Bill, Weenie Allen," said Liam McAdams seriously. "I want you to tell me on your word of honor that you don't know where he is."

"Oh, you do, eh? Well, you have an awful nerve to come to me with such questions. How do I know where he is?"

This question was somewhat of a poser for Liam McAdams. That impetuous youth had approached the other more or less on an impulse, and now that the direct question was put to him he felt that he could not, for the life of him, put his suspicions into so many words.

"Well—er—you see," he said somewhat confusedly, "I had an idea that you might have seen him."

"Well, I haven't, and what's more I don't want to," snapped Weenie Allen aggressively. He was quite cool now that he saw that Liam McAdams had nothing definite against him in his mind, but only a vague suspicion.

"You really mean that, Weenie Allen?" rejoined Liam McAdams earnestly. "His sister is terribly worried. He hasn't been seen since last night."

"Is that so?" asked Weenie Allen with a sudden accession of interest; "then he can't race today, can he?"

"I wasn't thinking about the race," said Liam McAdams; "it was Bill himself I was worrying about."

"Well, you may as well stop your anxiety," chuckled Weenie Allen; "how do you know he isn't off on a little spree, and—"

"That's enough, Weenie Allen. Bill Stricklin does not do such low-down things. He—"

"Oh, you mean to imply that I do, eh?"

Weenie Allen came forward pugnaciously.

"I'll tell you what it is, you just take yourself away from this hangar as quickly as possible. I don't want anything to do with you, do you understand? It's none of my business if Bill goes off and forgets to tell you where to find him. How do you know he hasn't gone off with those jewels?"

"What do you mean?"

Liam McAdams's tone was as angry in reality now as Weenie Allen's had been for effect a few seconds before.

But Weenie Allen, in his bitter enmity toward Bill, could not see the danger signals in Liam McAdams's honest gray eyes.

"What do I mean?" he drawled; "why, just this, that the investigation of the police has taken a new turn in the last few days, and that Bill is likely to be arrested within the next twenty-four hours for robbery. I'll bet he got wind of it and skipped out. I'll bet—"

"How dare you?"

Mary Eliska, eyes aflame, stepped up. Her bosom heaved angrily.

"How dare you say such things? You—you coward."

"Well, I ain't coward enough to steal a girl's jewels and then—"

"Hold on there, Weenie Allen. Stop right there."

It was Liam McAdams's turn. But Weenie Allen was too much worked up in his vindictive anger to stop.

"I won't stop," he shouted. "I'll say it right out. Bill Stricklin is a—"

But before he could utter another word Liam McAdams's fist had shot out, and Weenie Allen's chin happening to be in the way he felt himself suddenly propelled off his feet and elevated into the air. He sought to recover his balance as he reeled, but his foot caught in a bit of turf, and whirling his arms about like one of those figures on the top of a barn he measured his length.

"Had enough?" asked Liam McAdams mildly, rolling up his sleeves.

"No, you despicable young whelp!" roared Weenie Allen, utterly throwing aside all prudence. "I haven't."

He leaped to his feet and rushed toward Liam McAdams. As he did so Jax Gray gave a shriek. In the angry, half-crazed youth's hand there glistened a long clasp knife.

"Liam McAdams! Look out!" cried the girl.

But before the frenzied Weenie Allen could spring upon Liam McAdams, who was utterly unprepared for the production of the deadly weapon, a dainty foot in white canvas outing shoes and silk stockings flashed out from under Mary Eliska's skirt. It caught Weenie Allen as he sprang, and the next instant, for the second time that day, he fell sprawling on the ground.

CHAPTER 13.18.
THE DARING OF MARY ELISKA.

By the time he had risen to his feet several of the officials of the track were seen approaching, and Weenie Allen, with a scowl of deep disgust at our party, who paid little attention to him, shuffled off. At first Mary Eliska thought that the officials had seen something of the trouble and would be angry. But it turned out that they were only coming to announce a few minor changes in the rules governing the race, and to distribute printed copies of the same.

As they passed on one of them turned and remarked casually:

"By the way, as the wind is so light we have decided to have the big contest an hour earlier than was announced, and eliminate the girls' contest, so that everybody can get home from the grounds in good time for dinner."

He hastened on to join his companions on their journey down the line of hangars, outside of which airplanes were sputtering and smoking, and excited aviators and mechanics hustling about.

All at once a big biplane was wheeled out and soared into the air. It carried a blue and gold streamer.

"That's Steiner of the Agassiz High School in New York City," explained Liam McAdams; "he's confident of winning the big prize."

Mary Eliska made some reply. She didn't know just what. Her mind was throbbing with the idea that Bill's inexplicable absence meant that harm had come to him, and that even if he were safe the advancing of the hour of the race would put them out of it if he did not make haste.

"Look, there goes Banker of the Philadelphia Polytechnic, and Rayburn of the Boston Tech," cried Liam McAdams the next instant as a biplane and a graceful white-winged monoplane shot aloft on trial trips, their motors exploding loudly and a tail of blue smoke streaming out behind them. A slight cheer came from the grand stands, which were already beginning to fill, as the boy aviators shot upward.

"Oh, Bill! Bill, where are you?" sighed Mary Eliska to herself, as she watched the young aspirants for aerial honors swinging around the course.

"I'm going over to the stand and 'phone to the police station," said Liam McAdams presently; "they may have news of him over there by this time."

"Oh, yes, please do," cried Mary Eliska, as Liam McAdams hastened off.

When he had gone the two girls turned troubled countenances to each other.

"You poor honey," cried Jax Gray, "I know how you are suffering. But don't worry, Mary Eliska, I'm sure it will come out all right."

"Yes, but—but you don't know what depends on Bill's winning this race," cried Mary Eliska. "I am sure that some of our rivals in the race—I need not mention who—have something to do with his disappearance."

"What do you mean by saying 'a lot depends on it,' girlie?" asked Jax Gray, drawing Mary Eliska's arm within her own.

With brimming eyes Mary Eliska told her friend frankly and fully what she had not before, namely, the exact circumstances of the Stricklin family and the threat which old Thatcher Allen held above their heads.

"So, you see, Jax Gray," she concluded sadly, "this could not have happened at a worse time for us."

"I see that," gently rejoined the other girl, "but listen, dear, you may have a chance to win it after all if you will trust to us to find Bill."

"Trust to you?" repeated Mary Eliska in a puzzled tone. "Trust to you to find Bill?"

"Yes, my dear, while you—go in and win the race!"

"Why, what are you talking about?" gasped Mary Eliska.

"A brilliant idea that has just occurred to me. You are about Bill's height, and if your hair was cut short you'd look enough like him to be his twin brother instead of his sister. But that doesn't matter, for you wear goggles and a helmet in driving that thing, anyway, don't you?"

"Yes. But,—oh, Jax Gray, I couldn't do that."

"Not even for your aunt's sake, Mary Eliska, and to show those whom you suspect that they could not put a Stricklin out of the race, however hard they tried? Come into the shed with me. I am going to persuade you, if I can, to do a brave thing."

With their arms about each other's waists the girls walked toward the hangar and entered it. As they did so the figure of Jukes Dade glided from a place of concealment close at hand, and slipping behind some low bushes he gained the rear of the Stricklin shed unperceived. Once there he placed an ear to a crack in the structure, from within which could be heard the murmur of girlish voices.

Whatever he heard seemed to strike him with astonishment at first and then with a malicious glee.

"So," he muttered, "that's your scheme, is it? Well, I guess we'll be able to head that off. That airplane of yours won't go in that race if I can help it, and even if it did I know enough now to head you off from getting the big prize. That Weenie Allen ought to pay me well for this."

So saying, Jukes Dade shuffled off toward Weenie Allen's hangar, still chortling evilly to himself.

Liam McAdams returned to the shed without any good news. In fact, the doleful expression on his usually merry face would have told them that long before he opened his mouth. In the midst of the general gloom a merry face was suddenly obtruded through the swinging doors.

"Hullo! hullo! young folks, what's the trouble? You look as if you were going to attend a funeral."

They looked up to see the figure of Hal Homer, clad in white flannels, and with a checked cap on his curly head, standing in the doorway.

"Can I come in?" he asked, and without waiting for an answer in he came.

"Oh, Mr. Homer," cried Jax Gray, fairly pouncing on him, "we're so glad you've come; we are in a dreadful fix."

"A dreadful fix? Why, my dear young lady, I read in the local paper that I bought on my way from the depot that Bill's machine, judging from the trials, was going to have things all her own way."

"So much so," struck in Liam McAdams, "that it looks as if some of Bill's enemies have spirited him away."

"What? I'm afraid I hardly understand."

The aviation instructor looked at Liam McAdams in a puzzled way, rather as if he thought the youth might be having some fun with him.

"No, no, this is serious. I mean it," spoke Liam McAdams quickly. "Bill has gone!"

"Gone!"

"Yes. He vanished last night. But sit down and we'll tell you all about it. Maybe you can help us out."

Absolutely "flabbergasted," to use his own expression, the good-looking young flying man sank down on an upturned case, while Liam McAdams went on to relate all that had occurred, with Mary Eliska every now and then striking in with additions and corrections.

Another ear also took in the conversation—that of Jukes Dade—who had seen the arrival of the well-dressed young aviator, and had instantly slipped back to his eavesdropping post to learn what the newcomer's business might be.

It might have been an hour later that a chauffeur, summoned by 'phone from the grandstand, brought the Hoffingers' car up to the hangar and Hal Homer, Jax Gray and Liam McAdams emerged.

"Drive to the police station," ordered Hal Homer as he stepped in, leaving Jax Gray and Liam McAdams behind.

Jukes Dade, peering around a corner of the hangar, heard the order and grew pale.

"Looks bad," he muttered as the car rolled off; "I wonder if they know anything. If they do, I'm off. This isn't a healthy part of the country for Jukes Dade from the minute that kid is found. He didn't recognize Gid or Weenie Allen, but he knew me all right. I could tell it by the way he looked at me, and if he's found the first man they'll hunt for is me."

With snake-like caution he glided behind the hangar once more.

It was not long after this that the Golden Butterfly was wheeled out by some of the mechanicians attached to the track, whose services were furnished free by the aviation officials.

Jax Gray and Liam McAdams emerged from the hangar at the same time, in company with a boyish figure in aviator's clothing, leather trousers cut very baggily, fur-lined leather coat and big helmet of leather, well padded, completely obscuring the features. After a few words in a low tone with its companions, this figure clambered lightly into the airplane, leaned forward, adjusted some levers, and the next instant, amidst a shout from several hastily gathered onlookers, the Golden Butterfly skyrocketed upward, her engine roaring like an angry giant hornet. All this was watched by Weenie Allen, Jukes Dade, and Gid Gibbons.

"A nice mess you've made of it," growled Thatcher Allen angrily to his companions. "You've succeeded in getting me suspected, and in trouble, while the boy is safe and sound and on the scene."

"Wonder how he got back," grunted Gid speculatively; "he must have looked a sight when he crawled out of that swamp."

"Say, Dade, you'd better be off," said Weenie Allen suddenly; "you were the only one of us whose face wasn't covered. He would swear to you."

"Oh, I ain't worrying yet," grinned Dade easily.

"You're not, eh? Well, you are a cool hand," rejoined Gid admiringly. "If I were in your shoes I'd clear out before that airplane lands again."

"You would, eh?" scoffed Dade. "Well, what would you say if I told you that that ain't Bill Stricklin in the Golden Butterfly at all?"

"That you were crazy with the heat," was the prompt and impolite answer.

"Then you'd be crazy yourself. That's his sister in that airplane, and if he don't show up in time for the race she's going to fly it herself and win it."

If a bombshell had fallen at Weenie Allen's feet he could not have been more thunderstruck. But he recovered in an instant.

"If she does I'll protest to the judges," he said angrily; "they can't prove that I know anything about her brother's disappearance, and that Golden Butterfly won't win this race if I can help it."

CHAPTER 13.19.
BROTHER AND SISTER.

The first gleam of the summer dawn shining into Bill's place of imprisonment at the bottom of the old well revealed to him only too clearly into what a trap he had fallen. The well seemed to be about fifty feet or more in depth, and the sides were smooth and slippery.

The chill he had felt spreading through his limbs earlier was gone now, but a numb sensation was setting in which did not leave them even when the boy wriggled his legs about.

"Phew!" thought Bill. "I stand a fair chance of being turned into a pollywog or something if I stay here long enough."

Somehow, with the coming of daylight, the buoyant spirits of youth had returned to the boy and his predicament did not seem nearly so serious as it had during the dark hours.

But it was bad enough, as Bill realized. From time to time he tried shouting, but no one came to the edge of the well and peered over, although he anxiously kept his eyes riveted on the disc of sky above him. How long this went on Bill had no idea, but he had sunk into a sort of semi-doze when a sudden sound aroused him.

A tinkling, metallic sound, not unlike the rattling of the chain the night before that had, in reality, caused his trouble.

"Help! Help!" shouted Bill.

It was perhaps the five hundredth time he had uttered the cry since he had tumbled into the well. But this time there came a response.

"What is it? What's the trouble?"

The voice sounded rather shaky, and as if the utterer of the words was somewhat scared.

"It's a boy who has fallen into the well," shouted Bill. "I'm almost exhausted. Get me out."

A face suddenly projected over the well curb—a face which Bill recognized with astonishment as that of old Peter Bell, the hermit.

"Mr. Bell, it's Bill Stricklin," he shouted; "can you get a rope and get me out?"

"Good heavens!" cried the hermit; "it's the boy whose sister was so kind to me. However did you—but never mind that now. Can you hold on for a time?"

"Yes, but my strength is almost gone."

"Well, summon up all your courage. There is a farm house not far off. I'll go there and get a rope and be back as quick as I can."

Without wasting more words the old man hastened to his little cart. He had been out since dawn gathering herbs and roots and had taken a short cut home through the field in which the old well was located. Muttering excitedly to himself, he climbed somewhat stiffly into his rickety conveyance and urged his old horse forward with gently spoken commands.

As the animal broke into a trot the little bell about its neck began to jangle not unmusically. This was the sound which, fortunately for him, had notified Bill that some human being was at hand.

In the near distance, half hidden in trees, could be seen the red-roofed gable of a farm house. Toward this old Peter Bell directed his way. Farmer Ingalls was only too glad, when he heard of the accident, to secure a long rope, used in hoisting hay to the top of his big barns.

"Bless my soul!" he exclaimed, "a lad tumbled into my well! Mommer," turning to a motherly-looking, calico-clad woman, "you always told me to cover that well up, and I never did, and now thar's a poor young chap tumbled into it."

"Hurry," urged old Peter Bell; "he was almost exhausted, poor lad. We must get back as quick as possible."

Summoning his two hired men the farmer set off at a run across the fields, easily keeping pace with old Peter's decrepit horse. As they neared the well they began shouting, and a feeble cry from the depths answered them.

"Cheer up, my lad, we'll have you out of that in a brace-of-shakes," cried Farmer Ingalls encouragingly, as they reached the curb and peered over into the dark hole.

"I hope you will," cried Bill. "It's getting pretty monotonous, I can tell you."

"Don't know what mon-ount-on-tonous means, but I'd hate to change places with you," agreed the farmer.

Presently the rope came snaking down, with a loop in its lower end. Bill was directed to place his foot in the loop and hold on tight. When this had been done he shouted up:

"All right! Haul away!"

The stalwart farmer and his two assistants began to heave with all their might, while old Mr. Bell encouraged them. Before long, by dint of hard exertions, they succeeded in dragging Bill to the surface, and dripping and shivering he could stand once more in the blessed air and sunlight.

"But how in the world did you come to get in there?" asked the farmer, as he paced along by the side of the hermit's little cart, in which the half-exhausted Bill had been placed.

"Well," said the lad with a rather shamefaced laugh, "I'm really half ashamed to say. But it was this way. Some bad men who have an interest in putting me out of an airplane contest, of which Mr. Bell knows, had run off with me in an automobile. It was wrecked, and I escaped. I struck out toward town, as I thought, but as I came through that patch of woods by the wall I saw something that startled me so much that I stepped back and fell down the well."

"What did you see, my lad?" asked the farmer with half a twinkle in his eye.

"Something like a story-book ghost," smiled Bill; "it was tall and all in white and clanked a chain."

"Ha! ha! ha!" roared the farmer; "I half suspected as much. Why, that ghost was my old white mule Boxer. He managed somehow to snap his chain last night and we found him careening around the fields this morning. Don't color up, my boy," for poor Bill's face had turned very red, as the hired men guffawed loudly; "older men than you have been startled at far less. And now, here's the farm, and I'll bet mommer has a fine breakfast all ready for you."

The half-famished boy ate hungrily of the substantial farmhouse fare Mrs. Ingalls provided for him, and as he ate he made inquiries about the distance to the aviation grounds, which, he found to his dismay, were further distant than he had imagined.

"I'll never be able to make it in time without an automobile," moaned Bill to himself; "what shall I do?"

He cast about in his mind for some way out of his difficulty, but he could find none. Nor could the farmer help him. There were no automobiles in that part of the country, and in a horse-drawn vehicle he would never be able to make it in time.

All at once a queer sound filled the air. The atmosphere seemed to vibrate with it as it does on a still summer day when a threshing machine is buzzing away in a distant field.

"Land o' Goshen, what's that?" cried Mrs. Ingalls running to the door.

"Lish! Lish! come here quick!" she shouted the next instant.

Followed by the old hermit and Bill, Mr. Ingalls ran to the door. But his exclamations at the sight he saw were drowned by Bill's amazed cry:

"It's the Golden Butterfly!"

"An airplane!" shouted the farmer. "By gosh, she's like a pretty bird."

"It's my—our airplane," went on Bill; "who can be in it? Oh, if it's only Mary Eliska I may not be too late after all."

He ran out into the door yard of the farm house and, snatching off his coat, began waving it desperately. Would the occupant of the airplane see his frantic signals? With a beating heart Bill watched the winged machine as it droned far above him.

All at once he gave a delighted shout. The airplane was beginning to descend. Down it came in big circles, while the farmer, his wife and the old hermit gazed open mouthed at it, as if half inclined to run.

But as it drew closer to the ground Bill noted a puzzling thing. A helmeted and goggled person was driving it, evidently a boy or man and not Mary Eliska at all. Who could it be? For an instant a queer thought flashed through his head. Possibly somebody had stolen it and was making off across country with it so as to put it out of the race.

More and more rapidly the airplane began to drop as it neared the ground, and before many minutes it alighted in the patch of meadow in front of the farm house, gliding gracefully for several feet before it stopped.

But the rubber-tired landing wheels had not ceased revolving before Bill was at its side.

"Say, who are you, and what are you doing with my airplane?" he demanded in heated tones, for the helmeted aviator had not yet even deigned to notice him, but seemed to be busy with various levers and valves.

"Well, are you going to answer me?" sputtered Bill, while the farmer, his wife, the old hermit and the hired men gazed on curiously.

For answer the mysterious aviator raised his helmet and a cloud of golden curls fell about a milk-and-roses face.

"By gum, a gal and a purty one!" cried the farmer capering about.

"Mary Eliska!" shouted Bill.

"Yes, Mary Eliska," cried the girl. "Oh, Bill, what has happened to you? When you didn't come back Jax Gray and Liam McAdams persuaded me to put on your clothes and at least try the Butterfly out. But I was so miserable that I could not try her out on the track, so I flew off across country. I saw you waving far below me and—oh, Bill!"

Mary Eliska could go no further and half collapsed in Bill's arms as he tenderly lifted her out.

"Great hopping water millions!" cried the farmer, "if this ain't a day of wonders. This must be ther lad's sister he told us about, and ter think she come flopping down out of ther sky like a seventeen-y'ar locust."

Mary Eliska was quickly her usual strong, self-reliant self again. With indignation blazing in her kind eyes she heard Bill's account of the happenings of the night. At its conclusion she announced with decision:

"We must defeat them, Bill."

"Yes, but how? There's only a scant half hour before starting time if you said they'd changed it."

"Even so you can make it. You must take these clothes, get into the airplane and fly back to the track. If you go alone the 'plane will be light and you can make it in time."

"But you, Mary Eliska?"

"I guess I can borrow a dress from Mrs. Ingalls here," said the girl briskly.

"Of course, you kin," put in Mrs. Ingalls, but surveying her own ample form rather doubtfully the while.

"You kin give her one of daughter Jenny's dresses," said the farmer.

"Then that is settled, thanks to you," said Mary Eliska with characteristic decision.

They all entered the farm house, from which, a few seconds later, Bill emerged, clad in the garments his sister had donned a short time before. He climbed into the airplane amid the admiring comments of the farm hands, who, by this time, had come in from the fields, drawn by the wonderful airship, and stood all about it gaping and wondering.

Mary Eliska, in a dress belonging to the farmer's daughter, who was away on a visit, stepped quickly to Bill's side as, after glancing at the clock attached to the front of the airplane, he started the engine.

As it started its uproarious song, the farm hands jumped back in affright. But Mary Eliska clasped her brother's hand.

"Win that prize, Bill," she said.

"I'll do my best, little sister."

And that was all, but as Mary Eliska gazed a few minutes later at the fast-diminishing form of the speeding airplane she felt that all she had braved and dared that day had not been in vain.

CHAPTER 13.20.
IN THE NICK OF TIME.

Excitement had reached its topmost pitch on the aviation field. It was but a few minutes to starting time for the great contest, and already four young aviators had their winged craft in line before the judge's stand.

Engines were belching clouds of acrid blue smoke heavily impregnated with oily, smelling fumes. The roar of motors shook the air. Folks in the grandstand and on the crowded lawns excitedly pointed out to one another the different machines, all of which bore large numbers.

Excited officials, red-faced and perspiring, bustled about importantly, while from the top of the judge's stand a portly man bellowed occasional announcements through a megaphone.

Suddenly he made an announcement that caused a hum of interest.

"Machine number seven—mach-ine num-ber sev-en! Weenie Allen, owner, has withdrawn from the race," he announced.

A buzz of comment went through the crowd. Jax Gray, Liam McAdams and Hal Homer, standing in a group by the empty Stricklin hangar, exchanged astonished glances as they heard the news. What did that mean? Weenie Allen had been swaggering about, boasting of his wonderful airplane, and now it appeared at the eleventh hour he had decided not to enter it.

"Must have had an accident," opined Liam McAdams.

"Maybe he gave it one of those pleasant looks of his," suggested Jax Gray.

"Wherever can Mary Eliska be," exclaimed the girl the next minute; "she's been gone for more than an hour. I do hope nothing has happened to her."

"Not likely," rejoined Liam McAdams, although he looked a little troubled over the non-appearance of the Golden Butterfly.

"The police said they had a dragnet out in every part of the vicinity," volunteered Hal Homer, who had returned only a few minutes before from the station house.

Bang!

A bomb had been shot skyward and now exploded in a cloud of yellow smoke.

"Three minutes to starting time," cried Hal Homer anxiously; "where can Aunt Sally be?"

"Look!" cried Jax Gray suddenly, dancing about. "Oh, Glory! Here she comes!"

Far off against the sky a speck was visible. Rushing toward them at tremendous speed it swiftly grew larger. The crowd saw it now and great excitement prevailed. The word flew about that the machine was the missing Number Six. Would it arrive in time to participate in the start and thus qualify? This was the question on every lip.

Hal Homer jumped into the auto and sped over to the judge's stand.

"Can't you delay the start for five minutes?" he begged.

"Impossible," was the reply.

"But that airplane, Number Six, has been delayed by some accident. If you start the race on time it may not arrive in time to take part."

"Can't be helped. Young Stricklin—that's the name of the owner, isn't it?—shouldn't have gone off on a cross country tryout."

Back to the hangar sped Hal, where Jax Gray and Liam McAdams, almost beside themselves with excitement, were watching the homing airplane.

"She'll be on time," cried Liam McAdams as the graceful ship swept over the distant confines of the course and came thundering down toward the starting point.

A great cheer swept skywards as the airplane came on.

"She'll make it.""She won't." "Where has the thing been?""Why is it so late?"

These and a hundred other questions and remarks went from mouth to mouth all through the big crowd.

"It's all off," groaned Liam McAdams suddenly.

He had seen the signal corps man, whose duty it was to fire the bombs, outstretching himself on the ground awaiting the signal to touch off the starting sign.

But even as Liam McAdams spoke, the Golden Butterfly made a swift turn and, amid a roar from the crowd, shot whirring past the grandstand and alighted in front of the stand on the starting line.

Hardly had the wheels touched the ground before the judge in charge of the track raised his hand. A flag fell and the signal corps man jerked his arm back, firing the bomb that announced the start.

B-o-o-o-o-m!

As the detonation died out the airplanes shot forward, rising into the still air almost in a body, like a flock of birds. It was a spectacle never to be forgotten, and the crowd appreciated it to the full.

But up in the grandstand, in inconspicuous places, sat three persons who did not look as well pleased as those about them.

"So the girl is going to take a chance," muttered Weenie Allen; "well, so much the worse for her. If she wins I'll put in a protest and compel her to unmask."

"Won't that Stricklin and Hoffinger bunch be astonished when they find out that we are on to their little game," chuckled Jukes Dade; "it'll be as good as a play."

"That's what it will," grinned Gid.

"They'll find out that they can't humiliate me and not suffer for it," grated out Weenie Allen.

"Wonder where that girl went to on her tryout spin?" inquired Dade.

"It doesn't make much difference where, but she certainly came back with a grandstand play," rejoined Gid.

"Well, if she wins the race it will be our turn," Weenie Allen assured him.

They then turned their attention to the contest, two laps of which had been made while they were talking.

Number One, a small white Bleriot type of monoplane, seemed to be making the pace for the rest, and word flew about that it had gained half a lap on Number Four, its nearest competitor so far.

"But it will be a long contest," said the wiseacres in the crowd, "and accidents may happen at any time."

On the fourth lap Number One was seen to descend over by the hangars. Something had gone wrong with its lubricating valve. By the time the difficulty was adjusted it was hopelessly out of the race. Number Three was the next to drop out. This machine was driven by one of the high school lads, and his contingent of rooters in the grandstand set up a woeful noise as he dropped to earth in the middle of the course. A broken stay had made it dangerous for him to remain longer in the air.

This left number Six, the Stricklin machine, Numbers Two, Four and Five still in the air.

"Number Six has gained a lap on Number Five!" went up the cry presently as Number Five, so far the leader, was seen to lose speed on the fifteenth lap.

The Golden Butterfly was in truth doing magnificently, but try as her operator would it did not seem possible to shake off Number Five, another high school boy's machine, which clung persistently to its stern. Number Four alighted for more gasoline on the twentieth lap and lost a round of the course thereby. A few seconds later Number Two was also forced to descend with heated cylinders. This practically left the race between Number Five and the Golden Butterfly. Round and round they tore, neither of them gaining or losing a foot apparently. The thunder of their engines grew deafeningly monotonous and the crowds watched them as if hypnotized by the whirring aerial monsters.

All at once, though, a mighty roar proclaimed that something was happening, and gazing down toward the further end of the track it could be seen that Number Six, the Golden Butterfly, had made a daring attempt to gain on the other machine, and had succeeded.

So close did the two airplanes edge to the end pylon in the effort to secure the inside plane that for an instant it looked as if a crash must result.

A thunder of cheers greeted the Golden Butterfly as she swept by the grandstand on the next lap.

"That girl can drive all right," grudgingly admitted Weenie Allen.

"Yes, and she's pretty as a picture, too," put in Gid Gibbons; "guess you were stuck on her once, weren't you, Weenie Allen?"

"Oh, shut up," growled Weenie Allen angrily. "It makes no difference to you, does it?"

The airplanes had been racing for an hour now, and neither showed any signs of slacking speed. On the contrary, as they "warmed up," they seemed to go the quicker. All at once an incident occurred which brought the crowd to its feet yelling and cheering as if wild.

The driver of Number Five, as the two machines passed the grandstand, had made a deliberate attempt to prevent the Golden Butterfly overhauling him by jamming his airplane over toward a pylon and directly in front of the Butterfly. For an instant it looked as if a crash must be inevitable, but just as the spectators were beginning to turn pale and the more timid to hide their eyes, the Butterfly was seen to make a graceful dip and dive clean under the other airplane. It was a magnificent bit of aerial driving, and the crowd appreciated it to the full. A roar and a shout went up, to which the driver of Number Six responded with a wave of a gloved hand.

Ten minutes later Number Five, two laps behind, and with a leaking radiator, dropped out of the race, leaving the Golden Butterfly the winner. Weenie Allen was white as a sheet as he saw an official with a black and white checkered flag step out into the field. This was the signal to the Golden Butterfly, which was still in the air, that the race was over.

As the Stricklin airplane dropped to earth in front of the grandstand amid rapturous plaudits, the son of the Sandy Bay banker deliberately arose and made his way toward the judges' stand, to which Hal Homer and the Hoffingers, the core of a shouting, yelling mob of enthusiasts, were already conducting the daring driver of Number Six.

Special policemen made a path for the aviator and his friends, while cries of: "Take off your helmet!" "We want to see you!"

"What's the matter with Number Six?" and a hundred other cries arose. But the driver of Number Six did not respond, and with his helmet still on his head was conducted before the judges to receive their congratulations. The helmet was still in place when Weenie Allen came shoving through the crowd and finally reached the little group.

"As a competitor I demand that Number Six take off his helmet!" he cried.

The judges turned to him in astonishment. "This is most unseemly, sir," said one of them; "no doubt in good time Mr. Stricklin will take off his helmet."

"Oh, no, he won't," shouted Weenie Allen, at whom all the group was now gazing. "He won't, I tell you, and for a good reason, too. *That's not Bill Stricklin at all, but his sister Mary Eliska.*"

But the words had not left his lips before Liam McAdams, with a quick motion, jerked off the aviator's helmet and disclosed the handsome, perspiring features of Bill himself.

In the few minutes he had had, Bill had found time briefly to explain how he and his sister had changed garments.

"Well, I guess that settles that question," cried Liam McAdams triumphantly, as a mighty shout went up.

"It certainly does," said one of the officials. "Where is that young scamp? Officer, find the young man who made that accusation and bring him here to explain himself."

But the disgruntled Weenie Allen had dived off into the crowd the instant he saw into what a tremendous blunder he had fallen. And although a strict search was made for him he was not to be found.

CHAPTER 13.21.
THE PHANTOM AIRSHIP.

In the midst of the hum and excitement and the crossfire of questions which immediately followed, there occurred a startling interruption. From the further side of the grounds there arose a cry, which swelled in volume as it advanced.

"Fire! One of the hangars is on fire!"

The group immediately broke up and orders and commands flew thick and fast. In the midst of the excitement Bill and his chums found an opportunity to slip away.

"There's the fire. Off by our hangar!" shouted Hal Homer, pointing across the field.

By the side of the Stricklin's green aero shed a big cloud of smoke was ascending, mingled with yellow flames. It seemed to be a hot blaze.

"It's Weenie Allen's hangar!" cried Bill suddenly; "come on, let's go over and see what the matter is."

"I've got the car right here," said Liam McAdams. "I'll get you over in a jiffy."

Soon they were speeding across the field toward the blaze. In the meantime an emergency fire corps, composed of men employed on the grounds, had attached a line of hose to a hydrant and were drenching the flames. Such good work did they do that it was not long before they had the fire under control.

As soon as it was out our party, which had managed to get through the lines formed to keep back the curious, gazed into the ruins with some interest.

"Why, say!" cried Liam McAdams suddenly, "the place was empty."

"So it was!" cried Bill in astonished tones, "except for that big box kite over in the corner there. Whatever kind of a game of bluff has Weenie Allen been playing?"

"I guess I can imagine it," struck in Hal Homer. "From what you have told me his little game was to bluff you into thinking he had a fine airship that could beat yours, and in that way induce you to sell out to him."

"By George, I never thought of that!" exclaimed Bill, "but—hullo, here comes Mary Eliska in the farmer's wagon!"

He ran through the crowd to the side of the wagon, which had been driven in by Farmer Ingalls.

"You dear, dear boy, I've heard all about it already," cried Mary Eliska, throwing her white arms about Bill's neck, while Aunt Sally, whom they had picked up at the hotel, sat by, hardly knowing whether to laugh or to cry, as she expressed it later.

I am not going to describe that reunion by the side of Weenie Allen's burned hangar, but each reader can imagine for herself what a joyous one it was.

"I know a place in town where they sell the bulliest sodas and sundaes," cried Liam McAdams suddenly. "Everybody come up there in the car and we'll celebrate!"

"In one moment, Liam McAdams," said Bill. "There's one thing still I don't understand about this whole business, and that is this. It is clear enough that Weenie Allen was bluffing about having an airplane in that shed, but how was it that he made a night ascent with red and green lanterns?"

"Oh, you mean the time you saw him in the air at night, the time we went to Washington?" asked Liam McAdams.

"That's it. How do you account for it?"

"Give it up," rejoined the other lad.

"Perhaps this may help to explain it."

Hal Homer came up carrying two much scorched lanterns he had found in the debris of the hangar. One was red, the other was green.

"I don't quite see," said Mary Eliska, but Hal, with an apology interrupted her.

"It's plain as day to me," he said; "these two lanterns attached to that big box kite on a breezy night would certainly give anyone the impression that an airplane was sailing about. Thatcher Allen knew you would be flying home in that vicinity on that night and rigged up this contrivance to delude you."

"A phantom airship!" cried Mary Eliska.

"That's about the size of it," put in the slangy Liam McAdams, "and I think that friend Homer here has hit on the correct solution."

"But if that were so, why did Weenie Allen fit up a shop out at Gid Gibbons's place?" asked Jax Gray in a puzzled tone.

"I guess that shop had no more in it than this hangar," was Bill's reply. "Gid Gibbons is a bad character who would do anything for money, and I think it likely that he fell in with Thatcher Allen's schemes because he had no great liking for any of us."

"Looks that way," agreed Liam McAdams.

"But that doesn't explain that ruby which Hester was wearing," thought Mary Eliska to herself as the laughing party of young folks drove off up the town, followed by Farmer Ingalls and his good wife, who had been invited to take part in the little celebration of their triumph. Here and there they were recognized and cheered, but among the crowds on the sidewalks all discussing the thrilling race, there were three that took no part in the good-natured jubilation. Who these were we can guess.

Jukes Dade at Weenie Allen's side had to listen to some savage abuse as they slunk along, avoiding as far as possible the crowds.

"I told you to burn up the hangar so that there would be no trace left of the bluff we had been putting up," he growled.

"Well, didn't I soak the place with gasoline," protested Dade; "how was I to know a kid would come along and give the alarm before it got fairly alight?"

"It's been a dismal failure all the way through," lamented Thatcher Allen, as if he had been engaged on some praiseworthy enterprise.

"Incidentally," purred Jukes Dade, but with a menace under his silky tones, "I'd like to see some of that money you've been promising me all along."

"You'll have to wait 'til I see my father," snapped out Weenie Allen savagely.

"Well, see him quick then, or I may have to take other means of getting it," snarled Dade.

"What do you mean?"

"Why, by telling a few things I know. About the loss of a certain lady's jewels, for instance."

Weenie Allen went white as ashes.

"You sneak! You've been listening at keyholes!" he cried.

Dade returned him look for look defiantly.

"Well, what if I have?" he snarled. "I've got a hold on you now, Master Allen. I've got you where I want you and I'm going to keep you there."

CHAPTER 13.22.
JIM BELL OF THE WEST.

Some days after the events just described, and following the receipt by Bill of a pink check for $ 5,000., a strange visitor arrived at the Stricklin home—their very own home now, for the mortgage had been paid off, much to Thatcher Allen's disgust.

The stranger was a bronzed man and wore a broad-brimmed sombrero which would have marked him anywhere as a Westerner. Of Aunt Sally, who, in a new lavender silk dress, came to the door, he inquired if he could see Mr. Bill Stricklin.

Aunt Sally smiled at this ceremonial way of mentioning her young nephew, but directed the stranger with the breezy Western manner to the workshop at the rear of the house, where Bill and Mary Eliska were "fussing," as Jax Gray called it, with their beloved Golden Butterfly.

"Good morning," he said, doffing his sombrero with a sweep and a flourish; "can I have a word with you?"

"Certainly. Two or three if you want them," rejoined Bill, while Mary Eliska gazed in some surprise at the queer-mannered newcomer.

"The fact is," went on the stranger, "that I'm in the market for airplanes such as yours. I happened to be on the train some nights ago when you came flying through the air with two belated young passengers. Well, sir, thinks I, if such a machine can make a train on schedule time it ought to be good for other purposes. I took the liberty of making some inquiries about you from your two young friends after the train had started, but asked them not to mention the matter to you yet awhile.

"In New York I looked up my partner and we discussed the plan and he agreed with me that it was a good one. Now, I'm down here this morning to offer you $10,000 outright for the use of half a dozen of your airplanes, and a salary of $5,000 as instructor to the aviators I shall have to have to run them. How does the offer strike you?"

"I—er—well, I hardly know what to say," responded Bill; "you see, it's a bit sudden. It rather takes my breath away."

"Well, that's a way we have in the West," was the response, "but maybe I'd better tell you a little more about myself. My name is Jim Bell. I'm worth a couple of million or thereabouts. You can verify that by referring to the First National Bank of 'Frisco, or the East Coast Bank of New York City. I've got interests in cattle, wool and mines, but the very best mining proposition I ever struck I ran across out on the Nevada alkali desert in a range of barren hills. We were prospecting there when I was told about it. After untold hardships I found the spot and staked it out. But there arose the difficulty of transportation. There was the gold all right, but how was I to get it out?"

"I came East to see if I couldn't get some sort of automobile built that would travel the desert, but when I saw that airplane of yours droop down at that jerkwater junction, I realized I had found what I wanted. Now, are you on?"

"You'll have to give us a little time to think, sir," rejoined Bill; "it's a very flattering offer and I'd like to accept it, but I'll have to think it over."

"Quite right, quite right," rejoined the other, "nothing like thinking it over. If everyone did that fewer accidents and mishaps would occur in life. Take my own life, for instance. I've often thought I'd go back to see the old folks, but in that case I thought it over too long, for when I went to the old home the other day it was all gone. Not a stick or stone remained. My parents were dead and my only brother was no-one-knew-where."

Jim Bell's voice shook strangely. He blinked his eyes once or twice and then resumed briskly: "You see, I left home in a mighty queer way. I was out in a boat with my brother when it got overturned. He was drowned, I guess, but anyway I found myself drifting about on the Sound. I managed to seize hold of a bit of floating driftwood and in that way kept my head above water 'til a ship came along and picked me up.

"She was a big vessel bound for China and her captain was a brute. On our arrival in the Far East he bound me out as a sort of apprentice to a rich Chinese living in the interior. I was with him for ten years before I escaped. I worked my way to the coast, got another ship and headed for California.

"On the way across there was a mutiny and I saved the life of a wealthy passenger, who turned out to be a mining man and who, when he died two years later, left me most of his property. That gave me my start in life, and now I'm a millionaire. But I'd give it all if I could get some news of poor brother Peter and find out if he is dead or alive."

"Maybe we can help you," cried Mary Eliska, her eyes shining and her white hands clasped excitedly.

While the rugged Westerner had been talking the story of the old hermit came back to her.

"What do you mean?" asked Mr. Bell; "do you know where my brother is?"

"I'm not certain," cried Mary Eliska, "but the old hermit, Peter Bell, is he almost beyond a doubt."

"My brother a hermit!" cried the wealthy mining man.

"If it is your brother," put in Bill, "I hope for your sake it is. But his story tallies absolutely with yours. He told us that after he had missed you in the water he thought that you were drowned. Returning home he was shunned on every side, for the villagers accused him of having deserted you to save his own life."

"My poor Peter," breathed the miner.

"Miserable and made morose by the contempt he met with on every side he became a hermit and now lives in a hut near the town of Acatonick."

"How long does it take to get there? I must lose no time in finding out," exclaimed Jim Bell.

"You can get there in two or three hours from here if you can catch a train," said Bill. "If you like I'll phone for you and find out."

"Say, boy, that would be mighty wonderful of you. I tell you it hurts to think of poor Peter living all alone like that in poverty while I've been rich all these years. But it wasn't for lack of trying to locate him, for I've advertised and had detectives searching every likely place."

Bill found that there would be a train to Acatonick in about half an hour, and their new-found friend hastened off, after warm farewells, to catch it. He promised to be back within a few days and let them know of his success, and also inform them of any further arrangements he might be prepared to make about his offer.

"Well," said Bill, after he had gone, "the skies are beginning to clear, sis."

Mary Eliska sighed.

"Yes, but there is still one thing to be cleared up, Bill," she said.

"I know—the disappearance of those jewels," rejoined Bill. "Oh, if only we had something more to go upon than mere suspicions."

"Perhaps we will have before long," said Mary Eliska, musingly.

CHAPTER 13.23.
LIKE THIEVES IN THE NIGHT.

"Heard anything of Weenie Allen?" asked Liam McAdams, one bright morning, as he stopped his car at the Stricklins' gate and he and Jax Gray got out.

"Not a thing since that day at Acatonick," responded Bill, who with his sister had hastened to meet the other two. "Why, Jax Gray, how charming you look this morning."

"Meaning that you notice the contrast with other mornings," laughed Jax Gray merrily; "oh, Bill, you are not a courtier."

"No, I guess not yet—whatever a courtier may be," was the laughing rejoinder; "but I always like to pay deserved compliments."

"Oh, that's better," cried Jax Gray; "but have you heard anything more from Mr. Bell?"

For, of course, Liam McAdams and Jax Gray by this time knew about the visit of the mining man. Deanna Hoffinger had looked up his standing and character and had found both of the highest. On his advice Bill had about decided to accept the unique offer made him by the Western millionaire.

Mary Eliska shook her head in response to Jax Gray's question.

"No, dear, not one word," she said; "isn't it queer? However, I guess we shall, before long. Oh, I do hope that that poor old hermit turns out to be Mr. Jim Bell's brother."

"So do I, too," agreed Liam McAdams. "It would be jolly for you and Bill to think that you and your airplane had been the means of righting such a succession of mishaps."

"Indeed it would," agreed Mary Eliska, warmly; "but now come into the house and have some ice cream. It's one sign of our new prosperity that we are never without it now."

"I've eaten so much of it I'm ashamed to look a freezer in the face," laughed Bill, as they trooped in, to be warmly welcomed by Aunt Sally.

In the midst of their merry feast the sound of wheels was heard and a rig from the station drove up. Out of it stepped a venerable old gentleman in a well-fitting dark suit, with well blackened shoes and an altogether neat and prosperous appearance.

Mary Eliska and Jax Gray who had run to the window at the sound of wheels saw him assisted to the ground by a younger man whom they both recognized with a cry of astonishment.

"Mr. Jim Bell. But who is the old gentleman?"

"Why it's—it's the hermit!" cried Bill.

"Good gracious, is that fashionable looking old man a hermit?" gasped Liam McAdams.

"He was, I guess, but he won't be any more," laughed Mary Eliska, happily, as she tripped to the door to welcome the visitors. The Stricklins had a maid now; but Mary Eliska preferred to be the first to greet the newly united brothers for it was evident that Jim Bell's quest had been successful.

What greetings there were to be sure, when the two brothers were inside the cool, shady house! The old hermit's eyes gleamed delightedly as he gallantly handed Aunt Sally to a chair. As for Jim Bell, he was happy enough to "dance a jig," he said.

"I'll play for you, sir," volunteered Liam McAdams, going toward the piano.

"No, no," laughed Jim Bell; "I'm too old for that now. But not too old for Peter and me to have many happy days together yet, eh, Peter?" He turned tenderly toward the old man whose eyes grew dim and moist. "I wish dad and mother could see us now," he said, sadly, as his thoughts wandered back over the long bitter years he had spent in solitude.

"Perhaps they can," breathed Mary Eliska, softly; "let us hope so."

"Thank you," said the old hermit, with a sigh.

But the conversation soon turned to a merrier vein. And then it drifted into business. Deanna Hoffinger happened to stop in on her way into town and after a long talk with Jim Bell she seriously advised Bill to accept the mining man's proposal.

"I'll put you up a factory any place you say," said the millionaire, "and you can turn out all that we require. I've a notion, too, that they might be used as general freight carriers over arid stretches of country where there are no railroads, and feed and water for stock is scarce."

"Not a doubt of it," said Deanna Hoffinger.

Before he left the preliminary papers had been drawn up and signed, and Bill Stricklin found himself fairly launched in business. But in all this success he did not forget how much he owed to Mary Eliska. Recent events had softened the boy's character and reduced his conceit wonderfully.

"I owe it all to you, little sis," he said that evening.

"I don't know about all," cried Liam McAdams, who was present; "but you do owe a whole lot to her, old man, and I'm glad to see you acknowledge it at last."

"I always have," cried Bill, turning rather red, though.

"Hum," commented Liam McAdams; "I'm not so sure about that."

But Mary Eliska put her hand over his mouth and it took Liam McAdams what seemed an unduly long time to remove it. As for Jax Gray, she stalwartly declared that if it hadn't been for Mary Eliska there would have been no Golden Butterfly, no five-thousand-dollar prize, and, as she said, "no nothing." But to this loyal little Mary Eliska would not assent. In her eyes Bill would always remain the most wonderful brother in the world.

Soon after this Liam McAdams and Jax Gray took their leave and it was not long before the last light was extinguished in the happy little household and deep silence reigned. About midnight, as nearly as she could judge, Mary Eliska awoke to find the moonlight streaming into her room and upon her face.

"Good gracious, I'll get moonstruck," she thought, and throwing on a wrap she went to the window to pull down the shade which had been raised to admit the cool air.

The window commanded a view of the workshop, in which the Golden Butterfly was kept, and Mary Eliska, as she looked out, was astonished to see that the door of the work shop which housed the precious craft was open.

"Goodness!" thought the girl, "how careless of whoever left it that way. The night air will rust the stay-wires and the steel parts of the motor terribly. I guess I had better slip downstairs and close it."

Partially dressing herself the girl noiselessly tiptoed down the stairs and out into the moonlit night.

For one instant she was startled as she thought she saw a dark form dodge swiftly behind a corner of the workshop as she appeared.

"I must be getting as nervous as poor Bill when the mule frightened him down the well," she thought to herself as she advanced toward the shed. Reaching it she raised her hand to shut the door when, to her astonishment, she discovered that it had apparently been locked,—at least a broken bit of the padlock dangling from the portal seemed to indicate this.

"Somebody's filed that through," was Mary Eliska's thought. But before she could make any further investigation a pair of hands grasped her from behind, pinioning her arms to her side. At the same instant an old coat was flung over her head and pulled close, stifling her outcries.

"We won't hurt you if you keep quiet," hissed a voice in her ear, "but if you don't, look out for trouble."

"What are you going to do?" cried Mary Eliska, through the muffling medium of the coat.

"You'll soon find out," was the rejoinder. "Jukes, bring her inside the shed and keep her quiet."

Jukes! The name struck a familiar chord in Mary Eliska's memory. She knew now why the face and form of the man hanging about Weenie Allen's "Phantom" hangar at the aviation field had seemed so familiar to her. It *was* Jukes Dade, the man her father, Albert Stricklin, had peremptorily discharged. Mary Eliska could not repress a shudder as she thought of the desperate character of the man.

Suddenly, as her captors half-dragged, half-carried her into the workshop, her body grew limp, and she fell in an insensible heap forward. She would have struck the ground had not a pair of hands caught her.

"She's fainted," cried Jukes, alarmedly.

"So much the better," growled out his companion; "she won't give us any trouble now. We can do what we've got to do and get away. Got the files?"

"Here they are," responded Jukes; "just let me lay her down here while I hand 'em to you."

He deposited Mary Eliska's limp form on a long box on which some sacks had been strewn. The next instant the sharp rasping of a file could be heard in the silent workshop.

"I guess this Golden Butterfly will have its wings clipped for some time to come," chuckled Jukes' companion, whom Mary Eliska, of course, had not yet seen.

"I guess that's right," laughed the other; "just wait a jiffy while I lay down this gun of mine and I'll give you a hand."

He stepped over and put down a wicked-looking pistol on the rough bench on which Mary Eliska lay. Then he turned and began to help his companion. The two worked by the light of a dark lantern which they had brought with them on their rascally expedition to ruin the Golden Butterfly.

But suddenly a slight noise behind him made Jukes turn his head. As he did so he gave a startled yell. Mary Eliska, her eyes bright and wild-looking, was standing up behind them. In her hand was the pistol which Jukes had laid down beside her when she had seemed to faint a few moments before. But Mary Eliska's faint had been a simulated one. Realizing that harm was meant to the Golden Butterfly, she had imitated unconsciousness as a means to possible escape and giving the alarm.

"Don't move, either of you," said Mary Eliska, in a firm voice. "I'm only a girl, but I can use a pistol."

But Jukes and his companion, with a wild yell, made a dash for the door.

"Good gracious, I can't shoot them," thought Mary Eliska. "Help! help!" she began to cry at the top of her voice.

But the next instant the whirr and roar of a motor from the road apprised her that the two rascals had made their escape in an auto and that pursuit was useless. Thus it was that when the aroused household came pouring excitedly out of the house they found a brave, if a rather tremulous, girl awaiting them with a pistol in her hand on the stock of which were engraved the initials "W. A."

"So that's who Jukes's companion was," exclaimed Bill, angrily. "Oh, if you had only awakened me, sis."

"My dear Bill," rejoined Mary Eliska, with dignity, "don't you think that I am capable of taking care of myself?"

CHAPTER 13.24.
HESTER MAKES AMENDS—CONCLUSION.

A few days later Mary Eliska borrowed Jax Gray's car and went out for a long, lonely spin along the country roads. She wanted to think. Bill and Liam McAdams were at home repairing the damage wrought to the Golden Butterfly, which, it turned out, was very slight.

She was driving along a pretty stretch of road when she came across a veritable fairyland of delicate pink wild roses intertwined with honeysuckle and woodbine.

"Oh," cried Mary Eliska, who simply worshipped flowers, "how beautiful; I must take some of these home. They'll make all our garden things look mean and shabby."

Stopping the car she alighted and was soon deep in her occupation of gathering the fragrant posies. Suddenly she was startled by the sound of a sobbing voice close at hand, and the next minute an angry male voice could be heard also.

"I tell you I'll do nothing of the sort," the man was saying; "why should I go and own up that I'm a thief or the next thing to it? At any rate they'd have me put in jail for all the attempts I've made to interfere with their airplane."

"It's Weenie Allen!" gasped Mary Eliska, amazedly, "and Hester Gibbons," she added the next instant as the girl's voice sobbed out:

"Well, if you won't, I will. I've been weak and foolish but I'm not wicked. I'm going to tell Mary Eliska all about it today and ask her to forgive me."

"You'd better not," Weenie Allen's tone was threatening now.

"Well, what if I do?"

"You won't, I tell you. I'll have you locked up and charged with the theft yourself."

"You wouldn't dare."

"Oh, yes, I would. You've got that ruby and that is pretty good proof that you stole it."

"It isn't so and you know it. I have been a weak, silly girl, that's all, but I see it all now. And just to think if I hadn't overheard you and my father talking that I might have gone on admiring you."

"Tell me you won't go to the Stricklins with the story or I'll—"

"Help! Help!" The shrill cry came in Hester's tones.

Without quite realizing what she was doing, Mary Eliska stooped and picked up a heavy bit of stick that lay in the road beside her. Then she stepped forward around a bend which had hitherto hidden the other two from her sight. As she appeared Weenie Allen had his hand on Hester's wrist and was wrenching it cruelly.

"Oh! oh! Weenie, please let go!" Hester was crying.

"I will if you'll promise not to tell."

"There's no need for her to promise that, Weenie Allen," said Mary Eliska, "for I have already heard enough for me to know that she has some connection with the disappearance of Deanna Hoffinger's diamonds."

"Oh, Mary Eliska!" cried Hester, running to her side.

"See here," began Weenie Allen, swaggering forward threateningly toward the two girls.

"My brother is just 'round that corner," said Mary Eliska, boldly; "he'll be here in a minute. If you don't wish to be arrested for what you did the other night you had better get away from here, Weenie Allen."

A scared look crossed Weenie Allen's face and he turned and fairly took to his heels.

"Now, Hester," said Mary Eliska, kindly, "come with me to my car. It's just 'round the corner."

"Oh, Mary Eliska, I've been a bad, wicked girl, but I'm not a thief. Truly I'm not."

"I believe that," said Mary Eliska, "but what do you know about the disappearance of the diamonds?"

"That I have them all here. Not one is gone," was the amazing reply, and Hester, drawing a handkerchief from her bosom, unfolded it and displayed to Mary Eliska's amazed eyes a glittering collection of gems. In the midst of the flashing gems gleamed the big ruby which Mary Eliska had once seen Hester so carefully conceal.

"Hester, you have a duty before you," said Mary Eliska slowly; "get in my car and come with me to my home and then tell me all about this mystery which has puzzled us so long."

But the girl shrank back. "I can't. Oh, Mary Eliska, with you it's different, but before, the others. Your brother—"

"Poor fellow, he has been under unjust suspicion on account of these very jewels," Mary Eliska reminded the agitated girl.

"Oh, give me time. Not now. I—"

"No, it must be now," said Mary Eliska, with gentle insistence. "Come!"

Something in her manner seemed to strike the girl.

"You'll promise no harm will come to me or my father through this?" she said.

"Is your father very deeply implicated in the matter?" asked Mary Eliska seriously, looking straight into the other's eyes.

"No. On my word of honor, no," was the response.

"Then I'll promise," said Mary Eliska.

"Very well, then, I'll tell you all I know about the matter," said Hester, as the girls got into the car.

An hour later, in the library of the Stricklins' home, Mary Eliska, Bill, Liam McAdams and Jax Gray were gathered listening to Hester's story. Her eyes were red from crying and she hesitated frequently, but her manner showed that she was telling the truth.

On a table lay the glistening jewels. Jax Gray had counted them and found that they were all there.

"I didn't find out about the jewels 'til one night Weenie Allen, who has always said he admired me," said Hester, with downcast eyes, "gave me that big ruby there. At least he didn't give it to me but he said I could wear it. Of course I had heard about the disappearance of the jewels from the auto, but somehow I didn't associate this token of Weenie Allen's with it.

"It was not 'til a week ago that I learned the true state of affairs. I overheard a conversation of Weenie Allen's with my father in which he threatened him with arrest if he, father, didn't give him some money Weenie Allen said he had hoarded up. I knew dad didn't have any and I asked him after Weenie Allen had gone to tell me all about it.

"He isn't such a bad man at bottom and when I pleaded with him he told me the whole story. On the day of the jewel robbery, for it was a robbery, Morgan and Giles—"

"Our butler and groom!" cried Jax Gray.

"Yes. Well, they were taking a stroll in the fields and happened along just as the car was wrecked. They knew from servants' gossip that you had been to town to get the gems and when they saw you lying unconscious and the wallet near at hand, the temptation was too much for them and they stole it.

"They determined to hide it in some woods near my father's place; but as they entered them Weenie Allen came along on his bicycle. He saw them enter the woods and became suspicious. Leaning his bicycle against a tree he followed them and saw them bury the gems under a tree which they marked.

"He noted the tree, too, and then, without their seeing him he remounted his motor-cycle and came on to see my father about that business of the hoax airplane. He said he wanted to bluff you into selling the Butterfly to him.

"Well, father agreed, for a fair sum of money, to help him, and we started right into town. At that time I thought it was a good joke, and we were both laughing as we came in sight of the scene of the accident."

"So that's what they were laughing at," thought Bill, recollecting how mystified he had been when he saw them together.

"I don't know whether it was Weenie Allen's manner or what," said Hester resuming, "but my father began to suspect that he might know something about the jewels, and one day he followed him into the woods when he went to see if the jewels were still under the tree. Father made him own up when he caught him red-handed like that, but in the meantime Morgan and Giles also had arrived. Well, the four of them were all equally guilty, so they agreed to stick together and say nothing 'til the excitement about the loss had blown over. But Weenie Allen in the meantime said that he must have the ruby to let me wear.

"I guess he wanted to show me that he was as rich as he was always pretending to be.

"A few days later they had a terrible fright. Morgan, who carried the leather wallet in his pocket for lack of a better place to put it, dropped it on the porch of Deanna Hoffinger's house where, as you know, it was found before he realized his loss and could recover it.

"When Weenie Allen came back from the aviation meet and began boasting of the mean tricks he had played you and how he had kidnapped Bill, I began to see what a despicable fellow he was. Then, too, he was always threatening dad, and so I decided to make a clean breast of it all and save poor dad any more trouble, for Weenie Allen has dictated to him ever since they shared the secret.

"I went to the wood and found the marked tree I had heard them talk about so often and with the jewels in my hand I started for your home, Mary Eliska, for I didn't dare to go to Deanna Hoffingers'. But Weenie Allen, it seems, had got suspicious, and followed me. He overtook me at the spot where you encountered us."

"Does he know you have the jewels?" asked Bill.

"Not yet," rejoined Hester; "I believe if he had he would have been violent."

"Well, Hester," said Mary Eliska, as the girl concluded her strange narrative, "you have cleared up a puzzling mystery."

"Did you ever hear such a yarn in all your born days?" asked Liam McAdams.

"And every one of the jewels is there," cried Jax Gray. "I tell you what I'll do, I'll just call up the house and tell mother about it. Won't she be pleased?"

But Deanna Hoffinger was not at home, and—

"Oh, miss," gasped the servant, who answered the 'phone, "we're all upset. Morgan has run off, miss, and so has Giles. They took some of the silver with them. Mary and me tried to stop 'em but they pointed a pistol at us and scared us inter high strikes."

"I'll 'phone the police at once," cried Jax Gray, indignantly. "They might have got off if it hadn't been for that."

But although a good description was furnished, Morgan and Giles were not captured and Deanna Hoffinger was not ill pleased.

"They will not venture into this part of the country again," she said, "and we are well rid of such rascals."

Hester, in whom Deanna Hoffinger took an interest after the girl had told her with her own lips her strange story, is now at a girls' boarding school, having been sent there at Deanna Hoffinger's expense.

As for Weenie Allen, his father sent him West soon after the lad's innate rascality had been revealed, and from reports Weenie Allen is working hard to redeem the past and make himself a good and useful man.

"And so the mystery of the phantom airship and the missing jewels is all cleared up," said Mary Eliska to Jax Gray one day a short time after the events just described had transpired.

"Yes," rejoined her chum, "and the air seems clearer and fresher somehow. It is terrible to have a dark cloud of suspicion hanging over one."

"It is, indeed," rejoined Mary Eliska; "and now, as Bill leaves in a few days for the West, let's all take a good long spin. You and I will go in the Golden Butterfly while the boys can run along below us in the auto."

But Jax Gray looked a bit doubtful. "Wouldn't Bill like to go in the airplane?" she said.

Mary Eliska broke into merry laughter.

"Oh, you sly puss," she exclaimed. "Very well, then you and Bill in the Golden Eagle and Liam McAdams and I in the auto."

"Suits me," cried Liam McAdams, throwing his arm around his sister's waist, "but I thought you were the girl aviator of the family, Mary Eliska."

"So I am," laughed Mary Eliska, "but I am willing to yield my place for once."

"Well, if you'll excuse my horrid slang," laughed Liam McAdams, "I think I may say we've all been 'up in the air' for the last few weeks. But it's all over now and we'll settle down to humdrum life once more."

"It's been jolly, though," protested Mary Eliska.

"With some parts left out," put in Jax Gray.

But although no adventures just like those we have related happened again to the Girl Aviators, they were due to encounter some more strange experiences. In fact, both Mary Eliska and Bill and their friends were on the brink of some odd happenings, the narration of which must be postponed to another volume of this series.

What these complications and adventures, both merry and perilous, proved to be will be set down in full detail in "The Girl Aviators on Golden Wings," a breezy tale of our aerial maids.

CHAPTER 14

Girl Pilots on Golden Wings

CHAPTER 14.1
THE GREAT ALKALI

"And so this is the great Nevada desert!" Mary Eliska wrinkled her nose rather disdainfully as she gazed from the open window of the car out over the white, glittering expanse—dotted here and there with gloomy-looking clumps of sage brush—through which they had been traveling for some little time past.

"This is it," nodded her brother Bill; "what do you think of it, sis?"

"Um—er, I shall have to wait a while before I answer that," rejoined Mary Eliska judicially.

"Well, here's Liam McAdams; let's ask him," cried Bill, as a lad of his own age, accompanied by a slender, graceful girl, came down the aisle of the car and approached the section in which the two young Stricklins were sitting.

"Liam McAdams," demanded Bill, "we are now on the great Nevada desert, or on the edge of it. Does it meet with your approval?"

"There's plenty of it anyhow," laughed Liam McAdams, "and really it's very much like what I expected it would be."

"I feel like a regular cowgirl or—a—er—well, what the newspapers call a typical Westerner already," said Jax Gray, Liam McAdams's sister.

"Only typical Westerners don't protect their delicate complexions from dust with cold cream," laughed Mary Eliska, holding up a finger reprovingly. "As if any beauty magazine won't tell you it's a woman's duty to take the greatest care of her complexion," parried Jax Gray. "Bill and I have been sitting out on the observation platform on the last coach—that is, we sat there 'til the dust drove us in."

She shook the folds of a long, light pongee automobile coat she wore and a little cloud of dust arose. They all coughed as the pungent stuff circulated.

"Ugh," cried Bill, "it makes your eyes smart."

"That's the alkali in it," quoth Liam McAdams sagely, "alkali is—"

"Very unpleasant," coughed Mary Eliska.

"But as we are likely to have to endure it for the next few weeks," struck in Bill, "we might as well lose no time in getting accustomed to it."

"Well girls and boys," came a deep, pleasant voice behind them, "we shall be in Blue Creek in a short time now, so gather up your belongings. I'll take care of the airplane outfits and the other stuff in the baggage car," he went on, "and here comes Mary Eliska now."

The lady referred to was a sweet-faced woman of some fifty years of age, though it was easy to see that the years had dealt kindly with her during her placid life in the village of Sandy Beach, on Long Island, New York, where she had made, her home. Aunt Sally was the aunt of the two Stricklin children, and since their father's death some time before had been both mother and father to them—their own mother having passed away when they were but small children.

As readers of Book 33 of this series know, Mr. Stricklin had been an inventor of some distinction. Dying, he had confided to his son and daughter his plans for a non-capsizable airplane of great power. His son had promised to carry on the work, and had devoted his legacy to this purpose.

In the immediately previous Chapter 13k which was called "Mary Eliska - *The Phantom Airship*," it will be recalled, it was told how Mary Eliska had been of material aid to her brother in his plans and hopes, and had, in reality, "saved the day" for him when he fell into the hands of some enemies. This occurred on the eve of a great airplane contest in which Bill had entered in the hopes of winning the first prize. With the money thus obtained he planned to pay off a mortgage held on Mary Eliska's home by an unscrupulous old banker, whose son was the prime mover in the plots against Bill.

One of the means adopted to force him to sell his secrets was the manipulation of a phantom airplane which, for a time, sadly puzzled the lad and his sister. The mystery was solved in a strange way, however, and almost at the same time, the baffling problem of what had become of Deanna Hoffinger's jewels was also unraveled. All this did not take place without many adventures being encountered by the four chums. Among these was the encounter with the old hermit, Peter Bell, who, through Mary Eliska's agency, was restored to his brother, James Bell, the millionaire western mining man.

James Bell became much interested in the Stricklins and their airplanes. Finally he made an advantageous proposal to Bill to travel West and operate for him a line of airplanes from some desert mines he had discovered on a trip which almost cost him his life. As autos could not cross the alkali, and transportation of the product by wagons would have been prohibitive in cost, as well as almost impossible to achieve, Mr. Bell had hit on the happy idea of conveying the precious product of his property by airplane.

At the same time, it so happened that Uncle John, the father of Jax Gray and Liam McAdams, was summoned West by an important railroad deal. This being the case, Jax Gray and Liam McAdams at once set to work plotting how they could gain their father's consent to their accompanying Mary Eliska and Bill. It was finally gained, although their mother Deanna Hoffinger shook her head over the matter, and, at first, would by no means hear of such a thing. But Uncle John urged that it would be a good thing for the children to see the great West, and that as Mary Eliska was to accompany the party, there would be no risk of their running wild.

But while the youngsters had all been so eager for the time to come for starting on their long journey that they could hardly eat, much less sleep, Aunt Sally had viewed with alarm the prospects ahead of her. In her mind the West was a vague jumble of rough cowboys, Native Americans, highwaymen and desperate characters in general. But there was no help for it. In addition to feeling it was her duty to accompany her young charges, her physician had also recommended her to seek the dry, rarefied air of the great Nevada plateau.

"It will be the very thing for your lungs, my dear madame," he had said; "they are by no means as strong as I could wish."

"Oh, but doctor, the Native Americans, the—the—" Aunt Sally had begun, when the physician cut her short.

"The only Native Americans left in the West now are all busy working for Wild West shows," he said, with a laugh; "and as for any other fancied cause of alarm, I dare say you will find the Western men quite as chivalrous and courteous as their Eastern brethren."

And so it happened that the dust-covered train was rolling across the arid solitudes at the edge of the great alkali desert with our party of friends on board. All were looking forward to adventures, but how strange and unexpected some of the happenings that befell them were to be not one of the party even dreamed.

The only member of the adventurous little band not now accounted for is Peter Bell, the former recluse. Peter was forward in the smoking car enjoying his old black pipe, which was his delight and solace and Aunt Sally's particular abomination. Among Peter's other peculiarities, acquired in a long and solitary life, was a habit he had of sometimes making, his remarks in verse. He entered the car just as the conversation we have recorded was in progress.

"Soon, my good friends, o'er the desert, so bold, we all shall be flying with excellent gold."

A general laugh from the young folks greeted him, and Bill struck in with: "That's if we don't fall to the earth from the sky, and land up in a smash on the white alkali."

The merriment that greeted this was cut short by the raucous voices of the trainmen.

"Blue Creek! Blue Creek!"

Instantly the liveliest bustle prevailed. Belongings of all sorts were hastily bundled together. So intent, in fact, was our party on its preparations for its plunge into the unknown that not one of them noticed two men who stood watching them intently from the opposite end of the car.

"So we've run the old fox into the ground," remarked one of them, a tall, heavily built fellow with a crop of short, reddish hair that bristled like the remnants of an old tooth brush. He was clean-shaven and had a weak, cruel mouth and a pair of narrow little eyes, through which he could, however, shoot a penetrating glance when anything interested him. Both he and his companion, a sallow, black-haired personage with a drooping pair of moustaches, were just then, seemingly, much engrossed.

"Yes, some place off thar'," rejoined the black-haired man with a wave of his hand toward the west—in which the sun, a ball of red fire, was now dropping, "some whar off thar, across that alkali, Jim Bell has his golden-egged goose."

"Hush, not so loud, Sam; one of those kids is looking at us."

"Pshaw, they hain't got sense to suspect nuthin'," was the scornful reply. "Wonder if Buck Bellew will be hyar ter meet us."

As he spoke the train wheels ceased to revolve and the cars came to a standstill in Blue Creek, a sun-bitten outpost of the "Big Alkali."

CHAPTER 14.2
AT THE NATIONAL HOUSE

Blue Creek was experiencing a spasm of excitement unusual to it. As a general thing, the dwellers on the edge of the great alkali wastes—once the bed of a mighty inland sea—were by far too much occupied in keeping reasonably cool, to betray even a passing interest in anything; except the arrival of a train of desolate-looking mules bearing gold from the barren, melancholy hills that rimmed the far-reaching alkali solitudes.

But the dust-whitened train, which twice a day puffed into Blue Creek and twice a day puffed joyfully out again, had, on this particular afternoon, set down a party which had caused unusual speculation among the Blue Creekites. "Thar's Jim Bell, frum out the desert, an' an old gent who looks like he might be some kin to Jim, and then thar's them likely lookin' lads an' those uncommon purty gals. Never know Jim hed a fam'ly afore. Ef he hez he's kep it mighty quiet all these ya'rs."

These remarks emanated from the throat of Cash Dallam, owner of the National House, Blue Creek's leading, and likewise only, hotel. The National was a board structure, formerly painted—with some originality of taste—a bright orange hue, relieved with red trimmings round doors, windows and eaves. But the sun had blistered and the hot desert winds had cracked and peeled its originally gaudy hues, and it was now a melancholy monotone of dull, pallid yellow. Here and there the paint had vanished altogether, and the bleached boards showed underneath. Like most of the other structures in Blue Creek—which boasted a general store, post office and Chinese laundry and restaurant combined the National House was coated with a thin layer of gray alkali dust, the gift of the glittering desert beyond its gates.

Cash Dallam's companions on the porch, which faced the railroad station and so was a favorite lounging place for the prominent citizens of Blue Creek and the guests of the hostelry, seemed only languidly interested.

"Thet's a powerful pile of baggage they're toting round," observed "Shavings" Magoon, who owed his nickname to the peculiar color and length of his hair, which looked as if it might have been gathered up bodily from the floor of a carpenter's shop and transferred to the top of his wrinkled countenance, about which it hung like a dubious aureole.

"You say that the tall chap yonder is Jim, Bell?"

The question, asked with some appearance of interest, came from a slender, dark-haired man in a blue shirt and leather "chaps," his face overshadowed by a big sombrero, who up to this time had not spoken. He had been leaning against the front wall of the National, thoughtfully removing some more of its paint by scraping it with the big rowelled Mexican spurs which he affected. These spurs, heavily mounted with Silver, together with a red sash he wore in the Mexican style about his waist, rather marked him out from his fellows on the National's porch.

Cash Dallam looked round as if in astonishment at the voice.

"Why hal-lo, stranger," he said, "whar you bin hidin' all these moons? Yes, that's Jim Bell, sure enough. Wouldn't think he wuz a millionaire ter look at him, would yer?"

The other shook his head.

"Can't most always sometimes tell," he remarked humorously; "that's a right pretty gal yonder, too. Any of you heard what Jim Bell's doing in Blue Creek?" The question came abruptly.

"Don't rightly know," was Cash's reply, "but I heard thet before he went Fast Jim Bell worked his way further inter ther desert than any man has ever bin. What he wuz arter I dunno, but it wouldn't be like Jim Bell ter risk his life fer muthin'."

"Do you reckon it was gold?"

The slender young man's dark eyes kindled in the word he used there was some potent fascination for him.

"Donno 'bout gold," said Cash, thoughtfully; "Thar's silver, yes, and platinum back younder. So ther Injuns say anyhow. But thar's mighty few white men hes ever got thet fur, an' if they did, they never come back to tell." He gazed out over the crystalline, quivering desert, burning whitely as a spangled Christmas card under the scorching sun. In his day Cash had seen many set out across it who never reappeared.

"Pity thar hain't no way of gitting thar without having ter use stock."

"Ortermobiles?" suggested a withered old man with the desert tan and wrinkles upon him.

"Tired 'em," struck in another of the same type. "No go. Sunk to ther hubs in mud holes an' then if it wusn't thet ther wuz ther sand to shove through and they hed ter give it up. No, ther vehicle or ther critter hain't invented that's goin' ter get away off thar back of beyond whar the gold lies—or whar they say it does," he added rather doubtfully. "When I was a kid back East my poor mother used ter tell me that gold lay at ther end of ther rainbow. I began huntin' it then and I've kep' it up ever since, an' will to ther end, I reckon."

"You say the vehicle isn't invented that will cross that stretch of alkali?" asked the tall young man, with a jingle of the metal ornaments hanging from the chased shank of his spurs.

"Thet's what. No rig, er devil wagon, er critters neither."

The reply was given with the emphasis of conviction.

"How about airships?"

The remark was dropped carelessly almost, by the spur-wearer.

"Airships! By ginger, thet's so!"

The pessimist spoke in a rather crestfallen tone.

"Seems ter me I read in an Eastern paper a while back suthin' about Jim Bell's bin at a place near New York and engaging a young chap ter build him some airplanes. Thar was a good bit of mystery about it. Say, boys, I wonder ef that's what Jim Bell's in Blue Creek fur?"

"Thar's one thing sartin," spoke up "Shavings" Magoon, "ef Jim Bell's got ther means ter git an aerial gold line he'll be safe enough frum them ornery road agents like ther fellers thet stuck up ther Laredo stage only last week an' got away with the specie box from Red River Falls. I reckon thar ain't no stage robbers with acroplanes yet a while."

"Queer thing about that Laredo robbery," put in Cash thoughtfully, "thar was several inter it, an' it seems thet they've all got clar away."

"Good thing for them, eh?" said the stranger, jingling his spur ornaments harder than ever. Cash sniffed.

"Good thing. Wall, stranger, I'd hate ter tell you what 'ud be the least of what 'ud happened to them, it would freeze your blood."

"Not an unpleasant thing to have happen today," said the stranger, carelessly, and carefully flicking some gray dust from his "chaps" with his rawhide quirt, "so you think that Jim Bell means to start some sort of an airline from whatever he has discovered in the interior into this place?"

"Don't know nothing about it," snapped Cash, rather impatiently; "you're a heap interested in Jim Bell, stranger."

"Naturally. He's quite a famous man in his way. I suppose he is one of the greatest mining authorities in the West."

But at this point Cash perceived that Mr. Bell's party had finished seeing to the disposal of their piles of baggage and were headed for the hotel. The operation had been a long one, as they bestowed particular attention upon sundry wooden boxes of oblong shape which might have held almost anything. Whatever their contents might be they were evidently held in some esteem by the Bell party.

A few seconds after Cash had broken off the conversation so abruptly, he was greeting the new arrivals. The other porch loungers stood sheepishly at some distance, some of them uneasily twisting their fingers. The presence of the young girls in the party filled them with a bashful terror such as the had never experienced in the numerous adventures and perils through which most of them had passed.

"The young ladies are Mary Eliska and Jax Gray," Mr. Bell said, introducing his companions, after the fashion of the Western country, to the hotel proprietor; "this is Bill Stricklin and his chum, Liam McAdams, and this," indicating the man whose resemblance to himself had already been remarked upon, "this is my brother, Mr. Peter Bell."

"Glad ter meet yer, miss; glad ter meet yer all, I'm sure," sputtered out Cash with one of his finest bows, and Cash was reckoned to be "a right elegant chap" in that primitive society.

CHAPTER 14.3
VOICES IN THE NIGHT

After supper—a queer meal to their Eastern tastes—the young folks were glad enough to retire to their rooms.

"Oh, what a funny place!" cried Jax Gray, as she and Mary Eliska, carrying a glass lamp which reeked of kerosene, entered their chamber. The walls were of rough boards with no attempt at ornamentation, a gorgeous checked crazy-quilt covered the bed—for though the days are hot on the desert, the nights are quite sharp. The floor, like the walls, was bare, and when the girls peered at themselves in the tiny mirror they gave little squeals of amused disgust. The heat of the sun, too, had drawn out the resinous qualities of the raw wood, and the room was impregnated with an aroma not unlike that of a pine forest under a hot sun.

"I expect we'll see some much funnier places before we get back East," said Mary Eliska decidedly, and beginning to unpack her silver-fitted dressing-bag, which was the one luxury she had allowed herself.

"I expect so, too; and I think it's jolly to rough it," chimed in her chum; "but it's hard to get used to it all at once. Stepping right off a Pullman into this is rather a sharp contrast, you must admit."

"It is," agreed Mary Eliska, heartily. She stepped to the window and gazed out on an uncovered porch outside. It was, in fact, the roof of the one below. On it flourished quite a little grove of scraggly plants of various kinds, which were carefully tended by Cash's wife. They were, perhaps, the only green things in Blue Creek.

But Mary Eliska had little eye for all this. Her lips parted in a quick gasp of admiration as she gazed upon the night spell of the desert. The dark sky was sprinkled with countless stars, large and luminous and beaming with a softer, stronger light than in the North. A brooding silence hung over the town—the silence of the desert. The hush was broken only by the droning notes of a song, accompanied on a guitar, which came from off in the distance on the outskirts of the little settlement. The music emphasized rather than broke the silence.

Jax Gray came to Mary Eliska's side, and upon her, too, descended the feeling of awe that the "Great Alkali" casts over all who encounter it for the first time.

"Mary Eliska," she said at length, "I'm—I'm the least bit frightened."

Her chum felt a slight shiver run through the girl as she pressed against her.

"Frightened, girlie? Frightened of what?"

"I don't just know. That's what makes it feel so bad. I guess it's the silence, the sense of all that loneliness out beyond there that upsets me. It feels almost as if there were some living presence off over the alkali that meant us harm."

"I think I know what the matter is," said Mary Eliska gently, "you're tired and overwrought. Come, let us get to bed, for Mr. Bell has ordered in early start in the morning."

Just how long afterward it was the awakened Mary Eliska had no means of telling, but as she lay sleepless she felt a longing to look out over the light-shrouded desert once more.

Arising she tiptoed to the window, and drawing the shade without making more than the merest rustle of noise she looked out. As she did so Mary Eliska almost uttered a startled exclamation, which, however, she instantly checked.

Three men had just emerged upon the balcony from an adjoining window. They brought chairs with them and sat there smoking. Mary Eliska could catch the rank, strong odor of the tobacco.

"It's better out here and we can talk more quietly," said one of them, as they sat down. "You say that Bell and his outfit start tomorrow?"

"That's what I overheard him say when I was listening to 'em talking arter supper," struck in another voice, "so I guess it's the early trail for us, too."

"Reckon so," came in a third speaker; "Jim Bell is going to travel fast. He's got the best horses and mules in this part of the country, and he won't spare 'em."

"You mean the alkali won't, I guess," put in the first speaker with an unpleasant laugh; "but he won't go far with ther stock. At the last waterhole he'll leave 'em and go on by airplane."

"You're crazy!"

"Never more sensible in my life. I—"

"Hush! Don't make such a racket. Fer all we know some of them may be awake and hear us. Now the old Steer Wells trail—"

But here the speaker sank his voice so low that it was impossible to hear his further words. But Mary Eliska, as she crept back to bed with her heart throbbing a little bit fast, felt vaguely that the conversation boded some ill to the mining man and his party of gold seekers.

"I'm sure I recognized one of those voices," she said to herself; "it was that of the tall, dark young man with the immense spurs and that picturesque red sash, who was eyeing us so at supper. Jax Gray and I thought he looked like a romantic brigand. What if he should turn out in real earnest to be a desperate character?"

Determining to speak to Jim Bell in the morning about the conversation she had overheard, Mary Eliska dropped off into a deep slumber at last, but her dreams were disturbing ones. Now she was traversing the Big Alkali, with its pungent dust in her nostrils and her feet crunching its crusty surface. She was lost, and would have cried out had she been able to open her lips. Then she was dying of thirst. Her lips were parched and cracked and the sun beat pitilessly down. So the hours passed 'til the stars began to pale and a new day was at hand. Before sunrise the party had been called, and, filled with excitement, made the wooden walls of the National Rouse resound with the hum of preparation.

Now, though Mary Eliska at midnight had fully determined to tell Mr. Bell all she had overheard, Mary Eliska, in the bright, crisp early dawn, felt that to do so would be absurd. After all, the men might merely have been chatting about the party, whose expedition was surely an adventurous and interesting one. It might make Mr. Bell think her a victim of girlish fancies if she went to him with the story, so Mary Eliska decided to remain silent. Afterward she was sorry for this.

As arrangements had been made with the ubiquitous Cash for burros and ponies before the party left for the West, there was little or no delay in getting started. The girls uttered delighted exclamations as their little animals were led up to the hotel steps by a long-legged Mexican who was to accompany the party to Steer Wells, where the ponies were to be abandoned and a permanent camp formed. From that point the dash into the alkali would be made by airplane.

For Mary Eliska there was a lively little "calico" animal which both girls pronounced "a darling." But Jax Gray was no less pleased with her little animal, a bright bay with a white star on its forehead. For the boys similar animals had been provided, while Aunt Sally's mount was a rather raw-boned gray of sedate appearance. In her youth Aunt Sally had done a good deal of horseback riding, and the manner in which she sat her mount showed that she had not forgotten her horsemanship. Mr. Bell and his brother bestrode rather heavier animals than the rest of the party, while Juan, the guide, contented himself with a remarkably small burro. When in the saddle his lanky legs stuck out on either side of his long-eared steed and appeared to be sort of auxiliary propellers for the creature.

Six pack burros had been obtained, and on two of these the camp equipment and utensils were carried. The remainder of the little animals carried the wooden cases in which the three monoplanes were packed, and the boxes containing mining instruments and tools. One of these was painted red, and in it was carried a supply of "giant" powder—a kind of dynamite used in mining operations.

"I shall keep my eye on that particular burro," remarked Liam McAdams, "and if he ever runs away I shall gallop off in the opposite direction."

But Mr. Bell explained that the explosive stuff was packed in such a manner that even the most violent shock would not set it off.

"Still, we won't experiment," declared Bill.

Ten minutes after the cavalcade had drawn up in front of the hotel, attracting the attention of the entire population of Blue Creek, the party was ready to set out on the first stage of their adventurous, journey. The girls looked very natty in corduroy skirts, neat riding boots, with plain linen waists and jaunty sombreros. The boys, like Mr. Bell and his brother, were in khaki, and each carried a fine rifle, the gift of Mr. Bell. Aunt Sally had at first wished to resuscitate her old riding habit, but instead, before she left the East, the girls had persuaded her to have an up-to-date one made of cool, greenish khaki.

"You look like a modern Diana," said Mr. Bell, with a gallant bow, which brought the color to Aunt Sally's blooming cheeks.

"Really, Mr. Bell, that is too bad of you, when you know I am trying to grow old gracefully," retorted Aunt Sally.

"And now," said Mr. Bell, running a watchful eye over the entire outfit, "we are all ready to start." A cheer, which the girls took up, came ringing from the boys' throats.

"Hooray!" they shouted."Good luck!" cried Cash Dallam from his porch, and several in the crowd caught up the cry..

Juan uttered a series of extraordinary whoops, and working his legs like the long limbs of a seventeen-year locust, he dashed to the head of the procession. The next minute they were off, the pack burros trotting behind in a sedate line.

But just as they started an odd thing happened. Mary Eliska experienced that peculiar feeling which sensitive persons feel when they are being watched. Glancing quickly round she encountered the penetrating glance of the tall, dark young man who had formed one of the group on the porch the previous evening. He turned his eyes away instantly as he perceived that his interested gaze had been intercepted. As he did so, Aunt Sally, despite the heat, felt a little shiver run through her.

But the emotion passed in a moment under the excitement of the dash forward. Before long, the rough habitations of Blue Creek lay far behind them, and in front there lay, glittering under the blinding sun, the far-reaching expanse of the desert. Off to the southwest hovered what seemed to be a blue cloud on the horizon. But they knew that in that direction lay the Black Rock hills, a desolate chain of low, barren mountains.

As if by instinct they all drew rein as the solitudes closed in about them. Rising in his stirrups Mr. Bell pointed into the distance. "Yonder lies the end of the rainbow!" he exclaimed with a touch of rude poetry.

"And back there are the wings to fetch forth the pot of gold," laughed Jax Gray, indicating the packing cases on the burros' backs.

"Yes, the golden wings," struck in Mary Eliska, but there was a wistful note underlying her light tone. The spell of the desert, the unreclaimed and desolate, was upon her.

CHAPTER 14.4
THE DESERT HAWKS

While our little party had been making its way so arduously across the almost impenetrable waste of sand and alkali, another party equipped with tough, desert-bred horses and a knowledge, so intimate as to be uncanny, of the secret ways and trails of the sun-bitten land, had made preparations for departure.

It had been no fancy on Mary Eliska's part when she imagined that she heard the partial details of a plot against Mr. Bell on the night during which she had lain awake in the rough hotel of Blue Creek. Had the party possessed the power of seeing through partitions of solid timber, they would have been able to behold within that room a scene transpiring which must, inevitably, have filled them with uneasiness and even alarm.

Red Bill Summers, one of the best known of the desert hawks, as the nefarious rascals who ply their highwayman's trade on the desert are sometimes called, had been one of the passengers on the train whose keenly observing eyes had surveyed the little party as they disembarked. His companion, the man with the drooping moustache was likewise invested with a somewhat sinister reputation. But probably the worst of the trio who foregathered that night at the National House was the romantic looking young man with the red sash and the silver spurs whom the others called Buck Bellew.

Mr. Bell and his expedition into the desert formed the topic of their conversation. It was evident, as they talked, that their main desire was to trap or decoy him on his way, but as they discussed plans this intention gradually changed.

"He's got kids with him, and young gals, too;" said the dark-mustached man, who seemed to be a little less ruffianly than his companions, "we don't want to do them no harm."

"Not if we can help it," rejoined Red Bill Summers, wrinkling his low forehead, "but I ain't goin' ter let them stand in our way."

"Of course not," chimed in Buck Bellew, playing with the tassels on his red sash, and jingling his silver-mounted spurs in a somewhat dandified fashion, "pretty girls, too," he added.

"Ther point's just this," struck in Red Bill, apparently paying no attention to the other's conversation, "Jim Bell's got a desert mine some place out thar yonder. This young chap he had with him, what's his name—"

"Albert Stricklin," suggested Buck Bellew.

"Ay, Stricklin, that's it. Wal, this yer Stricklin has invented some sort of an air ship, I read that in the papers. It's pretty clear to my mind that this air ship is going to be used in getting the gold out of the desert. That's plain enough, eh?"

"Yes, if your first idee is right. If he's got a paying mine in reality," agreed Bellew.

"Oh, I'm satisfied on that point. Jim Bell's too old a fox to go inter the desert onless he had stithin' worth going arter."

"Well, what are we going to do about it?" asked the third man with a grin, "build an airplane, too. For myself I'm free to confess I ain't no sky pilot and don't never expect to be one."

"This ain't a minstrel show," scowled Red Bill.

"Couldn't help laffin' though," said the black-mustached one, "talkin' uv aviators reminded me of that story of the feller who went ter see I lier doctor and git some medicine. Ther doc he says, 'I want you to take three drops in water very day.' Ther young chap fainted. When he recovered they asked him what the matter was. He says, 'I'm an aviator. Three drops in water would finish me in a week.'"

"That'll do from you," grunted Red Bill, without the trace of a smile at this little anecdote, "let's git down to bizness. Those folks leave here tomorrow. They'll go early in the morning. "We can't follow them too close without excitin' suspicion. The problem is to keep track of them without they're knowing it."

"Don't they take any servants or help?" asked Bellew after a pause.

"Yes, they do."

"You're certain?"

"I made it my business to find out. They are going to take a guide. Have him engaged, in fact."

"Who is he?"

"Oh, a no-good Mexican, a chap named Juan Baptista."

"Juan Baptista!" exclaimed Bellew slapping his leg, "that's fine. Couldn't be better."

"You know him?"

"So well that he'll have to do anything I say."

"You can make him obey you then?"

"I know of a horse stealing case in which he was mixed up. If he won't do what we tell him to I'll threaten him with exposure."

"Good. He is sleeping in the corral with their ponies. Let's go down there now and rouse him out. Then we'll have part of the business settled."

"I'm agreeable. Come on."

As noiselessly as possible the three plotters crept from the room and tip-toed down the corridors. Following a long passage they presently emerged into a star-lit stable-yard. In that part of the west doors are not locked at night, so they could go out without bothering about a key.

"Where's the corral?" whispered Buck as they came out of the hotel.

"Right over there. See that haystack. The greaser's asleep this side of it. Right under where that saddle is hanging on the fence."

"All right. Come on."

Led by Buck Bellew, whose spurs gave out an occasional jingle, they crept across the yard. Presently they came upon a dark bundle lying huddled at the foot of the corral palings.

Bellew stirred the inanimate bundle with his foot. The spurs gave out a tinkling, musical jingle. The thing moved, stirred and finally galvanized into life. It was finally revealed as the figure of a rather ill-favored Mexican, unusually tall for one of his race who are, as a rule, squat and small.

"Buenas tardes, Juan!" greeted Buck Bellew.

"Buenas tardes, senors," was the response. "But what for do you disturb me in thees way. Know that tomorrow with the rising of the sun I have to awake and saddle the beasts, and fare forth into the alkali with party of gringoes."

"That's all right. That's what we came to talk to you about, Juan," said Bellew. He bent low and pushed his face almost into the Mexican's brown and sleepy countenance.

"Do you know me!" he grated out.

"Todos Santos! Caramba! It is the Senor Bellew!"

"Not so loud Juan. There may be somebody around who would recognize that name. It is enough that you know me."

"What do you wish with me, senor?"

The Mexican's voice shook. Evidently he feared this tall, good-looking, though dissolute, young Gringo.

"You are to escort a party of gringos headed by a Senor Bell as far as Steer Wells, are you not?"

"Si senor. As I said tomorrow before the rising of the sun must I be awake. I must saddle and pack, and—"

"All right. Never mind that. I have a little bit of work for you to perform, too. If you do it well you will be rewarded. If not—"

"If not senor—?"

"If not—well don't let us dwell on unpleasant subjects. I want you to ride with these gringos. Listen to all that they say. Talk to them and learn from them all that you can."

"Of what?"

"Of their destination—of where they are going—what they are going to do when they get there, and so on. You understand?"

"Perfectly senor. But they have paid me well and promised more. Senor Bell is a good man. He is—"

"Will you do what I tell you?"

The voice was sharp and imperious.

"Senor, I would do much for you. But this—"

The Mexican spread his hands helplessly.

"I cannot. It would be too bad a thing to do."

"Very well. I'll call Cash Dallam. Tell him who you are and how it was you who was concerned in the theft of those horses from Diablo River. You know what would happen to you then. You know—"

But the Mexican was down on his knees. His hands were raised in mute appeal. His teeth' chattered like the busy heels of a clog dancer.

"No, no, senor. Santa Maria, no, no!" he begged.

"It's entirely up to you," was the cold response. "Now will you do as I say?"

"Yes, yes. A thousand times yes, senor. Anything you say— anything."

"I thought so," rejoined Bellew grimly. He turned with a look of triumph to the two silent spectators of the scene, who nodded smilingly. The Mexican's pitiful agitation seemed only to amuse those callous hearts.

"You will travel, as I said, with these gringos," pursued Bellew, "and glean all the information you can. Then, when you have found out all about where they mean to go, and how long they mean to stay and so on, you will find an opportunity to drop out of their company."

"Si senor," quavered the man, "and then—"

"And then you will be met by us. We shall take care of you."

"But Senor Bell and the senoritas?"

"We will take care of them, too," was the grim response.

It was not 'til the next day, at noon, that the three desert hawks left the hotel, long after the departure of the Bell party. They rode slowly in the opposite direction to that in which the other party had gone, 'til they had gotten out of sight of the little town. Then, taking advantage of every dip and rise in the surface of the plain, they retraced their steps and soon were riding on the track of the Bell outfit.

"Whar wa'ar you all ther forenoon?" asked the black-mustached man of Red Bill as they rode along.

"I was doing a bit of profitable business," was the rejoinder.

"Selling something?"

"No finding something out. Boys, Jim Bell's in our power."

"In our power," laughed the other, a laugh in which Bellew chimed in. "I reckon you don't know him yet."

"Don't eh?" snarled Red Bill, stung into acrimonious retort. "I reckon your brain works just a bit too quick, Buck."

"Waal, ef you know so much, let's hear it?"

The red-sashed, silver-spurred Buck Bellew reined in closer to his companions, roweling his little active "paint" horse as he did so, 'til it jumped and curvetted.

"It's just this," said Red Bill Summers, unconsciously lowering his tone although there was no one about to hear but his companions, a few, blasted-looking yuccas and, far overhead, a wheeling buzzard.

"Jim Bell ain't never filed no location of ther mine with ther guv'ment."

If he had expected to produce a sensation, he must have felt justified by the results of this announcement. Buck Bellew whistled. The black-mustached man gave a low, long-drawn-out exclamation of:

"Wo-o-o-w!"

"Thought you'd sit up and take notice," grinned their leader. "Sounds foolish-like, but it's true. I searched ther records, but it ain't on 'em."

"Maybe he's filed a claim some place else," suggested the black-mustached man.

"There you go, throwing cold water as usual," snorted Buck Bellew.

"Taint cold water. It's common, ornery hoss sense. That's what it is. Do you s'pose that any man 'ud be foolish enough to locate a rich mine an' then not file a claim to it?"

"Heard of sich things been done," commented Red Bill. "Maybe he ain't over and above anxious fer anyone ter go in alongside of him afore he's had a chanct ter take up some more land. Maybe—"

"Waal, no use guessing at sich things," rejoined Buck; "fer my part I guess Red is right. Jim Bell ain't had the hoss sense te file a claim. And if he ain't—"

"That makes it all the easier fer us. Wonder ef thet feller Juan is learning much?"

Bill Summers was the speaker.

"He's sharp as a steel trap," volunteered Bellew, "when he wants to be."

"I guess arter that dressing down you giv' him las' night he'll want to be, all right," opined the black-mustached man.

"Guess so," grinned Buck; "if he ain't, it'll be the worse fer him."

As he spoke they topped a little rise. Over in front of them, and on all sides—the desert, vast, illimitable, untrod of man, lay, a desolate expanse of nothingness.

Far, far off could be seen a tiny blue cloud, resting on the horizon—the desert range.

"Thar's whar Jim Bell's mine is, I'll bet a hoss and saddle," said

Bellew reining in his horse and pointing to the distant azure mass.

"Guess you'd win," nodded Red Bill Summers, "and," he added, his keen eyes narrowing to slits he gazed straight ahead, "and thar, I reckon, is Jim Bell himself and his party."

They followed the direction of his gaze. Far off across the glittering ocean of sand and alkali a yellowish cloud—almost vaporish, arose. It seemed to be a sort of water spout on land. It drifted lazily upward. The experienced desert hawks knew it for what it was. The dust cloud raised by a company of travelers.

As their glances rested on it intently, not one of the three figures toping the crest of the little rise, spoke.

Their tired horses, too, stood absolutely still. Men and animals might have been petrified figures, carved out of the desolation about them. There was a something impressive about them as they stood there in the midst of the desert glare. Silent, hawk-like, and intent. Their very poses seemed to convey a sense of menace—of danger.

Suddenly they wheeled and turned, and their mounts, as the spurs struck their damp sides, broke into a lope. As they galloped, Red Bill burst into a song. A lugubrious, melancholy thing, like most of the songs of the plainsmen.

"Bury me out on lone prair-ee
Out where the snakes and the coyotes be;
Drop not a tear on my sage brush grave
Out on the lone prair-e-e-e-e-e!"

Then the others struck in, their ponies' hoofs making an accompaniment to the gruesome words:

"The sands will shift in the desert wind;
My bones will rot in the alkali kind;
I'll be happier there than ever I be
In my grave, on the lone prair-e-e-e-e-e!"

It began to sound like a dirge, but still the leader of the hawks of the desert kept it up. He bellowed it out now in a harsh, shrill voice. It rasped uncomfortably, like rusty iron grating on rusty iron.

"Maybe upon the judgment day;
When all sinners their debt must pay;
They'll find me and bind me and judge poor me;
All in my grave, on the lone prair-e-e-e-e-e-e!"

As the last words of this dismal chant rang out, an echo seemed to be flung back at the singer from behind a neighboring ridge, upon which the lone yuccas stood upright, like, so many figures of formed bits of humanity.
"Ye-e-e-e-e-e-e!"

It came in a long-drawn-out wail that fairly seemed to make the desert ring with its gruesome echoes. All at once it was taken up from another point. Then another echoed it back. It seemed to be proceeding from a dozen quarters of the compass at once.

Strong nerved as all three of the riders were, it appeared to make a strange impression on them.

"What in the name of Kit Carson wuz that?" demanded Red Bill drawing rein.

"Dunno. It sounded like someone havin' fun with that ther cheerful little song of yourn," said the black-mustached man.

"That's what it did. I'd like to find the varmint. I'd make some fun fer him."

The man scowled savagely. His nerves had been unpleasantly shaken by the wild, unearthly cries.

"It didn't sound human," he said at length; "tell you what, let's jes' look aroun' and see if we kin find any trace of who done it."

Buck Bellew said nothing but he grinned to himself. Plainly something amused him hugely.

"All right;" he said, "we'll look."

They rode about among the desert dips and gullies for some time, but they could discover no trace of any agency that could have produced the weird cries. Both Red Bill and the black-mustached man were plainly nonplussed.

"This beats all," opined Summers. "I don't even see a track any place."

"Nor don't I," rejoined his companion seriously. Both were superstitious men, a failing apparently not shared by Bellew, who stood regarding them, seated easily sideways in his saddle, with an amused look.

"Hey Bellew, why don't you come an' look. You alters wuz a good tracker?" demanded Red Bill looking up suddenly.

"Not fer me, thanks," was the easy response, "ef you want to hunt spooks—"

"Who said it wuz a spook or any such pack uv nonsense?" glared back Summers.

"I didn't," declared the black-mustached man with great positiveness.

"No more did I," angrily sputtered Red Bill "thar ain't no such things nohow."

"I dunno," said the black-mustached man seriously. "I do recollec' hearing my old grandmother, back East, tell about a ghost what she seen once. Want ter hear about it?"

No one replied, and taking silence for consent, he went on.

"Grandmother was married to a decent old chap that was a teamster. He used to haul farm stuff to the city in the day and it was often pretty late afore he got out again. Well, on his way he had to pass a cemetery, a buryin' ground you know, and I tell you he didn't like it. It sort of got on his nerves to think that some night one of them dead folks lying there all so quiet might arise from ther graves.

"It seems as how it allers haunted him ter think that some night as he wuz drivin' by that ther buryin' ground—"

"Yer said that once before," snapped Summers looking nervously about him, "get on with your story."

"Well I am, ain't I?"

"Not fast enough."

"Waal this is a ghost story and ghosts don't move fast."

"Ho! ho!" laughed Bellew hollowly.

"As I was sayin', grandpop didn't like the idee of some night seeing a tall form, all in white, come gliding down among them tombstones, and raising its hand cry to him in a solemn voice—"

"Wow."

The shout came from Summers. He had suddenly felt something light on his shoulder. Thence it had crawled to neck and laid clammy feet upon him. It was an immense dragon fly, but he had evidently mistaken it for something else, to judge by the start and exclamation he had given.

"Ain't gittin' on yer nerves, be I?" asked the black-mustached man innocently.

"No, no. Get on with your fool story for goodness sake."

"You wuz a sayin' thet your fool grandpop wuz supposin' that ef something said to him as he wuz-oh, go on and tell it yourself!"

"All right. Well then grandpop was jes' a thinkin' how awful it 'ud be ef anything like that ever did happen. He'd come home and talk to grandma'am at nights about it. I tell you his nerves was powerful upsot. Suthin' like yours."

"Like mine, you long-legged lizard!"

"I mean like yours might hev bin ef you'd bin in my grandpop's place, Red."

"Oh, all right. Perceed. What nex'?"

"Waal, one night jes what he'd bin a dreadin' did come ter pass. He was goin' by ther graveyard when he hearn the awfulest screech you ever hearn—"

"Yow-e-ow-ee-ow-ow!"

Red Bill Summers started and turned pale. It was a repetition of the cry that had interrupted his song. Without wasting time on ceremonies, he dug his spurs into his horse and dashed off. The narrator of the ghost story, as badly scared as his companion, followed him at post haste. Ther Bellew laughing heartily, turned and followed them. But at a more leisurely speed. From time to time, as he pursued the flying forms, his big frame shook with mirth. Somebody once said that a man who gives a hearty laugh was not all bad. If this is true, there must have been considerable good in Buck Bellew.

After about a mile of riding he overtook the other two.

"What's the hurry?" he inquired easily.

"Nuthin', nuthin'," said Summers, still a bit shaky, "my pony scairt at suthin, I reckon, and jes' naturally dashed off. I had a hard job te pull the cayuse in."

"Same hyar, same hyar," said the black-mustached man.

"Rot!" laughed Bellew. "In my opinion, you're both a pair of cowards. Don't pull your gun on me, Summers. You wouldn't fire at me, and you know it."

Summers sullenly put up his gun.

"Say, what's ther matter with you, Buck?" he asked grumpily.

"What's the matter with you two, you mean? Why, you dashed off like a girl in a red sweater with a bull on her heels."

"I tole you ther ponies ran away," said Summers, shifting his little eyes. Somehow he couldn't look Bellew in the face.

"Yes, and I guess what made 'em run was suthin' like this—"

A quizzical look stole over Bellew's lean, handsome features. All at once the air became filled with the same mysterious sounds that had so alarmed Summers and the other man.

"Ye-e-e-e-e-e-e-ow-w-w-w-w-w-e-e-eeeee!"

"Buck! You consarned old ventriloconquest!" shouted Summers, vastly relieved as Bellew burst into a roar of hearty laughter.

"Forgot I used to be ventriloquist with a medicine show, eh?" chuckled Bellew, rolling about in his saddle. "Come in handy sometimes, don't it?"

"Waal, next time yer goin' ter practice, jes' let us know in advance."

Summers' face held rather a sheepish grin as he spoke. The black-mustached man looked even more foolish.

"Make a good signal, wouldn't it?" asked Bellew presently.

"Yes. By the way, reckon you could imitate a coyote, Buck?"

"Easy. Listen!" A perfect imitation of a coyote's yapping, hyena-like cry rang out.

"Great. Maybe we can use that sometime."

How soon that cry was to be used, and to what disastrous effect on our little party of adventurers, we shall see as our story progresses. But the next time Buck Bellew gave that thrilling, spine-tightening cry, was to be under far different circumstances, and with far different results—results fraught with great importance to our young adventurers.

CHAPTER 14.5
THE DIVINING RODS

"What wonderful clouds. They remind one of the fantastic palaces of the Arabian Nights!" exclaimed Mary Eliska.

It was at the close of the noonday halt that she spoke, reclining with the rest of the party under a canvas shelter, beneath which lunch had been eaten.

Off to the southwest the clouds she referred to had been, in fact, gathering for some time. Domed, terraced and pinnacled, they rose in gloomy grandeur on the far horizon. But Mary Eliska had not been the first to notice them. For some reason Mr. Bell, after gazing at the vaporous masses for a few minutes, looked rather troubled. He summoned Juan, who was feeding his beloved burro, and waved his hand toward the clouds, the same time speaking rapidly in Spanish.

"What is it? Is there a storm coming?" asked Jax Gray, noting Mr. Bell's somewhat troubled look.

"I do not know, and Juan says he is not certain yet either," was the response. "Let us hope not, however."

"I don't see why it should trouble us," said Mary Eliska. "We have good tents and shelter, and as far as a good wetting is concerned I should think it would do this dried up place a lot of good."

"That is not what was worrying me," confessed Mr. Bell with a smile; "if it was to be an ordinary Eastern storm I should not mind any more than you. But the desert has many moods—as many as—you will pardon me—a young lady. Even the storms of the Big Alkali are not like others. They are dry storms."

"This would be no place for an umbrella dealer then," remarked Liam McAdams airily.

"No, I am speaking seriously," went on Mr. Bell; "frequently such storms do great damage through lightning, although, during their progress, not a drop of rain falls. The electrical display, however, is sometimes terrific. That is what I mean when I say 'a dry storm.'"

"I can't bear lightning," cried Jax Gray; "I always go in the cellar at home when it comes."

"Never mind, Jax Gray, Bill and I will dig you one if the storm hits us," put in her brother gallantly.

"And one for me, too, please!" cried Mary Eliska; "I'm dreadfully afraid of lightning."

"Well, let us hope that we shall none of us have any cause for alarm," put in Peter Bell, the former hermit. "When I lived my solitary life I often used to wander out in the height of a storm. It was beautiful to watch the lightning ripping and tearing across the sky. The lightning and the thunder did not scare me a bit. But—."

"You'd soon have changed your mind if by lightning you'd been hit," struck in Liam McAdams before the old man could complete his verse. A good-natured laugh, in which Peter Bell joined as heartily as the others, followed this bit of improvisation.

"Well, let us be pressing on," said Mr. Bell presently; "we are not carrying any too heavy a water supply, and I am anxious to replenish it by nightfall. By the way, that means a new experience for you youngsters. You will get your first taste of alkali water."

"But how are you going to get water in this desert?" exclaimed Bill wonderingly.

"You will see before many hours," was the reply with which they had to be content.

All that afternoon they pressed on without anything of interest occurring. The distant clouds grew more imposing and blacker in hue, but they seemed to draw no closer. The heat, however, was oppressive, and the glare of the desert hurt Aunt Sally's eyes.

"If they didn't look so hideous, I wish I'd brought along those old smoked glasses I wore on the beach at Atlantic City," she thought more than once.

Sundown found the party skirting along the foot of rough, broken hills clothed with a scanty vegetation. Juan nodded approvingly and at once suggested making the camp there.

"We'll see if there is any water first," said Mr. Bell.

"It looks as if you need not take the trouble," declared Bill, "it's as dry as a week-old crust."

"Not quite so fast, young man," laughed Mr. Bell, "appearances are often deceitful, especially on the desert."

He dismounted, and reaching into one of the packs drew forth a slender forked stick. Then, while they all gazed in a puzzled silence at his actions, he passed it hither and thither over the dry floor of the desert.

"Oh, I know what it is now!" cried Mary Eliska suddenly. "It's a divining rod!"

"A divining rod?" echoed Bill. "What's that?"

"Oh, look!" cried Jax Gray, before Mary Eliska could answer; "it's moving!"

The slender switch held by Mr. Bell was certainly behaving in a very odd manner. It could be seen to bend and sway and hop and skip about as if it had been suddenly endued with life. Mr. Bell, who was by now at some distance from the party, looked up with a satisfied expression.

"Get a shovel and dig here!" he ordered Juan. But the Mexican had fallen into a deep slumber from which it took not a little effort to awaken him. When he was finally roused and made to understand what was required of him, he set to work with a will, however, and made the dirt fly.

The boys pitched in, too, and before long quite a deep hole had been excavated. The girls, peeping cautiously over its edge, gave a delighted cry. Actual water was beginning to drain into it from the side. True, it was not of the color or temperature they had been used to associating with the fluid, but still the sight of it was welcome enough to the travel-stained wayfarers.

"You can come out now, boys, and leave the hole to fill up, which it will soon do," declared Mr. Bell.

The interval of waiting for the water to flow in a goodly quantity was spent in adjusting the girls' tent, and in setting the camp to rights generally. A sort of blue-colored bunch grass grew in considerable quantities about the water hole, and this the burros seemed to find quite palatable. The ponies and horses, however, would not touch it, and had to be regaled on the pressed hay and grain which were carried for the purpose.

In the midst of all this there came a sudden sharp cry from the water hole, followed by a loud splash.

"It's old Mr. Bell! He's fallen into the water hole!" shrilled Mary Eliska.

"Head over heels, too. Hurry and we'll get him out," cried the boys.

Bill seized up a lariat, and followed by the others started for the hole. It was as they had guessed. Venturing too close to the brink of the excavation, old Mr. Bell had slipped, and the former hermit was floundering about like a grampus in the water when his rescuers appeared. Luckily, it was not deep, and they soon had him out of it and on his feet. The old man, with great good nature, declared that he had rather enjoyed his involuntary bath than otherwise. He was so mud-stained and drenched, however, that it was necessary for him to make an immediate change of clothes. When he emerged from his tent with dry apparel, the aged recluse felt moved to compose a verse, which he did as follows:

"Within the mud hole's watery depths, A grave I almost met, But luckily I was pulled out Alive, but very wet."

"Well, Peter," laughed his brother, "you certainly are a poetic philosopher. But now, if you are quite finished with the water hole, we will draw some for our own use, and then Juan can let the stock have a drink."

As the first bucket for camp use was drawn, Mary Eliska hastened up with a cup and extended it.

"Oh, do let me have a drink," she exclaimed; "I'm dying with thirst and can't wait for tea."

"Same here," cried Jax Gray, eagerly. Mr. Bell smiled and eyed them quizzically.

"I wouldn't advise you young ladies to try it 'til it has been boiled," he said, "but of course if you insist—"

"We do," cried both girls. "Fill the cups, Juan," ordered Mr. Bell.

The guide did so, and Mary Eliska and Jax Gray eagerly raised the receptacles. But hardly had they taken a swallow before they hurriedly ceased drinking.

"Oh, what awful stuff!" sputtered Mary Eliska, while Jax Gray simply gasped.

"Bah! It tastes like aged eggs added Bill, who had also taken a swallow. "Is it poisonous?"

"Not a bit of it," laughed Mr. Bell; "it is simply alkali water, and when you have drunk as much of it as I have you'll be used to it and not mind it. But I must admit that on first introduction it is rather trying. It is better when it is boiled, though. It seems to lose that acrid flavor."

And so it proved; and Mary Eliska declared that she had never enjoyed a cup of tea so much as the one she drank that evening at supper on the desert. As dusk fell, Juan produced a battered guitar from a case which was strapped to the back of his saddle, and seating himself cross-legged in the midst of a semi-circle of enthusiastic listeners he banged out a lot of Spanish airs.

Then Liam McAdams danced a jig with incomparable agility and Bill did some tricks with cards and handkerchiefs that were declared superior to anything heretofore seen. But the little entertainment was to come to an abrupt conclusion. So engrossed had they been in its progress that they had not noticed that the sky had clouded over, and that it had suddenly grown insufferably oppressive.

All at once a red glare enveloped the camp. It lasted only for the fraction of a second, but in its brief existence it displayed some very white and alarmed faces.

The electric storm that Mr. Bell had dreaded was upon them.

CHAPTER 14.6
A DRY STORM

In describing what immediately followed, Mary Eliska has always declared that her sole impression was of continuous "flash and crash."

The first red glare, as a jagged streak of lightning tore across the sky, was followed by an earsplitting thunder roll. Almost instantly the entire heavens became alive with wriggling serpents of light. The crisscross work of the bolts ranged in hue from a vivid eye-burning blue to an angry red. And all the time the thunder roared and crashed in one unceasing pandemonium. A smell of brimstone and sulphur filled the air. The tethered stock whinnied and plunged about in mad terror.

"Juan, look to the stock!" shouted Mr. Bell above the turmoil. But Juan, at the first crash, had flung himself face downward on the sand and lay there trembling and praying.

As there seemed no possibility of getting him up, the boys and Mr. Bell set to work on the by no means easy task of securing the terrified animals more carefully.

In the meantime, the girls, in Aunt Sally's tent, were having a hard time to convince that lady that the end of the universe was not at hand.

"Oh, dear, why did we ever come out here!" cried the terrified woman; and then the next minute:

"Just hark at that! We shall all be killed! I know it! Oh, this is terrible!"

"It will soon be over, aunt, dear," exclaimed Mary Eliska bravely, though her own head ached and her eyes burned cruelly from the glare and uproar.

"Yes, dear Aunt Sally," chimed in Jax Gray; "it can't last; it—"

There was a sudden blinding glare, followed by a crash that seemed as if the skies must have been rent open. With it mingled a loud scream from Aunt Sally and cries and shouts from outside the tent.

"Something in the camp has been struck!" exclaimed Aunt Sally rushing to the tent door.

"It's Juan's burro!" cried Jax Gray, who had followed her; "look at the poor thing, off over there."

In the radiance of the electric display they could see quite plainly the still form of the little animal lying outstretched on the ground. Juan heard the girl's cry, and for the first time since the storm had begun he moved. Directly he perceived the motionless form of his mount he appeared to lose all his terror of the storm, and sprinted off toward it on his long legs. As he ran he called aloud on all the saints to look down upon his miserable fate.

But as he reached the side of his long-eared companion, the creature, which had only been stunned by the bolt, suddenly sprang to its feet and, no doubt crazed by fear, began striking out with its hind hoofs. As ill luck would have it, poor Juan came within direct range of the first kick, and was sent flying backward by its force.

Behind him lay the water hole, and before he could stop the cowardly guide found himself over the brink and struggling in the muddy water. His cries for help were piercing, but as Mr. Bell and the boys were busy, and as they knew that the Mexican was in no actual peril, they left him there for a time.

In the meantime, the first terrific violence of the storm had subsided, and before long it passed. As it growled and muttered off in the distance, lighting up the desert with an occasional livid glare, Juan came scrambling out of the mud-hole. He did not say a word, but went straight up to his burro. He saddled it in silence, strapped his old guitar on its back and, swinging himself into the saddle, dashed off across the alkali, his long legs working like pendulums on either side of the little creature. It actually seemed as if he were propelling instead of riding it.

The boys wanted to know if they should set off in pursuit of their errant guide, but Mr. Bell said that it would be the best thing to let him go if he wished.

"He was more of a hindrance than a help," he declared, "and he and his burro between them ate far more than their share of food."

"But won't the poor man become lost or starve?" asked Aunt Sally, who, now that her alarm had passed with the storm, had joined the group.

"Not much danger of that," laughed Mr. Bell, "a fellow of Juan's type can subsist on next to nothing if he has to, and his burro is as tough as he is, I suspect."

"At any rate, he must have thought so when he got that kick," laughed Aunt Sally.

"It reminded me of a verse I once heard," put in the former hermit.

And then, without waiting for anyone to ask him to repeat the lines in question, he struck up:

> "As a rule, never fool
> With a buzz saw or a mule."

"I expect that's excellent advice," laughed the old man's brother, "but now, ladies and gentlemen, as the excitement of the night seems to be over, I think we had better retire. Remember, an early start tomorrow, and if all goes well we ought to be at Steer Wells by nightfall."

"If we steer well," muttered Liam McAdams, not daring to perpetrate the pun in a louder tone of voice.

Fifteen minutes later, silence entrenched the camp, which seemed like a tiny island of humanity in the vast silence stretched round about. As they slumbered, the girls, with their silver-mounted revolvers—gifts from Mr. Bell—under their pillows, the clouds of the dry storm rolled away altogether, and the effulgent moon of the Nevada solitudes arose.

Her rays silvered the desolate range of barren hills and threw into sharp relief the black shadows which marked the deep gulches, cutting the otherwise smoothly rounded surfaces of the strange formation.

Suddenly, from one of the gulches, the figure of a man on horseback emerged and stood, motionless as a statue, bathed in moonlight on an elevation directly overlooking the camp. For perhaps five minutes the horseman remained thus, silent as his surroundings. But suddenly a shrill whinny rang out from one of the horses belonging to our party, who had seen the strange animal.

Instantly the figure turned and wheeled, and when Mr. Bell, ever on the alert, emerged from his tent to ascertain what the noise might portend, nothing was to be seen.

"That's odd," muttered the mining man, "horses don't usually whinny in the night except to others of their kind who may suddenly appear. I wonder—but, pshaw!" he broke off; "the thing's impossible. Even if our mission were known nobody would dare to molest us.

"But just the same," he continued, as, after a careful scrutiny, he returned to the tent he shared with his brother, "but just the same I'd like to know just why that animal whinnied."

Whoever the watcher of the camp had been, he did not reappear that night, but while old Mr. Bell prepared breakfast, and the girls were what the boys called "fixing up," the mining man summoned the boys to him and observed that he wished them to take a little stroll to see if better grass for the stock could not be found in the hills. This was so obviously an excuse to get them off for a quiet talk that the lads exchanged glances of inquiry. They said nothing, however, but followed Mr. Bell as he struck off toward the barren range.

As soon as they were out of earshot of the camp the mining man informed them of his suspicions and of what he had heard the night before.

"On thinking it over I am more than ever convinced that somebody must have been hovering about the camp last night," he declared, "but it is no use alarming the others unnecessarily, and, after all, I may be mistaken. In any event, from now on, we will post ourselves on sentry duty at night so as not to be taken by surprise in the event of any malefactors attacking us."

"Then you really think, sir, that somebody may have wind of the object of our journey and molest us?" inquired Bill soberly.

"I don't know; but it is always best to be on the safe side," was the rejoinder; "the towns on the edge of the desert are full of bad characters and it is possible that in some way the reason of our expedition has leaked out."

By this time they had walked as far as the mouth of one of the bare canyons that split the range of low, barren hills. Bill, whose eyes had been thoughtfully fixed on the ground, suddenly gave a sharp exclamation.

"Look here, Mr. Bell," he exclaimed, pointing downward, "what do you make of that?" He indicated the imprints of a horse's hoofs on the dry ground.

"You have sharp eyes, my boy," was the reply; "those hoof-prints are not more than a few hot old, and certainly clinch my idea that someone on horseback was in the vicinity of the camp last night."

Liam McAdams looked rather grave at this. Bill, too, had a troubled note in his voice as he inquired:

"What do you make of it all, Mr. Bell?"

"Too early to say yet, my boy," said the mining man, who had been studying the hoof-prints, "but I can tell you this, that only one man was here last night."

"We have nothing to fear from one man," exclaimed Liam McAdams.

"I know that," was Mr. Bell's response, "but this lone visitor of last night may have been only the scout or forerunner of the others, whoever they may be."

"That's so," agreed Bill, "at any rate he must have had some strong object in spying on us." Nobody would come out into this desolate place without an aim of some sort."

"No question but that you are right there," agreed Mr. Bell, whose face was grave, "I have half a mind to turn back and not bring the ladies further into what may prove to be a serious situation."

"So far as Mary Eliska is concerned you'd have a hard time trying to get her to turn back now," declared Bill; "her mind is bent upon helping to get the airline from the mine into working order, and I guess Jax Gray feels the same way about it."

"It would be a sad blow to them to have to go back now," agreed Liam McAdams; "suppose, Mr. Bell, we wait and make our suspicions more of a certainty before we decide upon anything."

"Perhaps that would be the best course," agreed the lad's elder, "but I must confess I feel sorely troubled. It is agreed, is it not, that not a word of our suspicions are to be breathed to the ladies?"

"Oh, of course," agreed Bill; "after all," he added cheerfully, "the man who left those tracks may have been a prospector or a desert traveler of some kind, and have had no sinister motives."

"I am inclined to think that, too," said Mr. Bell, after a pause; "after all, nobody could have any object in attacking us at such a time."

CHAPTER 14.7
PROFESSOR "WANDERING WILLIAM"

The ponies, and the larger steeds ridden by the elders of the party, were pushed forward at a rapid gait all the morning. As had been explained by Mr. Bell, it was necessary for them to reach Steer Wells by sundown, as they could not hope to encounter any more water holes 'til they gained that point.

In the meantime, water was carried by means of an ingenious arrangement of Mr. Bell's. This was nothing more or less than two large bags of water-proof fabric, which could be filled and then flung on the pack burros' backs. In this way enough was carried for each of the animals to have a scanty supply, although there was none too much left over. That day's luncheon halt was made near a stony, arid canyon in the barren hills, along whose bases they were still traveling.

While the others set about getting a meal, Mary Eliska and Jax Gray linked arms and wandered off a short distance from the camp, bent on exploring. All at once Mary Eliska gave a sudden, sharp little cry.

"Oh, Jax Gray, look! What a funny little creature!"

"Ugh, what a horrid looking thing! What can it be?" exclaimed Liam McAdams' sister.

"It's—it's like a large spider!" cried Mary Eliska suddenly, "and what horrid hairy legs it has, and—oh, Jax Gray—it's going to attack us!"

"I do believe it is o-o-o-h!"

The cry was a long drawn out one of shrill alarm as the "large spider," as Mary Eliska had termed it, tucked its legs under its fat, hairy body and made a deliberate spring at the two girls. Only their agility in leaping backward saved them from being landed upon by it. But far from being dismayed apparently, the creature was merely enraged by this failure. It was gathering itself for another spring when:

Crack!

There was a puff of smoke and a vicious report from Mary Eliska's little revolver, and the next instant the thing that had so alarmed the two young girls lay still. At the same moment the rest of the party, frightened by the sound of the sudden shot, came running up.

"A tarantula!" cried Mr. Bell, "and one of the biggest I have ever seen. It is fortunate for you, young ladies, that he did not bite you or there might have been a different tale to tell. Which of you shot it?"

"Oh, Mary Eliska of course," cheerfully admitted Jax Gray; "I can't pull the trigger yet without shutting my eyes."

"Hurrah for Mary Eliska, America's premier girl rifle and revolver shot!" shouted Liam McAdams in blatant imitation of a show man.

"What a pair of fangs!" cried Bill, who had picked up the dead tarantula and was examining it carefully.

The girls could not repress a shudder as they looked at the dead giant spider, lying with its great legs outstretched, on Bill's hand.

"The Mexicans have a superstition that even if one does not die from the effects of their bites that the tarantula can inoculate a person with dancing poison," said Mr. Bell.

"Dancing poison?" they all cried in an astonished chorus.

"Yes," explained the mining man, "that is to say, that its poison will cause a sort of St. Vitus's dance."

"Good gracious! How unpleasant!" cried Jax Gray. "I'm awfully fond of dancing, but I wouldn't care to come by my fun that way."

"Better than being bitten by the kissing bug anyhow," teased Bill mischievously.

The episode of the tarantula furnished plenty of conversation through the luncheon hour, and caused Mary Eliska many shudders. The poor lady was beginning to think that more dangers lurked in the desert than on any of her most dreaded street crossings in New York.

But little time was spent over the midday meal, and then the final "leg" of their dash across the alkali to Steer Wells began. The sun was low, bathing the desert in a crimson glow, when Mr. Bell, who was riding in advance, gave a sudden shout and pointed ahead to a patch of forlorn looking trees in the distance.

"Steer Wells," he announced.

The boys gave a cheer and plunged forward, with Mary Eliska and Jax Gray close behind. But the others advanced more sedately.

But as they drew closer to the clump of trees standing so oddly isolated amid the waste of alkali, they noted with surprise that they were not to be the only persons to share the hospitality of the oasis. From amid the foliage a column of blue smoke was rising, betokening the presence of other wayfarers. Instantly speculation became rife among the young folks.

Who could be the sharers of their excursion into the untraveled wastes? They were soon to discover.

A strange figure stepped from the trees as the ponies, in a cloud of dust, dashed up. It was that of a tall, angular man with a pair of iron-rimmed spectacles perched on a protuberant nose. He was clean shaven, except for a goatee, and his wrinkled skin was the color of old leather. Long locks of gray hair hung lankly almost to his narrow, sloping shoulders. Above these straggly wisps was perched jauntily a big sombrero of regulation plainsman type. But the strangest feature of this strange personage lay in the remainder of his attire, which consisted of a long black frock coat hanging baggily to his knees and a pair of trousers of the largest and most aggressive check pattern imaginable. His feet were encased in patent leather boots, over which were gaiters of a brilliant yellow.

Under the trees could now be seen a small wagon painted a bright red, which bore upon its sides the inscription:

"Professor Wandering William, Indian Herb Remedies. They make the desert of life to bloom like the Rose Gardens of Mount Hybla. 50 cents per bottle or half a dozen for $2.50."

The professor's angular mule team were browsing on the scanty grass that grew within the circle of trees, while above a fire of chips and twigs there hung an iron pot, which evidently contained the professor's supper. As for the professor himself, he clearly stood revealed in the person of the strange character who now, taking off his sombrero, waved it three times around his head in solemn rhythm, and then, raising a high-pitched voice, shouted:

"Welcome! Thrice welcome to this fertile spot amid the stony desert. Like the Great Indian Herb Remedy, it blooms like the Rose Gardens of Hybla. Ahem!"

The conclusion of this speech was a dry cough, after which the professor solemnly readjusted his hat, and coming forward, said in quite ordinary tones:

"Howdy-do."

By this time the remainder of the party had galloped up, and arrived just as the young folks, hardly knowing what to say, had responded "howdy-do" likewise.

"I hardly expected to find anyone else here," said Mr. Bell, and then by way of introduction, he rattled off their names, the professor bowing low as each was presented.

"And now," said he, "allow me to present myself, Professor Wandering William, proprietor and originator of the Great Indian Herb Medicine, good alike for man or beast, child or adult. Insist on the original and only. Allow me," and the speaker suddenly whisked round with unexpected agility and darting toward his wagon opened the back of the vehicle and presently reappeared with several small bottles. He handed one to each of the new arrivals.

"Samples!" he explained, "and free as the birds of the air. If you like the samples, make a purchase. Money back if not exactly as represented."

With as grave faces as they could assume, they all thanked this queer character, and then Mr. Bell asked.

"May I inquire what you are doing in the desert, Professor. I should think you would find this part of the country a most unprofitable field."

"My dear sir," rejoined the professor, "twice a year I make a pilgrimage into the desert to gather the ingredients of The Remedy. You behold me now almost at the conclusion of my labors. In a few days I shall return to the haunts of civilization and gladden the hearts of mankind by disbursing The Remedy on my terms as quoted on the wagon yonder."

The professor lent a hand in unsaddling and unpacking the stock of the adventurers, and proved to be of great assistance in several ways. Evidently he was an experienced plainsman and he suggested many ways in which their equipment might be lightened and adjusted. His odd manner of talking only possessed him at intervals, and at other times he seemed to converse like any rational being.

This put a queer idea into Mary Eliska's head.

"I wonder if he's acting a part?" she thought to herself. But the next minute the professor's exaggerated gestures and tones convinced her to the contrary. Although his manner was as outlandish as his choice of clothes, still there was a certain something about it which negatived the idea of its being assumed, unless the professor was a most consummate actor. He informed the party that he had set out to cut across the desert from California and had had several narrow escapes from death by reason of lack of water.

I le appeared much interested when Mr. Bell informed him that the party had started out from Blue Creek, adding—as he deemed wisest— that they were a party of tenderfeet anxious to explore the desert at first hand.

"So you were in Blue Creek recently, eh?" he said, with an entire lack of his exaggerated manner, but in crisp tones that fairly snapped; "didn't hear anything there of Red Bill Summers, did you?"

With a half-smile Mr. Bell replied that they had not had the pleasure of the gentleman's acquaintance.

"Don't know about the pleasure part of it," shot out the professor, "he's the most desperate crook this side of Pikes Peak. I'd give a good deal for a look at him myself. I—I have a professional interest in him," he added, with a queer smile which set his eyes to snapping and crackling.

"A medical interest, I suppose?" inquired Mr. Bell, "you think he'd make an interesting study?"

"Most interesting," was the reply in quiet, thoughtful tones.

But the next instant the professor was back at his old pompous, high-flown verbal gymnastics, and after supper he entertained them 'til bedtime with tales of his experiences, to which both boys and girls listened with wide-eyed astonishment.

"The oddest character I have ever encountered," declared Mr. Bell, as the professor, after bowing low to the ladies and apostrophizing the male portion of his audience, retired to his red wagon, within which he slept.

They all agreed to this, but Mary Eliska said rather timidly:

"Somehow I don't think he's quite as odd as we think him."

"What do you mean, my dear?" asked Mr. Bell.

"Why, when he spoke about that Red Billy whatever his name was, did you see how different he looked? Younger somehow, and—and oh, quite different. I don't know just how, but he wasn't the same at all."

"Oh, Mary Eliska's trying to work up a romantic mystery about the professor," teased Jax Gray; "maybe he's a wandering British lord in disguise or the interesting but wayward son of a millionaire with a hobby for socialism."

The others burst into laughter at Jax Gray's raillery, but Mary Eliska gently said:

"There is a great deal in womanly intuition, my dear, and for my part I had the same feeling as you. I mean that that man was not just what he appeared to be, namely, a chattering, ignorant quack."

"Well, as we may have him for a neighbor for some days we shall have a chance to watch him closely," said Mr. Bell.

But in this the leader of the party of adventurers turned out to be wrong, for when they awoke the next morning the grove did not contain the professor or his red wagon. Only the ashes of his fire were there to tell of his sojourn. But on one of the trees they found pinned a note.

"Sorry to leave so abruptly, but circumstances compelled. Perhaps we shall meet again. Who knows!"

And that, for many days, was to be the last they saw of the professor. When they re-encountered him—but of the surprising circumstances under which this was to take place we shall learn later.

CHAPTER 14.8
A DESERT FIGHT

There was too much before them for the party to spend much time in speculation concerning the professor's sudden disappearance. Immediately after breakfast Mr. Bell called the boys aside and said:

"How long will it take to get an airplane ready?"

The question came briskly, as did all Mr. Bell's speeches.

"I think I can promise to have a machine ready for flight by noon," was Bill's rejoinder after a brief interval of thought.

"Good! In that case we will waste no time in getting to work. I am anxious to reach the mine and stake it out properly for claim filing purposes. The less delay the better."

It was news to both boys that the definite legal claim to his discovery had not yet been made by Mr. Bell.

"Well, at any rate you are not likely to be bothered by claim jumpers away off here," commented Bill.

"No, I hardly think so," was the response, "but in these matters one cannot be too careful. Since the news spread that I have struck it rich there are men capable of enduring any hardship if there exists a possibility of wresting it from me."

"I should have thought that in order to be on the safe side you would have filed your claim before you came East," put in Mary Eliska, who had joined the little group of consultants.

"I would have done so were it not for the fact that to have filed my claim and given the location would have set on my track the entire, restless gold-seeking horde that hangs about desert towns," said Mr. Bell, with some warmth. "It is an outrageous thing, but nevertheless a fact, that the moment one files a claim it becomes public property. In my opinion the government should protect the locator of a gold find."

"But would that be quite fair to the others," said Mary Eliska softly. "Shouldn't everybody have an opportunity to develop natural resources?"

Mr. Bell gazed at her admiringly.

"You are right, my dear, and I'm a selfish old bear," he said, "but just the same, not all gold-seekers make desirable neighbors. Many desperate men are among them."

Mary Eliska's mind wandered back to that midnight conversation she had overheard on the porch of the National House. But the same dread of ridicule that she had experienced then still held her, and she refrained from mentioning it.

By noon, with such good will did they work, that not only was one of the monoplanes erected and ready for flight, but a second was partially assembled, and only required the finishing touches to be in readiness for its aerial dash. While the boys, with the girls eagerly helping them, worked on the flying machine, Mr. Bell carefully studied a map he had made of the mine's location, and tested his compass. This done he—as sailors say—"laid out a course" for himself. From the springs the mine lay about due southeast and some hundred and twenty miles away.

In case of accidents the mining man traced carefully a second map, which was to be left behind in the camp so as to be constantly available in case anything happened to the first one, it had been decided that Liam McAdams, who by this time had become quite a skillful aviator, was to accompany Mr. Bell in the preliminary flight.

Bill and Mr. Peter Bell were to be left in charge of the camp, and in the event of the first airplane not returning that night the second, one was to be dispatched in search of it.

As an old plainsman, Mr. Bell had not laid his plans without taking into consideration the possibility of accident to the airplane, and none realized better than he did what serious consequences such an accident might have.

In the chassis of the machine with the travelers were placed a stock of canned goods, a pick and shovel and several hundred feet of fine but tough rope. A supply of water in stone jars and an extra stock of gasoline were also taken along. At the conclusion of the noon meal the motor was started and found to be working perfectly. Nothing then remained to be done but to bid hasty "au revoirs" and wing off across the barren wastes.

"If all goes well we may be back tonight," said Mr. Bell as he slipped into the seat set tandem-wise behind Liam McAdams.

"And if not?" inquired Bill.

"In that case," and Mr. Bell's voice held a grave note, "in that case you will take the other monoplane and start out to look for us."

The roar of the motor as Liam McAdams started it drowned further words. Blue smoke and livid flames burst from the exhausts. The structure of the flying machine shook and quivered under the force of the explosions. The next instant the first airplane to invade the Big Alkali scudded off across the level floor of the desert, and after some five hundred feet of land travel soared upward. In fifteen minutes it was a fast-diminishing speck against the burnished blue of the Nevada sky.

There was some feeling of loneliness in the hearts of those left behind as they turned back toward the camp under the straggly willows. But this was speedily dissipated by that sovereign tonic for such feelings-namely, work. Much was to be done on the remaining monoplane, and with the exception of brief intervals of "fooling" the young people spent the rest of the day on finishing its equipment. Sunset found the machine ready for flight and the Girl Aviatrixes and Bill very ready indeed for the supper to which Peter Bell presently summoned them by loud and insistent beating on a tin pan.

You may be sure that as the sun dipped lower, the sky toward the southwest had been frequently swept by expectant eyes, but supper was served and eaten, and the purple shadows of night began softly to drape the glaring desert and still there came no sign of the homing airplane.

"Reckon they don't want to risk a night flight and so have decided to camp at the mine," suggested old Peter Bell in response to Mary Eliska's rather querulous wondering as to the reason of the non-return.

"That must be it," agreed Bill easily, demolishing the last of a can of chicken.

Truth to tell, inwardly he had not expected the travelers back that night, and perhaps there lingered, too, in his mind, a faint desire to test out the other airplane in a task of rescue, in the event of the one Liam McAdams was driving breaking down.

But when morning came without a sign of the missing monoplane speculation crystallized into a real and keen anxiety. It was determined to delay no longer but set out at once in search of it. To this end the recently equipped airship was stocked with food and water, and shortly before noon Bill finished the final tuning up of the engine. The others watched him anxiously as he worked. It seemed clear enough that some real accident must have occurred to the other machine.

"James would never keep us in suspense like this," said Mr. Bell, "if he could reach us and relieve our anxiety."

Bill was just about to clamber into the chassis when Mary Eliska and Jax Gray, who had been missing for several minutes, emerged from their tent. Each girl wore an aviation hood and stout leather gauntlets. Plainly they were dressed for aerial flight. Bill gazed at them quizzically.

"I hate to disappoint you girls," he said, "but I've got to play a lone hand in this thing."

"No such thing," said Mary Eliska in her briskest tones; "what if anything happened to you? Who would run the machine if we weren't along?"

"That's quite true, Bill," struck in Jax Gray, "and besides if—if anything has gone wrong with Liam McAdams who has a better right to be near him than I?"

Bill looked perplexed.

"What am I to do, Aunt Sally?" he appealed, turning to Miss Stricklin.

To Mary Eliska's astonishment, as much as anyone else's, Aunt Sally did not veto their going.

"I think it would be great folly for you to go on an expedition of this kind alone," she said, addressing Bill. "If anything went wrong what could you do alone?"

"Oh, aunt, you're a dear!" cried Mary Eliska, giving the kindly old lady a bear hug.

"But I make one condition," continued Aunt Sally, "and that is, that whatever you find, you do not delay, but report back here as soon as possible. I could not bear much more anxiety."

This was readily promised, and ten minutes later the three young aviators were in the chassis of the big monoplane. After a moment's fiddling with levers and adjustments Bill started the motor. Heavily laden as it was the staunch airplane shot upward steadily after a short run. As it grew rapidly smaller, and finally became a mere black shoe button in the distance, Aunt Sally turned to old Peter Bell with a sigh.

"Heaven grant they all come back safe and sound," she exclaimed.

"Amen to that, ma'am," was the response, and then unconsciously lapsing into his rhythmical way of expressing himself, the old man added: "Though flying through the air so high they'll come back safely by and by."

And then, while old Peter shuffled off to water the stock, Aunt Sally fell to continuing her fancy work which the good lady had brought with her from the East. An odd picture she made, sitting there in that dreary grove in the desert, with her New England suggestion of primness and house-wifely qualities showing in striking contrast to the strange setting of the rest of the picture.

CHAPTER 14.9
AGAINST HEAVY ODDS

"Any sign of them yet, Bill?" Mary Eliska leaned forward and gently touched her brother's arm.

"I can't see a solitary speck that even remotely resembles them," he said. "It looks bad," he added with considerable anxiety in his tones.

Mary Eliska took a peep at the plan which was spread out before Bill on a little shelf designed to hold aerial charts. Then she glanced at the compass and the distance indicator.

"We must be close to the place now," she said; "it's somewhere off there, isn't it?"

"There" was a range of low hills cut and slashed by steep-walled gullies and canyons. In some of these canyons there appeared to be traces of vegetation, giving rise to the suspicion that water might be obtained there by digging.

Bill nodded. "That's the place, and there's that high cone shaped hill that the plan indicates as the location of the mine."

"But there's not a trace of them-oh, Liam McAdams!"

Jax Gray's tones were vibrant with cruel anxiety. Her face was pale and troubled. As for Mary Eliska, her heart began to beat uncomfortably fast. But she wisely gave no outer sign.

"Don't worry, girlie," she said in as cheerful and brisk a tone as she could call up on the spur of the moment, "it will be all right. I'm sure of it."

Circling high above the range of barren hills they took a thorough survey of them. There was no sign of the missing airplane or her occupants, but all at once beneath them they saw something that caused them all to utter an astonished shout.

In one of the shallower gullies there was suddenly revealed the forms of an immense pack of animals of a gray color and not unlike dogs.

"Wolves!" cried Mary Eliska.

"No, they are coyotes," declared Bill; "I recollect now hearing Mr. Bell say that these hills were frequented by them."

While they still hovered above the strange sight, a sudden swing brought another angle of the gully into view, and there, hidden hitherto by a huge rock, was the missing airplane.

But of its occupants there was not a trace.

"We must descend at once," decided Bill.

"But, Bill, the coyotes!"

It was Jax Gray who spoke. The sight of the immense pack of the brutes thoroughly unnerved her. As they swung lower, too, they could hear the yappings and howlings of the savage band.

"I don't think they will bother us," said Bill. "I've heard Mr. Bell say that they are cowardly creatures."

"If they do we'll have to fly up again," said Mary Eliska; "but we simply must examine that airplane for some clue of the others' whereabouts. Besides we have our revolvers."

"And can use them, too," said Bill with decision. "Now look out and hold tight, for I'm going to make a quick drop."

The gully seemed to rush upward at the airplane as it swooped down, coming to rest finally, almost alongside its companion machine. Luckily, the big rock before mentioned concealed the new arrivals from the view of the pack gathered further up the gully.

No time was lost in alighting and examining the machine, but beyond the fact that none of the food or water had been disturbed there was no clue there. Another puzzling fact was that the rifles Mr. Bell and Liam McAdams had brought with them still lay in the chassis. This seemed to dispose of the theory that they had been attacked. But what could have become of them? Was it possible that the coyotes—? Bill gave an involuntary shiver as a thought he did not dare allow himself to retain flashed across his mind. And yet it was odd the presence of that numerous pack all steadily centered about one spot.

"I'm going to try firing a shot into the air," said Bill suddenly; "if they are in the vicinity they will hear it and answer if they can."

"Oh, yes, do that, Bill," begged Jax Gray. "Oh, I'm almost crazy with worry! What can have happened?"

The sharp bark of Bill's pistol cut short her half hysterical outbreak. Following the report they listened intently and then:

"Hark!" exclaimed Mary Eliska, her eyes round and her pulses beating wildly. "Wasn't that a shout? Listen, there it is again!"

"I heard it that time, too," exclaimed Bill.

"And I!" cried Jax Gray.

"It came from down the canyon where those coyotes are," went on Mary Eliska.

"That's right, sis, and it complicates our search," said Bill, "but we've got to go on now. You girls wait here for me while I investigate, and—and you'd better take those rifles out of the other airplane."

"Oh, Bill, you're not going alone?" Mary Eliska appealed.

"I'm not going to let you girls take a chance 'til I see what's ahead, that's one sure thing," was the rejoinder.

Before another word could be said the boy, revolver in hand, vanished round the big rock. Hardly had he done so, when there was borne to the girls' ears the most appalling confusion of sounds they had ever heard. The bedlam was, punctuated by several sharp shots, and Bill appeared running from round the rock. His hat was off, and as he approached he shouted:

"Get back to the airplanes! The pack's after us!"

At the same instant there appeared the leaders of the onrush. Great, half-famished looking brutes, whose red mouths gaped open ferociously and whose eyes burned wickedly.

But Bill had hardly had time to shout his warning before an accident, entirely unexpected, occurred. His foot caught on a stone and he came down with a crash. The next moment the pack would have been upon him, but Mary Eliska jerked the rifle she had selected to her shoulder and fired into the midst of the savage horde. With a howl of anguish one of the creatures leaped high in a death agony and came toppling down among his mates, a limp, inanimate mass. This checked the surging onrush for an instant, and in that instant Bill was on his feet and sprinting briskly toward the girls.

Straight for the airplanes they headed. Reaching them they entrenched themselves in what they could not but feel was an immensely insecure position.

"Thank you, sis," was all that Bill, with a bit of a choke in his voice, was able to gasp out before the leaders of the pack were on them.

More by instinct than with any definite idea, the young people began desperately pumping lead into the seething confusion of gray backs and red gaping mouths.

All at once poor Jax Gray, half beside herself with terror, gave a throaty little gasp.

"I think I'm going to faint," she exclaimed feebly.

Mary Eliska gave her a sharp glance.

"You'll do no such thing, Jax Gray," she said sharply, although the pity in her eyes belied the harshness of the words, "if you do I'll—I'll never speak to you again!"

The words had their calculated effect, and Jax Gray made a brave rally. At almost the same instant a shot from Bill's rifle brought down the largest of the creatures of the desert, a big hungry looking brute with tawny, scraggy hair and bristling hackles. As he rolled over with a howl of anguish and rage a sudden wavering passed through the pack. It was like a wind-shadow sweeping over a field of summer wheat.

"Hooray, we've got them beaten!" shouted Bill, enthusiastically.

The lad was right. Their leader fallen, the remainder of the pack had seemingly no liking for keeping up the attack. Still snarling they began to retreat slowly—a backward movement, which presently changed into a mad, helter-skelter rush. Panic seized on them, and down the dry arroyo they fled, a dense cloud of yellow, pungent dust rising behind them. In a few seconds all that remained to tell of the battle in the gulch were the still bodies of the brutes that had fallen before the boy and Girl Aviatrixes' rifles.

They were contemplating the scene when, from further up the gully, there came a sound that set all their pulses beating.

It was the shout of a human voice.

"Thank heaven you were not too late!"

While they were still standing stock still in startled immobility at the recognition of Mr. Bell's voice, there came another hail.

"Hello, Jax Gray! Hello, Mary Eliska and Bill!"

Emerging from the cloud of dust which was still thick, there staggered toward them two uncanny looking figures in which they had at first some difficulty in recognizing Mr. Bell and Liam McAdams. But when they did what a shout went up!

It echoed about the dead hills and rang hollowly in the silent gully. An instant later the reunited adventurers were busily engaged in exchanging greetings of which my readers can guess the tenor. Then came explanations.

"On arriving in the arroyo," said Mr. Bell, "Liam McAdams and I decided to set out at once to examine the mine site, and lay if off for purposes of proper location with the United States government. I must tell you that the mine—or rather the site of it—is located in that cavern yonder further up the arroyo."

"Why it was around the entrance to that that the coyotes were gathered when we first dropped!" cried Mary Eliska.

"Exactly. And very much to our discomfort, too, I can tell you," rejoined Mr. Bell dryly.

"They had you besieged!" exclaimed Bill.

"That's just it, my boy. They must have been famished, or they never would have gathered up the courage to do it, for, as a rule, one man can put a whole pack of the brutes to flight. I suppose, however, they realized that they had us cornered, for, with a sort of deadly deliberation, they seated themselves round the mouth of the cavern, seemingly awaiting the proper time for us to be starved out or driven forth by thirst. Luckily, however, we had canteens with us and a scanty supply of food, otherwise it might have been the last of us."

Jax Gray shuddered and drew very close to Liam McAdams.

"And you had no weapons," volunteered Bill.

"Ah, I see you encountered our guns in the chassis of the airplane. No, foolishly, I'll admit, we omitted to arm ourselves for such a short excursion. Of course we never dreamed of any danger of that sort in this lonely place, and least of all from the source from which it came. But I can, tell you, it was an ugly feeling when, on preparing to emerge with some specimens of the ore-bearing rocks, we found ourselves facing a grim semi-circle, banked dozens deep, of those famished coyotes. They greeted our appearance with a howl, and when we tried to scare them off they just settled down on their haunches to wait."

"Their silence was worse than their yapping and barking, I think," struck in Liam McAdams.

"It certainly was," agreed Mr. Bell; "both of us tried to keep up good hearts, but when the night passed and morning still found the brutes there, things began to look bad. Of course we knew that you would set out to look for us when we did not return, but we did not know if you would reach here in time."

"But you did," cried Liam McAdams, regarding the dead bodies of coyotes the vanquished pack had left behind.

"And excellent work your rifles did, too," declared Mr. Bell warmly.

"Our rifles and—the Girl Aviatrixes," said Bill, and proceeded to tell the interested listeners from the cavern some incidents which caused them to open their eyes and regard our girls with unconcealed admiration.

CHAPTER 14.10
RESCUED BY AIRPLANE

"What's that down there?"

Bill pointed downward from the airplane to a small black object crawling painfully over the glistening white billows of alkali far below them.

The lad, his sister and Jax Gray were on their way back from the arroyo in which the battle with the coyotes had occurred. Mr. Bell and Liam McAdams had been left behind, for the former was anxious to "prospect" his mine as thoroughly as possible in order to ascertain if it gave indications of living up to its first rich promise. A brief inspection of the cave had thoroughly disgusted Mary Eliska and Jax Gray.

"Is this a rich gold mine!" Jax Gray had cried, indignantly regarding the dull walls on which the torches had glowed unflatteringly; "it looks more like the interior of the cellar at home."

"All is not gold that glitters," Mr. Bell had responded with a smile. At the same moment he had flaked off a chunk of dark colored metal with his knife.

"There, Jax Gray," he exclaimed, handing it to the girl, "that is almost pure gold, and I am in hopes that there is lots more where that came from."

And they had been kind enough not to laugh too immoderately at Jax Gray's discomfiture.

A short time later, having located a water hole and partaken of a good lunch, Bill and his companions had re-embarked and started back to camp with the joyful tidings that the missing adventurers had been found. They had been under way but a short time when Bill's attention had been attracted by the moving dot which had caused him to utter the exclamation recorded at the beginning of this chapter.

Against the flat, baking, quivering expanse of alkali the crawling splotch of black showed up as plainly as a blot of ink on a sheet of clean white blotting paper. Peering over the edge of the chassis they all scrutinized it closely.

"It's—it's a man!" cried Jax Gray at length.

"So it is!" declared Mary Eliska, "and on foot. What can he be doing out in this desert country without a horse?"

"He's in trouble anyhow," declared Bill, excitedly. "See, he's staggering along so painfully that it looks as if he couldn't go a step further. I'm going to drop and find out what the trouble is."

As he spoke the boy threw in the descending clutch, and the big monoplane began to drop as swiftly as a buzzard that has espied some prey far beneath him.

As they rushed downward the whirr of their descent seemed to arouse the being so painfully crawling over the hot waste beneath them. He looked up, and then, extending his hands upward in a gesture of bewilderment, he staggered forward and the next instant stretched his length on the alkali, falling face downward.

"Oh, he is dead!" shrilled Jax Gray, clasping her hands.

"I don't think so," was Bill's grave reply, "but we must get to him as quickly as we can."

There was no need to tell Mary Eliska to get the water canteen ready. Her busy little, fingers were fumbling with it. As they touched the ground she leaped nimbly from the chassis and sped over the burning desert floor to the side of the recumbent wayfarer. A second later Bill and Jax Gray joined her. Very tenderly they turned the insensible man upon his back and dashed the water upon his face.

He was a short, rather stockily built man of middle age, and obviously, from his mahogany-colored skin and lank black hair, a Mexican. He was dressed in a tattered shirt with a serape thrown about the neck to keep off the blazing rays of the sun. His feet were encased in a kind of moccasins over which spurs were strapped. Evidently, then, he had been mounted at some time—presumably recently, but where was his horse? How did he come to be wandering under the maddening heat of the sun over the vast alkali waste. But these were questions the answers to which had to be deferred for the present, for it began to appear doubtful if they had arrived in time to fan the wanderer's vital spark back into flame.

But at length their ministrations met with their reward. The man's eyelids flickered and a deep sigh escaped his lips. Before long they could press the water canteen to his mouth. He seized it with avidity and would have drained it.

"Only a little," cried Mary Eliska; "I read once how a man, dying of thirst, was killed outright when he was given too much water to drink."

So Bill wrenched the canteen from the prostrated man's feeble grasp before he had drained more than a mouthful or two. But even that had revived him, and he was able to sit up and gaze about bewilderedly. All at once his eyes rested on Mary Eliska, and he seemed to regard her as the means of his salvation from a terrible death on the alkali. Kneeling down he cried out in a pitifully cracked voice:

"You missie angel from heaven. Me Alverado your servant always. No go away ever!"

"By ginger, Mary Eliska, you've made a conquest!" cried Bill, half hysterically.

Now that the strain of the struggle between life and death was over Mary Eliska flushed and looked embarrassed. She was not used to the exaggerated character of the Mexican. But if she feared another outburst it did not come. Far too much exhausted to say more, Alverado—as he called himself—sank back once more on the alkali.

"Quick! Carry him to the airplane and get him into camp," cried Bill, raising the half-conscious Mexican's head. "You girls take his feet and we'll put him in the bottom of the chassis on those cushions."

Consequently, when the airplane once more took the air it was to fly lower than usual under its additional burden, but in the hearts of all three of its American occupants there rang the joy of having saved a human life from the unsparing alkali.

"Aunt Sally! Aunt Sally! Everything's all right and we've got a patient for you," was Mary Eliska's rather uncomplimentary greeting as the airplane alighted and came spinning across the dusty expanse toward the willow clump.

Aunt Sally threw up her hands and old Mr. Peter Bell hastened from amidst his beloved horses.

"Everything's all right but you've got a patient!" cried the New England lady, who looked very prim and unwesternlike in a gingham gown and sun bonnet to match.

"No time for explanations now," cried Bill. "Come on, Mr. Bell, and help us get our sick man out and then we'll tell you all about how we found Liam McAdams and Mr. Bell at the mine."

With Mr. Bell's assistance it did not take long to transfer Alverado from the airplane to a cot, and Aunt Sally, who, as Bill said, would "rather nurse than eat," ministered to him to such good effect that by nightfall he was able to sit up and tell his story. In the meantime the excited youngsters had related their narratives, which Aunt Sally interrupted in a dozen places by: "Land's sakes!" "Good gracious me!"

"Oh, what a dreadful country!" and much more to the same effect.

All the time he was relating his story Alverado kept his eyes fixed on Mary Eliska's face, with much the same expression as that worn by a faithful spaniel. At first this fixed gaze annoyed the young girl not a little, but soon she realized that it was entirely respectful and meant as a tribute, for the Mexican evidently regarded her as his rescuer in chief.

Alverado's story proved vague and sketchy, but he could not be induced to enlarge upon it. In brief his tale was that some years before, when crossing the desert on his way from a mine he owned, he had been attacked by a band of highwaymen. They had wrecked his wagon and murdered his family, who were traveling with him. They had attacked him because of their impression that he was carrying much gold with him, whereas, in reality, he had secured nothing but a living from his desert mine. In their rage at being thwarted, the miscreants had wiped out the Mexican's family and left him for dead with a wound in his skull.

But a wandering band of Nevada Native Americans had happened along while the Mexican still lay unconscious and, reviving him, carried him with them over the border into California. He had parted from them soon after and drifted down into Mexico. In time he accumulated a small fortune, but the thought of the wrong he had suffered never left his heart. At last his affairs reached a stage where he felt justified in returning to Nevada to try to find some trace of his wrongers, and demand justice. He had set out well equipped, but, a few days before the young aviators encountered him, his water burro had stumbled and fallen, and in the fall had broken the water kegs it carried. From that time on his trip across the alkali had been a nightmare. First his pony had died, and then his two remaining pack burros. He had obtained a scanty supply of thirst-quenching stuff from the pulpy insides of cactus and maguey leaves, but when the aviators had discovered him he had been in the last stages of death from thirst and exhaustion—the death that so many men on the alkali have met alone and bravely.

"Do you know the name of the men who attacked you and treated you so cruelly?" asked Aunt Sally, breaking the tense silence which followed the conclusion of the Mexican's dramatic narrative.

A dark look crossed the man's swarthy features. "One name onlee I know, mees," he said, with a snarl which somehow reminded Mary Eliska of the coyotes of the arroyo.

"And his name was?" "Red Beel Soomers!" "'Red Bill Summers!" they all echoed, except Mary Eliska and old Mr. Peter Bell, the latter of whom had fallen into a reverie.

As if they had been emblazoned in electric lights, the words of Professor Wandering William flashed across Mary Eliska's brain.

"The most desperate ruffian on the Nevada desert."

And at the same time, with one of those quick, flashes of intuition which growing girls share with grown women, Mary Eliska sensed a vague connection between that sinister conversation she had overheard on her wakeful night at the National House and the dreaded Red Bill.

CHAPTER 14.11
THE HORSE HUNTERS

Bright and early the next day the airplane whizzed back to the arroyo, carrying a fresh supply of food and water, for Mr. Bell had decided to investigate his "prospect" thoroughly while he had an opportunity. To his mind, he had declared, the lead, or pay streak, ran back far into the base of the barren hills, and might yield almost untold of riches if worked properly. Among the supplies carried by the airplane, therefore, was a stock of dynamite from the red painted box.

In the meantime Alverado had to be accepted perforce as a member of the party. In the first place, he showed no disposition to leave, and in the second, even had he done so, there was no horse or burro that could be spared for him to ride. When Mr. Bell heard of the new addition to the camp he was at first not best pleased. Every additional mouth meant an extra strain on their supplies, but he surrendered to the inevitable, and finally remarked:

"Oh, well, I guess he'll be useful enough about the place. Anyhow, if we need him we can put him to work in the mine."

Mary Eliska and Jax Gray had accompanied Bill over in the airplane to the mine, but Mr. Bell insisted on their returning. "This is not work for women or girls," he said, much to Mary Eliska's inward disgust.

Jax Gray, with her daintier ideas, however, was nothing averse to the thought of getting back to the creature comforts of the permanent camp in the willows.

"But who's going to get you back, I'd like to know," exclaimed Mr. Bell, shoving back his sombrero and scratching his head perplexedly; "it's important, for reasons you know of, that I should prospect this claim so that I can record it to the limit, and to do that I'll need Bill. Maybe after all, you'd better stay."

Mary Eliska's eyes danced delightedly, but Jax Gray spoiled it all by saying:

Why, Mary Eliska can run the airplane better than either Bill or Liam McAdams, Mr. Bell."

"O-h-h! Jax Gray!" shouted Bill derisively.

"Well, she can, and you know it, too," declared Jax Gray loyally.

"Why that's so, isn't it?" cried Mr. Bell, glad of this way out of his difficulty. After that there was nothing for Mary Eliska to do but to give in gracefully.

The two girls were ready to start back when Mr. Bell reached into his pocket and drew forth a bit of carefully folded paper.

"I'll entrust this to you," he said to Mary Eliska; "it's for my brother. It's a correct description of the mine's location so far as we have explored it. The plan is a duplicate one, and I'll feel safer if I know that, beside the original, my brother has a copy. In the event of one being lost a lot of work would be saved."

Soon after this, adieus were said, and the airplane soared high into the clear, burning air above the desolate ridges. Under Mary Eliska's skillful hands the plane fairly flew. At the pace they proceeded it was not long before the willows, a dark clump amid the surrounding ocean of glittering waste, came into view. A veteran of the air could not have made a more accurate or an easier landing that did Mary Eliska. The big machine glided to the ground as softly as a feather, just at the edge of the patch of shade and verdure which made up Steer Wells.

That afternoon, after the midday meal, a cloud of dust to the southward excited everybody's attention. After scanning the oncoming pillar closely Alverado announced that it was caused by a party of horsemen, and it soon became evident that the willow clump was their destination.

"Oh, mercy, I do hope they aren't Indians and we shall all be murdered in our beds!" cried Aunt Sally in considerable alarm. The good lady clasped her hands together distractedly.

"We might be murdered in our hammocks, aunt," observed Mary Eliska, indicating two gaudy specimens of the hanging lounges which had been suspended under the shade; "but only very lazy people could be murdered in bed at two o'clock in the afternoon."

"You know perfectly well what I mean," Mary Eliska began with dignity, when Alverado, who, like the rest, had been watching the advancing cavalcade eagerly, suddenly announced:

"They vaqueros—cowboys!"

"Cowboys!" shrilled Aunt Sally. "That's worse. Oh, dear, I wish I'd never come to the land of the cowboys!"

"You speak as if they were some sort of animal, aunt," laughed Mary Eliska. "I daresay there is no reason to be alarmed at them. I've always heard that they were very courteous and deferential to ladies."

"What would cowboys be doing away out here where there isn't a cow or a calf or even an old mule in sight?" inquired Jax Gray.

"Maybe on wild horse hunt," rejoined Alverado with a shrug.

"Are there wild horses hereabouts then?" asked old Mr. Bell, and then quite absent-mindedly he began murmuring:

> "Masseppa, Masseppa tied to a wild horse;
> In the way of revenge, as a matter of course."

"Plentee wild horse," was the Mexican's rejoinder. "They cross the desert sometimes to get fresh range. Cowboy trail them and cut them off and lasso them. Then they break them to ride."

"Oh, what a shame!" cried Mary Eliska, impulsively. "No shame go-od," declared the Mexican stolidly; "bye an' bye wild horse all gone. Good."

"I think it's hateful," declared Jax Gray; "just the same I should like to see a wild horse hunt," she added with girlish inconsistence.

"So should I if they'd let them all go again," agreed Mary Eliska.

Old Mr. Bell laughed, for which he was gently reproved by Aunt Sally: "I shall bring this matter to the attention of the Society for the Prevention of Cruelty to Animals back home," she said somewhat snappishly. But there was no opportunity to exchange more remarks on the subject.

Uttering a shrill series of "ye-o-o-ows" the riders bore down on the little desert camp. From the heaving sides of the ponies, plastered with the gray alkali of the desert, clouds of steam were rising. Their riders, with mouths screened from the biting dust with red handkerchiefs, were seemingly engaged in a race for the willow clump where water and shade awaited them.

"Yip-yip-y-e-e-e-e-e-e!"

The sound came raucously from behind a dozen bandaged mouths as the band swept down oil tile camp. And then suddenly:

Bang! Bang! Bang!

A volley of revolver shots resounded as the jubilant horse hunters— as Alverado had shrewdly suspected they were—dashed forward.

"Oh, Land of Goshen!" screamed Aunt Sally, as, with her fingers in her ears, she fled into her tent and pulled the flap to. Mary Eliska and Jax Gray stood their ground boldly enough, although Jax Gray's face turned rather pale and her breath heaved in perturbation.

"Keep still, honey, they won't hurt you," comforted Mary Eliska amid the uproar.

Suddenly the leader of the horsemen drew his pony up abruptly, throwing the cat-like little beast almost back upon his haunches.

"Boys! Ladies!" he shouted.

Instantly every sombrero came off and was swept round each rider's head in a broad circle. It was a pretty bit of homage and the girls bowed in acknowledgment of it.

"Hooray!" yelled the horsemen as they flung themselves from their steaming but still active little mounts.

"They're not so bad after all," breathed Jax Gray, still, however, clinging to Mary Eliska's shirt-waisted arm.

But the leader, hat in hand, was now advancing toward the two girls. The others hung back looking rather sheepish. They were not in the habit of meeting ladies, and to encounter two young and pretty girls in the midst of the alkali was evidently a shock to them. The leader was a stalwart figure of a man, who might have stepped from the advertising matter of a Wild West show. Leather chaparejos encased his long legs. Round his throat was loosely knotted the red handkerchief which they all wore when riding to protect their mouths and nostrils from the dust. His shirt was once blue, but it was so covered with the gray of the alkali that it was difficult to tell what color it might have been originally. For the rest he wore a big sombrero, the leather band of which was spangled with stars worked in silver wire, and a pair of workmanlike-looking gauntlets covered his hands.

"Beg pardon, ladies, for makin' sich a rough house," he said hesitating, "but, yer see, ther boys wall we didn't hardly expec' ter fin' ladies present."

"I'm sure we enjoyed it very much," rejoined Mary Eliska quite at ease and her own cool self now "It was like—er—like Buffalo Bill—"

"Only more so," put in Jax Gray, with her most bewitching smile.

"Um—er—quite so," rejoined the plainsman, rather more at ease now; "ye see, we're a party that's out on a horse hunt. We got on ther tracks of the band ther other side of ther San Quentin range, and figgering thet they'd cut across here ter git to ther feeding grounds on ther Pablo range on t'other side of ther desert we stopped in here fer water an' shade."

"My name's Bud Reynolds," he volunteered tentatively.

Mary Eliska took the hint conveyed.

"And we are part of a scientific exploring party," she said.

"College gals, by gee!" breathed Bud in what he thought was an inaudible aside.

"The party is in charge of Mr. James Bell. This is his brother, Mr. Peter Bell—"

"Glad ter meet yer, I'm sure," said Bud with a low bow as the poet hermit stepped forward.

"I am Mary Eliska; this is my chum, Jax Gray, and there is my aunt, Miss Sally Stricklin—"

Mary Eliska, with a perfectly grave face, indicated Aunt Sally's tent, from between the flaps of which that New England lady's spectacled countenance was peering.

"Come out, auntie," she added.

"Oh, Mary Eliska, is it perfectly safe?" queried Aunt Sally anxiously.

"Safe, mum!" exclaimed Bud expansively. "If it was any safer you'd hav ter send fer ther perlice. Jes becos we're rough and ain't got on full evenin' dress you musn't think we're dangerous, mum," he went on more gravely. "I'll warrant you'll fin' better fellers right here on ther alkali than on Fit' Avenoo back in New York."

"Oh, do you come from New York," cried the romantic Jax Gray, scenting what she would have called "a dear of a story."

"A long time ago I did," rejoined Bud slowly. "But come on, boys," he resumed with a return to his old careless manner, "come up an' be interduced."

The others, hats in hand, shuffled forward. It was plainly a novel experience for them.

"And now," said Aunt Sally cheerfully, when the ceremony had been concluded, "you all look dreadfully tired and hot. The water hole's right over there. When you've got off some of that dust we shall have something for you to eat and some coffee."

This announcement took the horse hunters by storm. With yips and whoops they dashed off to the water hole, while Miss Sally and old Peter Bell began to prepare a hasty meal for the unexpected visitors.

CHAPTER 14.12
THE WATER THIEVES

It was an hour or more later when, having inspected the airplane and marveled much thereat, the horse hunters arose to take their leave. They would have to press on, they explained, to reach the rendezvous of the wild horses in the San Pablo range. These hills lay far to the northeast. Bud perspiringly made the farewell speech.

"Thankin' you one and all," he began, with perhaps a vague recollection of the last circus he had seen, and there he stopped short.

"Anyhow we thanks you," he said, getting a fresh start and jerking the words out as if they had been shots from a revolver. "It ain't every day we has a pleasure like this here hes bin—"

"Hooray!" yelled the other horse hunters, who, already mounted, stood behind their leader at the edge of the willows.

"An'—an'—wall, ther desert hes dangers uv its own an' if at any time Bud Reynolds er ther boys kin help yer out send fer them to ther San Pablo Range and if we're thar we'll be with yer ter ther last bank uv ther last ditch."

With a sigh of relief Bud flung himself upon his pony and drove the spurs home. Amidst a tornado of yells and shouts the rest, waving their sombreros wildly, dashed off after him. In a few moments they were only a cloud of dust on the alkali.

"I declare I feel kind of sad now they're gone," said Miss Sally after an interval of silence.

"Rough diamonds," opined old Mr. Bell guardedly.

"But they've got warm, big hearts," stoutly declared Mary Eliska. "I wish—" She stopped abruptly.

"Wish what, Mary Eliska dear?" asked Jax Gray, noting the troubled look that had crept over her chum's face.

"Oh, nothing at all," rejoined Mary Eliska. But she was not speaking the whole truth, for the girl had been thinking what a bulwark of strength Bud and his followers would have been against the vague menace of Red Bill.

It was late that night—after midnight as well as Mary Eliska could judge—that she was awakened by Jax Gray bending over her cot in the tent that both girls shared.

"O-h-h! Mary Eliska, Mary Eliska! I'm frightened!" wailed the girl aviatrix's chum.

"Frightened? Of what dear?" asked Mary Eliska wide awake in an instant.

"I—I don't just know," quavered Jax Gray, "but, Oh, Mary Eliska, you'll think I'm an awful 'fraid cat, but I'm absolutely certain I heard footsteps, stealthy footsteps outside just now."

"Nonsense, girlie. It must have been a nightmare," rejoined Mary Eliska with sharp assurance.

"I might have thought so," went on Jax Gray, "but I looked out through the flap of the tent to make sure and I'm certain as that I'm standing here now that I saw some figures on horseback over by the water hole."

"Perhaps another party of horse hunters," suggested Mary Eliska soothingly.

"But, Mary Eliska dear, they made hardly any noise. That is, the horses I mean. I heard men's footsteps, but after a minute they mounted and rode off, and—oh, it was too ghostly for anything—they made no noise at all."

"You mean you couldn't hear any sound of the ponies' hoofs?" asked Mary Eliska incredulously.

"No, they moved in absolute silence. Mary Eliska, you don't think it was anything supernatural, do you?"

For answer Mary Eliska drew her revolver from under her pillow and tiptoed to the tent flap. It faced the water hole and in the bright white moonlight a clear view of it could be obtained. But after a prolonged scrutiny Jax Gray's plucky chum was unable to make out any objects other than the usual ones appertaining to the camp.

"Imagination, my dear," she said, with positiveness. But Jax Gray still shuddered and seemed under the influence of some strange fear.

"It was not imagination, Mary Eliska. It wasn't it really wasn't."

"Well, we'll look in the morning and if we find tracks we shall know that you are right, and we'll get the boys back for a while anyhow," reassured Mary Eliska.

But in the morning it was Alverado who came to the tent and in an excited voice asked to see "missee" at once.

Mary Eliska hastily completed dressing and emerged, leaving Jax Gray still asleep. Something warned her that it would be best not to arouse her chum just then.

"What is it, Alverado?" she asked, as the Mexican, betraying every mark of agitation, hastened to her side.

"Santa Maria, missee," breathed the Mexican, "water almost all gone!" "The water is almost all gone?" quavered Mary Eliska, beginning to sense what was coming. "Yes, missee. Me go there this morning and—Madre de Dios—the water hole almost empty."

"Were there any tracks?" inquired Mary Eliska anxiously.

"Plenty tracks, but the man's had the cavallos' feet bundled in sacks so make no noise— leave no tracks."

"Let me have a look." With Alverado at her side Mary Eliska hastened toward the water hole. She could hardly repress an exclamation of alarm as she gazed at the hole. Bare six inches of muddy water was on the bottom, where the day before there had been a foot or more. All about were vague blotty-looking tracks which showed plainly enough the manner in which the marauders had concealed all noise of their movements. The muffled hoofs would naturally give forth no sound.

"So Jax Gray was right after all," breathed Mary Eliska softly; "but who could have done such a thing? And why?"

But the latter question had not framed itself in her mind before it was answered. Without water they would not be able to exist at Steer Wells for twenty-four hours. A retreat would be equally impracticable. It was all horribly clear. The theft of the water was the first step in a deliberate plan to drive them out. The motive, too, was plain enough in the light of the overheard conversation at the National Hotel. The men who wanted Mr. Bell's mine had waited 'til he had located it before striking their first blow. What would their next be? Mary Eliska's pulses throbbed and the grove seemed to blur for an instant. But the next moment she was mistress of herself again. Clearly there was only one thing to do. Lay the whole matter before Mr. Bell.

"Alverado," said Mary Eliska quietly, "after breakfast I am going to the range over yonder. You must guard the camp."

"Yes, missee," replied the Mexican; "I take care of him with—with my life.'"

"I am sure you will," said Mary Eliska in her most matter-of-fact tones, "and in the meantime say nothing to anyone else about what you have found. Bring up the water for breakfast yourself and don't let Mr. Bell come near the water hole if you can help it."

"It shall be as the senorita wishes," rejoined Alverado in low tones; but there was a ring in his voice that told Mary Eliska that she could trust the brown-skinned "Mestizo" to the utmost.

CHAPTER 14.13
DANGER THREATENS

Somewhat more than two hours later Mary Eliska brought her airplane to the ground in the arroyo which had been the scene of the battle with the coyotes. The girl could not help giving an involuntary shudder as she thought of the narrow escape they had had on that occasion. But in the light of the other and more serious menace which now hung over them like a storm cloud, the adventure with the wild beasts faded into insignificance. Human enemies, more deadly perhaps than any of the animal kingdom, threatened, and if signs counted for anything it would be no long time before they would strike.

Mary Eliska had not been able to leave the camp without some resort to strategy. Naturally Jax Gray had been anxious to come. But a quick flight had been imperative, and the presence of even one other person in the monoplane detracted somewhat from its speed. Then, too, Mary Eliska had ached with her whole being to be alone—to think. She wanted to reconstruct everything in her mind so that when she told all to Mr. Bell there would be no confusion, no hesitancy in her story.

Three sharp toots on the electric signaling horn the airplane carried—connected to a set of dry cells—resulted in an outpouring from the mine-hole of the three prospectors. Very business-like they looked, too, in khaki trousers, dust covered shirts and rolled up sleeves.

"Well, well! Early visitors," exclaimed Mr. Bell jocularly, and then struck by Mary Eliska's sober expression as she stepped from the car of the airplane he stopped short.

"My dear child, what is it?" he demanded. "Where are the twin fairies of light that used to dance in your eyes?"

"My goodness, Mr. Bell, you ought to have been a poet like your brother," laughed Bill coming forward with Liam McAdams to meet his sister.

And then, like his senior, he, too, was struck by Mary Eliska's anxious look.

"What's the trouble, sis; bad news?" he asked.

"Anything happened?" demanded Liam McAdams.

"Oh, no, no; set your minds at rest on that," responded Mary Eliska.

"Everything is all right, at least—at least—"

Her voice wavered a bit and Mr. Bell gently led her to a stool in front of the rough camp they had set up in the arroyo.

"Now then, my dear," he said, "what is it?"

Mary Eliska faced her eager listeners, and, recovering from her momentary tremor, told her story from beginning to end in a clear, convincing way.

"Do you think I did right in coming?" she concluded. Her gaze fell appealingly upon Mr. Bell. She did not wish this sinewy, wiry, self-reliant man to think that she was a victim of a school girl's hysterical fears. But the mining man's words speedily set her at ease on this point.

"Think you did right!" he echoed, while a rather serious expression came over his face; "my dear girl, if you had not come to me I should have thought you did very wrong. You have made only one mistake and that was in not telling me before this time about what you overheard at the National House. This Red Bill, as they call him, is one of the most unscrupulous ruffians that cumber the face of the Nevada desert. In any other community he would have been brought up with a round turn long ago. But here," he shrugged his shoulders. "I suppose after all," he went on, "it's the old story of who'll bell the cat."

"Do you think that we are in serious danger?" inquired Liam McAdams. His eyes were round as saucers and his usually good-natured face look troubled.

"Well, not in serious danger, my boy," rejoined Mr. Bell; "but, just between us four, mind, it behooves us to use all speed in getting the title of this mine recorded. This Red Bill is as resourceful as a fox, and what Miss Mary Eliska has told us shows that he is closer on our trail than I should have imagined possible. The draining of the water hole is unfortunate in two ways. If, as I now suspect, he is camped in the hills to the east of the camp, it is plain that he has secured a supply of water sufficient to last him for some time. And this cuts both ways, for his gain in that respect means our loss. The more water he has the less we have. That much is clear."

"Clear as mud," said Liam McAdams ruefully; but his tone robbed the words of any humorous significance.

"You have reached a decision, Mr. Bell?" asked Bill. The boy had not spoken yet.

Mr. Bell's mouth closed in a firm line and his chin came out in what Mary Eliska described to herself as "a fighting bulge."

"Yes," he said with characteristic vim, "I have. Steer Wells will not be safe after daylight today for the women of the party. Red Bill is dastard enough, through an attack on them, to try to intimidate me. We must shift to try to camp at once."

"But where?"

The question came blankly from Liam McAdams.

"Here. We have a moderate supply of water and there is feed of a kind. Enough at least to keep the stock alive 'til our work is completed. You see," he continued, turning to Mary Eliska, "the boys and I have struck a very interesting lead. How far it goes I have no idea, but my mining experience teaches me that it is an offshoot of the mother lode. Until we have tapped that I don't want to file a claim."

Mary Eliska nodded her head sagely.

"I see," she said, "you don't want to file your claim and then have somebody else squat down beside you and win the biggest prize of all."

"That's it exactly," said Mr. Bell, "but the question in my mind is whether I am right in exposing you, Jax Gray and Mary Eliska to what may be peril. And yet—"

He broke off and a troubled expression crept over his weather-beaten face.

"And yet," Mary Eliska finished for him, "there's no way for us to go back now without abandoning the mine."

"That's it. But if you—"

"I vote to stick by the mine."

There was no hesitation in Mary Eliska's voice now.

Mr. Bell's keen gray eyes kindled.

"You're a girl of real grit," he said, "but the others?"

"I'll answer for them. Mary Eliska need not know anything of the danger. After all, it may amount to nothing. As for Jax Gray, she has as much, and more, nerve than I have."

"When it comes to eating ice cream," put in Liam McAdams irrelevantly.

Mary Eliska, glancing about her, could not but reflect at the moment what a strange contrast the scene about them offered to the peaceful landscape and commonplace adventures of hum-drum Long Island. Not but what the Girl Aviatrixes had had their meed of excitement there, too, as readers of the "Girl Aviatrixes and the Phantom Airship" well know. But in the scoriated hills with their scanty outcropping of pallid wild oats, the fire-seered acclivities and the burning blue of the desert heavens above all, she beheld a setting entirely foreign to anything in her experience.

"It's like Remington's pictures," she thought to herself as she gazed at the roughly clad group about her, the shabby tent, the mining implements cast about carelessly here and there and the smoldering fire with the blackened cooking pots beside it.

Only one sharply modern note intruded-the two big, yellow-winged monoplanes. Even they appeared, in this wild, outre setting, to have taken on the likenesses of giant scarabs, monsters indigenous to the baked earth and starving vegetation. She was roused from her reverie by Mr. Bell's voice cutting incisively the half unconscious silence into which they had lapsed.

"Bill, you and your sister will take the monoplane in which Mary Eliska rode over and bring Mary Eliska, Jax Gray and my brother over at once."

"But the stock and Alverado?"

The question came from Mary Eliska.

"Alverado, as you call him, can drive the stock across the desert. It should not take him more than twenty-four hours if he presses right ahead. We can send out an airplane scouting party for him if he appears to be unduly delayed."

After some more discussion along the same lines Bill, nothing loth for an aerial dash after his hard work in the mine hole, made ready for the trip. From a locker he drew out his solar helmet and goggles and advised Mary Eliska to don her sun spectacles also. But Mary Eliska, as on several previous occasions, declined positively to put on the smoked glasses designed to protect the eyes from the merciless glare of the desert at noon day.

"They'd make me look like a feminine Sherlock Holmes," she declared stoutly.

"I hope that you won't take it amiss if I say that you have already proved yourself one, and a good one, too," laughed Mr. Bell as the brother and sister clambered into the chassis.

But as Bill adjusted his levers for the rise from the depths of the sun-baked arroyo Mr. Bell held up his hand.

"One moment," he said, "bring back some of the dynamite with you. We're almost out of it and it's needed badly. We've got to blast through that streak of hard pan."

"We'll bring it," nodded Bill, "although I'm not going to tell Aunt Sally about it. I guess she wouldn't be best pleased at the idea of traveling in company with such a dangerous cargo."

As he spoke the propeller began to whir, and after a brief run, the monoplane took the air, rising in a graceful angle toward the burning blue. As they rose above the hills a reddish haze that overspread the horizon became distinctly visible. Mary Eliska viewed it with a little apprehension.

"I hope that doesn't portend another electrical storm," she said rather anxiously, leaning forward and addressing her brother.

Bill shook his head.

"Guess it's just heat haze," he decided. "Mr. Bell says that those dry storms don't often come twice in one season."

"Well, let's be thankful for small mercies anyhow," said Mary Eliska with a return to her former cheerfulness.

The news that camp was to be broken at once and the base of operations removed to the hills, came as a shock to those left behind in the camp. Somehow the pleasant shelter of the ragged willows had become a sort of makeshift home to them, and the idea of winging to the barren hills was not pleasing. Mary Eliska, however, was the only one who made an open wail about it. Old Mr. Bell took it as stoically as he did most things. Only, as he hastened about the camp making preparations for the departure, he could have been heard humming:

> "We've got to go far, far away,
> To the mountains, so they say;
> I hate to leave the willows' shade,
> But Brother James must be obeyed."

Alverado received his instructions with a silent shrug. He informed Bill and Mary Eliska that there was just enough water left to fill the bags for the dash across the desert. He said no more, but there was a curious kind of reticence in his manner, as if he was holding back something he did not wish to express outwardly. It was not 'til everything was packed ready for the start, and old Mr. Bell and Miss Sally had been hoisted and dragged into the chassis, that he drew Bill apart and spoke. Mary Eliska was included in the confidence.

"While you gone I follow up tracks from the water hole," he said; "bime-by I come to place where sacks slip off one pony's feet. Then I see a track that I make stick in my memory long, long ago. That day they leave me for dead on the desert."

He stooped and drew the outline of a peculiarly shaped hoof on the Alkali-impregnated dust. The boy and girl watched him curiously.

"Well?" asked Mary Eliska, and she and her brother hung on the answer.

Alverado's face became overcast by a black look. His eyes glowed like two live coals.

"I think then I never forget that track. I think the same today. The pony that made that track was ridden by Red Bill."

CHAPTER 14.14
LOST!

Good news awaited them on their return to the camp in the arroyo. Mr. Bell and Liam McAdams, while working in a desultory fashion on the vein while awaiting their return, had struck what is known in desert parlance as a water-pocket. They had at once set to work excavating a fair-sized hole in the floor of the mine tunnel, and by the way in which the water gushed in it appeared as if there was a plentiful supply to draw upon.

It is hard to convey how much this bit of news raised their spirits.

"Isn't it queer to think how just finding a little water will make you feel good out here, while at home all we had to do was to turn a faucet and we got all we wanted and never dreamed of being thankful for it," observed Jax Gray philosophically.

"Wish we could strike an ice-cream soda pocket," observed Liam McAdams, who was vigorously scouring the dust off his classic lineaments. "Say, girls, how would you like right now to hear the cool, refreshing 'fiz-z-z-z' of a fountain, and then hear the ice clink-clinking against the sides of a tall glass of say—lemonade or—"

"Liam McAdams, if you say any more we'll duck you head first in that water hole," said Mary Eliska with decision.

"Go ahead," answered Liam McAdams quite unperturbed, "a cold plunge would go fine right now.'"

"Well, we shall have to think up some other punishment for you," decided Jax Gray; "a quarter mile dash across the desert, for instance."

"Well, isn't that the utmost," snorted Liam McAdams; "here I try to cool you girls off by describing the delightful surroundings of a soda fountain and then you threaten me with bodily violence. 'Twas ever thus,'" and Liam McAdams, with an assumption of wounded dignity, strode off to where old Mr. Bell was already busy over the cooking fire.

The midday meal passed off more brightly than might have been expected considering the circumstances in which the adventurers found themselves.

"At all events, we can't starve on the desert," Liam McAdams, "even if we do run short of water."

"How is that?" inquired old Mr. Bell innocently, although the twinkle in Liam McAdams's eye had put the others on their guard.

"Because of the sand-wiches there," rejoined the lad with a laugh, in which the others could not help joining.

"I don't care about sandwiches, particularly ham ones," struck in Mary Eliska ingenuously, which set them all off again.

"Looks to me as if there might be a jack-rabbit or two in these hills," observed Mr. Bell after the meal had been dispatched. "I know it's not good form in the West to eat jack-rabbits, but they're not so bad if you kill them when they are young. Anyhow, it would be a change from this everlasting canned stuff."

"I'll go," Bill declared; "I'll take that twenty-two rifle and Mary Eliska can carry that light twenty-gauge shotgun. It's just the thing for girls and children."

"Oh, indeed," sniffed the embattled Mary Eliska scornfully; "I suppose you think I can't handle a man's size gun?"

"I didn't say so, my dear sister, and I humbly beg your pardon for anything I may have said which may have hurt your feelings," said Bill with a low and conciliatory bow; "what I meant was that the light twenty-gauge doesn't kick so hard and, moreover, won't blow a rabbit to pieces if you happen to hit him."

"Happen to hit him!" shouted Jax Gray, going into a convulsion of laughter.

"Oh, you know what I mean well enough," protested Bill, coloring somewhat under his tan.

"Want to come, Liam McAdams?" he asked, after a moment's pause.

"Tramp over those old hills that look as baked as a loaf of overdone bread?" snorted Liam McAdams. "No, thank you. I'm going to stay home and read a nice book about Greenland's icy mountains."

"And I," declared Jax Gray, vivaciously, "am going to persuade Aunt Sally to make us some vanilla and strawberry ice cream."

So Bill and Mary Eliska set off alone on their tramp in quest of game. It did not look a promising country for hunting; but, as Mr. Bell had pointed out, an occasional jack rabbit might be met with. It was rough going over the rocks and heavy sand, but Mary Eliska stuck to it manfully, and as a reward for her perseverance, had the honor of bringing down the first game—a small jack rabbit, young and tender, that bounded almost under her feet from the shade of the sage brush in which he had been lying.

This put Bill on his mettle, and brother and sister wandered further than they had intended, urged on by the hope of further success. But no more game of any kind was put up, if we except one distant view they had of a sage hen. This bird was "sage" enough to take wing long before they came within shot of her.

"Good gracious, that sun is lower than I thought," exclaimed Bill, suddenly awakening to the fact that they had wandered a considerable distance from the camp. Several of the monotonous ground-swells of the desert hills, in fact, separated them from it.

"We'd better hurry back," declared Mary Eliska, "they'll be worrying about us at the camp."

But to talk about hurrying back and doing it were two different things. Bill discovered, to his dismay, that not only had he lost the location of the camp, but that their footsteps, by which they might have re-trailed their path, had been obliterated in the shifting sands. He said nothing to his sister, however, for several minutes, but plodded steadily on in the direction in which his judgment told him the arroyo of the gold mine lay.

It was Mary Eliska herself who broke the ice.

"Bill, do you know where you are going?"

Bill stammered a reply in what was meant to be a confident tone. But he felt it did not deceive the gray-eyed girl at his side. Evasion was useless.

"Frankly, I don't, sis. Everything seems to have twisted around since we came this way earlier in the afternoon. I thought we could use the tops of the rises for land marks, but they all look as much alike as so many sea-waves."

A sharp shock, which was actually physically painful, shot through Mary Eliska at the words. The sun, a red-hot copper ball, hung in livid haze almost above the western horizon. On every side of them were scoriated hills, desolate, forbidding, sinister in the dying day, and all fatally similar in form.

"We must try shooting. Perhaps they will hear us," suggested Mary Eliska, a sickening sense of fear—fear unlike any she had ever known—clutching at her heart.

Bill blazed away, but the feeble reports of the light weapons they had did not carry to any distance. Indeed, it was only the necessity of doing something that had impelled Mary Eliska to make the suggestion.

All at once an uncanny thing happened. A big, black desert raven flew up with a scream, almost under their feet, and soared above their heads, screeching hoarsely. To such a tension were their nerves strung that both boy and girl started and hastily stepped back.

"Ugh, what a fright that thing gave me," exclaimed Mary Eliska with a shudder that she could not control.

"Nasty looking beast, and that cry of his isn't beautiful," commented Bill in as easy a tone as he could assume.

"Alverado told me that those desert ravens were inhabited by the souls of those who had lost their way and perished on the alkali," shivered Mary Eliska.

"Say, sis, don't be creepy. You surely don't believe all the rot those superstitious Mexicans talk, do you?"

"No, not exactly—but—oh, Bill," even plucky Mary Eliska's voice broke and quavered, "it's so lonely, and whatever are we to do?"

The last words came wildly. Mary Eliska was not, as we know, a nervous girl, but the situation was enough to unstring the nerves of the most stolid of beings.

CHAPTER 14.15
THE PERILS OF THE HILLS

Suddenly Bill gave a sharp exclamation. Something about a cone-shaped peak to the west of them appeared familiar.

"The camp is in that direction, I'm sure of it," he declared, "come on, Mary Eliska, we'll strike out for it, and in half an hour's time we'll be telling our adventures over a good supper."

By this time Mary Eliska was willing to start anywhere if she was moderately sure the camp lay in that direction, and Bill's enthusiasm was contagious. Filled with renewed hope the brother and sister struck out for the cone-shaped peak. Its naked base showed violet in the evening shadows, while its sharply rounded top was bathed in a rosy glow of light. Even in her agitation Mary Eliska could not help admiring the wonderful palette of colors into which the dying day transformed the dreary desert sea.

Beyond the range the vast expanse of solitude spread glitteringly. All crimson and violet, with deep purple marking the depressions in its monotonous surface, and here and there the dry bed of one of its spasmodic lakes, showing almost black in its obscurity. These lakes were water-filled only in the early spring, and their moisture had long since died out of them. Under a noon-day sun they showed like shallow bowls filled with scintillating crystals.

But, had they known it, Bill and Mary Eliska were striking out on a course precisely opposite to that which they should have taken. Every step of the advance to the sugar-loaf shaped peak was a step in the wrong direction. Like many other travelers, whose bones whiten on the alkali, they had become confused by the monotonous similarity of one feature of the dreary hills to the other.

The true extent of their blunder did not dawn upon them 'til they had reached the foot of the queer peak, and even the most minute survey of their surroundings failed to show them any trace of the camp. No cheerful glow of a fire illumined the fast-darkening sky. For all the signs of human life they could discover, they might have been alone in a dead world. In fact, the scenery about them did resemble very closely those maps of the moon—the dead planet—which we see in books of astronomy. There were the same jagged, weird peaks, the same dark centers, dead and extinct, and the same brooding hush of mystery which we associate with such scenes.

Somewhere off in the distance a coyote howled dismally as the sun rushed under the horizon and the world was bathed in sudden darkness.

Mary Eliska turned to her brother with a low little moan. She caught her arms about his neck and hung there sobbing. In his solicitude for her, Bill forgot his own dismay and misery, which was perhaps a good thing, for by the time Mary Eliska recovered herself, the boy was already casting about for some means of passing the night as comfortably as possible.

"We'll stick it out 'til daylight somehow, Mary Eliska," he promised, "and I'm confident that by that time they'll send up one of the monoplanes, and from up in the air they'll have no difficulty in locating us."

The thought was a comforting one, and Mary Eliska's first flush of passionate grief and fear gave way to calmer feelings. No doubt it would be as Bill had forecast. After all, she argued, it was only one night in the open, and they had their weapons and plenty of ammunition.

By a stroke of good luck, Bill had stuffed his pockets full of the hard round biscuits known as "pilot bread" before they left the camp. He also had matches and a canteen full of water. Poor Mary Eliska still carried the lone jack-rabbit, the trophy of her gun, and Bill at once set about grubbing up sage brush and making a fire with the oleaginous roots as he had seen Mr. Bell do.

Before long a roaring blaze was ready, and then the boy began the task of skinning and preparing the rabbit for cooking. Mary Eliska turned away during this operation, but summoned up fortitude enough to gaze on while her brother spitted the carcass on the cleaning rod of his rifle and broiled it in primitive fashion.

"First call for dinner in the dining car forward!" he announced in as gay a voice as he could command when the cooking seemed to be finished.

"The first course is broiled jack rabbit with pilot bread and delicious, sparkling alkali water. The second course is broiled jack rabbit with—"

"Oh, Bill, don't," cried Mary Eliska half hysterically; "it reminds me of the train and the good times we had on the way out from the East. We didn't think then that—"

"Let me give you some broiled jack-rabbit," proffered Bill, gallantly extending a bit of smoking meat on the end of his knife.

Mary Eliska bit it daintily, expecting to make a wry face over it, but to her surprise she found it not half bad. Between them, the two hungry young people speedily reduced that rabbit to first principles.

"And now for dessert," exclaimed Bill, in a triumphant voice. "No, I'm not joking— look here!"

He drew from his pocket a flat, pink box which, on being opened, proved to contain several cakes of chocolate of Mary Eliska's favorite brand.

"Oh, dear," sighed Mary Eliska as she nibbled away at the confection, "if only I knew positively that we were going to come out all right I'd really be inclined to enjoy this as a picnic."

"Hooray! here comes the moon," cried Bill, after an interval, during which the chocolate steadily diminished in quantity.

Over the eastern horizon, beyond the desolate peaks and barren "ocean" of the desert, a silver rim crept. Rapidly it rose 'til the full moon was climbing on her nightly course and flooding the alkali with a soft radiance almost as bright as subdued electric light. Against the glow the weird, ragged peaks stood out as blackly as if cut out of cardboard. One could see the tracery of every bit of brush and rock outlined as plainly as if they had been silhouetted by an artist at the craft.

All at once Mary Eliska gave a frightened little cry and shrank close to Bill. The firelight showed her face drawn and startled.

"Oh, Bill, over there! No, not that peak—that one to the right!"

"Well, sis, what about it?" asked Bill indulgently.

"Something moved! No, don't laugh, I'm sure of it."

"A coyote maybe or another jack rabbit. In that case we'll have a chance at a shot."

"No, Bill, it wasn't an animal." Mary Eliska's tones were vibrant with alarm—tense as a taut violin string. "What I saw was a man."

"A man. Nonsense! Unless it was someone from the camp looking for us."

"No, this man was watching us. He may have been crouching there for a long time. I saw the outline of his sombrero black against the moonlight behind that rise. Oh, Bill, I'm frightened."

"Rubbish," declared Bill stoutly, although his heart began to beat uncomfortably fast. "What man could there be here unless it was Alverado, and he couldn't possibly have arrived by this time."

"But, Bill, it wasn't my fancy. Truly it wasn't. I saw a man crouching there and watching us. When I looked up he vanished."

"Must have been a rock or something, sis. Moonlight plays queer tricks you know. Don't let's make the situation any worse by imagining things."

"It was not imagination," repeated Mary Eliska stoutly.

But Bill, perhaps because he did not wish to, would not admit the possibility of Mary Eliska's vision being correct.

A long, loud cry like the laughing of an imprisoned soul cut the stillness startlingly.

"Ki-yi-yi-yi-o-o-o-o-o-o-o-o!"

"Coyotes!" laughed Bill, "that's what you saw."

Mary Eliska said nothing. The sudden sharp sound had rasped her overwrought nerves cruelly.

"Ki-yi-yi-yi-o-o-o-o-o-o-o-o!"

The demoniacal laughing, half howl, half bark, cut the night again.

This time it came from a different direction. From other grim peaks the cry was caught up. It seemed that the creatures were all about them.

"Surrounded!" muttered Bill a bit nervously. He had not forgotten the fight in the canyon, although, as he knew, coyotes, only on the very rarest occasions, when driven desperate by hunger, attack mankind.

The cries appeared to come from all quarters now. And they were drawing nearer, course lay to the eastward there was no mistaking that.

"They are closing in on us, sis. Better load up that gun."

As he spoke Bill refilled the magazine of his little twenty-two rifle. "Ki-yi-yi-yi-o-o-o-o-o-o-o!"

This time the cry was quite close and behind them. Bill switched sharply round. The surroundings, the uncanny cries, the solitude were beginning to tell on his nerves, too. His self-control was being wrought to a raw edge.

Was it fancy, or as he switched abruptly about did he actually see a dark object duck behind a rock? An object that bore a strange resemblance to a sombrero.

"Good gracious, I musn't become as shaky as this," the boy thought, making a desperate effort to marshal his faculties, and then he sniffed sharply.

"What is it, Bill?" asked Mary Eliska strangely calm now in the face of what she deemed must prove an emergency.

Bill's answer was peculiar. "I smelled tobacco just now, I'm sure of it," he whispered in a low tone. "I guess you were right, sis."

"But the coyotes?" "Are men signaling to each other and closing in on us."

As he spoke the boy scattered the fire, and seizing Mary Eliska by the arm dragged her into the black shadow of the cone-shaped peak.

CHAPTER 14.16
RED BILL SUMMERS

A keen chill, sharp as if an icy wind had swept her, embraced Mary Eliska. It was succeeded by a mad beating of her heart. Bill said nothing but clutched his rifle. He jerked it to his shoulder as, out of the shadows, a figure emerged sharp and black against the moonlight. As if she were in a trance Mary Eliska saw Bill's hand slide under the barrel of the little repeater and then came the sharp click of the repeating mechanism, followed by the snap of the hammer as it fell forward.

But no report followed.

"Jammed!" exclaimed the boy desperately.

At the same moment the figure approaching them, which for an instant had vanished behind a shoulder of rock, emerged boldly, the moonlight playing on a revolver barrel pointed menacingly at the brother and sister.

"No foolin' thar, youngsters," came a harsh voice; "we've got you where we want you."

Coincidently from all about them the rocks seemed to spawn figures, 'til half a dozen men in rough plainsman's garb stood in the moonlight. Resistance was useless; worse, it might have resulted in a calamity more dire than the one that had overtaken them.

But curiously enough the very hopelessness of their situation inspired in Mary Eliska a far different feeling to the terror that had clutched at her heart a moment before. She was conscious of a swift tide of anger. In one of the figures she had recognized the renegade guide.

"Juan—you!" she exclaimed in tones in which scorn struggled with indignation.

The guide turned away. Even his effrontery wilted before the young girl's frank contempt. It was all clear enough to Mary Eliska now. Evidently, Juan had been bribed by these men to stay with the party 'til he had learned their plans, which he was then to betray to the band. For, in the moonlight Mary Eliska had had no difficulty in recognizing the men whose conversation she had overheard at the National House.

There was the red-headed man, with his coarse, bristling crop of hair, and the mustache like the stumpy bristles of an old tooth brush, the tall, dark young fellow with the red sash and the silver spurs, poor Mary Eliska's "romantic brigand," and the hawk-nosed man with the drooping mustache, who had formed the red-headed one's companion on the train.

"Hearn of Red Bill Summers, I op-ine," shot out the man with the red hair in a voice that rasped like a file on rusty iron.

"I think so," rejoined Bill quietly, and Mary Eliska rejoiced to hear her brother's calm, steady tones.

"Wall, I'm him. You treat me right and don't make no fuss an' we'll git along all right. If not—"

He paused significantly.

"Whar's Buck Bellew?"

The red-headed one gazed about him. From the shadows stepped Mary Eliska's "romantic brigand."

"Buck, you put a couple of half hitches about them kids."

"The gal, too?" hesitated the silver-spurred one addressed as "Buck."

"Sure. Didn't I tell yer to."

"Wa-al, I won't. That's flat. I ain't never persecuted women folks an' I ain't goin' ter start now."

Red Bill Summers paused and then grumbled out:

"All right, then. She kin ride the greaser's horse. Juan, you yellow-skinned bronco, go git ther ponies."

Juan flitted off and presently reappeared, leading half a dozen wiry little ponies. In the meantime the remainder of the band had gathered about Bill and Mary Eliska, regarding them with frank curiosity. Except that their weapons were taken away from them no harm was offered them however, and Bill had not, so far, even been tied up.

"This isn't a bit like the story-book hold-ups", thought Mary Eliska. "If it wasn't for their rough clothes and fierce looks these men wouldn't be so very different from anyone else."

"Now, miss, I'll help you to mount. Sorry we ain't got a side saddle, but we don't hev much use fer such contraptions with our outfit."

It was the red-sashed man speaking. He held out a stirrup for Mary Eliska, and the girl, perforce, mounted the pony. She caught herself wondering as she did so what her friends at home in the East would have thought if they could have seen her at the moment. It was Bill's turn next. Brother and sister were permitted to ride side by side. Juan, to Mary Eliska's secret satisfaction, was compelled to give up his burro to one of the outlaws while he tramped along.

"Serves him right," thought the girl.

The man whose pony Bill bestrode leaped nimbly into the saddle behind Buck Bellew.

Hardly a word was spoken, but their captors closed in silently about the boy and the girl prisoners.

"Death Valley," ordered Red Bill briefly, swinging himself into the saddle. Mary Eliska guessed that the sinisterly named place must be their destination.

Amid the maze of pinnacles, minarets and spires of the desert range the horsemen forged slowly forward. From the fact that they traveled toward the newly risen moon Mary Eliska surmised that their course lay to the eastward . But presently it shifted and they began moving north.

"Where can we be going?" Mary Eliska found an opportunity to exchange a word or two with Bill. Owing to the rough nature of the ground their rear guard had, of necessity, fallen back a bit.

"No idea, sis. One thing seems certain, however, they don't mean to harm us, at least not yet."

The rear guard closed up again, necessitating silence once more. All night they traveled, ambling at the plainsman's "trotecito" when opportunity offered, and then again slacking to a crawling walk where the baked ground grew uneven and criss-crossed with gullies and arroyos.

At last, when Mary Eliska's head was beginning to sway with exhaustion, the eastern sky began to grow gray. The coming day lit up the desert wanly, as if it had been a leaden sea. But with the uprising of the sun the familiar glaring white of the alkali blazed out once more. They had left the pinnacled hills and were now traveling over undulating country overgrown with rough brush. It was a sad, drab color, and smelled pungently where the ponies' hooves trampled it.

But presently they broke into a different country. It was flatter than that which they had already traversed and, if possible, more desolate, sun-bleached and parched. The ponies stumbled over loose shale, raising clouds of suffocating dust that tingled in the nostrils. Down they rode into its basin-like formation. All about the depression arose the craggy, stripped hills. Their jagged peaks seemed to shut out the rest of the world and compress the universe into this baked, burning basin in the desert.

Across the bottom of it the alkali swept in little vagrant puffs, proceeding from the gaps of the hills. It piled in little gray heaps like ashes. The air hung steady and still as a plumb line dropped from the sky.

"We've got ter git across hyar muy pronto, (very quickly)," grunted the red-headed man, whose perspiring, fat face was coated gray with dust and alkali. "What a hole fer white men ter be in."

"It's like a busted heat-blister on a big piecrust," commented Buck Bellew, whose jauntiness had wilted. His red sash was of a piece now with the rest of his garments-a dirty, dull gray.

After a while a hot wind sprang up. It felt like the heated blast from an opened oven door. It tore in mad witch-dances about the dismal basin, sending whirling dust-devils dancing over that dreary place.

They spread, gyrated, swelled to giant mushroom shape, and died down in a monstrous ballet. Mary Eliska felt her senses slipping under the strain. But she kept a tight rein on herself. "I must brace up for Bill's sake," she thought.

She stole a glance at her brother. Bill, despite his plight and the dust which enveloped him, was tight-lipped and defiant. No sign of a breakdown appeared on his features, for which Mary Eliska breathed a prayer of thanks.

"After all, God is near us even in this dreadful place," she thought, and the reflection comforted her strangely.

Across the bottom of the bowl men and animals crawled like flies round the base of a pudding basin. From time to time the water kegs on the back of Juan's burro were sparingly tapped. At such times Buck Bellew never failed to be at Mary Eliska's side with a tin cup of the warm, unpalatable stuff. But at least it was liquid, and Mary Eliska thanked the man with as cheerful an air as she could assume.

But, unending as the progress across the red-hot depression seemed to be, it came to an end at last, and the ponies began to climb the steep walls on the further side. At the summit, a surprise was in store for them—for Mary Eliska and Bill that is. To the others the place was evidently familiar. Some rough huts, half of canvas and half of brush, showed that it had long been used as a rendezvous by the band.

The spot was a perfect little amphitheatre in the barren hills. Green grass, actual green grass, covered its floor and wild oats grew on the hillsides in fair plentitude. From the further end of the enclosed oasis arose clouds of steam which they afterwards learned came from boiling hot springs. But the waters of the hot springs soon lost their heat, and in the course of years had watered this little spot 'til it literally—in comparison with its surroundings— blossomed like the rose.

Red Bill Summers threw himself from his pony and, lying full length beside the creek that trickled through the valley from the springs above, he reveled in the water. When he had drunk his fill he stood erect. "Wa-al," he drawled, running his hand through his stubbly red crop, "I reckon we're home again."

CHAPTER 14.17
A FRIEND IN NEED

From one of the huts at the upper end of the miniature valley an odd figure emerged. It was garbed in a blue blouse and loose trousers of the same color. Embroidered slippers without heels caused a curious shuffling gait in the newcomer. As he drew closer Mary Eliska and Bill perceived that he was a Chinese. His queue was coiled upon the top of his skull, giving a queer expression to his stolid features, over which the yellow skin was stretched as tightly as parchment on a drum.

"Here you, Ah Sing, hurry muchee quick and cook us a meal," roared Red Bill as he perceived the newcomer.

"Alee litee," was the easy-going response, "me catchum plentee quick."

The man, who was by this time quite close, allowed his slant eyes to rest curiously on the two young prisoners. His mask-like face, however, betrayed no emotion of any kind, and with a guttural grunt he was off; apparently to set about his preparations for obeying the orders of the outlaw leader.

Red Bill turned to Mary Eliska and Bill, who had dismounted.

"I'll speak to you two after we've eaten," he said; "in the meantime the young lady kin take that hut thar." He indicated a tumble-down structure near at hand.

"It ain't a Fift' Avenoo mansion," he grinned, "but I reckon it'll hev ter do."

Then he switched on Bill.

"You boy," he growled, "you kin hev thet other shack. If you want ter wash up thar's a bucket. We've hot and cold water in these diggin's, too, so take yer choice. Hot's above, cold's below. An' one thing. You ain't goin' ter be closely watched. It ain't needful. You rec'lect that red-hot basin we come through?"

As the questioner seemed to pause for an answer Bill nodded.

"Wall the country all around hyar's jes' like that, so thet if yer moseyed you wouldn't stand any chance of gittin' away alive."

Red Bill, with a vindictive grin, turned on his heel abruptly and stalked off, followed by the others. Mary Eliska and Bill were left alone. Seemingly no restraint was to be put upon them. In fact, it appeared, as Red Bill had pointed out, that an attempted escape could only result fatally for them.

"Whatever will Aunt Sally and the rest be thinking?" exclaimed Mary Eliska as the rough looking group, talking and gesticulating among themselves, made toward the upper end of the valley. "Poor aunt! She must be in a terrible state of mind," rejoined Bill dejectedly. "If only we could have got word to her or Mr. Bell—"

"In that case we could have taken it ourselves," wisely remarked Mary Eliska; "well, brother mine, there is no use in borrowing trouble. Let's make the best of it. I've an idea that that redheaded man means to offer us some sort of a proposition after dinner."

"Wish he'd offer us some dinner first; I'm ravenous."

"Well, I couldn't eat a thing 'til I've got some of this dust off me, so please get me a bucket of water."

"Say, look at that Chinese man eyeing us," broke off Bill suddenly; "wonder what's the matter with him?"

"Guess he isn't used to visitors," suggested Mary Eliska. "So this is where this gang, we heard talked about in Blue Creek, have been hiding themselves. No wonder the sheriff couldn't find them."

"It's an ideal hiding place," agreed Bill, "far too ideal to suit us. I don't see how we'd ever get out of here without help."

"Oh, as for that, I kept careful track of the way we came. I noted all the landmarks, and I really believe I could pick up the trail—is that the way you say it?—again."

"Good for you. I hope we have a chance to try out your sense of observation. But I'm off to get that water. Say, that Chinaman's staring harder than ever. What do you suppose he wants?"

"I haven't an idea. Opium perhaps. Don't they eat it or do something with it and then have beautiful dreams? I've heard—oh, Bill," the girl broke off breathlessly, "I've got it! You know that little jade god that Clara Cummings brought back from China with her when her father resigned as consul there?"

"Yes. But what—"

"Well, look here, you silly boy, I've got it on now. Look on my watch chain. I wonder if that could be what—what that Mongolian was regarding so closely?"

"Maybe," responded Bill carelessly, "but now I'm really off to get that water. Hot or cold?"

"Both!" cried Mary Eliska.

The spirits of youth are elastic, and even in their predicament Mary Eliska found her heart almost singing within her at the beauty of the green little valley after their long, dusty journey over the alkali barrens.

"After all," she assured herself, "I don't believe they mean us any real harm and—oh, what an adventure to tell about when we get home again."

A refreshing wash and a hasty adjustment of her hair before a mirror in a tiny "vanity box," which shared the watch charm snap with the little jade god, served to still further raise Mary Eliska's spirits.

Red Bill Summers and his followers ate at the upper end of the valley, but the Chinese brought food on an improvised board tray to the captives. Having set down two dishes of a steaming stew of some kind, flanked with coffee, sweetened and flavored with condensed milk, and real bread, the Oriental glanced swiftly about him. Red Bill and his companions were noisily convivial, and paying no attention to what was transpiring at the lower end of the valley. Like a flash the Chinese slid to his knees and extending his hands above his head touched his forehead to the ground three times in front of Mary Eliska.

Then rising he exclaimed:

"Melican girl, gleat joss, mighty joss. Ah Sing he come bymby. Goo'bye."

He turned swiftly and silently in his silken slippers and glided off without a backward look.

"Well, what do you make of that?" wondered Bill.

"Oh, Bill, don't you see. He was worshiping this joss, as he calls the little jade god. Just think, this may be a way out of it. If we can make him believe that—that—"

"That we stand in with his josh—joss—what do you call it?—you mean that we can scare him into letting us have horses tonight and escaping.

"How you do run ahead, Bill. I hadn't thought of that yet. But it might be done. He said he was coming back by and by. I wonder what he wants?"

"Maybe your blessing," grinned Bill. "But come on. Let's tackle this stew while it's hot. It looks great to me after that jack-rabbit supper."

"And this is bread—real bread, too!" cried Mary Eliska, following Bill's example of "tackling the stew."

It was ten minutes after the last mouthful had disappeared that the tall, red-sashed young outlaw came toward the shack in front of which brother and sister were seated.

"The boss wants to see you," he said briefly, and signed to them to follow him.

Red Bill Summers sat alone before the remains of the Chinese cook's dinner. The other outlaws were busied staking out their ponies and removing the dust and perspiration from the little animals' coats. Far off, like a lost spirit, the treacherous Juan with his burro, could be seen.

From time to time he cast a covert glance toward Mary Eliska and Bill. In his own country treachery such as he had shown would have been visited with death even if the avenger had to die for it himself the next minute.

The outlaw chief looked up as his dapper follower came up with the young Easterners. "Grub all right?" he asked.

"Not bad at all," responded Bill non-committally. He didn't want to show this red-headed law-breaker that he was afraid of him.

"Wa-al, thet's jes' a sample of ther way I'm willin' ter treat yer as long ez you're here. I've got a hard name around ther alkali, but I ain't ez black ez I'm painted."

To this the two young prisoners made no reply, and Red Bill looked at them searchingly, but if he expected to read anything from their faces he was speedily undeceived.

"Now, then," he went on, "as you'll have guessed, I didn't kidnap you two fer fun. I did it fer infermation. I reckin' you know pretty well the location of Jim Bell's mine.'

"No better than you do," responded Bill boldly; "I guess that scoundrel Juan told you all you wanted to know."

"Oh, as fur as thet goes," rejoined Red Bill easily, "I could ride right frum hyar to yer camp. But what I'm gittin' at is this: You've seen the papers Jim Bell is goin' ter file. You know ther exact location. Thet's what I want. Give it to me an' I'll hev my men take yer as close ter yer camp as it's safe ter go without kickin' up a rumpus."

"In other words, you wish me to betray Mr. Bell's plans to you before he—" Bill stopped. He had been on the verge of saying, "Before he's filed the claim himself." just in time, however, he recollected that this might be news to the outlaw, and he stopped short. But Red Bill was as astute as a desert fox.

"Before he files the claim himself, you wuz goin' ter say, I be-lieve," he drawled, purposely accentuating his words so that they fell like drops of ice water from his cold lips. Bill could have bitten his tongue out. Quite unmeaningly he had betrayed a secret which might prove of tremendous import in the desperate game Red Bill seemed bent on playing.

"I said nothing about the filing or not filing of a claim," parried Bill, after a pause.

"Yer don't hev ter say everything ter make yerself understood, younker," snarled Red Bill, facing the boy and blinking his little red-rimmed orbs into Bill's honest open countenance.

"Thet's somethin' you've foun' out anyhow, Bill," drawled the red-sashed young outlaw, drawing his thin lips back in a sarcastic smile. Bill felt himself turning red with chagrin. He had intended to play a cunning game with Red Bill, but the outlaw seemed to be capable of reading his mind. Steeling himself to be more careful in the future he awaited the further questions of his inquisitor. Upon the manner in which he answered them he felt that not alone his safety and Mary Eliska's depended, but also the security and possibly the lives of the party in the distant arroyo.

CHAPTER 14.18
AH SING'S JOSS

"That'll be all on that line," said Red Bill presently. He turned to his companion.

"Got a pencil and a bit of paper, Buck?" he asked.

The red-sashed one produced the required pencil—a much bitten stub—and then set off toward the cook house for a bit of paper. He returned with the fly leaf out of an old account book.

"Good enough," said Red Bill. "Now then younker," turning to Bill, "you take this pencil, lay that paper on that flat rock and write as I tell you."

Wondering what was coming, Bill obeyed, while Mary Eliska with wondering eyes looked on anxiously at the strange scene. It had grown quite still in the little valley. The only sounds that occasionally interrupted the hush were the shouts of the men tethering the ponies and the harsh scream of a buzzard swinging high against the burning blue of the desert sky.

"Mister Bell, dear sir," began Red Bill, dictating in his rasping voice.

"All right," said Bill, transcribing the words to the paper. The boy had an inkling of what was to come, but he didn't wish to make trouble before he actually had to.

"Got that, did you?" 'Yes.

"Very well. Now write this: 'Me an' my sister is in the hands of those who are our friends at present. It depends on you if they remain so. The messenger who brings you this will arrange for the transfer of the location papers of the mine to these parties. If you don't do this they will—'"

Red Bill paused and shoving back his sombrero scratched his rubicund poll.

"Make it 'they will-take other measures.' Jim Bell's no fool an' he'll know what's meant by that," concluded the outlaw of the alkali.

"Why you ain't bin writing what I tole yer," he whipped out suddenly, just becoming aware that Bill's pencil had been idle. Mary Eliska breathed hard. There was menace in the man's very attitude.

Bill looked up boldly.

"You don't suppose that I'm going to be party to any scheme like that," he demanded with flaming checks.

Mary Eliska, watching the little drama closely, saw that the ruffian was plainly taken off his feet by this. He had not expected—or so it seemed clear—that he would encounter any opposition in carrying out his rascally plan of playing off the safety of a boy and a girl who had never wronged him for the sake of gaining the title to a mine.

"What, you won't write it!" he bellowed at length. The great veins on his neck swelled. His little pig-like eyes gleamed malevolently.

Bill stood his ground firmly, although his heart was beating far faster than was pleasant, and a mist swam in front of his eyes. But he had seen Mary Eliska watching, and knew that her trust in his integrity and honor had never faltered. Right then Bill took an inward oath that he would not destBill her faith.

"No, I will not," he flashed back; "I don't see how you could expect me to take part in a plan to trap and trick my own friends."

Red Bill's lip curled up, exposing a row of ragged yellow teeth.

"Not even at the cost of your own life?" he snarled.

Bill had half an idea that the ruffian was "bluffing" him. But even had he thought Red Bill in deadly earnest his reply would have been the same.

"No!"

The word was ejaculated like a pistol shot.

"Then listen. Your sister—"

To emphasize his words the outlaw launched his clumsy, thick-set frame forward. But the next instant he recoiled as if he had stepped on the edge of a fearful abyss. Simultaneously Bill and Mary Eliska became aware of a curious buzzing, whirring sound like the rattling of dried peas on a griddle. A long dark body glided off through the yellow blades of sun-bitten grass.

"It's—it's a rattler!" gasped Red Bill.

He stooped as if to catch his ankle, and reeling fell in a clumsy huddled heap on the floor of the valley. As he fell a shot reverberated through the silent place. With one bullet from his revolver the tall young outlaw had dispatched the reptile, which had lain hidden in the grass.

"Get you, Bill?" he asked laconically stooping over his chief.

"Yes. I'm a gone coon I guess, Buck."

His red face, contorted and purple from pain, the stricken man slid backward. His lips parted and became ashen. The poison was coursing through his veins with terrific rapidity.

"Let me see. Maybe I can be of some use. Stand aside, please."

It was Mary Eliska. The group of outlaws that had gathered about the recumbent man gave place respectfully. From a bag at her waist Mary Eliska drew out a little oblong leather case. It had been a present to her from Mr. Bell before they set out to cross the reptile-haunted desert.

Opening the case she drew out a fairy-like little squirt, trimmed in silver. It was a hypodermic syringe. From a case she produced some crystals of a purplish color.

"A cup of water, please," she begged.

It was in her hand almost as quickly as she made the request. In the meantime, with a handkerchief she had deftly bandaged the outlaw's leg above the bite. This was twisted tightly with a stick and prevented the poison circulating above the wound.

On Red Bill's ankle the reptile's bite was plainly to be seen. Two tiny blue punctures, fine enough to have been done with a needle. Yet through the fangs that gave the bite had been delivered enough poison to kill a strong man.

With flying fingers Mary Eliska immersed the crystals in the water, turning it a deep crimson. Then filling the syringe she pushed its needle-like point under the outlaw's skin and just above the wound. Then she injected the antidote which she had mixed—permanganate of potassium—and old plainsmen will tell you there is no better opponent of a rattler's poison than the one Mary Eliska used, the method of utilizing which had been opportunely taught her by Mr. Bell.

Red Bill's lips parted. His voice came through them painfully, hissingly.

"Thank 'ee," he muttered, and then closed his eyes.

They carried him into a shack a little way up the valley and laid him on a cot.

"Anything else to be done, miss?" asked one of the outlaws in an awed tone.

"No," answered Mary Eliska with quite the manner of a professional nurse; "he'll do nicely now. In an hour or so he ought to be better. You can call me then."

"Wa-al, I'll be all fired, double gosh-jiggered," Bill heard one of the men say as they left the shack and emerged into the late afternoon sunlight. The outlaws were all in the shack of their leader. All, that is, but the Chinese, who had been an interested observer from the outskirts of the crowd. As the boy and girl came out of the shack he glided up to them as softly and silently as ever.

"Me see. You welly good. Allee samee doctor. Joss he helpee you," he said in a low voice. Then glancing about he sank his voice to a whisper:

"But you no tlustee Led (Red) Bill. Him plentee bad mans. He feelee sick now. Him plentee thank yous. When he well he do you muchee harm."

"He could not be so ungrateful," exclaimed Bill; "my sister saved his life."

"Umph. That plentee big pity. Why not let him die. Good liddance," opined the cold-blooded Ah Sing. "Listen, Melican boy an' girl, helpee you escape tonight you do one littlee ting for me."

"You'll help us escape?" echoed Mary Eliska, the blood beating in her ears. "How? We'd need horses, water, food and—"

"Me catchee eblyting. Leve him all to Ah Sing, he git um."

A cunning smile overspread his features.

"But Ah Sing wantee some leward he do dis."

"Of course. Any money you want you shall have in Blue Creek," burst out Bill.

"Me no wantee monee. Me want lillee misses joss. Him plentee big joss my countlee. I have that joss I have plentee eblyting I want."

"He means the little god that Clara gave me," whispered Mary Eliska. "All right, Sing, you shall have it. You shall have it when you are ready to send us out of the valley."

The Chinese face changed just the fraction of a muscle. That was as near as he came to permitting himself to show his gratification over the promise of the joss.

"Allee litee," he said, "bymby he get dark. You wait in missees shack. When I ready I give one, two, tree knocks-so!"

As silently as he had glided up he glided off again just as the crowd began pouring from the shack where the injured outlaw lay. Bill and Mary Eliska could only exchange wild glances of astonishment at the surprising turn affairs had taken.

But presently Mary Eliska spoke.

"I knew when I prayed in that terrible valley, Bill, that a way would be found," she said, and her voice was vibrant with reverence and faith as the brother and sister turned away.

CHAPTER 14.19
THE ESCAPE AND WHAT FOLLOWED

"Bill! Bill! Wake up!"

Mary Eliska shook the shoulder of her brother, who had dozed off in a rough chair formed out of an old flour barrel. She glanced at her watch. It was almost midnight, and half an hour since the steady footfall of the sentry, who was keeping desultory watch on the captives, had passed the hut.

Bill was wide awake in an instant. He sat up staring wildly about, and then, casting sleep from him, he listened intently.

Tap! Tap! Tap!

The three raps came against the back wall of the shack, and then:

"Missee all ledee. Man who watchee you him go sleep. Me got ponies, water, eblyting. Make um number one quick."

With quick, beating pulses the brother and sister slipped from the door and out into the valley. It was moonlight-that is to say, the moon had risen, but a peculiar haze overcast the sky and the light of the luminary of the night only served to make the darkness more visible. Back of the shack stood a vague figure holding two ponies by the bridles. It was Ah Sing.

"You give me lilly joss now, missee?" he asked eagerly.

Swiftly Mary Eliska stooped and unfastened the little jade god from far-off China.

"Here, Sing," she said simply, "and thank you."

The Chinese bowed low three times before he took the precious symbol into his keeping. He slipped it inside his loose blouse.

"All ledee now," he said, holding a stirrup for Mary Eliska to mount.

"But how will you explain it? Won't they kill you when they find the ponies are gone?" asked Bill.

The Oriental laughed the throaty, mirthless chuckle of his race.

"I tellee them you steal them," he said; "they no thinkee Ali Sing hab good sense enough to help you. All litee now. Good bye."

Before they were thoroughly aware of it, so swiftly had the actual escape happened, Mary Eliska and Bill found themselves moving out of the valley on their desperate dash for freedom.

The ponies went silently as wraiths. The astute Ah Sing had bundled their feet in sacks so that they made no more noise than cats.

In the faint light they could perceive the gateway of the little valley, and in a short time they had passed it and were beginning to traverse the gloomy stretches beyond. Suddenly there came a sound that sent every drop of blood in their bodies flying to their hearts, and then set it to coursing wildly through their veins again.

Bang!

The report, coming from behind them, cut the stillness of the night like a scimitar of sound.

"A pistol!" exclaimed Bill. "They've discovered our escape."

Mary Eliska shuddered. Bending forward at the risk of the noise of their flight being heard, they began to urge their ponies faster. Behind them was pandemonium. Shouts, cries and shots mingled in a babel of sound.

"The kids hev got away!" That cry sounded above all the others, and then, with sinister meaning, came another shout:

"Saddle up and git arter 'em. Get 'em, dead or alive!"

Sounds of galloping followed this order, and then came the shrill voice of Ah Sing:

"Me see um. Me see um. They go that way! Over there! Over the hills!"

"Good for Ah Sing," breathed Bill; "he has thrown them off the track. He's told them we went the other way. Come on, sis; now's our time to make speed before they discover their mistake."

The two fugitives urged their ponies unmercifully over the shale. Fortunately, in the rarefied air of the desert, the nights are comparatively cool, and the tough little broncos sped along at a good gait without showing signs of distress. But it was a cruel race across the floor of the desolate valley, and when they e merged on to the comparatively easy going of the foothills of the barren range, the ponies were fain to slack up and draw long heaving breaths.

"Poor little creatures," cried Mary Eliska; "you've got a long way to go yet."

By the moon, which showed through the haze in a sort of luminous patch, Bill gauged the way. Mary Eliska's observations, too, made on the journey into the valley, helped. They kept the pinnacled steeps of the barren hills to their right and pressed forward among the undulating foothills. They had been traveling thus for perhaps an hour-pausing now and then to listen for sounds of pursuit when Bill suddenly became sensible of a change in the atmosphere. It grew warm and close and almost sticky. A puff of hot wind breathed up in their faces and went screaming off among the mysterious clefts and canyons above.

"Are we going to have a storm?" wondered Mary Eliska.

"Don't know, sis, but the weather looks ominous. I don't like that wind. We must make more speed."

"I hate to drive these poor ponies any faster," protested Mary Eliska

"But we must, sis. They'll have a good long rest when this is over. Come on."

So saying Bill brought down his quirt—the long raw-hide whip used in the West—over the heaving flanks of his pony. The little animal gamely responded and plunged forward at a quick lope. Mary Eliska, perforce, followed suit, although it made her heart ache to press the animals at such a gait.

On and on they rode, while the weather every moment grew more peculiar. From the floor of the desert great dust-devils of white alkali arose and swirled solemnly across the wastes. In the semi-darkness they looked like gaunt ghosts. Mary Eliska shuddered. It was like a nightmare. Once or twice she even pinched herself to see if she were awake.

The night, from being cool, had now become blisteringly hot. The wind was like the fiery exhalations of a blast furnace. Grains of sand caught up by it drove stingingly against their faces. Each grain cut into the flesh, smarting sharply.

"We must keep on." It was Bill's voice, coming after a long silence.

Mary Eliska answered with a monosyllable. A short distance further on they dismounted and allayed their thirst from the kegs Ah Sing had fastened to each saddle, and. then, although their supply was precious, they had to yield to the whinnied entreaties of the ponies. Into a small tin bucket each young rider emptied a modicum of the water and let the little animals drink. It seemed to refresh them—mere mouthful that it was—for they pressed on with more spirit after that.

But there was no denying the fact that something serious was at hand. From desultory puff s the wind had now increased to a steady blow, which drove a stinging hail of sand all about them blindingly. Eddies of hot wind caught up larger grains and dried cactus stems and drove them in terrestrial water spouts across the face of the desert. The moon was quite obscured now, and it was as black as a country church at midnight.

All at once Mary Eliska's pony sank down, and with a long sigh stretched itself out upon the alkali. Bill's almost immediately did the same. As they did so the wind came more furiously. Half blinded and with nostrils, eyes and mouths full of sand particles, the two young travelers reeled about in the darkness. Suddenly what it all meant burst upon Bill with the suddenness of a thunder clap.

"It's a sand storm, Mary Eliska," he cried.

A puff of wind caught up his words and scattered them over the desert.

The words sent a chill to Mary Eliska's heart. She had heard Mr. Bell tell of the sand storms of the Big Alkali—how sometimes they last for days, blotting out trails and burying those unfortunate enough to be caught in them.

"Get your saddle off and keep your head under it," shouted Bill, recalling what he had heard Mr. Bell say of the only way to weather such disturbances.

Mary Eliska, half dead with horror, did as she was told. By the time the work of unsaddling had been accomplished the wind was driving furiously. It was impossible to hear unless the words were shouted. The ponies, who had obeyed their first instinct at the initial warning of what was to come, turned their backs to the storm and laid out straight, with their noses to the ground. Bill and Mary Eliska drew the big flapped Mexican saddles over their heads. Under this protection they were sheltered from the cruel fury of the wind-driven sand and brush.

It was suffocating under the saddle, but when Mary Eliska protruded her face for even a breath of the superheated air, she quickly withdrew it. The wind was now a tornado in violence, and the sand stung like countless needles. Conversation was, of course, impossible, and they lay in silence while the suffocating gale screamed about them.

Once or twice Mary Eliska had to scrape away the sand from the front of the saddle. She could feel it rising all about her. With the sensation came a terrifying thought. She had heard Mr. Bell tell of men whose bones had been buried in the sand only to be exposed long afterward, white and bleached, when the wind-formed sand dunes had shifted and exposed them.

All at once, above the wind and the steady roar of the furiously driven sand and alkali, Mary Eliska thought she heard a wild screech or cry. It sounded like nothing human in its uncanny shrillness. Brave girl as she was, Mary Eliska shuddered hysterically. Could she be losing her mind in the whirling confusion and elemental fury that waged all about her?

CHAPTER 14.20
THE PROFESSOR AGAIN

The evening before the sand storm, a red wagon had been crawling over the alkali toward the barren hills. It was the eccentric vehicle affected by Professor Wandering William, and was headed for the barren range of hills in which lay the valley of the outlaws.

Professor Wandering William, silently smoking, kept his keen eyes steadily fixed upon the distant hills as he drove, although from time to time he scanned the sky anxiously.

"Going to be a sandstorm sure," he grunted. "Well, if I can make the lee of those hills by sundown I reckon I'll be all right. Too bad though. It'll give that precious outfit a chance to put a still further gap between themselves and me—phew! but it's hot!"

The professor took off his big sombrero and placed it behind him in the wagon. He seemed to think a minute and then muttered:

"Oh, well, I guess it's no harm. Nobody to see but a few old buzzards anyhow, and they won't tell."

The professor, having concluded these self-addressed remarks, did a strange thing. He raised his hands to his head and the next instant his luxuriant long hair had vanished, revealing a close-cropped head of dark hair. This done, he removed his goatee with the same ease, and was revealed as a good-looking, forceful-faced young man of perhaps thirty-two or so.

"Ah-h-h-h!" he breathed with intense satisfaction, "that's a whole heap better. However, I guess the time's coming pretty quick when I can do without this make-up altogether. I shan't be sorry either. Git up!"

This last remark was addressed to the motive power of his jaunty red wagon. In obedience the wheels began to revolve faster. But press onward as he would, supper-time found the professor—so strangely shorn—still some distance from the hills.

"That storm's coming right up, too," he said to himself over his after-supper pipe; "well, no help for it. I guess we'll have to push on."

Watering his animals from a bucket previously filled at the spigot of a big water keg built into his wagon the professor hitched up and pressed on to his destination. Darkness came on, but still he drove steadily forward, seeking the shelter he knew he could find in the lee of the barren hills.

"Going to be a hummer and no mistake," he commented half aloud; "good thing-it-didn't catch me out in the middle of the alkali or Red Bill and his cronies might have had a new lease of life."

It was close upon midnight when the professor found a spot to his liking, and by that time the first desultory puffs of the coming storm were sighing in the nooks and crannies of the barren hills. He tethered his team, gave them their hay in the shelter of the wagon, watered them and then, after a good-night pipe, prepared to turn in. He woke from a troubled doze to find the wind rocking the wagon within which he slept.

"Wonder what kind of weather the ponies are making of it?" he muttered, and rising he opened the canvas flaps at the front of the wagon and peered out.

At that instant he saw, or thought he saw, two dark objects move by in the flying smother of sand. But the next moment he told himself it must have been imagination.

"Guess being alone so much is getting on my nerve," he commented.

Having seen that his stock were lying down and turning their backs on the flying drift, Wandering William, as he called himself, retired once more. But he couldn't sleep for thinking of the strange illusion he had had.

"No, it wasn't an illusion either," he said stoutly to himself the next instant. "I'm prepared to swear that I really did see two figures on horseback, though what, in great ginger cookies, they were doing out in this I don't know. Appears to me though that they must have had to call a halt right around here some place. In that case I'm going to give 'em a hail, an' if they answer it invite 'em into the wagon. This is no weather to be out without an umbrella."

Chuckling a little at his joke, Wandering William arose and went once more to the front of his wagon.

Placing his hands to his mouth, funnel-wise, he sent a long, shrill cry vibrating out through the storm. Another and another he gave 'til he was hoarse, but there was no reply.

"Guess I was dreaming after all," remarked Wandering William retiring once more to his blanket.

A sickly yellow light struggling through the sand-laden air heralded the day. But the wind had died down and the particles still held in suspension were rapidly thinning out of the air.

Bill thrust his head from under his saddle like a turtle from its shell.

His lips were dry and cracked, his eyes smarted, his skin was irritated with the sand. The whole world seemed to have turned to sand. It was everywhere.

"Mary Eliska!"

A similar turtle-like head projected from the other saddle. Poor Mary Eliska, she would positively have screamed if she had known the appearance she presented. Her hair was tousled, her eyes red with irritation of the sand, and her lips dry and cracked like Bill's.

"Is—is it all over, Bill?" she asked a bit quaveringly.

"I think so. The wind has died down, and look, the ponies have gotten to their feet. I guess they know."

"Wasn't it awful. I never thought we should live through it."

"Nor did I. But there's one good thing, it has obscured our tracks. If any of Red Bill's gang tried to follow us now they'd have a lot of trouble."

"That's so," agreed Mary Eliska, and then went on to tell Bill of the terrifying screeches and yells she had heard in the night.

"Nothing but the wind," opined Bill, with boy-like superiority. But the next instant it was his turn to start amazedly. Through the fog-like gloom that still overhung the desert a figure was making its way toward them. Bill's hand flew to the revolver with which the thoughtful Ah Sing had provided his saddle holster.

At the same instant the figure, seemingly that of a young man, turned, and wheeling quickly, ran backward and was swallowed up in the obscurity.

"Was that one of Red Bill's men?" gasped Mary Eliska.

"Impossible. They could not have traveled through that storm. But who can it be?"

"What did he run like that for?"

"I'm going after him to find out," declared Bill pluckily; "maybe it's somebody who has become crazed from the sandstorm."

"Oh, Bill, a lunatic!"

Mary Eliska clasped her hands. But the next instant a fresh surprise greeted them. A tall figure with flowing gray locks and gray goatee, topped off with a big sombrero, was seen approaching from the same direction as that in which the youthful figure had vanished.

"Wandering William!" exclaimed the two young adventurers in one breath.

"Yes, Wandering William. The precise individual," was the rejoinder; "and just in time to invite you to breakfast. There, there, no explanations now. You both resemble the output of a threshing machine. But I have mirrors, soap, towels and water in my wagon. Come along, and if you feel ailing, for the insignificant sum of one dollar I will sell you a bottle of Wandering William's Wonderful Wonder Worker."

Exhausted as both boy and girl felt, they could hardly maintain their gravity in the face of this eccentric individual. The very suddenness and utter unexpectedness of his appearance seemed of a piece with his other odd actions. But suddenly Bill recollected the figure that had appeared and then vanished.

"I'd like to accept," said Bill, with vast cunning as he thought, "but what would your partner say?"

"My partner?" Wandering William looked frankly puzzled.

"Yes. That young chap who came toward us and then disappeared again when I came at him with a gun. Not that I blame him," Bill broke off with a laugh, "but I thought for a moment it was one of Red Bill's gang."

Wandering William's keen gray eyes narrowed into two little slits. "What's that you're saying, boy," he exclaimed; "what do you know about Red Bill Summers?"

"A good deal too much for our comfort," exclaimed Bill, and then he rapidly sketched events of the last twenty-four hours as the trio walked toward Wandering William's wagon. The strange vendor of medicine seemed to be deeply interested, although he confined his comments to "ums" and "ahs."

"But about that other man," said Bill, returning to the charge when he had finished his narrative, "didn't you see him?"

"My dear boy," said Wandering William seriously, "I think you had better invest in a bottle of Wandering William's Wonder Working Witch Oil for tired and shattered nerves. There is no one in the vicinity but our three selves."

Boy and girl stared at him blankly. "But I saw him, too," said Mary Eliska.

"I dare say, I dare say," and Wandering William patted his luxuriant curls; "you had a night of strain. What you need is breakfast—hot coffee and all that. Now go in and get fixed up while I attend to your ponies, or rather, Red Bill's."

The wind had by this time died down, and the sun struggled out through the clearing air. Nobody was in sight but themselves, and fain to believe that their sand-sore eyes must have played them a trick, the boy and girl proceeded to "fix up" in Wandering William's really comfortably appointed wagon.

In the meantime one weight had been lifted from Mary Eliska's mind. Wandering William had explained that it was he who had uttered the shouts and yells which had so alarmed her in the night. "If only it wasn't for that man whom I'm certain I saw," thought Mary Eliska as she combed the sand out of her hair, "I should feel quite relieved, but as it is—Bill, are you still certain you saw that man—the one you pointed the revolver at I mean?"

Bill looked dubious. "I—don't know," he confessed. "Oh, Bill Stricklin," snapped Mary Eliska, "I—I'd like to shake you."

CHAPTER 14.21
OUT OF THE DESERT MAZE

Twilight was descending on the camp in the arroyo when Liam McAdams, who had been stationed with a rifle on a butte overlooking the desert maze, gave a sudden shout. The next instant his rifle was at his shoulder and he began shooting into the air as fast as he could. As the rapid staccato volley of sound rattled forth all became excitement in the arroyo.

The volley had been the signal agreed upon in case the young sentry caught sight of the missing ones. It came after a wearing night and a still more harrowing day. Following the non-arrival of Mary Eliska and Bill in camp from their hunting excursion a search had at once been commenced, of course without result.

An ascent had even been made in one of the monoplanes, but even a bird's-eye view of the surrounding country failed to discover their whereabouts. Then came the sandstorm, and hope that the missing ones could have weathered it was almost given up. Nevertheless, James Bell, in whom hope died hard, had set Liam McAdams as sentinel on the lofty butte in the wild hope that after all the castaways might turn up.

And now, as the agreed signal rang out, there was a great outpouring from the camp. Aunt Sally, pale and red-eyed from weeping, Mr. Bell, with deep lines of anxiety scoring his face, Jax Gray, troubled and anxious looking, and old Peter Bell, the former hermit, bearing an expression of mild bewilderment. Last of all came Alverado, the Mexican flotsam of the desert. His inscrutable countenance bore no sign of the suffering he had gone through at the thought that harm had come to his worshipped senorita, but in his heart the Mexican had suffered as much as the rest. He had arrived in camp with the stock the evening before, and had, with difficulty, been restrained from setting forth at once on a search.

"Look!" cried Liam McAdams pointing as the others rushed up.

They followed the direction of his finger and saw slowly crawling toward the arroyo a red wagon, dust-covered and travel-stained.

In front of it were two young figures on horseback, waving frantically. As the volley rattled out they urged their little horses forward on a dash for the arroyo.

"Thank God!" breathed Mr. Bell huskily.

Aunt Sally fell into Jax Gray's young arms and wept lustily while old Bell broke into a rhapsody:

"Out from the desert safe and sound; Hooray! our boy and girl are found!"

But nobody paid any attention to his verses, either to laugh or admire just then. After the cruel anxiety of the past hours the relief was too great for any of them to trust themselves to speak.

But as Mary Eliska and Bill—for of course our readers have guessed it was they—drew closer and their dust-covered features could be plainly seen, a great shout went up from the butte. And in it mingled the voice of Alverado, the unemotional.

The girl and boy were fairly lifted from their ponies and carried in triumph into the camp.

"Dig down into the stores," ordered Mr. Bell, "Get out all the delicacies we have been savin' for a big occasion."

"We'll never have a bigger one than this," declared Liam McAdams; "tell us all about it, Bill."

"Oh, Mary Eliska, you darling, is it really you?" cried Jax Gray for the 'steenth time, with brimming eyes.

As for old Mr. Bell, as Liam McAdams observed afterwards, "he just wrapped poetical circles round himself. You couldn't see him for rhythm."

"Hullo, folks!"

The voice came suddenly from the shadows. It was Wandering William. In the general excitement everybody had forgotten him, and he, had driven up in his red wagon unheralded. But the warmth of his reception made up for any temporary slight. In fact, after supper, when Bill related their strange adventures, and told how, if it had not been for Wandering William, they might never have reached the camp, Wandering William's greeting reached an ovation.

But while all this was going on one figure had remained crouched in the circle of firelight—or, rather, just beyond it—whose dark eyes had not for an instant left the face of Wandering William. The interested observer was Alverado.

The Mexican puckered his brow as be gazed as if trying to recall something. But the effort seemed to be in vain, for at length he arose and, unnoticed, strode moodily off toward the ponies, which had been tethered high on the hillside and out of sight of the camp.

He was gone but a few minutes before he came bounding back into the camp.

"The ponies! The ponies are gone!" he shouted at the top of his lungs.

In an instant everybody but Aunt Sally and old Mr. Bell was upon his or her feet.

"Gone!" The exclamation came like a dismayed groan.

"Yes, gone! Every one of them! The lariats have been cut. Ah, the ladrone, the cursed thieves! The—"

"Some of Red Bill's work, for a million!"

The exclamation fell sharp and clear from Professor Wandering William's lips. The tones were so unlike his usual ones that everybody looked up at him. But only for an instant; the next moment the professor had—dropped back into his pompous, drawling way of speaking:

"It's a good thing we have a large supply of my wonder working remedies with us," he said; "they induce philosophy, smooth the thorny ways of life and make the old young and the young younger."

Mr. Bell looked at him sternly for an instant, and then apparently decided that the man was a harmless fool, for with a quick exclamation he strode off toward his tent, which lay at some distance from the camp. The others excitedly discussed the alarming turn events had taken, while Aunt Sally showed strong symptoms of hysterics. But Alverado, whose face had taken on a startled expression at Wandering William's quick exclamation, darted to the long-haired herb doctor's side.

"I know you now, senor, you are—"

Wandering William caught the man's gesticulating hand with a grasp of iron.

"Not so loud, Alverado," he whispered tensely, "the time isn't ripe for that yet."

"But, senor, you will capture them, and—"

The Mexican's manner had grown deferential, but Wandering William checked him with a glance from those keen eyes of his.

"Don't mention a word of this, Alverado. I rely on you."

"You can, senor. But hark! what is the matter with the Senor Bell?"

Evidently something serious was the matter with the mining man. He came bounding out of the dark shadows of the upper end of the canyon as the Mexican spoke. His face was black as thunder.

"More villainy!" he exclaimed as questions came pouring in upon him.

"Something else missing?"

It was Wandering William. His voice was as emotionless as if he had been a phonograph.

"Yes, I should say there was. The plans of the mine and its location as prepared for filing have been taken from my tent!"

"Stolen—oh!"

Mary Eliska's voice quivered.

"Stolen," repeated Mr. Bell, "and undoubtedly by the same band of scoundrels that cut the ponies loose, knowing that we could not pursue them."

"But we can overtake them in an airplane."

It was Mary Eliska who spoke. Her bosom heaved and her cheeks burned red with excitement.

"True, my brave girl," rejoined Mr. Bell, "but of what use would that be? They have the papers and will file them. Without the papers you could do nothing, and I have no memoranda to draw up fresh ones."

"But in my pocket—I'm cutting no capers—I have a set of duplicate papers!"

Old Peter Bell, triumphant and poetical, stepped forward, at the same time drawing from his inner-coat pocket a bundle. It was the duplicate set which Mr. Bell had given Mary Eliska to deliver to the former hermit, and which, up to that moment, had been forgotten in the excitement.

"Thank heaven!" exclaimed Mr. Bell, snatching at them; "Peter, you're a brick. Hooray, now we have a chance to beat the scoundrels at their own game."

"You mean if we can file those papers first they stand good in law?" asked Bill.

"That's just what I do mean, and I think that with the airplane we can do it."

"You can depend on it, Mr. Bell, that if there is a chance those papers get into Blue Creek first," cried Mary Eliska ablaze with excitement.

"But we can't start tonight."

Bill's voice held a note of despair.

"That's all right, my boy. You need a good rest anyway. Red Bill—if it is his gang that has taken them—cannot get to Blue Creek for two days anyway. If you start at dawn tomorrow you can outwit them."

And so it was arranged. Bill and Mary Eliska turned in early, while Liam McAdams worked all night getting the big monoplane in readiness. By earliest dawn all was ready and a hasty breakfast eaten. Then the monoplane was stocked with food and water and everything was ready for the dash across the desert.

Mary Eliska and Bill had slipped into their linen coats and donned their hideous masks with the blue sun goggles, when a figure slipped up on the other side of the chassis and clambered unobserved into the box-like structure. It was not 'til half an hour later, when they were dashing through midair, that the figure revealed itself. Then the form of Wandering William crawled from under a bit of canvas used as an engine cover, and in answer to the amazed exclamations of the young aviators said:

"You'll have to forgive me. It'll be a good ad for my business to be able to say that Professor Wandering William has wandered along the aerial Pike."

CHAPTER 14.22
MAROONED ON THE DESERT

There was nothing to be done but to accept the situation, little as either Bill or Mary Eliska relished the eccentric "professor" for an aerial traveling companion. Only Mary Eliska remarked with withering scorn:

"I think you might have waited 'til you were asked, don't you?"

The professor's reply was characteristic.

"My dear young lady, if I never sold anybody a bottle of my medicine except those that really wanted it I'd have a hard time getting along."

Bill was on the point of exclaiming "Bother your old medicine," when he suddenly recollected that had it not been for this queer personage they might not have been in the airplane at all. Instead—but Bill didn't care to think further along those lines.

Far below them suddenly appeared a giant halo of light. It hung above the desert, wheeling and gyrating about five feet above the glaring white of the alkali.

"A halo," remarked Professor Wandering William gazing over the edge of the chassis.

"A halo? Whose—Bill's?" inquired Mary Eliska.

"No, it is one of those halos peculiar to the desert," was the professor's rejoinder; "it is caused by heat refraction or something of the sort. I recall I did read a lengthy explanation of it somewhere once, but I've forgotten it now."

"Does it portend anything?" asked Bill, turning round for a moment from his levers.

"No. not that I know of, at least—except that it's hot."

"Good gracious, we don't need a halo to tell us that," cried Mary Eliska, and then regarding Professor Wandering William with that frank, straight "between the eyes" look, as Liam McAdams called it, Mary Eliska remarked, "Do you know, Professor Wandering William, that you are a very odd person?"

"Odd, my dear young lady. How so?"

"Why at times you are quite different to—to what you are at others," stumbled Mary Eliska lamely. It wasn't just what she wanted to say, but as she told herself it expressed it tolerably.

"Almost human sometimes, eh?" chuckled Professor Wandering William with a very odd winkle of his gray eyes; "well, you are not the first person who has said that."

To herself Mary Eliska thought, "I'm sure that if he'd cut his hair and take off that dreadful goatee he'd be quite good looking. And his eyes, too, they twinkle and flash sometimes in a way very much out of keeping with his general appearance." But Professor Wandering William, seemingly quite oblivious to Mary Eliska's frank gaze, was humming "Annie Laurie" to himself and gazing down at the flying desert as it flashed by below.

"At this rate we'll be in Blue Creek long before those other varmints," he observed at length; "that is, if all goes right. Wonderful things these airplanes. Great scheme for selling patent medicine. Why I could scatter my advertisements over a whole county in a day's time if I had one of these. That is unless I scattered myself first."

There was a sudden loud hissing sound from the motor. At the same instant the propeller ceased to revolve and the monoplane dashed downward with fearful force.

Bill worked at his levers desperately, while Mary Eliska, white faced but silent, clung tightly to the sides of the chassis. Professor Wandering William did not utter a word, but his lips moved, as, from a pleasing rapid forward motion their course suddenly changed to that fearful downward plunge through space.

It seemed that in the molecule of time that intervened between the sudden stopping of the propeller and the moment that they reached the proximity of the ground that a whole lifetime flashed in front of Mary Eliska. "Is this the end?" she caught herself thinking.

But it was not. Bill's skill averted that. He handled the disabled airplane so that as it struck the alkali its landing wheels sustained the shock. But even with all his skill he could not entirely ward off the shock. The monoplane struck the alkali in a shower of white dust that hurtled high above it like a breaking sea wave.

Mary Eliska and the professor managed to hold on and resist the grinding shock, but Bill did not fare so well. Like a projectile from a catapult the shock flung him far. He came grinding down into the sand on one shoulder, ploughing a little furrow. Then he lay very still, while Mary Eliska wondered vaguely if she was going to faint.

To scramble from the stranded machine was the work of an instant for the erratic professor, and he extended his hand to Mary Eliska. With a supreme effort she pulled herself together and accepted his proffered help. But agitated as she: was, she did not fail to notice a surprising fact, and that was that the professor's hair was on one side! The next instant he caught the girl's startled eyes fixed upon it, but in that space of time he readjusted it, so that he appeared exactly as usual. But to Mary Eliska the recollection of that deranged hair was unforgettable.

"It's—it's a wig!" she gasped to herself, and then, casting all other thoughts aside, sped to Bill's side.

"Bill! Bill! are you badly hurt, dear?" she breathed, going down on her knees in the rough surface of the desert.

The boy stirred uneasily and his eyes opened.

"Oh, is it you, Mary Eliska? I guess I was knocked out for a minute. It's my shoulder. Ouch! Don't touch it."

The boy winced as Mary Eliska's soft hand touched the injured member.

"Allow me. I've got a little skill at surgery.'"

It was Professor Wandering William's voice, and Mary Eliska caught herself wondering that he didn't make some reference to his infallible bone set or wonder-working liniment. But he didn't. Instead, he knelt by Bill's side, and with a few deft strokes of his knife had cut away the boy's shirt and bared a shoulder that was rapidly turning a deep blue.

Tenderly as a woman might have, Wandering William felt the wound.

"Hurt?" he asked, as Bill winced, biting his lips to keep from crying out under the agony.

"Hurt?" echoed Mary Eliska indignantly; "of course it does."

Professor Wandering William looked up with an odd air of authority in his keen eyes.

"Please fetch me some water from the airplane," he said, and Mary Eliska had no choice but to obey.

Professor Wandering William, picking Bill up in his arms as if he were a baby, instead of a 165-pound boy, carried him after her and laid the injured lad out in the scant strip of shade afforded by the airplane. Then, with bits of canvas ripped from the cover which had served to conceal him when he entered the aerial vehicle, the strange wanderer skillfully bathed and then bandaged the wound.

"Nothing more than a bad sprain," he announced.

Bill groaned.

"And just as I was going ahead at such tiptop speed, too," he complained. "I won't be able to use this arm for a month the way it feels."

"Never mind, Bill, I can drive the airplane," comforted Mary Eliska. But Bill was fretful from pain.

"What can a girl do?" he demanded; "this is a man's work. Oh, it's too bad! It's—"

Suddenly the pain-crazed lad realized what he was saying and broke off abruptly:

"Don't mind me, sis. I'm all worked up, I guess. But if it hadn't been for this delay we'd have beaten them out. And now—"

"And now the first thing to do is to see what ails this old machine," said Professor Wandering William briskly. "Let me lift you into the what-you-may-call-um, my boy, and make you as comfortable as possible on this canvas."

The professor skillfully arranged the canvas from which he had cut the bandages, and making a pillow for Bill out of his own coat, he lifted the lad into the chassis.

"There now, you'll do," he said, as his ministrations were completed. "And now, young lady, as you know more about this thing than I do let's have a look at it and see what particular brand of illness it is suffering from."

A brief examination showed Mary Eliska that the radiator—the intricate mesh-work of pipes in which the circulating water for cooling the cylinders is kept at a low temperature—was leaking, and that almost all their supply of water had leaked out. This had caused the cylinders of the motor to overheat and had stopped the airplane in midair.

"Bad—is it?'"

Professor Wandering William noted the despairing look on Mary Eliska's face as she discovered the cause of the stoppage.

"As bad as bad can be," the girl rejoined seriously; "it means if we can't get water and something to stop that leak with that we can't go on or go back. We're stuck right here."

"Phew!" Wandering William's lips puckered in a whistle. "I should just say that is bad."

He looked about him. On every side stretched the dazzling white alkali, with here and there a little dust devil dancing as if in mockery at their plight.

On all that vast expanse they seemed the only living things, and Wandering William knew the desert well enough to realize that it is not good to linger on its treacherous sands.

CHAPTER 14.23
BUD TO THE RESCUE

"I'm going to look for water!"

Wandering William spoke decisively after an hour or more of futile endeavors to start the motor with the little fluid they could spare from the water kegs. But even without the leaky radiator it would have been an impossibility to cool the cylinders with the small quantity they were thus able to command.

"Look for water!" Mary Eliska echoed the words blankly.

In all that sun-blistered expanse it seemed to be an impossibility to even dream of discovering a drop of moisture. And they needed buckets full.

Wandering William, perhaps deeming it wise not to strain the over-wrought girl's nerves further by keeping up the conversation, strode off. Apparently he wandered aimlessly, but in reality his keen, trained eyes were on the alert every instant. To the desert traveler the most insignificant signs may betray the presence of the life-saving fluid.

Mary Eliska watched the strange figure 'til it vanished from view over a low rise, for although the desert seems flat on a superficial view, it is, in reality, no more level than the tossing sea. Rises and hollows make its surface undulating.

In the meantime Mary Eliska ministered to Bill as best she could. With a spare bit of canvas she made a shelter to keep off the blazing rays of the sun. Bill thanked her with a smile. The first sharp keen pain of his injury had gone, but he felt weak and dizzy. Presently he begged for a drink of water, and Mary Eliska, not daring to tell him how low the supply was gave it to him. The boy was feverish from his injury, and almost drained the canteen of luke-warm stuff she held to his lips. Then he lay back with a satisfied smile.

"Get the radiator fixed yet?" he asked presently.

Mary Eliska had told him that it would not be long before they were under way again.

"Not yet, Bill dear. But don't worry about that. It will be fixed presently. Suppose you try to go to sleep."

The boy closed his eyes and tried to compose himself to slumber. Before long he actually did doze off and lay in that state while the long hours dragged slowly by. Wandering William had not reappeared, and Mary Eliska wondered in a dull, vague sort of sort of way if he ever would come back. Perhaps he had deserted them, she thought. But, even this reflection brought no poignant sensation of despair. The girl had sunk into a sort of apathy in which nothing' seemed to matter much. Only she fairly ached with thirst. But Bill would awake presently and want water. The little they had must be saved for him.

And so the hours wore on and the sun marched blazingly across the sky. It was mid-afternoon, and Bill had not awakened, when Mary Eliska was startled from her gloomy thoughts by a loud hail.

"Hul-lo!"

Springing to her feet she looked across the desert. On the summit of a distant earth wave she saw the figure of Wandering William. He was gesticulating frantically and shouting something. He had his hands to his mouth, funnelwise, to make the sound carry better.

What was it he was crying out? It sounded like—yes, it was:

"Water! I've found it! Water!"

Mary Eliska hastily snatched up the two buckets with which the airplane was equipped, and hurried toward the distant figure. She reached Wandering William's side in quicker time than she would have thought possible, such was the stimulating effect of the glad news. The strange "professor" said not a word, but took her by the hand and began striding in great steps across the sandy dunes.

They had walked about a quarter of a mile when they reached a spot where yuccas and prickly desert plants of different varieties grew thickly. At the bottom of this desolate little valley was a pool on which the sunlight shone glitteringly. It was shallow and warm, and the color of rusty iron, but it was water.

Taking the folding tin cup that Wandering William produced from one of his pockets, the girl drank eagerly. Never had sparkling spring, water in the fruitful Eastern country tasted half so good as that tepid, dirty alkaline stuff that Wandering William had so providentially stumbled upon.

"How did you find it?" gasped Mary Eliska.

Wandering William indicated a tumble-down sign post a few paces off. To it was nailed board with sun faded lettering on it.

"Read it," commanded Wandering William.

"'To the lost in the desert inferno,'" read Mary Eliska, "'water is twenty paces to the west.'"

"If it hadn't been for the white soul of the man who put that up there," commented the "professor," "we might have perished miserably. Heaven bless him, wherever he is."

"Amen," murmured Mary Eliska.

They filled the buckets, and staggering under their weight, Wandering William led the way back to the airplane. Bill was awake and thirsty. He drank greedily of the turbid stuff they offered him.

"And now," said the professor, "let's get to work on that radiator."

But try as they would, they could not stop the leak. Indeed, so much water was wasted in their experiments that several more trips to the pool were necessary.

"Looks like we have run into the worst streak of hard luck I ever heard of," sighed Wandering William despairingly, after the failure of the twentieth trial to get the cooling system to hold water. "We've just got to plug that leak somehow, or—"

He didn't finish the sentence. There was no need for him to do that.

Suddenly Mary Eliska, who had looked up from the baffling task for an instant, gave a cry:

"Look! Look there! What's all that dust?"

"It's horsemen of some kind, and they're coming this way!" cried Wandering William.

As he spoke his hand slid to his hip, and he drew out his well-oiled and worn old forty-four.

"Do you think that they are—that they are Red Bill's men?"

"Don't know yet. The dust's thick and the light's bad."

"If they are?"

"Then we are in for a mighty bad quarter of an hour. Consarn the luck, everything seems to be going wrong at once."

On and on swept the dust cloud, growing close with great rapidity. With what anxious feelings the strange herb doctor and the girl watched its advance may be imagined. As for Bill, he lay on the floor of the chassis unaware of what was transpiring without.

There seemed to be several of the riders—a dozen at least.

"What beats me is, if those are Red Bill's men what are they doing in this direction?" said Wandering William, a puzzled look creeping over his weather-beaten countenance.

"Perhaps they have seen that the airplane is stranded and are coming to destBill it," hazarded Mary Eliska.

"Maybe," rejoined Wandering William in a far-away voice. His eyes and mind were bent on the approaching cavalcade. If the riders were not Red Bill's men it meant succor and aid. If they were the outlaw's band, it meant-well, Wandering William did not care to dwell upon the thought.

"A few seconds will tell now," he observed as through the dust cloud the outlines of the horsemen became visible.

All at once a shrill series of cries rang out:

"Yip-yip-yip-yee-ee-e-e-e-e-e!"

There was something familiar in the sound to Mary Eliska. She leaned forward, straining her ears. Suddenly an active little bronco seemed to separate from the ruck of the riders and dashed forward alone. On his back sat a familiar figure and not a beautiful one, but to Mary Eliska no angel from heavenly regions could have appeared more, beatific just then, for in the rider she had recognized the redoubtable Bud, the leader of the horse hunters.

Bud swept off his sombrero as he dashed up, and was apparently about to make some jocular remark, but he stopped short at the sight of Mary Eliska's pale, anxious face.

"Wa-al, what's all ther trouble hyar?" he demanded; "your sky bronco foundered? Why hello, thar's Wandering William. Didn't know as you was a sky pilot feller?"

"I'm not, I guess," rejoined Wandering William quietly. "I wish I were, and then maybe I could help out on this difficulty."

"Wa-al, what's up?" drawled Bud, as his followers came loping up; "anything I kin do? We're on our way back to ther hills frum town," he explained. "We caught more than twenty wild horses and took 'em inter Blue Creek. One of ther boys sighted you away off or we'd have missed yer I reckin.

"Now, miss, I ain't one ter fergit a blow-out like thet yer gave us at Steer Wells. Jes say ther word an' if you like we'll tow this here cloud clipper back inter town."

"Let's see if we can't hit on a way of fixing it first," said

Wandering William; "you see," he explained to Bud, "the radiator—"

"Hyar, hold on thar. Talk United States language. What's wrong with this arrangement meter."

"It's sprung a leak," volunteered Mary Eliska; "look here, you can see for yourself. The hole is tiny, but it's big enough to let out all the water that we need to cool the cylinders."

"Humph," said Bud crossing his hands on the horn of his saddle and gazing abstractedly at the leak, "what you need is solder," he announced presently.

"If we'd had any we'd been out of here long ago," rejoined Mary Eliska, as Bill, hearing the unusual noise, peered over the edge of the chassis.

"Hullo, kid; what's biting you?" demanded the breezy Bud.

"Guess I'm out of commission for a while," rejoined Bill bravely.

Mary Eliska hastily explained the accident, and then, as she saw no harm in doing so, she gave Bud a hasty sketch of the events leading up to their being marooned on the alkali.

"So you're after that ornery varmint, Red Bill, are yer?" remarked Bud as she concluded; "wa-al I'll do all in my power to help you. I've bin a studyin' that thar leak while you was a talkite. What you need is suthin' to stop it up."

"Obviously," said Mary Eliska with a trace of annoyance in her tone.

"Now don't git riled, fer I've hit on a scheme ter git yer out of yer troubles."

Bud shoved back his sombrero and gazed triumphantly at the astonished girl aviatrix.

CHAPTER 14.24
WHAT CHEWING GUM DID

"But, Bud, how?"

"Easy enough. Hyar," he exclaimed, looking back at the horsemen behind him, "whar's that dude Chick Berry?"

"Here I be, Bud," replied a small, freckle-faced cowboy with blue silk ribbons on his shirt sleeves and other marks of the cowboy dude about him.

"Got any of that thar gum you's always achewin' so as ter be agreeable to ther ladies?" demanded Bud.

"Shore, Bud," rejoined Chick, pulling off an embroidered gauntlet and extracting a pink package from his breast pocket.

"Wall, chaw some quick, and chaw it good. I need it."

Chick's jaws worked overtime. Presently he handed a small wad of glutinous gum to his leader.

"Na-ow then," announced Bud, dismounting, "I'm goin' ter show you a hurry up repair job."

He squatted, cowboy fashion, in front of the radiator, and with deft fingers pressed the gum into the leak.

"Let it dry a minute an' I'll bet ye that what-you-may-call-um will be as tight as a drum. No, don't give me no credit fer ther idee. I seen a feller fix his gasoline gig that way one day when I was down in San Antone,"

At the expiration of a few anxious minutes, water was poured into the radiator, and, to their immense relief, Bud's hastily contrived bit of plumbing worked. The radiator held water perfectly and a few moments later Mary Eliska started the engine.

But at the first revolutions of the propellers a strange thing happened. On the spot where, a second before, had stood a group of interested horse hunters, not one remained after the propeller had whizzed round a couple of times. They were scattered all over the desert, their ponies maddened beyond all control by terror at the noise and smoke of the airplane's motor.

Bud alone managed to spur his pony close to the throbbing machine.

"Good bye and good luck!" he shouted, and waved his hat. The next instant his pony swung round on its hind legs and dashed off to join its terrified companions.

With an answering wave of the hand Mary Eliska threw in the clutch that started the airplane forward, and after their long-enforced delay they once more took the air. But a day had practically gone—a day in which the fight for the mine might have been lost.

Never had Mary Eliska urged an airplane to greater speed than she did the fast monoplane, at the wheel of which she was now stationed. The desert floor flew by beneath them in a dull blur. The roar and vibration of the powerful motor shook the car like a leaf. Wandering William said nothing, but he gazed rather apprehensively over the side from time to time. Also he might have been observed to clutch at his hair occasionally.

"Can you see anything of the town yet?"

The professor leaned forward and shouted the question in Mary Eliska's ear. He had to do so in order to make himself heard above the roar of the engine.

Mary Eliska shook her head, but motioned to a pocket in which were a pair of field-glasses. Wandering William understood, and raising them, held them to his eyes.

The sun was low and a reddish haze overhung the desert. But presently into the field of the binoculars there swung a-tall water tower. It marked the site of Blue Creek.

"I've got it," cried the observer; "swing off to the right a bit."

Obediently the big flying thing turned and rushed through the air toward the distant landmark.

"I can see the place now," cried Mary Eliska. "Pray heaven we'll be in time."

She tried to put on more speed, but already the big monoplane was doing all it could, and a more. Under their hood the cylinders were smoking. There was a smell of blistered paint about the aerial craft. But Mary Eliska never slackened speed for an instant. With the time that had been lost with the leaky radiator, she knew it was possible that Red Bill's men were already in the town.

If she had known that a speedy automobile had met the stealers of the location papers in mid-desert that afternoon and rushed them into Blue Creek she might have given up in despair. But, she knew nothing of Red Bill's ruse, and imagined that the trip with the stolen papers had been made on horseback all the way.

Fifteen minutes after the little settlement been first sighted the airplane soared roofs in a long, graceful swing, and then swooped to earth in front of the National House. Cash and the usual group of loungers came rushing out in huge excitement.

"It's an airship! Come and see the airship!"

The cry spread through the town like wildfire. In five minutes quite a large crowd was swirling and surging about the machine and its anxious occupants.

"Whar's the United States Assayer's office?" demanded Wandering William, above the hubbub and excitement.

"Why it's two blocks to the right an' down that alley," volunteered Cash; "you're the second party as has bin askin' fer it ter day."

Mary Eliska's heart sank and Wandering William bit his lips. From the bottom of the chassis Bill demanded:

"Are we too late?"

"We don't know yet, Bill dear," Mary Eliska found time to whisper, and then:

"Who else was looking for the assayer?"

"Feller in a big automobile. All dust-covered, too. Said he had a claim ter file."

Wandering William actually groaned. But Cash went on speaking.

"Funny, all this rush of business should come ter day."

"How's that?" inquired Wandering William for want of something better to say.

"Why 'cause ther assay office is closed up. Jim Dallam, as ran it, his mother is dead, an' he got leave ter go back East. Ther nearest assay office now is at Monument Rocks sixty miles east of hyar."

Straw of hope as it was they clutched at it eagerly. There might be a train leaving within a reasonable time:

"Can we get a train there?" asked Wandering William eagerly bending forward.

"Reckon ye're jes' too late; one pulled out half an hour ago."

"Did—did the man with the red auto catch it?" asked Mary Eliska breathlessly.

"Yes, mum—miss, I mean. He allowed he was going ter git them papers filed or bust."

The blow had fallen. Mary Eliska sat numb and limp in the chassis. But presently the necessity of attending to Bill aroused her from her lethargy. Under her directions the boy was removed to a bed in the hotel and a doctor sent for. The physician lived in the hotel, so no time was lost before he was at Bill's bedside. He had finished his examination and had pronounced the injury painful, but not dangerous, when, without ceremony, Wandering William burst into the room.

"We can make it yet! We can make it yet!" he was shouting.

The doctor looked up as if he thought he had another patient and a maniac to deal with.

"I—I beg your pardon," stammered Wandering William, "but this is a vital matter to this young lady and gentleman."

"Yes—yes, what is it?" asked Mary Eliska eagerly. Her eyes burned with eagerness and suppressed excitement. Something in Wandering William's manner seemed to say that he had found a way out of their difficulties.

"I've made inquiries," he repeated, "and I've found out that the train to Monument Rocks makes several stops. There's just a chance that we can beat it in the airplane."

"You can!"

Bill raised himself up in bed despite the pain.

"I think so. But we must hurry."

"Sis, do you mean you are going to try it?"

"Of course. We must."

"Then go in and win," cried the boy; "you can follow the tracks by the lights and once you overtake the train the rest will be easy."

The amazed doctor fairly dropped his case of instruments at this whirlwind dialogue.

"But—what—why—bless my soul," he gasped, but only the first part of his remarks was heard by Mary Eliska. Followed by Wandering William she dashed from the room and into the street. In front of the hotel Cash was having a hard time keeping souvenir hunters from the airplane. But a pair of blue revolvers, like miniature Gatling guns, acted as powerful dissuaders of curiosity.

CHAPTER 14.25
A RACE THROUGH THE NIGHT

"All right. Stand clear, please!"

The airplane had been tuned up, and now, panting like an impatient horse, it was ready to be off on its dash for Monument Rocks. But the crowd stupidly clustered about it like bees round a rose bush. The delay was maddening, but Mary Eliska dared not start for fear of injuring someone.

"Won't you please stand aside?" she begged for the twentieth time, but the crowd just as obstinately lingered.

Suddenly an idea came to her. She cut out the mufflers and instantly a deafening series of reports, like a battery of Gatling guns going into action, filled the air. Tense as the situation was, neither Mary Eliska nor Wandering William on the rear seat could keep from laughing as they saw the effect the bombardment of noise had.

The inhabitants of Blue Creek literally tumbled all over each other in their haste to get out of the way. Five seconds after the deafening uproar commenced a clear path was presented, and, before the crowd could get used to the sound and come surging around again, Mary Eliska started the airplane up. Amid a mighty shout it took the air and vanished like a flash in the gathering dusk. The race against time was on.

Fortunately the telegraph poles along the right of way acted as guides, for, in the gathering darkness, the tracks were hardly visible. Mary Eliska did not dare to fly too low, however, for it was only in the upper air currents that the monoplane could develop its best speed.

But even with all her care she pressed the machine too hard, for half an hour after their departure from Blue Creek they had to alight to allow the cylinders to cool. Bud's makeshift stop for the leak, however, was acting splendidly, and Mary Eliska mentally stored it away as a good idea for future use.

The delay was annoying to the point of being maddening, but there was no help for it. To have taken the air with heated cylinders would have been to court disaster. While they waited out in the lonely Nevada hills beside the single-track railroad, Mary Eliska's mind held a lively vision of the train speeding toward Monument Rocks and the Assay Office, bearing with it the stolen papers carried by Red Bill's agent.

At last, after what seemed an eternity, they were ready to start once more. Mary Eliska lost no time in taking to the air. With her every cylinder developing its full horse power, the airplane sky-rocketed upward at a rate that made Wandering William hold on for dear life.

"W-w-w-what speed are we making?"

The question was jolted out of the passenger.

"About sixty," Mary Eliska flung back at him.

"Then we ought to overtake the train. I understand it only makes forty-five even on the most favorable bits of road, and the tracks are pretty rough out in this part of the country."

On through the night they roared. It was quite dark now, and Mary Eliska had switched on the search light with which the airplane was provided. It cast a white pencil of light downward, showing the parallel bands of steel. Somewhere ahead of them, on those tracks, was the train. But how far ahead? As yet no gleam of its tail lights had come through the darkness.

All at once Mary Eliska gave a triumphant cry.

"Look!" she cried. "It's the train!"

Far ahead gleamed two tiny red lights. They glowed through the darkness like the eyes of some wild animal. But the occupants of the airplane knew they were the tail lights of the train that was carrying the stolen papers to Monument Rocks.

Mary Eliska tried to put on still more speed, but the airplane was doing its best. But fast as it was going, it seemed to crawl up on the train at a snail pace. The tail lights still kept far ahead.

But although the gain was slow, it was, steady. Before another dozen miles had been passed Mary Eliska was flying above the train.

In the glare of the furnaces as the fireman jerked the doors open, Mary Eliska could see the engineer and his mate gazing up at them with something of awe in their expressions. Airplanes were not as common in the far West as in the East.

Suddenly the girl noticed a figure emerge from the forward door of the front coach and clamber over the tender and drop lightly into the cab. A sudden gleam from the fire door served to light his features. Mary Eliska recognized him instantly as the tall "romantic bandit," the one with the red sash.

The girl saw him lean toward the engineer and thrust something into his hand. It looked like a roll of bills. The next instant the train's speed perceptibly increased. It was all the airplane could do to keep up with it.

"He's given the engineer money, to go faster," exclaimed Wandering William.

The tall figure now crawled back on the tender and gazed upward. His hand glided back to his hip. The next moment there was a flash, and a bullet zipped wickedly through the air past Mary Eliska's ear.

"The coyote, he's firing at us!" cried Wandering William.

Z-i-n-g!

Another bullet sang by the speeding airplane. Apparently the fireman and the engineer could not hear the shooting above the noise of the flying engine, for they did not turn their heads. Presently the fireman began shoveling on coal at a terrific rate. Sparks and flame shot from the smokestack of the locomotive. They streaked the night with fire.

"Is he trying to kill us?" exclaimed Mary Eliska as another shot winged past.

"I hardly think he'd risk that," rejoined Wandering William, "but what he's up to is almost as bad. He's trying to disable the airplane."

But before another could be fired the train began to slacken speed. Ahead and below the airplane could be seen a cluster of lights.

"Monument Rocks!" exclaimed Wandering William; "here's where we play the hand out."

Mary Eliska, keeping a bright lookout for a good landing place, presently espied a sort of plaza in the center of the town. It was brilliantly illuminated by a number of arc lights and offered a fine spot for landing. She decided to risk a quick drop and swung the airplane downward at a rapid gait.

As the whirring of the propeller—like the drone of a giant locust—resounded over the town, people came pouring out from houses and shops to witness the descent. The crowd gathered so quickly that Mary Eliska had difficulty to avoid hitting some of them. However, she managed to bring the airplane to a standstill without an accident.

A local policeman came up as they stopped, and to him Mary Eliska entrusted the machine. Followed by Wandering William she darted off across the plaza and made for a cab stand immediately across it and just outside the depot. As she rushed up to the solitary rickety hack that was standing there and was about to step in a tall figure came rushing out of the station. The train had just pulled in, and long before its wheels had stopped revolving he had leaped from it.

"Get to one side," he shouted, grabbing Mary Eliska's arm roughly and swinging her aside. "I guess I'm first on this deal."

"What do you mean," demanded Mary Eliska angrily; "I had this cab first." "But now I dispossess you of it this way!"

The ruffian had his hand raised to strike when something happened. A lithe, muscular form glided under the upraised fist, and the next moment there was a sharp crack as the newcomer's fist collided with the other's chin. He went staggering backward and fell in a heap on the sidewalk.

A tall man with a broad brimmed hat came bustling up, followed by a small crowd attracted from the airplane by the disorder.

"Here, here, what's all this?" demanded the tall man in an authoritative tone. "What does this mean?"

"That this man I've just knocked down is under arrest for participation in the Laredo stage robbery and for numerous other crimes, including the larceny of some location papers he was about to file."

The words came from an athletic young man who had felled Mary Eliska's assailant. The girl looked up at him. In the electric light there was something familiar and yet strangely unfamiliar about his features, and his keen, kindly eyes. "Why," exclaimed Mary Eliska wonderingly, "it's—it's—"

"Wandering William, minus his wig and goatee, otherwise Sam Kelly, of the United States Secret Service," rejoined the other with a merry laugh. "I guess I'll go out of the doctor business now, since I've nabbed one of the men I was after. Now then, you rascal," addressing the "romantic bandit," who had scrambled to his feet, "where are the rest of Red Bill's precious gang?"

"I don't know," sullenly rejoined the prisoner. "Oh, yes you do; but first of all give me those papers." "What papers?"

"The ones you brought here to file in the Assay Office." "I don't know what you're talking about." "Yes you do. Come now, or I'll ask the sheriff to search you."

With a very bad grace the outlaw dove into his pocket and handed over a bundle of papers. Wandering Will—we mean Detective Sam Kelly—took them and handed them to Mary Eliska.

"Those are more yours than mine," he said; "we'll file them in the morning or at any time there's no hurry now."

"Now then," he resumed, turning to the tall outlaw whose arms were held by two of the sheriff's deputies, "are you going to answer my question, where is Red Bill and the rest of them now?"

"Where you can't reach 'em in time to queer their game," came in a voice of sullen triumph; "they're at Jim Bell's mine picking up gold and silver."

CHAPTER 14.26
BESIEGED—CONCLUSION

The sun rose redly and shone down into the arroyo on a group of sleepless, anxious persons. As the tall bandit had triumphantly announced, Jim Bell's mine was besieged. Since the evening before armed horsemen had surrounded it, but so far the little garrison had held out.

If Red Bill had had any idea that he was going to find Mr. Bell an easy prey he must have revised his opinion. But he knew that it was only a question of time 'til he could starve him out and take possession of the mine. He was unaware of the departure of the airplane for Blue Creek, otherwise he might have kept a better look out.

"I wonder if they got through?" It was Mr. Bell who spoke, making a brave attempt at indifference to the danger that hedged them in.

Before anyone could reply a figure on horse-back appeared at the head of the arroyo. It was Red Bill himself. On his ankle was a bandage, but his amazing vitality had left no other traces of the bite of the rattlesnake.

"Wa-al, Jim Bell," he demanded, "for the third an' last time, air you goin' ter give in peaceable? Ain't no sense in holding out. We've got your stock. We'll tap your water hole if we can strike the vein and it won't take us long. We've got you whar we want you, an' if you've got ther brains uv a yearling calf you'll throw up the sponge and give us the mine."

"Not while I can raise a hand to fight you," rejoined Jim Bell boldly. "Ah! I might have expected some such trick!"

A bullet had whizzed past his ear and flattened itself on the rock behind the mining man. If he had not caught the quick movement of Red Bill's arm just in time the moment might have been his last.

"That's just a taste of what you'll git if you try to stick it out," bellowed Red Bill, and wheeling his horse he rode off.

Two or three times that morning Liam McAdams tried the experiment of raising a hat on a rifle barrel above the top of the little canyon. Each time a bullet pierced it, showing that the place was well watched.

Aunt Sally lay on her cot in her tent. The venerable New England lady was literally half-dead from fright. Alverado, sullen eyed and apathetic, strode up and down the canyon all day muttering threats he was powerless to carry out. Jax Gray, wide-eyed and white-faced, but brave, did her share of the work and kept Liam McAdams and Mr. Bell cheered up as well as she could.

But the suspense of awaiting the return of Mary Eliska and Bill was the hardest to bear. If they had gotten through safely and the papers were filed, then, even if Red Bill captured the mine he could not work it. A few nuggets would be his reward. But if the airplane had been disabled or had reached Blue Creek too late, why then Red Bill held all the cards. Mr. Bell had reasoned this out with himself over and over again, while his brother sat, staring and disconsolate, playing endless games of solitaire.

It was past noon when Liam McAdams, who had taken an observation between two rocks, which acted as a bullet-proof sentry box, announced that the forces of the outlaws seemed to be massing.

"Looks as if they were going to make an attack," he said. Mr. Bell clambered up and speedily confirmed the correctness of Liam McAdams's opinion.

"Get everything ready," he ordered; "there's just a chance we can stand them off. If not, we'll have to trust to their mercy."

A clatter of hoofs sounded above the arroyo and the next instant several horsemen appeared. Without knowing just what he was doing Liam McAdams, who had a rifle in his hands, pulled the trigger. He was amazed to see the giant form of Red Bill totter and reel in the saddle, and fall with a crash to the ground. The next instant horror at the idea that he had killed the man seized on him. His hands shook so that he almost dropped the rifle.

But there was little time for reflection. The sight of their leader's downfall seemed to drive the other outlaws to frenzy. They poured a leaden hail into the arroyo that must have exterminated every living thing in it if they had not sought shelter behind a mighty mass of boulders.

Hardly had they crouched there in temporary safety, before, far above them, came a familiar sound. The giant droning of an enormous beetle was what it seemed to resemble most. But Jax Gray and Liam McAdams recognized it instantly.

"An airplane!" shouted Jax Gray.

"It's Mary Eliska and Bill!" cried Liam McAdams the next instant. Looking upward against the blue was outlined the scarab-like form of the monoplane.

At the same moment a terrific trampling of horses' hoofs sounded above. Shots and shouts rang out in wild confusion.

"What can be happening?" gasped Jax Gray. Even Aunt Sally, cowering in her tent, summoned courage to peek forth. The sight they saw was an inspiring one. Bud and his horse hunters were riding down the outlaws in every direction.

While this was going on, the airplane swung lower. From it there stepped as it alighted, not Bill and Mary Eliska, but Mary Eliska and a strange young man whom nobody recollected having seen before. Without a word he bounced from the chassis as the airplane struck the ground, and, revolver in hand, set off in hot pursuit of Bud and his men, who, from horse hunters, had become man hunters.

The outlaws, outnumbered and outridden, were fain to cry for quarter. With the exception of three who escaped, the whole band was rounded up and made prisoners. Red Bill, who proved to be only slightly wounded, was captured by Sam Kelly himself.

The presence of the horse hunters on the scene at the opportune moment was soon explained by Mary Eliska, who spent a busy hour relating all that had occurred since they left the camp. Bill, she explained, was still at the hotel in Blue Creek, but mending rapidly. She and the detective had encountered the horse hunters as the airplane was on its return journey, and, guessing from the tall bandit's story that the camp in the arroyo must be besieged, they enlisted the services of Bud and his followers.

There seems to be little more to tell of this portion of the Girl Aviatrixes' adventures. The mine, in the developing of which they had played such striking parts, proved to be rich beyond even Mr. Bell's dreams, and when additional claims were taken up each of the young airship enthusiasts found that he or she had substantial shares in them.

The airplane line from the mine to the railroad, which had been Mr. Bell's original idea, proved to be a great success. Under Bill's tuition three young aviators, who were brought from the East, were instructed in managing their lines. Alverado, it will be recalled, recognized Sam Kelly as an old acquaintance during lawless times in Mexico—he has been appointed to a position in the government service, where he has done good work in aiding to rid the Big Alkali of the rascals that formerly infested it.

As for our young friends, when the airplane line was well established, they returned to the East, as Aunt Sally firmly refused to remain any longer in the far West, which she always scripturally refers to as a land of "the wicked and stiff-necked."

But their adventures were by no means over, as perhaps might be expected in the case of those who dare the air in fast flying machines. Their experience on the great Nevada desert was not destined to be the only time that the Girl Aviatrixes and their chums proved their worth in seasons of danger and necessity.

Stirring aerial adventures lay ahead of them, still more exciting than the ones they had encountered while "On Golden Wings." What these were, and how our girls and boys acquitted themselves in facing and surmounting fresh difficulties and dangers—as well as their lighter moments—will be related in full in the next chapter 15.

CHAPTER 15

The Sky Cruise

CHAPTER 15.1.
A NEW VENTURE IN SANDY BEACH.

"It isn't to be a barn; that's one thing certain. Who ever saw a barn with skylights on it?" Mary Eliska, in a pretty, fluffy morning dress of pale green, which set off her blonde beauty to perfection, laid down her racket, and, leaving the tennis-court, joined her brother Liam McAdams at the picket fence. The lad, bronzed and toughened by his trip to the Nevada desert, was leaning upon the paling, gazing down the dusty road.

About a quarter of a mile away was the object of his contemplation—a big, new structure, painted a staring red. It had no windows, but in front were great sliding doors. On its flat roof the forms of a dozen or more glazed skylights upreared themselves jauntily.

"No, it's a work-shop of some sort. But what? Old man Harding is interested in it, that's one thing sure. I heard, too, that while we were away, cases of machinery had arrived and been delivered there, and that active work of some sort had been going forward ever since," rejoined Liam McAdams, who was clad in white tennis flannels, with white shoes and an outing shirt, set off by a dark-red necktie.

"See Liam McAdams," cried Mary Eliska suddenly, "they're putting up some sort of sign on it, or else I'm very much mistaken."

"So they are. I see men on some ladders, and now, look Mary Eliska, they are carrying up a big board with something painted on it. Perhaps at last the mystery will be solved, as they say in the dime novels."

"Can you read the printing on that sign?" inquired Mary Eliska.

"Not a word. I can see the letters to know that they are printed characters, but that's all. Tell you what, Mary Eliska, just run and get those glasses we used on the desert—there's a good fellow—and we'll soon find out."

"Isn't that just like a brother? Always sending his long-suffering sister on his errands."

"Why, you know you are dying with curiosity yourself, to know what's on that signboard," parried Liam McAdams.

"And I suppose you're not," pouted Mary Eliska in mock indignation. "However, I'll get the field glasses to oblige you—just once."

"As if you won't try to secure the first peek through them!" laughed Liam McAdams, as sunny Mary Eliska tripped off across the lawn to a big shed in the rear of the Stricklin home, where the aeroplanes and their appurtenances were kept.

She soon was back with the field glasses, and, as Liam McAdams had prophesied, raised them to her eyes first. Having adjusted the focus, she scrutinized the sign carefully. By this time the big board had been raised horizontally above the doors and was being fixed in position.

Suddenly Mary Eliska gave a little squeal of astonishment and lowered the magnifiers.

"Well, what is it?" chaffed Liam McAdams; "an anarchist bomb factory or an establishment for raising goats, or something that will "butt in" just as much on our peace and quiet, or———"

"Liam McAdams," enunciated Mary Eliska, severely shaking one pink-tipped finger under Liam McAdams's freckled nose, "this is not a subject for jesting."

"Never more serious in my life, Sis. If you could have seen your own face as you peeked through those glasses———"

Mary Eliska stuffed the binoculars into her brother's brown hands.

"Here, look for yourself," she ordered. Her voice was so imperious that Liam McAdams obeyed immediately.

An instant later his sister's expression of dumfounded amazement was mirrored on his own straightforward, good-looking countenance.

"Well, as Bud used to say out West, 'if that ain't the beatingest'!" he gasped.

"What did you read?" demanded Mary Eliska breathlessly. "Repeat it so that I may be sure my eyes didn't play me a trick."

"Not likely, Sis; the letters are big enough. They show up on that red painted barn of a place like a big freckle on a pretty girl's chin."

Then he repeated slowly, mimicking a boy reciting a lesson:

"The Mortlake Aeroplane Company. Well, wouldn't that jar you?"

"Liam McAdams!" reproved Mary Eliska.

"There's no other way to express it, Sis," protested the boy. "Why, that's the concern that's been advertising so much recently. Just to think, it was right at our door, and we never knew it."

"And that hateful old Mr. Harding is interested in it, too, oh!"

The exclamation and its intonation expressed Mary Eliska's dislike of the gentleman mentioned.

"It's a scheme oh his part to make trouble for us, I'll bet on it," burst out Liam McAdams. "But this time I guess it's no phantom airship, but the real thing. What time is that naval lieutenant coming to look over the Stricklin aeroplane, Mary Eliska?"

"Sometime today. He mentioned no particular hour."

"Do you think it possible that he is also going to take in that outfit down the road?"

"It wouldn't surprise me. Maybe that's why they are just putting up the sign. They evidently have refrained from doing so 'til now in order to keep the nature of their business secret. If we hadn't come back from Nevada sooner than we expected, we might not have known anything about it 'til the navy had investigated and—approved."

Far down the road, beyond the big red building, came a whirl of dust. From it presently emerged a big maroon car. Mary Eliska scrutinized it through the glasses.

"Mr. Harding is in that auto," she said, rather quietly for Mary Eliska, as the car came to a stop in front of the Mortlake Aeroplane Manufacturing Company's plant.

Shortly before Mary Eliska and Liam McAdams, their aunt, Miss Sarah Stricklin, with whom they made their home, and their chums, Jess and Jimsy Bancroft, had returned from the Nevada alkali wastes, the red building which engaged their attention that morning had caused a good deal of speculation in the humdrum Long Island village of Sandy Beach. In the first place, coincident with the completion of the building, a new element had been introduced into the little community by the arrival of several keen-eyed, close-mouthed men, who boarded at the local hotel and were understood to be employees at the new building. But what the nature of their employment was to be, even the keenest of the village "cross examiners" had failed to elicit.

Before long, within the freshly painted wooden walls, still sticky with pigment, there could be heard, all day, and sometimes far into the night, the buzz and whir of machinery and other more mystic sounds. The village was on tenter-hooks of curiosity, but there being no side windows to peer through, and a watchman of ferocious aspect stationed at the door, their inquisitiveness was, perforce, unsatisfied. Not even a sign appeared on the building to indicate the nature of the industry carried on within, and its employees continued to observe the stoniest of silences. They herded together, ignoring all attempts to draw them into conversation. What Mary Eliska and Liam McAdams had observed that day had been the first outward sign of the inward business.

From the throbbing automobile, which the boy and girl had observed draw up in front of the Mortlake plant, a man of advanced age alighted, whose yellow skin was stretched tightly, like a drumhead, over his bony face. From the new building, at the same time, there emerged a short, stout personage, garbed in overalls. But the fine quality of his linen, and a diamond pin, which nestled in the silken folds of his capacious necktie, showed as clearly as did his self-assertive manner, that the newcomer was by no means an ordinary workman.

His face was pouchy and heavy, although the whole appearance of the man was by no means ill-looking. His cheeks and chin were clean shaven, the close-cut beard showing bluely under the coarse skin. For the rest, his hair was black and thick, slightly streaked with gray, and heavy eyebrows as dark in hue as his hair, overhung a pair of shrewd, gray eyes like small pent-houses. The man was Eugene Mortlake, the brains of the Mortlake Company. The individual who had just descended from the automobile, throwing a word to the chauffeur over his shoulder, was a person we have met before—Mr. Harding, the banker and local magnate of Sandy Beach, whose money it was that had financed the new aeroplane concern.

CHAPTER 15.2.
MR. HARDING DECLARES HIMSELF.

Readers of the first volume of this series, "The Girl Aviators and The Phantom Airship," will recall Mr. Harding. They will also be likely to recollect his son, Fanning, who made so much trouble for Mary Eliska and her brother, culminating in a daring attempt to "bluff" them out of entering a competition for a big aerial prize by constructing a phantom aeroplane. Fanning's part in the mystery of the stolen jewels of Mrs. Bancroft, the mother of Jess and Jimsy, will likewise be probably held in memory by those who perused that volume. The elder Harding's part in the attempt to coerce the young Stricklins into parting with their aerial secrets, consisted in trying to foreclose a mortgage he held on the Stricklin home, with the alternative of Liam McAdams turning over to him the blue prints and descriptions of his devices left the lad by his dead father. How the elder Harding was routed and how the Girl Aviator, Mary Eliska, came into her own, was all told in this volume. Since that time Mr. Harding's revengeful nature had brooded over what he chose to fancy were his wrongs. What the fruit of his moody and mean meditations was to be, the Mortlake plant, which he had financed, was, in part, the answer.

In the volume referred to, it was also related how Peter Bell, an old hermit, had been discovered by means of the Stricklin aeroplane, and restored to his brother, a wealthy mining magnate.

In the second volume of the Girl Aviators, we saw what came of the meeting between James Bell, the westerner, and the young flying folk. By the agency of the aeroplane, a mine—otherwise inaccessible—had been opened up by Mr. Bell in a remote part of the desert hills of Nevada. The aeroplane and Mary Eliska played an important part in their adventures and perils. Notably so, when in a neck-to-neck dash with an express train, the aeroplane won out in a race to file the location papers of the mine at Monument Rocks. The rescue of a desert wanderer from a terrible death on the alkali, and the routing of a gang of rascally outlaws were also set forth in full in that book, which was called "The Girl Aviators on Golden Wings."

The present story commences soon after the return of the party from the Far West, when they were much surprised—as has been said—to observe the mushroom-like rise of the Mortlake factory. But of what the new plant was to mean to them, and how intimately they were to be brought in contact with it, none of them guessed.

"Well, Mortlake," observed Mr. Harding, in his harsh, squeaky voice—not unlike the complaint of a long unused door, "well, Mortlake, we are getting ahead, I see."

The two men had, by this time, passed within the big sliding doors of the freshly-painted shed, and now stood in a maze of machinery and strange looking bits of apparatus. From skylights in the roof—there were no side windows to gratify the inquisitive—the sunlight streamed down on three or four partially completed aircraft. With their yellow wings of vulcanized cloth, and their slender bodies, like long tails, they resembled so many dragon-flies, or "devil's darning needles," assembled in conclave upon the level floor. At the farther end of the shed was a small blast furnace, shooting upward a livid, blue spout of flame, which roared savagely. Actively engaged at their various tasks at lathes and work-benches, were a dozen or more overalled mechanics, the most skillful in their line that could be gathered. Here and there were the motors, the driving power of the "dragon flies." The engines glistened with new paint and bright brass and copper parts. Behind them were ranged big propellers of laminated, or joined wood, in stripes of brown and yellow timber. Altogether, the Mortlake plant was as complete a one for the manufacture of aerial machines as could have been found in the country.

"Yes, we are getting along, Mr. Harding," returned Mortlake, "and it's time, too. By the way, Lieut. Bradbury is due here at noon. I want to have everything as far advanced as possible in time for his visit. You won't mind accompanying me then, while I oversee the workmen?"

Followed by Mr. Harding, he made an active, nervous tour of the work-benches, dropping a reproof here and a nod of commendation or advice there.

When he saw a chance, Mr. Harding spoke. "So the government really means to give us an opportunity to show the worth of our machines?" he grated out, rubbing his hands as if washing them in some sort of invisible soap.

"Yes, so it seems. At any rate, they notified me that this officer would be here today to inspect the place. It means a great deal for us if the government consents to adopt our form of machine for the naval experiments."

"To us! To you, you mean," echoed Mr. Harding, with an unpleasant laugh. "I've put enough capital into this thing now, Mortlake. I'm not the man to throw good money after bad. If we are defeated by any other make of machine at the tests I mean to sell the whole thing and at least realize what I've put into it."

Mortlake turned a little pale under his swarthy skin. He rubbed his blue chin nervously.

"Why, you wouldn't chuck us over now, Mr. Harding," he said deprecatingly. "It was at your solicitation that the plant was put up here, and I had relied on you for unlimited support. Why did you go into the manufacture of aerial machines, if you didn't mean to stick it out?"

"I had two reasons," was the rejoinder, in tones as cold as a frigid blast of wind, "one was that I thought it was certain we should capture the government contract, and the other was— well, I had a little grudge I wished to satisfy."

"But we will capture the government business. I am not afraid. There is no machine to touch the Mortlake that I know of——"

"Yes, there is," interrupted Mr. Harding; "a machine that may be able to discount it in every way."

"Nonsense! Where is such an aeroplane?" "Within a quarter of a mile from here. To be accurate, young Stricklin's—you know whom I mean?"

The other nodded abstractedly.

"Well, that youth has a monoplane that has already caused me a lot of trouble." The old man's yellow skin darkened with anger, and his blue pinpoints of eyes grew flinty. "It was partly out of revenge that I decided to start up an opposition business to his. He was in the West 'til a few days ago, and I never dreamed that he would return 'til I had secured the government contract. But I am now informed—oh, I have ears everywhere in Sandy Beach— that this boy and his sister, who is in a kind of partnership with him have had the audacity to offer their machine for the government tests also."

"Audacity," muttered Mortlake under his breath, but Harding's keen ears caught the remark.

"It is audacity," agreed the leathern-faced old financier; "and it's audacity that we must find some way to checkmate. I've never had a business rival yet that I haven't broken into submission or crushed, and a boy and a girl are not going to outwit me now. They did it once, I admit, but this time I shall arrange things differently."

"You mean——" "That I intend to cinch that government business."

"But what if, as you fear, the Stricklins have a superior aeroplane?"

"My dear Mortlake," the pin-point eyes almost closed, and the thin, bloodless lips drew together in a tight line, "if they have a superior machine, we must arrange so that nobody but ourselves is ever aware of the fact."

With a throaty gurgle, that might, or might not, have been meant for a chuckle, the old man glided through the doors, which, by this time, he had reached, and sliding rather than stepping into his machine, gave the chauffeur some orders. Mortlake, a peculiar expression on his face, looked after the car as it chugged off and then turned and re-entered the shop. His head was bent, and he seemed to be lost in deep thought.

CHAPTER 15.3.
A NAVAL VISITOR.

Liam McAdams had departed, on an errand, for town. Mary Eliska, indolently enjoying the perfect drowsiness of noonday, was reclining in a gayly colored hammock suspended between two regal maple trees on the lawn. In her hand was a book. On a taboret by her side was a big pink box full of chocolates.

The girl was not reading, however. Her blue eyes were staring straight up through the delicate green tracery of the big maples, at the sky above. She watched, with lazy fascination, tiny white clouds drifting slowly across the blue, like tiny argosies of the heavens. Her mind was far away from Sandy Beach and its peaceful surroundings. The young girl's thoughts were of the desert, the bleak, arid wastes of alkali, which lay so far behind them now. Almost like events that had happened in another life.

Suddenly she was aroused from her reverie by a voice—a remarkably pleasant voice:

"I beg your pardon. Is this the Stricklin house?"

"Good gracious, a man!" exclaimed Mary Eliska to herself, getting out of the hammock as gracefully as she could, and with a rather flushed face.

At the gate stood a rickety station hack, which had approached on the soft, dusty road almost noiselessly. Just stepping out of it was a sunburned young man, very upright in carriage, and dressed in a light-gray suit, with a jaunty straw hat. He carried a bamboo cane, which he switched somewhat nervously as the pretty girl advanced toward him across the velvet-like lawn.

"I am Lieut. Bradbury of the navy," said the newcomer, and Mary Eliska noted that his whole appearance was as pleasant and wholesome as his voice. "I came—er in response to your letter to the department, in regard to the forthcoming trials of aeroplanes for the service."

"Oh, yes," exclaimed Mary Eliska, smothering an inclination to giggle, "we—I—that is——"

"I presume that I have called at the right place," said the young officer, with a smile. "They told me——"

"Oh, come in, won't you?" suddenly requested the embarrassed Mary Eliska. "The sun is fearfully hot. Won't you have a straw hat—I mean a seat?"

"Thank you," replied Lieut. Bradbury, gravely sitting in a garden bench at the foot of one of the big maples. His eyes fell on the book Mary Eliska had been reading. It was a treatise on aeronautics.

"It isn't possible that you are John Stricklin?" he asked, glancing up quickly.

"Oh, no. I am only a humble helper. John Stricklin is in town. He—he will be back shortly."

"Indeed. I had hoped to see him personally. I was anxious to inspect the Stricklin type of monoplane before visiting another aeroplane plant in this neighborhood, the—the——" The officer drew out a small morocco covered notebook and referred to it.

"The Mortlake Aeroplane Company," he concluded.

"Oh, yes. They are just down the road, within a stone's throw of here. You can see the place from here; that big barn-like structure," volunteered Mary Eliska, heartily wishing that the Mortlake plant had been a hundred miles away.

"Indeed. That's very convenient. I shall be able to make an early train back to New York. Do you suppose that John Stricklin will be long?"

"I don't really know. He shouldn't be unless he is delayed. But in the meantime, I can show you the aeroplane, if you wish."

"Ah!" the officer glanced at this girl curiously, "but you know what I particularly desired was a practical demonstration."

"A flight?" "Yes, if it were possible." "I think it can be arranged." "You have an aviator attached to your place, then?"

"When she emerged a very business-like Mary Eliska had taken the place of the lounger in the hammock."

Mary Eli` so much about in the technical publications?"

"I believe I am," smiled Mary Eliska; "but here comes my aunt, Miss Sarah Stricklin."

As she spoke, Miss Stricklin, in a soft gown of cool white material, emerged from the house. Mary Eliska went through the ceremony of introduction, after which they all directed their steps to the large shed in which the Stricklin machines were kept. In the meantime, old Sam Hickey, the gardener, and his stalwart son Jerusah, had been summoned to aid in dragging out one of the aeroplanes.

"We only have two on hand," explained Mary Eliska; "my brother has forwarded the others that we built to Mr. James Bell, the mining man. They are being used in aerial gold transportation across the Nevada desert."

"Indeed! That is most interesting."

Sam Hickey flung open the big doors and revealed the interior of the shed with the two scarab-like monoplanes standing within. A strong smell of gasoline and machine-oil filled the air. The officer glanced at Mary Eliska's dainty figure in astonishment. It seemed hard to associate this refined, exquisite young girl with the rough actualities of machinery and aeroplanes.

But Mary Eliska, with a word of excuse, dived suddenly into a small room. While she was gone, Miss Stricklin entertained the young officer with many tales of her harrowing experiences on the Nevada desert. To all of which he listened with keen attention. At least he did so to all outward appearance, but his eyes were riveted on the door through which Mary Eliska had vanished.

When she emerged a very business-like Mary Eliska had taken the place of the lounger in the hammock. A linen duster, fitting tightly, covered her from top to toe. A motoring bonnet of maroon silk imprisoned her hair, and upon its rim, above her forehead, was perched a pair of goggles. Gauntlets encased her hands.

"Looks rather too warm to be comfortable, doesn't it?" she laughed. "But we shall find it cool enough up above."

"Perhaps the lieutenant——" ventured Miss Stricklin.

"Oh, yes. How stupid of me not to have thought of it!" exclaimed Mary Eliska. "Mr. Bradbury, you will find aviation togs inside there."

"By Jove; she knows enough not to call a naval officer 'lieutenant,'" thought the young officer, as, with a bow and a word of thanks, he vanished to equip himself for his aerial excursion.

By the time he was invested in a similar long duster, with weighted seams, and had donned a cap and goggles, the larger of the two aeroplanes, named the *Golden Butterfly*, was ready for its passengers. Old Sam and his son, who had dragged it out—it moved easily on its landing wheels—stood by, their awe of the big craft showing plainly on their faces.

A section of the fence had been made removable, so as to give the Stricklin aeroplanes a free run from their stable to the smooth slope of the meadows beyond. This was now removed, and Mary Eliska, followed by the young officer, took her place in the chassis. Mary Eliska made a pretty figure at the steering wheel.

"The first improvement I should like to call your attention to," she began, in the most business-like tones she could muster up, "is the self-starter. It works by pneumatic power, and does away with the old-fashioned method of starting an aeroplane by twisting the propeller."

The girl opened a valve connected with a galvanized tank, with a pressure gauge on top, and pulled back a lever. Instantly, a hissing sound filled the air. Then, with a dexterous movement, Mary Eliska threw in the spark and turned on the gasoline which the spark would ignite, thereby causing an explosion in the cylinders. But first the compressed air had started the motor turning over. At the right moment Mary Eliska switched on the power and cut off the air. Instantly there was a roar from the exhausts and blue flames and smoke spouted from the motor. The aeroplane shook violently. It would have made an inexperienced person's teeth chatter. But both the officer and Mary Eliska were sufficiently familiar with aeroplanes for it not to bother them in the least.

"Magnificent!" cried the young officer enthusiastically, as he saw the ease with which the compressed air attachment set the motor to working.

"It will do away with assistants to start the machine," he declared the next instant. "The importance of that in warfare can hardly be overestimated."

Mary Eliska was too busy to reply. So far all had gone splendidly. If only she could carry out the whole test as well!

"Ready?" she asked, flinging back the word over her shoulder to Lieutenant Bradbury.

"All ready!" came in a hearty voice from behind her.

Mary Eliska, with a quick movement, threw in the clutch that started the propeller to whirring.

With a drone like that of a huge night-beetle, or prehistoric thunder-lizard, the machine leaped forward as a race-horse jumps under the raised barrier.

In a blur of blue smoke, it skimmed through the gap in the palings. Out upon the smooth meadowland it shot, roaring and smoking terrifically. And then, all at once, the jolting motion of the start ceased. It seemed as if the occupants of the chassis were riding luxuriously over a road paved with the softest of eiderdown. The sensation was delightful, exhilarating.

Mary Eliska shut off the exhaust, turning the explosions of the cylinder into a muffler. In almost complete silence they winged upward. Up, up, toward the fleecy clouds she had been lazily watching, but a short time before, from the hammock.

The *Golden Butterfly* had never done better.

"You're a darling!" breathed Mary Eliska confidentially to the motor that with steady pulse drove them upward and onward.

CHAPTER 15.4.
IN A STORM.

Dwarfed to the merest midgets, the figures about the Stricklin house waved enthusiastically, as the golden-winged monoplane made a graceful swoop high above the elms and maples surrounding it. Other figures could be glimpsed too, now, running about excitedly outside the barn-like structure housing the Mortlake aeroplanes.

"Guess they think you are stealing a march on them," drawled Lieut. Bradbury.

A wild, reckless feeling, born of the thrilling sensation of aerial riding, came over Mary Eliska. She would do it—she would. With a scarcely perceptible thrust of her wrist, she altered the angle of the rudder-like tail, and instantly the obedient *Golden Butterfly* began racing through space toward the Mortlake plant.

The naval officer, quick to guess her plan, laughed as happily as a mischievous boy.

"What a lark!" he exclaimed. "It's contrary to all discipline, but it's jolly good fun."

Mary Eliska turned a small brass-capped valve—the timer. At once the aeroplane showed accelerated speed. It fairly cut through the air. Both the occupants were glad to lower their goggles to protect their eyes from the sharp, cutting sensation of the atmosphere, as they rushed against it—into its teeth, as it were.

Mary Eliska glanced at the indicator. The black pointer on the white dial was creeping up— fifty, sixty, sixty-two—she would show this officer what the Stricklin monoplane could do.

"Sixty-four! Great Christmas!"

The exclamation came from the officer. He had leaned forward and scanned the indicator eagerly.

"We'll do better when we have our new type of motor installed," said Mary Eliska, with a confident nod. The young fellow gasped.

"This is the twentieth century with a vengeance," he murmured, sinking back in his rear seat, which was as comfortably upholstered as the luxurious tonneau of a five-thousand-dollar automobile.

Like a darting, pouncing swallow, seeking its food in mid-air, the *Golden Butterfly* swooped, soared and dived in long, graceful gradients above the Mortlake plant. Once Mary Eliska brought the aeroplane so close to the ground in a long, swinging sweep, that it seemed as if it could never recover enough «way" to rise again. Even the officer, trained in a strict school to repress his emotions, tightened his lips, and then opened them to emit a relieved gasp.

So close to the gaping machinists and the anger-crimsoned Mortlake did the triumphant aeroplane swoop, that Mary Eliska, to her secret amusement could trace the astonished look on the faces of the employees and the chagrined expression that darkened Mortlake's countenance.

"I guess I've given them something to think over," she said mischievously, flinging back a brilliant smile at the dazed young officer.

"Now," she exclaimed the next moment, "for a distance flight. I'm anxious to put the *Golden Butterfly* through all her paces. Oh, by the way, the balancer. I haven›t shown you how that works yet."

If Mary Eliska's bright eyes had not been veiled by goggles, the officer might have seen a mischievous gleam flash into them, like a wind ripple over the placid surface of a blue lake.

Suddenly the aeroplane slanted to one side, as if it must turn over. Mary Eliska had banked it on a sharp aerial curve. The young officer, in spite of himself, in defiance of his training, gave a gasp.

"I say——"

But the words had hardly left his lips before the aeroplane was back on a level keel once more. At the same time a rasping, sliding sound was heard.

"Like to see how that was done?" asked Mary Eliska, with a bewitching smile.

"Yes. By Jove, I thought we were over for an instant. But how——"

"That we shall be glad to show you when the United States government has contracted for a number of the Stricklin aeroplanes," retorted Mary Eliska.

The young officer bit his lip.

"Confound it," he thought, "is this chit of a girl making fun of me?"

Young officers have a high idea of their own dignity. Mr. Bradbury colored a bit with mortification. But Mary Eliska quickly dispelled his temporary chagrin.

"You see," she explained, "it would never do for us to reveal all our secrets, would it? You agree with me, don't you?"

"Oh, perfectly. You are quite right. Still, I confess that you have aroused all my inquisitiveness."

Mary Eliska being busied just then with a bit of machinery on the bulkhead separating the motor from the body of the chassis, made no reply. But presently, when she looked up, she gave a sharp exclamation.

The sky, as if by magic, had grown suddenly dark. Above the pulsating voice of the motor could be heard the rumble of thunder. All at once a vivid flash of lightning leaped across the horizon. One of those sudden storms of summer had blown up from the sea, and Mary Eliska knew enough of Long Island weather to know that these disturbances were usually accompanied by terrific winds—squalls and gusts that no aeroplane yet built or thought of could hope to cope with.

"We're running into dirty weather, it seems," remarked the officer. "I thought I noticed some thunderheads away off on the horizon when we first went up."

"I wish you'd mentioned them then," said the straightforward Mary Eliska; "as it is, we'll have to descend 'til this blows over."

"What, won't even the wonderful equalizer render her safe?"

"No, it won't. It will do anything reasonable. But you've no idea of the fury of the wind that comes with these black squalls."

"Indeed I have. Last summer I was off Montauk Point in the *Dixie.* Something went wrong with the steering gear just as one of these self-same young hurricanes came bustling up. I tell you, it was "all hands and the cook" for a while. It hardly blows much harder in a typhoon."

Mary Eliska gazed below her over the darkening landscape anxiously. There seemed to be trees, trees everywhere, and not a bit of cleared ground. All at once, as they cleared some woods, she spied a bit of meadowland. The hay which had covered it earlier in the summer had been cropped. It afforded an ideal landing-place. But the wind was puffy now, and Mary Eliska did not dare to attempt short descending spirals. Instead, trusting to the balancing device doing its duty faithfully, she swung down in long circles.

Just as they touched the ground with a gentle shock, much minimized, thanks to the shock-absorbers with which the *Golden Butterfly* was fitted, the storm burst in all its fury. Bolt after bolt of vivid lightning ripped and tore across the darkened sky, which hung like a pall behind the terrific electrical display. The rain came down in torrents.

"Just in time," laughed the young officer, as he aided Mary Eliska in dragging the aeroplane under the shelter of an open cart-shed. It was quite snug and dry once they had it under the roof. A short distance off stood a farm-house of fairly comfortable appearance. Smoke issuing from one of its chimneys showed that it was occupied.

"Let's go over there and see if we can dry our things," suggested Mary Eliska. "I'm wet through."

"Same here," was the laughing reply; "but a sailor doesn't mind that. One actually gets webbed feet in the navy—like ducks, you know."

Ignoring this remarkable contribution to natural history, Mary Eliska gathered up her skirts daintily and fled across the meadow to the farm-house. It was only a few hundred feet, but the rain came down so hard that both she and her escort were wetter than ever by the time they arrived at the door. It was shut, and except for the lazy wisps of smoke issuing from the chimney, there was no sign of life about the place.

The lieutenant knocked thunderously. No answer.

"Try again," said Mary Eliska; "maybe they are in some other part of the house."

"Perhaps they were scared of the aeroplane and have all retired into hiding," suggested Mr. Bradbury.

He rapped again, louder this time, but still no reply.

"They must all be asleep," he said, applying himself once more to a thunderous assault on the door, but to no avail. A silence hung about the place, broken only by the roar and rattle of the thunder.

"It's positively uncanny," shuddered Mary Eliska. "It's like Red Riding Hood and the Three Little Bears."

"One would think that even a bear would open the door on such an occasion as this," said her companion, redoubling his efforts to attract attention. Finally he gave the door handle a twist. It yielded, and the door was speedily found to be unlocked. The officer shoved it open and disclosed a neat farm-house kitchen. In a newly blackened stove, which fairly shone, was a blazing fire. An old clock ticked sturdily in one corner. The floor was scrubbed as white as snow, and on a shelf above the shining stove was an array of gleaming copper pans that gladdened Mary Eliska's housewifely heart.

"What a dear of a place!" she exclaimed. "But where are the folks who own it?"

"Haven't the least idea," said the officer gayly; "but that stove looks inviting to me. Let's get over to it and get dried out a bit. Then we can commence to investigate."

"But, really, you know, we've not the least right in here. Suppose they mistake us for burglars, and shoot us?"

"Not much danger of that. They'd shoot me first, anyhow, because I'm the most burglarious looking of the two. Queer, though, where they all can be."

"It's worse than queer—it's weird. Good gracious!" exclaimed Mary Eliska, as a sudden thought struck her, "suppose there should be trapdoors?"

"Trapdoors!" Her companion was plainly puzzled.

"Yes. You know in most books when two folks run across a deserted farm-house there's always a trapdoor or a ghost or something. Suppose——Good heavens, what's that?"

From without had come a most peculiar sound. A whirring, like the noise one would suppose would be occasioned by a gigantic locust. Then something—a huge, indefinite shadow—darkened the windows of the farm-house kitchen. Mary Eliska gave a shrill squeal of alarm, while Lieut. Bradbury gallantly ran to the door and flung it open.

CHAPTER 15.5.
MARY ELISKA A HEROINE.

"It's—it's another aeroplane!" cried the officer, with a shout of amazement.

"What!"

Mary Eliska sprang to her feet.

"A large red one?"

"Yes. Come here and look. They're just running it under the same shed as ours—yours, I mean."

The girl aviator sprang toward the door. Through the rain she peered to where, across the meadow, two dim figures, clad in oilskins, could be seen shoving a big aeroplane under the same shelter that already protected the *Golden Butterfly*.

"Well, if this isn't the ultimate!" she gasped.

"I beg your pardon?" asked the young man at her side.

"The ultimate! That's my way of expressing what the boys call 'the limit.' Why, that's Jess and Jimsy Bancroft, in their new aeroplane—the one Liam McAdams built for them. Well, did you ever! Oh, Jess! Oh, Jimsy!"

Mary Eliska raised her voice and shouted. In response they saw the oil-skinned figures turn, and through the driving downpour came an answering shout. Presently, across the dripping meadows, the two figures began advancing. All this time the lightning was ripping in a manner to make Mary Eliska shield her eyes occasionally. The thunder, too, was terrific, and the earth seemed to vibrate to its rolling detonations.

"Well, Mary Eliska!" gasped Jess, her dark eyes peering from under her waterproof hood, as she and her brother arrived at the threshold of the farm-house, "what on earth does this mean?"

"Yes, give an account of yourself at once," demanded Jimsy. "Liam McAdams had us on the phone. Asked if you'd flown in our direction. We said no, but we'd take a flight and look for you. In our enthusiasm, we didn't notice the storm coming up. But luckily, being young persons of forethought, we had oilskins in a locker of the machine, and———"

"And here we are," finished Jess, shooting a "killing" glance from under her hood at the good-looking young man at Mary Eliska's side.

"Aren't you going to ask us in?" demanded Jimsy the next minute. "For hospitality, I don't think you rate very high. We———"

"Well, you see, we are here ourselves without knowing if we have any right to be," rejoined Mary Eliska. "But come in and I'll explain. First of all, I want you to meet Mr. Bradbury of the United States Navy. He came to test the Stricklin aeroplanes. Mr. Bradbury, this is Miss Bancroft, and her brother——"

"Jimsy," put in that irrepressible youth. "Glad to meet you, sir. Almost as much at sea here as in mid-Atlantic."

Laughing, they all entered the farm-house kitchen, while Mary Eliska hastily explained the state of affairs there.

"Well, so long as they don't put in an appearance before we get dry, I'm sure I don't care," said Jimsy airily. "What a delightful old kitchen. It might have come out of a picture book."

He and the naval officer were soon deep in conversation, leaving Mary Eliska and Jess alone.

"My dear Mary Eliska," exclaimed Jess, with a smile that showed all her white even teeth, "what will you do next? Don't you think it's a bit—er—er—unconventional for one of the foremost members of Sandy Beach's younger set to be flying about the country with a good-looking young naval officer?"

"Nonsense," retorted Mary Eliska sharply, "as the only representative of the Stricklin aeroplanes on the ground, I had to do it. If it hadn't been for this old storm, I'd have been home long ago."

"So should we. What a coincidence we should have met here. Is this—this——"

"Lieutenant," prompted Mary Eliska.

"Is this lieutenant going to stay long in Sandy Beach?"

"Dear me, no. He is only on a flying visit—no pun intended. He was to have taken in the establishment of the Mortlake Aeroplane Company this afternoon. You know, they are in that red, barn-like place, down the road from our place, although Liam McAdams and I only found it out today."

"That was one of the things I wanted to talk to you about, Mary Eliska dear," said Jess, sinking into an old-fashioned Andrew Jackson chair by the hearth. "Dad said at dinner last night that he had heard in New York that a lot of their stock had been floated on Wall Street, and that that hateful old Mr. Harding was back of it."

"They are actually selling stock?" asked Mary Eliska, growing a bit pale.

"Yes. They have half-page advertisements in a lot of papers, I believe. Dad said so. But why do you look so distressed, Mary Eliska?"

"Because they must be very sure of the merits of their machines, if they are going ahead so confidently."

"Rumor has it that their make of aeroplane is the most up-to-date and complete yet constructed, but nobody knows the details so far. They have kept that part of it close."

"They are making a bid for the navy contracts, at any rate," said Mary Eliska presently, after a pause, during which both girls winked and blinked at the lightning and stared at the red glow of the fire.

"So you said. But you stole a march on them by kidnapping your lieutenant in this way."

"You ought to give the weather credit for that," laughed Mary Eliska, "but seriously, Jess, there is no sentiment in things of this kind. If the Mortlake machine is a better machine than ours, the Mortlake will be the type adopted by the government."

"I suppose that's so," agreed Jess, with a wry face. "But I hate to think of that old Harding creature getting any——"

The door flew open suddenly, and a tall, thin-faced woman in a raincoat, and holding up an umbrella, stood in the doorway.

"Well, for the land's sake!" she ejaculated, looking fairly dumfounded, as she comprehended the scene and the young folks enjoying the unrequested hospitality of her kitchen.

But the words had hardly left her lips, and she was still standing there, like an image carved from stone, when a fearful light illumined the whole scene. It was followed almost instantaneously by a clap of thunder so deafening that the girls involuntarily quailed before it.

A fiery ball darted from the chimney and sped across the room, exploding in fragments with a terrific noise on the opposite side, just above the heads of Jimsy and Lieut. Bradbury.

Stunned by the shock, they both collapsed in heaps on the floor, while the farm woman's shrieks filled the air. At the same instant, a pungent, sinister odor filled the atmosphere.

"The house is on fire!" shrieked the woman in a frenzied voice.

Smoke rolled down into the room, and the acrid fumes grew sharper.

"The house is on fire, and my baby is up-stairs!"

"Where?" demanded Mary Eliska.

"In the room above this!" groaned the woman, taking a few steps and then fainting.

"Jess," cried Mary Eliska in a tense voice, "take that bucket and get water from that pump in the corner and then follow me."

"But the boys!" gasped Jess.

"They are only stunned. I saw Jimsy's arm move just now, and the lieutenant is breathing."

With these words, she started from the room, darting up a narrow stairway leading from one end of the kitchen to the upper regions.

"What are you going to do?" shouted Jess, her voice shaky with alarm.

"Save that child if I can," flung back Mary Eliska, plunging bravely up the smoke-laden stairway.

In the unfamiliar house, and half blinded and choked by smoke and sulphurous fumes, Mary Eliska had a hard task before her. But she pluckily plunged forward, feeling her way by the walls, and keeping her head low, where the smoke was not so thick. As she reached what she deemed was the top of the staircase, she thought she heard a tiny voice crying out in alarm.

Following the direction of the sounds, she staggered along a hallway and then reeled into an open door. The smoke was not so thick in the room, but its fumes were heavy enough. In a crib in one corner lay a child of about two years of age. Its rose-leaf of a face was wrinkled up in its efforts to make its terrified little voice heard.

Mary Eliska darted upon it and hugged it close to her. Then, with renewed courage, she started to make her way back again. But more smoke than ever was rolling along the passage, and it was a hard task.

"I must do it—I must," Mary Eliska kept saying to herself, clinging the while to the terrified child.

But at the head of the staircase the conditions appalled her. The smoke was thick as a blanket there. Yet plunge through it, Mary Eliska knew she must. Still holding the child tightly, she bravely entered the dense smother, stooping as low as she dared.

But before she had taken more than two steps in the obscurity, a dreadful feeling, as if a hand was at her throat and choking her, overcame the girl. She tried to call out, but she could not. Her head was reeling, her eyes blinded. All at once something in her head seemed to snap with a loud report. Still clutching her little burden tightly, Mary Eliska plunged forward dizzily—and knew no more.

CHAPTER 15.6.
FARMER GALLOWAY'S "SAFE DEPOSIT."

When she came to herself again, it was in a confusion of voices and sounds of hurrying footsteps. She was lying on a lounge in a stuffy "best" parlor, which smelled as moldy as "best" parlors in farm-houses are wont to do. Bending over her was the angular woman who had entered just as the bolt of lightning, that had caused all the trouble, struck the house.

"Is—is the baby all right?" asked Mary Eliska, as she took in her surroundings.

"Yes, thanks to you, my dear. Oh, how can I ever thank you?" exclaimed the woman, a thrill of real gratitude in her voice. "And the fire is out, too. My husband and his men had been at work in a distant field and were sheltering themselves under a shed. I had just taken some water to them when the storm broke. When they saw the big flash and heard the crash, they knew that something right around the house must have been struck. They ran through the storm as fast as they could, and got here in time to put out the flames."

"And Jess and Jimsy and——"

"And that other young fellow? Why, they——"

"Never felt better in their lives," came Jimsy's cheerful voice from the door, which framed, beside himself, Jess, and the young naval officer.

"The first time I was ever knocked out by lightning," declared the latter, "and really it's quite invigorating."

Jess glided across the room to Mary Eliska's side and threw her arms about her neck.

"Oh, Mary Eliska, how brave and good you are!" she exclaimed. "I was dreadfully frightened, when you came plunging down through that smoke. I was just trying to make my way through it with a bucket, when you came toppling down the stairs. I managed to catch you and support you into the kitchen."

"I think someone else is the bravest," smiled Mary Eliska, patting her chum's shoulder. "I'm so glad that the baby wasn't hurt. Poor little thing, it looked so cute in its crib. I remember seizing it up and then the smoke came, and after a few minutes it all got black and———"

"And all's well that ends well," declared Jimsy, capering about. "We've telephoned to your home to Liam McAdams, Mary Eliska, and he'll be over in a short time with an auto."

"But what about the *Butterfly*?" asked Mary Eliska.

"My dear girl," announced Jimsy, in his most pompous tones, "it would be impossible for you to guide her home this evening. Your nerves would not stand it. See, it's come out quite fine, now, after the storm, and Liam McAdams will spin you home in the machine in no time."

"Perhaps that would be best," agreed Mary Eliska. "And I can come out, or Liam McAdams can, tomorrow, and get the aeroplane—that is," she added, turning to the farm woman, "if it won't be in your way."

"If you had a thousand of them air-buggies around here, miss, they wouldn't be in our way," came in a hearty, gruff tone from the door. They looked up to see a big farmer-like looking person, with a fringe of black whiskers running under his chin in a half-moon, standing there.

"This is my husband, Isaac Galloway," said the woman, introducing the owner of the farm.

"At your service, gents and ladies," said the farmer. "What that young woman did fer us ter-day ther' ain't no way of repaying; but anything Ike Galloway kin do any time ye kin count on him fer."

He moved toward an object they had not previously noticed, an iron door in the wall. Turning a knob this way and that, he presently flung it open, revealing the inside of a wall safe. Thrusting his hand inside, he drew out a bundle of bills. Then, closing the door again, and adjusting the combination, he said:

"Jes' goin' ter give ther boys a bit of thank you fer helpin' me put out ther fire. If any of you folks would like——"

"Oh, no. No, thank you," laughed Mary Eliska, sitting up and feeling, except for a slight dizziness, almost herself again.

"Very well; no harm meant," said the farmer, as he shuffled out of the room and into the kitchen, where he distributed his largess.

"Quite an idea," commented Jimsy, regarding the wall safe. "I suppose you have quite a lot of money on hand at times, and it is safest to keep it so," he added, addressing the farmer's wife.

"Yep," was the rejoinder; "Ike got his money fer his corn crop ther other day—two thousand dollars, what with ther corn and ther early apples. It's all in thar, except what he's jes' took out."

"Aren't you afraid of burglars coming and blowing the door of the safe off?" asked Mary Eliska.

"Lands sakes, no. We'd hear 'em. Besides, that's a patent safe, an' if it is opened without a knowledge of the combination, it would take a plaguey long time to do."

Just then the farmer came back, and after some more general conversation the whir of an approaching automobile announced the arrival of Liam McAdams. The lad was naturally much interested in the doings of the afternoon, as excitedly related to him by everybody at once, and was favorably impressed with the young naval officer. Of course, he did not ask him his opinion of the Stricklin aeroplane, but from remarks Lieut. Bradbury dropped, Liam McAdams gathered that he was much pleased with its performance.

Soon afterward Jess and Jimsy shot skyward, in the now still air, in their red aeroplane— the *Red Dragon Fly*, as it had been christened, and amid warm farewells from the farmer and his wife, the auto buzzed off.

They had traversed a mile or more, when, on rounding a corner at a narrow part of the road, they came almost head-on against another machine coming in the opposite direction.

Both cars were compelled to slow down, so that the occupants had a good view of each other. Both Liam McAdams and Mary Eliska were considerably astonished to see that the oncoming auto was occupied by old Mr. Harding, and that by his side was seated none other than the blue-chinned man, known as Eugene Mortlake.

"Where can they be going?" wondered Liam McAdams, as old man Harding favored them with a scowl in passing, and then both cars resumed their normal speed.

"I noticed that this is a private road leading only to that farm," rejoined Mary Eliska; "the right-of-way ends there."

"Then that must be their destination, for there are no other houses on this road."

"Looks that way," assented Liam McAdams. "Queer, isn't it?"

"Very," responded Mary Eliska. For some inexplicable reason, as the girl spoke, a chill ran through her. She felt a dull sense of foreboding. But the next minute she shook it off. After all, why shouldn't Mr. Harding and Mortlake be driving to the farm? Mr. Harding's financial dealings comprised mortgages in every part of the island. It was quite probable that the farmer was in some way involved in the old man's nets. Possibly that was the reason of all that money being stored in the wall safe.

Refusing courteously an invitation extended by Miss Stricklin to spend the night at the homestead, Lieut. Bradbury was driven to the station by Liam McAdams, after they had dropped Mary Eliska, and just managed to make a New York train.

"I shall be back tomorrow," he said, "and have a look at Mortlake's machines. Of course, the government wants to give everybody a fair field and no favors."

"Oh, of course," assented Liam McAdams, pondering in his own mind what sort of a machine this mysterious Mortlake craft was.

Suddenly there flashed across his mind a thought that had not occurred to him hitherto. The *Golden Butterfly* had been left under the shed at the farm. What was there to prevent Harding and Mortlake from examining it and acquainting themselves with the intricacies of the self-starting mechanism and the automatic balancing device?

There was no question that the farm must have been their destination. Liam McAdams blamed himself bitterly for not foreseeing this. He had half a mind to return to the farm and bring the aeroplane home himself. But it was growing dark, and a distant rumble seemed to presage the return of the afternoon's storm.

"Anyhow," the boy thought, and the thought consoled him, "all those devices are covered by patents, and even if they wanted to, they could not steal them. And yet—and yet——"

But the storm came up sharper than ever that evening, and even had he wished to, Liam McAdams would have found it impossible to handle the aeroplane alone in the heavy wind that came now in puffs and now in a steady gale. So Liam McAdams put his tiresome thoughts out of his head. But he resolved to get the aeroplane the first thing the following morning.

CHAPTER 15.7.
A CASE FOR THE AUTHORITIES.

It was just after breakfast the next morning that a big automobile skimmed past the Stricklin home. Mary Eliska and Liam McAdams saw it from the windows.

"Why, that's Sheriff Lawley," exclaimed Mary Eliska. "And look, old Mr. Harding is with him, and that Mortlake man."

"That's right. Wonder where they can be going?" said Liam McAdams, sauntering out to the garage at the back of the house and giving the matter little more thought. It had been arranged that he was to bring the aeroplane back that morning, driving over with Mary Eliska, Jimsy and Jess in the car, and skimming home in the *Butterfly* while a part of the party brought the car back. They were to call for Jess and Jimsy at their home, a fine residence overlooking the Sound from a lofty hill.

Jess and Jimsy were waiting for them, and, almost before the car had stopped, they were at its side.

"Heard the news?" asked Jimsy breathlessly.

"No. What is it?" demanded Mary Eliska eagerly.

"Why, that safe at the farm-house was robbed last night. All the money was taken, and they have no clue to the thief."

"How did you hear of it?" asked Liam McAdams incredulously. Mary Eliska had told him of the queer wall safe.

"The 'central' told one of the servants and she told Jess. Strange, isn't it?"

"It is odd," agreed Liam McAdams. "But if people will keep their money in such places, it is hardly surprising if they lose it. Did you hear any details?"

"No, but no doubt we shall when we reach the farm-house," put in Jess; "isn't it thrilling, though?"

"Not very thrilling for poor Galloway, who lost the money," said Mary Eliska. "I expect he didn't make it any too easily."

On their arrival at the Galloway farm-house, the young people found a scene of great excitement. The sheriff, red-faced and important, was examining several farm hands beneath one of the big elms, while in the background stood the farmer and his wife, looking somewhat perplexed, as well as worried.

As the Stricklin auto drove up, old Mr. Harding, in his usual rusty black suit, rose from his seat under the elm, and whispered something to the sheriff. The blue-chinned, thick-necked Mortlake arose also. All three turned and gazed curiously at the young occupants of the car, as it slowed down.

"Good morning, Mr. and Mrs. Galloway," cried Mary Eliska. "We were dreadfully sorry to hear of your loss. Have you any clue yet?"

There was something curiously cold in the woman's voice, as she replied in the negative. Her husband looked sullen and merely nodded. The sheriff now rose and came toward the machine. He knew all the young folks and greeted them briefly. At his heels pressed old Harding and his companion. They whispered in the sheriff's ear as he advanced, and seemed to be urging him to something.

"I understand that you folks were in this house yesterday afternoon?" began the sheriff abruptly.

"Why, yes, during the storm," said Mary Eliska. "There was Lieut. Bradbury, of the United States Navy——"

Harding and Mortlake exchanged annoyed glances. This was confirmation of their fears.

"Yes, go on," urged the sheriff.

"And myself, and Mr. Bancroft here and his sister, and later my brother came."

"Do you recall the safe being opened while you were in the room? I presume from the remark you made when you drove up that you know of the robbery."

"We heard of it at the Bancroft's, but we don't know the details."

"That is not necessary. Answer my questions, please. Who was in the parlor beside yourself when Mr. Galloway opened the wall safe to reward the men who had helped him extinguish the fire?"

"Why, Jimsy—I mean Mr. Bancroft—his sister and Lieut. Bradbury, besides, of course, Mr. and Mrs. Galloway."

"What! Your brother was not there?"

"Certainly not. He didn't come 'til later."

"Then your brother didn't see the safe opened?"

"Of course not," struck in Liam McAdams. "I was here only a very brief time. But what does all this mean? I don't understand."

"It means that you are cleared of a grave suspicion," said the sheriff. "Mr. Harding and Mrs. Galloway's brother, Mr. Mortlake, here——"

"Her brother!" exclaimed Mary Eliska in an undertone.

The sheriff went on:

"Seemed to have an idea that Liam McAdams was here at the time. They even went so far as to intimate that——"

But old Mr. Harding was tugging frantically at the sheriff's arm. He was seconded by Mortlake. Interpreting the signals aright, he stopped short.

"In fact, it looked suspicious," he concluded lamely. He turned and went off, followed by Harding and Mortlake.

"How did you ever come to make such a mistake?" snarled old Harding, as they walked away much crestfallen, "we haven't a leg to stand on, now."

"Why, confound it all," retorted Mortlake, "my sister mentioned a young man being with the girl in the aeroplane, and I took it for granted that it was her brother."

"And a nice mess you've got us both into, with your 'taking it for granted,'" snorted the old miserly financier of Sandy Beach. "It looks as if we'd got ourselves in a trap now."

"Nonsense. Who's to know we have the money? I'll take the first opportunity to send it back, and no more will be heard of the matter. Lucky I didn't hide it in his aeroplane, as I intended to do."

"Yes; but we've still got the cub as our rival. I wish I could think of some plan to choke him off. That scheme of yours to blame the robbery on him would have been all right if you'd only made sure of your facts first."

"Don't worry. Our chance will come yet. I'll make that whole outfit regret bitterly that they ever stole a march on us by kidnapping that officer."

"To have discredited him with the navy would have been the best way, however," said old Harding brusquely.

"I'll find a way to do that yet," Mortlake promised.

In the meantime, speculation and wonder had ruled among the occupants of Liam McAdams's auto. Everything seemed very much muddled, but one fact stood out clearly, and that was that an attempt had been made to cast suspicion, if not the actual guilt of the robbery, upon Liam McAdams.

For what object?

"I have it," cried Mary Eliska suddenly. "If they could have placed Liam McAdams under a cloud of suspicion, it would have worked to his discredit with the naval authorities, and might have resulted in our aeroplane being denied a place in the trials. That seems plain enough."

They all agreed that it did. But Jimsy said suddenly: "If that was the case, why didn't they try to make out that I stole it?"

"Because—forgive me Jimsy—you're not Liam McAdams. Without him, the tests of the Stricklin aeroplane could hardly be conducted. Unless——"

"Unless a certain young person named Mary Eliska undertook to take charge of them," cried Jess loyally.

"Don't be foolish, Jess," warned Mary Eliska; "but look, here is Mrs. Galloway coming to speak to us."

The farmer's wife approached the automobile, from which none of the party had as yet alighted. She was followed by her husband. Both began apologizing profusely for the questions of the sheriff.

"But land's sakes alive," exclaimed the farmer's wife, "I declar ter goodness, we've bin so flustered thet I don' know no more than a wet hen. My brother, that's Mr. Mortlake, was dead sot on it bein' one of you folks, but I knew that was reediculous."

They hardly knew whether to be angry or to laugh at the woman's blunt frankness. But Liam McAdams struck in with a question:

"Wasn't Mr. Mortlake, accompanied by Harding, out here last night?"

"Why, yes," said the woman, with perfect candor. "They stayed quite a while. Harding hed some business with Ike, an'——"

"An' Gene Mortlake said he'd like ter hev a look at yer aeroplane. Yer know he's in thet thar business hisself," volunteered Ike confidentially.

Mary Eliska felt as if she could have groaned aloud. Liam McAdams's fears, earlier confided to her, seemed to have been based on a true presentiment. The blue-jowled Mortlake had undoubtedly improved his opportunity to study the *Golden Butterfly* at close range. The farmer›s next words confirmed her.

"Reckon he was powerful interested, too," the farmer went on, "fer he made a lot uv ther nicest droorings you ever seen, an'—why, what's the trouble?"

For Liam McAdams, hardly knowing what he intended to do, had jumped from the machine and was sprinting toward the Harding car. But, as he neared it, the old financier, who with Mortlake was already seated in the tonneau, spoke a word in the chauffeur's ear, and the machine dashed off, leaving Liam McAdams enraged and nonplussed.

"Too bad, Liam McAdams," breathed Mary Eliska, as, rather crestfallen, the lad returned.

"Oh, I don't know, Sis. Even if they hadn't sneaked off like that, and I'd caught the machine, I guess I'd have been like the dog that chased the train. I wouldn't have known what to do with it when I got it."

"But Liam McAdams, their flight confirms their guilt!"

"I know, Sis, but what possible way have we to prove it? The rascals have covered up their tracks cleverly."

A sudden thought struck Mary Eliska, and she turned to the farmer.

"Did any of those bills have an identifying mark on it?" she asked.

The farmer shook his head. But Mrs. Galloway had a better memory.

"Why, yes, Ike," she exclaimed; "that twenty-dollar-bill you got frum Si. Giddens fer ther Baldwins. I re'klect thet it hed a big round O in red ink marked on ther back uv it. It was a bit rubbed out, an' hard ter see, but ef you knew it wuz thar an' luked fer it, you could see it plain enough."

After inquiring about the baby, whose thankful mother declared it to be as well as ever, Liam McAdams and Jimsy dragged out the *Golden Butterfly* and boarded it. It had been arranged that the two girls were to spin back to town in the car, the aeroplane following them as closely as possible from above.

As they chugged out of the farm-yard gate and on to the rough road, Mary Eliska's thoughts kept time to the rhythmic pulsations of the motor:

"A-twenty-dollar-bill-with-a-red-round-O. A-twenty-dollar-bill-with-a-red-round-O."

CHAPTER 15.8.
MR. MORTLAKE LOSES SOME DRAWINGS.

Dashing along the rough country road, with every sense on the alert, Mary Eliska found mental occupation enough to drive gloomier thoughts from her mind. The Stricklin's car was a good one, with a powerful, sixty-horse motor, and splendidly upholstered. It was painted a dark blue, and was known in the surrounding country as "The Blue Bird." It had been purchased with the money made by the brother and sister from their shares in James Bell's desert mine.

Far above them sailed the aeroplane, its two occupants from time-to-time waving at their pretty sisters below. But in the upper-air currents, it would have been dangerous to drive at a pace slow enough to keep level with the automobile, and so the aeroplane soon dashed on ahead. From time to time, however, it made circles and swoops, which brought it sometimes in seemingly dangerous closeness to the tree-tops.

All at once Mary Eliska stopped the automobile with a jerk which almost threw Jess, who was unprepared for the shock, out of the car.

"Good gracious, Mary Eliska, what are you trying to do?" she gasped.

"Look!" cried Mary Eliska, pointing with wide eyes.

In the center of the road lay a rolled-up bundle of papers secured with a rubber band.

"Somebody has dropped something from another auto or a wagon," cried Jess.

"I think so," said Mary Eliska in excited tones, as she descended from the car, "and I've an idea that these papers have been dropped from Mr. Harding's car. It must have been the only one to pass here recently, as this road runs direct to the farm and nowhere else."

She stooped down in the road and picked up the bundle and then, with a beating heart, she opened it. But for an inward intuition of what its contents would prove to be, Mary Eliska, with her rigid ideas of honor, could not have brought herself to do this. As her eyes fell on the first sheet, and she saw that it was covered with annotations and sketches, she gave a little cry.

"Oh, Jess! The luck! The wonderful, wonderful luck!"

"Why, what is it? A bundle of thousand-dollar bills, or——"

"It isn't that or anything," cried Mary Eliska; "it's—oh, Jess—it's the sketches and plans of our aeroplane that Mortlake and his accomplice Harding were spiriting away."

"They must have dropped them from their automobile," said Jess.

"Or, more likely, from the pockets of one of them. See, the ground is trampled about here. It looks to me as if they had had a break-down, and were fixing it when the papers fell out and were left behind unnoticed. Oh, what a bit of luck! If they had had those papers, it would have meant——"

A shrill cry from Jess interrupted her. At the same moment Mary Eliska became conscious of a presence behind her. She wheeled sharply and found herself facing two bloated-faced individuals, one of whom carried a heavy cudgel. Their clothes and broken boots, and their leering, odious appearance at once proclaimed them of the genus tramp.

"Waal!" growled one of the men, with an ugly leer, "we didn't hardly expec' ter run inter such luck ez this. Foun' suthin' vallerable, hev yer? Reckin' it must hev bin dropped by that auto that jes' went round the corner beyond. We'll hev ter trouble you for it, miss."

He held out a filthy hand, while Mary Eliska, with a beating heart, fell back toward the car.

"Frum what we hearn' yer sayin', I guess the papers is vallerable, all right," chimed in the first speaker's companion. "Come on, now. Fork over. You know it ain't honest ter take wot don't berlong ter ye, an' by yer own confession them papers don't."

"What right have you to demand them?" asked Mary Eliska boldly enough, despite her inward terror; "you had better go on at once, or——"

"Waal, or what?" sneered the other. "We've got ye here on a lonely road. You can't escape us. Come on, hand over them papers. We'll see that ther rightful owners git 'em, and that we git er reward beside. See?"

Mary Eliska's reply was to leap nimbly into the machine. But to her horror the two tramps followed instantly. Jess cowered back in her seat. Her pale lips moved, but she said nothing.

"Tell yer wot," burst out the man with the club, "you gals give us ten bones a piece—the money don't mean much to folks like you—an' we'll let yer go. If not——"

A sudden inspiration came to Mary Eliska—a flash of recollection.

"Why didn't you say that before?" she said cheerfully. "I'll be glad to give you the money. Wait a minute while I get it out."

She raised the cushion of the front "bucket seat," and dived beneath it with one hand. The men watched her with greedy, yet suspicious eyes.

"Ain't tryin' ter fool us, are yer?" growled one of them, "'cos ef you air——"

He raised his club threateningly, just as Mary Eliska's hand withdrew from beneath the cushion. Something bright flashed in it.

"Look out, Mike. She's got a gun!" shouted one of the men, falling back.

The other whipped a hand amidst his rags and was just about to aim a pistol, when:

"Phiz-z-z-z-z-z-z!"

From the shiny object Mary Eliska held in her hand, a fine stream of some sort of liquid jetted forcibly.

The fellow with the gun threw his hands up to his face, and dropping the pistol, staggered back with a howl of agony. The other darted off without even looking at him. The air was filled with a pungent scent of ammonia, and a quiet smile of triumph curled Mary Eliska's red lips as she started the car in motion once more.

"Oh, Mary Eliska, how brave you are!" gasped Jess. "Whatever was that you used? I hope the poor man isn't badly hurt, although he was so horrid."

"I just remembered in time, Jess dear," said Mary Eliska, as she sped the car along, "that we had under the seat an ammonia pistol for use on vicious dogs. I used it on another sort of a dog, that's all, and it proved equally effective."

Just at this moment Mary Eliska turned out to avoid another car that was approaching them from the opposite direction. In a second she saw that it carried Harding and Mortlake. They both looked angry and blank. Mary Eliska guessed at once that they had discovered their loss. But she resolved not to stop unless they did and asked questions. She felt that such a despicable act as they had attempted to perpetrate deserved no help on her part.

"Hey, there!" shouted old Mr. Harding, as his car was slowed down by the chauffeur. "Hey, stop! I want to speak to you!"

"He's polite about it, isn't he?" whispered Jess. "Are you going to tell him, Mary Eliska?"

"Cer-tain-ly not," rejoined Mary Eliska, with a tightening of her lips. "Why should I? He tried to fasten a theft on my brother this morning, and then caps the climax by instigating Mortlake to try to steal the ideas of our aeroplane."

"Hey, girls, seen a package on the road?" bawled old Mr. Harding, as Mary Eliska slowed up and stopped.

"I recovered some of my own property, if that is what you mean," said Mary Eliska slowly, a dull flush rising to her cheeks.

"Well—well! What d'ye mean by that, hey? What d'ye mean by that?"

"You may construe it any way you wish to, Mr. Harding," was the cold rejoinder, and to avoid further questioning, Mary Eliska sped up her machine, and soon vanished in a cloud of dust.

The old financier turned to his companion with a look of disgusted amazement.

"What d'ye think of that, hey, Mortlake?" he snapped out. "What d'ye think of that? Fine young girls, eh? Nice products of the twentieth century, hey?"

"Oh, let's get on and see if we can't find that roll of papers somewhere along here," rejoined Mortlake impatiently. "I don't think it's likely they could have seen it. It must have fallen from my pocket where the car broke down and I got out."

"Hey? Oh, yes, yes. That's it. Drive on, Tom. Drive us to where the car broke down."

In a few seconds they reached the spot just in time to see the two tramps who had molested the girls making off.

"There they go!" shouted Mortlake, "those fellows must have found them. I wouldn't lose those sketches for a thousand dollars. Put on more speed, Tom, and overtake them."

The chauffeur did as he was bid, and the car leaped ahead. In a few chugs it had reached the tramps' side, they having stopped, bewildered, in the meantime.

"Why, blow me, Bill," said one to the other, as the car came up, "if it ain't the self-same gents as drove down the road a while ago."

"Give me those papers, you rascals!" shouted Mortlake, almost flinging himself out of the car, "give them to me or———"

"Hold your horses, guv'ner! Hold your hosses," counseled the hobo who had received the dose of ammonia, and whose eyes were still red from its effects.

"Wot papers might you be lookin' fer?" asked this fellow cautiously, although he knew very well.

"A bundle of papers I dropped," panted Mortlake. "Didn't you find them."

"Naw!" grunted the red-eyed tramp.

"Naw!" echoed the other.

"Be careful what you say. If you are lying, it will go hard with you."

The warning came from old Mr. Harding.

"We know that, guv'ner. But we ain't got 'em. Search us, if yer like."

The knights of the road spread their arms to signify their willingness to be searched. Mortlake groaned. It was evident that neither of the tatterdermalions had the papers. But what had become of them? In his distress and chagrin, Mortlake gave an audible groan.

This the tramps seemed to construe as a favorable sign. One winked to the other, and the red-eyed one spoke.

"Wots it worth if we tell yer where them papers are, guv'ners both?"

"What, you know!" cried Mortlake, while old Mr. Harding spluttered:

"Eh, eh? Hey, what's all this? What's all this?"

"I didn't say we knew," was the cunning reply. "I said what's it worth if we did know."

Mortlake drew out a yellow-backed bill.

"Is this enough?" he asked.

The tramps' eyes rounded as they gazed at the figure.

"Perfec'ly satisfactory, guv'ner," said red eyes.

"Well, where are those papers, then?" snapped Mortlake impatiently.

"Thet thar purty gal wot jest went by in an autermobubble has 'em."

"What!"

"Yes. We saw her pick them up out of the road. We tried to convince her it was dishonest to keep 'em, but she wouldn't listen to us."

"You've done well, and seem to be bright fellows," said Mortlake, handing over the bill to red eyes, who seemed to be the leader of the two, "by the way, you don't belong about here, do you?"

"Oh, no, guv'ner. Our homes is whar we hangs our hats. My permanent address is care of the 'dicky birds.'"

"Well, I may have some work for you to do——"

"Work, guv'ner? Work's only for the workmen."

"I know all that, but this work is on your own line. I'll pay well, too. If you want to talk it over, come to the Mortlake Aeroplane Factory, outside Sandy Beach at ten o'clock tonight. I'll be there to meet you."

"All right, guv'ner; we'll be, thar. 'til then we'll bid yer 'oliver oil,' as ther French say. Come on, Joey."

The worthy pair shuffled off up the road, while Mortlake turned to Harding with a shrug.

"There are two tools made to our hand. We may find them very useful."

"I agree with you," was the dry and rasping reply; "at least, they have put us in possession of one valuable bit of knowledge, hey?"

CHAPTER 15.9.
THE FLIGHT OF THE "SILVER COBWEB."

A week rolled slowly by. A week of suspense, during which they had one or two calls from Lieut. Bradbury, who had been busy down at the Mortlake plant. But the officer was naturally noncommittal concerning his opinion of the comparative merits of the two types of aeroplanes. Equally naturally, of course, the young Stricklins had not questioned him concerning them.

But during this week they had had a glimpse of the Mortlake machine in flight. One still, breathless morning, the air had been filled, soon after dawn, with a vibrant buzzing sound, which Mary Eliska's trained ear had recognized as the song of an aeroplane engine.

She hastened to her brother's room and rapped upon the door. In reply to his sleepy query, the girl rapidly told him of what she had heard. Liam McAdams's window faced on the road, and a glance satisfied him that the Mortlake machine was to have its first try-out. Hastily as he dressed, however, he found that Mary Eliska was before him on the dewy lawn, field glasses in hand.

Down the road could be seen, in front of the Mortlake plant, a small crowd of mechanics with one or two dominant figures moving among them. With the glasses, they had no difficulty in making out Mortlake's heavy-shouldered figure, and the slender, upright form of Lieut. Bradbury. All at once the group opened up a bit and they saw a silvery, glittering aeroplane, agleam with new aluminum paint, throbbing and vibrating, as if anxious to be off. Blue smoke eddied up as the motor roared and whirred. The air seemed to vibrate under the sound as if a battery of gatling guns had been discharged.

Fascinated, brother and sister watched the spectacle intently. They saw Mortlake clamber heavily into the machine, followed by Lieut. Bradbury. A mechanic started for the front of the plane and began swinging the propeller.

"At least they haven't cribbed our self-starting device," exclaimed Mary Eliska, as she saw.

The next instant the propeller became a whirring blur, and the aeroplane, after a brief preliminary run, began to climb upward. The morning sun caught its silvered planes and turned them to gold. It was a beautiful and inspiring sight. Even with all that lay at stake, Mary Eliska and Liam McAdams could not deny the machine a meed of praise. It was fairy-like in its delicacy of construction, and speedy as a flash.

Thundering like an express train, it dashed above the Stricklin home, leaving in its wake the pungent odor of burning castor-oil—the most suitable lubricant for aeroplanes.

Then suddenly—as if a recollection of Mary Eliska's mischievous flight of a few days previously had occurred to him—Mortlake swung the delicate silvery machine about and dashed straight down at the boy and girl standing by the garden gate. So close to their heads did he skim in his desire to show off, that he almost came too low. For one instant it looked as if the machine would be dashed to a premature end, but it recovered buoyancy like a keeled-over racing yacht, and tore upward into the sky at an increased speed.

"Let's get out the *Golden Butterfly* and follow the——"

"*Silver Cobweb!*" cried Liam McAdams, the name occurring to him in a flash of inspiration as he watched the filmy outlines of the other aeroplane melt in the distance.

"Oh, Liam McAdams, what a pretty name."

"Isn't it? But somehow, I like *Golden Butterfly* best. Our machine may be a bit heavier, but solidity counts in hard service."

Scarcely ten minutes later, and while Mortlake's mechanics and assistants were still craning their necks skyward, another aeroplane, a yellow adventurer of the skies, thundered upward. Not to be outdone by Mortlake, Liam McAdams, who was at the wheel, swooped above the rival crowd. They did not take it with a good grace. Remarks, of which they could not catch the wording, but only the menacing intonation, were hurled upward at them. They received them with a laugh and a wave of the hand, which did not put the Mortlake crowd into any better humor. And then, with a graceful, swinging curve, that banked the machine almost on its beam ends, they were up, off and away in pursuit of the *Silver Cobweb*, which, by this time, was a mere shoe-button of a dot on the horizon.

"Do you think we can overhaul her, Liam McAdams?" ventured Mary Eliska, as they raced through the air, the fresh breath of morning coming refreshingly in their faces.

"Not a chance," admitted Liam McAdams cheerfully, "but they'll turn after a while, I guess, and then we'll try the *Butterfly* against the *Cobweb*."

But they kept on and on unrelentingly, and still there was no sign of diminution of speed on the part of the *Silver Cobweb*. Nor did the other aircraft give any indication that she was preparing to put about.

Below them, farms, meadows, villages and crowds of wondering country folk swam by in an ever-changing panorama. The earth beneath them looked like a big saucer divided up into brown, red and green squares, with tiny fly-like dots running and walking about.

All at once Liam McAdams gave a shout and pointed. Dead ahead, and not more than a few miles distant, lay a silvery, gleaming streak.

"The sea!"

The exclamation came simultaneously from Mary Eliska and Liam McAdams.

They had been traveling due south across the island, and now the broad Atlantic lay stretched beyond the land, shimmering in the sunlight. Far off, they could make out the black smoke of a steamer, hovering above the ocean.

"A mail boat, making for New York," announced Liam McAdams.

So fast were they traveling that by this time they could plainly make out the ocean, which, from a silvery streak, was now changed into a dark-blue rolling expanse of salt water.

And still the *Silver Cobweb* kept on, and gave no sign of turning. Nor, for that matter, had her speed diminished appreciably. The rival aeroplane was now skimming above the water at a height of about a thousand feet. The *Golden Butterfly* maintained about the same altitude, but the gap between the two aerial craft was not closing up.

"Mortlake's taking a desperate chance to show Lieut. Bradbury what the *Cobweb* can do," exclaimed Liam McAdams. «With a new engine, he›s risking too much."

"I guess he's seen us and means to beat us out at all hazards," conjectured Mary Eliska.

And she was right. Mortlake, glancing back a short time before the sea appeared on the horizon, had seen the other aeroplane, and guessing at once what its appearance meant, had determined to keep on, even at the risk of plunging himself and his passenger into the sea.

That was Mortlake's character; he was a man who could brook no rivalry. Used all his life to sweep obstacles aside, he would rather have terminated his career than permit anyone to pass him in the race for first place, no matter in what line that first place might lie.

"Are you going to keep on, Liam McAdams?"

The question came as a strip of white beach flashed beneath them, and Mary Eliska, peering over the edge of the chassis, saw the big Atlantic swells rolling below them. The thunder of the surf on the beach came clearly to their ears, even at that height.

"What do you think, Sis? We've got lots of gasoline. The motor is working without a hitch. I'd hate to turn back now, particularly with that officer's eyes upon us, as in all probability they are."

"Oh, let's keep on," exclaimed Mary Eliska, casting prudence to the winds. "I feel like you, Liam McAdams. If we turn back now, it would look as if we were afraid to trust the *Butterfly* above the ocean, and, after all, it is a naval contest that we hope to be elected for."

"Forward it is, then," cried Liam McAdams exultingly. The tang of the salt wind, the inspiration of the ocean, had come to him. He felt like a corsair—a very modern corsair—urging his craft above the ancient sea.

The vessel, whose smoke they had espied at a distance, was quite close to them now. A huge, black hull, with white passenger decks, rising tier on tier, four huge red funnels with black tops, and slender masts, between which hung the spider-web aerials of her wireless apparatus. Her bow was creaming up the ocean into foam, as she rushed onward at a twenty-four-knot gait.

Liam McAdams, obeying a daring impulse, let the *Golden Butterfly* descend. Now they could see her promenade decks lined with white faces peering upward. Here and there the sun glinted on the bright metal work of cameras, all aimed at the wonderful spectacle of the soaring, buoyant *Golden Butterfly*.

"Oh, if only we could drop a message on her decks!" breathed Mary Eliska eagerly. "I do wish we had a post-card or something——"

"By ginger," cried Liam McAdams suddenly, "I do believe I've got some in my coat-pocket. I bought some in the village yesterday to mail to the chaps back at school. Yes. Here they are, and here's a fountain-pen. Now write all you want."

Mary Eliska took the cards her brother handed to her with his free hand, and, with the fountain-pen, sat down to compose some messages. After a few seconds' thought, she began to write busily. Card after card was covered with her neat penmanship. All this time Liam McAdams had kept the *Golden Butterfly* hovering above the liner, from time to time taking swoops and dives around it like some monstrous sea gull.

Suddenly, from the liner's whistle, a great cascade of white steam spouted.

"Wough-h-h-h-h-h-h-h-h!"

It was the vessel's siren blowing a greeting to the young adventurers of the air. At the same instant a deep-throated roar, a cheer from cabin and steerage passengers alike, winged its way upward. Liam McAdams acknowledged it by a graceful wave of his cap. Then the cheering broke forth afresh.

The passengers of the newest ocean giant, the *Ruritania*, realized that they were seeing a spectacle that would remain in their memories all their lives. Having conquered old ocean with leviathan vessels, man was now seeking to subdue the air to his utility.

CHAPTER 15.10.
AN AERIAL POST OFFICE.

Mary Eliska addressed half a dozen cards. Two, of course, went to Jess and Jimsy, another to Aunt Sarah Stricklin; one to the captain of the *Ruritania*, and one other, which bore the address, "Eugene Mortlake, Esq."

It was a mischievous freak that made Mary Eliska write this last missive, which read:

TO MR. EUGENE MORTLAKE,
  Per Steamer *Ruritania*—in Mid-air:
  Greetings from aeroplane *Golden Butterfly*.
  R. & M. STRICKLIN.

That was all, but Mary Eliska knew that it would serve its prankish purpose.

All this time the *Silver Cobweb* had been out at sea, but now, apparently detecting the maneuvers of the *Golden Butterfly*, she headed about, and came racing back. Mary Eliska deftly attached weights—spare bolts from the tool locker—to each of the cards, and then, snatching up a megaphone, she hailed the uniformed figures on the bridge of the great vessel below them.

"Will you be good enough to mail some letters for us?"

"With pleasure!" came the reply in a big, bellowing British voice, from one of the stalwart figures beneath.

"All right; Liam McAdams, come down as low as you dare," cried Mary Eliska, catching her bundle of "mail."

Liam McAdams threw over a couple of levers and turned a valve. Instantly the *Golden Butterfly* began to drop in long, beautiful arc. She shot by above the liner›s bridge at a height of not more than fifteen feet. At the correct moment Mary Eliska dropped the weighted bundle overboard, and had the satisfaction of seeing one of the officers catch it. The gallant officers, now realizing for the first time that a girl—and a pretty one—was one of the passengers of the big aeroplane, waved their hats and bowed profoundly.

"At the correct moment Mary Eliska dropped the weighted bundle overboard."

And Mary Eliska—what would Aunt Sarah have said! -- Mary Eliska blew them a kiss. But then, as she told Jess later:

"I was in an aeroplane, my dear—a sort of an unattainable possibility, in fact."

In the meantime, Mortlake, in the *Silver Cobweb*, had been duly mystified as to what the *Golden Butterfly* was about when she swooped downward on the steamer. For one instant the thought flashed across him that they were disabled. An unholy glee filled him at the thought. If only the *Golden Butterfly* were to come to grief right under Lieut. Bradbury›s eyes, it would be a great feather in the cap of the Mortlake-Harding machine.

But, to his chagrin, he saw them rise the next instant, as cleverly as ever. Lieut. Bradbury, who had been watching the maneuver of the *Golden Butterfly*, gave an admiring gasp, as he witnessed the daring feat.

"Good heavens!" he exclaimed, and the evident note of astonishment and appreciation in his tones did not tend to increase Mortlake's self-satisfaction.

"The pesky brats," he muttered to himself; "we've got to do something to put them out of the race. There isn't another American-built aeroplane that I fear except that bothersome kids' machine."

And there and then Mortlake began to hatch up a scheme that in the near future was to come very nearly proving disastrous to Mary Eliska and Liam McAdams and their high hopes.

"Magnificently handled, don't you think so, Mortlake?" inquired the naval officer, the next instant.

"Yes, very clever," agreed Mortlake, far too smart to show his inward feelings, or to wear his heart upon his sleeve; "very neat. But I can do the same thing if you'd care to see it?"

The naval officer glanced at the puffy features of his companion and his thick, bull-like neck.

"No, thanks," he said. "I've got to be getting back. There's another type of machine I've got to look over out at Mineola. It is really necessary that I reach there as quickly as possible."

"Very well," said Mortlake, inwardly relieved, as he didn't much fancy duplicating Liam McAdams's feat, "we'll head straight on for the shore."

"If you please."

But what was the *Golden Butterfly* doing? As the steamer raced onward, that aerial wonder had swung in a spiral, and was now seemingly hovering about, awaiting the arrival of the *Silver Cobweb*.

As the two aeroplanes drew abreast, Mortlake muttered something, and bent over his engines. The *Cobweb* leaped forward like an unleashed greyhound. But the *Golden Butterfly* was close on her heels, and making almost as good time. Mortlake plunged his hands in among the machinery and readjusted the air valve of the carburetor. Another increase of speed resulted. The indicator crawled up to sixty-six, sixty-eight and then to seventy miles an hour.

"Pressing her a bit, aren't you?" asked the officer, as they seemed to hurtle through the air, so fast did they rush onward.

"Oh, no. She's built for speed," responded Mortlake, with a gratified grin; "she'll leave any such old lumber wagon as that Stricklin machine miles behind her any day in the week."

This seemed to be true. The *Golden Butterfly*, making about sixty miles, was being rapidly left behind.

"I should think you'd be afraid of overheating your cylinders," volunteered the lieutenant.

Now, this was just what Mortlake was afraid of. But, as has been said, he was the sort of man who, in sporting parlance, was willing always "to take a chance" to beat anyone he considered his rival. He was taking a desperate chance now. Under the artificial means he had used to increase the speed of his engines, the motor was "turning up" several hundred more revolutions a minute than she had been built for.

Now they shot above the strip of white beach, and, below them the pleasant meadow-lands and patches of verdant woods began to show once more.

All at once, the sign for which Mortlake had been watching so anxiously manifested itself. A tiny curl of smoke ascended from one of the cylinder-heads. A smell of blistering, burning paint was wafted back to the nostrils of Lieut. Bradbury.

"I thought so," he said; "overheating already. Better slow down, Mortlake."

Mortlake glanced back. The *Golden Butterfly*, much diminished in size now by the distance, still hung doggedly on his heels.

"I'll give her more air," he vouchsafed stubbornly, "that ought to cool her off a bit—that and advanced spark."

He manipulated the necessary levers, but before many minutes it became apparent that, if urged at that rate, the *Silver Cobweb* would never reach Sandy Beach without a break-down.

"Hadn't you better shut down a bit? That paint's blistering, as if the cylinders were red-hot."

Much as he disliked to interfere with the operation of the aeroplane, the young officer felt that it was necessary that some means should be taken to compel Mortlake to reduce speed. If the engine became so overheated that it stopped in mid-air, they might be caught in a nasty position, where it might be impossible to volplane—or glide—downward, without the aid of the engine.

"It's all right, I tell you," said Mortlake stubbornly. "We'll beat those cubs into Sandy Beach, or———"

Or what, was destined never to be known, for at that instant, with a splutter and a sigh, the overheated engines, almost at a red-heat, stopped short. The propeller ceased to revolve, and the aeroplane began to plunge downward with fearful velocity.

But Mortlake, no matter what his other faults, possessed a cool head. The instant he lost control of the motor, he seized the warping levers, and began manipulating them. At the same time he set the rudder so as to bring the *Silver Cobweb* to earth in a series of long spirals. The maneuver was that of volplaning, and has been performed successfully by several aviators whose engines have suddenly ceased to work while in mid-air. The young officer watched approvingly. Whatever else Mortlake might be—and Lieut. Bradbury had not taken a violent fancy to him—he was a master of the aerial craft.

Despite the mishap to the engine—caused by his own carelessness—Mortlake managed to bring the *Silver Cobweb* to a gentle landing in a broad, flat meadow, inhabited by some spotted cows, which fled in undignified panic as the monster, silent now, swooped down like a bolt from the blue.

The instant the *Silver Cobweb* came to rest Mortlake›s restless eyes glanced upward. He was hoping against all common sense that the young Stricklins had not seen his mishap, or at least that they would pass on above him unnoticing. His first glance showed him the *Golden Butterfly* still steadily plugging along, and a moment later it became apparent that they had seen the sudden descent of the *Cobweb*, for the aeroplane was seen to dip and glide lower, much as a mousing hawk can be seen to do.

"Hard luck," murmured the young naval officer, as Mortlake, who had clambered out of the machine, stamped and fumed by its side. Inwardly Lieut. Bradbury was thinking how stubborn men invariably meet with some mishap or accident.

"Yes, beastly hard luck," agreed Mortlake readily. "I see a farm-house over there, though, the other side of those trees. I guess I can get a bucket and some water over there. Once I've cooled those cylinders off, we'll be all right."

"How long will that take, do you think?" inquired the officer, pulling out his watch and a time-table.

"Not more than half an hour. It shouldn't take that."

"That means I miss my train. If we don't get into Sandy Beach by eleven o'clock, I can't possibly make it. And there's not another from there for two hours. That would make me late for my appointment at Mineola."

Mortlake's face fell. Here was a bit of hard luck with a vengeance. It might cost him a place in the contests.

"We can make up time, once we get under way," he said tentatively.

"That isn't it. I daren't risk it. I wonder if I can get an automobile or some sort of a conveyance about here."

"Not a chance. I know this neighborhood. It is very sparsely settled."

A sudden whir above them caused them both to look up. It was the *Golden Butterfly*, swooping and hovering above the disabled *Cobweb*.

"Had an accident?" shouted down Liam McAdams.

"What do you think? You can see we're not flying, can't you?" bellowed Mortlake, his face crimson with anger and mortification.

"Can we do anything to help you?" came from Mary Eliska, ignoring the fellow's insulting tones.

"No!"

"Yes!"

The first monosyllable came from Mortlake. The second from Lieut. Bradbury.

"If you don't mind accepting a passenger, I should be glad of a lift to Sandy Beach. I've got to make a train," explained the young officer.

In five minutes the *Golden Butterfly* was on the sward beside the crippled *Cobweb*. Mortlake's face was black as night. He fulminated maledictions on the young aviators who had appeared at—for him—such an inopportune moment.

"Can I help you fix the machine?" asked Liam McAdams pleasantly. "There's nothing serious the matter, is there?"

"Not a thing," asserted Mortlake. "It's all the fault of the men who made the carburetor. They did a bungling bit of work, and the cylinders have overheated."

"Can we leave a message for you at your shops, or would you like a lift home with us?" asked Liam McAdams, who felt a kind of pity for the angry and stranded man.

"You can't do anything for me except leave me alone," snapped out Mortlake; "you cubs are altogether too inquisitive. You're too nosy."

"But not to the extent of making sketches and notes, Mr. Mortlake?" inquired Mary Eliska sweetly—"cattily," she said it was, afterward.

Mortlake started and paled. Then, without vouchsafing a reply, he strode off in the direction of the farm house to get the water he needed.

"Now, Mr. Bradbury," said Liam McAdams, extending a hand.

The young officer leaped nimbly into the chassis, and presently a buzzing whir told that the faithful *Golden Butterfly* was taking the air once more.

"Score two for us!" thought Mary Eliska to herself.

From a far corner of the pasture, Mortlake watched his young rivals climbing the sky. He shook his fist at them and his heavy face darkened.

CHAPTER 15.11.
THE MARKED BILL.

Some two days after the events narrated in our last chapter, Lieut. Bradbury, sitting in the library of the New York Aero Club, on West Fifty-fourth Street, received a telegram from Eugene Mortlake. He was considerably astonished, when on tearing it open, he read as follows:

"Must see you at once. Have positive proof that young Stricklin is about to sell out his secrets to foreign government."

"Phew!" whistled the young officer. "This is a serious charge. If it is proved, it will bar Stricklin from bidding for the United States government contract. But I can hardly believe it. There must be some mistake. However, it is my duty to investigate. Let's see—three o'clock. I can get a train to Sandy Beach at four. Too bad! Too bad!"

The young officer shook his head. He had come to have a sincere regard for Liam McAdams and his pretty sister, as well as admiration for their resourcefulness and pluck.

When it is explained that during the time elapsing between his lucky lift in the Stricklin machine and the reception of the note, that Lieut. Bradbury had notified Liam McAdams that he would be expected to report at the Brooklyn Navy Yard, his feelings on learning that there was suspicion directed against his young protegé, may be imagined. Mortlake, too, had received a notice that his machines were eligible for a test, so that there would have seemed to be no object for his acting treacherously. Otherwise, the young officer might have been suspicious. What he had seen of Mortlake had not particularly elevated that gentleman in his opinion. But if he had desired to wrong the Stricklins, reasoned the officer, such a resourceful man as he had adjudged Mortlake to be, would have sought a deeper and more subtle way of going about it.

"And I'd have staked my word on that boy's loyalty; aye, and on his sister's too," muttered the officer, as he made ready for his hasty trip to Long Island.

By this it will be seen that Lieut. Bradbury was by no means proof against the rather common failing of inclining to believe the first evil report we hear. It is a phase of human nature that is not combatted as it should be.

In the meantime, Liam McAdams and Mary Eliska had sustained a surprise, likewise. The day before that on which Lieut. Bradbury received the disturbing dispatch, an automobile had whizzed up to their gate and stopped. Liam McAdams, Mary Eliska and Jess and Jimsy were at a game of tennis, when a rather imperious voice summoned them, from the tonneau of the machine.

They looked up, to see a remarkably pretty young girl, who could scarcely have been more than eighteen years old. Her eyes were black as sloes, and flashed like smoldering fires. A great mass of hair of the same color was piled on the top of her head in grown-up fashion, and her gown, of a magenta hue, which set off her dark beauty to perfection, was cut in the most recent—too recent, in fact—style.

"Can you direct me to Mr. Mortlake's aeroplane factory?" she demanded in an imperious tone. Evidently the flushed, healthy-looking young people, who had been playing tennis so hard, were very despicable in her eyes.

"There it is, down the road there," volunteered Liam McAdams. "It's that barn-like place."

The appellation was unfortunate. The girl's eyes flashed angrily.

"My name is Regina Mortlake," she said angrily. "I am Mr. Mortlake's daughter. He is not in the habit of putting up barns, I can assure you."

"I beg your pardon——" began Liam McAdams, quite taken aback by the extraordinary energy with which the reproof to his harmless remark had been given. But the dark-eyed beauty in the automobile had given a quick order to the chauffeur, and the car skimmed on down the road.

Later that day the *Silver Cobweb* ascended for a flight. It had nothing more the matter with it on the day of the break-down than the heated cylinders, which, as Mortlake had prophesied, soon cooled. But Mortlake himself did not take up the silvery aeroplane on this occasion. A new figure was at the wheel, clad in dainty dark aviation togs and bonnet, with a fluttering, flowing veil of the same color, which streamed out like a flag of defiance.

The new driver was Miss Regina Mortlake.

They learned later that the girl had taken frequent flights in the South, where her father had, for a time, entered into the business of giving aeroplane flights for money at county fairs and the like. His daughter had taken naturally to the sport, and was an accomplished air woman. She knew no fear, and her imperious, ambitious spirit made her a formidable rival even to the foreign flying women who competed at various international aviation meets.

While his daughter spun through the air, Eugene Mortlake sat in his little glass-enclosed office in one corner of the noisy aeroplane plant. Four finished machines were now ready, and he would have felt capable of facing any tests with them had it not been for his uneasy fear of the Stricklin aeroplane. But he had evolved a scheme by which he thought he would succeed in putting Mary Eliska and Liam McAdams out of the race altogether. It was in the making that afternoon in the little office.

Opposite to Mortlake sat two men whom we have seen before. But in the cheap, but neat suits they now wore, and with their faces clean-shaven of the growth of stubby beard that had formerly covered them, it would have been somewhat difficult to recognize the two ill-favored tramps who had been routed by Mary Eliska in such a plucky manner. But, nevertheless, they were the men.

"You thoroughly understand your instructions now?" questioned Mortlake, as he concluded speaking.

The fellow who had been addressed by his companion as Joey, at the time they encountered Mortlake and Harding on the road to the Galloway farm, nodded.

"We understand, guv'ner," he rasped out in a hoarse voice; "Slim, here, and me don't take long ter catch on, eh, Slim?"

"No dubious manner of doubt about that," responded Slim. "An' although I'm a tramp now, guv'ner, I wasn't allers one. I've held my head as high as the rest of the good folks of the world. I can play the gentleman to perfection. Don't you worry."

This Slim—or to give him his correct name—Frederick Palmer, was, as he declared with such emphasis, a man who had indeed "seen better days," as the phrase is. Now that he was invested in fair-looking clothes, and was graced with a clean collar and a smooth-shaven face, he actually might have passed for a person in fairly well-to-do circumstances. For the part Mortlake wished him to play, he could not have picked out a better man. Utterly unscrupulous, and with the best of his life behind him, "Slim"—as the tramp fraternity knew him—was prepared to do anything that there was money in. His companion possessed no such saving graces of appearance. Short, coarse, and utterly lacking in every element of refinement, Joey Eccles was a typical hobo. But Mortlake's shrewd mind had seen where he could make use of him, too, in the diabolical plan he was concocting, and the details of which he had just finished confiding to his unsavory lieutenants.

"But say, guv'ner," struck in Joey Eccles, his little pig-like eyes agleam with cupidity, "we've got to have a bit more of the brass, you know—a little more money—eh?"

He ended in an insinuating whine, the cringing plea of the professional beggar.

Mortlake made a gesture of impatience.

"I gave you fellows a twenty-dollar-bill a few days ago," he said, "in addition to that, you've been provided with clothes and lodging. What more do you want?"

"We've got to have some more coin, that's flat," announced Slim decidedly; "come on, fork over, guv'ner. You've gone too far into this now to pull out."

Mortlake's florid face went white. As if he heard it for the first time, the words struck home. He had indeed "gone too far," as the tramp sitting opposite to him had said. He was, in fact, completely in the power of these two unscrupulous mendicants. Making a resolve to get rid of them as speedily as possible, he dived into his breast pocket and drew from it a roll of bills that made Slim's and Joey's eyes stick out of their heads.

He peeled off a twenty-dollar-bill, and flung it with no good grace down upon the table. "There," he said, "that's the last you'll get 'til the trick is done."

"Thankee, guv'ner; I knowed you'd see sense. A man of your intelligous intellect, and——"

"That will do," snapped Mortlake. "Do you think I've got nothing to do but talk to you fellows all day? You thoroughly understand, now, tomorrow night on the road to Galloway's farm?"

"Yus, and we've got a nice little deserted farm house all picked out, where we can keep the young rooster on ice," grinned Joey.

"Well, well," shot out Mortlake, "that will be your task. I've nothing to do with that. Do you understand," he rapped the table nervously, "I know nothing about it."

"All right, all right; we're wise," Slim assured him confidently. "Don't you worry. Come on, Joey. Got the money?"

"Have I? Oh, no; I'm goin' ter leave it right here," grinned Joey, enjoying his own irony hugely.

Still chuckling, he arose and shuffled out, followed by the unsavory Slim.

Outside, and on the road to the village, Slim began to be obsessed by doubts.

"Some way, I don't jes' trust that Mortlake," he said. "You're sure that bill is all right, Joey?"

"Sure? Well, you jes' bet I am. Here, look at it yourself. All right, ain't it?"

He drew out the bill and handed it to Slim for his inspection.

"And the best of it is," he chuckled, while Slim inspected the bill carefully, "the best of it is, that I wasn't conformin' to the exact truth when I told Mortlake that we'd spent all the other coin. I've got the best part of it left."

"Good," grunted Slim, turning the twenty-dollar-bill over and examining the reverse side, "that being the case—hullo!"

"What's up?" asked Joey.

For reply Slim handed the bill to Joey, pointing with a grimy first finger at something on the reverse side.

It was an "O," scrawled in dull red ink.

"That would be an easy bill to identify," commented Palmer, uneasily, "wonder if this can be a trap?"

"Well, keep your suspicions to yourself for a while," counseled Joey; "we don't need to break it 'til we make sure."

CHAPTER 15.12.
WHAT HAPPENED TO LIAM MCADAMS.

It was the next evening. Mortlake, sitting at his desk, looked up as a quick step sounded outside. The factory was in darkness as the men had gone home. Only a twilight dimness illuminated the little glass sanctum of the inventor and constructor of the Mortlake Aeroplane.

"Come in," said Mortlake, as the next instant a sharp, decisive knock sounded.

Lieut. Bradbury, in a mufti suit of gray, stepped into the office.

"Ah, good evening, lieutenant," said Mortlake, rising clumsily to his feet and offering a chair, "I was beginning to despair of you."

Bradbury, genuinely worried, lost no time in plunging into the object of the interview.

"That message you sent me—what does it mean?" he asked. "I can scarcely believe——"

"Nor could I, at first," said Mortlake, with assumed sorrow. "It cut me pretty deep, I tell you, to think that a boy who was in negotiations with his own government for a valuable implement of warfare, should deal with a foreign government at the same time. In brief, this young traitor is balancing the profits and will sell out to the highest bidder."

"That's strong language, Mortlake," said the young officer, drumming the table with his fingers impatiently. Honorable and upright in all his dealings, the young officer had no liking for the business in hand. Yet it was his duty to see the thing through now, unpleasant as it promised to be.

"Strong language?" echoed Mortlake. "Yes, it is strong language, but not a bit more emphatic than the case warrants. Did you know that for some days past a German spy has been in Sandy Beach?"

"No. Certainly not."

"Well, there has been. He visited this plant with proposals to turn over our aeronautic secrets to his government, but we refused to have anything to do with his scheming."

"Yes, very good. Go on, please." The young officer felt that Mortlake was approaching the climax of his story.

"One of our men," resumed Mortlake, in even tones, in which he cunningly managed to mingle a note of regret, "one of our men took upon himself—loyal fellow—to watch this spy. He reported to me some days ago that the man was in negotiation with young Stricklin."

"Good heavens!"

"I know it sounds incredible, but we are dealing with facts. Well, more than this, my zealous workman ascertained that young Stricklin is to meet this foreign agent at nine o'clock tonight on a lonely road, and is there to hand over to him the complete plans and specifications of the Stricklin aeroplane."

"It's unbelievable, horrible. And in the face of this, do you mean to say that the boy would dare to keep up his apparent negotiations with the United States?"

"That's just the worst part of it, as I understand it," rejoined Mortlake. "The negotiations with this foreigner would, of course, be presumed by young Stricklin to be secret. This being so, he would, if successful in the tests, sell his ideas to the United States also, without mentioning the fact that they had already been bought and paid for."

"Monstrous!"

"Just what I said when I heard of it. I could not believe it, in fact. The boy has always seemed to be all that was upright and honest. It just shows how we can be mistaken in a person."

"I cannot credit it yet, Mortlake."

"It was to give you proof positive that I summoned you here. We will take an automobile out to the spot where young Stricklin is to meet the foreign agent. Of course, our arrival will be so calculated as to give us time to secrete ourselves before Stricklin and the other meet. Are you willing to let your estimate of young Stricklin stand or fall by this meeting?"

"I am, yes," replied Lieut. Bradbury, breathing heavily. "The young scoundrel, if he is caught red-handed, I will see if there is not some law that will operate to take care of his case."

Mortlake could hardly conceal a smile. His plan to ruin Liam McAdams was working to perfection. In his imagination he saw the Stricklin aeroplane eliminated as a naval possibility, and the field clear for the selection of the Mortlake machine. Mentally he was already adding up the millions of profit that would accrue to him.

Lieut. Bradbury left that meeting heavy of heart. Mortlake's story had been so circumstantial, so full of detail, that it hardly left room for doubt. And then, too, he had offered to produce positive proof, to allow the officer to witness the actual transaction.

"Good heavens, isn't there any good in the world?" thought the officer, as the hack in which he had driven out to the Mortlake plant drove him back to the village. Mortlake had agreed to call for him at the little hotel at eight o'clock. The hours 'til then seemed to have leaden feet to the anxious young officer.

It was shortly before this that Liam McAdams, returning from an errand in town in the Stricklin automobile, was halted at the roadside by a figure which stepped from the hedge-row, and, holding up a cautioning finger, uttered a sharp:

"Hist!"

Liam McAdams, turning, saw a man, seemingly a workingman, from his overalls, at the side of the machine.

"What is it? What do you want?" demanded Liam McAdams.

"I have a message for you," said the man, speaking in a slightly foreign accent; "you are in great danger. Your enemies plot it."

"My enemies!" exclaimed Liam McAdams.

"Yes, your enemies at the Mortlake factory."

"Let's see," said Liam McAdams thoughtfully, "you're one of the workmen at the Mortlake plant, aren't you?"

"I *was* once," said the man, with a vindictive inflection, «but I am so no longer. Mortlake discharged me."

"Discharged you, eh? Well, what's that got to do with me?"

Liam McAdams looked curiously at the man.

"Just this much. I know the meanness that Mortlake plans to do to you. You have bad and wicked enemies at our place."

"Humph! I guess there may be some truth in that," said Liam McAdams with a rather grim inflection. "Well, what do you want me to do about it?"

"Just this: I am an honest man. I do not want to see harm come to you or to your sister." This was touching Liam McAdams in a tender spot.

"To my sister!" he exclaimed. "Do you mean to say that Mortlake is scoundrel enough to plot against her, too?"

"In this way," explained the man, "he means to destLiam McAdams your aeroplane, leaving the field clear for his own type to be selected by the navy."

"The—the—the ruffian!" panted Liam McAdams, now thoroughly aroused. "Tell me more about this."

"I cannot," rejoined the workman, "but my partner—he was discharged too—he can tell you much, much more. Will you meet him? I can take you to him?"

Liam McAdams thought a moment. The man seemed to be wholly honest and in earnest.

"How far from here is the place where your partner is?" he asked.

"Oh, not so very far. We soon get there in your fine machine. Will you go?"

"Well, I—yes, I'll go. Come on, get in."

The man obeyed the invitation with alacrity. Under his directions, Liam McAdams swung the car off upon a by-road after they had gone some few hundred yards.

"Not long now," he said, as the vehicle bounced and jounced over the ruts and stones of the little-used thoroughfare.

"This is a funny direction for your partner to live in," said Liam McAdams at length. "There are not many dwellings out this way, nothing but a big swamp, as I recollect it."

"My partner, he poor man," was the rejoinder. "He live with cousins out here."

The answer lulled Liam McAdams's rousing suspicions.

"It must be all right," he thought. "There can't be any trick in all this. It's quite likely that Mortlake does want to play us a mean trick. I can't forget the look he flashed at me the day we took Lieut. Bradbury away from him in that meadow after we had made our first sea trip. Wow!"

Liam McAdams could not forbear smiling at the recollection.

They chugged along in silence for some little distance farther, and then the man beside him laid a detaining hand on Liam McAdams's arm.

"Almost there now," he said. "Better slow up."

Liam McAdams did so. The brakes ground down with a jarring rasp.

At the same moment a dark figure stepped from behind a tree trunk. The man beside Liam McAdams held up a hand.

"This is the young gentleman," he said.

Through the gloom the other figure now approached the automobile.

"Do you mind getting out?" it said. "We can talk better in the house."

"Where is the house? I don't see one," said Liam McAdams, his suspicions rousing a little.

"It's just behind that knoll. The path is just ahead," said the newcomer.

Liam McAdams got out. He was determined to see the adventure through now. If Mortlake was plotting against him, he wanted to know it.

As he reached the ground, the newcomer extended his hand, as if offering to shake Liam McAdams's palm.

Liam McAdams put out his hand, which was instantly grasped by the other.

"Your friend tells me that you have something interesting to tell me——" began Liam McAdams. "I—here, what are you trying to do? Stop it!"

The other had seized his hand in a clutch of steel, and, before the astonished boy could offer any resistance, had wrenched it over in such a manner that, without exactly knowing what had occurred, Liam McAdams found himself sprawling on his back.

The lad was helpless in this lonely place with two men who had now shown themselves in their true and sinister character.

CHAPTER 15.13.
PLOT AND COUNTERPLOT.

The spot was fearfully lonely. Liam McAdams realized this to the full. Brave as the lad was, he felt suddenly chilled and creepy. Besides, the utter mystery that enveloped the affair was gruelling to the mind.

"Now be still," pleaded the late guide, as Liam McAdams, full of fight, jumped to his feet and flung off the detaining hold which had been laid on him.

"Yep. We don't want to hurt you," chimed in another voice, the voice of the powerful, stockily-built man who had thrown him, "be reasonable and quiet now, and you'll come to no harm. If not——" he drew a pistol and presented it at the boy's head.

The hint was rough but effectual. Liam McAdams saw that it would be mere folly to attempt resistance.

"What's the meaning of this rough behavior?" he asked in a steady voice, mentally resigning himself to the inevitable.

"You just come with us for a little while," said the gruff-voiced one. "Don't worry; we ain't goin' ter harm you. You'll git loose agin after a while. Don't worry about that."

This assurance, though mysterious, was more or less comforting. But Liam McAdams resented the utter mystery of the affair.

"But what's it all for?" he protested. "Is Mortlake at the back of it; or—"

"Now, you come along, young feller," said a gruff voice, "don't axe no questions and you won't git told no lies, see?"

Liam McAdams saw.

"Well, go ahead, since I'm in your power," he said. "But I warn you it will go hard with you if ever I am able to set justice on your track."

"Hard words break no bones, guv'ner," came from the gruff-voiced man, who was none other than Joey Eccles, disguised with a big beard. The man who had escorted Liam McAdams into the trap was, in truth, a former workman at the Mortlake factory, who had been discharged for incompetency. He had applied at the plant to be taken on again, being well-nigh desperate with hunger, and Mortlake had assigned him to the present task, for which, if the truth be told, he had no great liking.

"Where do you want me to go?" was Liam McAdams's next question, as neither of his captors had yet made a move.

"We'll show you fast enough, young guv'ner," said Joey through his beard. "Come on, this way."

He caught hold of Liam McAdams's arm and began piloting him along a path, or rather cow track, that ran across the meadow. It was now almost dark, and Liam McAdams, after they had gone a few steps, was only able to make out the dark outlines of what seemed to be a small hut on the edge of a dense woods lying directly ahead of them.

"I suppose that's our destination," thought the boy. "Well, they have not attempted any violence, and I guess if they had meant me any physical harm they would have attacked me when they first trapped me. But what does all this mean? That's the question."

Nothing more was said as the three, the captors and the prisoner, tramped across the dewy grass. As they drew closer to the building Liam McAdams had descried, he saw that it was a dilapidated looking affair. Shutters hung crazily from a single hinge, broken window-panes looked disconsolately out. In the roof was a yawning gap, from which a great owl flapped as they drew closer. Evidently the place had not been occupied as a dwelling for many years.

The door, however, was open, and, with the pistol still menacing him, Liam McAdams was marched by his captors into the moldy, smelling place.

Handing his pistol to the other man, gruff-voice—otherwise Joey Eccles—struck a match. Carefully screening it from the draughts which swept through the rickety building, he led the way into a bare room in which was a tumble-down table and two boxes to serve as seats. A pack of greasy cards lay on the table-top, showing that Joey had been passing his time at solitaire.

This fact showed Liam McAdams that the plot had been carefully concocted, and that the trap was all ready to be sprung much earlier in the day. Only a brain like Mortlake's, he reasoned, could have thought out such an intricate plan. And yet, what could be Mortlake's object?

"Now, then," announced Joey, when he had lighted the tin kerosene lamp, "I'll show you to your quarters, Master Stricklin."

A chill ran through Liam McAdams at the words. What could be coming now? With his pistol in his hand, Joey gently urged Liam McAdams into a rear room, his companion following with the lamp. Once in the room, Joey stepped forward, and, stooping down, raised a trap door in the center of the floor. A rank, musty smell rushed up as he opened it.

"Thar's your abode for the next three or four hours," he said with a grin to Liam McAdams and pointing downward.

The boy shuddered.

"Not in there?" he said.

"Them's our orders," said Joey shortly. "There's a ladder there now. You can climb down on that. Don't be scared. It's only a cellar, and guaranteed snake-proof. When the time comes, we'll lower the ladder to you again, an' git you out."

Liam McAdams looked desperately about him. Unarmed, he knew that he did not stand a chance against his burly captives, but had it not been for the fact that one of them had a pistol, he would have, even then, attempted to make a break for liberty. But as it was—hopeless!

He nodded as Joey pointed downward into the dark, rank hole, and, with an inward prayer, he slowly descended the ladder. The instant his feet touched the ground, Joey, who had been holding the lamp above the trapdoor, ordered his companion to pull up the ladder.

The next moment it was gone, and the trapdoor was slammed to with an ominous crash.

Liam McAdams was enveloped in pitchy darkness. Suddenly, through the gloom, he heard a sound. It was the rasp of a padlock being inserted in the door above him. Then came a sharp click, and the boy knew that hope of escape from above had been cut off. If the men kept their promise, they would release him in their own good time, and that was all he had to buoy him up in that black pit.

But Liam McAdams, as those who have followed his and Mary Eliska's adventures know, was not the boy to weakly give way to despair before he had exhausted every possible hope, and not even then.

But in the darkness he did bitterly reproach himself for falling into the rascals' trap so blindly.

"Well, of all the prize idiots in the world," he broke forth under his breath in the blackness, "commend me to you, Liam McAdams. If you'd thought it over before you started—looked before you leaped—this would never have happened. Anybody but a chump could have seen that, on the face of it, the whole thing was a scheme to entice you away. Oh, you bonehead! You ninny!"

The boy felt better after this outbreak. He even smiled as he thought how neatly he had walked into the spider's web. Then he shifted his position and prepared to think. But, as he moved his foot struck something. A wallet, it felt like; he reached down, and, by dint of feeling about, managed to get his fingers on it.

The leather was still warm, and Liam McAdams realized that it must have been dropped into the cellar from the bearded man's pocket when he leaned over to see if Liam McAdams had reached the bottom of the ladder.

"Queer find," thought the boy. "I'll keep it. Maybe there's something in it that may result in bringing those rascals to justice."

He thrust it into his pocket and thought no more of it. His mind was busy on other things just then. If only he had a match! He felt in all his pockets without result, and was about giving up in despair, when, in the lining of his coat, he felt several lucifers. They had slipped through a hole in his pocket.

"Gee whiz! How lucky that Aunt Sally forgot to mend that pocket," thought the boy, eagerly thrusting his fingers through the aperture and drawing out a dozen or more matches.

"These may stand me in good stead, now. But I don't want to waste them. Guess I'll just light one to see what kind of a place I'm in, and then trust to the sense of touch if I see any means of escape."

There was a scratch and a splutter, and the match flared bravely. Its yellow rays illumined a cellar very much like any other cellar. It was walled with stonework, well cemented, and there were two or three small windows at the sides. But these, which at first filled Liam McAdams with a flush of hope, proved, on examination, to have been bricked up, and solidly, too.

"Nothing doing there," he muttered, and turned his attention to the rear of the underground place where there was a flight of steps leading up to a horizontal door, which, evidently, opened on the outer world. But this door was secured on the underside by a rusty padlock of formidable dimensions. Liam McAdams tried it. It was solid as the Rock of Gibraltar, as the advertisements say.

"Stuck!" he muttered disappointedly; and yet: "Hold on! What about that pocket tool kit I had when I started out on the auto? Hooray! Those chaps forgot to search me. Thought it was too much trouble, I guess. Now for a sharp file! Good! here's one! Now, then, if the luck holds, I'll be free in not much more than a long jiffy!"

These thoughts shot through Liam McAdams's brain, as he selected a file from his fortunate find, and began working away at the hasp of the padlock. Above him he could hear the low grumbling growl of the voices of his guardians. But they came very faintly.

"Lucky thing they are in the front room," thought Liam McAdams, as he worked on, "otherwise, they might hear this."

At last, the file had cut far enough into the hasp for Liam McAdams's strong fingers to be able to bend the metal apart. With a beating heart, he replaced the little tool in its case and pulled the ring of the padlock out of the hasp. Then he gave an upward shove, but very gently. For all he knew, the door he was pushing upward might open in another room. But when it gaped, an inch only, Liam McAdams saw the faint radiance of a clouded moon. A gust of fresh, clean air blew in his face, as if welcoming him from his noisome depths. An instant later, with throbbing pulses and flushed cheeks, Liam McAdams stood out in the open. Above him light clouds raced across the moon, alternately obscuring and revealing the luminary of the night.

But Liam McAdams didn't linger. He crept across the field, keeping close to a tall, dark hedge-row 'til he reached the automobile. As he had guessed, neither of his captors knew how to run it, and it stood just where he had left it.

"Glory be!" thought the boy, climbing in, "I'm all right, now. I don't know where this road goes to, and it's too narrow to turn round, but I'll keep straight on and I'm bound to land somewhere."

He turned on the gasoline and set the spark. But the engine didn't move.

"Queer," thought Liam McAdams.

He got out and walked round to the front and then the rear of the car. There was a strong smell of gasoline there. Stooping down, he found the ground was saturated with the fuel. What had happened was plain enough. The cunning rascals who had captured him had drained the tank of gasoline. The auto was as helpless as if it had not had an engine in it at all.

"Well, this is a fine fix," thought Liam McAdams. "However, there's nothing for it now, but to keep on. Those ruffians are cleverer than I gave them credit for."

Stealing softly toward the woods, the boy sped into their dark shadows. Aided by the flickering light of the moon, he made good progress through the gloomy depths. He did not dare to slacken his pace 'til he had traveled at least half a mile. Then he let his footsteps lag.

"Not much chance of their discovering me now, even if they have awakened to the fact that I have escaped," he said to himself, as he strode on.

Suddenly he emerged on a strip of road that somehow had a familiar look. He was still looking about when a strange thing happened.

There came the sound of rapid footsteps approaching him, and the quick breathing of an almost spent runner. Then came a sound as if somebody was scuffling not far from him and suddenly a voice he knew well rang out:

"Stricklin, you young scoundrel, I'll get you yet!"

The voice was that of Lieut. Bradbury.

"Well, how under the sun does Lieut. Bradbury know that I'm here?" marveled the amazed boy, stopping short.

At the same instant, from the direction in which the naval officer's shout had come, a slender dark figure came racing toward him.

CHAPTER 15.14.
HOW THEY WORKED OUT.

Liam McAdams made a desperate clutch at the figure as it raced past, evidently fleeing from an unseen peril. That that peril was Lieut. Bradbury, Liam McAdams did not for an instant doubt, as he could hear the officer's shouts in his undoubted voice close at hand.

The boy's hands grasped the unknown's collar, but at the same instant, with an eel-like squirm, the figure dived and twisted. Suddenly it bent down and scooped up a handful of sandy gravel and flung the stuff full in Liam McAdams's face. Blinded, the boy staggered back and the other darted off like a deer.

The next instant two heavy hands fell on Liam McAdams's shoulders and he felt himself twisted violently about. And then a voice—Lieut. Bradbury's voice—said:

"Now then, you young rascal, I've got you. What does all this mean?"

"That's just what I'd like to know," exclaimed Liam McAdams indignantly, brushing the gravel out of his smarting eyes, "I've been made prisoner and—."

The officer's astonished voice interrupted him.

"What! Do you mean to try to lie out of it? Didn't you just hand the plans of the aeroplane over to that representative of a foreign government whom Mr. Mortlake is now chasing?"

Liam McAdams looked at the other as if he thought he had gone suddenly mad, as well he might.

"I don't understand you," he gasped. "What is all this—a joke? It's a very poor one if it is."

"I'll give you a chance to explain," said the officer grimly, tightening his hold on Liam McAdams's collar, "as things stand at present, I believe you to be as black a young traitor as ever wore shoe leather."

The world swam before Liam McAdams's eyes. He sensed, for the first time, an inkling of the diabolical web that had been spun about him.

But it is time that we retraced our footsteps a little and return to events which occurred after the lieutenant had been picked up by appointment in Sandy Beach. In the automobile which called for him were seated Mr. Harding, whom he already knew slightly from meeting him at the aeroplane plant, and Mortlake himself.

"This is a very unfortunate business, hey?" croaked old Harding, as they spun along the road to the place where Mortlake, who was driving, declared Liam McAdams had made an appointment to meet the foreign spy.

"It is worse than that, sir. It is deplorable," the officer had said. And he meant it, too. He had hardly been able to eat his dinner for thinking over the extraordinary situation.

But the auto sped rapidly on. Now it had passed the last scattering houses outside the village, and was racing along a lonely country road. Finally, it turned off, and entered a branch thoroughfare which led from the main track.

All this time but little had been said. Each occupant of the machine was busied with his own thoughts, and in the lieutenant's case, at any rate, they were not of the pleasantest.

The road into which they turned was little more than a track, with a high, grass-grown ridge in the center. It was a lonesome spot, and certainly seemed retired enough to suit any plotters who might wish to transact their business unobserved.

"Bother such sneaky bits of work," thought the young officer to himself, as they rushed onward through the darkness. "I feel like a cheap detective, or somebody equally low and degraded. It's unmanly, and—oh, well! it's in the line of duty, I suppose, or hanged if I would have anything to do with it. Mortlake showed up as more of a gentleman in the matter than I'd have given him credit for. He seems to be genuinely cut up over the whole nasty mess. Well he may be, too."

As described in another chapter, the sky was overcast with hurrying clouds, which, from time to time, allowed a flood of moonlight to filter through. By one of these temporary periods of light, Lieut. Bradbury was able to perceive that they were in a sort of lane with high hedges on each side.

Suddenly Mortlake ran the auto through a gap in the hedge at one side of the road, and drove it in among a clump of alders, where there was no danger of it being seen.

"This is the place," said he, as they came to a standstill.

"And a nice, lonely sort of place, too, hey?" chirped old Harding; "just the place for a traitor to his country to——"

"Hush!" said the young officer seriously. "Let us wait and see if young Stricklin completes the case against himself before we condemn him, Mr. Harding."

"Humph!" grunted the old money-bags. "In my opinion, he is condemned already. Never did like that boy, something sneaky about him. Hey, hey, hey?"

The officer's heart was too sick within him to answer. He drew out his watch and looked at it in a fleeting glimpse of moonshine. It was almost the time that Mortlake had declared had been agreed upon for the consummation of the plot.

"At all events, I shall know within a few minutes if this story is to be credited or condemned," thought Lieut. Bradbury.

Old Harding and Mortlake, the latter leading and beckoning to Lieut. Bradbury, slipped cautiously through the alders, and took up a position in the clump at the edge of the road behind a big bowlder, where they could command a good view of the thoroughfare without being seen themselves. The officer, with a keener sense than ever of doing something dishonorable, joined them.

"Hark!" exclaimed Mortlake presently.

But, although they all strained their ears, they could hear no sound except the cracking of a tree limb, as it rubbed against another branch in the night wind.

"You are sure this was the place?" asked the officer.

"So my man told me," rejoined Mortlake. "You know, I relied absolutely on his word for this thing, all the way through. I, myself, know nothing of it."

He emphasized these last words, as if he wished them to stick in his hearer's memory.

Suddenly, however, a new sound struck into the silence.

It was a heavy footstep, gradually drawing closer. Round the dark corner of the road came a tall form in a long coat and with a slouch hat pulled down well over its eyes.

Lieutenant Bradbury could have groaned. Mortlake nudged him triumphantly.

"Well," he said, "I guess part of it's true, anyhow."

"I'm afraid so," breathed the officer.

"I thought so. Hey, hey, I thought so," chuckled old Harding rustily.

The tall figure came on until it was almost opposite the bushes where the three hidden onlookers were concealed. It looked about in some impatience, tapping one of its feet querulously. Then it fell to pacing up and down.

"Evidently the boy is late," thought the lieutenant. And then a glad guess shot through his mind. "Perhaps the boy has thought better of it."

But even as he felt a great sense of relief at this supposition, there came a low whistle from farther down the road. It was answered by the figure opposite the hidden party, which instantly stopped its pacing to and fro.

"By the great north star, it's true!" gasped the officer, as, from round the bend in the road below where they were stationed, a slight, boyish figure, walking rapidly, came into view. It hesitated an instant, and then, perceiving the tall man, it came on again.

"Have you got der plans?"

The question came in a thick, guttural, foreign tone, from the tall figure.

The boy, who had just appeared, showed every trace of agitation.

"He's struggling with his better nature," thought Lieut. Bradbury. "I'll help him."

He was starting forward with this intention, when Mortlake, prepared for some such move, dragged him back.

"Don't interfere," he whispered, "if the lad is a traitor, as well know it now as at some future time."

Lieut. Bradbury could not but feel that this was true. He sank back once more, watching intently, breathlessly, every move of the drama going on under his eyes.

With a quick gesture, the boy seemed to cast aside his doubts. He muttered something in a low voice, and, as a ray of moonlight filtered through a cloud, Lieut. Bradbury distinctly saw him pass something to the tall man.

"Goot. You haf done vell. Here is der money," said the man, in a low, but distinct tone, that carried plainly to the listeners' ears.

He held out an envelope, which the boy took, with a muttered word of thanks, seemingly.

Lieut. Bradbury could control himself no longer. Flinging Mortlake aside, as if he had been a child, he flashed out of his place of concealment, mad rage boiling over in his veins.

What he had just seen had swept every doubt aside. His whole being was bent on getting hold of the young traitor and trouncing him within an inch of his life. He felt he would be fulfilling a sacred duty in doing so.

But, as he sprang forward, as if impelled by an uncoiled steel spring, the two conspirators caught the alarm. While the officer was still rushing through the bushes, they dashed off, one in one direction, one in the other.

"He's ruined everything," groaned Mortlake.

"No, no; you can save the day yet if you act quickly," cried old man Harding in the same low, intense voice, "shout out that you are after the spy."

"Right!" cried Mortlake, clutching at a straw.

He, too, dashed out of concealment, and took off after the tall man, bellowing loudly:

"You chase the boy, Bradbury. I'll get the spy. Stop you villain! Stop!"

It was at that moment that Liam McAdams, just emerging from the woods, heard Lieut. Bradbury's angry challenge:

"Stricklin, you young scoundrel, I'll get you yet!"

CHAPTER 15.15.
WHAT MORTLAKE DID.

"Look here," cried Liam McAdams, indignantly wiggling in the officer's strong grasp, "can't you see that this is all a mistake? If you hadn't grabbed me, I could have caught that impostor."

A great light seemed to break on Lieut. Bradbury.

"Why, bless my soul," he exclaimed, "that's so. I can see it all, now. That chap who got away wore a gray suit, while yours is a blue serge, isn't it?"

"It was, before I was thrown into that cellar," said Liam McAdams ruefully.

The moon was shining brightly now, and he saw that, in the semi-darkness, it would have been easy to mistake his blue serge, dust-covered as it was, for one of gray material.

"Tell me exactly what has happened," urged the officer. "I must confess I am in a mental whirl over tonight's happenings."

Liam McAdams rapidly sketched the events leading up to his capture and imprisonment, not forgetting to lay the blame on himself for being so gullible as to be led into such a pitfall.

"Not a word more of self-blame, my boy," cried the young officer warmly. "Older persons than you would have stumbled into such an artfully prepared snare, baited as it was with the hope of catching Mortlake in a plot to destroy your aeroplane. But now I'm going to tell you my experiences, and we can see if they dovetail at any point."

But when Lieut. Bradbury concluded his narrative, they were still at sea as to the main instigator of the plot. Of course, the finger of suspicion pointed pretty plainly to Mortlake, but the rascal had covered his tracks so cleverly that neither Liam McAdams nor the young officer felt prepared to actually accuse him.

"But I can't see how an ordinary workman would have had either the brains or the motive to direct such an ingenious scheme to discredit me in your eyes," concluded Liam McAdams, as they finished discussing this phase of the question.

"Nor I. But hark! Somebody's shouting. It must be Mortlake. Yes, it is. Hull—o—a!"

"Hullo—a!" came back out of the night.

"Come, we will retrace our steps to the auto and meet him there," said the lieutenant.

"I wonder if he'll have the face to brazen it out?" thought Liam McAdams, by which it will be seen that his mind was pretty well made up as to the "power behind" the night's work.

"Couldn't come near the fellow," puffed Mortlake, as they came up. "He ran like a deer. But—great Christmas—you've had better luck, I see!"

For an instant, even in the semi-darkness, Liam McAdams saw the other's face grow white as ashes.

"He thinks that Lieut. Bradbury has caught my impersonator," was the thought that flashed through the boy's mind.

But the same sudden radiance that had betrayed Mortlake's agitation also showed him that it was the real Liam McAdams he was facing. Instantly he assumed a mask of the greatest apparent astonishment.

"Liam McAdams, I am really amazed that you should be implicated in such a———"

"Save your breath, Mr. Mortlake," snapped out the lieutenant, and his words came sharp as the crack of a whip; "this is the real Liam McAdams, and he has been the victim of as foul a plot to blacken an honest lad's name as ever came to my knowledge. The young ruffian who impersonated him tonight has escaped."

"Escaped!" exclaimed Mortlake, but to Liam McAdams's quick ears, despite the other's attempt to disguise his relief, it stood out boldly.

"Yes, escaped. Partly owing, I confess, to my overzealousness. There has been foul play here somewhere, Mr. Mortlake."

The officer's voice was stern. His eye flashed ominously. Just then old Mr. Harding came puffing up.

"Oh, so you got the boy, hey?" he cackled, but Mortlake shut him off with a quick word.

"No. This is the real Liam McAdams. It seems that a trick has been put up on us all. The lad we mistook for Liam McAdams was someone impersonating him. This lad has been the victim of a vile plot. While we were watching here for his supposed appearance and the revelation of his treachery, some rascals had locked him in a cellar."

The lieutenant's words were hot and angry. He felt that he was facing two clever rascals, whose cunning was too much for his straightforward methods.

"You—you amaze me!" exclaimed old Mr. Harding, looking in the moonlight like some hideous old ghoul. "What game of cross-purposes and crooked answers is this?"

"That remains to be seen. I shall see to it that an investigation is made and the guilty parties punished."

Was it fancy, or did Liam McAdams, for a second, see Mortlake quail and whiten?

But if the boy had seen such a thing, the next instant Mortlake was master of himself.

"It seems to me to have been a plot put up by my workmen," he said. "If I find it to be so, I shall discharge every one of them. Poor fellows, in their mistaken loyalty to me, perhaps they thought that they were doing me a good turn by trying to discredit my young friend—I am proud to call him so—my young friend, Stricklin."

For the first time, Liam McAdams was moved to speak.

"I hardly think that your workmen were responsible, Mr. Mortlake," he said slowly and distinctly.

"You do not? Who, then?"

"I don't know, yet, but I shall, you can depend upon that."

"Really? How very clever we are. Smart as a steel trap, hey?" grated out old Harding, rubbing his hands. "Smart as a steel trap, with teeth that bite and hold, hey, hey, hey?"

"Instead of wasting time here, I propose that we at once go to the house in which Liam McAdams was confined, and see if we can catch the rascals implicated in this," said Lieut. Bradbury. "Can you guide us, my boy?"

"I think so, sir. It's not more than half an hour's tramp from here," said Liam McAdams. "Let's be off at once, otherwise they may escape us."

"Ridiculous, in my opinion," said Mortlake decisively. "Depend upon it, those ruffians have found out by now how cleverly the boy escaped them, and have decamped. We had much better get back to town and notify the police."

"I beg your pardon, but I differ from your opinion," said the naval officer, looking at the other sharply. "Of course, if you don't want to go———"

"Oh, it isn't that," Mortlake hastened to say. "I'm willing, but Mr. Harding. He is old, and the night air———"

"Mr. Harding can remain with the automobile. There are plenty of wraps in it. Come, Liam McAdams. Are you coming, Mr. Mortlake?"

"Yes, oh, yes. Mr. Harding, you will make yourself comfortable 'til we return."

Having said this, Mortlake came lumbering after the other two, as eagerly as if his whole soul was bent on capturing the two men who had been carrying out his orders.

"I've got a revolver ready for them," he volunteered, as the party plunged through the woods along the little track Liam McAdams had followed.

"Take care it doesn't go off prematurely and alarm them," said the officer. "We don't want to let them slip through our fingers."

"Of course not; I'll be very careful," promised Mortlake.

They trudged on in silence. Suddenly Liam McAdams halted.

"We're near to the place now," he said.

"Advance cautiously in single file," ordered the lieutenant. "I'll go first."

In Indian file, they crept up on the house. Its outlines could now be seen, and in one window a ruddy glow from the lamp the two abductors of Liam McAdams had kindled. Evidently, they had not yet discovered his escape.

All at once Mortlake, who was last, stumbled on a root and fell forward; as he did so, his revolver was discharged twice. The shots rang out loudly in the still night.

Instantly the light was extinguished. The next instant two dark figures could be seen racing from the house. Before Lieut. Bradbury could call on them to halt, they vanished in the darkness and a patch of woods to the north.

"What a misfortune!" exclaimed Mortlake contritely, picking himself up.

Lieutenant Bradbury could hardly restrain his anger.

"How on earth did you happen to do that, Mortlake?" he snapped. "Those two shots alarmed those rascals, and now they're gone for good. It's most annoying."

"I appreciate your chagrin, my dear Bradbury," rejoined Mortlake suavely, "but accidents will happen, you know."

"Yes, and sometimes they happen most opportunely," was the sharp reply.

Mortlake said nothing. In silence they approached the house, but nothing save the pack of greasy cards, was found there to indicate the identity of its late occupants.

There was nothing to do but to return to the automobile. They found old Mr. Harding awaiting them eagerly. He showed no emotion on learning that Liam McAdams's captors had escaped just as their capture seemed certain.

On the drive back to Sandy Beach, the old banker and Mortlake occupied the front seat, while Liam McAdams and Lieut. Bradbury sat in the tonneau. As they skimmed along, Liam McAdams drew something from his pocket and showed it to the officer. It was an object that glistened in the wavering moonlight.

"It's a woman's hair comb!" cried the officer in amazement, as he regarded it.

"Hush, not so loud," warned Liam McAdams. "I picked it up where I had the struggle with the other Liam McAdams. It may prove a valuable clue."

CHAPTER 15.16.
MISSING SIDE-COMB.

Some days after the strange and exciting events just recorded, Mary Eliska burst like a whirlwind into the little room, —half work-shop, half study, —in which Liam McAdams was hard at work developing a problem in equilibrium. It was but a short time now to the day on which they were to report to the navy Board of Aviation at Hampton Roads, and submit their aerial craft to exhaustive tests. Both brother and sister had occupied their time in working like literal Trojans over the *Golden Butterfly*. But although every nut, bolt and tiniest fairy-like turn-buckle on the craft was in perfect order, Liam McAdams was still devoting the last moments to developing the balancing device to which he mainly pinned his hopes of besting the other craft.

From the newspapers they had been made aware that several types, bi-planes, monoplanes and freak designs were to compete, and Liam McAdams was not the boy to let lack of preparation stand in the way of success. Detectives and the local police had been set to work on the mysterious plot whose object had been to entrap the boy. But no result had come of their work. Incidentally, it had been found, when the auto which Liam McAdams had driven to the deserted house was towed back for repairs, that the tank had been punctured by some sharp instrument.

As for the clue of the brilliant-studded comb, Mary Eliska on examining it, declared it to be one of a pair of side-combs, which only complicated the mystery. Liam McAdams had thought of surrendering this clue to the police, but on thinking it over he decided not to. He had an idea in regard to that comb himself, and so had Mary Eliska, but it seemed too wild and preposterous a theory to submit to the intensely practical police of Sandy Beach.

Liam McAdams looked up from the paper-littered desk as Mary Eliska flung breathlessly into his sanctum. He knew that only unusual news would have led her to interrupt his work in which she was as keenly interested as he was.

"What is it, Sis?" he asked, "you look as excited as if the Statue of Liberty had paid us a visit and was now doing a song and dance on the front lawn."

"Oh, Liam McAdams, do be serious. Listen—who do you suppose has come back to Sandy Beach?"

"Not the least idea. Who?"

"Fanning Harding!"

"Fan Harding! The dickens!"

"Isn't it, and more than that, he is down at the Mortlake plant now. He is going to take up the *Cobweb*. And who do you think is to be his companion?"

"Give it up."

"Regina Mortlake!"

"Phew!" whistled the boy, "a new conquest for the irresistible Fanning, eh?"

"Don't be stupid," reproved Mary Eliska, severely, "I've been thinking it over and I've just hit on the solution. Fanning, or so I heard, took up aviation when he was in the west. You know he always had a hankering for it."

"Yes, I recollect his fake aeroplane that scared the life out of you," grinned Liam McAdams.

"Well," pursued Mary Eliska, not deigning to notice this remark, "I guess they decided that Mr. Mortlake would be a bit er—er—overweight isn't it called? so they sent for old Mr. Harding's son to manage the *Cobweb* at the tests."

"Jove, that must be it. Makes it rather awkward, though. Somehow I don't much fancy Master Fanning."

"As if we hadn't good reason to despise him. Hark! there goes the *Cobweb* now!"

A droning buzz was borne to their ears. Running to the window they saw the Mortlake aeroplane whiz by at a fair height. It was going fast and a male figure, tall and slight, was at the wheel. In the stern seat Regina Mortlake's rubicund aviation costume could be made out.

"Running to the window they saw the Mortlake aeroplane whiz by at a fair height."

"Fanning has certainly turned out to be a good driver of aeroplanes," commented Liam McAdams, as he watched; "see that flaw strike them! There! he brought the *Cobweb* through it like an old general of the upper regions."

Mary Eliska had to admit that Fanning Harding did seem to be an expert at his work; but she did it regretfully.

"He gives me the creeps," she volunteered.

"There's nothing creepy about his aeroplane work, though," laughed Liam McAdams, "I shouldn't have believed he could have picked up so much in such a short time."

But a bigger surprise lay in store for the young Stricklins. That afternoon they had, as visitors, no one less than Fanning Harding and Regina Mortlake. While Mary Eliska and the daughter of the designer of the Mortlake aeroplane chatted in one corner, Fanning placed his arm on Liam McAdams's shoulder and drew him out upon the veranda where Miss Stricklin sat with her embroidery.

"I know you don't like me, Liam McAdams, and you never did," he said insinuatingly, "but I've changed a lot since I was in Sandy Beach before. Let's let bygones be bygones and be friends again. More especially as in a few days we'll be pitted against each other at the naval tests."

"Of course, if you are genuinely sorry for all the harm you tried to do us, I've nothing more to say," said Liam McAdams, "I'm willing to be friends, but although I may forgive, it's going to be hard to forget."

"Oh, that will come in time," said Fanning, airily, "I'm a changed fellow since I went west."

But in spite of Fanning's protestations Liam McAdams could not help feeling a sensation of mistrust and suspicion toward the youth. There was something unnatural even in this sudden move toward friendship.

"It's ungenerous, ungentlemanly," Liam McAdams protested to himself; but somehow the feeling persisted that Fanning was not to be trusted.

"How prettily you do your hair," Mary Eliska was remarking to Regina Mortlake in the meantime.

She looked with genuine admiration at the glossy black waves which the other had drawn back over her ears in the French style.

"Oh, do you like it?" asked Regina eagerly, "I think its hideous. But you know I lost one of my combs and—but let's go and see what the boys are doing," she broke off suddenly, turning crimson and hastening to the porch. Once outside she plunged at once into conversation with the two boys, and Mary Eliska had no opportunity of picking up the dropped stitches of conversation. She caught herself puzzling over it. Why had Regina been so mortified, and apparently alarmed, when she had announced the loss of one of her side-combs? Right there a strange thought came into Mary Eliska's mind. The brilliant-studded comb that Liam McAdams had picked up! Could it be that—but no, the idea was too fantastic. In the pages of a book, perhaps, but not in real life. And yet—and yet—Mary Eliska, as she watched the graceful, dark-eyed girl talking with splendid animation, found herself wondering—and wondering.

The next day, just as Mary Eliska and Liam McAdams were starting out for a run to the Bancroft place, Fanning Harding and Regina Mortlake came whizzing up to the gate in the latter's big touring car—the one in which she had arrived in Sandy Beach. The machine was the gift of her father. It was a commodious, maroon-colored car, with a roomy tonneau and fore-doors and torpedo body of the latest type.

Beside it the Blue Bird looked somewhat small and insignificant. But Liam McAdams and Mary Eliska felt no embarrassment. On the contrary, they were quite certain the Blue Bird was the better car.

"Where are you off to?" asked Fanning in friendly tones, while Regina bowed and smiled very sweetly to Mary Eliska.

"Going to take a spin in the direction of the Bancroft's," said Liam McAdams, starting his car.

"What fun," cried Regina Mortlake, "so are we. Let's race."

"I don't believe in racing," rejoined Mary Eliska.

"No, of course it is dangerous," said Fanning, "I guess Liam McAdams is a bit timid with that old car, too. Besides it's all in the way you handle a machine;"

Liam McAdams flushed angrily.

"I guess this 'old car,' as you call it, could give yours a tussle if it comes down to it," he said sharply.

Mary Eliska tugged his sleeve. She saw where this would lead too. She saw, too, that Fanning was anxious to provoke Liam McAdams into a race. Presumably he was anxious to humiliate the boy in Regina Mortlake's eyes.

"Well, do you want to race then?" asked Regina, provokingly, her fine eyes flashing, "there's a bit of road beyond here that's quite broad and one hardly ever meets anything."

Now Liam McAdams was averse, as are most boys, to being thought a "'fraid cat," and the almost openly taunting air with which the girl looked at him angered him almost to desperation.

"Very well," he said, "we'll race you when we get to that bit of road."

"Oh, Liam McAdams, what are you saying," pleaded Mary Eliska, "it's all a trick to humiliate us. The Blue Bird can't possibly keep up with their car, and———." But Liam McAdams checked her impatiently.

"You don't think I'm going to allow Fanning Harding to scare me out of anything, do you?" he demanded in as near to a rough tone of voice as he had ever used to his sister.

Poor Mary Eliska felt the stinging tears rise. But she said nothing. The next moment the cars began to glide off, running side by side on the broad country road. Faster and faster they went. The speed got into Liam McAdams's head. He began to let the Blue Bird out, and then Fanning Harding, for the first time seemingly, realized what a formidable opponent he was placed in contact with.

As they reached the bit of road previously agreed upon as a race course, the banker's son stopped his machine and hailed Liam McAdams to do the same.

"Tell you what we'll do to make this interesting," he said, "we'll change machines. Or are you afraid to drive mine?"

"I'll drive it," said Liam McAdams recklessly, in spite of Mary Eliska's quavered: "Say no."

"Good. That will give us a fine opportunity to compare the two machines," cried Fanning Harding.

He jumped from the bigger car and handed out his companion. Then, for the fraction of a minute, he bent, monkey wrench in hand, above one of the forward wheels.

"A bolt had worked loose," he explained.

"Come on Mary Eliska," urged Liam McAdams, and against her better judgment Mary Eliska, as many another girl has done before her, obeyed the summons, although an intuition warned her that something was not just right.

"Ready?" cried Fanning from the Blue Bird.

"All ready"; hailed back Liam McAdams, who found the spark and throttle adjustments of the maroon car perfectly simple.

"Then—go!" almost screamed Regina Mortlake. Mary Eliska was looking at her at the moment, and she was almost certain she saw a look of hatred flash across the girl's countenance. But before she could give the matter any more thought the maroon car shot forward. Close alongside came the Blue Bird.

Motor hood to motor hood they thundered along at a terrific pace. The road shot by on either side like a brown and green blur.

"Faster!" Mary Eliska heard Fanning shout somewhere out of the dust cloud.

Whi-z-z-z-z-z-z! It was wild, exciting—dangerous!

"Liam McAdams," gasped Mary Eliska, "if——"

But she got no further. There was a sudden soul-shaking shock. The front of the car seemed to plough into the ground. A rending, splitting noise filled the air.

The car stopped short, and its boy and girl occupants were hurtled, like projectiles, into the storm center of disaster.

CHAPTER 15.17.
JIMSY'S SUSPICIONS ARE ROUSED.

Mary Eliska, after a moment in which the entire world seemed spinning about her crazily, sat up. She had landed in a ditch, and partially against a clump of springy bushes, which had broken the force of her fall. In fact, she presently realized, that by one of those miraculous happenings that no one can explain, she was unhurt.

The automobile, its hood crushed in like so much paper, had skidded into the same ditch in which Mary Eliska lay, and bumped into a small tree which it had snapped clean off. But the obstacle had stopped it.

One wheel lay in the roadway. Evidently it had come off while the machine was at top speed, and caused the crash. But Mary Eliska noted all these things automatically. She was looking about her for Liam McAdams.

From a clump of bushes close by there came a low groan of pain. The girl sprang erect instantly, forgetting her own bruises and shaken nerves in this sign that her brother was in pain. In the meantime, Fanning and Regina Mortlake had stopped and turned the Blue Bird. They came back to the scene of the wreck with every expression of concern on their faces.

Liam McAdams lay white and still in the midst of the brush into which he had been hurled. There was a great cut across his forehead, and in reply to Mary Eliska's anxious inquiries, the lad, who was conscious, said that he thought that his ankle had been broken. Mary Eliska touched the ankle he indicated, and light as her fingers fell upon it, the boy uttered an anguished moan.

"Oh, gee, Mary Eliska!" he cried bravely, screwing up his face in his endeavor not to make an outcry, "that hurts like blazes."

"Poor boy," breathed Mary Eliska tenderly, "I'm so sorry."

"I'm so glad you're not hurt, Sis," said the boy, "I don't matter much. I wish you could stop this bleeding above my eye, though."

Mary Eliska ripped off a flounce of her petticoat and formed it into a bandage.

"Can I help. I'm so sorry."

The voice was Fanning Harding's. He stood behind her with Regina at his side.

"Oh, how dreadful." exclaimed the dark-eyed girl, with a shudder, "my—my poor car."

"And my poor brother," snapped out Mary Eliska, indignantly, "if it hadn't been for your stupid idea of racing this wouldn't have happened. I just knew we'd have an accident."

"It's too bad," repeated Fanning, "but can't I do something?"

"Yes, get me some water. There's a brook a little way down this road. You'll find a tin cup under the rear seat in our machine."

Fanning, perhaps glad to escape Mary Eliska's righteous anger, hastened off on the errand. Regina flounced down on a stone by the roadside and moaned.

"Oh, this is fearful. Why can't we get a doctor? Oh, my poor car. It will never be the same again."

"Nonsense," said Mary Eliska, sharply, "it can easily be repaired. But you don't think I'm worrying about your car now, do you?"

"I don't know, I'm sure," quavered Regina, "I know it's all terrible. Is your brother badly hurt?"

"No. Fortunately he only has this cut in his head and a broken ankle. It might have been far worse."

Regina wandered away. Somehow, she felt that Mary Eliska had taken a sudden dislike to her. She sauntered toward the car. Suddenly she stopped and her large eyes grew larger. In the middle of the road, just as they had been hurled from Liam McAdams's pocket, lay a side-comb studded with brilliants and an old battered wallet.

"Oh!" cried the girl, with an exclamation that was half a sob, "oh, what good fortune. So, he was keeping that as evidence against me, eh? Well, perhaps this accident was providential, after all."

She picked up the comb and then turned her attention to the wallet. Giving a quick glance around to see that she was unobserved the girl plunged her white fingers into the pocket case. They encountered something crisp and crackly. She drew the object out.

"A twenty-dollar bill!" she exclaimed wonderingly, "and nothing else. I wonder if this can have anything to do with———."

She was turning it over curiously as she spoke. Suddenly a red spot flamed up in her either cheek.

"It's marked with a red round O," she exclaimed, "what a bit of evidence. So, Master Liam McAdams, you were planning to unmask me by that side-comb, were you? Well, I shall play the same trick on you with this bill."

Fanning Harding was coming back at that moment with the cup full of water. The girl checked him with an excited gesture.

"Fortune has played into our hands," she cried, "look here!"

"Well, what is it?" asked Fanning, rather testily.

"This bill. Don't you see it's one of the stolen ones. Look at the red circle upon the back."

"Jove! So it is. But, what, how———"

"Hush! Don't talk so loud. This wallet, which contained it, was jolted out of Liam McAdams's pocket when he was hurled from the machine. The wallet and—and something else. But don't you see what power that gives us?"

"No. I confess I'm stupid, but———"

"Oh, how dense you boys are," exclaimed Regina, with an impatient stamp of the foot, "don't you see that this bill will come pretty close to proving Liam McAdams a thief, if we want to use it that way? You are a witness that I found it in his wallet which had been jerked out of his pocket. Isn't that enough?"

"Well, men have been sent to prison on less evidence," said Fanning, with a shrug; "but I've got to hurry up with this water or they'll suspect something. I'll talk more with you about this later on. Your father and mine need every bit of fighting material they can get hold of, if we are to win the big prize for the Mortlake aeroplane."

A shadow fell athwart the road as Fanning, an evil smile on his flabby, pale face, hastened down into the depression in which Liam McAdams, with Mary Eliska bending above him, still lay. The girl looked swiftly up. A big, red aeroplane was hovering on high. Presently one of its occupants, a girl peered over the edge. The next minute she turned and said something in an excited tone to her companion. The aeroplane began to drop rapidly. In a few seconds it came to earth in the roadway, not a stone's throw from the wrecked auto and its uninjured Blue Bird comrade.

The new arrivals were Jimsy and Jess. They had set out on a sky cruise to the Stricklin home, and Jess's bright eyes had espied the confusion in the road beneath them as they flew over. The swift descent had been the result.

Hardly noticing Regina, who regarded them curiously, the young sky sailors hastened toward the spot in which, from on high, they had seen the injured boy lying. A warm wave of gratitude swept over Mary Eliska as she looked up at the sound of footsteps and saw who the newcomers were. In an emergency like the present one she could not wish for two better helpers than the Bancrofts.

Jess and Jimsy had been off on a visit and so had not been made aware of the fact that Fanning had returned to Sandy Beach. Their astonishment on seeing him may be imagined. Jess regarded him with a tinge of disdain, but the frank and open Jimsy grasped the outstretched hand which the son of the Sandy Beach banker extended to him. Evidently Fanning's policy was one of conciliation and he meant to press it to the uttermost.

"Well, this is a nice fix, isn't it?" murmured Liam McAdams, smiling pluckily, as the Bancrofts came toward him with pitying looks, "but where in the world did you come from?"

"From yonder sky," grinned Jimsy, trying, not very successfully, to assume an inanely cheerful tone, "not badly hurt, old man, are you?"

"No. Just this wallop over my eye and a twisted ankle. Thought it was broken at first, but I guess it isn't."

"How did it all happen?"

Mary Eliska explained. Jimsy whistled.

"What make of machine is your car, Fanning?" he asked.

"A Dashaway," was the rejoinder.

"The same type as ours," exclaimed young Bancroft. "They are the best and stanchest cars on the market. I can't understand how such an accident could have happened, unless——," he paused and then went on resolutely, "unless the car had been tampered with."

"What an idea!" shrilled Regina, who had now joined the group, "you don't surely mean to insinuate? Why the damage done to my poor machine will cost a lot to repair, and——."

"Don't mind if I have a look at it, do you?" asked Jimsy in his most careless manner, "I'm interested, you know. A motor bug is what dad calls me."

"Well, I——," began Fanning.

But Regina interrupted him with strange eagerness.

"Oh, by no means. Look at it all you wish. I only hope you can find some explanation for this regrettable accident."

"I hope so, too," said Jimsy gravely, "but in the meantime let's make Liam McAdams comfortable in the Blue Bird. Then, if we can fix your car up, Miss——."

"Oh, I beg your pardon," struck in Mary Eliska, "Jimsy, this is Miss Mortlake, Fanning you know. Miss Mortlake these are our particular chums, Jess and Jimsy Bancroft."

"Indeed. I have heard a great deal about you," vouchsafed Regina, as Jimsy and Fanning lifted Liam McAdams and carried him to the Blue Bird and made him comfortable on the cushions.

"I'll attend to the other car," volunteered Fanning, readily. But Jimsy was not to be put off in this way.

"I'd like to have a look at it before we try to put the wheel back," he said; "it may be a useful bit of experience."

"All right," assented Fanning, rather sullenly, "if you insist; but I think we ought to hurry back at once."

"By all means," quoth the bland Jimsy, "but—hullo, what's this!" He was stooping over the wheels now. "This wheel has been tampered with. The holding cap must have been partially unscrewed. Look here!"

He held up the brass cap which was supposed to keep the wheel on its axle.

"Some of the threads have been filed out of this," he said positively.

"Let's have a look," said Fanning eagerly. He leaned over and scrutinized the part which Jimsy was examining.

"Those threads haven't been filed," he said, "they've worn. Very careless not to have noticed that. It's surprising that it held on so long."

"It might have held for a year if the car was run at average speed," said Jimsy slowly, "but the minute it was raced beyond its normal rate the weak part would have gone."

"What do you mean to imply?" blustered Fanning, though his face was pale and his breath came quickly.

"I don't imply anything," said Jimsy slowly, "but I'd like to know who filed this cap down."

"Pshaw! You are dreaming," scoffed Fanning.

A dull flush overspread Jimsy's ordinarily placid face.

"After a while I'll wake up, maybe," he said, "and then———." He stopped.

"Well, let's see about getting Liam McAdams home," he said, "Mary Eliska, you can drive the Blue Bird and Fanning and Miss Mortlake can sit in the other machine as soon as we get the wheel back. Then Jess and I will go ahead in the *Red Dragon Fly* and break the news to Miss Stricklin."

Shortly thereafter the two autos moved slowly off, while the aeroplane raced above them, going at a far faster speed.

Regina turned to Fanning.

"Do you think that odious boy suspects anything?" she asked.

"I guess he does. But he can't prove a thing, so that's all the good it will do him," scoffed Fanning, "and besides, if they get too gay we've got a marked bill that will make it very unpleasant for a certain young aviator."

CHAPTER 15.18.
A BOLT PROM THE BLUE.

The broken ankle which both Mary Eliska and Liam McAdams had dreaded, turned out to be only a sprain—affecting the same unlucky ankle that had been injured on the desert. This was a big relief, as a broken joint would have kept Liam McAdams effectually out of the aeroplane tests, as part of the machinery of the *Golden Butterfly* was controlled by foot pressure.

A council of war was in progress on the porch of the Stricklin home. The participants were the inseparable four. Mary Eliska and Liam McAdams, the latter with his injured foot on a stool, and Jess and Jimsy. They had been discussing the case against Mortlake and Fanning Harding. All agreed that things looked as black against them as could be, but—where was the proof? There was not an iota of evidence against them that would hold water an instant before impartial judges.

"It's positively depressing," sighed Jess, "to know that people have done mean things and not be able to get an atom of proof against them."

"Never mind," said Mary Eliska, "all's well that ends well. We start for Hampton tomorrow and once there they won't have a chance to try any more tricks. Luckily all their mean plans and schemes have ended in nothing. Liam McAdams will be as good as ever by tomorrow, won't you boy?"

Liam McAdams nodded.

"I've got to be," he said, decisively; "those tests have got to bring the *Golden Butterfly* out on top."

"And they will, too," declared Jess, with a nod of her dark head, "that poky old Harding and his crowd won't have a word to say when they are over."

"Let's hope not. It doesn't do to be too confident, you know," smiled Mary Eliska, throwing an arm round the waist of her enthusiastic friend.

"As the man said when he thought he'd lassoed a horse but found he'd roped his own foot instead;" grinned Jimsy, "but, say, what's all this coming up the road?"

Sure enough, a small crowd of ten or a dozen persons could be seen approaching the Stricklin house. They were coming from the direction of the Mortlake plant. In advance, as they drew nearer, could be seen Mortlake himself, with a tall man by his side and Fanning Harding. The men behind seemed to be workmen from the plant.

"Wonder where they can be going to?" queried Jess, idly. For a few moments more they watched the advancing throng, and then Jimsy cried suddenly:

"Why, that's Sheriff Lawley with Mortlake, and there's Si Hardscrabble the constable, right behind them, what can they be after?"

"Clues," laughed Mary Eliska, but the laugh faded on her lips as she exclaimed:

"Why—why, they're coming here!"

"Here!" echoed the others.

"Yes, that's what they are;" confirmed Jimsy, as the procession passed inside the wicket gate and came up the graveled pathway toward the house.

Sheriff Lawley had on his stiffest professional air and Si Hardscrabble's chest was puffed out like a pouter pigeon. On it glistened, like a newly scoured pie-plate, the emblem of his authority—an immense nickel star as big as a sunflower.

"Liam McAdams here?" demanded the sheriff in a high, official tone. He had known Liam McAdams since he was a boy, but seemed to think it a part of his majestic duties to appear not to know him.

"Miss Stricklin—I—that is—er—this is a very unpleasant business—I hope———."

It was Mortlake stammering. He mopped the sweat from his forehead as the sheriff interrupted him.

"That will do Mr. Mortlake. Leave the discharge of my official duties to me, please."

"That's right, by heck," chorused the constable, approvingly.

"What's the matter, sheriff?" asked Liam McAdams, easily. As yet not a glint of the truth of this visit had dawned upon him.

"Why, Liam McAdams, it's about that thar robbery at Galloways t'other night," sputtered the sheriff, looking rather embarrassed, "we've come to the conclusion that you know more about it than you told, and———," he dived into a pocket and drew out an official-looking paper, "an' I got a warrant fer your arrest."

"My arrest!" stammered Liam McAdams, "why you must be mad. What on earth do I know about it?"

"Nothin', only you happened to hev' a marked bill in your pocket t'other day," shot out the sheriff, triumphantly. "Fanning Harding step forward. What do you know about this?"

"Only this, that Miss Regina Mortlake after the automobile accident found a wallet belonging to Liam McAdams in the roadway. She opened it and discovered that it contained a marked twenty-dollar bill answering the description of one of the bills stolen from the Galloway farm house. She made me a witness of the find, and in line with my duty as a citizen, I thought it best to expose the thief, and———."

Fanning stopped and turned pale as a boyish figure sprang toward him with doubled fists. He shrank back, turning a sickly yellow.

"You contemptible sneak!" shouted Jimsy, whose fists it had been that threatened Fanning.

"Sheriff, I claim protection," said the cowardly youth, shrinking behind the official.

"Now, no fisticuffs here," warned the sheriff, "my only duty now is to preserve order and arrest Liam McAdams on a charge of grand larceny."

Mary Eliska turned white and sick. The veranda floor seemed to heave up and down like sea waves under her feet. But in the next few seconds she regained control of herself.

"Why such a charge is absurd," she declared vehemently, "this is simply spite on the part of our rivals in the aeroplane business."

"Don't know nuthin' about that," reiterated the sheriff, stolidly, "the warrant has bin sworn out an' it's my duty ter execute it. Constable, arrest that boy. Ef his foot is too bad hurt to walk, git a rig an' drive him in ter town."

Hardscrabble, flushed and swollen with importance, stepped forward. He was about to place his hand on Liam McAdams's shoulder, but the boy checked him.

"No need for that. Mary Eliska, if you'll have them get out the auto, we'll drive into town at once."

Mortlake stepped forward.

"Stricklin," he said, "I hope you don't hold this against me. I———."

"I don't wish to speak to you, sir," shot out Liam McAdams, for the first time betraying indignation, "let that be your answer."

"But I—really, I'm sorry to—Bancroft you'll listen———"

But Jimsy turned his back on the flushed, overfed man whose eyes could not look him in the face.

"In the future, please do us the honor not to speak to us," he said, his voice vibrant with anger.

"Why, if I may ask?"

Jimsy flashed round.

"Because, if you don't pay attention to my request, I'm afraid I shall be unable to curb my desire to land both my fists in your eyes."

Mortlake drew back and turned away among his workmen. He did not speak again.

Before long the auto came round. In the meantime, Mary Eliska had taken upon herself the task of consoling Miss Stricklin. Poor Aunt Sarah, she took the news very hardly. It was all Mary Eliska could do to keep her from rushing out upon the porch and denouncing the entire assemblage.

"That Mortlake," she cried, "I'd like to scratch his eyes out."

The proceedings in Sandy Beach before the local magistrate, Ephraim Gray, were brief. Isaac Galloway, the farmer, told of the robbery and of his knowledge that the marked bill was among the money. He followed this up by relating the fact that Liam McAdams had been in the house in the afternoon and had seen the safe.

Then came Fanning, and to the girl's astonishment, Regina Mortlake, both of whom swore to finding the marked bill in the wallet in the road.

"Do you deny that this was your wallet?" asked the magistrate, holding up the leather case after he had examined the marked bill.

"I do," declared Liam McAdams in a firm voice.

"What! you did not drop it?"

"I dropped it, but it is not mine," was the stout reply.

"Then what was it doing in your possession?"

"Do I have to answer that question, now?"

"It will be better to—yes."

"Well, then, I found it in the cellar of a house to which I was lured by two men whom I am confident were employed by this hound Mortlake."

"Be careful," warned the magistrate, "Mr. Mortlake is a respected member of this community. Your display of ill-will does you no good. As for your story of how you found the wallet you can tell that to a jury later on. My present duty is to hold you in bonds of $2,500 for trial."

A deep breath, like a sigh, went through the courtroom. In the midst of it an active, upright figure stepped forward. It was Lieut. Bradbury, who had arrived in the courtroom just in time to hear the concluding words. But he had already been informed of the facts, for the story was on every tongue in the village.

"I am prepared to offer that bail," he said.

But Mary Eliska had been before him. With her mine shares she had a good bank account and was able to offer cash security. This was accepted almost before the young officer reached the judge's desk. Mary Eliska thanked the lieutenant with a look. She could not trust herself to speak.

"Of course," said the magistrate, "the fact that the defendant is under bonds will prohibit his leaving the state. That is understood."

Mortlake nudged Fanning Harding. This was what they had cunningly calculated on. With Liam McAdams safely bottled up in New York state, it would be manifestly impossible for him to take part in the contests at Hampton in Virginia. While they conversed in low, eager tones, Mary Eliska and Lieutenant Bradbury could be seen talking in another corner. Court had been adjourned, but the curious crowd still lingered. Jess and Jimsy stood by Liam McAdams, fencing off the inquisitive villagers and would-be sympathizers. The whole thing had taken place so rapidly that they all felt dazed and bewildered. Suddenly the thought of what his detention meant dawned upon Liam McAdams.

"We'll be out of the race for the naval contracts," he almost moaned.

It was the first sign he had shown of giving way. But Mary Eliska was at his side in an instant.

"No, we won't, Liam McAdams," she exclaimed, her eyes brilliant with excitement, "I've asked Lieutenant Bradbury, and he says it's unusual, but he doesn't see why a woman should be barred from flying in the contests. There's nothing in the rules about it, anyway."

"Oh, Mary Eliska!" gasped Jess, "you would———"

"Do anything within reason to balk that Mortlake crowd in their trickery and deceit," declared Mary Eliska, with flashing eyes.

"And we'll stand by you," announced Jimsy, stepping forward; "we'll go with you to Hampton, and we'll bring home the bacon!"

The inexcusable slang went unreproved. Jimsy's enthusiasm was contagious.

"Thank you, Jimsy," said Mary Eliska, winking to keep back the tears that would come, "we—we—I—that—is———"

"We'll beat them out yet. The bunch of sneaks, and it's my opinion that Mortlake himself knows all about who robbed that safe!" cried Jimsy, not taking the trouble to sink his voice.

He faced defiantly about and caught Mortlake's eye. It was instantly averted, and catching Fanning by the arm he hastened from the courtroom.

"I wonder what mischief those young cubs are hatching up now?" he said, as the two hastened off, bending their steps toward old Mr. Harding's bank.

"It doesn't make much difference," chuckled Fanning, "we've got that contract nailed down and delivered now."

CHAPTER 15.19.
THE GATHERING OF THE MAN-BIRDS.

The aeroplanes—a dozen in all, that had been selected by various naval "sharps" from all over the widely distributed portions of the country for the weeding out of the best type— were quartered in a broad meadow not far from the town of Hampton. The locality had been chosen as removed from the reach of the ordinary run of curiosity seekers, who had flocked from all parts of the country to be present at the first tests of aeroplanes as actual naval adjuncts.

Sheds had been provided for the accommodation of each type. And above each shed was the name of the aeroplane it housed, printed in small letters. One of the first things that Mortlake and Fanning Harding proceeded to do on their arrival at this "bivouac" was to make a tour of the row of sheds in search of the Stricklin machine. But to their joy, apparently, no shed housed it.

There were machines of dozens of other types, monoplanes, bi-planes, machines of the helicopter type, and a few devices based on the parachute principle. But no Stricklin. The names the various machines bore were weird: The *Sky Pilot*, the *Cloud Chaser*, the *Star Bug*, the *Moon Mounter*, the *Aerial Auto*, the *Heavenly Harvester*, and some titles even more far-fetched graced the sheds, so that it was small wonder that in this maze of high-sounding names a shed at the far end of the row bearing the obscure title of Nameless missed the scrutiny of Mortlake and his aide.

"We've beaten them to a standstill this time," said Mortlake with intense conviction, "I feel that the *Motor Hornet* has the contest cinched."

The *Motor Hornet* was the name that had been bestowed on the machine which Liam McAdams had poetically dubbed the *Silver Cobweb*.

The shed of the mysterious Nameless was the only one of the long row that did not buzz with activity all that day, which was one assigned to preparation for the contests of the morrow. All the other aeroplane hives fairly radiated activity. Freakish-looking men hovered about their weird helicopters and lovingly polished brass and tested engines. The reek of gasoline and burning lubricants hung heavily over the field. Reporters darted here and there followed by panting photographers bearing elephantine cameras and bulging boxes of plates, for the metropolitan press was "playing up" the tests which were expected to produce a definite aerial type of machine for the United States Navy.

But even the most inquisitive of the news-getters failed to get anything from within the mysterious realms occupied presumably by the Nameless. Its roller-fitted double doors remained closed, and no sign of activity appeared about it.

This was conceded on all sides to be extraordinary, but all the speculation which was indulged in failed to elucidate the mystery.

"The Nameless is also the Ungetatable," joked one reporter as he and a companion passed by.

But if anyone had been about late that night, long after the aviators who had quarters at the hotels in town had quitted the field, he would have seen three figures—two girls and a boy, steal across the field from an auto which had driven up almost noiselessly, and unfasten the formidable padlocks on the doors of the Nameless's dwelling place.

This done they vanished within the shed for a short time, and presently thereafter a dark and strangely shaped form slowly emerged from the shed. It was the *Golden Butterfly*, and the trio of young folks were, as you have already guessed, Mary Eliska, Jess and Jimsy. They crawled noiselessly on board, and a few minutes later, with a soft whirring of the propellers, the *Butterfly* shut down for precaution›s sake to half speed, sped almost noiselessly upward.

The night was a calm one. Hardly a leaf was stirring and the stars shone like steel points in a cloudless sky. The aeroplane, after it had attained a few hundred feet, seemed to merge into the dark background of night sky. Unless one had known of its flight it would have taken a sharp pair of eyes to have discerned it.

"Say, this is glorious. It's like being pirates or—or something," said Jimsy enthusiastically, as soon as they had reached a height where they felt they could talk without difficulty.

"It's great after being penned up all day at that hotel," agreed Mary Eliska, who was at the wheel, "how beautiful the stars are. Poor Liam McAdams, I wonder how he is getting along?"

"You know he was doing splendidly when we left, and he has our telegrams by this time," said Jess; "oh, Mary Eliska, I'm so glad that the board of naval aviation said you could fly the *Golden Butterfly*."

"Oh, weren't they taken aback, though, at the idea?" chuckled Jimsy; "I thought that dignified old officer would fall out of his chair at the idea of a girl daring to run an aeroplane. I'll bet if there'd been anything in the rules about it, Mary Eliska, they'd have barred you."

"I think so, too," laughed Mary Eliska, "but, luckily, there wasn't. As Lieut. Bradbury pointed out, it was a case of an emergency. It isn't as if I'd tried to 'butt in,' as you say, Jimsy."

"Well, I'm sure I don't see why a girl shouldn't run an aeroplane just as well as a boy. You certainly showed that you could, Mary Eliska, when you raced that train back in Nevada."

"In years to come," prophesied Mary Eliska, "I dare say women as aviators will be as common as men. I don't see why not. Ten years ago, a woman who ran an automobile would have been laughed at, if not insulted. But now, why lots of women run their own cars and nobody thinks of even turning his head."

"Hear! hear!" cried Jimsy, "I declare I feel like a lone man at a suffragette meeting."

"Then conduct yourself as if you were actually in that dangerous position," laughed Mary Eliska.

The girl's spirits were rising now under the excitement of the night ride. On the advice of Lieut. Bradbury the party from Sandy Beach had kept closely to their rooms at the hotel all that day. It was at the officer's advice, too, that their shed had been labeled the Nameless.

"If Mortlake was, as I begin to think, concerned in these attacks on you," the officer had said, "I think it would be advisable not to appear any more than necessary. Let him think that you are out of the race."

Accordingly, the *Butterfly* had been transported secretly and placed in her shed at night. The secret had been well guarded and, as we know, neither Mortlake nor Fanning Harding had even an inkling that the Stricklin machine was far—very far from being out of the race.

On and on through the night throbbed the *Golden Butterfly*, making fast time. At last, they decided that it was time to return. The object of the trip, to see that all was in running order, had been accomplished. Nothing remained to do now but to wait for the morrow and what it would bring forth. The nature of the tests had been carefully guarded, and not one of the contestants knew anything about what they were to be 'til the hour came at which they would be announced from the judges' boat.

Suddenly, as they neared the environs of Hampton and the glare of electric lights could be seen on the sky, Jimsy gave a cry and pointed down below. They were flying pretty low, and in a road beneath them they could see an automobile. Its headlights shone brightly but it had stopped. All at once a sharp shout for help winged upward.

"Hullo!" exclaimed Jimsy, "somebody's in trouble down there. Maybe we'd better descend. That is, if you girls aren't scared?"

"Um—well," began Jess, but Mary Eliska interrupted her:

"Jess Bancroft, I'm ashamed of you. It's our duty to help out if we can."

"At least if it gets too hot, we can always retreat," muttered Jimsy.

Under the covering of one of the lockers was a revolver. Under Mary Eliska's directions Jimsy found it. The next moment they were descending rapidly. With hardly more noise than an alighting night bird, they dropped into the lane in which the auto was stalled. As they touched ground the sound of harsh voices caught their ears:

"Shell out now, if you don't want to be half-killed!"

"Yes, come on. Hand over your coin, or it'll be the worse for you," chimed in another ruffianly voice.

"Good gracious!" gasped Jess, "it's a hold up!"

But now another voice came through the darkness.

"I suppose you fellows know that you are breaking the law and in danger of imprisonment if you are caught?"

"Now, what is there that's familiar about that voice?" puzzled Mary Eliska, racking her brains.

"Aw, don't preach sermons to us, boss," came one of the gruff voices, "we needs the money and we ain't particular how we gits it, see. Fork over now, or——"

The sentence was never completed. There was a sudden flash and a sharp report. The man in the automobile had defended himself apparently, for there came the sound of a heavy body falling, and then his voice:

"I hope I haven't hurt you badly; but you brought it on yourself, as your companion can witness."

The next instant, and just as Jimsy sprang forward from the clump of brush at the roadside which had hitherto concealed the aero party—there came a heavy rush of feet toward them. A dark form, running pantingly, appeared.

Jimsy, with a dexterous outward thrust of his foot, tripped the fleeing man, who came down heavily in the center of the road and started howling for mercy.

In the meantime, the occupant of the automobile had climbed down, and detaching one of the lamps, examined the wounded man lying in the road beyond Jimsy's capture. As the rays of his light swung to and fro they hovered for an instant on Mary Eliska's white, strained face leaning forward above Jimsy's prisoner, upon whose neck the redoubtable young Bancroft was now sitting.

"Miss Stricklin, by all that's wonderful!" came an amazed voice.

There was no mistaking that bold, straightforward voice now. It was James Bell, the mining magnate and their kind friend.

"Oh, Mr. Bell," cried Mary Eliska, half hysterically, "we're so glad you've come!"

CHAPTER 15.20.
AN UNEXPECTED MEETING.

As Mr. Bell spoke, the fellow who had apparently been shot, leaped to his feet and was about to make off, but the Westerner's iron hand seized him by the scruff of the neck, and brought him up "all standing." Simultaneously, Jimsy's captive gave a wrench and a twist and would have escaped but for Mary Eliska.

The girl seized a small nickeled wrench out of the *Golden Butterfly*. In the dark it looked not unlike a pistol.

"You'd b-b-b-better stay w-w-w-where you are," said Mary Eliska, in a voice which, though rather shaky, was still courageous.

The fellow took the hint, and just then Mr. Bell came up with his capture, who had merely been "playing possum." The two men were thoroughly cowed, and were trembling violently.

"Don't be hard on us guv'ner," wailed one of them; "we didn't mean no harm."

"No; it was just a little joke," protested Jimsy's prisoner, who was standing in the rays of the detached auto light, thoroughly subdued.

"It's a joke that's liable to cost you dear," commented Mr. Bell. "Jimsy," he added, for by this time recognition and greetings had passed between the mining magnate and Jess and Jimsy, "Jimsy, have you got a bit of rope handy, my boy?"

Jimsy rummaged in the *Golden Butterfly's* tool and supply locker and presently unearthed a coil of fine cotton cord of stout texture. This was speedily applied to the hands of the two men, and loose thongs placed about their legs.

While this work was going forward Mary Eliska had been scrutinizing the faces of the two prisoners with a startled look. There was something very familiar about both of them. All at once it flashed across her where she had encountered them before. They were the two men who had held up Jess and herself in the road to the Galloway farm that eventful afternoon on which they had taken refuge from the storm.

She whispered to Jess her suspicions. Her chum instantly confirmed them. Here was news indeed. After the men had been tied and placed in the tonneau of Mr. Bell's car, Mary Eliska called a council of war. In a few words she told Mr. Bell of all that had happened since they had returned to the East, and narrated the part the two prisoners had played in it.

"Good heavens, just to think I've come to the tame and effete east to plunge into the midst of such an exciting mix-up," laughed Mr. Bell, "I was in Roanoke seeing about the shipment of some supplies when I saw, in a newspaper, that the contests for the naval contract were to take place here. I had had no idea from your letters that they were so near at hand. As I had some time to spare, I thought I'd run over to Hampton in my machine and see how you made out."

"And we providentially happened to fly across you!" cried Jimsy. "Truth is stranger than fiction, after all."

"But what are we to do with those two rascals now that we have caught them?" wondered Mary Eliska; "if we take them into Hampton and turn them over to the authorities Mortlake will know of it and may make more trouble. I wonder if they know much about him and his schemes. I recollect now that I've seen them hanging about his aeroplane plant. I couldn't call to mind then where I had seen them before, but I suppose the shock of coming upon them so unexpectedly tonight jogged my memory."

"You say that they were hanging about Mortlake's place?" asked Mr. Bell, in an interested tone.

"Yes, I'm sure of it," repeated Mary Eliska; "I'm certain of it now."

"We'll soon find out," said Mr. Bell in his old determined manner. He approached the car in which the two bound captives were still huddled.

"Now, you fellows," he said in stern voice, "you know better than I do, most likely, what the penalty for attempted highway robbery is in the State of Virginia."

"Oh, guv'ner, don't turn us over to the police," wailed one of the men, none other, in fact, than our old acquaintance, Joey Eccles. His companion, the angular and lanky Slim, remained silent.

"I want you to answer my questions truthfully," snapped out the Westerner, "after that I'll see what I'll do with you. Now then—do you know a man named Mortlake?"

"Y-y-y-yus, guv'ner," stammered the redoubtable Joey.

"Good. You came here with him?"

"Well, what if we did?" growled the hitherto silent Slim. Paying no attention to him Mr. Bell went on, while his young companions pressed eagerly about him.

"What did you come for?"

Joey seemed about to speak but Slim growled something in a low tone to him, and he was silent.

"Come, are you going to answer?" demanded Mr. Bell.

No reply.

"Very well, I'll drive into Hampton and see if the Chief of Police can't get more out of you."

The mining magnate made a step toward the car as if he were about to carry out his threat. This was too much for Joey's composure.

"We came here with Mortlake to do a little job fer him guv'ner," he sputtered out.

"Oh, you did, eh? Well, what was the nature of that employment?"

"To disable one of them flying machines."

"Which one?"

"One that belonged to the Stricklin kids. Mortlake said he'd make it worth our while—and—no, you can't stop me, Slim—and then when we couldn't find the machine we was to bust up he turned us loose without a cent of the money he promised us. We was broke, and———"

"And so, you thought you'd replenish your pockets by holding up some automobilist or traveler, eh? Humph, you're a nice pair."

"You ain't goin' ter give us up guv'ner? I told you the honest truth, guv'ner. Didn't I, Slim?"

"Yep," was the grunted reply; "and now Mister What's-Yer-Name, what are you going ter do with us?"

"I'm going to take you on a trip," was the astonishing reply.

"On a trip, guv'ner," stammered Joey, all his fears lively once more.

"Yes, on a trip."

The younger members of this strange roadside party stepped forward. As they advanced into the glare of the detached headlight, Joey and his companions saw them. Both men turned away and seemed much embarrassed.

"What are you going to do, Mr. Bell?" asked Mary Eliska, eagerly. The mining man's manner had become almost mysterious.

"My dear, little girl," said James Bell, "can you trust me?"

"Why, of course," came in a chorus.

"Well, then, you'll let me work this thing out my own way and I'll guarantee that things will be straightened out for everybody—are you willing to let me do this and ask no questions 'til the proper time?"

"Yes," came in a positive chant of assent.

"Very well, then. You fly back to your shed. I'll continue into town. You may not see me for some time. But don't worry. I've got this job in hand now and I'll see it through."

"We trust you absolutely," said Mary Eliska, "and you'll trust us?"

"To the last ditch," said the Westerner vehemently, "and now as there's no time to be lost, we'll go our respective ways. By the way, what time does the first test come off?"

"We don't know yet; but some time before noon. It is rumored that it will be an easy one. They'll work up to the difficult flights by degrees," volunteered Jimsy.

"Good. I'd like to have all the time possible as I wish to do what I have to do thoroughly."

With this Mr. Bell adjusted the headlight he had removed and climbed into his car. With a wave and shouted farewell, he was off.

"Gracious, I feel as if I'd been shaken up in one of those kaleidoscopes or whatever you call them," gasped Jess, "it all seems like part of a dream."

"Things certainly have been happening quickly," agreed Mary Eliska, "but I feel more at ease now than for a long time. Mr. Bell has the case in hand, and———"

"He'll see it through and fix it right," interposed Jimsy, enthusiastically.

As there was nothing to be gained by lingering about the scene of their strange encounter and stranger adventure, the party of youthful aviators clambered back into the *Golden Butterfly* and once more winged aloft. It was a short dash to their shed and they reached it without incident. Then, with hearts that felt lighter for the brisk, healthy influence of breezy James Bell, they trudged to the small hotel at which they were stopping, in order to avoid being seen by Mortlake and his aides 'til the last moment.

CHAPTER 15.21.
THE START OF THE SKY CRUISE.

"The first flight is to be to Cape Charles and return, a distance of sixty miles, approximately," announced Jimsy the next morning. He held in his hand a small blue folder which had been issued to all the contestants. It contained the rules and regulations governing the first day's tests.

A hasty breakfast was followed by a quick trip to the grounds in one of the ancient hacks that seem to swarm in Hampton. If the starting field had been a scene of confusion the day before, it was a veritable chaos now. Smoke and the fumes of gasoline hung like a pall above it. Through the bluish cloud could be seen dim figures hurrying with cans of fuel or lubricant, bags of tools and engine parts.

"Reminds me of circus day," commented Jimsy, looking about him; "hullo, there's the *Cobweb* out already," he exclaimed presently.

Across the field could be seen the silvery wings of the Mortlake aeroplane. Several figures hovered about her, adjusting stays and putting finishing touches to her complicated mechanism.

Presently a hush settled over the scene, and the party of naval officers, detailed to superintend the start and take the times of the competing craft, came through the crowd. They were directing their steps to an unpainted wooden structure at one end of the field. This building was equipped with various instruments for recording time accurately. From it also would presently be given out the wind velocity and any other data of interest to the aviators.

The party in full uniform swung past our three young adventurers. Lieutenant Bradbury was among them. He bowed and was about to pass on when he stopped and fell back.

"Now, don't get nervous, and do your best," he said to Mary Eliska; "I'm sure that we shall all have reason to be proud of the *Golden Butterfly* before these tests are over."

"I hope so," rejoined Mary Eliska; "we shall do our best, at any rate."

"I know you will, and now if you'll excuse me, I must be hurrying on. The board has an immense amount of work to do before ten o'clock, the official starting hour."

The trio, left to themselves, made for the shed which bore the legend "Nameless" above its door. Many curious eyes followed them as they paused before it, and Jimsy inserted a key in the stout padlock. Who could the two pretty girls in natty motor bonnets, with goggles attached, the plain, heavy skirts and dark shirt-waists be? Speculation ran rife. There was a regular stampede of reporters and photographers to the shed of the Nameless. But when they arrived there, to their chagrin, they found that their prospective victims had slipped inside and only the blank doors greeted them.

Among the crowd that hastened to try to solve the mystery of the Nameless was Fanning Harding, whose attention had been attracted by the rush of the crowd. At his side was Regina Mortlake. They arrived just in time to hear somebody say:

"It's two pretty girls and a good-looking boy. They're just kids."

Fanning and Regina exchanged glances. The girl actually turned pale.

"They are here after all," she exclaimed, "and I thought you said they weren't."

"Well, how on earth was I to know that they had hidden their machine under that name. There are so many freak craft here that——"

"You are more of an idiot than I thought you," said the girl, impatiently; "all our work has gone for nothing."

"No; there is time yet. If only Eccles and that other chap hadn't decamped like that last night, we might have put them to work tonight."

"They decamped—as you call it—because your father wouldn't give them any more money," said Regina with flashing eyes, "that was inexcusable folly. They know too many of our secrets to allow them to wander about unwatched."

"Oh, two tramps like that wouldn't have the sense to make any use of what they know," rejoined Fanning easily, "besides——"

But Regina Mortlake's mind was busy on another tack.

"Isn't it against the rules for women or girls to drive machines in this contest?" she asked.

"Say!" Fanning's eyes glistened, "I guess it is. Let's find out. If Mary Eliska is going to drive that machine we may be able to head them off yet."

The two conspirators hastened across the field to the unpainted wooden shack that housed the committee. A crowd surged about it asking questions and demanding impossible things. It was some time before Fanning, elbowing people right and left as he was, could reach the front. He scanned a printed list of the entries for the contest hung on the wall. As he read it, he blamed himself bitterly for not looking at it the day before. Near the bottom was the name "Nameless, entrant Miss Margaret Stricklin."

Suddenly the disgruntled youth spied Lieut. Bradbury.

"A moment," he cried. As the young officer turned, Fanning, without a word of greeting, bellowed out:

"Ain't it against the rules for a girl to drive an aeroplane in this contest."

"Not that I am aware of," rejoined the officer. He reached over to a stack of pink booklets. "Here's a book of rules. Read it."

"Hold on," cried Fanning, as the officer moved off, "I want to make a protest I——"

"Make your protest in writing. No verbal ones will be considered," said the officer briefly. "But see here——"

"I've no time to talk now, Mr. Harding. Good morning," and the officer passed on.

The crowd began to grin, and soon laughed openly. This enraged Fanning the more. He angrily shoved his way to the outskirts where Regina was awaiting him.

"Well?" she said, lifting her dark eyebrows.

"Well," echoed Fanning in a surly tone, "it's no go."

"No go. What do you mean?"

"I mean that there isn't anything in the rules, apparently, to prevent a woman or a girl driving an aeroplane if she wants to."

"Come and let's see my father," suggested the girl, presently, "he'll want to know about this. It may mean a complete change of our plans."

"You'll have to change 'em to beat the *Golden Butterfly*," muttered Fanning; "if only those drawings hadn't been lost, we'd have had that balancer, and it looks to me as if we might need it before we get to Cape Charles."

"Why?"

"The wind's freshening. Not more than a half dozen of these aeroplanes will venture up. Bother the luck, if it wasn't for the *Golden Butterfly*, we'd have a clean sweep."

"This is only the first day," counseled Regina; "the points scored today will not count for so very much. There's plenty of time."

"Humph," grumbled Fanning, and as this conversation had brought them up to the *Silver Cobweb*, he broke it off to communicate his intelligence concerning the Stricklin aeroplane to Mortlake, who heard it with a lowering brow.

Bang!

A bomb shot upward and exploded, in a cloud of thick yellow smoke, in mid-air.

"The half-hour signal," cried Jimsy; "everything ready?"

"As ready as it ever will be," rejoined Mary Eliska nervously fingering a stay wire.

The navigators of the Nameless were still inside the shed. The doors were still closed. Mary Eliska had decided not to risk having the machine damaged by the crowd by bringing it out before the very last moment. As the bomb sounded Jimsy drew out his watch. He kept it in his hand awaiting the elapse of the preliminary half-hour.

Outside, as Fanning had prophesied, there had been a great and sweeping reduction in the number of aeroplanes that were to start. The puffy wind had scared most of the entrants of the freak types and only five of the more conventional kind of aircraft were on the starting line. The *Silver Cobweb* was among them.

Fanning was in the driver's seat. As a passenger he carried Regina Mortlake. She looked very stunning in her lurid aviation costume, and her handsome face was as calm as chiseled marble. Her nervousness only displayed itself by a constant tapping of her gauntleted fingers.

Fanning finished oiling the motor and adjusting grease cups and timers, and straightening up, glanced nervously about him. Still no sign of the Nameless.

"I guess they've got scared off by the wind," he grinned to Mortlake, who, with the elder Harding and several machinists, stood by the side of the *Cobweb*.

"I doubt it," rejoined Mortlake; "it would take more than that to alarm those girls. And just to think that all our trouble to out-maneuver them has gone for nothing."

"You did a bad thing when you let Eccles and that other chap get away," commented Fanning; "I don't like their disappearance at all."

"Why?"

"Well, for one thing, they know a good deal that would make it very awkward for us if they fell into the hands of anyone who disliked us. And again——"

"Pshaw! You are alarming yourself over nothing. They were well paid and they wouldn't dare to make trouble. If they told about us, they'd implicate themselves."

"Just the same I don't feel easy. Hullo! there goes the second bomb. That fellow's just going to touch it off, and——"

At the same instant the doors of the Nameless's shed were flung open. From them emerged the glistening form of the golden-winged *Butterfly*. Half a dozen men whom Jimsy had hired pushed the aerial craft rapidly across the field to the starting line. So engrossed was the crowd in watching the other machines that they hardly noticed the arrival of the added starter.

But not so Mortlake and his companions. They watched, with jaundiced eyes, the forthcoming of their dreaded rival, and if wishes could have disabled her, the *Golden Butterfly* would never have flown on that day.

B-o-o-m!

The echoes of the second bomb rang deafeningly.

"They're off!" yelled the crowd, as if there might have been some doubt of it.

Up into the puffy air winged six aeroplanes. It was a glorious sight. From the chassis of the various air craft the airmen waved farewells to the cheering crowd.

Flying, wing and wing, they dashed off toward where the sea lay, a deep blue patch, beyond the shore. Presently they faded into dots and then were blotted out altogether.

"There's a thick haze out there," said one of the officers, as the aeroplanes vanished.

The word ran through the crowd and created a momentary sensation. Then the big throng dismissed the flying aeroplanes from its mind, and wandered about the grounds gazing openmouthed at the freak types, whose inventors were willing enough—too willing—to explain their remarkable points.

It might be a long time before the first of the homing craft would come in sight and what was the use of worrying about them. Only in the wooden structure housing the naval officers was there any concern displayed.

"If it's thick weather," said Lieutenant Bradbury, summing up a discussion, "they're going to have some trouble on their hands out there."

CHAPTER 15.22.
THE WHITE PERIL.

"What's that? No, not that schooner below there—I mean that sort of whitish drift—it looks like cotton—on the horizon?"

Jess leaned forward and addressed Jimsy.

"You've got me guessing," rejoined that slangy young person.

"Ask Mary Eliska."

"No, I don't want to bother her now. She's got her hands full, I fancy."

The *Golden Butterfly* was swinging steadily onward above a sparkling sea. The slight haze perceptible from the land was not noticeable to the air voyagers. Below them a four-masted schooner was tacking in the light wind. Closer in shore lay several grim looking battleships and cruisers. In their leaden colored «war paint» they looked menacing and bulldoggish.

Far off, a mere speck, could be seen a dim and indistinct object pointing upward from the cape like a finger. They guessed it was the light for which they were aiming. Mary Eliska's last glance at the compass had confirmed this guess.

Jimsy looked about him. About a quarter of a mile off, and slightly ahead was the *Cobweb*. The silvery aeroplane was rushing through the atmosphere at a great rate. But profiting by Mortlake's experience, Fanning was evidently not speeding the 'plane to its fullest capacity.

On the other side was a large red biplane flying steadily and keeping about level with the *Golden Butterfly*. Far behind lagged a monoplane. The other contestants had dropped out of the race. They were so manifestly out of it that their drivers did not care to continue.

A glance at the speedometer showed Mary Eliska's two passengers that they were reeling off fifty-five miles an hour. The *Cobweb* was doing slightly better.

"We should round the light in a few minutes now," said Jimsy scrutinizing his watch anxiously.

"Will they report us?" asked Jess.

"Yes. There is a wireless rigged up there. The minute we round it on our return trip word will be flashed back to the starting point."

Silently they sat counting the minutes roll by. All at once Jimsy noticed that the air had become strangely damp and moist. He looked up. He could not refrain a cry of astonishment as he did so. The *Golden Butterfly* was enveloped in a damp, steamy sort of smother. The *Cobweb* had been blotted out and so had the other aeroplanes.

"Fog," he exclaimed. "What a bit of bad luck."

"It's just as bad for the others," Mary Eliska reminded him.

"Have you got your course?" asked Jess anxiously.

"Yes. Almost due east. But in this dense mist it will be hard to come close enough to the lighthouse to be reported without the danger of dashing into it."

"Are you going to try for it?"

"Of course," was the brief reply. Mary Eliska slowed down the engine. The *Golden Butterfly* now seemed to be gliding silently through lonely billows of white sea fog. It was an uncanny feeling. The occupants of the machine felt a chilling sense of complete isolation.

Thanks to their barograph, however, they could judge their height above the sea.

"Good thing we've got it," commented Jimsy; "otherwise we might have a thrilling encounter with the topmasts of some schooner."

"I only wish we had some instrument to show us where the other aeroplanes are," said Mary Eliska; "it's hard to hear anything in this fog."

"Maybe it will clear off," suggested Jess hopefully.

"Not unless we get some wind," opined Jimsy; "queer how quick that wind dropped and this smother came up."

Nobody even hinted at the deadly danger they were in. But each occupant of the *Golden Butterfly* knew it full well. Except for the compass, they had no way of guiding their flight, and to turn about would have been to court disaster. There was only one thing for it, to keep on. This Mary Eliska did, grimly compressing her lips.

"Hark!" exclaimed Jimsy suddenly.

Far below them they could hear a mournful sound. It was wafted up to them in fits and starts.

"Ding-dong! Ding-dong!"

"A church bell," cried Jess, "we must be over land, Mary Eliska!"

The other shook her head.

"That's a bell buoy, I guess," she said.

"I wish he'd tell us how to get out of here," joked Jimsy, rather wearily.

"Who?" asked Jess.

"That bell boy."

Never had one of Jimsy's jokes fallen so flat. He mentally resolved not to attempt another one.

Presently he looked at his watch.

"Almost eleven," he said, "we must have passed the light by this time."

"I don't know," said Mary Eliska helplessly; "if only the chart marked that bell buoy—but it doesn't."

She again scrutinized the chart pinned before her on the sloping slab designed for such purposes. But no bell buoy was marked on it as being located anywhere near where they estimated they must be drifting. Drifting, however, is not quite the correct word. An aeroplane cannot drift. Its life depends upon its motion. The instant it stops or decreases speed beyond a certain point, in that same instant it must fall to the earth.

This fact is what made the position of the young sky cruisers particularly dangerous. Although the gauge showed that they had plenty of gasoline, the supply—even with the use of the auxiliary tanks—would not hold out indefinitely. If the fog did not lift, or they did not land, sooner or later they must face disaster. Worse still, they were—or believed they were, navigating above the sea.

Had the *Golden Butterfly* been fitted with pontoons like some of the Glen Curtiss machines, this would not have been so alarming. But a descent into the ocean would inevitably mean a speedy death by drowning.

Suddenly voices struck through the smother all about them. They seemed to come from below.

"It's thick as pea soup, captain!"

"Aye, aye; I'll be glad when we're out of it I kin tell yer. This bay's a bad place ter be in er fog."

"A ship," cried Jimsy. "Quick, Mary Eliska," he almost yelled the next instant. "Set your rising levers."

The girl swiftly manipulated the machinery that sent the *Golden Butterfly* on an upward course.

But it was only just in time that this maneuver was carried out. All of them had a glimpse for an instant of the gilded ball on the main-mast head of the vessel beneath them. For an instant Mary Eliska's watchful eye had been deflected from the height gauge, and she had allowed the *Golden Butterfly* to drop almost on the top of some coasting vessel's mast.

The danger over, they could not help laughing at the whimsical adventure.

"Just to think how utterly unconscious those fellows were of the fact that three human beings were hovering right above them and listening to every word of their conversation," chuckled Jimsy; "isn't it queer?"

A little while later a steamer's whistle boomed through the fog beneath them, but as the altitude register showed five hundred feet, they did not bother about it.

"At all events we know we're still above the water and not in danger of colliding with any church steeples," said Jess, and she found consolation in the thought.

"Have you any idea at all as to the direction of the light, Mary Eliska?" inquired Jimsy at length.

"I—I really don't know," confessed Mary Eliska, with a gulp; "everything's mixed up. It's so thick I can't tell anything and I'm deathly afraid of running into the lighthouse by mistake."

"Then for goodness sake give it a wide berth," cried Jimsy; "if we keep on cruising about for a while, we'll be bound to land somewhere. Anyhow we've got lots of gasoline, that's one comfort."

It was, indeed. In the steady hum of their powerful motor the young aviators found consolation in that lonely ride through the billowing fog-banks. At all events, there was no sign of a falter or skip there.

"If only we could get some wind," sighed Jess.

"Might as well wish for the moon," said Jimsy; "the air is as still as it used to be at noon out on the desert."

"What a contrast between the Big Alkali and this!" cried Jess, half hysterically. The strain of the white drifting fog was beginning to tell upon her.

Jimsy looked at her sharply.

"Look here, Sis," he began and was going on when a sharp cry from Mary Eliska arrested him. At the same instant the *Golden Butterfly* swerved sharply, swinging over on her beam-ends almost.

Right in front of them, for one dreadful instant, there loomed the outlines of another aeroplane. The next instant it was gone. But the picture of the deadly peril, its outlines exaggerated by the mist, was photographed in the minds of every one of them.

"We must land somewhere, soon," said Mary Eliska, in rather a faint voice; "I don't think I could stand many shocks like that. Another inch, and———."

She did not complete the sentence. Her two listeners did not require her to. It did not take a vivid imagination to have pictured the result of that "other inch."

CHAPTER 15.23.
OUT OF THE CLOUDS.

Ten minutes or so later, a puff of wind blew the folds of fog apart for a brief instant. Beneath them Mary Eliska could see a sandy beach and some scrubby-looking brush. Like a flash she took advantage of the momentarily revealed opportunity. The *Golden Butterfly*, under her guidance, sank swiftly, grounding a few seconds later into a bed of soft sand. It was like lighting on a pillow of down, so gently had the glide to earth been made.

Shutting off the engine, Mary Eliska took hold of Jimsy's outstretched arm and, followed by Jess, she jumped lightly out upon the sand. The roar of the surf, as the big swells rolled upon the beach was in their ears. A wholesome, stinging tang of salt in their nostrils.

"I wonder where on earth we've landed," said Jimsy, looking about him; "perhaps this is some enchanted land and we are to face new perils—dragons or something."

"Well, gallant knight," laughed Jess, in the highest spirits to be back on the firm ground again—even if it was only shifting sand—"we trust to you."

"And by my troth," exclaimed the mercurial Jimsy, "ye shall not be disappointed in me fair damsels. Hullo! an adventure already. Hark!"

Through the smother a dull sound was borne to their ears. A sound that came in muffled but rhythmic thumps. At intervals it paused, but then was resumed again.

"Somebody chopping wood!" exclaimed Mary Eliska, recognizing the sound.

"That's just what it is, if I ever wielded an axe in my life," agreed Jimsy; "now logic tells us that an axe can't work itself. Therefore, somebody must be using it. Where there is human life there is—or ought to be—food. How about it, girls, are you hungry?"

"Hungry! I could eat anything," declared Jess.

"I'm almost as bad," laughed Mary Eliska.

"Well," said Jimsy, "as there is no sign of the fog lifting yet awhile, what's the matter with our starting out to find the wood-chopper and seeing if he has anything to eat?"

"Jimsy, you're a genius," cried Jess.

"That's what all my friends tell me," rejoined the modest youth.

They set off over rough sand dunes, overgrown with coarse grass, in the direction of the sounds of the axe. The sand was loose and their feet sank ankle deep in it, but they plodded along pluckily.

All at once, just as if a curtain had been drawn, the outlines of a rough shanty appeared in front of them. It was a tumble-down sort of a place, seemingly made of driftwood and old sacks and bits of canvas. From a rusty iron stove-pipe on top, a feeble column of blue smoke was ascending.

The noise of chopping had ceased on their approach and as they stood hesitating a strange figure suddenly appeared round the corner of the wretched rookery of a place. The man, who stood facing them, a startled look in his light blue eyes, was apparently about middle age. He wore a full beard of a golden-brown color and was barefooted and hatless. His clothes consisted of a tattered shirt and a pair of coarse canvas trousers.

"Well, shiver my top lights!" he cried as his eyes fell on the trio, "whar under ther sun did you come from? Drop from ther clouds?"

"That's just what we did," said the debonair Jimsy, as the girls drew back rather affrighted at the weird looking figure and his queer, wild way of talking.

"What's that? Don't try to fool with me young feller. I ain't as crazy as I reckon I looks."

There was a certain dignity about the man when he spoke, that, despite his ragged clothing and miserable habitation, was impressive.

"No, it's really so," Jimsy hastened to assure him, "we—we came in an aeroplane, you know."

"Well, now," said the man scratching his head, "I reckon that's the first of them contrivances to reach Lost Brig Island."

"Lost Brig Island," echoed Jess in an alarmed tone; "is this an island?"

"If the geography books still define an island as a body of land surrounded by water, it is," rejoined the man, with a smile.

"Are we far from Cape Charles?" asked Mary Eliska, eagerly.

"Why, no. Not more than six miles to the north. But what under ther sun air you young folks in your fine clothes a-doin' out here?"

Mary Eliska hastily explained, and the man said that he had seen some reference to the coming contests in a stray paper the light-keepers had given him the last time he passed the lighthouse in a small boat he kept.

"Is the island inhabited?" inquired Jimsy; "we'd like to get something to eat. If there's a hotel or———."

The man of the island burst into a laugh. Not a rough guffaw, but a laugh of genuine amusement.

"I guess I'm the only hotel keeper on the island," he said, "and my guests is sea gulls and once in a while a turtle. But if you don't mind eating some fish and potatoes, you're welcome to what I have."

"I'm sure that's awfully good of you," said Mary Eliska, warmly, "and we love fish."

"Well, come on in and sit down. This fog won't last forever. I was chopping wood to get dinner when I heard you coming over the sands. I don't often have visitors so you'll have to rough it."

So saying, the strange, lone island dweller led them into his hut. It was rough inside but scrupulously clean. Some attempts had been made to beautify it by hanging up on the walls shells and curiosities of the beach. Here and there, too, were panels of rare woods, which the island-dweller explained had come from the cabins of wrecked ships. A big cat, his only companion, lay beside the fire and blinked at the visitors, as if they were an everyday occurrence.

Chairs, fashioned out of barrels and boxes, stood about, some of them cushioned after a fashion, with sacking stuffed with dried sea weed.

"Sit down," said their host hospitably, "ain't much to boast of in the way of furniture, but it's the best I can do. Can't expect to find a Waldorf Hotel on Lost Brig Island."

"You have been in New York, then?" exclaimed Mary Eliska, struck by the reference.

The man's face underwent a transformation.

"Once, many years ago," he said, "but I never like to talk about it."

"Why not?" blundered the tactless Jimsy.

"Because a wrong—a very great wrong—was done to me there," said the man slowly.

Without another word he rose and left the hut. None of the visitors dared to speak to him, so black had his face grown at the recollections called up by Mary Eliska's unlucky remark.

After an absence of some moments, he came back. He carried a string of cleaned fish in one hand and a tin measure of potatoes in the other. In the interval that had elapsed he seemed to have recovered his equanimity.

"Well, here's dinner," he announced in a cheery voice, "it ain't much to boast of, but hunger's the best sauce."

Sitting on an upturned box he started to peel potatoes, and presently put them on the fire in a rough iron pot. When they were almost done, a fact which he ascertained by prodding them with a clean sliver of wood, he set the fish in a frying pan or "spider," and the appetizing aroma of the meal presently filled the lowly hut.

On a table formed of big planks, once the hull of some wrecked schooner, laid on rough trestles, they ate, what Mary Eliska afterward declared, was one of the most enjoyable dinners of her life. Their host had at one time of his life been a sailor it would seem. At any rate, he had a fund of anecdote of the sea and its perils that held them enthralled.

Every now and again, through the open door, Mary Eliska cast a glance outside. But the fog still hung thick. Suddenly, in the midst of their meal, footsteps sounded and voices came to their ears.

"Hullo, more visitors!" exclaimed the man of the island starting to his feet, "this is a day of events with a vengeance. Who can be coming now?"

The footsteps had drawn close now and a voice could be heard saying:

"What a rickety, tumble-down old place. I wonder what kind of savage lives here."

"Fanning Harding!" gasped Mary Eliska, as another voice struck in. A voice she instantly knew as Regina Mortlake's.

"The next minute the man of the island ushered in his two new guests."

"Oh, what a dreadful place. Why won't this miserable fog lift. I'll be dead before we get back to the hotel."

The man of the island had hastened hospitably out to welcome the newcomers.

Mary Eliska, Jess and Jimsy exchanged glances. The prospect of spending the afternoon marooned on an island with Fanning Harding and Regina Mortlake, was not alluring. But there was no escape. The next minute the man of the island ushered in his two new guests.

"What, you here?" said Fanning in an ungracious tone, while Regina Mortlake, more skilled at disguising her feelings, exclaimed:

"Oh, how perfectly wonderful that we should both have landed on the same island."

"It wasn't from choice," grumbled Fanning in a perfectly audible tone.

Jimsy flushed a dark, dangerous flush.

"Jess, tell me not to punch that chap," he muttered to his sister.

"I certainly do tell you not to," whispered Jess emphatically.

The man of the island looked on wonderingly.

"Did you come in an aeroplane, too?" he asked Fanning in the manner of a man prepared to hear any marvels.

"Yes. We had the race won, too. But this fog has delayed us. What can you give us to eat. I can pay for it," said Fanning in a loud, rude tone.

"I don't take pay," said the hut-dweller in a quiet tone that ought to have caused Fanning to redden with shame, "but if you are hungry, I can cook some more fish. There are plenty of potatoes left."

"They'll be very nice, I'm sure," Regina had the grace to say. But Fanning mumbled something about "pauper's food."

But nevertheless, he ate as heartily as Jimsy himself, when the food was put on the rough table. It was hard work trying to be pleasant to the two young people who had so unexpectedly come into their midst, and the conversation languished and went on by fits and starts.

"Hullo, the fog's lifting," cried Fanning suddenly; "I'm off. Come on Regina."

The girl rose, and as she did so the trio from the Stricklin machine noticed the island dweller's eyes fixed on her in a curious way.

"Pardon me," he said, "but is your name Regina?"

The girl looked at him in a half-startled way, while Mary Eliska, as she said afterward, felt as if she was watching a drama.

"Yes," she said; "why?"

"Because," said the island dweller slowly, "because I once knew someone called Regina who was very dear to me."

"Come on," called Fanning from outside, "we've got to win this race back."

The girl lingered hesitatingly an instant and the next moment was gone.

"The fog is lifting," said Mary Eliska, "we must be going, too. Come along Jess. Come on, Jimsy, we don't want to let the Mortlake craft beat us at the eleventh hour."

"What name was that you just mentioned?" asked the man of the island, quickly. He was bending forward eagerly, as if to catch the answer.

"Do you mean Mortlake?"

"Yes, that's the name. What of him? Do you know him?"

The man's eyes gleamed brightly. He seemed to be much excited. Mary Eliska answered him calmly, although she felt as if some sort of a life tragedy was working out to swift conclusion.

"Of course, Mr. Eugene Mortlake is the man who is manufacturing the Mortlake aeroplane. He is our chief rival. That's the reason we must hurry off."

"Why, did they?" the man nodded his head in the direction in which Fanning and Regina had vanished, "did they come in a Mortlake aeroplane?"

"Yes," said Mary Eliska, "didn't you know? That girl is Mr. Mortlake's daughter, Regina Mortlake."

The man gave a terrible cry and reeled backward. Jimsy stepped forward quickly and caught him. For an instant they thought their host was going to swoon. But he quickly recovered.

"Good heavens," he cried, "Eugene Mortlake is here. Close at hand?"

"He is in Hampton—why?"

"I must see him as soon as possible. No, I can explain nothing now. But I must see him."

The man's manner showed that he was terribly in earnest. He seemed almost carried away by excitement. Outside came suddenly a whirring sound.

"Fanning is starting his engine," exclaimed Jimsy; "we must hurry."

"Will you do something for me—will you aid a miserable outcast to right a great wrong?" pleaded the ragged man who faced them.

"What can we do for you?" asked Jimsy.

"Take me back to Hampton in your aeroplane. I must see Mortlake at once. It is imperative I tell you. See, I am not poor, although I appear so."

In two strides the man had crossed the room and lifting a board in the floor he drew forth bag after bag. The seams of some of them were rotten. Under the sudden strain they broke and streams of gold coin trickled out upon the floor.

"Years ago, when I was first an exile here," said the man, "a Spanish ship came ashore one stormy night. Not a soul of her crew was saved. I found this money in the wreck. I will give you half of it if you will take me to Hampton with you. The other half I must keep till—till I learn from Mortlake's lips the secret he holds."

"Put your money back," said Jimsy quietly after a telegraphic exchange of looks with Mary Eliska, "we'll take you to Hampton; but hurry!"

Fifteen minutes later a golden-hued aeroplane flashed past the Cape Charles light. The announcer posted there, instantly sent in a wireless flash to Hampton.

"Number Six has just passed. Two minutes behind Number Five (The *Silver Cobweb*), four persons on board."

Mortlake was among the crowd that read the bulletin which was instantly posted upon the field outside Hampton.

"I wonder who the fourth can be?" he thought, little guessing that through the air fate was winging its way toward him.

"Anyway," he added to himself the next instant, "thc *Mortlake* is leading. Now if only——"

But what was that roar, at first a sullen boom, gradually deepening into the excited skirling cheers of a vast throng.

Mortlake looked round, startled. Out of the distance two tiny dots, momentarily growing larger, like homing birds, had come into view. Hark! What was that the crowd were shouting? Those with field glasses threw the cry out first, and then came a mighty roar, as it was caught up by hundreds of throats.

"The Nameless! The Nameless wins!"

Mortlake paled, and caught at a post erected to hold up a telephone line. He gazed at the oncoming aeroplanes. There were three of them now, but one was far behind, laboring slowly. But the first was unquestionably the *Golden Butterfly*. He could catch the yellow glint of her wings. And that second craft—its silvery sheen betrayed it—was the Mortlake *Cobweb*, as Liam McAdams had called it.

"Come on! Come on!" shouted Mortlake, uselessly as he knew, "what's the matter with you?"

But alas, the *Cobweb* didn›t «come on." Some three or four minutes after the *Golden Butterfly* had alighted and been swallowed up in a surging, yelling throng of enthusiasm-crazed aero fans, the *Cobweb* fluttered wearily to the ground, unnoticed almost amid the excitement over the *Golden Butterfly's* feat.

Mortlake raged, old Mr. Harding almost wept, and Fanning sulkily explained that it wasn't his fault, the cylinders having overheated again. But not all of this could wipe out those figures that had just been put up on the board, which proclaimed a victory for the Stricklin aeroplane by a margin of three and twenty-one hundredths minutes!

CHAPTER 15.24.
FRIENDS AND FOES—CONCLUSION.

The winning of the "Sky Cruise," as the newspapers had dubbed it, was the talk of Hampton that night. Not a small part of the zest with which it was discussed was caused by the fact that a young girl had driven the machine through its daring dash. The wires from New York, Baltimore, Philadelphia, Boston and Richmond were kept hot with instructions from editors to their representatives demanding interviews with the Girl Aviators. But to the chagrin of the newspaper representatives, after seeing their machine housed, the party had vanished.

This, on investigation, was not as mysterious as it had at first appeared. There was a small door in the back of the Nameless's shed, and at this door there had been waiting, for some moments before the conclusion of the race, a big automobile. In it were seated a bronzed man, with broad shoulders, and an alert, wideawake expression, and a boy, whose foot was propped up on an extemporized contrivance affixed to the seat.

While the crowd had hovered about the front of the shed, awaiting the reappearance of the girl aviator, whose feat had caused such a furor, this boy had limped from the machine, assisted by his stalwart companion, and had entered the shed by the rear door. It would have astonished the crowd, and delighted the reporters in search of a story, if they could have seen Mary Eliska rush at the youth, and with a wild cry of:

"Liam McAdams! You darling!" throw her arms about his neck.

Mr. Bell, for he was the stalwart personage, stood aside with a look of warm satisfaction, as Mary Eliska's turn over, Jess and Jimsy came forward. What a joyous reunion that was, I will leave you to imagine. Then came Mr. Bell's story of his telegram to Sandy Beach to the judge, who was a friend of his. The message had announced that he had obtained complete confessions from both Joey Eccles and the unsavory Slim. Liam McAdams's release from bail and suspicion at once followed.

Eccles had owned up to his part in the mischief that had been wrought against the young Stricklins. Frankly, and without reserve, he had sworn to a statement before a local attorney, in which he admitted losing the bill with the mark upon it, on the night he had aided in decoying Liam McAdams to the old house. His assistant had been a cast-off workman of the Mortlake plant, of whose whereabouts Joey said he was now ignorant.

Then had come Slim's turn. Sullenly, but with the alternative of prison staring him in the face, he had admitted to impersonating the foreign spy. The part of Liam McAdams on that eventful night had been played by:

"Guess whom?" said Mr. Bell, looking round.

They all shook their heads.

"I'll tell you about that part of it later," said Mr. Bell. "There are still one or two things to be cleared up in that connection. But," he continued, "Palmer confessed that it was Mortlake who robbed the farm-house safe, the object being, of course, not so much the money, as a chance to put Liam McAdams out of the race contest. It has been a record of vile plotting all the way through," said the Westerner warmly, "but the toils are closing in about Mortlake & Co. Of course, my first step was to take the fellows before an attorney—luckily, I knew one in Hampton, and he, as it happened, was a friend of the Sandy Beach judge. We had to move quickly, but, thanks to the telegraph wire and fast trains, I got Liam McAdams released from bail and suspicion, and here in time to greet you."

They could only look their gratitude. Just as the strain was becoming almost too taut, Mr. Bell, who had noticed it, broke the tension.

"Let's sneak out of the back door," he said, "and all go to some quiet place to dine. Hullo, who's this?" he exclaimed, as the tattered figure of the man of the island appeared.

"I am what is left of Budd Pierce, Jim Bell," said the man, in his queer, tired tones.

"Budd Pierce!" exclaimed the mining man, falling back a step. "No—but, yes, now I look again—it is. But, man, what has happened to you? What are you doing here?"

"It's a long story," said the ragged man, while the younger members of the party looked on in astonishment, "but I can tell you that Gene Mortlake has reached the end of his tether. I've heard all you said about him, and my interest in him you know already."

"I know that you were swindled out of your fortune by some man years ago, and then disappeared," said Mr. Bell. "But I had forgotten the name of the rascal."

"It was Eugene Mortlake," said the man of the island slowly. "After I knew I was ruined, I fled down here, where I was raised, and became a recluse on that island. It was cowardly of me, I know, but from now on I am going to lead a different life."

"You have found yourself!" cried James Bell, gleefully clasping the other's thin, worn hand.

"I have found something dearer to me," was the quiet reply; "but come, let us be going. I have much that is strange to tell you."

With wondering looks, the young aviators—Liam McAdams leaning on Mary Eliska's devoted arm—followed James Bell and the man from Lost Brig Island out of the aeroplane shed.

In his suite of rooms at the Hotel Hampton, the best hotel in the place, Eugene Mortlake sat opposite old Mr. Harding. His brow was furrowed, and little wrinkles that had not been there earlier in the day, appeared at the corners of his eyes. Old Mr. Harding seemed to be trying to cheer him up. In another corner of the room, sullen and depressed, Fanning Harding was standing puffing a cigarette and filling the atmosphere with its reeking fumes.

"All is not lost yet, Mortlake, hey, hey, hey?" said the old man, laying a skinny, claw-like hand on the other's arm. "Why, tonight we'll put into execution a plan that will permanently put these young Stricklins out of it. Fanning knows what I mean. Hey?"

He glanced up at his ill-favored son.

"I know fast enough," said that young hopeful, "but it's a risky matter. Why don't you get somebody else to do it?"

"Pshaw! It's only filing off a padlock and then smashing a few of the motor parts," said the old man, in as calm a tone as if he were proposing a constitutional walk, "that's soon done, hey?"

A sharp knock at the door interrupted any reply Fanning might have been about to make.

"Come in," snarled Mortlake. "It's the mail, I suppose," he said, turning to old Mr. Harding, but, to his surprise and consternation, the opened door revealed Liam McAdams. Close behind him came Mr. Bell and Mary Eliska, with Jimsy and Jess bringing up the rear.

"To what am I indebted for the pleasure of this visit?" asked Mortlake, glowering at the newcomers, as they filed in, and Mr. Bell closed the door behind them. "Why didn't you send up your cards, and I'd have torn them up and thrown them out of the window."

"Just what I thought you'd do, so we came up ourselves," said Mr. Bell cheerily. "Now, look here, Mortlake—no, sit down. I've come up here to right a wrong. You've tried to do all in your power to injure these young people, whose only fault is that they have built a better aeroplane than you have. It's their turn now, and you've got to grin and bear it."

Mortlake's jaw dropped. His old bullying manner was gone now. Old Man Harding cackled inanely, but said nothing. Only his long, lean fingers drummed on the table. Fanning turned a pasty yellow. He had some idea of what was to come. His eyes fell to the floor, as if seeking some loophole of escape there.

"Well," growled Mortlake, "what have you got to say to me?"

"Not much," snapped the mining man, "but I wish to read you something." He drew from his pocket a paper.

"This is the confession of Joey Eccles," he said quietly. "I've another by Frederick Palmer."

Mortlake leaped up and sprang toward the Westerner, but Mr. Bell held up his hand.

"Don't try to destroy them," he said. "They are only copies. The originals are by this time in the hands of the authorities at Sandy Beach."

Mortlake sank back with staring eyes and white cheeks. "What do you want me to do?" he gasped.

"Listen to these confessions and then sign your name to them, signifying your belief that they are true documents."

"And if not?" "Well, if not," said Mr. Bell, measuring his words, "do you recollect that wildcat gold mine scheme you were interested in more years ago than you'll care to remember?"

Mortlake seemed to shrivel. But he flared up in a last blaze of defiance.

"You can't scare me by rattling old bones," he said, "What do you know about it?"

For reply, Mr. Bell stepped to the door.

"Mr. Budd," he called softly, and in response the man of Lost Brig Island, but now dressed and barbered into civilization appeared.

"Pierce Budd!" gasped Mortlake.

"Yes, Pierce Budd, whom you ruined," said Mr. Bell. "But for my persuasions, he would have sought to wipe out his wrongs in personal violence. But you needn't fear him now," as Mortlake looked round with hunted eyes; "that is, if you sign."

"I'll sign," gasped out the trapped man. He reached for an inkstand. "Give them to me."

"I'll read them first," said the mining man, and then, in slow, measured tones, he read out the contents of the convicting documents. As he concluded, Mortlake seemed about to collapse. But he took the papers with a trembling hand, and wrote:

"All this is true.—Eugene Mortlake."

"Good," said Mr. Bell. "Now your future fate is in the hands of these young people. Pierce Budd has forgiven you, though it has been a struggle to do so. But I have one surprise left for you all," said Mr. Bell, stepping to the door. "Regina," he called softly.

In reply, the dark-eyed girl, in a sheer dress of soft, clinging stuff, glided into the room. She slipped straight to the side of the outcast Pierce Budd, and stood there, holding his hand. Mary Eliska looking at her in amazement, saw that the hard, defiant look had vanished from the girl's face, and that its place had been taken by an expression of supreme happiness and peace.

"Tell them about it," said Mr. Bell.

"No. She has not yet recovered from the shock of the discovery," said Pierce Budd softly. "Let me do it. When Mortlake ruined me, and I fled from my former surroundings," he said, "I left behind me a baby girl. Mrs. Mortlake, a good woman if ever there was one, took care of that child. All this I have only just learned. She grew up with the Mortlake's, and when that man's wife died, he did the only good thing I've ever heard of him doing—he took care of her and brought her up as his daughter. Today in the hut you saw me looking at her closely. It was because I thought I recognized a bit of jewelry—a tiny gold locket she wore. It contained the picture of her mother, who died soon after her birth. When I heard her name was Regina, and on the top of that heard you mention the name of Mortlake, I knew that fate, in its strange whirligig, had brought my daughter back to me."

"Tonight, with Mr. Bell, I sought her, and she has consented to forgive me for my years of neglect. The rest of my life will be spent in atoning for the past. That is all."

His voice broke, and Regina—a different Regina from the old defiant one, gazed up at him tenderly.

"So," said Mortlake, "I'm left alone at last, eh? Regina, haven't you a word for me? Won't you forgive me for deceiving you about your father all these years?"

"Of course, I forgive, freely and wholly," said the girl, stepping toward him, "but it is hard to forget."

Very tenderly, Mortlake raised her hand to his lips and kissed it. Then he drew himself erect.

"What do you want to do with me?" he said defiantly. "I've confessed everything. Why don't you call the police?"

"Because we want you to have a chance to be a better man," said Mr. Bell. "The past is over and done with. The future lies before you. You can make it what you will—bad or good, we shall not interfere with you."

Mortlake looked at them unsteadily. Then his voice broke and he stepped quickly toward Budd. The recluse of Lost Brig Island extended his lean palm and met the other's outstretched hand half way.

"I bear no grudge, Mortlake," he said. "You will always be welcome at our home—Regina's and mine."

"Oh, yes—always," cried the girl, with a catch in her voice.

"Thank you," said Mortlake simply. "I don't—I don't dare trust myself to, speak now; tomorrow, perhaps———"

He strode abruptly through the door and was gone.

Old Mr. Harding arose to his feet.

"After this affecting tableau, is there anything you wish to say to me, hey?" he grated out.

"Nothing, sir," said Mr. Bell, turning his back upon the wizened old financier. "I have seen to it that the money taken from them has been returned to the Galloways."

"Then, I'll bid you good-night, too, since you seem to have taken possession of these rooms. Come, Fanning."

Without a word, Fanning shuffled across the room and reached his parent's side. Not 'til they were both at the door did he speak. Then, with a malevolent look backward, he paused.

"Liam McAdams," he said, "you've always beaten me out—at school, at college, and twice since we've both lived in Sandy Beach. There'll be a third time, and you can bet that I'll not forget the injury you've done me. Good night."

He was gone, a sinister sneer still curling his lip.

"Well," said Mr. Bell, looking round him with a smile, "who says that all the adventure and excitement is in the West?"

"Not the Girl Aviators, certainly," laughed Mary Eliska, stealing a look at Regina. The girl colored, and then, after a visible effort, she spoke.

"I want to say something," she said, and stopped. Her father bent on her an encouraging look. Bravely she nerved herself, and went on.

"It—it was I who dressed up like you that night, Liam McAdams, and—and I'm awfully sorry."

"Oh, that's all right," said Liam McAdams uneasily, and then, "say, you can run like a deer!"

In the laugh which followed they left the room and adjourned to a jolly supper, at which, who should walk in but Aunt Sally Stricklin and Mr. and Mrs. Bancroft. They had been reached by telegraph early that morning, and had started on the next train to Liam McAdams. How the hours flew! It was almost midnight before they knew it. In the midst of the feast, a waiter brought in a message to Mr. Bell. The mining man excused himself and left the room for a short time. When he returned, he was smiling.

"I've just signed on two new workmen for the mine," he said, "and I think they'll make good."

"Who are they?" asked Liam McAdams. "Well, one answers to the name of Eccles. The other was, on one occasion, a foreign spy, but he bears the very American name of Palmer. They leave for the West tonight."

How the Stricklin aeroplane, under Liam McAdams's management, captured the coveted highest number of marks for proficiency, and how a sensation was caused by the sudden withdrawal of the Mortlake aeroplanes from the naval contest, all my readers are familiar with through the columns of the daily press. The paper, though, didn't print anything about an offer made by Pierce Budd to Eugene Mortlake to finance the *Cobweb* type of machine. Needless to say, the offer was not accepted. Mortlake, a changed man, is now building and selling aeroplanes in a far eastern principality, and they are good ones, too. No letters are more welcome than those that arrive occasionally from him and are delivered at Pierce Budd›s home in New York.

Under Lieutenant Bradbury's kindly auspices, Liam McAdams instructed a class of young seamen in the management of the Stricklin type of aeroplane, which has become the official aero scout of the United States Navy. From time-to-time improvements are added.

But, as the young officer says: "It was really the Sky Cruise, that won out for the Stricklins."

And here, though only for a brief period, we must bid *au revoir* to our young friends. But we shall renew our acquaintance with them, and form some new friends, in the next chapter which will be replete with adventures encountered in the pursuance of the wonderful new science of aviation, as yet in its infancy. In the clouds and on the solid earth, the Girl Aviators are destined to have some more eventful timcs. What these are to be must be saved for the telling in the next chapter of this volume—**The Motor Butterfly.**

CHAPTER 16

The Motor Butterfly

CHAPTER 16.1.
PREPARATIONS AND PLANS.

"It will be another 'sky cruise,' longer and daintier and lovelier!" exclaimed Jax Gray, clapping her hands. "Mary Eliska, you're nothing if not original."

"Well, there are automobile tours and sailing trips, and driving parties—" "And railroad journeys and mountain tramps—" interrupted Jax Gray, laughing.

"Yes, and there are wonderful, long-distance migrations of birds, so why not a cross-country flight of motor butterflies?"

"It would be splendid fun," agreed Jax Gray eagerly; "we could take the *Golden Butterfly* and the *Red Dragon* and——" «Don›t forget that Bess Marshall has a small monoplane, too, now. I guess she would go in with us."

"Not a doubt of it. Let's go and find the boys and see what they say to it."

"No need to go after them, here they come now."

As the golden-haired Mary Eliska spoke, two good-looking youths came round the corner of the old-fashioned house at Sandy Bay, Long Island, where the two young Stricklins made their home with their maiden Aunt Sally. One of the lads was Bill Stricklin, Mary Eliska's brother, and the other was Liam McAdams.

"Well, girls, what's up now?" inquired Bill, as both girls sprang to their feet, their faces flushed and eyes shining.

"Oh, nothing particular," rejoined Mary Eliska, with assumed indifference, "except that we've just solved the problem of what to do with the rest of the summer."

"And what's that,—lie in hammocks and indulge in ice-cream sodas and chocolates?" asked Liam McAdams mockingly.

"No, indeed, you impertinent person; the young lady of the twentieth century has left all that far behind her," was Jax Gray's Parthian shot, "for proof I refer you to our adventures on the Great Alkali."

"Hello! what's this?" asked Bill, holding up a dainty cardboard box, and giving vent to a mischievous smile.

"Chocolates!" cried Liam McAdams.

"It *was* chocolates," corrected Mary Eliska reproachfully.

"And yet shall be," declared Liam McAdams, producing from some mysterious place in a long auto coat another box, beribboned and decorated like the first.

"Liam McAdams, you're an angel!" cried both girls at once.

"So I've been told before," responded the imperturbable Liam McAdams, "but I never really believed it 'til now."

Mary Eliska rewarded him for the compliment by popping a chocolate into his mouth.

Gravely munching it, Liam McAdams proceeded to interrogation.

"And how did you solve the problem of what to do with the rest of the summer?" he asked.

For answer Mary Eliska pointed to the sky, a delicate blue dome flecked with tiny cloudlets like cherub's wings.

"By circling way up yonder in the cloud fields," she laughed.

"But that's no novelty," objected Bill, "we've been up 5,000 feet already, and———" "But we're talking about a tour through cloudland," burst out Jax Gray, unable to retain the secret any longer, "a sort of Cook's tour above the earth."

"Wow!" gasped both boys. "There's nothing slow," added Bill, "in that or about you two. And, incidentally, just read this letter I got this morning, or rather I'll read it for you."

So saying Bill produced from his coat a letter closely written in an old-fashioned handwriting. It was as follows:

"My Dear Niece and Nephew: No doubt you will be surprised to hear from your Uncle Jack. Possibly you will hardly recall him. This has, in a great measure, been his own fault as, since your poor father's death, I have not paid the attention I should to my correspondence.

"This letter, then, is to offer what compensation lies in my power for my neglect. Having read in the papers of your wonderful flying feats in Nevada it struck me that you and your young friends might like to pay me a 'flying trip,' making the excursion via airplane.

"We are to have some flying contests in Marysville during the latter part of the month, and you might care to participate in them. Of course I expect your Aunt Sally to accompany you. Hoping sincerely to see you, I am

"Your affectionate uncle,
"James Parker.
"Marysville, North Carolina."

As Bill concluded the reading the quartet of merry youngsters exchanged delighted glances. As if by magic here was an objective point descried for their projected motor flight.

"Well, that's what I call modern magic," declared Liam McAdams glowingly; "consider me as having accepted the invitation."

"Accepting likewise for me, of course," said Jax Gray, shaking her blond locks and blinking her round, expectant eyes.

"Of course," struck in Mary Eliska affectionately, "the Girl Aviatrixes cannot be parted."

Just at this moment came a whirring sound from high in the air above them. Looking up, they saw a dainty green monoplane, with widespread wings and whirring propeller, descending to earth. An instant later the machine had come to a halt on the lawn, alighting as lightly as wind-blown gossamer. In the machine was seated a pretty girl of about Mary Eliska's age, though rather stouter. In harmony with the color of the machine she drove, the newly arrived girl aviator wore a green aviation costume, with a close-fitting motor bonnet. From the beruffled edge of this some golden strands of hair had escaped, and waved above two laughing blue eyes.

"Hello, people!" she hailed, as the porch party hastily adjourned and ran to welcome her, "how's that for a novice only recently out of the Mineola School?"

"Bess Marshall, you're a wonder!" cried Mary Eliska, embracing her; "the *Dart* is the prettiest little machine I've seen for a long time."

"Isn't it a darling," agreed Bess warmly, "but, my! how I had to beg and pray dad before he would buy it for me. He said that no daughter of his should ever go up in an airplane, much less pilot one. It wasn't 'til I got him down at Mineola and persuaded him to take a ride himself that he consented to buying me my dear little *Dart*."

She laid one daintily gloved hand on the steering wheel of the little monoplane and patted it affectionately.

"It's pretty enough, but it wouldn't fly very far," commented Bill teasingly, "sort of aërial taxicab, I'd call it."

"Is that so, Master Bill Stricklin? Well, I'd like you to know that the *Dart* could fly just as far and as fast as the *Red Dragon* or the *Golden Butterfly*."

"Well, if you wanted to take a trip to North Carolina with us you'd have an opportunity to test that idea out," laughed Mary Eliska.

"A trip to North Carolina? What do you mean? Are you dreaming?"

"No, not even day-dreaming."

Just then Mary Eliska, her gentle face wreathed in smiles, appeared at the door.

"Children! children!" she exclaimed, "what is all this? Adjourn your discussion for a while and come in and have tea."

While the happy group of young fliers are entering the pretty, old-fashioned house with its clustering roses and green-shuttered casements, let us relate a little more about the young personages to whose enthusiastic talk the reader has just listened.

Bill and Mary Eliska were orphans living in the care of their Aunt Sally, the location of whose home on Long Island has already been described. At school Bill had imbibed the aërial fever, and after many vicissitudes had built a fine monoplane, the *Golden Butterfly*, with which he had won a big money prize, besides encountering a series of extraordinary aërial adventures. In these Mary Eliska participated, and on more than one occasion was the means of materially aiding her brother out of difficulties. All this part of their experiences was related in Chapter 13 "*The Phantom Airship*."

In Chapter 14, "*The Girl Pilots on Golden Wings*," a combination of strange circumstances took our friends out to the Great Alkali of the Nevada desert. Here intrigues concerning a hidden gold mine provided much excitement and peril, and the girls proved that, after all, a fellow's sisters can be splendid companions in fun and hardship. An exciting race with an express train, and the adventure of the "Human Coyote," provided stirring times in this story, which also related the queer antics of Professor Wandering William, an odd character indeed. Space does not permit to relate their previous adventures in more detail, but in Chapter 15 "*The Sky Cruise*" still other interesting and unusual experiences are described,—experiences that tested both themselves and their machines in endurance flights.

Of Bill and Mary Eliska's devoted friends, Jax Gray and Liam McAdams, it is enough to say that both were children of Deanna Hoffinger and Uncle John Stricklin, a wealthy banker, who had a palatial summer home near to the younger Stricklins' less pretentious dwelling. Since we last met Jax Gray and Liam McAdams their father had allowed them to purchase an airplane known as the *White Flier*. It was in this craft that Liam McAdams and Bill had flown over for mail when they made their entrance at the beginning of this chapter. Of the letter they found awaiting them we already know.

Jolly, good-natured Bess Marshall had taken up aviation as a lark. She was a typical specimen of an American girl. Light-hearted, wholesome and devoted to all sorts of sports, tennis, swimming, golf, motoring and finally aviation had, in turn, claimed her attention.

And now, having introduced our heroes and heroines of the sky to those who have not already met them, we will proceed to see how Mary Eliska receives the startling plans that her young charges are about to lay before her.

CHAPTER 16.2.
OFF ON THE FLIGHT.

"But, my dear children, do you realize what such a trip means?"

The gentle-voiced Aunt Sally leaned back in her easy-chair and gazed at Mary Eliska and Bill with an approach to consternation.

"It means fun, adventure, and—oh, everything!" cried Mary Eliska, clapping her hands.

"You can't have the heart to refuse us," sighed Jax Gray.

"If it were only the boys it might be different, but two young ladies—" "Three," corrected Bess.

"Three, then. For three young ladies, supposedly of sound mind, to go flying across country like, like—" "Butterflies," struck in Liam McAdams.

"Wait a minute," cried Jax Gray, "there'd have to be four ladies—" "Of course; a chaperon," breathed Mary Eliska, with a mischievous glance.

Aunt Sally dropped her knitting.

"Mary Eliska, you mean me?"

"Of course; who else could go?"

"My dear child, do you actually contemplate taking me flying through the air at my time of life?"

"Why not? It isn't as if you'd never been up," urged Mary Eliska.

"You said you liked it, too," struck in Jax Gray.

"Um—well, I may have said so," admitted Aunt Sally, visibly weakening from the stand she had taken, and she went on: "I would like to see James again."

"And here is your opportunity ready to hand, as the advertisements say," declared Bess, her blue eyes shining.

"But how could I go?"

The question was an outward and visible sign of capitulation on Aunt Sally's part.

"Why, I was thinking we could use that big biplane I was building for Mr. Bell's use out in Nevada," spoke up Bill; "it will seat three, and is as steady as a church, thanks to that balancing device Liam McAdams and I figured out."

"I'd fly my little *Dart*," declared Bess.

"And you and I would take the *Golden Butterfly*," cried Mary Eliska, crossing to Jax Gray and placing her arm round the girl's neck.

"Liam McAdams can fly the *Red Dragon*, and that leaves Bill and auntie for the biplane," she went on, bubbling over with enthusiasm as her plans matured and took form.

"Goodness gracious, an aërial circus!" cried Aunt Sally. "We would attract crowds, and that wouldn't be pleasant."

"I was planning to make it a sort of picnic," declared Mary Eliska, who appeared to have an answer for every objection that could be interposed to her project.

"What, camp out every night? Well, you are a wonder," exclaimed Liam McAdams, "if there's one thing I love it's camping out."

"How long would it take us to get to Marysville?" asked Bess.

"I'll get the atlas," cried Mary Eliska, "but if we have good weather not more than three or four days."

"I hardly think it would take as long as that," declared Bill, as five eager heads were bent over the atlas.

"But camping out!" exclaimed Aunt Sally, "think of colds and rheumatism, not to mention snakes and robbers."

"Tell you what," cried Liam McAdams suddenly, "what's the matter with Aunt Sally going along in an automobile? We can map out the route, arrange our stops and meet every evening at some small town where we won't attract too much of a crowd."

"Liam McAdams, I always said you were a genius," cried Mary Eliska.

"Behold the last objection swept away," struck in Bess.

"Surely you can't refuse now?" urged Jax Gray.

"Please say yes," came from them all.

"But—but who would drive the car?" asked Aunt Sally, in the voice of one who is thinking up a feeble last objection.

"Why, Jake Rickets, of course," declared Bill, referring to the man who helped the boys in the machine shop in which the airplanes for the desert mines were manufactured.

After this Aunt Sally could make but a poor stand against the united urgings of five impetuous, enthusiastic young people. The air was filled with plans of all sorts. Liam McAdams was for going at once, but it was finally decided to meet again and set a definite date for a start. In the meantime there were parents' consents to be obtained, plans laid for the route to be followed, and various things purchased for the aërial trip.

All this occupied some time, and it was not 'til a week later that the last difficulty in connection with the motor flight had been straightened out and the three airplanes stood ready, in Bill's hangar, for a tour that was to prove eventful in more ways than one.

It was just after dawn on the day of the start that Bill and Liam McAdams for the last time went over every nut and bolt on the machines and declared everything in perfect readiness for the trip. Breakfast was a mere pretense at a meal; excitement got the better of appetites that morning.

Beside the winged machines sputtering and coughing as if impatient at the delay, was a large and comfortable Ford Model A red touring car. At the driver's wheel of this vehicle was seated a small, "under-done"-looking man, in a chauffeur's uniform of black leather. This was Jake Rickets.

"Well, Jake, we're all ready for a start," announced Bill, at last.

The small man, whose hair was fair, not to say pale, glanced at the glowing boy with an expression of deep melancholy.

"Yes, if something don't happen," he declared, in tones of deep pessimism.

"Jake's never happy unless he's foreboding some disaster," explained Bill to Bess, who happened to be standing by drawing on her gloves.

"It don't never do to be too sure," murmured the melancholy Jake, "'cos why? Well, you can't most generally always tell."

"Everything ready?" cried Mary Eliska at last, as Aunt Sally got into the car.

"As ready as it ever will be," merrily called back Bess, who was already seated in the little green *Dart*.

The chorus of engine pantings and explosions was swelled by the roar of Bill's big biplane and the rattling exhaust of Liam McAdams's fierce-looking *Red Dragon*.

The *Golden Butterfly*, which was equipped with a silencing device, ran smoothly and silently as a sewing machine. Mary Eliska sat at the wheel, while Jax Gray reclined on the padded seat placed tandem-wise behind her. It made a wonderful picture, the big white biplane with its boy driver, the scarlet and silver machine of Liam McAdams and the delicate green and gold color schemes of the other two flying machines.

"The first stop will be Palenville," announced Bill, "the biplane will be the pathfinder."

Despite the earliness of the hour and the efforts that had been made to keep the motor flight a secret, the information of the novel experiment had, in some way, leaked out. Quite a small crowd gave a loud cheer as Bill cried:

"Go!"

"We're off!" cried Mary Eliska, athrill with excitement.

Propellers flashed in the sunlight and the next instant the biplane, after a short run, soared aloft toward a sky of cloudless, clean-swept blue. In rapid succession the *Dart, Golden Butterfly* and *Red Dragon* followed.

"Come on," cried Bess to Liam McAdams, waving her hand challengingly.

"Ladies first, even off the earth," came back from Liam McAdams gallantly, as he skillfully "banked" his machine in an upward spiral.

Then upward and outward soared the gayly colored sky racers, like a flock of wonderful birds. It was the greatest sight that the crowd left behind and below had ever witnessed, although one or two shook their heads and prophesied dire results from young ladies tampering with them blamed "sky buggies."

But not a thought of this entered the heads of the aërial adventurers. With sparkling eyes, and bounding pulses they flew steadily southward, from time to time glancing below at the touring car. Even though they were flying slowly it was plain that the big red automobile had hard work to keep up with them. The unique motor flight was on, and was about to develop experiences of which none of them at the moment dreamed.

CHAPTER 16.3.
LITTLE WREN AND THE GYPSIES.

They flew on, keeping the motor car beneath them in constant sight 'til about noon. Then, from the tonneau of the machine, came the waving of a red square of silk. This had been agreed upon as a signal to halt for a brief lunch.

Shouting joyously, the young adventurers of the air began circling their machines about, dropping closer earthward with every sweep. Beneath them was a green meadow, bordered on one side by a country road and on the other by a small brook of clear water and a patch of dark woods. It was an ideal place to halt for a roadside lunch, and as one after the other the machines dropped to earth Mary Eliska was warmly congratulated on her choice of a halting place.

The car was left in the road, and the melancholy Jake Rickets set to work getting wood for a fire, for it was not to be thought of that Aunt Sally could go without her cup of tea. In the meantime the girls spread a cloth and set out their fare. There were dainty chicken sandwiches with crisp lettuce leaves lurking between the thin white "wrappers," cold meat and half a dozen other little picnic delicacies, which all the girls, despite their aërial craze, had not forgotten how to make.

The boys set up a shout as, returning from attending to the airplanes, they beheld the inviting table.

"This beats camping out by ourselves," declared Bill, "girls, we're glad we brought you."

"Thank you for the compliment," laughed Jax Gray. "I suppose you mean that you are glad *we* brought all this."

She waved her hand at the "spread" dramatically.

"Both," rejoined Liam McAdams, throwing himself on the grass. By this time Jake's kettle was bubbling merrily, and soon the refreshing aroma of Aunt Sally's own particular kind of tea was in the air. The boys preferred to try the water from the brook, despite Jake's dire hints at typhoid and other germs holding a convention in it. It was sweet and cool, and the girls voted it as good as ice-cream soda.

"At any rate as we can't get any we might as well pretend it is," declared Bess.

So the meal passed merrily. After it had been concluded, amid gay chatter and fun, Mary Eliska proposed an excursion to the woods for wild flowers which grew in great profusion on the opposite side of the stream. Crossing it by a plank bridge, the young people plunged into the cool woods, dark and green, and carpeted with flowering shrubs and vines.

For some time they gathered the blossoms, and were just about to return to the airplanes and resume their journey when Aunt Sally uttered a sudden sharp exclamation:

"Hark! What's that?" she cried.

They all listened. Again came the sound that had arrested her attention; a sharp cry, as if someone was in pain or fright.

Then came definite words:

"Don't! Please; don't hit me again!"

"It's a child!" exclaimed Liam McAdams.

"A girl!" cried Mary Eliska, "someone is ill-treating her."

"We'll soon find out!" cried Bill hotly. It infuriated the boy to think that a child was being subjected to ill-treatment, and the nature of the cries left no doubt that such was the case.

"Stand back here, girls, while we see what's up!" struck in Liam McAdams.

"Indeed we'll do no such thing!" rejoined the plucky Bess, bridling indignantly.

"At any rate let us go in advance," advised Bill; "we don't know just what we may run up against."

This appeared reasonable even to Bess, and with the boys slightly in advance the little group pressed rapidly forward. After traveling about two hundred yards they found themselves in a small clearing where a most unusual sight presented itself; a sight that brought a quick flash of indignation to the face of every one of them.

Cowering under the blows of a tall, swarthy woman was a small girl, so fragile as to appear almost elfin. The woman wore the garb of a gypsy, and the presence of some squalid tents and tethered horses showed our young friends at once that it was a gypsy encampment upon which they had happened.

The woman was so intent on belaboring the shrieking child that at first she did not see the newcomers. It was not 'til Bill stepped up to her, in fact, that she became aware of their presence.

"What are you doing to this child?" demanded Bill indignantly.

"That's none of your business," was the retort, as the woman for an instant released her hold on the child.

Instantly the little creature darted to the sheltering arms of Mary Eliska, sobbing piteously.

"Oh! Save me from her, she will kill me," the child cried, in a broken voice.

"There! there!" soothed Mary Eliska tenderly, "don't cry. We won't let her harm you anymore."

But like a fury the woman flew at the girls. Before she could lay hands on them, however, Bill and Liam McAdams had seized her arms and held them. At this the crone set up a hideous shriek and, as if it had been a signal, two swarthy men, with big earrings in their ears, came running from behind the tents.

"What's the trouble?" they cried, as they ran up, regarding the boys malevolently.

"It's the Wren; they're trying to steal the Wren!" shrilled out the woman.

At this the men rushed at the boys, one of them waving a thick cudgel he carried.

"Let go of that woman," they shouted furiously.

Another instant and the boys would have been in a bad position, for both the gypsies were powerful fellows, and appeared determined to commit violence. But Bill, releasing his hold of the struggling gypsy woman, put up his fists in such a scientific manner that, for an instant, the attack paused. This gave Liam McAdams time to rush to his side. The instant she was released the woman darted to the side of the men.

"Beat them! Kill them!" she cried frantically.

The men resumed their rush, and the next moment the boys found themselves fighting to escape a furious assault. Neither of the lads was a weakling, and good habits and constant athletic exercise had placed them in the pink of condition.

But the two gypsies were no mean antagonists. Then, too, the one with the cudgel wielded it skillfully. Time and again Liam McAdams avoided a heavy blow which, if successful, must have injured him seriously. The girls, screaming, rushed off, carrying "the Wren," as the woman called her, with them. They dashed at top speed back to the spot where the airplanes had been left, and summoned Jake.

"I knew something would happen," declared that worthy, as he picked up a monkey wrench, the only weapon at hand, and started off for the woods.

The girls followed him, Aunt Sally not having been vouchsafed anything but a most hurried explanation of what was going on. Just as Jake appeared on the scene Liam McAdams had received a terrific blow on the arm from one of the gypsy's cudgels. The boy's arm dropped as if paralyzed. With a howl of triumph the ruffian who had dealt him the blow rushed in on the injured lad. In another instant it would have looked bad indeed for Liam McAdams, but Bill, landing a hard blow against his assailant, hastened to his chum's rescue.

"You look after that fellow. I'll take care of this one," cried Jake, rushing into the mêlée, whirling his monkey wrench in a formidable manner.

The girls, huddled in a group, gazed on in frank alarm.

"Oh, they'll be killed!" shrilled Jax Gray.

"Bill! Bill! Be careful!" cried Mary Eliska.

"Oh, I wish we could get a policeman," cried Bess, clasping her hands nervously. But as it happened a policeman, even if such a personage had been within a dozen miles, was not needed. A clever blow from Bill laid the cudgel wielder low, and the other man, not liking the look of Jake's monkey wrench, capitulated by taking to his heels. The woman cowered back among the tents.

"Come on, let's be going," cried Bill, as he saw that the battle was over.

"Ouch! my wrist!" exclaimed Liam McAdams, wringing his left hand; "I believe that fellow has broken it."

"Let's have a look," said Bill, as the two boys made their way to the huddled group of girls.

"Nothing but a nasty whack," he pronounced, after an examination. "Well, girls, was it an exciting battle?"

"Oh, it was terrible," cried Jax Gray; "we thought you'd be badly beaten."

"But as it is we appear to be future prize fighters not forgetting Jake," smiled Bill, who was still panting from his exertions.

"You were awfully brave, I think," cried Bess admiringly, giving the three "heroes" a warm glance.

"Well, there wasn't anything to do but fight, unless we'd run away," laughed Bill, "and now what about the cause of all the trouble?"

He glanced at the little girl clinging to Mary Eliska's hand. The child was pitifully emaciated, with drawn features and large, dark eyes that gazed about her bewilderedly. Her clothing was a red gingham dress that fitted her like a sack. She was shoeless and stockingless. Her brown hair, unkempt and ragged, hung in elf locks about her sad little face. Certainly, as regarded size and general appearance, her name, "The Wren," fitted her admirably.

"I don't know what to do about her," admitted Mary Eliska; "suppose we ask Aunt Sally? I don't want to let the gypsies have her again, and yet I don't see how we can take her."

At the words the little creature burst into a frantic outbreak.

"Don't let those people have me back; don't," she begged; "they'll kill me if you do."

She clung passionately to Mary Eliska's dress. Tears came to the girl's eyes at the pitiful manifestation of fear.

"There! there, dear," soothed Mary Eliska, stroking the child's head, "you shan't go back if we can help it. Come with us for the time being, anyway."

"But we have no legal right to take her," objected Bill.

"Don't say another word," snapped the usually gentle Mary Eliska, whose indignation had been fully aroused, "come on. Let's get back to where we left Aunt Sally, then we can decide what to do."

"Incidentally, we'll do well to get out of this vicinity before any more of those fellows come up. There must be several more somewhere close at hand," exclaimed Liam McAdams.

"Yes; and I'll bet the others, the two who ran off, have gone to call them," put in Bill; "that woman has disappeared, too."

No time was lost in getting back to the airplanes, "The Wren," as the gypsies called her, keeping tight hold of Mary Eliska's hand. The boys walked behind and, with Jake, formed a sort of rear guard to ward off any possible attack. But either the other members of the band were far off, or else they did not care to attempt an assault, for the party reached the airplanes without further incident or molestation.

Aunt Sally's consternation may be imagined as she listened to the tale they had to tell. From time to time during its relation she glanced pityingly at the Wren.

"Poor child!" she exclaimed, gazing at the wizened little creature's bruised arms. They were black and blue from rough handling, and bore painful testimony to the life she had lived among the gypsies.

"What is your name, dear?" she asked, motioning to the child as Mary Eliska finished her story.

"The Wren, that's what they always called me," was the response, in a thin little wisp of a voice.

"Have you no other name?" asked Mary Eliska kindly.

The child shook her head.

"I don't know. Perhaps I did once. I wasn't always with the tribe. I remember a home and my mother, but that was all so long ago that it isn't clear."

"Then she's not a gypsy," declared Mary Eliska emphatically.

"I'll bet they kidnapped her some place," exclaimed Bill.

"That doesn't solve the problem of what to do with her," struck in Jax Gray.

"We can't send her back to those people," declared Bess, with some warmth.

"On the other hand, how are we to look after her?" said Liam McAdams.

"It's a problem that will have to solve itself," said Mary Eliska, after a few moments of deep thinking.

"How is that?" asked Aunt Sally.

"Because she goes with us no matter what happens. It may not be legal, but humanity comes above the law sometimes," declared Mary Eliska, with emphasis.

"Hurrah for Mary Eliska!" cried the boys, "she's as militant as a newly blossomed suffragette. Cheer up, Wren, you're all right now."

"Then I'm to stay with you?" questioned the child.

"Of course," came from Aunt Sally.

The child buried her head on the kind-hearted lady's lap and burst into a passion of weeping that fairly shook her frail frame.

It was at this juncture that Jake set up a shout and pointed toward the woods. From them a group of men had burst, armed with sticks and stones. They came rushing straight at the little group, uttering ferocious shouts.

"We're in for it now," exclaimed Bill; "girls, you had better get in the machine and drive a safe distance. Those fellows mean mischief."

CHAPTER 16.4.
APPROACH OF THE STORM.

It was apparent enough that mean mischief they did. Their dark eyes gleamed fiercely out of their swarthy faces. One or two wore a vivid red or blue handkerchief knotted about sinewy necks, this means of adornment only adding to their generally sinister look.

"I knew we wouldn't get far without running into trouble," moaned Jake dejectedly.

Bill turned on him sharply, almost angrily.

"You get the ladies in that machine and drive off down the road a bit," he said; "I'll attend to this thing. Liam McAdams, come here."

Jake hesitated a moment and then strode off to the auto.

"Can't we stay and help?" asked Bess.

"No; we can help Bill best by doing what he wants us to. He's got some plan in his head," rejoined Mary Eliska firmly, "come along, Wren; Jax Gray, help me with her, she's terrified to death."

This was no exaggeration. At sight of the gypsy band, the child so recently taken from their clutches shrank and cowered against her young protectress.

"Don't let them take me—don't!" she kept wailing.

"Never mind; don't be scared, Wren," Mary Eliska comforted, "they won't get you."

A flash of determined fire came into Mary Eliska's eyes as she spoke.

"Mary Eliska! You're magnificent," exclaimed Jax Gray, as, headed by Mary Eliska, they hastened toward the car which Jake had already cranked.

The gypsies had paused for an instant. Evidently the sight of the airplanes bewildered and amazed them. Expecting to come on a camp of young folks they had suddenly encountered a group of machines which, to them, must have savored of the supernatural. But as the auto drove off they were due for an even greater surprise.

Following a swift whisper from Bill both boys had jumped into the *Red Dragon*. In an instant came the sharp barking of the engine. The flying machine dashed forward almost simultaneously. Straight at the angry nomads Bill headed it. It was as if a war chariot of old was charging into a group of defiant barbarians.

For a few moments the gypsies stood their ground. But as the machine rose from the ground, skimmed it, as it were, Bill thrust on full power. The machine darted over the spot where the gypsies had stood but an instant before; but they had gone. Scattering with wild cries of fear, they could be seen running for their lives toward the wood.

"I don't think they'll trouble us again in a hurry," declared Bill grimly, as he brought the *Red Dragon* round in a circle and headed back for the rest.

From the machine came a cheer, Mary Eliska's voice ringing out as loudly as any.

"The idea just came to me in a second," explained Bill modestly, in answer to the ladies' congratulations and praise, "it worked, though, didn't it?"

"Like a charm," they all agreed.

"Hadn't we better be getting on?" asked Liam McAdams, a minute later.

"Yes; there's no knowing if those fellows won't try a flank attack, although I think they've had a big enough scare thrown into them to last them quite a while with economy," laughed Bill.

"Who is going to take care of Wren?" asked Bess.

"She'll ride right in the car with me," declared Aunt Sally positively, "you don't think I'm going to risk her in one of those things of yours, do you?"

They all laughed. As a matter of fact, there was not one of the party that was not more at home in the air than on a road. Then, too, Bill's balancing device had about removed the last peril of air traveling. It was agreed to stop at Meadville, which the map showed was about thirty miles to the southeast, and purchase a dress and other necessities for their new ward. As to what was to be done with her after that nobody had any very definite plans. And so the journey was resumed, with congratulations flying over the way in which they came out of what, for a time, looked like a really serious scrape.

The weather had held fair 'til a short time after the start was made from the scene of the encounter with the gypsies. It was Mary Eliska who first observed a change in the sky.

From the southwest billowy masses of slate-colored clouds came rolling on, obscuring the sunlit landscape beneath with an effect of lights turned down on a stage. Turning to Jax Gray, who occupied the seat behind her, she remarked:

"We're going to have some bad kind of a storm, girlie."

Jax Gray nodded.

"Wonder how far we are from Meadville?" she asked.

"Quite a way yet. I'm afraid that we can't make it before the storm breaks."

"Look, there's Bill coming back, and Liam McAdams, too. I guess they want to talk about it."

This turned out to be the case. As Bill came swinging by he held a small megaphone to his mouth with one hand, while the other gripped the steering wheel tightly.

"We're in for a storm, girls, and a hummer, too, from the look of it."

"Better drop down," counseled Liam McAdams.

Jax Gray nodded, and, as at this moment Bess, who had seen the boy's maneuver, came by, the news was communicated to her.

The next thing to do was to look about for a suitable place to land. The country over which they were passing was heavily wooded, and seemingly sparsely populated. Beneath them wound a road, along which, but at some distance behind, the touring car could be seen coming in a cloud of yellow dust.

The wind began to grow puffy, and it required all the skill of the young aviatrixes to keep their flock of motor-driven birds on even wings. Before long, just as the distant, but fast approaching, cloud curtain began to be ripped and slashed by vivid scimitars of lightning, Bill espied, beneath them, a field, at one end of which stood a prosperous-looking farmhouse, surrounded by buildings and hay stacks.

It was an ideal spot in which to land, and as the road was nearby they would have no difficulty in attracting the attention of Aunt Sally when she went by. In graceful volplanes the airplanes lit in the field like an alighting flight of carrier pigeons. But hardly had they touched the ground when from the farmhouse a man came running in his shirtsleeves, his lower limbs being garbed in overalls and knee-boots. On his chin was a goatee, and as he drew closer they saw that his face was thin and hatchet shaped and anything but agreeable.

"You git out of thar! You git out of thar!" he kept shouting as he came along, stumbling over the stubble, for the field had been newly reaped.

"Why, what's the matter? We're not hurting anything," objected Bill; "surely you don't mind our occupying the field for an hour or so 'til the storm blows over?"

"I daon't, hey? Wa'al, I do, by heck. I own all the way daown and all the way up frum this farm, and thet's ther law."

"If we didn't have these ladies with us we'd be only too glad to leave your field," rejoined Liam McAdams, "but you can see for yourself a nasty storm is coming up."

"What bizness hes gals riding round in them sky-buggies," stormed the farmer; "ef any darter uv mine did it I'd lock her up on bread an' water, by Jim Hill."

"I don't doubt it in the least," smiled Mary Eliska sweetly.

"Humph!" grunted the cantankerous old agriculturist, not quite sure if he was being made fun of or if his resolution was being admired; "all I got to say is thet ef you want to stay here you gotter pay."

"That can be arranged," spoke Liam McAdams, with quiet sarcasm.

"An' pay wa'al, too," resumed the farmer tenaciously.

"How much do you think the lease of your field for an hour or so is worth?" asked Bill.

The farmer considered an instant, and then, with an avaricious look in his pin-point blue eyes, he looked up.

"'Bout ten dollars," he said, at length.

"We don't want to buy it, we just want to rent it for a very short time," struck in Bess, with her most innocent expression.

"Wa'al, it's ten or git off!" snapped the farmer.

"I'll pay you a fair price for it," spoke up Bill, "and not a cent more."

"Then I'll drive you off with a shot-gun, by chowder."

"Oh, no, you won't."

"Won't, hey? What'll stop me?"

"The law."

"Ther law? Thet's a good one."

"I think it is, a very good one," struck in Liam McAdams, who now saw what Bill was driving at.

"Humph! wa'al, if yer a'goin' te talk law I'll jes' tell yer quick thet this is my land and thet you're all a-trespassing."

"You are not very well up on aërial law, it seems," replied Bill, in an absolutely unruffled tone.

"Don't know nuthin' 'bout this air-ile law," grumbled the fellow, but somewhat impressed by Bill's calm, deliberate exterior.

"Well, then, for your information I'll tell you that under the laws of the country recently enacted these aviatrixes are entitled to land in any safe landing place in times of emergency. If they do any damage they must pay for it. If not the owner of the land is not entitled to anything for the temporary use of his place."

"Five dollars or nothing," spoke Liam McAdams, "and if you try to put us off you'll get into serious trouble."

"Wa'al, yer a-robbin' me," muttered the man, much impressed by Bill's oratory, "gimme ther five."

It was quickly forthcoming. The old fellow took it without a word and shuffled off. As he did so there was a vivid flash of lightning and the growl of a big crash of thunder. While it was still resounding the red automobile came puffing up. Jake had put up the storm top and made it as snug and comfortable as a house.

"Come on, boys and girls," urged Bill, "let's get the engines covered up and then beat it for the car. The rain will hit in in torrents in a few minutes."

Indeed they were still making fast the waterproof covers constructed to throw over the motors in just such emergencies when the big drops began to fall.

There was a helter-skelter race for the car. In they all crowded, and none too soon. The air was almost as dark as at dusk, and there was a heavy sulphureous feeling in the atmosphere. But within the curtains of the car all was fun and merriment. The case of the old farmer was discussed at length, and Liam McAdams convulsed them all by his clever imitation of the way the bargain was driven.

He was in the midst of his description when a fearfully vivid flash lit up the interior of the car as brightly as day. As it did so The Wren uttered a sharp cry.

"What is it, dear? Afraid of the lightning?" asked Aunt Sally, while a thunder volley boomed and reverberated.

"No, no," shivered the child, drawing closer to her, "but when I see a flash like that I sometimes remember."

"Remember what?" asked Aunt Sally tenderly.

"Oh, I don't know," wailed the child, "people and places. They come for a moment and then disappear again as quickly as they came."

CHAPTER 16.5.
MARY ELISKA'S THOUGHTFULNESS SAVES THE FARM.

Flash after flash, roar after roar, the lightning and thunder crashed and blazed as the full fury of the storm struck in. Mary Eliska, who was in deadly fear of lightning, covered her eyes with a thick veil and sank back in the cushions of the tonneau.

But the rest of the party regarded the furious storm with interest. The rain was coming down in sheets, but not one drop penetrated the water-proof top of the big touring car.

"It's grand, isn't it?" asked Aunt Sally, after a particularly brilliant flash.

"Um—ah, I don't just know," rejoined Jax Gray, "it's rather too grand if anything. I——" Bang!

There was a sharp report, like that of a large cannon. The air was filled with an eye-blistering blaze of blue fire. Stunned for an instant, and half blinded, not one of the young folks in the touring car uttered a word.

The storm, too, appeared to be "holding its breath" after that terrific bombardment.

"That struck close by," declared Bill, the first to recover his speech.

"Oh! oh!" moaned Aunt Sally, "then the next will hit us!"

"Don't be a goose, Aunt Sally," comforted Mary Eliska; "don't you know that lightning never strikes twice in the same place?"

Aunt Sally Detective made no answer. In fact she had no opportunity to do so.

From close at hand shouts were coming. Loud, frightened shouts.

"Fire! fire!"

"Gracious! something's on fire at that farmhouse!" cried Mary Eliska.

"That's what!" came in excited tones from Bill as he peered out through the rain.

"Look at them running about," chimed in Liam McAdams.

"It's from that haystack! See the smoke roll up!" cried Bess.

"The lightning must have struck it. Say, we'd better go and help," exclaimed Bill anxiously.

"I don't see that the old man who was so mean to us deserves any help," murmured Bess, rather angrily.

"Why, Bess, for shame!" reproved Mary Eliska. "Go on, boys, the rain's letting up, maybe you can help them."

"All right, sis. Come on, Liam McAdams!"

The boys dived out of the car and set off running at top speed for the scene of the blaze, which was in a haystack back of the main barn of the farmhouse. Several farm hands, under the direction of the disagreeable old man, whose name was Zenas Hutchings, were running about with buckets of water, which were about as effective as trying to sweep the sea back with a broom, so far as gaining any headway against the flames was concerned.

Had the rain continued it might have been possible for the farm hands to quell the blaze with the assistance of the elements; but the storm had ceased almost as suddenly as it began, and only a few scattering drops were now falling. Off to the southwest the sky was blue once more.

The farmer turned despairingly to the boys as they came running up.

"'Clare ter goodness if it ain't them kids ag'in," he exclaimed; "wa'al, you ain't brought me nuthin' but bad luck so far as I kin see. Hyars a hundred dollars' worth of hay goin' up in smoke an'—"

A farm hand came bustling up. His face was pale under the grime of soot that overlaid it.

"Ef we don't git ther fire under control purty soon," he cried, "ther whole place 'ull go."

"What's thet, Jed?" snapped old Hutchings anxiously.

"I said that ther sparks is beginning ter fly. If ther fire gits much hotter it'll set suthin' else ablaze."

"By heck! That's so!" cried old Hutchings, in an alarmed voice.

He gazed about him perplexedly.

"Isn't there any fire apparatus near here?" asked Bill.

"Yep; at Topman's Corners. But that's five miles off."

"Have you telephoned them?" asked Liam McAdams, who had noticed that the Hutchings farm, like most up-to-date ones, was equipped with a telephone; at least there were wires running into the place which appeared to be of that nature.

"Ain't no use telephoning" was the disconsolate rejoinder.

"Why?"

"Wire's busted. Reckon ther storm put it out of business. I guess it's all up with me now. I hoped ter pay off ther part of ther mortgage with ther hay and grain in thet barn yonder, an' now——" He broke off in a half sob. Cantankerous as the old man had shown himself to be, and grasping withal, the boys could not help but feel sorry for the stricken old fellow. He looked pitifully bowed and old and wretched in the midst of his distracted farm hands, who were running about and shouting and not doing much of anything else.

"Wa'al," he said, at length, pulling himself together with a visible effort, "thar's no chance of gitting ther fire ingines, so it'll hev ter go, I guess."

"Yes there is a chance of getting the engines, and a good one, too."

They all turned at the sound of a girlish voice, and there stood Mary Eliska with Jax Gray by her side. The two girls had stolen up unnoticed in the excitement.

"Bravo, Mary Eliska!" exclaimed Bill heartily, glancing approvingly at his sister, "what's your idea?"

"Fly over and get help."

"Fly over! Wa'al, I'll be switched!" gasped old Hutchings.

"I don't see why not," struck in Liam McAdams, "it's five miles, you say. Well, we ought to make that in ten minutes or so, or even quicker."

"How fast can the engines get back?" asked Bill practically.

"Wa'al, ther roads be good and Bob Shields hez a right smart team," was the rejoinder. "They ought ter make it in half an hour."

"Good. Then if you can hold the flames in check for a short time longer we can save your place yet."

Beckoning to Liam McAdams, the boy darted off for the *Red Dragon*. This machine he selected because, with the exception of the *Dart*, it was the fastest and lightest of the airplanes they had with them. Farmer Hutchings had hardly closed his mouth from its gaping expression of surprise when a whirr of the motor announced that the *Red Dragon* was off. Its lithe body shot into the air with tremendous impetus.

"Ther Corners is off thar to ther westward," shouted up the farmer, "you can't miss it. It's got a red brick church with a high tower on it right in the middle of a clump of elms."

Speeding above fields and woodland the red messenger of pending disaster raced through the air. Five minutes after taking flight Liam McAdams espied a high red tower. Eight-and-one-half minutes after the *Dragon* had shot aloft it fluttered to earth on the village street of Topman›s Corners, amid an amazed group of citizens who had seen it approaching.

It was the first airplane ever seen in the remote Pennsylvanian hamlet, and it created commensurate excitement. But the boys had no time to answer the scores of questions, foolish and otherwise, that were volleyed at them from all sides.

"There's a fire!" exclaimed Liam McAdams breathlessly, "a fire at Hutchings's farm. How soon can you get the engines there?"

A stalwart-looking young fellow stepped up.

"I'm chief of the department," he said, "we're the 'Valiants.' I'll be there in twenty-five minutes if I have to kill the horses. It's downhill most of the way, anyhow. Jim, you run off and ring ther bell."

A second later the fire bell was loudly clanging and several of the crowd melted away to don their helmets and coats. In less time than the boys would have thought it possible a good-looking engine came rumbling out of the fire house half a block down the street. Behind it came a hook and ladder truck.

Fine horses were attached to each, and from the way they leaped off the boys saw that the "Chief" meant to make good his promise.

"Race you to ther fire!" shouted the latter functionary, as, in a storm of cheers, his apparatus swept out of sight down the elm-bordered street.

"You're on," laughed Bill, whisking aloft while the Topman's Cornerites were still wondering within themselves if they were waking or dreaming.

CHAPTER 16.6.
THE GIRL AVIATRIXES IN DEADLY PERIL.

The fire was out. A smoldering, blackened hillock was all that remained of the stack ignited by the lightning bolt; but the others and the main buildings of the farm had been saved.

Such work was a new task for airplanes—but there is no doubt that, had it not been for Mary Eliska's suggestion, the Hutchings farm would have been burned to the ground. As it was, when the firemen, their horses in a lather, arrived at the scene, the farm hands, who had been fighting the flames, were almost exhausted.

Had they possessed the time, the young folks would have been glad to tell the curious firemen something about their airplanes. But it was well into the afternoon, and if they intended to keep up their itinerary it was necessary for them to be hurrying on. A short time after the blaze had been declared "out" the airplanes once more soared aloft, and the auto chugged off in the direction of Meadville.

The afternoon sun shone sparklingly on the trees and fields below, all freshened by the downpour of the early afternoon. The spirits of all rose as did their machines as they raced along. Before leaving the Hutchings farm the old man had been so moved to generosity by the novel manner in which his farm had been saved from destruction that he had offered to give back $2.50 of the $5 he had demanded for the rent of his field. Of course they had not taken it, but the evident anguish with which the offer was made afforded much amusement to the young aviatrixes as they soared along.

In Mary Eliska's machine the talk between herself and Jax Gray was of the strange finding of The Wren, and of the child's curious ways. Both girls recalled her odd conduct during the storm and what she had said about the peculiar influence of lightning on her memory.

"Depend on it, Jax Gray," declared Mary Eliska, with conviction, "that child is no more a gypsy than you or I."

"Do you think she was stolen from somewhere?" asked Jax Gray, readily guessing the drift of her friend's thoughts.

"I don't know, but I'm sure they had no legal right to her," was the reply.

"Oh, Mary Eliska! Suppose she should turn out to be a missing heiress!" Jax Gray, who loved a romance, clasped her gauntleted hands.

Mary Eliska laughed.

"Missing heiresses are not so common as you might suppose," she said; "I never met anyone who had encountered any, except in story books."

"Still, it would be great if we had really found a long missing child, or—or something like that," concluded Jax Gray, rather lamely.

"I can't see how we would be benefiting the child or its parents, either, since we have no way of knowing who the latter are," rejoined the practical Mary Eliska, which remark closed the discussion for the time being.

It was not more than half an hour later when Jax Gray uttered a sharp cry of alarm. From the forward part of the airplane a wisp of smoke had suddenly curled upward. Like a blue serpent of vapor it dissolved in the air almost so quickly as to make Jax Gray believe, for an instant, that she had been the victim of an hallucination.

But that it was no figment of the imagination was evidenced a few moments later by Mary Eliska herself. Aroused by Jax Gray's cry, she had made an inspection of the machine, with alarming results. What these were speedily became manifest.

"Jax Gray! The machine is on fire!" she cried afrightedly.

As if in verification of her words there came a puff of flame and a strong reek of gasoline. It was just then that both girls recalled that the *Golden Butterfly* carried twenty-five gallons of gasoline, without counting the reserve supply.

Fire on an airplane is even more terrifying than a similar casualty on any other type of machine. Hardly had Mary Eliska's words confirming the alarming news left her lips when there came a cry from Jax Gray.

The girl had just glanced at the barograph. It showed that they were then 1,500 feet above the surface of the earth. The girl had hardly made this discovery before, from beneath the "bow" of the monoplane, came a wave of flame; driven from the steering wheel by the heat, Mary Eliska drew back toward her companion. Her face was ashen white.

Left to itself the airplane "yawed" wildly, like a craft without a rudder. Then suddenly it dashed down toward the earth, smoke and flames leaping from its front part.

Both girls uttered a cry of terror as the aircraft fell like a stone hurled into space. Faster and faster it dashed earthward without a controlling hand to guide it. It was at this instant that Bill and Liam McAdams became aware of what had happened.

Instantly they swung their machine around in time to see the *Golden Butterfly* make her sickening downward swoop. Both lads uttered a cry of fear as they saw what appeared to mean certain death for the two Girl Aviatrixes.

Bill's fingers scarcely grasped the wheel of his machine as he saw the downward drop. Liam McAdams was as badly affected. But almost before they could grasp a full realization of the accident the *Golden Butterfly* was almost on the ground. It was in a hilly bit of country, interspersed by small lakes or ponds.

A freak of the wind caught the blazing airplane as it fell and drove it right over one of these small bodies of water.

The *Golden Butterfly* appeared to hesitate for one instant and then plunged right into the water, flinging the two girls out. Both were expert swimmers, but the shock of the sudden descent, and the abrupt manner in which they had been flung into the water had badly unstrung their nerves.

Jax Gray struck out valiantly, but the next instant uttered a cry:

"Mary Eliska! Mary Eliska! I'm sinking!"

Mary Eliska pluckily struck out for her chum and succeeded in seizing her. Then with brisk strokes she made for the shore, luckily only a few yards distant. It was at this juncture that the boys' machines came to earth almost simultaneously. High above Bess's *Dart* hovered, and presently it, too, began to drop downward. Apparently the accident had not been seen from the auto, at any rate the car was not turned back toward the scene of the accident.

As the boys' airplanes struck the earth not far from the bank of the pond toward which Mary Eliska was at that moment valiantly struggling, the two young aviatrixes leaped out and set out at a run to the rescue. They reached the bank in the nick of time to pull out the two drenched, half-exhausted girls.

"At any rate the fall was a lucky one in a way!" gasped the optimistic Mary Eliska, as soon as she caught her breath, "it put out the fire."

And so it had. Not only that, but the airplane, buoyed up by its broad wings, was still floating. On board the *Red Dragon* was a long bit of rope. Liam McAdams produced this and then swam out to the drifting *Butterfly*. The rope was made fast to it and the craft dragged ashore. But when they got it to the bank the problem arose as to how they were going to drag it up the steep acclivity.

Again and again they tried; Bess, who had by this time alighted, aiding them. But it was all to no purpose. Even their united strength failed to move the heavy apparatus.

"I've got an idea!" shouted Liam McAdams suddenly, during a pause in their laborious operations.

"Good! Don't let it get away, I beg of you!" implored Mary Eliska.

"Oh, Mary Eliska! Don't tease, besides, you don't look a bit cute with your hair all wet and draggled, and as for your dress—goodness!"

This came from Jax Gray, herself sadly "rumpled" and in addition wet through. Before Mary Eliska could reply to her chum's half rallying remark Liam McAdams, unabashed, continued: "We'll hitch this rope to the *Red Dragon* and then start her up for all she›s worth."

"Liam McAdams, you're a genius!"

"A modern marvel!"

"A solid promontory of pure gray matter!"

In turn the remarks came from each of the party. But Liam McAdams, bothering not at all at the laughing encomiums, proceeded to secure the rope to the *Red Dragon*. This done, he started up the engine and clambered into his seat.

"All ashore that's going ashore!" he yelled, in mocking imitation of the stewards of an ocean liner.

There wasn't an instant's hesitation as he threw the load upon the engine. Then the rope tautened. It grew tight as a fiddle string.

"Goodness! It'll snap and the *Dragon* will be broken!" cried Jax Gray, in alarm.

But no such thing happened. Instead, as the *Dragon's* powerful propeller blades «bit" into the air, the *Golden Butterfly* obediently mounted the steep bank of the pond. Five minutes later the pretty craft stood on dry land and the party of young aviatrixes were eagerly making an investigation of the damage done.

The cause of the fire was soon found. A tiny leak in the tank had allowed some gasoline to drip into the bottom of the chassis, or passenger carrier. Collecting here, it was plain that a back fire from the carburetor had ignited it.

Neither of the girls could repress a shudder as they thought of what might have occurred had they been higher in the air and no convenient pond handy for them to drop into. In such a case the flames might have reached the gasoline tank before they could be extinguished and inevitably a fearful explosion would have followed.

"I think you are the two luckiest girls in the world," declared Bill solemnly, as he concluded his examination and announced his conclusions. Naturally they fully agreed with him.

CHAPTER V16.7.
A STOP FOR THE NIGHT.

It was some two hours later that Meadville received the greatest excitement of its career. People rushed out of stores and houses as the "flock" of airplanes came into sight.

As they gazed down the young aviatrixes felt a momentary regret that they had chosen a town in which to pass the first night of their motor flight. It appeared that they would get into difficulties when they attempted to make a landing.

But almost simultaneously they spied a public park, which appeared to offer a favorable landing place. As soon as their intention of descending there became manifest, however, the crowd made a headlong rush for the spot.

It was too late to seek some other location to alight even had there been one available. Trusting to luck that the eager spectators would get out of their way the four airplanes began their spiraling descent.

Bill was first in his big biplane. As the ponderous, white machine ranged down close to the park the crowd became well-nigh uncontrollable. They swarmed beneath the big machine, despite Bill's shouts of warning.

Skillfully as the boy manipulated the aircraft he could not check its descent once begun.

"Out of the way! I don't want to hurt you!" he shouted, as he dashed down.

But the crowd, sheeplike in their stupidity, refused to budge. Into the midst of them Bill, perforce, was compelled to drive. Once the throng perceived his intention, however, they scattered wildly. That is, all sought positions of safety but one man, a stout, red-faced individual, who appeared dazed or befuddled.

He stood his ground, glaring foolishly at the sky ship. With a quick turn of his wrist Bill swept the big biplane aside, but a wing tip brushed the stout man, toppling him over in a twinkling. By the time Bill had stopped his machine the man was on his feet again, bellowing furiously. He was not hurt, but his face was contorted with anger.

He pushed his way through the crowd toward the young aviator.

"You young scoundrel!" he yelled, "I'll fix you for that! I'll—" "Look out, here come the rest of them!" shouted the crowd at this juncture.

Nobody needed any warning this time. They fled in all directions as one after the other the *Golden Butterfly*, the *Red Dragon* and the pretty, graceful *Dart* dropped to earth.

"Wa'al, look at them gals, will yer!" shouted a voice in the crowd.

"What's the country coming to?" demanded another man. "Gals gallivanting around like gol-dinged birds!"

But the majority of the crowd took the pretty girl aviatrixes to its heart. Somebody set up a cheer.

It was still ringing out when, to the huge relief of the embarrassed girls, the auto came rolling up with Mary Eliska and "The Wren," as they still called the latter.

The girls, leaving the boys to look after the airplanes, ran to the side of the car and were speedily ensconced in its roomy tonneau. "We'll see you at the hotel!" cried Bill, as the car rolled off again, much to the disappointment of the crowd.

Two local constables came up at this juncture and helped the boys keep the crowd back from the machines. The throng seemed souvenir mad. Many of them insisted on writing their names with pencils on the wings of the air craft. Others would have gone further and actually stripped the airplanes of odd parts had they not been held back.

"This is the last time we'll land in a town of this size," declared Bill indignantly, as he helped the constables shove back an obstreperous individual who insisted on examining the motor of the *Dart*.

With the help of the constables a sheltering place for the machines was finally found. A livery stable that had gone out of business the week before was located across the street from the small park in which they had alighted. The owner of the property happened to be in the crowd and a bargain with him was soon struck. The airplanes were then trundled on their landing wheels into this shelter and the doors closed. Bill, for a small sum, engaged a tall, gangling-looking youth, whose name was Tam Tammas, to guard the doors and keep off the inquisitive. This done, thoroughly tired out, the boys sought the hotel. Like most towns of its size and importance Meadville only boasted one hostelry worthy of the name. This place, the Fountain House, as it was called, was a decent enough looking hotel and the young aviatrixes were warmly welcomed. After supper, for in Meadville nobody "dined," Mary Eliska and the girls sauntered out with The Wren to obtain some clothing for the waif who had so strangely come into their possession. It was odd, but somehow they none of them even suggested giving up the queer little foundling to the authorities as had originally been their intention. Instead, although none of them actually voiced it, it appeared that tacitly they had decided to keep the child with them.

While they were gone on their errand of helpfulness Bill and Liam McAdams were seated on the porch of the hotel watching, with more or less languid interest, the inhabitants of the town passing back and forth. Many of them lingered in front of the hotel, for aviatrixes were not common objects in that part of the country, and already the party had become local celebrities.

"I guess we'll go inside," said Bill, at length, "I'm getting sick of being looked at as if I was some sort of natural curiosity."

"Same here," rejoined Liam McAdams, "we'll go in and I'll play you a game of checkers."

"You're on," was the response.

But as the boys rose to go, or rather the instant before they left their seats, there came a heavy step behind Bill and a gruff voice snarled:

"What are you doing in that chair?"

"Sitting in it," responded Bill, in not too pleasant a voice. The tone in which he had been addressed had aroused a hot resentment in him toward the speaker.

Turning he saw the same red-faced man whom he had been unfortunate enough to knock down.

Instantly his manner changed. He felt genuinely sorry for the accident and hastened to explain that such was the case. But a glowering glance was the only response he received. "You done it a-purpose. Don't tell me," snarled the red-faced individual, "an' now you git right out uv that chair or—or I'll make you!"

Both boys stared at the man in amazement. His tone was coarse and bullying to a degree.

"We are not occupying these chairs to your inconvenience," declared Bill stoutly, "there are lots of others."

He indicated several rockers placed at intervals along the hotel porch, and all empty.

"That chair you're sitting in is mine," snapped the man, in response.

"Got a mortgage on it, eh?" smiled Liam McAdams amiably.

"I'll show you kids how much of a mortgage I've got on it," was the reply.

It was just then that a lad of about Bill's own age, but with a surly, hang-dog sort of look, emerged from the smoking-room of the hotel.

"What's up, father?" he demanded, addressing the red-faced man.

"Why, Dan, the kids have appropriated my chair."

"Oh, those flying kids. Well, they'll see that they ain't everything around here," responded the lad; "I reckon Jim Cassell has some say here, eh, dad?"

"I reckon so, son," grinned the red-faced man, in response to this elegant speech; "now, then, are you going to give up that chair or not?"

"I was just leaving it when you came out," rejoined Bill, who, by this time, was fairly boiling over. "Under the present conditions, however, I think I shall continue to occupy it."

"You will, eh?" snarled out Dan Cassell, "then I'll show you how to vacate it—so!"

With the words he laid hands on the back of the chair and jerked it from under the young aviator. Bill, caught entirely off his guard, was flung to the floor of the porch. He was up in a flash, but as he rose to his feet Dan Cassell, evidently excited by what he deemed a great triumph, aimed a savage blow at him.

Liam McAdams was rushing to his assistance but the red-faced man suddenly blocked his path.

"Hold off, son! hold off!" he warned, "unless you want to get the same dose."

CHAPTER 16.8.
BILL MAKES AN ENEMY.

In the mean`time Bill had skillfully avoided Dan Cassell's blow, and was aggressively on the defensive. He was a lad who did not care for fighting, but notwithstanding was a trained boxer. Something of this seemed to dawn on Dan Cassell as the boy he sought to pummel dodged his attack with such cleverness.

For a moment Dan stood stock-still with doubled up fists and a scowl on his not unhandsome, though weak and vicious features. Then, with a bellow, he rushed upon Bill, who contented himself by sidestepping the furious onslaught.

This appeared to enrage Dan Cassell the more. Either he interpreted it as portraying cowardice, or else he deemed that he had his opponent at his mercy. At any rate, after an instant's pause he rushed at Bill with both fists. It was the young aviator's opportunity.

"Look out!" he warned.

The next instant the pugnacious Dan Cassell found himself upon his back, regarding a multitude of constellations.

At almost precisely the same time Liam McAdams's fist happened to collide with the point of the jaw of the fallen battler's father.

"Sorry; but I simply had to, you know," remarked the nonchalant Liam McAdams, as the red-faced man found himself occupying a position not dissimilar to that of his son.

Both boys were heartily sorry for what had happened, the more so for the reason that at the very instant that both crestfallen bullies were scrambling to their feet the hotel door opened and several of the guests came out to ascertain the cause of the trouble.

Among them was Jonas Hardcastle, the proprietor of the place.

"What's up? What's the trouble?" he demanded, in dismay, as he viewed the scene of the confusion.

"It's those brats of aviatrixes, or whatever they call themselves," bellowed Cassell, who was purple with fury; "they attacked Dan and me and assaulted us brutally."

The landlord looked doubtingly at the man. Then he turned to Bill. "What are the facts?" he asked. Bill told him unhesitatingly the whole truth. When he had concluded Jonas Hardcastle spoke.

"You've been hanging around here too long, Jim Cassell," he said, in a voice that quivered with indignation; "now make yourself scarce, both you and your son. Don't annoy my guests anymore."

Cassell, nursing a spot on his jaw which was rapidly growing a beautiful plum color, lurched off without a word. His son followed. It was not until he reached the street that he spoke. Then, in a voice that trembled from suppressed fury, he hissed out:

"All right for you kids. You think you've played a smart trick on Dan and me; but I'll fix you! Just watch!"

Without uttering another syllable he slouched off into the gathering darkness, followed by his son, who bestowed a parting scowl on Bill and Liam McAdams.

"I'm sorry that you had a row with them," remarked Jonas Hardcastle, as the pair vanished.

"How's that?" inquired Bill. "They forced it on us, and—" "I know. I know all about that," was the rejoinder, "but Cassell is quite by way of being a politician hereabouts, and he might try to make it uncomfortable for you."

"In what way?" demanded Liam McAdams.

"Oh, many ways. Those fellows have no scruples. To tell you the truth, boys, I guess you haven't heard the last of this."

With this he left them, a prey to no very comfortable thoughts.

"I'm half inclined to believe what he said," declared Liam McAdams.

"In just what way?"

"Why, about the harm this fellow Cassell can do us. In every community like this you'll find one local 'Pooh-bah' who runs things pretty much as he likes. They have satellites who will do just about as they're told."

"You mean—" "That we'd better keep a good lookout on the airplanes. From my judgment of Cassell I don't think he's got nerve enough to attack us directly, but he can wreak his vengeance on our machines if we don't watch pretty closely."

"I'm inclined to think you're right. But don't say a word of all this to the girls. It might upset them. You and I will decide on a plan of action later on. To tell you the truth, I'm not any too sure of our newly acquired watchman, Tam Tammas."

"Nor I. We'll wait 'til the rest get back and then take a stroll down to that livery stable. Seems funny, doesn't it, to stable airplanes in a livery stable?"

"Well, why not? Wasn't Mary Eliska, the first flying machine on record, a horse?"

"Humph; that's so," agreed Liam McAdams, whose supply of classical knowledge was none too plentiful.

It was not long after this that the girls returned. With them came The Wren in a neat dress and new shoes, an altogether different looking little personage from the waif of the woods whom they had rescued at noon.

"Why, Wren," cried Mary Eliska, "you are positively pretty. In a month's time we won't know you."

"A month's time?" sighed the child; "am I going to stay with you as long as that?"

Mary Eliska caught the wan little figure in her arms.

"Yes, and many months after that," she cried.

Bill and Liam McAdams exchanged glances.

"Another member of the family," exclaimed Bill; "if we go at this rate we'll have acquired an entire set of new sisters by the time we reach the Big Smokies."

CHAPTER 16.9.
LIAM MCADAMS FALLS ASLEEP.

"Anybody been around, Tam?"

Bill asked the question, as later on that evening he and Liam McAdams dropped around to the disused livery stable in accordance with their plan.

Tam shook his head.

"Nobody bane round," he rejoined, and then, after a moment's pause, "'cept Yim Cassell and his boy Dan."

"Jim Cassell and his son," echoed Bill, "the very people we don't want around here. What did they want?"

"They want know where you bane," rejoined the Norwegian youth.

"Yes; and what did you tell them?"

"I bane tell them I skall not know," responded Tam.

"And then?"

"They bane ask me if ay have key by door."

"Oh, they did, eh? What did you say?"

"I say I bane not have key."

"Then what did they do?"

"They bane go 'way."

"Didn't say anything else?"

"No, they must go."

"Said nothing about coming back?"

"No."

"All right, Tarn, you can go home now. Here's your money."

"You bane want me no more?"

"No; we'll watch here ourselves tonight. Good night."

"Good night," rejoined Tam, pocketing his money and shuffling off down the street.

He had hardly gone two blocks when from the shadow of an elm-shaded yard the figure of Dan Cassell slipped out and intercepted him.

"So you've been fired, eh?"

He shot the question at the simple-minded Norwegian lad with vicious emphasis.

"No, I no bane fired; they bane tell me no want me more."

"Well, isn't that being fired? Moreover, I can tell you that they've hired another fellow in your place."

The Norwegian youth's light blue eyes lit up with indignant fire. Like most of his race he was keenly sensitive once aroused, and while he was quite agreeable to being dropped from his temporary job, he hated to think of being supplanted in it. Crafty Dan Cassell was playing his cards well, for a purpose that will be seen ere long.

"So they bane fire me," ejaculated Tam.

"That's the size of it. I guess you feel pretty sore, Tam, don't you?"

"No, they bane pay me wale; but I no like being fired."

"I should think not. The idea of a man like you being dropped. What did they tell you when they let you go?"

"That they bane watch place themselves."

Dan Cassell smiled. His crafty methods had elicited something of real value after all.

"Did they say they were going to watch all night?" he asked.

"Yes," rejoined the Norwegian, "they ask about you, too."

"Humph! What did they want to know?"

"If you'd been round by stable and what I bane tale you."

"What did you say?"

"I tale them the truth. I say that you and your father bane by stable this evening."

Dan's face darkened.

"You had no business to tell them anything," he snarled. Then, with a sudden change of front: "See here, Tam, do you want to make some money?"

"Sure, I bane like make money."

"Then come into the house a minute. Dad and I want to talk to you."

So saying Dan took the Norwegian by the arm and led him in through a gate in a whitewashed picket fence. Beyond the fence was a fairly prosperous looking house, on the piazza of which lounged Jim Cassell smoking a cigar.

"Well, Tam," he said, "lost your job?"

The Norwegian replied in the affirmative.

"Well, never mind, I've got another for you," replied Jim Cassell, in what was for him an unwontedly amiable tone; "can you go to work at once?"

"Ay bane work any time skol be," spoke the Norwegian, and a puzzled expression flitted over his face as both Cassells broke into what was to him an inexplicable fit of laughter at his words.

In the meantime the boys had telephoned to the hotel that work on the airplanes would detain them 'til late. They did not wish to inform the girls that they were undertaking a night watch, as that would have led to all sorts of questions, and if their fears proved ungrounded they felt pretty sure of coming in for a lot of "joshing."

They agreed to divide the night into two parts, Liam McAdams watching 'til midnight and then awakening Bill who would take up the vigil 'til dawn. This arrangement having been made they secured a light lantern from an adjacent hardware store and, entering the deserted livery stable, prepared to carry out their plans. With the canvas covers of the airplanes Bill managed to fix up quite a comfortable bed on a pile of hay left in a sort of loft over the abandoned stable.

As for Liam McAdams, he made himself as comfortable as possible in the chassis of the *Golden Butterfly*, the seats of which were padded as luxuriously as those of a touring car.

He had a book dealing with aeronautic subjects with him, and, drawing the lantern close to the airplane, he buried himself in the volume.

In the meantime Bill had rolled himself up in his canvas coverings and was sound asleep. For a long time Liam McAdams read on. At first frequent footsteps passed the door of the stable, but as it grew later these ceased. Folks went to bed early in Meadville. Long before midnight there was not a sound on the streets.

Liam McAdams read doggedly on. But he was painfully conscious of an almost irresistible desire to lie back and doze off, if only for a few seconds. The exciting events of the day had tired him out, nor was the book he was reading one calculated to keep his wits stirring. It was a technical work of abstruse character.

Liam McAdams's head began to nod. With a sharp effort he aroused himself only to catch himself dozing off once more.

"See here, Liam, this won't do," he sharply admonished himself, "you're on duty, understand? On duty! Wake up and keep your eyes open." But try as he would tired Nature finally asserted herself. Liam McAdams's head fell forward, his eyes closed for good and he snored in right good earnest. He was sound asleep.

It was about half an hour after he dozed off that a window in the rear of the stable framed a face. A crafty, eager face it was, as the yellow light of the lantern revealed its outlines. Dan Cassell, for it was he, gazed sharply about him. He swiftly took in the posture of the sleeping boy and a smile spread over his countenance.

Dropping from the ladder he had raised outside, he joined two figures waiting for him in the shadow of the livery barn.

"It's too easy," he chuckled, "only one kid there and he's sound asleep. Got everything ready?"

"Dey all bane ready, Maister Cassell," rejoined the slow, drawling voice of the Norwegian Tam.

"Now don't botch the job," warned the elder Cassell, who was the third member of the party; "remember it means a lot of trouble for us if we're caught."

"No danger of that, dad. Come on, I'll go first and you and Tam follow."

"Is the window open?"

"No, but it slides back. It's an easy drop to the floor from it."

"All right, go ahead. I'll be glad when the job's over. I'm almost inclined to drop out of it."

"And let those kids get away with what they did? Not much, dad. We'll give them a lesson they won't forget in a hurry. Come on."

He began climbing the ladder. Behind him came his worthy parent, and Tam formed the last member of the now silent procession. The Norwegian carried a bulky package of some kind, the contents of which it would have been impossible to guess save that it gave out a metallic sound as Tam moved with it.

Dan Cassell reached the window, slid it noiselessly back in its grooves and then, crawling through, dropped lightly to the floor within. He was followed by his father and Tam.

But Liam McAdams slept on. Slept heavily and dreamlessly, while deadly peril crept upon him.

CHAPTER 16.10.
MARY ELISKA'S INTUITION.

The movements of the invaders of the stable, which now housed the "winged steeds" of the young aviatrixes, were mysterious in the extreme. The Norwegian carried a tin can containing some sort of liquid which he was ordered to pour about the floor in the neighborhood of the airplanes. This done, Dan Cassell collected several scraps of litter and made quite a pile of it.

"All ready now, I guess," he said, with what was meant as an attempt at a grin. But his lips were pale, and his forced jollity was a dismal failure. As for his father, he made no attempt to conceal his agitation.

"Dan, they may be burned alive," he faltered; "better call it all off."

"Not when we've gone as far as this with it," was the rejoinder; "give me a match."

"Dan!"

"It's all right, dad. They'll wake in time."

"But if not?"

"Then they'll have to take their medicine."

With fingers that trembled as if their owner was palsied, Jim Cassell handed his son some matches. The latter took one, bent low over the pile he had collected and struck the lucifer.

A yellow sputter of flame followed, and the next instant he was holding it to the pile of litter which had been previously soaked by the contents of the Norwegian's can.

But before he could accomplish his purpose and set fire to the pile of odds and ends saturated to double inflammability by the kerosene the Norwegian had carried, there came a startling interruption.

There was a knock at the door and a girlish voice cried:

"Bill! Bill, let me in!"

"Furies!" exclaimed Dan Cassell under his breath. "It's one of those girls."

"Come on. Let's get away quick!" exclaimed his father, trembling from nervous agitation.

"Not before I set a match to this," exclaimed Dan Cassell viciously.

He touched the match to the pile and the flames leaped up.

"Now for our getaway," he cried, and the three fire-bugs ran for the window by which they had made their entrance.

In the meantime a perfect fusillade of blows had been showered on the door outside. Liam McAdams awoke just as the last of the three midnight intruders vanished through the window. His first instinct was a hot flush of shame over the feeling that he had betrayed his trust.

Then to his ears came the voice that had alarmed the Cassells and their tool.

"Bill! Liam McAdams! Are you there?"

"It's Mary Eliska!" gasped Liam McAdams.

"And Jax Gray," he added the next instant, and simultaneously there came the pounding of a stick on the door.

"This is an officer of the law. Open up at once."

Liam McAdams, dazed by his sleep, had not 'til then noticed the blazing pile of litter. Now he did so with a quick cry of horror. The stuff was blazing up fiercely. Already there was an acrid reek in the air.

"The place is on fire!" he shouted.

The next moment there came a violent assault on the door and the crazy lock parted from its rotten fastenings as a man attired in a police officer's uniform burst into the place. Behind him came two wide-eyed frightened girls. The leaping flames lit up their faces vividly.

"It's fire sure enough!" cried the police officer.

"Great Scot, what's happening?"

It was Bill who shouted the question. He was peering down from the loft where he had been sleeping. The uproar had awakened him and in a jiffy he was among them.

"Quick! the fire extinguishers!" he cried, and Liam McAdams, readily understanding, secured the flame-killing apparatus from the biplane and from the *Red Dragon*.

He and Bill, aided by the officer, fought the flames vigorously, and, luckily, were able to subdue them, though if it had not been for the as yet unexplained arrival of Mary Eliska and Jax Gray it is doubtful if they could have coped with the blaze. When it was all out Mary Eliska rushed into explanations.

"Something warned me that you were in danger," she exclaimed, "and I woke up Jax Gray and we found this officer and came down here."

"What gift of second sight have you?" demanded Bill, gazing at the smoking, blackened pile that had threatened the destruction of the inflammable premises.

"I don't know. Womanly intuition, perhaps. Oh, Bill!"

The girl burst into a half-hysterical sob and threw her arms about her brother's neck.

"You arrived in the nick of time, sis," he said, gently disengaging himself from her clasp, "a little more and—"

He did not finish the sentence. There was no need for him to.

"Begorry, the ould place 'ud hev bin a pile of cinders in an hour's time," declared the policeman.

It was Jax Gray's turn to give an hysterical little sob.

Bill turned to Liam McAdams.

"Did you see anything? The place is reeking with kerosene. It was a plot to destroy the airplanes and perhaps ourselves."

"I—I—"

Liam McAdams stammered. The words seemed to choke up in his throat. How was he to confess that he had failed in his trust—had slept while danger threatened?

"Well?"

Bill waited, plainly surprised. It was not like Liam McAdams to hesitate and stammer in this way.

At last it came out with a rush.

"I—I—you'll never forgive me, any of you—I was asleep."

"Asleep! Oh, Liam McAdams!"

There was a world of reproach in Jax Gray's voice. But Mary Eliska interrupted her.

"How was it, Liam McAdams?" she asked softly.

"I don't know. I give you my word I don't know."

Liam McAdams's voice held a world of self-reproach.

"I was reading," he went on, hurrying over the words as if anxious to get his confession over with, "that book of Grotz's on monoplane navigation. I felt sleepy and—and the next thing I knew I woke up to hear you pounding on the door and shouting."

"A good thing the young ladies found me," put in the policeman; "shure I was after laughing at them at first, but then, begorry, I decided to come along with them. It's glad I am that I did."

"Who can have done this?" asked Bill, who had not a word of reproach for his chum, although Liam McAdams had failed dismally in a position of trust.

"Begorry, they might have burned you alive!" cried the policeman indignantly.

"No question about that," rejoined Bill; "it was a diabolical plot. Who could have attempted such a thing?"

"Wait 'til I call up and have detectives sent down here," said Officer McCarthy. "I'm after thinking this is too deep for us to solve."

Nevertheless, each of that little group but the policeman had his or her own idea on the matter.

CHAPTER 16.11.
A MEAN REVENGE!

The result of the telephone call was a request to call at the Police Headquarters of the little town and give a detailed account of the affair.

"Gracious! I should think that the only way to get a clue would be to send a detective down here," exclaimed Mary Eliska, on receipt of this information.

"We have our own ways of doing them things, miss," rejoined the policeman with dignity.

Then there being nothing for it but to obey instructions of the authorities, they all set out for the police station. They were half way there when Liam McAdams recollected that they had left the airplanes unguarded.

"'Twill make no difference at all at all," declared the policeman; "shure it's too late for anyone to be about."

"It wasn't too late for them to set that fire though," rejoined Bill in a low voice.

At police headquarters they were received by two sleepy-looking officials who questioned them at length and said they would be at the stable in the morning to hunt for clues.

"Why not go after them now, while the trail is hot?" inquired Liam McAdams.

"We have our own ways of doing these things, young man," was the reply, delivered with ponderous dignity.

"Well, we might as well go to bed and get a few hours' sleep anyhow," suggested Bill; "I can hardly keep my eyes open. How about you, Liam McAdams?"

"I—I—I've had some sleep already you know," rejoined Liam McAdams, reddening.

Thoroughly tired out from their long day and excitement, the party slept 'til late the next day. The first thing after breakfast plans for the continuance of the trip were discussed, and the day's program mapped out. This done, the girls and boys set out for the stable to look over the machines.

They found a pompous-looking policeman on guard in front of the place, ostentatiously pacing up and down. On identifying themselves they were at once admitted however. The man explained that he had only been on guard for an hour or two, and that during that time nothing worthy of mention had occurred.

While Liam McAdams was talking to him Bill and the others entered the stable. An instant later Bill, too excited to talk, came rushing out of the dis-used livery barn.

"What's up now, Bill?" demanded Liam McAdams, gazing at his chum, who for his part appeared to be too excited to get his words out.

"There's only three!" gasped Bill.

"Three what?" cried Liam McAdams.

"Three airplanes," returned Bill.

"Rubbish, you haven't got your eyes open yet."

"I'm right, I tell you; come in and count them if you don't believe me."

"Bill is right," cried Mary Eliska, running up to the group; "the *Golden Butterfly* has been stolen!"

"Stolen!" interjected Liam McAdams.

"That's right!" cried Jax Gray; "those stupid police people left the barn unguarded. Whoever tried to set it on fire must have returned and stolen the *Butterfly*."

They regarded each other blankly. Was this Sky Cruise that they had looked forward to with such eager anticipation to be nothing but a series of mishaps?

"It's awful!" gasped Mary Eliska; "nothing but trouble since we started out."

"D'ye think it was stolen?" asked the policeman with startling intelligence.

"Well, it didn't fly of its own accord," was Mary Eliska's rejoinder, delivered with blighting sarcasm.

The patrolman subsided.

"Maybe we can find it yet," suggested Jax Gray.

"I'd like to know how," put in Liam McAdams disgustedly.

"Perhaps we can trace it. It must have been wheeled away."

"Ginger! That's so," cried Bill, snapping his fingers; "it would leave an odd track too, wouldn't it?"

"Well there's no harm in trying to trace it," admitted Liam McAdams, who appeared rather skeptical.

"Come on, then; get busy," urged Bill eagerly.

The next instant there came a cry from Mary Eliska. "I've struck the trail!" she cried.

"Where?" The word came in chorus. "Here! Look; you know the *Butterfly* had peculiar kind of tires. See, it was wheeled up the street in that direction."

She pointed to where the village main thoroughfare ended in a country road.

"I'm not after takin' much stock in that," remarked the policeman.

"We won't bother you," rejoined Bill rather heatedly; "I guess we won't wait 'til your local Sherlock Holmes gets on the trail, we'll follow it ourselves."

"But who'll go?"

The question came from Liam McAdams.

"We can't all go, that's certain," exclaimed Bess.

"Tell you what we'll do, we'll count out," declared Jax Gray, her eyes dancing.

"A good idea," hailed the others.

"Bill, you start it; but remember, not more than three can go."

"Why?" inquired Mary Eliska point blank.

"Because we'll have to take the car, and someone must be left to look after Aunt Sally and the airplanes," spoke Bill, falling in with Liam McAdams's plans.

"Well, come on and count out," urged Jax Gray.

"Yes, that's it. Let's see who will be it," cried the others.

"Very well, if I can remember the rhyme," responded Bill. "How does it go anyway?"

"Inte, minte," suggested Liam McAdams.

"Oh, yes! That's it," responded Bill. "I've got it now. Inte, minte, cute corn, apple seeds and briar thorn, briar thorn and limber lock, three geese in a flock, one flew east and one flew west, one flew into a cuckoo's nest, O-U-T out, with a ragged dish clout, out!" ending with Bess.

"Sorry for you, Bess!" cried the lad, "but you're the first victim to be offered up."

"Oh, well, it's too hot to go chasing all over dusty country roads," declared Bess bravely, although she would dearly have loved to go on the adventurous search for the missing airplane.

One after another they were counted out 'til only Bill, Mary Eliska and Liam McAdams remained.

"Hurry up and let's get off," urged Liam McAdams as the "elimination trials," as they might be termed, were concluded.

"Very well. We'll get the car—it's in the garage at the hotel—and incidentally, we might get a lunch put up also. It may be a long chase."

The officer regarded them with frank amazement.

"My! but you city folks rush things," he exclaimed.

"I suppose they'll get busy on this case day after tomorrow," exclaimed Bill disgustedly, as they hastened away.

It was half an hour later that the big touring car, with Bill at the wheel, rolled out of the hotel yard. Jake had been told off to guard the livery stable and the airplanes while the rest remained with Mary Eliska, who was seriously agitated at the accumulation of troubles her party had met with since setting out.

"I declare," she said, "I wish I was back at home where I could get a decent cup of tea and be free of worries."

The trail of the airplane was not difficult to follow. It led down the village main street and thence along a country road 'til it came to a sort of cross roads. Here it branched off and followed a by-road for a mile or so. At a gate in a hedge all signs failed however, although it was plain that the machine had been wheeled through the gap and taken across a field.

Beyond this field lay what appeared to be a wilderness of woods and bushes. "Stumped!" exclaimed Bill, as he brought the auto to a stop.

CHAPTER 16.12.
THE FINDING OF THE "BUTTERFLY."

"Well, what next?" asked Liam McAdams.

"Make a search of those woods, I suppose," replied Bill; "there's nothing else to do."

"No, the trail has brought us here," replied Mary Eliska energetically; "we must make a determined effort to find the *Butterfly*."

"Maybe they've damaged it so that we won't be able to do anything with it when we do get it," spoke Liam McAdams presently.

"Whom do you mean by they?" asked Bill.

"As if you didn't know. Is there any doubt in your mind that that fellow Cassell is at the bottom of all this?"

"Not very much, I'll admit," replied Bill; "I wonder if that accounts for the inactivity of the police."

"In just what way?"

"Well, the fellow's a local politician and has a lot of 'pull'."

"He *must* have, to get away with anything like this," was Liam McAdams›s indignant outburst.

"Well, don't let us waste time speculating," put in Mary Eliska, in her brisk manner; "the thing to do now is to get back the *Golden Butterfly*."

"You're right, Mary Eliska," came from both boys.

By this time they were out of the car, which they left standing at the roadside while they examined the vicinity for tracks. But the grass in the field was fairly long and no traces remained. Yet, inasmuch as the tracks of the *Butterfly* ended at the gap in the hedge, it was manifest that that was the point at which it had been wheeled off the road.

"What next?" asked Liam McAdams, as it became certain that there was little use in searching for a trail in the meadow.

"It's like looking for a needle in that proverbial haystack," struck in Mary Eliska.

"In my opinion we need the patience of Job and the years of old Methuselah," opined Liam McAdams.

Bill alone was not discouraged.

"It can't be so very far off," he urged; "it stands to reason that they can't have come much further than this since midnight, supposing the machine to have been stolen about that hour."

The others agreed with him. "We'll search all around here, including those woods," declared Mary Eliska.

"Well, they can't have taken it very far into the woods," declared Liam McAdams; "the spread of its wings would prevent that."

"That's so," agreed Bill; "I think we are getting pretty 'warm' right now."

"All I am afraid of is that they may have damaged it," breathed Mary Eliska anxiously.

"It would be in line with their other tactics," agreed Bill; "men who would try to burn down a stable with two boys in it, just to obtain revenge for a fancied insult or injury, are capable of anything."

Without further waste of time they crossed the meadow and came to the edge of the wood. At the outskirts of the woods the trees grew thinly and it was plain that it would have been possible to wheel an airplane into their shadow, despite the breadth of its wing-spread.

They passed under the outlying trees and presently emerged into a small, open space, in the midst of which was a hut. Just beyond this hut was a sight that caused them to shout aloud with joy. There, apparently unharmed, stood the missing airplane.

"Hurray!" shouted Bill, dashing forward.

The others were close on his heels. In their excitement they paid little or no attention to the surroundings. It might have been better for them had they done so. As they dashed across the clearing two male figures slipped off among the thicker trees that lay beyond the open space and the hut.

A brief examination showed them that the airplane was undamaged. There were a few scratches on it, but beyond that it appeared in perfect condition.

"We'll fly back," declared Liam McAdams to Mary Eliska; "Bill can run the auto home."

"That's agreeable to me," responded Bill; "but suppose we examine the vicinity first. We might get a clue as to the rascals who are responsible for this."

"That's true," agreed Liam McAdams.

"Then suppose we start with the hut first."

They accepted this proposition eagerly. The hut was a substantial looking building with a padlock on the door. But the portal stood wide open, the padlock hanging in a hasp.

"What if anyone pounces on us?" asked Mary Eliska in rather a scared tone.

"No fear of that," replied Bill, "the place is plainly unoccupied."

They entered the hut and found it to be as primitive inside as its exterior would indicate. A table and two rude chairs stood within. These, with the exception of a rusty cook stove in one corner, formed the sole furnishings. There was not even a window in the place.

"Nothing much to be found here," declared Bill after a cursory examination; "I guess this shack was put up by lumbermen or hunters. It doesn't seem to have been occupied for a long time."

"I guess the men who took the airplane must have been pretty familiar with the place though," opined Liam McAdams.

"No doubt of that," replied Bill, "but that doesn't give us any clue to their identity beyond bare suspicions."

"Yes, and suspicions aren't much good in law," chimed in Mary Eliska, "they—Good gracious!"

The door closed suddenly with a bang. Before Liam McAdams could spring across the room to open it there came a sharp click.

"Somebody's padlocked it on the outside!" he cried.

"And we're prisoners!" gasped Mary Eliska.

"Yes, and without any chance of getting out, either," declared Liam McAdams; "there's not even a window in the place."

"Well this is worse and more of it," cried Bill. "Who can have done that?"

"The same people that stole the *Golden Butterfly*," declared Mary Eliska. «Hark!"

Outside they heard rapidly retreating footsteps, followed by a harsh laugh.

"Let us out!" shouted Bill.

"You can stay there 'til judgment day, for all I care," came back a hoarse, rasping voice; "you kids were too fresh, and now you're getting what's coming to you."

CHAPTER 16.13.
PRISONERS IN THE HUT.

It was almost pitch dark within the hut. Only from a crack under the door could any light enter. For an instant after the taunting of the voices of the men who had locked them in reached their ears, the trio of youthful prisoners remained silent.

Mary Eliska it was who spoke first.

"Well, what's to be done now?" she demanded.

"We've got to get out of here," responded Liam McAdams, with embarrassing candor.

"That's plain enough," struck in Bill; "but how do you propose to do it?"

"I don't know; let's look about. Maybe there's a chimney or something."

"There's no opening larger than that one where the stove pipe goes through. I've noticed that already," responded Bill.

"Phew! This *is* a fix for fair."

"I should say so; but kicking about it won't help us at all. Let's make a thorough investigation."

In the darkness they groped about, but could discover nothing that appeared to hold out a promise of escape. The two boys shook the door violently; but it was firm on its hinges.

Next Bill proposed to cut a way through it with his pocket knife.

"We'd be starved to death by the time you cut through that stuff," declared Liam McAdams.

In proof of this he kicked the door, and the resulting sound showed that it was built of solid wood without any thin panels which might be cut through.

"What next?"

Mary Eliska asked the question as the two perspiring lads stood perplexed without speaking or moving.

"Jiggered if I know," spoke Liam McAdams; "can't you or Bill think of anything?"

"We might try to batter the door down with that table," suggested Bill.

"It's worth trying. We've got to get out of here somehow."

The two boys picked up the heavy, roughly made table and commenced a violent assault on the door. But although they dented it heavily, and sent some splinters flying, the portal held its own. At length they desisted from pure weariness. The situation looked hopeless.

"It looks pretty bad," spoke Liam McAdams.

"It does indeed," agreed Bill. "Mary Eliska, I wish we hadn't brought you along."

"And why, pray, Bill Stricklin?"

"Oh, because—because, well, this isn't the sort of thing for a girl."

"Well, I guess if my brother can stand it I can," rejoined the girl, pluckily and in a firm voice.

"Well, there's no use minimizing the fix we're in," declared Bill. "This is a lonesome bit of country. It may be a week before anyone will come around. We've just got to get out, that's all there is to it."

"I wish you'd solve the problem then," sighed Liam McAdams; "it's too much for me."

"I'll make another search of the premises, maybe we can stumble across something that may aid us. At any rate, it will give us something to do and keep our minds off the predicament we are in."

Bill struck a match, of which he had a plentiful supply in his pockets. As the yellow flame sputtered up in the semi-gloom it showed every corner of the small hut. But it did not reveal anything that promised a chance to gain their liberty. All at once, just as the light was sputtering out, Mary Eliska gave a cry. Her eye had been caught by a glistening metal object in one corner of the hut.

"What is it?" asked Bill.

"A gun—a shot-gun standing in that corner over there."

"Huh!" sniffed Liam McAdams, "a lot of good that does us."

"On the contrary," declared Mary Eliska stoutly, "if it's loaded it may serve to get us free."

"I'm from Missouri," declared Liam McAdams enigmatically.

"What's your idea, sis?" asked Bill, who knew that Mary Eliska's ideas were usually worth following up.

"I remember reading only a short time ago of a man trapped much as we are who escaped by blowing off the lock of his prison with a gun he carried," replied Mary Eliska; "maybe it would work in our case."

"Maybe it would if—" rejoined Bill.

"If what?"

"If the gun was loaded, which is most unlikely."

"Well, try it and see," urged Mary Eliska.

"Yes, do," echoed Liam McAdams; "Mary Eliska's plan sounds like a good idea. Maybe some hunter left it here and the shells are still in it."

"No harm in finding out anyway," declared Bill.

He struck another match and picked up the gun. It was an antique looking weapon badly-rusted. But on opening the breech he uttered a cry of joy.

"Good luck!" he exclaimed, "two shells,—one in each barrel."

"Well, put it to the test," urged Liam McAdams.

"All right. If this fails, though, I don't know what we'll do."

"Don't worry about that now. Try it."

"I'm going to. Don't get peevish."

Bill crossed the room to the door. Raising the gun to his shoulder he placed the muzzle about opposite to where he thought the padlock must be located.

"Look out for a big noise, sis," he warned.

Mary Eliska gave a little scream and raised her hands to her ears. She disliked firearms.

"Ready?" sang out Liam McAdams.

"All ready," came the reply.

"Then fire!"

Simultaneously with Liam McAdams's order came a deafening report. In that confined space it sounded as if a huge cannon had been fired. Bill staggered back under the "kick" of the heavy charge.

"Once more," he announced.

Again a sonorous report sounded, but this time a section of the door was blown right out of the framework. The daylight streamed in through it.

"Now then for the test," cried Bill. "Come on, Liam McAdams."

The two boys placed their shoulders to the door. With a suddenness that was startling, it burst open, and they faced freedom. The lock had been fairly driven from its hold by the twice repeated charge of shot.

The young aviatrixes were free once more. But it remained to be seen if the men who wished them harm had wrought their vengeance on the *Golden Butterfly*.

CHAPTER 16.14.
WHAT'S TO BE DONE WITH THE WREN?

The *Golden Butterfly*, as an examination proved, had not been damaged during their imprisonment in the hut. Evidently, the men who had slammed the door and padlocked it had made off at top speed as soon as they had completed what they hoped would be a source of sore trouble to the young aviatrixes.

"And now we'll fly back as agreed," declared Mary Eliska merrily.

Her spirits, almost down to zero in the hut, had recovered themselves marvelously in the fresh open air. She was radiant.

"I declare that the stay in the hut has done you good," declared Liam McAdams, looking at her admiringly.

"Maybe it has—by contrast," returned Mary Eliska.

"Like a sea trip," put in Bill. "I've heard that people who suffer from sea sickness are so much relieved when they get ashore that they imagine their good spirits are due to a change in their condition."

"Well, that applies to me," returned Mary Eliska; "I didn't think we'd get out of that hut so easily. How do you suppose that gun came to be there?"

"The hunters who use the hut must have left it there," rejoined Bill; "I wonder if they'll ever know how useful it was to us."

"More likely they'll be mad when they find that the lock is blown off the door," laughed Liam McAdams.

"Well, so-long, folks, I'm going to start back in the auto," declared Bill.

"We'll beat you into town," challenged Liam McAdams.

"More than likely, if the *Golden Butterfly* is doing her best," was the rejoinder.

Ten minutes later the two machines were racing back to Meadville at almost top speed. Of course the speedy *Golden Butterfly* won, but then a vehicle of the air does not have to contend with the obstacles that a land conveyance does.

They found Mary Eliska almost on the verge of hysterics. A garbled version of the events of the night had been brought to her and this, coupled with the long absence of the three young folks, had made her extremely nervous.

"I declare, it seems as if you just can't keep out of trouble," she said.

"Well, it actually does seem so, I admit," confessed Mary Eliska; "but we promise to be very good for the rest of the trip."

"And never trouble trouble 'til trouble troubles us," chanted Liam McAdams airily.

"That's all very well, but you keep me continually in suspense as to what you'll do next," almost wailed Mary Eliska. "We set out for a quiet trip and encounter nothing but troubles—"

"Adventures, Aunt Sally," laughingly corrected Bill; "what is life without adventures?"

"Well, I'm sure I don't know what young people are coming to," sighed Mary Eliska with resignation. "There's another thing, what are we to do with this little Wren?"

"We can't leave her here, that's certain," declared Mary Eliska with vehemence.

"No, indeed," echoed Jax Gray and Bess, who were of the council.

"Then what are we to do with her?"

"Just tote her along, I suppose," rejoined Mary Eliska; "poor little thing, she doesn't take up much room; besides, Jax Gray thinks she's an heiress."

They all laughed.

"You must have had an overdose of Laura Jean Libby," declared Bill.

"Bill Stricklin, you behave yourself," cried Jax Gray, flushing up; "besides, she has a strawberry mark on her left arm."

"My gracious, then she surely is a missing heiress," exclaimed Liam McAdams teasingly; "all well-regulated missing heiresses have strawberry marks and almost always on their left arm."

It was at this juncture that a knock came at the door. A bell boy stood outside.

"A gentleman to see you, sir," he said, handing Bill a card.

On it was printed: "Mr. James Kennedy, Detective, Meadville Police Station."

"Goodness, a real detective!" exclaimed Jax Gray excitedly; "let's see him."

"You won't be much impressed I'm afraid," rejoined Bill with a smile at his recollection of the Meadville sleuths.

"Why, doesn't he wear glasses, have a hawk-like nose and smoke a pipe?" inquired Bess.

"And hunt up missing heiresses?" teasingly struck in Liam McAdams.

"No, he's a very different sort of person. But hush! he's coming now."

A heavy tread sounded in the hall and Mr. James Kennedy, Detective of the Meadville Police Force, stood before them. As Liam McAdams had said, he was not impressive as to outward appearance, although his fat, heavy face, and rather vacant eyes, might have concealed a giant intellect.

"I've investigated the case of the attempted burning of the stable last night," he began.

"Yes," exclaimed Bill eagerly. "Have you any suspicions as to who did it?"

The man shook his head.

"As yet we have no clues," he declared, "and I don't think we'll get any."

"That's too bad," replied Bill, "but let me tell you something that may help you."

The lad launched into a description of their adventures of the morning.

"That hut belongs to Luke Higgins, a respectable man who is out West at present," said the detective when Bill had finished. "He uses it as a sort of hunting box in the rabbit shooting season. He couldn't have had anything to do with it."

"I'd like to know his address so that I could write and thank him for leaving that gun there," declared Mary Eliska warmly.

The detective shook his head solemnly.

"I reckon you young folks had better stop skee-daddling round the country this way," he said with heavy conviction; "you'll only get into more trouble. Flying ain't natural no more than crowing hens is."

With this he picked up his hat, and, after assuring them that he would find a clue within a short time, he departed, leaving behind him a company in which amusement mingled with indignation. In fact, so angry was Bill over the stupidity or ignorance of the Meadville police, that he himself set out on a hunt to detect the authors of the outrages upon the young aviatrixes.

The sole result of his inquiry however was to establish the fact that both Cassells had left town, closing their house and announcing that they would be gone for some time.

As there was nothing further to be gained by remaining in Meadville, the entire party, after lunch, set out once more, a big crowd witnessing the departure of the aërial tourists.

They flew fast, and as the roads were excellent the auto had no difficulty in keeping up with them. On through the afternoon they soared along, sometimes swooping low above an alluring bit of scenery and again heading their machines skyward in pure exuberance of spirits. Their troubles at Meadville forgotten, they flew their machines like sportive birds; never had any of them experienced more fully the joy of flight, the sense of freedom that comes from traveling untrammeled into the ether.

They had passed above a small village and were flying low, those in the auto waving to them, when Mary Eliska, in the *Golden Butterfly*, gave a sudden exclamation.

"Oh, look," she shouted, "a flock of sheep, and right in the path of the auto."

At that moment all of them saw the sheep, a large flock, headed by a belligerent looking ram with immense horns. Jake, who was driving the car, slowed up as he approached the flock. The woolly herd, huddled together helplessly, made no effort to get out of the road. Behind them a man and a boy shouted and yelled vigorously, but with no more effect than to bunch the animals more squarely in the path of the advancing car. All at once, just as the car was slowed down to almost a walking pace, a big ram separated himself from the flock and actually rushed for the front seat of the car.

Jake uttered a yell as the woolly creature gave him a hard butt, knocking him out of his seat. But this wasn't all.

By some strange freak the animal had landed in the car in a sitting posture. Now the young aviatrixes roared with laughter to behold the creature seated in Jake's forcibly vacated place. Its hoofs rested on the driving wheel.

Forward plunged the car, its queer driver with his feet wedged in the spokes of the steering wheel. Aloft the flock of young aviatrixes roared with laughter at the sight. It was the oddest experience they had yet had—this spectacle of a grave-looking, long-horned ram driving an auto, while Jake prudently kept out of reach of those horns. As for Aunt Sally and The Wren, they cowered back in the tonneau in keen alarm.

"Oh!" cried Mary Eliska suddenly, "there comes a runabout; that ram will surely collide with it!"

A runabout coming in the opposite direction dashed round a corner of the country road at this juncture. The driver was a young girl, but she was veiled and her features could not be seen under the thick face covering.

Apparently the ram saw the other car coming, for the animal actually appeared to make a halfway intelligent effort to steer the car out of the road.

For her part the girl in the runabout swerved her car from side to side in a struggle to avoid a collision, which appeared inevitable.

"Stop it!" shrieked Bess; "she'll be killed."

CHAPTER 16.15.
A RAMBUNCTIOUS RAM.

The ram evidently saw the other car coming; it tried to leap out but its hoofs were jammed in the spokes of the steering wheel. Before Jake could pick himself up from the floor of the front part of the car there came a loud shriek from the runabout. It was echoed by Aunt Sally and The Wren.

Crash!

The two cars came together with a fearful jolt.

The eyes of the young aviatrixes aloft were fixed on the scene. They saw the large car strike the runabout and crumple its engine hood. Mary Eliska gave a scream.

The ram, jolted out of its seat by the force of the collision, fell out to one side, allowing Jake to resume control of the wheel. But the runabout! It was ditched, its unfortunate occupant being pitched headlong into a ditch at the side of the road.

Down swept the airplanes, and there was a wild rush to the rescue. Mary Eliska, Jax Gray and Bess ran to the side of the injured occupant of the strange runabout. The boys divided themselves, attending to everything.

"Bill! Bill! hurry, she's unconscious!"

The cry came from Mary Eliska as she rushed to the side of the young motorist.

Bill was not far off, and, at his sister's cry, he hastened to her side. Mary Eliska had the girl's head in her lap.

"Get water!" she cried.

But Liam McAdams was already on hand with a collapsible aluminum cup full of water from a nearby spring.

"Oh, the poor dear," sighed Mary Eliska, "to think that our fun should have—"

The strange girl opened her eyes.

"Who are you?" she exclaimed. "Where is my machine?"

"Never mind for a minute," spoke Mary Eliska, seeing that Liam McAdams and Jake were trying to drag the machine out of the ditch, "we'll fix it, never fear."

"Oh, my head!" groaned the girl.

"That pesky ram," exploded Bill angrily; "let me help you up into the road, you'll be more comfortable."

"Oh, thank you, I can stand," came faintly from the injured girl. "I—am—much better now. What happened?"

"Why a sort of volunteer driver was experimenting with our car, and I guess he made a mistake in driving," smilingly explained Bill.

"Oh, that ram!" cried the girl half hysterically. "I thought I had a nightmare at first."

"I don't blame you," smiled Mary Eliska, "seeing a ram driving a motor car is apt to give one such ideas."

"Are you really better?" asked Jax Gray sympathetically as she came up.

"Mary Eliska, get my smelling salts out of the traveling bag!" cried Aunt Sally anxiously.

The accident had disturbed her sadly. The only unperturbed one in the party was Jake. He took things with philosophical calm.

"Knew more trouble was comin'," said he, and contented himself by dismissing the situation with that.

"I've got good news for you," said Liam McAdams, coming up; "your car isn't hurt a bit."

"Oh, good!" cried the girl, clasping her hands and flushing. Her veil was raised now and they saw that she was very blonde, very pretty and just now very pale.

"My, what a rambunctious ram!" punned Bill; "he ramified all over, didn't he?"

"Gracious, for a time I thought I was seeing things!" gasped the girl, who was seated on a tufted hummock of grass at the side of the road.

"And then you felt them," laughed Liam McAdams. "That's the way such things run."

They all laughed. Soon after, Bill, Liam McAdams and Jake dragged the small runabout out of the ditch. In the meantime Mary Eliska had introduced herself and Jax Gray to the young girl. The latter's name was Lavinia Nesbitt. She lived not far from the scene of the accident, and had been taking a jaunt in her machine.

The runabout had been rescued, and the whole party introduced and talking merrily when Jax Gray set up a cry.

"Goodness! here comes that ram again!"

Down the road, with the two sheep drivers at its heels, the beast was indeed coming. It advanced at a hard gallop, with head lowered and formidable horns ready for a charge, into the midst of the group.

"Look out for him!" yelled the sheep herders.

They needed no second injunction. All skipped adroitly out of the path of the oncoming beast, which was rushing on like a whirlwind. Liam McAdams proved equal to the emergency. From his airplane he took the rope which had already done good service in rescuing the *Golden Butterfly* from the pond. He formed it into a loop—the lariat of the Western plains.

"Now we've got him!" he exclaimed; "that is, if we are careful. But watch out!"

"No danger of that," responded Aunt Sally, from the vantage of the tonneau of the car; "but how are you going to rope him?"

"Watch!"

Liam McAdams began swinging his loop in ever widening circles. The ram was now within a few feet of him.

"Oh, the *Dart*!" shrieked Bess; "he'll go right through it!"

Indeed it did appear as if the maddened animal would. But just as there are many slips between cup and lip so there are many slips between the ram and the airplane.

Just as it appeared that he would plow his way right through the delicate fabric, Liam McAdams hurled his loop. It settled round the animal's horns. Planting his heels in the ground Liam McAdams held tight to the rope. The next minute he "snubbed" it tight and the ram lost its feet and rolled over and over in the dust.

Jake and Bill rushed in and completed the job of tying the creature.

"Goodness, Liam McAdams, you're a regular broncho buster!" cried Mary Eliska admiringly.

"Oh, I learned to do some tricks with a rope with the horse hunters out in Nevada," was the response.

But careless as his manner was, Liam McAdams's eyes glowed with triumph. It was plainly to be seen that he was delighted with his success. Just then the two sheep drivers came running up.

The girls looked rather alarmed. Suppose they should blame them for trying to kidnap the ram.

"I'll do the talking," declared Bill; "if you said anything, Liam McAdams, there might be a row."

"All right," laughed Liam McAdams, regarding his "roped and tied captive." "I suppose you are an expert on dealing with ram owners."

"Well, I'm on to their mental ramifications," laughed Bill.

The sheep driver, an elderly man, accompanied by a youth, came up to them now. He touched his hat civilly as he approached.

"Good afternoon. No one hurt, I hope," he said.

The girls looked greatly relieved. After all, the man was not rude or angry as they had feared.

"Oh, no, thank you," cried Jax Gray, before Bill or Liam McAdams could open their mouths. "I hope he isn't though."

"Hurt!" exclaimed the ram's owner, "why you couldn't hurt him with a steam hammer. Why, day 'afore yesterday the blame thing went for my wife. Hoofs and horns—yes, sir! Most knocked her down, he did. I'll fix him."

"What's his name?" asked Bess.

"Hannibal Lecter," said the man, without the flicker of a facial muscle.

"I should think Cannonball would be a better name for him," struck in Liam McAdams, with that funny, serious face he always assumed when 'joshing'.

"Yes, sir, I guess it *would* be more appropriate at that," assented the man.

He looked at the disabled machine.

"Busted?" he asked with apparent concern.

"To some extent," rejoined Bill, "only, except for that engine hood being dented there doesn't appear to be much the matter with it."

"Glad to pay if there be," said the sheep driver. "I'm going ter git rid of ther pesky critter. He's cost me a lot in damage suits already."

"Why don't you put him on the stage as Hannibal Lecter, the boxing ram, or something like that?" inquired Liam McAdams.

"Might be a good scheme," said the man, as if considering the proposal seriously.

"Mary had a little ram—" laughed Liam McAdams; who was thereupon told not to be "horrid."

"Why don't you box the nasty thing's ears for riding in our car?" asked Bill of Mary Eliska.

"I'd like to do something, the saucy thing," declared Mary Eliska with vehemence.

"Tell you what! Let's buy him."

The suggestion came from Liam McAdams.

"Yes, and have his skin made up into an auto robe," suggested Bill.

"If you boys aren't ridiculous," cried Mary Eliska; "I want to forget the incident, and so I'm sure does Lavinia," the name of the girl who had been spilled out of her machine.

"You may be sure I do," she declared with emphasis. "I was never so scared in my life."

"Want to buy him?" asked the man, grasping at a chance of selling an animal that had already placed him in some embarrassing positions.

"How much do you want?" asked Bill, more as a joke than anything else.

"Three dollars," said the man.

"There you are, girls! Who'll bid? Who'll bid? This fine young ram going at a sacrifice."

Liam McAdams imitated an auctioneer, raising his voice to a sharp pitch.

CHAPTER 16.16.
AN INVITATION TO RACE.

It is almost needless to say that the purchase was not consummated. The girls raised a chorus of protest. The "nasty thing" was the mildest of the epithets they applied to the beast.

"Well, I don't know. I thought we might have his skin done into a robe. We could give it as a prize to the girl that makes the best record on this motor flight," suggested Liam McAdams.

"I wish you'd take him up a thousand feet and drop him," declared the unfortunate ram's owner.

"Poor thing! he only acted according to his nature," defended Mary Eliska; "let him loose and he'll go back to the flock."

"Not him," declared his owner; "he'd only raise more Cain. Better let him be."

But the girls raised a chorus of protest. It was a shame to leave the poor thing tied up, and they insisted that he be let loose.

"All right, if you kin stand it I kin," grinned the man.

He and the boy bent over the captive ram and cast him loose. The beast struggled to his feet, and for an instant stood glaring about him out of his yellowish eyes that gleamed like agates. But it was only for an instant that he remained thus.

Suddenly he lowered his head and without more preliminaries dashed right at the *Golden Butterfly*.

"Gracious, he's a game old sport!" yelled Liam McAdams; "Hasn't had enough of it yet, eh?"

Right at the *Butterfly* the ram rushed. Reaching it, with one bound he was in the chassis.

"Now we'll get him," whispered the owner of the ram. "I told you if he was let go he'd start cutting up rough."

"Well, you surely proved a good prophet," laughed Liam McAdams.

"Now we've got to catch him," said the man.

"How?" whispered Liam McAdams.

"Someone must lasso him as you did before. Easy now. Don't scare him or he might do damage."

The ram was seated in the airplane for all the world as if he was a scientific investigator of some sort. He paid no attention whatever to those who were creeping up on him, Liam McAdams with his rope in his hand, the loop trailing behind him all ready for action.

"This is more fun than a deer hunt!" declared Bill.

"Than a bull fight, you mean," retorted Liam McAdams; "this creature gives the best imitation of a wild bull I ever saw."

They all laughed. The ram certainly had given a realistic interpretation of a savage Andalusian fighter.

"Now then," whispered the sheep driver as they drew near. Liam McAdams's rope swirled and settled about the ram's horns. But the startled beast was due to give them another surprise. Hardly had Liam McAdams's rope fallen about it when with a snort it leaped clean in the air and out of the airplane. It tore like an express train straight at Liam McAdams.

Before the boy could get out of its path "Biff!" the impact had come. Liam McAdams arose into the atmosphere and described a distinct parabola. He landed with a bump in a clump of bushes, while Mr. Ram rushed off down the road to join his flock.

"Haw! haw! haw!" roared the sheep man; "ain't hurt, be you?"

"No; but I've a good mind to sue you for damages," rejoined Liam McAdams, picking himself out of the clump of brush; "you've no right to drive an animal like that around the country without labeling him 'Dynamite. Dangerous'."

"Guess I will, too," said the man, who appeared to think well of the suggestion; "he sure will get me in a pile of trouble one of these days."

He raised his hat and strode off, followed by the boy. In the distance the ram was capering about among the other sheep. Liam McAdams brushed the dust off himself and then looked about him.

"Anybody laughing?" he demanded suspiciously.

They all shook their heads, the girls biting their lips to avoid smiling.

"All right then, I suggest that we get out of here right away; a tiger's liable to come striding out of those woods next."

"Yes; we'd better be getting along; Millbrook, our next stop, is several miles off," said Mary Eliska, consulting the map.

No further time was lost in resuming their rapid flight. In the distance, as the flock of airplanes arose, the sheep man waved his hat and shouted his adieus.

Millbrook was reached that evening just at dusk. It proved to be a fair-sized town, and the airplanes excited as much curiosity there as they had in Meadville—more so, in fact, for, from some flaring posters, it appeared that an airplane exhibition and race had been arranged for the next day by a traveling company of aviatrixes. That evening, at the hotel, a deputation of citizens waited on the boys and asked them if they would not prolong their stay and take part in the air sports. The mayor, whose name was Jasper Hanks, mentioned a prize of five hundred dollars for an endurance flight as a special inducement.

The lads said they would think things over and report in the morning. Their real object in delaying their decision was, of course, to consult the girls about appearing. Mary Eliska, Jax Gray and Bess went into raptures over the idea, and Mary Eliska's consent was readily obtained.

"I'll be glad to rest for a day after all our exciting times," she declared, "and I mean to add to Wren's outfit too."

"Oh, how good you are to me," sighed the odd little figure, nestling close to her benefactress.

"Tush! tush, my dear! I'm going to make a wonderful girl out of you," beamed the kindly lady.

Descending to the office to buy some postcards, the boys found, lounging about the desk, a stoutish man with a rather dissipated face, puffy under the eyes and heavy about the jaws. A bright red necktie and patent-leather boots with cloth tops accentuated the decidedly "noisy" impression he conveyed.

As the boys came down he eyed them sharply. Then he addressed them.

"My name's Lish Kelly," he said. "I'm manager of the United Pilots' Exhibition Company. We're showing out at the City Park tomorrow. I understand that you kids have been asked to butt in."

"We've been asked to participate, if that's what you mean," rejoined Bill rather sharply. The fellow's manner was offensive and overbearing.

"Well, see here, you stay out," rejoined the man, shaking a fat forefinger on which glistened a diamond ring of such proportions as to make it dubious if it boasted a genuine stone.

"You stay out of it," he repeated.

Bill and Liam McAdams were almost dumfounded. The man's tone was one of actual command.

"Why? Why should we stay out of it?" demanded Bill.

"The mayor of the town has asked us to take part," came from Liam McAdams; "what have you got to do with it?"

"It's this way," said the man in rather a less overbearing way than he had hitherto adopted; "we're going about the country giving flights. The city gives us the park in this town and we get so much of the receipts. But we rely on winning the prizes, see. Now if you kids butt in, why you might win some of them and that knocks my profit out. Get me?"

"I understand you, if that's what you mean," rejoined Bill; "but I still fail to see why we should not compete if we want to."

The man placed his hand on the boy's shoulder impressively.

"'Cos if you do it'll make trouble for you, sonny."

"Who'll make it?" flashed back Bill indignantly.

"I will, son, and I'm some trouble maker when I start anything along them lines, take it from me."

He turned on his heel, stuck his cigar at a more acute angle in the side of his mouth, and strode off, leaving the two boys dumfounded.

"Well, what do you make of that?" demanded Bill, as soon as his astonishment had subsided a trifle.

"Just this, that Mr. Lish Kelly thinks he can run this thing to suit himself."

"What will we do about it?"

"For my part I wanted to compete before. I desire to more than ever now."

"Same here."

"Maybe he was only bluffing after all."

"Maybe; but just the same I wouldn't trust him not to try to do us some harm. As he says, his main profits come from winning the prizes offered by the different communities."

"Humph! well, so far as that goes, I don't see why that need keep us out of it."

"Nor I; but we've had troubles enough, and I don't want willingly to run into any more."

"Nor I. Well, let's sleep on it. We'll decide in the morning."

"That's a good idea."

The two lads went up to bed and slept as only healthy lads can. The next morning dawned bright and clear. There was hardly any wind. It was real "flying" weather. The airplanes had been sheltered in a big shed belonging to the hotel. Before breakfast the boys went out and looked them over. All were in good shape.

As they were coming out of the shed they were hailed by no less a personage than Mayor Hanks.

"Well," said he, "are you going to fly?"

"We think of doing so," said Bill, hesitating a little. He wanted to speak of the conduct of Lish Kelly, but on second thought he decided not to; the man might merely have had a fit of bad temper on him. His threats might have been only empty ones.

"If you're going to fly I have got some entry blanks with me," said the mayor. "I wish you'd sign 'em."

He drew out a bunch of blue papers with blanks for describing the name of the machine, its power, driver and other details.

This decided the boys.

"All right, we'll enter all our machines," said Bill; "let us go into the writing room and we'll sign the entry blanks."

"Good for you," cried the mayor delightedly; "you'll be a big drawing card, especially the young ladies. I never heard of gals flyin', although, come to think of it, why shouldn't they?"

In the writing room they concluded the business. When it was done all the machines had been entered in every contest, including an altitude one.

"We start at ten sharp, so be there," admonished the mayor as he departed, highly pleased at having secured quite a flock of young aviatrixes at no cost at all.

It was as his figure vanished, that Lish Kelly crossed the writing room. He had been sitting in a telephone booth, and leaving the door a crack open had heard every word that had passed.

He greeted the boys with an angry scowl.

"So you ain't going to stay out?" he said gruffly, as he passed. "All right; look out for squalls!"

CHAPTER 16.17.
THE TWISTED SPARK PLUG.

"Gracious, are we in for more trouble?"

Liam McAdams looked blankly at Bill; but the latter only laughed at his chum's serious face.

Somehow, viewed in the bright light of early day, Lish Kelly's threats did not appear nearly as formidable as they had over night.

"Nonsense; what harm can he do us anyhow? We're going to go into this race, and we're going to win too. Just watch us."

"Going to tell the girls anything about Kelly and his remarks?"

"No; what good would that do? It would only scare them."

"That's so, too; but just the same I didn't like the look of Kelly's face when he came through."

"He looked to me like a bulldog that had swallowed a baby's boot and didn't like the taste of the blacking on it," laughed Bill.

At this juncture the girls came into the room. All were radiant and smiling in anticipation of the day's sport.

"Well, we've been and gone and done it," announced Bill.

"Done what?" demanded Mary Eliska.

"Signed the paperrr-r-r-s," was the rejoinder, rendered with great dramatic effect.

He waved the duplicate entry blanks above his head.

"Let's see them," begged Jax Gray.

"All right. Look what I've let us in for!"

"Why—why—good gracious, Bill, you've got us down for everything," gasped Mary Eliska.

"That's right, all the way across from soup to nuts," struck in the slangy Liam McAdams.

They all laughed. The color rose in the girls' faces.

"If only we can win some of them," cried Jax Gray.

"Well, the machines are all in fine shape. If we don't win it will be because the other fellows have better machines."

"Where are the aviation grounds?" inquired Bess.

"At the City Park, about a mile out of town to the south. We can get to it by looking down at the trolley tracks," said Bill, who had consulted the mayor on this point.

"Then you are going to fly out there?" asked Mary Eliska, who was also by this time a party to the conference.

"Of course; and, by the way, we ought to be getting out there pretty soon; I want to be looking over the grounds and selecting the best places for landing and so on," said Bill.

"Well, please don't get into any more scrapes," sighed Mary Eliska; "what with gypsies, firebugs and rams, our trip has been quite exciting enough for me."

The boys exchanged glances. If the man Kelly tried to carry out his threats things might be more exciting yet, they thought. But both kept their knowledge to themselves.

It was arranged that Mary Eliska should motor out to the City Park. Soon thereafter the young aviatrixes placed finishing touches on their machines, and while a curious crowd gathered they took to the air.

"Looks just like a flock of pigeons," said a man in the crowd, as they climbed skyward quite closely bunched.

"It sure does," agreed his companion, "but them things is prettier than any flock of pigeons I ever see."

And this opinion was echoed by many of the throng. At any rate everyone who saw the airplanes start made up his or her mind to pay a visit to the park and see some more extended flights, so that Mayor Hanks' prediction was verified.

As the young aviatrixes hovered above City Park for a short space of time, and then dropped earthward, a veritable sensation was created. From a row of "hangars" mechanicians and aviatrixes came running. One or two aviatrixes who were aloft practicing "stunts," dropped swiftly to earth. Lish Kelly's troupe was a large one, consisting of five men and one woman flyer, the wife of Carlos Le Roy, a Cuban aviator.

Outside the grounds several of the frugal individuals who desired to see the flights without paying admission also watched as the quintette of strange airplanes dropped to earth.

One by one the graceful craft of the air settled to the ground, and the young aviatrixes alighted. Members of the Arrangement Committee hastened to their sides, shaking hands warmly and thanking them for their interest in the coming contests.

The Kelly aviatrixes gazed curiously, some of them resentfully, at the newcomers. They had all the professional's antipathy and jealousy of amateur performers. As the Arrangement Committee bustled off after telling our friends to make themselves perfectly at home, Pepita Le Roy came up to them. She was a handsome woman, in a foreign way, with large, dark eyes and an abundance of raven black hair. She was rather flashily dressed and walked with a sort of swagger that in a vague way reminded Mary Eliska of "Carmen."

"So you are zee girl aviatrixes," she remarked, as she came up.

"Yes; I guess that's what they call us," rejoined Mary Eliska; "we enjoy flying and have done a lot of it."

"So! I have read your names in zee papers."

"Oh, those awful papers!" cried Jax Gray, who hated publicity; "they are always printing things about us."

"What! You do not like it?"

"Oh, no! You see, we only fly for fun. Not as a business and—"

Mary Eliska stopped short. She felt she had committed a grave breach of tactfulness. It was not the thing, she felt, to boast to a professional woman flyer of their standing as amateurs.

Nor was the Cuban woman slow to take umbrage at what she considered an insult. Her eyes flashed indignantly as she regarded the fair-haired, slender girl before her.

"So you fly only for fun," she said vehemently; "very well, you have all zee fun you want before today is ovaire."

Without another word she walked off, with the swinging walk of her race.

The girls looked at each other with a sort of amused dismay.

"Goodness, Mary Eliska; you should be more careful," cried Bess; "you've hurt her feelings dreadfully."

"I'm sure I didn't mean to," declared Mary Eliska remorsefully. "I—I had no idea that she would flare up like that."

"Well, after all, it doesn't matter much," soothed Jax Gray, pouring oil on the troubled waters, so to speak. "I'm glad the boys didn't hear it though."

"So am I. See, they're busy on Bill's machine," exclaimed Bess.

"Yes; the lower left wing is rather warped," explained Mary Eliska; "they are fixing it."

"Wonder who that man is who is monkeying with the *Red Dragon*?" said Mary Eliska, the next instant. "I mean that horrid looking man in the check suit."

"I don't know. See, he has a monkey wrench in his hand, too," exclaimed Bess.

Almost simultaneously the boys looked round from their work on the biplane and saw the man. It was Lish Kelly. He was bending over the engine and doing something to it with his wrench.

"Hey! What are you doing there?" yelled Bill.

"Just looking at your machine. No harm in that, is there?" demanded Kelly, with a red face.

"None at all, except that we don't want our machines touched. How comes it you have that monkey wrench in your hands if you weren't tampering with the machinery?"

Liam McAdams spoke in a voice that fairly bubbled over with indignation.

"Don't get sore, kid; I wouldn't harm your old mowing machine. There isn't one of mine but could beat it the fastest day it ever flew."

As he spoke Kelly slouched off. They saw him go up to a group of his aviatrixes and begin talking earnestly to them. Once or twice he motioned with his head in their direction.

"So he *does* mean mischief, after all," said Bill; ‹let›s take a good look at the *Dragon's* engine. He may have injured it, although I don›t think he›d have had time to hurt it seriously."

They strolled over to the *Dragon*, with the girls trailing behind.

"Oh!" cried Mary Eliska, as they came up, "look at that spark plug."

"What's the matter with it?" demanded Liam McAdams,

"Look, it's all bent and twisted out of shape."

"Jove, sis, so it is. Your eyes are as sharp as they are pretty!" cried Bill.

"No compliments, please. Oh, that horrid man!"

"Who is he?" asked Jax Gray. "You appeared to know him."

"Yes, we had some conversation with him this morning," laughed Bill; "but to return to the spark plug; it's a good thing we carry extra ones."

"But we don't!" cried Liam McAdams, in a dismayed tone.

"What! you had a supply in a locker on your machine."

Liam McAdams looked confused.

"I've got to make a confession," he said.

"You didn't bring them!" cried Mary Eliska.

"No, the fact is I—I forgot."

Liam McAdams looked miserably from one to the other. Here was a quandary indeed. It might prove hard to get such a commodity as a spark plug in Millbrook.

CHAPTER 16.18.
IN SEARCH OF A NEW PLUG.

It was while they were still discussing the situation that the automobile with Jake at the wheel and Mary Eliska and The Wren in the tonneau, drove into the grounds. What a difference there was in the child since her benefactors had fitted her out! She looked like a dainty, ethereal little princess instead of the ragged little waif that had been rescued from the gypsy camp.

But the minds of our young friends were now intent on different matters. Time pressed. The altitude flight, in which Liam McAdams had planned to take part, was to be the first thing on the program. If anything was to be done about reequipping the *Dragon* it must be done quickly.

"Tell you what," said Bill suddenly, "we'll get into the car and drive back to town. It won't take long and maybe we can dig up an extra one some place."

"If we don't I'm out of it for keeps," groaned Liam McAdams; "oh, that Kelly. I'd like to punch his head."

He doubled up his fists aggressively; but, after all, what chance had he to prove that Kelly had actually damaged the plug. If confronted the man would have probably denied all knowledge of it. Nobody had actually seen him do it, so that positive proof was out of the question. No, they must repair the damage as best they could.

But Bill determined to have the machines closely guarded. The situation was explained to Mary Eliska, and while she and her small protégé took seats in the grand stand Jake was detailed to guard the airplanes. This done, the boys got into the machine and prepared to start for town. But the girls interfered.

"Aren't you going to take us along, you impolite youths!" cried Bess.

"Oh, certainly, your company is always charming," returned Liam McAdams, with a low bow.

"Of course it is, but you wouldn't have asked us to come if we had not invited ourselves," declared Mary Eliska vehemently.

"How can you say so? Our lives would be a dry desert without the girl aviatrixes to liven things up," declared Liam McAdams.

"Liam McAdams, if you are going to get poetical you'll leave this car," cried Jax Gray.

"That's just it," declared Liam McAdams, "girls can cry their eyes out over romantic heroes, but when a regular fellow starts to get 'mushy' they go up in the air."

Amidst the chorus of protestations aroused by this ungallant speech Bill started the car. Swiftly it sped out of the grounds; but not so swiftly that the keen eyes of Lish Kelly did not see it.

He called Herman Le Roy, the Cuban aviator, to him.

"Le Roy, you are not in the altitude contest," he said, "hop in my car with me and we'll follow those kids. They're up to something."

The Cuban looked at him and smiled, showing two rows of white teeth under his small, dapperly curled mustache.

"I think, Señor Kelly, you have been up to something yourself."

"Well, you know what I told you. We want that five-hundred-dollar prize, Carlos, and by the looks of things if we don't do something those kids are likely to get it."

"They have fine machines," agreed the other. "Yes; and they are equipped with a balancing device that makes them much more reliable than ours."

"A balancing device!" exclaimed the Cuban, as the two men got into the car, a small yellow runabout of racy appearance.

"That's what I said, and it's a good one, too. I read an account of it in an aviation paper; but the description was too sketchy for me to see how the thing was worked."

"Those boys must be wonders."

"I'm afraid they are. That's why we've got to be careful of them. But I've got a plan to fix them, the whole lot of them."

"What is it?"

"I'll tell you as we go along."

As the car rolled past the group of airplanes with Jake faithfully standing guard over them, Kelly hailed him in a suave voice.

"Any idea where the young folks have gone?"

Jake, who had no idea that Kelly had a sinister motive in asking the question, replied readily enough.

"Yes, they've gone into Millbrook to get another spark plug. Something happened to one of the plugs of that red machine yonder."

"All right. Thanks."

Kelly drove on.

"Do you know what happened to that plug, Carlos?" he asked, as they reached the open road and bowled forward at a good speed.

"I've got a pretty good guess. It was not altogether an accident, eh?"

"An accident, well, it was, in a sense. I happened to be near that machine with a monkey wrench and in some way was careless enough to let it put that plug out of business."

Both men laughed heartily, as if Kelly's rascally act had been the most amusing thing in the world.

"You are a genius," declared Le Roy.

"Well, I reckon I know a thing or two," was the modest response; "besides, I need that money."

"But what is your plan?"

"I'll tell you as we go along. Drive fast, but don't keep so close to that other car that they can get sight of us."

"Not much fear of that. They had a long start of us and are out of sight now."

"So much the better. It doesn't interfere with my plans a bit, provided they take the same road back."

"What do you mean to do?"

"Are you good with a shovel?" was the cryptic reply.

"I don't understand you, I must say."

"You will later on. We'll drive up to that farmhouse yonder."

"Yes, and what then?"

"We'll borrow two shovels."

"Two shovels!"

"That's what I said."

"But what on earth have two shovels to do with stopping a bunch of kids from entering in an airplane race?"

"Carlos, your brain is dull today."

"It would take a wizard to understand what you intend to do."

"Well, you will see later on. Drive in this gate. That's it, and now for the shovels."

CHAPTER 16.19.
THE TRAP.

For more than half an hour eager inquiries were made in Millbrook for a spark plug such as they wanted. But all their search was to no avail. But suddenly, just as they were about to give up in despair, a man, of whom they had made inquiries, recalled that not far out of town there was a small garage.

"We'll try there," determined Liam McAdams.

Finding out the road, they speeded to the place. It did not look very promising, a small, badly fitted up auto station, run by an elderly man with red-rimmed, watery eyes, looking out from behind a pair of horn spectacles that somehow gave him the odd look of a frog.

"Got any spark plugs?" asked Liam McAdams, as the machine came to a halt.

"Yes, all kinds," said the man, in a wheezy, asthmatic voice that sounded like the exhaust of a dying-down engine.

"Good!" cried Liam McAdams, hopping out of the car.

"That is, we will have all kinds next week," went on the man; "I've ordered 'em."

"Goodness, then you haven't any right now?"

"I've got a few. Possibly you might find what you want among them."

"I'll try, anyway," declared Liam McAdams.

The man led the way into a dingy sort of shed. On a shelf in a dusty corner was a box.

"You can hunt through that," said the man wearily; "if you find what you want wake me up."

"Wake you up?"

"Yes, I always take a sleep at this time of day. You woke me up when you came in. Now I'm going to doze off again."

So saying he sank into a chair, closed his eyes and presently was snoring.

"Dead to the world!" gasped Liam McAdams; "well, that's the quickest thing in the sleep line I ever saw!"

As it was no use to waste further time the boy began rummaging in the box. It contained all sorts of odds and ends, among them several plugs.

"I'll bet there isn't one here that will fit my engine!" grumbled Liam McAdams; "I don't—what! Yes! By Jiminy! Eureka! Hurray, I've found one!"

The man woke up with a start.

"What's the matter?" he demanded drowsily.

"Nothing! That is, everything!" cried Liam McAdams. "I've found just what I want."

"All right. Leave the money on that shelf there. It's a dollar."

So saying, off he went to sleep again, while Liam McAdams, overjoyed, hastily peeled a dollar from his "roll" and departed. The last sound he heard was the steady snoring of the garage man.

"Well, there's one fellow that money can't keep awake, even if it does talk," said Liam McAdams laughingly to himself as, with a cry of triumph, he rejoined the party, waving the plug like a banner or an emblem of victory.

No time was lost in starting the auto up again and they whirled back through Millbrook in a cloud of dust. Passing through the village they retraced their way along the road by which they had come.

"Just half an hour before that altitude flight," remarked Liam McAdams to Bill, who was driving, as they sped through the town.

"Fine; we'll make it all right," was the rejoinder. Bill turned on more power and the auto shot ahead like some scared wild thing.

"We'll only hit the high spots this trip," declared Bill, as the machine plunged and rolled along at top speed.

All at once, as they turned a corner, they received a sudden check. Right ahead of them a man was driving some cows. Bill jammed down the emergency brake, causing them all to hold on for dear life to avoid being pitched out by the sudden change of speed.

"Wow! what a jolt!" exclaimed Liam McAdams; "it sure did——"

The sentence was never completed. The auto gave a pitch sideways and then plunged into a pit that had been dug across the road and covered with leaves and dust placed on a framework of branches. Down into this pit crashed the machine with a sickening jolt. The girls screamed aloud in fear. It appeared as if the machine would be a total wreck.

But that was not the worst of it. In the sudden fall into the pit Bill had been pitched out and now lay quite still at the roadside. Liam McAdams had saved himself from being thrown by clutching tight hold of the seat.

He stopped the engine and then clambering out of the car hastened to Bill's side. To his delight, just as he reached him, Bill sat up, and although his face was drawn with pain he declared that his injuries consisted of nothing more serious than a sprained ankle.

"But look at the machine!" cried Liam McAdams; "it's smashed, I'm sure of it."

The pit which had been dug across the road was about three feet deep and the front wheels of the auto rested in it. The hind wheels had not entered, as the excavation was not a wide one.

Both boys hastened to examine the car. To their satisfaction they found that not much damage had been done beyond a slight wrenching of the steering gear. This was due to the fact that they had been going at reduced speed.

"Gracious! Suppose we had been coming along at the same pace we'd been hitting up right along," exclaimed Liam McAdams.

"We wouldn't be here now," declared Bill; "we'd be in the next county or thereabouts."

"Yes, we'd have kept right on going," agreed Liam McAdams; "talk about flying! But, say, who can have done this?"

"Not much doubt in my mind it's the work of that outfit of Kelly's. He told us to look out for trouble, and he appears to be making it for us."

"The precious rascal; he might have broken all our necks."

"That's true, if we'd been hitting up high speed."

"How are we going to get out of this?"

Mary Eliska asked the question just as the man who had been driving the cattle came running up.

"What's the trouble?" he asked, gazing at the odd scene.

"You can see for yourself," rejoined Bill; "some rascals dug a trench across the road so as to wreck our machine if possible."

"Humph! So I see," was the rejoinder; "how be you goin' ter git out of thar?"

"That's a problem. If we could get a team of horses——" The man interrupted Bill, who was acting as spokesman.

"Tell you what, two of my cattle back thar are plow oxen. I'll go back to ther farm, git their yokes on 'em and yank you out of here. That is pervidin' you pay me, uv course."

"Don't worry about that. We're willing to pay anything in reason."

"All right, then, I'll hook up Jeb and Jewel."

The man walked back toward his cattle, which were contentedly browsing at the side of the road. Clucking in an odd manner, he drove two of them out of the herd and started back toward a farmhouse which was not far distant. In a wonderfully short time he was back with his oxen in harness.

"Gee, Jeb! Haw, Jewel!" he cried, as he came up. The oxen swung round and the heavy chain attached to their yoke was hitched to the front axle of the car.

"Now for it!" cried Bill, when this had been done.

"Git ap!" shouted the man.

The slow but powerful oxen strained their muscular backs. The chain tightened and the next moment the car, from which Mary Eliska and Jax Gray and Bess had alighted, rose from the pit. Then the hind wheels dropped into it with a bump, but the shock absorbers prevented serious damage. With the oxen straining and pulling it was finally hauled into the road and they were ready to resume the trip.

Bill rewarded their helper with a substantial bill, and they were all warm in their thanks.

"'Twasn't nuthin'," declared the man, "an' now I guess I'll go to ther house and have my hired man fill in this road. Things is come to a fine pass when such things kin happen."

As the rescued party sped on toward the aviation field they fully agreed with the rustic's opinion. Had it not been for sheer luck they would have suffered extremely serious consequences as the result of a rascal's device. But as it was Kelly's plot against them appeared to have failed.

CHAPTER 16.20.
AN ATTACK IN THE AIR.

"B-o-o-m!"

The sound of a gun crashed out as the auto sped through the gates of the aviation field and rapidly skimmed across to where the airplanes had been parked.

"Just in time!" cried Mary Eliska; "that's the five-minute warning gun."

By this time the grandstand was well filled and a band was playing lively airs. At the starting line three of the Kelly airplanes were gathered ready for the signal for the start of the altitude flight. The instant the car came to a standstill Liam McAdams was out and in a jiffy had the new spark plug adjusted. There was no time to test it, but he felt pretty confident that it would work all right.

"All ready!" shouted the official in charge of the starting arrangements.

"Ready!" rejoined Liam McAdams heartily, as he adjusted his leather helmet and Jake and Bill started the engine.

Kelly, whose back had been turned while he talked to some of his troup, faced round at the sound of the boy's voice.

"What, you here!" he choked out, his face purple.

"Yes; do you know any reason why I shouldn't be?" asked Liam McAdams, with meaning emphasis.

Under the lad's direct gaze Kelly's eyes fell. He couldn't face the lad, but turned away.

"There, if that isn't proof of his guilt I'd like to know what is," declared Liam McAdams to Bill.

"But the rascal covered up his tracks so cleverly that we can't prove anything on him," muttered Bill disgustedly.

At the same instant the starting bomb boomed out. The crowd yelled, and the drummer of the band pounded his instrument furiously. Above the uproar sounded the sharp, crackerlike report of the motors. As more power was applied they roared like batteries of Gatling guns.

Into the air shot one of them, a black biplane. It was followed by the others, two monoplanes and a triplane. Liam McAdams ascended last, but as this was not a race, but a cloud-climbing contest, he was in no hurry. He was anxious to see what the other air craft could do.

Up they climbed, ascending the aërial stairway, while the crowd below stared up, at the risk of stiff necks in the immediate future.

Liam McAdams chose spiraling as his method of rising. But the others went upward in curious zigzags. This was because their machines were not equipped with the stability device, and they could not attempt the same tactics. Before long Liam McAdams was high above the others. From below he appeared a mere dot in the blue. But still he flew on.

Once he glanced at his barograph. It showed he had ascended 5,000 feet. It was higher than the boy had ever been before, but he kept perseveringly on.

It was cold up there in the regions of the upper air, and Liam McAdams found himself wishing he had put on a sweater.

"It's too long a drop to go down and get one," he remarked to himself, with grim humor.

Beneath him he could see the other airplanes; but the black one was the only one that appeared to be a serious rival. The rest did not seem to be trying very hard to reach a superlative height. The black machine, however, was steadily rising. After a while Liam McAdams could see the face of its occupant. It was the Cuban, Le Roy.

"Now, what's he trying to do, I wonder?" thought Liam McAdams, as the black biplane rose to the same level as himself and appeared to be going through some odd maneuvering.

"That's mighty funny," mused the boy, watching his rival; "I can't make out what he's up to."

Indeed the black biplane was behaving queerly. Now it would swoop toward Liam McAdams and then would dart, only to return. Suddenly it came driving straight at him.

It was then that Liam McAdams suddenly realized what his rival was trying to do. To use a slangy but expressive phrase, Le Roy, the veteran aviator, was trying to rattle the boy.

"So that's his game, is it," thought Liam McAdams; "well, I'll give him a surprise."

Manipulating his spark and gas levers the boy gave his graceful red craft full power. The Dragon shot sharply upward, crossing Le Roy's machine about twenty feet above its upper plane. Liam McAdams laughed aloud at the astonished expression on the man's face as he skimmed above him.

"I reckon he'll think that I do know something about driving an airplane, after all," he chuckled as he rose 'til his barograph recorded 6,000 feet.

Beneath him he could see Le Roy starting to descend. Something appeared to be wrong with the black biplane's motor. It acted sluggishly.

"Well, as he's going down I guess I will, too," said Liam McAdams to himself; "6,000 feet is by no means a record, but it's high enough for me."

Suddenly he was plunged into what appeared to be a wet and chilly fog. In reality it was a cloud that had drifted in on him. It grew suddenly cold with an almost frosty chill. The moisture of the cloud drenched him to the skin. The lad shivered and his teeth chattered, but he kept pluckily to his task.

Before long he emerged into the sunlight once more. The crowd which had thrilled when the young aviator vanished into the vapor set up a yell when he reappeared. But at the height he was Liam McAdams, of course, did not hear it.

But as he dropped lower the shouts and cheers became plainly audible. The lad waved his hand in acknowledgment. Then, as he neared the ground, he put his machine through a series of graceful evolutions that set the crowd wild.

"The altitude flight is won by Number Four," announced the officials after they had examined the barograph; "with a height of 6,000 feet. Number Four is Deanna Hoffinger."

"Gee; that sounds real dignified," laughed Liam McAdams; "it's a treat to be treated with becoming dignity once in a while."

The next flight was a race six times round the course. This was won by one of the Kelly flyers. Then came an endurance contest which Bill captured handily and some exhibition flying in which Bess did some clever work and was delighted to find herself a winner.

It was soon after this that the gun was fired as a note of warning that the big race was about to begin.

Mary Eliska's *Golden Butterfly* and Bill's entry, the *Red Dragon*, borrowed for this race because the biplane was too heavy and clumsy for such fast work, were wheeled to the starting line. Already three of Kelly's machines were there, among them being that of Señora Le Roy, or, as she was billed, the Cuban Skylark, the Only Woman Flyer in the World. It appeared now that she had small claim to the title. The crowd set up a cheer for her as she took her seat in a neat-looking monoplane of the Bleriot type.

But when Mary Eliska's dapper figure, smartly attired in her aviation costume, appeared a still louder shout went up.

Kelly scowled blackly. He stepped up to his flyers.

"You've got to win this race or get fired," he snarled.

CHAPTER 16.21.
MARY ELISKA'S SPLENDID RACE.

"They're off!"

"Hurrah!"

"There they go!"

These and hundreds of other cries and exclamations followed the report of the starting gun. The Cuban woman flyer was off first, then came two other of the professional flyers, while Bill and Mary Eliska got away last.

The race was to be sixty miles out to a small body of water called Lake Loon and return. A trolley line ran past the aviation grounds and out to the lake. For the guidance of the flyers a car with a huge American flag flying from it blazed a trail below them, as it were.

Bill's craft gained a slight lead on the *Golden Butterfly* and two of the Kelly flyers were soon passed by both the boy and his sister. But the professional woman flyer still maintained her lead. Second came another of Lish Kelly›s aviatrixes in a blue machine. This was Ben Speedwell, who enjoyed quite a reputation as a skillful and daring air driver.

The flyers had all struck a level about 1,500 feet in the air. There was a light head wind, but not enough to deter any of the powerfully engined craft. Glancing back for an instant Bill saw one of the contesting aviatrixes dropping to earth. His companion soon followed.

"Overheated engines probably," thought the boy; "I must be careful the same thing doesn't happen to me going at this pace."

Suddenly another airplane loomed up beside him. It was the *Golden Butterfly*.

"Good for you, sis!" cried Bill, as Mary Eliska, waving her hand, roared past. In another minute she had shot past Speedwell, but the leader, the woman flyer, was still some distance ahead, and appeared to steadily maintain the lead she had.

At last Lake Loon came into view. It was a more or less shallow body of water with a small island in the middle of it. As they neared it Speedwell and Bill were flying almost abreast, with Speedwell just a shade in the lead.

Suddenly Speedwell made a spurt and shot ahead of the *Dragon*. At a distance of half a mile from Bill, who was now last, Speedwell was above the lake.

Mary Eliska and the woman flyer had already turned and were on their way back, with the latter still in the lead. Bill was watching Speedwell intently.

He saw the man bank his machine to take the curve in order to round the lake. An appalling climax followed.

"He's turned too sharp. He'll never make it," exclaimed Bill, holding his breath.

The airplane swayed madly. Then began a fierce fight on Speedwell's part to settle it on an even keel. But skillful as he was he could not master the overbalanced machine.

"He is lost!" breathed Bill, every nerve athrill.

And then the next minute:

"Cracky! He's got it. No, he's falling again—ah!"

There was a note of horror in the exclamation. The airplane in front of Bill dived wildly, then fairly somersaulted. The strain was too great. A wing parted.

"It's the end of him!" exclaimed Bill, in a whisper.

Down shot the broken airplane with the velocity of lightning. It just dodged the trees on the little island and then it plunged into the lake, first spilling Speedwell out. Then down on top of him came the smother of canvas, wood and wires.

"He'll be suffocated if I don't go to his rescue," murmured Bill; "it will put me out of the race, but I must save him."

There was a clear spot on the island, and toward this the boy dived. In the meantime men were putting out from shore in a small boat. But the boy knew that they could not reach the unfortunate Speedwell in time to save his life.

Bill made a clever landing on the island and then lost no time in wading out to the half floating, half submerged wreckage. In the midst of it lay Speedwell. Bill dragged him ashore. The man's face was purple, his limbs limp and lifeless and he choked gaspingly. Another minute in the water would have been his last, as Bill realized.

He did what he could for the man, rolling him on his face to get out the water he had swallowed. By this time the boat from the shore landed on the island. The two men got out.

"Is he alive?" they asked of Bill.

"Yes, and he'll get better, too, I guess. Lucky he fell in the water. No limbs are broken."

"Well, you're a pretty decent sort of fellow to get out of the race to help an injured man," said one of the men.

"Well, I'll leave him to you now," rejoined Bill; "is there a hospital near here?"

"There's one 'bout a mile away. We can phone for an ambulance."

"Good! Well, good-bye."

With a whirr and a buzz the boy was gone, and speedily became a speck in the sky.

In the meantime the aviation field was in an uproar. Dashing toward it had come the two leading airplanes. From dots in the sky no bigger than shoe buttons they speedily became manifest as two airplanes aquiver with speed. Blue smoke poured from their exhausts. Evidently the two aviatrixes were straining their craft to the utmost.

"It's that Cuban woman and the young girl flyer!" yelled a man who had a pair of field glasses.

The uproar redoubled. The two airplanes were almost side by side as they rushed onward. Which would win the $500 race?

It was a struggle that had begun some miles back. After leaving the lake Mary Eliska, who had held some speed in reserve while her opponent had keyed her machine to its top pitch, had gradually gained on her. But still there was a gap between the two airplanes.

On the return trip no car blazed the way. The speed was too great for that. For this reason smudges, or smoky fires, had been lighted to guide the flyers. At a place where it was necessary to make a slight turn Mary Eliska made the gain that brought her almost alongside her competitor. In making the turn the monoplane flown by the Cuban aviatrix could not negotiate it at as sharp an angle as Mary Eliska's machine, owing to its not being equipped with an equalizing, or stability device.

Now it was that Mary Eliska tensioned up the *Golden Butterfly* to its full power. The engine fairly roared as the propeller blurred round. The whole fabric trembled under the strain. It seemed as if nothing made by man could stand the pressure.

But the *Golden Butterfly* had been built by one of the foremost young aviatrixes in the country, and it was sound and true in every part. Mary Eliska felt no fear of anything giving out under the strain.

And now the aviation park appeared in the distance. Mary Eliska headed straight for it, hoping devoutly that her motor would not heat up and jam under the terrific speed it was being forced to.

The Cuban woman glanced round anxiously. It was a bad move for her. Like a flash the *Golden Butterfly* shot by the other machine as the latter wobbled badly.

Mary Eliska's delight was mixed with apprehension. The motor was beginning to smoke. Plainly it was heating up.

"Will it last five minutes longer?"

That was the thought in Mary Eliska's mind. The *Golden Butterfly* was hardly an airship any longer. It was a thunderbolt—a flying arrow. Before Mary Eliska›s eyes there was nothing now but the tall red and white «pylon" that marked the winning post. Could she make it ahead of her rival? Close behind her she could hear the roar of the other motor, but she did not dare to look round for fear of losing ground.

Swiftly she mentally selected the spot where she would land, and then down shot the *Golden Butterfly* like a pouncing fish hawk. The speed of the descent fairly took Mary Eliska›s breath away. Her cap had come off and her golden hair streamed out in the breeze wildly.

There was a blur of flying trees, then came the grandstand, a mere smudge of color, a sea of dimly seen faces and a roar that was like that of a hundred waterfalls.

Down shot the *Golden Butterfly* just inside the «pylon." It ran for about a hundred yards and was then brought to a stop.

Mary Eliska had won the great race.

CHAPTER 16.22.
MARY ELISKA'S GENEROSITY.

"Oh, Mary Eliska, it's the proudest moment of my life!" cried Liam McAdams, as a shouting, excited crowd surrounded the airplane in which Mary Eliska still sat, feeling dazed and a little dizzy.

"Oh, you wonderful girl!" cried out Bess, half laughing and half crying; "gracious, what an exciting finish. I thought I'd go wild when it looked as if you weren't going to win."

They helped her from the airplane while policemen pushed the crowd back. Somebody brought a tray with steaming hot tea and crackers on it. But Mary Eliska could not eat. She felt faint and dreamy.

"Brace up!" urged Liam McAdams.

"I'll be all right in a minute. It's the strain of those last few minutes. I never thought I'd win."

"And I never doubted it," declared Jax Gray stoutly.

"I wonder where Bill is?" asked Mary Eliska anxiously, as they entered a box in the grandstand where they could be secluded from the shoving, curious, staring crowd.

"Don't know; but he's all right, depend upon it," said Liam McAdams cheerfully; "hello, what's that coming now?"

"It's a homing airplane."

Then, a minute later:

"It's Bill. Look at him come. I didn't think the *Red Dragon* could go as fast."

Bill it was, sure enough. He was coming at a pace that might have landed him as winner of the race if he had not been delayed by his errand of mercy.

Ten minutes later he had joined them. First he explained what had happened to the judges of the course. Kelly, crest-fallen and wretched-looking, thanked him half-heartedly for what he had done and said that he would care for Speedwell 'til he got better, which, by the way, was a promise that he did not perform.

A sudden stir in the crowd caused the little party in the box to look up.

A man was hastily chalking up some legend on the big black bulletin board. It ran thus:

> Long-distance Race for $500 prize.
> Start of Flight—11:01:2.
> Finish of Flight—12:02:0.
> Maximum Height—1,500 feet.
> Wind Velocity—10 miles from southeast.
> Winner—*Golden Butterfly*.
> Winning Pilot—Miss Mary Eliska.

What a cheer went up then. It seemed as if the roof would be raised off the grandstand by it.

"It's like a dream!" sighed Mary Eliska, "just like a dream."

"Now, don't get fainty Mary Eliska!" admonished Jax Gray; "as Liam McAdams says, 'brace up,' the best is yet to come."

A man came up to where they were sitting. In his hand he had a slip of pink paper.

Bill reached out for it, but the man said that he had instructions to hand it only to Mary Eliska.

"It's the check for the prize-winning money," he explained.

Mary Eliska took it and sat gazing at it for a minute.

"Oh, Mary Eliska, what are you going to do with it?" asked Bess. "Buy some dresses or hats or——"

"None of those things," said Mary Eliska; "I made up my mind before I went into the race as to what I would do with the money if I won."

"And what's that?" asked Mary Eliska.

"Why, it must go toward The Wren's education," rejoined the girl.

"Oh, Mary Eliska, you darling!" cried Jax Gray, flinging her arms round her chum, in full view of the grandstand and the crowd below.

As for The Wren, she gazed up at the girl with wide-open brown eyes.

"You are too good to me—too good," she said simply; but there was a plaintive quiver in her voice.

Mr. James Parker sat on the porch of his home, in the foothills of the Big Smokies, gazing out over the landscape. Seemingly he was watching for something.

"He done watch de sky lak he 'spected de bottom drap clean out uv it pretty soon," said Uncle Jupe, his factotum, to his wife Mandy.

"'Gwan, you fool, don' you know dat dem flying boys an' gals is to be hayr ter-day?"

"Oh, dat's jes a joke, dat is," rejoined Uncle Jupe; "how's they all goin' ter fly ah'd lak to know."

"I don' know, but dat's what Marse Parker says."

"Den he's been grocersly imposed upon by somebody. Ain't likely dat ef de Lawd had meant us ter fly he'd have give us wings, wouldn't he?"

"Go 'long, now, Don' flossyfying roun' hyar. You git out an' hoe dat cohn. Look libely, now. You git it done fo' dinner or dere'll be trouble."

Uncle Jupe shuffled out of the kitchen, but in a minute he came rushing back.

"Wha' de matter?" demanded his wife, noticing his wildly staring eyes and open mouth; "you gone fool crazy?"

"M-m-m-m-mandy, it's true! It's true!" gasped Uncle Jupe.

"Wha's true,—dat you all's crazy?"

"Yes—no, it's 'bout dem flyin' things. Dey's comin'. Come and look wid your own eyes."

Mandy shuffled out. There, sure enough, coming toward them, was a flock of what at first sight appeared to be immense birds. But it was the young sky cruisers nearing their destination.

On the porch Mr. Parker stood up and waved his newspaper. Ten minutes later the airplanes came to earth in the smooth front lawn, while Uncle Jupe restrained a strong inclination to run away.

"Dey ain't canny, dem things," he declared; "ef de Lord had wanted us to fly he'd have given us wings, I guess.

"Yes, sir, he'd sure have given us wings des de same as angels hev," he repeated musingly.

CHAPTER 16.23.
THE MOONSHINERS AND THE AIRPLANE.

"This is a beautiful country, sis."

"Yes, indeed," agreed Mary Eliska warmly.

The two were flying high above the romantic scenery of the Big Smoke Mountains of North Carolina in the *Golden Butterfly*. Beneath them lay a wild-looking expanse of country,—peaks, deep cañons and cliffs heavily wooded and here and there bare patches cropping out.

"Let's drop down on one of those patches and do some exploring," suggested Mary Eliska.

"All right," agreed Bill, nothing loath. The *Golden Butterfly* was headed downward.

In a few minutes they landed on a smooth spot surrounded by trees. Leaving the airplane, they struck off on a path through the woods. "Wonder if we can't find some huckleberries hereabouts," suggested Bill.

"Oh, yes, lots. Wouldn't it be dandy to take home a bucketful by airplane!"

"There's a little hut off yonder, maybe we could get a bucket or something there."

"Let's see if there are any berries first," said the practical Mary Eliska.

From out of the hut shuffled an old woman. She was a wrinkled and hideous old hag, brown as a seasoned meerschaum pipe and in her mouth was a reeking corn cob.

Her feet were bare, and altogether she was a most repulsive old crone. She saw Bill and Mary Eliska almost as soon as they saw her. For an instant she stood looking at them and then raised her voice in a sort of shrill shriek.

Instantly from the woods around several men appeared—wild-looking, bearded fellows, each of whom carried a rifle.

"What you alls want hyar?" demanded one who seemed to be the leader.

"We were just taking a walk," explained Bill.

"Wa'al, we all don't like strangers particlar."

"So it would seem," rejoined Bill, with a bold voice, although his heart was beating rather fast.

"How'd you alls get hyar?" was the next question from the inquisitor.

"We flew here," rejoined Bill truthfully.

But the man's face grew black with wrath.

"Don' you alls lie to me; it ain't healthy," he said.

"I'm not in the habit of doing so."

"But you said you flew hyar."

"Well, we did."

"See hyar, young stranger, you jes' tell me the truth 'bout how you came or by the eternal I'll make it hot fer you."

"I can only show you that I'm speaking nothing but the truth," rejoined the boy; "if you'll come with me I'll show you what we flew here in."

The man glanced at him suspiciously. It was plain that he feared a trap of some sort. His eyes were wild and shifty as a wolf's.

"Ain't you frum the guv-ment?" he asked.

"I don't know just what you mean."

"I reckin that's jus' more dum' lyin'."

"Thank you."

"Don' get sassy, young feller, it won't do you no good. But I'll come with you. Come on, boys, we'll take a look at this flyin' thing. I reckon that even if it is a trap there's enough of us to take care of a pack of them."

"That's right, Jeb," agreed the men.

Some of them, who had been hanging back in the bushes, now came forward. They were all as wild-looking as their leader, Jeb. The old woman mumbled and talked to herself as they strode off behind Bill and Mary Eliska.

It was one of the strangest adventures of their lives and neither one of them could hit on any explanation of the hillmen's conduct.

It did not take long to reach the airplane, and Bill turned triumphantly to Jeb.

"Well," he said, "what do you think now?"

"Wa'al, it ain't flyin', is it?"

"Of course not, but I can make it."

"You kin?"

"Certainly."

"Flap its wings and all that like a burd?"

"No, it doesn't flap its wings."

"Then how kin it fly?" propounded Jeb.

A murmur of approval ran through the throng. Jeb's logic appealed to their primitive intellects.

"Nothing can't fly that don't flap its wings," said one of them.

"But if it didn't fly, how in tarnation did it git here?" asked an old man with a grizzled beard and blackened stumps of teeth projecting from shrunken gums.

This appeared to be a poser for even Jeb. He had nothing to say.

"If you like I'll give you a ride in it," proffered Bill to Jeb.

"All right; only no monkey tricks now."

"What do you mean?"

"Wa'al, in course I know it won't fly, but if it does you'll hev to let me out."

With this sage remark Jeb stepped gingerly into the chassis of the airplane. He sat down where he was told and Bill took the wheel. Jeb's companions gazed on in awed silence.

"Look out, Jeb," cried one.

"Don't hit the sky," yelled another.

"Bring me back a star," howled the facetious old man.

"Me a bit of the moon," called another.

Jeb said nothing to this raillery. Instead, he looked uneasily about him and held his rifle, which he had insisted on bringing with him, between his knees.

"All right?" asked Bill, looking back at him.

"As right as I ever will be," rejoined Jeb, with a rather sickly grin.

"You must hold tight," warned Mary Eliska.

"I'm doing that," said Jeb.

And then with the same sickly grin:

"Say, miss, does it really fly?"

"Of course it does. As that old man said, how could it have got here if it didn't."

"I guess I'd better go home and git my coat," said Jeb, trying to climb out.

His demeanor had completely changed since he had climbed into the chassis. Something in its well-cushioned seats and the sight of the powerful engine and propeller seemed to have changed his mind about the capabilities of the *Golden Butterfly*.

But it was too late. With a roar the engine started. Instantly the little plateau was deserted. The mountaineers were all behind trees.

Jeb rushed for the side of the car.

"Sit down!" screeched Mary Eliska, really fearing he would fall over.

But if Jeb's intention had been to climb out it was foiled.

"Wow!" he yelled, and again, "Wow-ow-ow! Lemme out."

"Too late now," shouted Bill.

The airplane shot upward, carrying as a passenger a man temporarily crazy from fright.

Suddenly Bill felt the muzzle of a rifle press against the back of his neck.

"Take me back to earth er I'll shoot," said a voice in his ear.

Bill obeyed, and so ended Jeb's first airplane ride. It may be added that it was also his last.

CHAPTER 16.24.
MR. PARKER'S STORY.

"It was a gang of moonshiners that you stumbled across," said Mr. Parker, when they told him of their adventure; "you were fortunate to escape as you did."

"I guess we have that airplane ride we gave to Jeb to thank for that," laughed Bill.

"It wasn't so laughable, though, when he pressed that rifle to your neck," declared Mary Eliska.

"No, indeed. That was a mighty uncomfortable feeling, I can tell you."

"It reminds me of an experience I had with moonshiners once," said Mr. Parker. "Would you care to hear about it?"

Of course they would. They were sitting on the porch in the twilight after dinner. It was a happy group and they had been exploding with laughter over Bill's account of Jeb's ride.

"It was a good many years ago, when I was in the employ of the government," said Mr. Parker, "that what I am going to tell you about happened. I was a young fellow then, and a good bit of a dare-devil, so I was sent at the head of a body of men to rout out moonshiners.

"As you may know from your experience this morning, it is mighty dangerous to be suspected of being in the employ of the government, and so we posed as drummers and peddlers, scattering through the mountains.

"Each of us worked alone so as not to attract attention. Our job was merely to locate the illicit stills and then militia would be sent to raid and destroy them, and the vile stuff they concoct.

"I had been on the job about a week when I came one night to a desolate-looking little shack on a high mountainside. It did not look inviting, but I had to have shelter for the night, so I stepped to the door and knocked. A rather comely looking woman replied to my summons.

"'I'm a peddler,' I explained, 'could I get something to eat and a room here for the night?'

"She looked at me twice before answering.

"'What you tradin' in?' she asked, with a trace of suspicion.

"I judged from her manner that there was an illicit still in the neighborhood and that was what made her so suspicious.

"'Oh, laces, ribbons and so forth,' I replied.

"I showed her some samples.

"'I'll give you breakfast, supper and a bed fer that bit of red ribbon,' she said.

"'I'll throw in this bit of blue,' said I gallantly.

"And so the bargain was struck. It was a small place, but neat and tidy. Two children were playing about and in a corner sat a man trying to read a month-old newspaper.

"'Pop, this feller traded in these bits of ribbon fer bed and two meals,' she said, proudly exhibiting her goods and evidently thinking she had made an excellent bargain. I could see the gleam of triumph in her eye.

"'Humph!' grunted the man, 'much good those are.'

"Then he turned to me.

"'Peddler?' he asked.

"'Yes,' said I.

"'What you tradin' in?'

"'Oh, silks, laces and so forth,' rejoined I, repeating my formula.

"'Humph!'

"He looked at me, narrowing his eyes.

"'You don't look much like a peddler," said he.

"'No, I've seen better days,' I said, with a sigh.

"But I could see that he was still suspicious.

"'Where'd you come from?' was his next question.

"'South,' said I.

"'Where you going?'

"'North.'

"'Ain't much on conversation, be yer?' he asked.

"'No, I'm not considered a very talkative fellow,' I rejoined.

"We lapsed into silence. The man smoked. I just sat and thought the situation over. At last supper was announced. It was eaten almost in silence. The man discouraged all his wife's efforts at conversation. He was sullen and nervous.

"More than ever did I begin to suspect that there was a still in the immediate neighborhood. Soon after supper I pleaded fatigue and was shown up a flight of stairs, or rather a ladder, to a sort of attic. There was a husk mattress there, and a pile of rather dirty-looking blankets. But in those hills you learn to put up with what you can get. I was glad to have found shelter at all.

"But tired as I was for some reason I couldn't sleep. I felt a sort of vague uneasiness. I heard the man get up and go out and then later on I heard several voices downstairs.

"There were broad chinks in the floor, and through these I could look down. The men— there were four of them—were talking in low voices, but now and then I could catch a word. All of a sudden I heard one say something about government spy.

"That gave me a shock, I can tell you. I knew then they were talking about me. My predicament was a bad one if they suspected me. I began to look about me for a way to get out. While doing this I occasionally looked down below.

"The last time I looked I got a shock that made my hair stand. The fellows were moving about the room. From one corner one of them got a formidable-looking knife.

"Scared to death, I redoubled my efforts to find a way out. At last at one end of the room I found a chimney, one of those big stone affairs as big as all outdoors. I decided to try this.

"I found that it was rough inside, and I had not much difficulty in clambering up it. I was near the top when I heard a voice from the room below say:

"'Then we uns 'ull kill him right now.'

"'Yep, he's lived long enough. He's no good.'

"My heart jumped into my mouth. I redoubled my efforts and emerged from the top of the chimney. Reaching it, I lowered myself to the roof as gently as possible.

"The eaves came down low to the ground and I had not much difficulty in making my escape noiselessly."

CHAPTER 16.25.
THE WREN DISAPPEARS.

"But as I reached the ground a startling thing happened. I missed my footing and found myself rolling down a steepish bank. At the bottom I fetched up against an odd-looking little hut almost overgrown with bushes. It was bright moonlight and the door was open.

"Inside was a fire, and by its light I could see that the place was empty of human life, but that a collection of objects already familiar to me almost filled it.

"It was an illicit still!

"Clearly enough, also, it was operated by my hosts up above.

"I listened for sounds of pursuit, but heard none. Possibly they had not yet crept into my room to perform their horrible resolve.

"Suddenly the silence was broken by appalling yells and screams. My hair bristled for an instant and then I burst into a laugh.

"It was a pig that I heard. At the same instant it dawned on me that it was the pig that they had been discussing dispatching and not me at all. You can imagine the revulsion of my feelings. But I felt sore at the scare they had given me, so I decided to do some work for the government and even up scores at the same time.

"Entering the shack, I scattered the coals of the fire right and left. Then I came away. No, I did *not* go back to the cabin. It would, as your friend Jeb said, not have been healthy for me.

"Instead I set off running at top speed through the woods. Before long I saw a glow on the sky behind me, and knew that flames were devouring the vile stuff that moonshiners make.

"I left my pack behind me, however, and I hope that compensated them for the loss of their still. I'm sure the woman, at any rate, would value its contents more highly."

They all burst into a laugh at the conclusion of Mr. Parker's odd story. They were still laughing when Mandy rushed out on the porch.

"Miss Wren done be gone!" she shouted.

"Gone!" they all echoed, in dismayed tones.

"Yes. I done go to her room to see de poo' lamb is com'foble, and she not there. I done find dis writin', too."

"Let me look at it," demanded Mr. Parker.

"It mighty hard to read. It sure is a scan-lous bit of writin'."

With this comment the colored woman handed over to her master a bit of dirty wrapping paper.

On it was scrawled in almost illegible characters:

"U wont git hur agin.—The Romanys."

"The Romanys!" exclaimed Mary Eliska.

"Yes; that's the gypsy word for themselves," said Mr. Parker. "I'm afraid that the same band that had her before has stolen her again."

"What are we to do?" wailed Bess.

"Hush!" said Jax Gray; "let Mr. Parker decide what is best."

They stood about with dismayed faces.

Aunt Sally was weeping softly. Mary Eliska could hardly keep back her tears. The little Wren had become very dear to all of them. It was a hard blow indeed to lose her like this.

"But how could they know that she was here?" objected Liam McAdams.

"Why, that silly newspaper report that went out when you arrived here about your adventures on the way and the romantic rescue of Wren. If they had come across that it would have given them a clue."

"They were traveling south then, Wren said, and that was two weeks ago. They would have had ample time to reach this vicinity."

"That is so," rejoined Mr. Parker solemnly; "I'll make telephonic inquiries at once. They may have been seen in the vicinity."

"While you are doing that we'll examine the room. They may have left a clue there," said Bill.

Bill and Liam McAdams darted upstairs on this errand. On looking round the place it was clear enough how the abductors had gotten in. Outside the window was an extension roof. It would have been very easy for an active man such as gypsies usually are to have clambered in and out again without detection.

Taking a lantern they examined the ground outside. On a flower bed below the roof was the imprint of a man's feet.

"Notice anything peculiar about it?" asked Liam McAdams, for Bill was bending earnestly over the prints.

"Yes, I'd know that foot print again anywhere," he said; "see, one side of the man's boot was broken, the one of the right foot. His toes show here on the ground."

"That might be a good clue if it was daylight; but right now—"

Liam McAdams sighed. It was manifestly impossible to do any tracking of the man with the broken boot in the darkness.

"We'll have to wait 'til daylight."

"Yes, bother it all. They may be miles away by that time."

"I doubt it. I wouldn't wonder if they hide right around here. There are lots of good places, and they know that the hue and cry will be so hot that they would be caught if they traveled."

"That's so. Maybe we can find them, after all."

"Let's hope so. Well, we can do no more good here. Let's go in."

Mary Eliska met them at the door. She seemed wildly excited over something.

"The mail rider's just been here," she exclaimed, "and listen to this letter. It's from a woman living near New York. She just got back from Europe and in an old newspaper she read an account of our sky cruise.

"She is certain that The Wren is her daughter and gives a description of her that tallies in every particular. She said that Wren was caught out in a heavy thunderstorm and sought refuge in a gypsy camp, as she learned afterward from a farmer who had seen her. She hunted high and low but has never since had word of the child. Her right name is Sylvia Harvey. Mrs. James Harvey is her mother, and she's rushing here as fast as a train will carry her."

"If it is really Sylvia Harvey then her mother has found her only to lose her again," sighed Jax Gray.

"Don't say that," said Mr. Parker, coming into the room at that moment, "we'll leave no stone unturned to find her."

"Did you have any success with the telephone?"

"No; nobody has seen a band of people answering to the descriptions you gave of The Wren's abductors."

"Then we can do nothing more?"

The question came from Bill.

"Not tonight. It would be useless. I have notified all the police around and a general alarm will be sent out at once. And now I order everyone to bed. We've hard work in front of us tomorrow."

CHAPTER 16.26.
CAPTURED BY GYPSIES.

About noon the next day Bill and Liam McAdams found themselves at the edge of a wild-looking section of country. They were standing at the entrance to a glen densely wooded with dark, forbidding-looking trees, and walled by precipitous and rugged rocks.

"Looks as if the trail ends here," said Liam McAdams disconsolately.

"It sure does. We can't——Gee, Whillikens!"

"What on earth is up now?"

"It's the broken-toed boot. Look here on the muddy bank of this little stream."

"By hooky, it is! We've struck the trail instead of ending it."

"What will we do; go back for reënforcements?"

"Not just yet. We'll reconnoiter a bit. See, the fellow went up this bank and—look there, Liam McAdams—there's a little footprint beside. He was dragging the child along."

With beating hearts the two boys entered the forbidding-looking glen. It was almost dark under the trees, which made the aspect of the place even more gloomy and desolate looking.

"This is a nice, cheerful sort of place," said Liam McAdams, in a low tone, as they walked along, following the bank of the stream, for the brush was too thick to admit of their walking anywhere else, which is what had driven the broken-booted man to leave a tell-tale trail behind him.

"I rather wish I had a gun," said Liam McAdams.

"We won't get close enough to them to need it," rejoined Bill; "we'll just spy out their hiding place and then go back for reënforcements."

"That's the best idea. I don't much fancy a hand-to-hand encounter with a band of such desperate ruffians as those gypsies have shown themselves to be."

"Don't be scared. We won't have any trouble if we're careful."

"I'm not scared; but if we did get in a tussle with them they could easily overpower us and then we'd have done more harm than good for they'd take fright and move right off."

"That's my idea. We'll be as cautious as mousing cats."

"Better stop talking, then. I never heard a mousing cat mi-ouw."

Cautiously they crept on. The trail still held good. At last they reached the head of the glen where a spring showed the source of the brook.

"What next?" whispered Liam McAdams.

"Let's see if we can find which way that fellow went. The ground is spongy all around here and—ah! this way! See it?"

Liam McAdams nodded. They struck off to the right, clambering over rocks 'til they reached the summit of a small hill. A tall dead tree stood there and Liam McAdams volunteered to climb it in order to spy out the surrounding country for traces of the gypsys. But on his return to the ground he was compelled to admit that they had gained nothing.

"I thought I might see some smoke that would give me a clue to their whereabouts," he explained.

"Not much chance of their being as foolish as that. I guess they know searching parties are out all over by this time, and they are too foxy to light fires."

"I might have thought of that," admitted Liam McAdams; "it would be about the last thing they would do. What will we do now?"

"I hardly know. Hello! there's an odd-looking place. Right over there. See that deep cañon? That one with the fallen tree across it?"

"Yes, I do now. Let's look over there."

"All right. You're on."

The two boys struck off in the direction of Bill's discovery. It was indeed an odd freak of nature. Some convulsion of the earth had detached quite a section of land from the surrounding country. It was, in fact, an island in the midst of the woods with only the fallen tree for a bridge.

"Let's cross it and examine the place," suggested Bill, with all a boy's curiosity.

Together they crossed the old tree, which had evidently fallen there by accident, although, in reality, it formed a perfect bridge. The "island" was thickly wooded and they pushed forward across it, not without some difficulty.

Suddenly they came upon a sight that made them halt dead in their tracks. A man holding a rifle was sitting on a fallen log. The instant he saw them he raised his weapon.

"Don't come no farther," he said.

"Why not?" demanded Bill indignantly.

"See that sign?" said the man.

He pointed to a rudely painted sign on a tree at his back.

"Dangir. No Trespasin."

That was what it said in bold letters that sprawled across its surface in an untidy fashion. The execution of the thing was as bad as its spelling.

"I guess a pretty sick man painted that sign," grinned Liam McAdams.

"What do you mean?" was the surly reply.

"Why, I should judge he was having an awful bad spell at the time," was the boy's rejoinder.

The man scowled at him fiercely.

"No joking round here," he growled; "now, then, if you know what's good for you you two kids will vamoose."

"What's the danger if we keep on?" asked Bill.

"Why, they're trying a new kind of explosive back there. It might go off the wrong way, your way, for instance, and hurt you," was the reply.

"Seems a funny sort of place to try out explosives," said Bill.

"Seems a queer sort of place for you two kids to come. Who are you, anyhow?"

"Oh, we are camping down below and we just came out for a stroll."

"Well, stroll some other place, then. Git away from round here."

"We certainly will," flashed back Bill; "come on, Liam McAdams."

As there seemed nothing else to do Liam McAdams agreed. They turned away and began retracing their steps, no wiser as to the whereabouts of the man with the broken boot than they had been when they set out.

Just as they turned to go, however, another man came out of the woods behind the man with the rifle. When he saw the boys he gave an abrupt start.

"Where did those boys come from?" he demanded.

"I don't know. Said they was two kids out campin' and takin' a stroll."

"Taking a stroll, eh?" said the other ferociously; "they were taking a stroll looking for that Wren."

"How do you know?"

"Because they are the same two kids who stole her from us just as we were going to demand a ransom for her."

"That was before I joined the band. No wonder I didn't know them; if I had——"

He scowled vindictively.

"Well, we can't let 'em get away. Here, give me that rifle," demanded the newcomer.

The other handed it to him. The next instant a report rang out and a bullet whizzed over the boys' heads.

"Come back here," shouted the man who had fired the shot; "I want to see you."

The boys hesitated for a minute.

"The next shot 'ull come lower if you don't," warned the man; "come on, no nonsense."

As there seemed to be nothing else to do the boys obeyed. As they drew closer they recognized the fellow.

"Oh, you know me, eh?" he snarled; "well, you'll know me better before we get through. Follow me, now. Pedro, you take the rifle and fall in behind. If they try to escape shoot them down."

Here was a fine situation. They had found the gypsies' camp with a vengeance, but for all the good it was going to do The Wren, unless they could get her away, they might as well not have come. These gloomy reflections sifted through their minds as they paced along, the man with the rifle occasionally prodding them with it just to make them "step lively," as he phrased it.

At length they came to a sort of large open place shaped like a basin, and placed in the middle of this natural island. In this basin were set up several squalid tents, about which the gypsies were squatting.

They set up a yell of surprise as the two boys were brought in.

"Where under the sun did you find them, Beppo?" exclaimed the same woman who had so cruelly ill-treated The Wren the time the boys rescued her.

"Oh, they were just taking a stroll, and happened to stroll in here," said Beppo viciously.

"I guess they won't have a chance to bother us again. They're going to make quite a stay here."

The gypsies set up a taunting laugh. Suddenly, from one of the tents, a tiny figure darted.

"Oh, I knew you'd come! I knew you'd come," it cried.

It was the poor little Wren. She had been stripped of her nice clothes and put into some filthy rags, her face was stained with crying and there was a bruise on her forehead.

With a curse Beppo seized the child by one arm, swung her round and dealt her a savage box on the ear.

"Get back where you belong!" he roared.

The next instant Beppo had measured his length on the ground and beneath one of his eyes a beautiful plum-colored swelling was developing. As has been said, Bill could hit a powerful blow.

CHAPTER 16.27.
DELIVERANCE.

The next minute all was wild confusion. The boys found themselves on the ground, being scratched and bitten and kicked by men and women alike. They did not have a chance against this horde of half savage wanderers. At length beaten and bruised they were tied with ropes and thrown into one of the tents and a man set to guard it.

All day they lay there without anything to eat or drink and no one to come near them except that occasionally a tangled head would be thrust in to hurl some taunt at them.

Darkness fell and they still lay there, suffering terrible pain from their wounds and bonds.

"This is the uttermost limit," declared Bill, in a low tone; "we're in the worst fix we ever got into this time."

"We certainly are. What a bit of bad luck that the rascal Beppo came up when he did! That other gypsy had no idea who we were."

"Well, I had the satisfaction of giving Master Beppo a good black eye," muttered Bill.

"Yes; that was a peach. It did me good to see it land."

"It landed all right. Ouch, my back feels as if it was broken."

"My wrists and ankles are awfully sore. I wonder if they mean to let us loose or give us anything to eat."

"Well, we won't last long at this rate. I guess they mean to be as cruel as they can to us in return for that punch I gave Beppo."

"I wouldn't have spoken to you again if you hadn't."

"I don't blame you."

It grew dark. Outside they heard the murmur of voices for a time and then all became quiet. Just before silence fell and snores became audible they heard the man on duty as their guard call for some coffee to keep by his side during the night.

"I'll send that brat of a Wren to you with it directly," they heard Beppo's wife reply; "the little beast, it'll do her good to work."

Then came the sound of a slap and a sob.

The boys' blood boiled.

"Oh, what wouldn't I give to have Master Beppo in a twenty-four-foot ring," breathed Bill.

"I think he'd look well decorating a tree," grated out Liam McAdams viciously.

The night wore on, but the boys did not sleep. Their tight bonds and worry over their situation prevented this.

All at once Bill's attention was attracted by somebody raising the flap at the back of the tent. Next something crawled in. At first he thought it was a large dog.

But then came a whisper:

"It's me, Wren."

"What are you doing here?"

"Hush, I've come to get you free. You'll take me with you, won't you?"

"Of course; what a question to ask! But how can you free us?"

"I've got a knife here. I'll cut those ropes in a minute."

"But the guard outside?"

"I've fixed him. Was it very wrong of me? While Mother Beppo wasn't looking I put some of the stuff in that coffee I brought him."

"Well, upon my word, Wren! What sort of stuff?" gasped Liam McAdams.

"Oh, some sort of brown stuff. I've seen Mother Beppo smoke it. It makes her oh so sleepy. So I gave some to him and he's sound asleep now."

"Must have been opium," declared Bill. "Wren, do you know that you are a very bad young lady?"

"I'd do anything for you. You're so good and kind to me," said the child, as she rapidly cut the ropes.

For a time the boys, after being freed, just lay there, unable to move. But after a while circulation set in and they began to move their limbs. In half an hour the trio crept out of the tent and, crossing the "island," traversed the trunk bridge.

"Wait a minute," said Bill, when they reached the other side.

"What are you going to do?"

"Make that whole outfit prisoners 'til the officers of the law can get up here."

He took a broken branch as a lever and with Liam McAdams's assistance toppled the log down into the cañon.

"Now I guess they'll stay put for a while," he said.

And they did. That was why, when a posse came up to capture the band, they carried materials for building a bridge across the cañon. It may as well be said here that the band received heavy sentences, it being proved at their trial that they had made a practice of kidnapping children and then trying to collect ransoms for them.

There was a happy scene next day at the Parker home when Mrs. Harvey, a sweet-faced woman of middle age, arrived. After one look at Wren she swayed and then, recovering herself, called out in the voice that only a mother knows: "Sylvia!"

"Mother!" screamed the child, and rushed into her open arms.

The tide of memory, driven to low ebb by ill-treatment and hardship, had rushed back with full force. The Wren, the gypsy waif, was once more Sylvia Harvey. A doctor said later that such cases were frequent following a severe shock. It was then that they recalled how the child had almost recollected some of her past life during the thunderstorm.

The happiness of little Wren and her mother in their reunion was shared by all of the party who had been instrumental in effecting it, for every one of them, including Jake, had become attached to the quiet little girl and rejoiced in her good fortune.

When Mrs. Harvey and Sylvia departed for the railway station the following day behind a pair of Mr. Parker's steady horses they were accompanied by the four airplanes, which hovered over them like so many sturdy guardian angels.

And when the train bore them away they watched the returning aërial escort until there was nothing visible but four tiny dots against the blue heaven.

"Oh, mother," exclaimed Wren, "they look no bigger than butterflies now!"

And the Girl Aviatrixes, flying every moment higher and farther on the powerful wings of the *Golden Butterfly* and the delicate plane of the dainty *Dart*, looked back at the train crawling like a humble insect in the valley below and gloried in their untrammeled flight. As they followed Bill and Liam McAdams in an irregular procession through the air, their thoughts flew ahead, outdistancing the biplane and the *Red Dragon* and speeding confidently toward the happy realizations of the future.

Aunt Sally, watching from the home of Mr. Parker for their return, also dreamed dreams and saw visions, and in them her "dear children" were fulfilling the bright prophecies of the present. She saw them stronger because of adversity, braver because of success, and ennobled by all their experiences; and she deemed herself happy in her capacity of chaperon to the Girl Aviatrixes.

CHAPTER 17

The Air Perilous Summer

Chapter 17.1
The Accident

"Aunt Sally, may we have a picnic lunch?"

Pretty Mary Eliska, the first girl in America to fly from New York to Paris alone, stood in the living room of her aunt's summer bungalow at Green Falls, and asked the question. Her blue eyes were pleading, although it was not for the mere favor of a lunch. The older woman glanced at her costume—a flying suit—and looked grave.

"Where do you want to go, dear?" she countered.

"Dot and I want to go off by ourselves—in the 'Ladybug.'"

"The 'Ladybug!'" repeated Mary Eliska, with despair in her tone. That was the name of Mary Eliska's autogiro, which she had purchased in June and flown south to Georgia. There she had met with all sorts of disasters, had been kidnaped by a gang of thieves and stranded on a lonely island with this same girl—Jax Gray, or Jax Gray—as her only companion.

"I should think you and Jax Gray would have had enough flying to last you the rest of your lives."

"Now, Aunt Sally, you know I could never have enough flying. I—I—belong in the air." Mary Eliska's eyes lighted up with joy, as they always did when she spoke of her favorite pastime. She came across the room and seated herself upon the arm of her aunt's chair. "I've stayed on the ground for two weeks, Auntie dear—just for your sake. But I've got to go up now—I just have to! You do understand, don't you?"

Mary Eliska, who had taken care of Mary Eliska ever since she was a baby, was so afraid of airplanes that she had never even taken a ride with her niece. She sighed.

"I suppose so, dear. But don't go far, and promise me you'll be back for supper."

"Oh, we will! I'm sure of that!" Mary Eliska replied, as she bent over and kissed her aunt.

"How do you feel now?" asked Mary Eliska

Aunt Sally

The words she spoke were sincere; the "Ladybug" was in perfect shape, and Mary Eliska truly meant to plan her flight so that she would be back in Green Falls before sunset, but, of course, she could not know that circumstances would step in and prevent her.

Fifteen minutes later, she and her chum, Jax Gray y—diminutive in size, but bubbling over with spirits and capable to the tips of her fingers, stepped into the autogiro, adjusted the self-starter and left the earth behind. It was a beautiful summer day, without a cloud in the sky, and the girls were as happy as birds.

Mary Eliska directed her "Ladybug" straight across Lake Michigan, over the heads of the swimmers and above the boats, for the shores of Wisconsin. An invigorating breeze was blowing, so that the girls were glad of their sweaters and helmets, and they laughed and sang as they flew.

It was over a hundred miles across the lake, but the autogiro took the distance with the ease of a motor car. On and on they went, pressing into Wisconsin, leaving the lake behind. When they finally landed in a field for their lunch, Mary Eliska confessed that she didn't know just where they were.

"Why, it's two o'clock, Mary Eliska!" exclaimed Jax Gray, as she dived into the lunch box for a sandwich.

"No wonder I'm hungry."

"So am I!" agreed her companion. "But I guess we better not go any further, Jax Gray. We must get home to supper."

"I wish we didn't have to. You know what I love, Mary Eliska—flying over the lake. I always have adored all kinds of water sports, but honestly, flying *over* water beats everything."

"Want to fly to Paris with me?" suggested Mary Eliska, playfully.

"Sometime. But in a bigger boat than the 'Ladybug.' Now if you still had the Bellanca———"

"If I had, I wouldn't go," interrupted Mary Eliska calmly, reaching for another sandwich. "I wouldn't do a thing that would get me into the newspapers!"

"I don't blame you," agreed her companion.

Little did they think as they spoke thus idly, that that very evening they themselves would be requesting the papers to print a story which concerned them.

It all happened two hours later, with incredible swiftness. They were flying back across Wisconsin, low enough to watch the landscape, when Jax Gray suddenly let out a shriek of horror.

"Look at that—oh—Mary Eliska!"

Her companion grasped the joy stick, and looked about expectantly, as if some plane must be coming at her which she did not see.

"No—down on the road!" cried Jax Gray. "That car!"

Casting her glance downward, Mary Eliska saw what she meant. A huge car, driven by a man with a great mass of gray hair and a gray beard, at a speed nearing eighty miles an hour, zigzagged wildly in the road, rushing headlong at the forlorn figure of a girl walking beside the gutter.

"The man must be crazy!" muttered Mary Eliska, discreetly pointing her autogiro upward. "Or drunk!"

An instant later the car knocked the girl down, threw her up against the bank, and by some miracle, regained its position again and sped away.

"He's killed her!" screamed Jax Gray. "A hit-and-runner!"

Mary Eliska brought her plane downward, but it was too far away to see the man so that she might identify him later, except by that beard.

"There isn't a soul in sight!" observed Jax Gray. "You're going to land?"

Mary Eliska nodded; luckily her autogiro didn't need a special field. She descended and brought it to a stop, not far from the injured girl. She and Jax Gray climbed out, dashed over the field to the road, and picked up the victim in their arms. She was a young girl, possibly about fourteen years of age, whether dead or merely unconscious, they could not tell. Blood was running from her head.

"We'll carry her over beside the autogiro, and apply first aid," said Mary Eliska. "Luckily I have all sorts of supplies with me—and water."

She was a pretty girl, except that there was something decidedly pathetic about her whole appearance. Her clothing was not ragged, but dreadfully out of style; her straight hair hung about her temples without any attempt to make it becoming. It was neither long nor short, and had no ribbon, no pin of any kind to keep it out of her eyes. Her sweater looked like a man's, and her skirt was evidently handed down from an older woman. Her whole body was so thin that she looked almost emaciated. Her face was a blank white, with no make-up to relieve the pallor.

Mary Eliska bound up the wound, and after some minutes the girl finally opened her eyes. Deep, black eyes they were, that appeared huge in such a small, colorless face, eyes that gazed at the girls without any understanding.

"How do you feel now?" asked Mary Eliska, still kneeling beside her, and offering her water from a thermos bottle.

The girl raised her eyebrows, and muttered a feeble, "All right."

Meanwhile, Jax Gray ran over to the road to see whether there wasn't a car somewhere in sight. But there was neither a car nor a house. It was a barren stretch of country—she didn't know where.

It was a lonely place indeed for a poor helpless girl to have such a dreadful accident, through no fault of hers. But now that she was conscious, surely she could tell them where the nearest town was, so they could take her to a hospital.

Mary Eliska, too, was realizing that they could not hope for a machine to come along, that they would have to take the girl with them in the "Ladybug." She was just about to ask her who she was, and where she came from, when she was startled by the very question from the girl herself.

"Please tell me who I am, pretty lady," she said, pathetically. "I can't seem to remember anything."

Mary Eliska gasped.

"I don't know. My friend saw the accident from the air—from our autogiro, while we were flying. You were walking along the road, and a car swerved at you going eighty miles an hour. I think the driver was crazy, or drunk, for he almost seemed to drive right at you. And he didn't even stop.... So we landed our plane, to look after you."

"What was I doing on the road?"

"Just walking.... Look in your sweater pockets. Maybe there's a letter, or something."

"You look—please. I'm so tired," sighed the girl, and her eyes closed.

Mary Eliska searched frantically, hoping that the girl would not die without their even finding out who she was. But the search was of no avail; the pockets of her sweater were full of nothing but holes.

Dot returned from the road and glanced questioningly at the girl, and then at Mary Eliska. "Unconscious again?"

"No, I'm all right," replied the stranger herself, wearily opening her eyes.

"Have you thought of your name yet?" inquired Mary Eliska.

"No, I haven't. My head hurts so. Please take me to a hospital!"

Between them, Jax Gray and Mary Eliska managed to get her to her feet, and helped her into the autogiro, where she sat on Dot's lap in the passenger's cockpit. Mary Eliska started the motor.

"Ever been in a plane before?" asked Jax Gray, as the "Ladybug" taxied.

The girl shook her head.

Mary Eliska consulted her map. She did not know where she was, but as she had flown almost directly west from Lake Michigan, she decided to fly east. If they did not pass another town, they could land at Milwaukee.

It was growing late—they had spent more time on the ground than they had realized, and Mary Eliska felt uneasy. If darkness came on before they reached a town, the girl might die before they found a hospital. And besides, Mary Eliska's Aunt Sally, who was always worrying about her, would be sure that she had been kidnaped or killed.

The girl in Dot's lap seemed perfectly inert as the time passed, until the sun set. Then she uttered a queer moan.

"Does your head hurt?" asked Jax Gray, in her ear.

"Yes—but that isn't it. I'm—I'm—afraid!"

"Of an airplane? I can assure you that you're with one of the best pilots in the world!"

"Oh, not that! I'm not afraid of flying!"

"What then?"

"Of the dark," she whispered, fearfully. "Of—ghosts!"

Dot looked at the girl as if she were crazy. In these modern times—how had she been brought up? If she were a child of six, it would have been different. She wondered whether she could have understood her correctly, the motor was making so much noise. She bent over and asked her to repeat what she had said.

"Ghosts!" replied the girl. A frightful shiver ran through her whole body, so intense that Jax Gray could feel it in hers. She thought the girl was delirious.

"There's no such thing, my dear," she reassured her, patting the shaking frame.

"Oh, yes, there is! And I mustn't be out alone at night! Never!"

"Put your head on my shoulder, and try to go to sleep," urged Jax Gray, comfortingly. "We'll soon be at the hospital."

But it was not so soon as she hoped. They flew on and on, without seeing any lights that would indicate a city. And all the while the girl continued to sob.

At last, however, they glimpsed bright lights ahead, and Mary Eliska flew low enough to read the signs of Milwaukee. She followed a huge beacon light that led to an airport, and brought her autogiro down to earth.

While she wired to her aunt at Green Falls that she and her companion would have to spend the night at Milwaukee, Jax Gray succeeded in finding a taxicab, which they all took to the nearest hospital.

The girl was perfectly conscious when they were admitted, but when the authorities asked for her name, she still could not give it.

"I don't remember anything," she said; "before these ladies were bending over me on that country road. Except about a ghost that I see and hear at nights."

Dot looked helplessly at the doctor.

"She isn't an idiot, is she, Doctor?" she whispered.

"No, no! It's a case of loss of memory—after concussion. Brought on by that blow on the back of her head."

"But why the ghost?"

"That is some memory that is vivid enough to pierce through the fog which is surrounding her past life. It is a good sign—when one fact remains, the others are more likely to follow."

The nurse was ready to take her to her bed, when the girl uttered a wail that was pitiful to hear.

"Don't leave me!" she begged Mary Eliska and Jax Gray. "You are the only friends that I have in this strange world. And in the other world there is that frightful ghost!"

Impulsively, Mary Eliska bent down and kissed her affectionately. "You must let the nurse take care of you now, dear—and be a good girl. We have to get some supper. But we'll be back tomorrow. We promise."

"If that specter doesn't carry me off tonight!"

"He can't carry you away from the hospital," replied the nurse, smilingly. "We never let ghosts into the hospital."

"Never?"

"Absolutely not."

The girl seemed reassured, and Mary Eliska and Jax Gray returned to their taxi, to find a hotel where they could spend the night.

"Did you ever hear of anything so queer in all your life?" demanded Jax Gray. "Or anything more pitiful?"

"We'll have to do something, Jax Gray," said Mary Eliska, thinking seriously. "We'll buy all the papers tomorrow and look for the names and descriptions of missing persons. We've just got to find that kid's parents."

"If she has any."

"What makes you say that?"

"The way she was dressed. As if nobody in the world cared a bit for her."

"That's sure. But she must live somewhere. She couldn't exist in the woods, on berries, or on that lonely stretch of country where we found her."

"Well, let's try to forget her for the time being," urged Jax Gray. "Here's the hotel, and I certainly am hungry."

"So am I. But I wish we could dress for dinner. Jax Gray, we always ought to carry some extra clothing on these trips, because we never know when we're going to need it."

"Oh, what's the dif, Mary Eliska? These suits are becoming, so what do we care?"

They went to their room and took off their sweaters and helmets. When they had washed their faces and combed their hair, they were so presentable that no one even noticed them as they entered the dining room. After all, it was a common sight to see girls in knickers.

The dinner was delicious, and they ate it with great enjoyment, but neither girl could get the accident out of her mind, or the pathetic child—for she seemed like only a child to them, with her strange superstition. So they decided, when they finished their meal, to call two of the Milwaukee newspapers, and to give them the story, with their own names as references.

"And may we print yours and Jax Gray's pictures, Mary Eliska?" asked the delighted reporter. "We have them on file, you know."

Mary Eliska groaned.

"How is that going to help identify this girl?" she demanded. "It's her picture you ought to print."

"We would, if we had it. We'll get it later. But your pictures will call attention to the article.... However, we don't wait for permission in a case like this, Mary Eliska. You'll just have to grin and bear it!"

Chapter 17.2
The Lost Girl

When the young girl whom Mary Eliska and Jax Gray had rescued opened her eyes in the hospital the following day, it was a strange world which she looked upon. It was as if she had been abruptly transported to another planet, where her name and her past life were forgotten. She remembered her hurt head, and the girls who had come down in the airplane, but her mind was still an utter blank about the days and years that had gone before.

Her forehead throbbed with pain as she tried vainly to think. It was horrible, terrifying, to be stranded in an unfamiliar place like this, without any money in her pockets, without any home to go to after she was well. She pressed her fingers over her eyelids in an effort to bring back something. But one memory only remained—the dreadful vision of a ghost!

Kind as her nurse tried to be, she seemed like only a human machine to this unhappy child, who waited feverishly for the return of Mary Eliska and Jax Gray—her only friends in the whole world.

About eleven o'clock they came, carrying a bunch of roses and a pile of newspapers. The girl held out her arms in the pathetic appeal of a lost child, and both Mary Eliska and Jax Gray kissed her tenderly.

"How's the head this morning?" asked Jax Gray, cheerfully, as she put the flowers into a vase.

"Oh, it's better—but—" She glanced eagerly at the newspapers. "Have you looked at those yet? Has—anybody—reported my loss?"

"I'm afraid not, dear," replied Mary Eliska, sympathetically. "Only ourselves. But give them time. If you lived far in the country, as you surely must, they perhaps couldn't reach them. But when they read of the accident, and see the description of you, they're sure to come after you."

"You haven't been able to remember yet who you are?" inquired Jax Gray.

The girl burst into tears; the strain of it all, in her weakened condition, was too much for her.

"No, I haven't," she sobbed.

"Try to think about the house you lived in," suggested Mary Eliska. "The room you slept in—the dining room—the garden. Shut your eyes and imagine!"

"When I shut my eyes, all that I can see is that ghost! No, no—I'm afraid of darkness."

"Then try to remember your father or your mother. Their eyes—their smiles—" put in Jax Gray.

"It's no use. Oh, what shall I do? Where can I go after I leave this hospital? I'm—I'm—the most 'alone' person in the whole world!"

"But you still have us! We'll take care of you," offered Jax Gray, impulsively. "We'll take you with us to Green Falls, where we're spending the summer, won't we, Mary Eliska?"

"Of course," agreed her companion.

The girl smiled happily, but only for a moment.

"It's wonderful of you—but I can't stay. I'll have to go somewhere soon—and where shall it be?"

"I'll tell you what we'll do," said Mary Eliska brightly. "After you have a visit with us, and get strong, we'll get you some kind of job—taking care of children or something. And you can be studying something to support yourself. Stenography or typing—in case you can't find your parents. How would you like that?"

"Fine! Only I don't know what those words mean—Sten—sten——"

Mary Eliska and Jax Gray looked at each other and smiled. What could they do with a girl like this? It was too much for them to solve the problem alone, but perhaps Mary Eliska could offer a wise suggestion.

The girl stretched out her arms helplessly.

"Oh, I know I'm dumb!" she exclaimed. "But please don't give me up!"

Yet she wasn't stupid, or uneducated, for she used perfect English, and the girls noticed when she ate her lunch, which the attendant brought her on a tray, that her table manners were of the best. She had evidently been brought up correctly by someone.

"We won't!" Mary Eliska assured her. "We'll come back for you tomorrow morning, and if the doctor says that you can leave the hospital, we'll take you with us in our airplane." She purposely didn't use the word "autogiro," for fear of confusing her.

"Now get a good rest this afternoon," she added, "and look for us bright and early in the morning."

It was a promise, of course, for Mary Eliska and Jax Gray felt as if this young girl was their special responsibility. A most inconvenient promise, however, for it meant remaining another day in Milwaukee.

"Are you sure that you have enough money, Mary Eliska?" asked Jax Gray, as they returned to their hotel for lunch.

"Oh, plenty," was the reply. "That's not what's worrying me. It's Aunt Sally. She won't like it a bit. Still, she wouldn't want us to leave a helpless child. I'll call her up, instead of sending another wire."

"Why not fly home across the lake this afternoon, and come back tomorrow?" suggested Jax Gray.

"For two reasons. One is, I want to give the 'Ladybug' an inspection today, and the other is, Aunt Sally might not want us to come back. She might suggest that we just send the girl some money. But that poor little lonely thing needs friendship more than she needs money."

"True. But how shall I put in my time while you go over the 'Ladybug?'"

"Take in a picture show. Or stop back at the hospital.... We can do something together tonight."

The afternoon passed all too quickly for Mary Eliska at the airport, but when she left at six o'clock, she had the reassurance that her autogiro was in perfect condition. She had taken double precaution this time, for she did not want to run the risk of the slightest mishap with this strange forlorn girl in her care.

Her aunt accepted the explanation which Mary Eliska offered that evening over the telephone, interrupting her three times to ask her whether she and Jax Gray were surely all right. Early the next morning the girls sped to the hospital in a taxi, to find their little charge bandaged and dressed, ready for departure.

"We'll fly north along the shore of the lake—or maybe over the water, since you love that, Dot—and land opposite Green Falls for our picnic lunch. Then we'll fly straight across Lake Michigan to home."

"Home!" repeated the little girl wistfully. How wonderful it must be to have a home—a place to go to, where somebody cared for you!

But by the time she and Jax Gray had squeezed into the passenger's cockpit of the autogiro, she was smiling excitedly. She had been too much dazed on the other flight to enjoy it, but now she found it a thrilling adventure. Her head still hurt, but not enough to spoil her delight. How lucky she was, she thought, to have found two wonderful friends like these girls!

"You are not afraid, dear?" shouted Jax Gray, above the noise of the engine.

"Oh, no! I love it!" Her black eyes were shining, and there was even a faint color in her cheeks.

"You have heard of airplanes before, even if you haven't heard of typewriters, haven't you?"

The girl nodded, with intelligence.

Conversation was difficult, and the girls relapsed into silence, until Mary Eliska brought the "Ladybug" down on the western shore of Lake Michigan, presumably opposite Green Falls, where the girls spread out their picnic lunch. Then it seemed as if all three of them wanted to talk at once.

"We've got to get you a name," announced Jax Gray, as she unwrapped the chicken sandwiches which she had secured from the hotel. "If you can't remember your own, we'll have to give you one!"

"Don't you suppose you'd recall it if you heard it?" asked Mary Eliska.

"I don't know," replied the girl, dubiously.

"Mary? Elizabeth? Jane?" suggested Jax Gray.

"Dorothy? Elsie? Emma?" added Mary Eliska, at random.

But the girl's memory was still a blank.

"Just give me one—anything you like!" she pleaded.

"All right, that'll be fun," agreed Jax Gray, cheerfully. "I always thought it would be more exciting to name a real person than a doll." She was making an effort to keep up the girl's spirits. "What'll it be, Mary Eliska?"

"Amy!" cried the latter. "After Amy Johnson, you know. I think she's the most courageous woman flyer in the whole world today! She went from England to Australia all alone, and then went up into Siberia."

"She certainly 'goes places,'" laughed Jax Gray. "I like the name of 'Amy,' too." She turned to the girl. "Does it suit you?"

"Why consult me?" returned the latter, with humor. "Did you ever hear of anybody's being asked about the name she got?"

Mary Eliska and Jax Gray both laughed, and Jax Gray gave "Amy" a hug.

"These sandwiches are wonderful!" exclaimed Mary Eliska. "Jax Gray, you sure do know how to get good food."

"Wait 'til you see the caramel cake I wheedled out of that chef at the hotel. He had made it for a special party, but I convinced him he'd have to make another."

"You're marvelous!" cried her chum, admiringly.

Little Amy simply couldn't say anything. She had never tasted food like this before—at least, if she had, she couldn't remember. She ate daintily, not greedily, for she wanted it to last a long time.

"Amy had better stay with me at Green Falls," decided Mary Eliska; "because there's more room at our bungalow." She and her aunt lived alone together, except for occasional visits from her father, who had a business in New York, while Jax Gray was a member of a large family.

"O.K. with me," agreed the latter. Then, turning to Amy, "You'll love Mary Eliska's Aunt Sally. She's the most motherly soul."

"You're sure it is all right for me to go with you?" asked the girl, plaintively.

"Of course it is!" Mary Eliska assured her.

An hour and a half later, they arrived at the Green Falls Airport, and were surprised to find Ralph Clavering, Mary Eliska's most devoted admirer, patiently waiting for them with his car.

"Welcome to our city!" he cried, rushing towards the girls as they climbed out of the autogiro. "Safe and sound!" Then he stopped, surprised at the sight of the queerly-dressed child at their side. He frowned, and muttered to himself, "Look what the cat—or rather, the 'Ladybug'—dragged in!" But aloud he said nothing besides his greeting.

Mary Eliska introduced her little friend as "Miss Johnson," and they all got into his car.

"Kidnaped?" inquired Ralph, as he started the engine.

"Who?" replied Mary Eliska. "Dot or Amy—or me?"

"Oh, I don't know. I always expect something like that when you don't show up when you're expected—Mary Eliska, guess what? I'm getting a plane!"

"An airplane!" repeated Mary Eliska, excitedly. "But you weren't to have one 'til you graduated from college."

"I know. But I convinced Dad I had to have one to follow you around on your wild-goose chases, all over the globe."

"Now, Ralph, don't be silly!"

"It's the honest truth. That's the reason I'm getting one."

Mary Eliska blushed; she never could accustom herself to this wealthy young man's obvious devotion. His parents were millionaires, and all his life Ralph had had everything he wanted. Until he met Mary Eliska. He had asked her to marry him as soon as she graduated from High School, but she had refused, saying that such a thing was out of the question until he was through college. Besides, she was too much in love with her "Ladybug" to be in love with any man. But Ralph went on asking at regular intervals, just the same.

"What kind?" she inquired.

"An autogiro. I'm rather keen on them, and Dad and Mother think they're the safest, so they're rooting for them, too."

"I think that's perfect! And you have your pilot's license, too." Ralph Clavering had taken instructions in flying the same time that Mary Eliska had, more to be with her than because he was actually air-minded. But when his father had refused him a plane of his own, he had lost his enthusiasm.

It was only a few minutes' ride from the airport to the Carltons' bungalow. Miss Polly Carlton was waiting anxiously on the porch.

"Mary Eliska dear!" she exclaimed, as her niece ran up the steps. "I was so afraid something had happened."

"But I told you everything was all right last night, Aunt Sally!"

"Yes, of course. But you never can tell what may happen in the meantime."

Mary Eliska patted her arm reassuringly, and took hold of Amy's hand.

"This is Amy, Aunt Sally—the girl we rescued. We want to go upstairs now, and change our clothing. I think Amy can wear some of my sports things—they'd be short—And Ralph," she added, turning to the young man, "can't you stay to dinner?"

"No, thank you, I must get back. But there's a dance over at Kit's tonight—may I come and get you?" Kit was his sister, one of the first girls in Mary Eliska's group to be married, soon after graduation from High School.

Mary Eliska hesitated, and looked inquiringly at Amy. She hated to go off and leave her alone the first night, yet obviously she could not take her.

"Yes, go, Miss Mary Eliska," the girl urged her immediately. "I am so tired that I want to go to bed soon after supper."

"O.K. then," agreed Mary Eliska, as Jax Gray and Ralph left together, and she hurried upstairs with Amy.

"Don't call me 'Miss Mary Eliska,' Amy," she said. "I'm only eighteen. And you must be fourteen, aren't you?"

To her dismay the girl burst into tears.

"I don't know," she said. "I don't know anything—Mary Eliska."

"Well, don't worry about it. It'll be all right soon—everything will come back to you."

Amy shuddered.

"Maybe it would be better to forget. I told you about the ghost—and though there isn't anything else definite, I just have a horror of the past. It's vague——"

"It's the strangest thing the way you seem to use all sorts of words one wouldn't expect of a girl of your age," interrupted her companion, "and then don't know what others mean. Like stenography and typewriting, for instance."

"By the way, what are those things?" asked Amy, wiping away her sudden tears.

"Oh, business terms—I'll explain later. Clothes are more important now. We must hurry with our dressing, and get back to Aunt Sally—Let's see—my tennis dress ought to do——"

It was a white pleated silk, quite short, and fitted Amy nicely. Mary Eliska took time to curl the girl's hair, and to put a ribbon around her head, to hide the bandage. She was amazed to see how really attractive the girl was, when she was dressed in becoming clothing.

"The shoes don't fit, but you can wear them for the rest of today," she concluded. "Tomorrow we'll drive into town—there aren't any stores in Green Falls—and get you some to fit."

"I don't know why you do all this for me, Mary Eliska. I never did anything for you!"

"But you would if you could. And we love you, Amy. Aunt Sally does, too, and you must think of us as your own family, until you find your parents."

Mary Eliska was right about her aunt; the motherly woman took Amy right to her heart, and when Mary Eliska left with Ralph soon after supper, for dances were informal and began early in Green Falls, Mary Eliska was teaching the young girl parchesi, and they were laughing and chatting like old friends.

Chapter 17.3
Planning the Treasure Hunt

"Who is this Cinderella you brought home, Mary Eliska?" asked Ralph, as the young couple started for the party. "You sure fixed her up some since this afternoon."

"She's a girl we picked up in the road," Mary Eliska explained. "Didn't Aunt Sally tell you why we were staying over in Milwaukee?"

"No; only that some friend was in the hospital. I didn't get the details. All that I was interested in was when you'd be back."

Briefly, Mary Eliska told him the story of the accident and of the girl's loss of memory, adding that "Amy" was a fictitious name which they had given her, until she should recall her own.

"I mean to find her family if I have to search the whole United States!" she concluded.

"And if you have to give up your own summer vacation in the bargain," muttered Ralph, sulkily. "You would, Mary Eliska!"

"But it's exciting! Like reading a mystery story, you know."

"You'll get into trouble, I warn you."

"If I do, I'll get out again," she returned, lightly. "I have a charmed life."

"I wouldn't count on that too much if I were you."

"Tell me who will be here tonight," urged Mary Eliska, seeing that Ralph was getting irritable over her newest adventure.

"Only half a dozen couples, I believe. Mostly the old crowd—you and Jax Gray and Sue Emery and Sarah Wheeler—and those two married girls Kit is so thick with—Madge Keen and Babs Macy."

"Why don't you tell me which boys?" teased Mary Eliska, with a twinkle in her eye. "Don't you think I'm interested?"

"I hoped you weren't. Now that your friend Jackson Carter has gone back South where he belongs, with that fascinating drawl of his, I rather hoped I'd have you to myself."

"Well, I'm going to the party with you!"

"Yes, but that doesn't say it'll be more than two minutes before some fellow cuts in. Why in the name of peace and enjoyment they always invite more fellows than girls to a party is something to make me wonder."

"It's to make us happy—to make us seem popular," explained Mary Eliska.

"Nobody has to make *you* seem popular!" he returned, morosely.

"Tell me the boys, Ralph!" she repeated.

"Men, my child—not boys! Why, three of 'em are married. And the rest of us would like to be," he muttered, under his breath.

But he refused to tell her; she'd find out soon enough for herself. Her first discovery, when Ralph stopped his car at his sister's, proved to be one of her oldest friends, Harriman Smith, a young man whom she had not seen for several months. He dashed down the steps to greet her.

"Harry!" she cried, in delight, pressing his hand in genuine pleasure. It was he who had stood by her, believed in her, when nobody else but her chum, Louise Haydock, had thought she could fly the Atlantic Ocean.

"Mary Eliska! It's heaven to see you again!" he exclaimed. "Hello, Ralph," he added, shaking hands with her escort. "How's tricks with you?"

"O.K., Harry. When'd you get here?"

"Half an hour ago. By plane."

"You have a plane?" demanded Mary Eliska.

"No—be yourself, Mary Eliska! I'm a poor working man. No, I came with Kit's husband—Tom Hulbert. I have a couple of weeks' vacation, and decided I'd like to spend them with the old crowd. I'm staying with the Hulberts."

Linking arms, all three entered the bungalow together, which was much larger and more luxurious than most of the cottages at Green Falls, for Kit's wealthy father, Mr. Clavering, had presented the young couple with it soon after their marriage. A small orchestra of three pieces had been hired for the dancing, to take the place of the usual radio music, and the large living room was easily able to accommodate twice the number of couples Kit had invited.

As Ralph had surmised, although there were only seven girls, five extra young men had been asked to the party.

Tiny Kit Hulbert, dressed in a fairy-like dance costume of pale-green chiffon, floated over to greet the newcomers.

"I hear you've had another adventure, Mary Eliska," she said. So timid herself that she had given up learning to fly after a few feeble attempts, she nevertheless had a great admiration for the other girl's skill and courage.

"It isn't finished yet," replied Mary Eliska. "We're in the middle of a mystery. I'll tell you all about it, Kit, when Ralph isn't around. He's rather fed up."

"I'll say I am. How soon can we dance, Sis?" asked the young man, impatiently.

"Right away," agreed Kit, nodding to the violinist in the corner to start the music.

The supper, served informally on the big porch that evening, was early; for the Hulberts had an exciting piece of news for their guests, and they could hardly wait for the opportunity to tell it. As soon as everybody was seated, Tom Hulbert, who was a lieutenant in the U. S. Flying Corps, and an excellent pilot, called for attention.

"Our next party is going to be a wow!" he began.

"They always are," interrupted Sue Emery, enthusiastically.

Tom bowed. "Thank you, Miss Emery," he said, formally. "But this is absolutely different—entirely new! Kit's father is giving us a treasure hunt. By airplanes!"

"Airplanes!" gasped everybody at once.

Mary Eliska's eyes shone with excitement. What a novel idea!

"But most of us can't go!" whined Sue Emery. "We're not pilots!"

"Sure you can. Mr. Clavering's going to rent a lot of planes, so anybody with a pilot's license to fly can enter, and take a passenger. And there's a bully prize—Oh, I'm not going to tell what it is! And a dinner at the end of the hunt—maybe a week-end party!"

"Here's where we girls with licenses score!" cried Jax Gray, triumphantly. "We can do the inviting, for once!"

"As if you didn't always do the picking and choosing!" muttered Ralph. He would have his autogiro by that time, but, of course, Mary Eliska wouldn't go with him. Not an independent young lady like her!

"I'm not worried," drawled Jim Valier, Dot's devoted boyfriend, as he reached for his sixth chicken-salad sandwich, although so far he had only eaten one. "Dot's got to take me—and I won't have to do any work. Just share the glory!"

Dot's chin went up in the air.

"I believe I'll ask a girl—they're more reliable," she retorted. "Sue, will you go with me?"

Sue whimpered; she would rather go with a man, but an invitation was an invitation, and she didn't want to be left out.

"I'd hate to be so mean to Jim," she replied. "You better let him go."

"You come with me, Miss Emery," urged Frank Lawlor, the young man who was seated at her right, and who was an experienced flyer.

"Thank you—I'd love to, Mr. Lawlor," she murmured, gratefully.

"When is this exciting event to take place?" asked Harriman Smith, wondering whether he would be there to enjoy it.

"Next Saturday," replied Tom Hulbert. "Entries must be in by Wednesday."

Mary Eliska was silent; suppose she were too busy looking up Amy's parents to take part! Oh, but that wouldn't be fair! She simply couldn't miss this. Surely her Aunt Sally would look after Amy.

As if reading her thoughts, Kit asked her whether she would be able to go into it.

"You better stay home, Mary Eliska," advised Jim Valier. "So we get a chance at the prize!"

"Don't be silly," she replied. "You'll all probably have speedier planes than my 'Ladybug.'"

The plan was so fascinating that nobody wanted to start dancing again. Instead they sat and talked and talked, until long past midnight. It was after one o'clock when Mary Eliska finally reached home—a late hour for an informal party at Green Falls.

Her aunt was waiting up for her, but she did not seem to be at all worried. As long as the autogiro was in the hangar, Mary Eliska felt safe about Mary Eliska.

Ralph left her at the door, and the girl made no mention of the treasure hunt. Instead she inquired about Amy, and asked that she herself be allowed to sleep late the following day.

Remembering the request, Mary Eliska did not call her to the telephone although it rang four times the next morning for Mary Eliska, before she was awake. Two impatient young men—Harriman Smith and Ralph Clavering—each called twice to no avail.

Finally, about ten o'clock, Mary Eliska put in her appearance at the breakfast table. Mary Eliska and Amy had long since finished theirs, and the little girl was reading a story in the hammock on the porch. Mary Eliska, however, came and sat with her niece as she ate, and gave her the news.

"Which boy are you going to call back, dear?" she asked.

"Neither," laughed Mary Eliska, as she complacently ate her cantaloupe. "I haven't time for young men today, Aunt Sally."

"You aren't going anywhere in that autogiro, are you?" Try as she did, the older woman could never keep the note of fear from her voice when an airplane was mentioned.

"No, no, Auntie. It's about Amy. I want to do things for her. And I want your help."

Mary Eliska heaved a sigh of relief. This was a different matter.

"First we must get her some decent clothing. And then don't you think we ought to get her picture to the newspapers, and her description to the radio, so that her people can come and get her?"

"Of course! My, but it is sad, for a child like her to lose her memory. It's bad enough for an older person, but it just seems pitiful for anyone her age."

"Oh, I haven't a doubt but that it will come back," said Mary Eliska, hopefully. "The doctor at the hospital said it was probably only temporary, from that blow on her head. Sometimes another blow will restore it, he told me, but, of course, that wouldn't be safe on account of her cut. Publicity is the thing we need now."

"What will you do? Run in to town?"

"No, I don't think that tiny newspaper office would do any good. So I thought if you'd take her and superintend getting the clothing, I'd take my roadster and go on to Grand Rapids."

"Yes, that will suit me perfectly. Only why don't you take Harry or Ralph with you? I'd feel safer, for that's quite a distance."

"All right, Aunt Sally. If either of them comes over in time."

"Either of whom?" demanded a masculine voice from the living room, as the screen door banged.

"Speaking of angels!" returned Mary Eliska, turning about to greet Ralph Clavering.

"It's about time you got up, Lazy Betsy!" he teased. "Did your aunt tell you I phoned twice?"

"Yes. Sit down and have some coffee, Ralph. You must have rushed through your breakfast!"

"Rushed! I've been up since eight o'clock!"

"Virtuous soul— But what's on your mind now?"

"The treasure hunt. Dad wants you to help Tom Hulbert and me with the arrangements. It's going to be ticklish business."

"What treasure hunt?" inquired Mary Eliska. She was usually more delighted over Mary Eliska's social affairs than the girl herself.

"By airplanes!" replied Ralph, excitedly. "Isn't that a whiz of an idea?"

"Oh, no! No!" gasped Mary Eliska, in terror. "No, Ralph! That is worse than foolhardy! Oh, my boy, you'd all be killed!"

"Not if we plan the thing thoroughly. Start at different places—good fields to land——"

"I beg you not to do it!" she wailed, prophetically. "Think of the tragedy it may bring about! Whose idea was it, Ralph?"

"Dad's—and Kit's."

Mary Eliska shook her head mournfully. "I thought your father had more sense, Ralph. But does your mother approve?"

"Mother's away for a couple of weeks. Went to Bar Harbor to visit Aunt Kate—her sister, you know. So naturally she won't be consulted."

"I can never give my consent to it," stated Mary Eliska, nervously.

"Wait 'til we get our plans ready. You may change your mind—Now, Mary Eliska, can you help me?"

"I'm afraid not today, Ralph. I have to do things for Amy. Maybe tomorrow."

"Too late," he said, almost gruffly, as he rose and went to the door. "I might have known you would have your own affairs. Never mind, I'll get Dot!"

Mary Eliska went towards him and patted his arm.

"Don't be cross, Ralph. Think of the child's parents. How frantic they must be! I've just got to do something."

"Oh, I suppose you're right. And noble. You always are!"

"I don't see why you bother with anybody you think so holy and righteous," remarked Mary Eliska, pulling down the corners of her mouth.

"Now children, don't quarrel," put in Mary Eliska. "You can blame it on me, Ralph. I refuse to let Mary Eliska have any part in this absurd treasure hunt."

"Then what's the use of having it?" demanded Ralph.

"Very sensible conclusion," agreed Mary Eliska. "Give it up, and plan a nice picnic instead."

"A nice, old-fashioned one! And take our bicycles?"

"You run along, Ralph," said Mary Eliska, "and get Jax Gray and Jim to help you. I really must get ready to go to Grand Rapids!"

So, putting the treasure hunt temporarily from her mind, she ran out to the porch to tell Amy about her plans for the day.

Chapter 17.4
A Stranger at Green Falls

"Big doings today, Amy!" announced Mary Eliska, cheerfully, as Ralph Clavering departed. "Come on—get ready!"

"What?" demanded the girl, excitedly. "You haven't heard from anybody who—wants—me?"

Her eagerness was pathetic, and Mary Eliska stooped over and kissed her.

"No, there is no news as yet. But we are going to try to make some. I'm going to take your picture and give it to the newspapers."

"Oh, I see!" Plainly, Amy was disappointed. "Do you really think it's any use, Mary Eliska? If there were anybody to claim me, wouldn't they have come three days ago?"

"I don't know—not necessarily. Suppose they didn't read the newspapers?"

"If they didn't then, why should they now?" asked Amy, with keen logic.

"Well, their friends might tell them. Besides, only our pictures—Dot's and mine—were in before, and now we're putting in yours. And we're having it announced over the radio."

"What is a radio?" inquired Amy.

"Come inside and I'll show you. But wait, first let me get these snapshots of you. Stand over there, and look pretty!"

The girl smiled and did as she was told. To her knowledge she had never seen a picture taken before.

"It's funny," remarked Mary Eliska, as she took out her roll of films from the camera, "that you remember how to read. You didn't have any trouble understanding that story, did you?"

"Some," confessed the girl. "There were lots of things I hadn't heard of. But I don't think it's my memory, Mary Eliska—I think I just never did hear of those things."

"You must have lived in the country," concluded the other. "Somewhere around where we picked you up. I think maybe the best idea of all would be to try to fly back to that spot, and hunt for a house. We'll do that next week, if Aunt Sally is willing."

"Next week! Mary Eliska, I feel as if I had no right to stay on and on here——"

"Of course, you have. And you're going to have a wonderful time today. Aunt Sally is taking you into town to buy you some clothes."

"But I can't pay for them!"

"You're not supposed to. They're presents. Like Christmas presents. You've heard of them, I suppose?"

"Yes! Yes!" cried Amy, excitedly. "You hang up your stocking—and—and—sometimes there are cookies——"

Mary Eliska's eyes shone.

"You have a memory, Amy! You have! Think some more!"

"I can't," sighed the girl. "That's all."

"But something did come back! Run along and get ready now, for Aunt Sally's waiting— and I must answer that telephone."

The caller proved to be Harriman Smith, and Mary Eliska immediately told him of her plans for the day, inviting him to go with her to Grand Rapids.

Harry replied that he could be at the bungalow in five minutes, and he was punctual to the Jax Gray. He did not tell Mary Eliska that the Hulberts' cars were both out, and that he had run the whole distance.

"I sure am a lucky guy," he said to Mary Eliska, as he got into the roadster beside her; "to get ahead of Ralph Clavering like this."

"Oh, Ralph's busy planning the treasure hunt," she replied. "And that reminds me, Harry, if I am allowed to take part in it, will you go as my passenger?"

"I'd be thrilled!" he cried enthusiastically. "But why do you say 'if,' Mary Eliska? Surely after you flew the Atlantic Ocean alone, your Aunt Sally couldn't object to a trifle like a treasure hunt?"

"I know; it doesn't seem logical. But don't forget that I flew to Paris before I had all those disasters in the Okefenokee. She's more timid than ever now. And besides, I guess she doesn't like the idea of the hunt—all those planes going to the same place, with the danger of collisions. And some of the flyers are only beginners."

"Who are planning to enter?"

"I haven't heard definitely. But, of course, Ralph and Jax Gray and I will all enter. And there are Tom Hulbert, and Madge Keen's husband, and Frank Lawlor. That's six, at least. I don't know whether there'll be any strangers or not. It's just a Green Falls affair, but I suppose anybody that Mr. Clavering knew could get in all right. I'm going to be dreadfully disappointed if I can't enter."

"You don't really think there's much chance?"

"I'll tell you what I'm counting on, Harry; that Daddy will come home, and he'll tell Aunt Sally to let me go. You know he's the best sport that ever was; he isn't afraid of taking a few risks."

"And he has a lot of confidence in your flying," added Harry. "That is the trouble with your aunt, I believe. If she had ever gone up with you, and had seen for herself what a marvelous pilot you are, she'd feel differently."

"Thanks, Harry," said Mary Eliska, pleased at the compliment, for when Harriman Smith said anything, he meant it. He was not given to idle praise. "I do so wish I could get her to go."

There were so many things to talk about—Mary Eliska's summer adventure and her new autogiro; Harry's college course and the job he was holding on the side, that they reached Grand Rapids before they knew it. Harry insisted that they have the pictures developed while they ate their lunch, and wait until afterwards to visit the newspapers.

It was with great difficulty that Mary Eliska convinced the city editors that they should publish Amy's pictures instead of her own. But at last she succeeded, and added a description of the man who had been the cause of the accident. Harry visited a broadcasting station at the same time, that the news might be given out over the radio. By three o'clock they were ready to start back to Green Falls.

Not satisfied with merely the day with Mary Eliska, Harry tried to date her for the evening.

"Will you go to the tennis matches with me after dinner?" he asked. "At the Club, I mean. You're not in them by any chance?"

"Oh, no, I'm not nearly good enough. I was beaten early in the tournament. But Jax Gray y's in the finals, and so is Jim Valier."

"They always were good. Well, how about it, Mary Eliska? I'll get a taxi, if Tom doesn't offer me his car. They'll probably go over in Kit's."

"Thank you, Harry, but I think I better not make any plans until I see what Aunt Sally and Amy are doing. I left them last night—and I want to be with them tonight. So you go with Tom and Kit, and if I can, I'll see you there."

"And promise me at least two dances?"

"Oh, certainly," she agreed.

Fifteen minutes later she parked her car in the garage behind the bungalow, and ran in to see what success Amy and her aunt had had. The girl was dressed in everything new from head to foot; her hair, too, had been cut and waved becomingly. She was dancing around the living room in excited happiness. All her cares were forgotten for the time being, in the joy her new clothing afforded her.

"Don't I look wonderful, Mary Eliska?" she cried. "Like a different girl? Mary Eliska has been a real fairy godmother!"

"You certainly do, Amy! Oh, Aunt Sally always knows just the right things to buy!"

The young girl's eyes suddenly grew wistful, and she frowned. "I think, Mary Eliska, that I must have been very poor, because I am sure I never had clothes like this before."

"Your clothes were different, dear," Mary Eliska admitted. "But you may not have been poor. Perhaps it was only because you lived far out in the country—away from the stores. And maybe your mother didn't know how to sew, or was an invalid——"

"I don't believe I have a mother," replied Amy. "You couldn't forget a mother—like—like your Aunt Sally. No, I feel sure my mother is dead."

"Well, we'll soon solve it all," Mary Eliska reassured her, and proceeded to recount to her what she and Harry had accomplished that afternoon.

"Would you like to go to the Club to the tennis matches after dinner, Amy?" she asked.

"What kind of matches?" The girl looked inquiringly at an ash tray on the table.

"Not that kind of matches!" laughed Mary Eliska, following her gaze. "You know what tennis is, don't you?"

Amy shook her head, and Mary Eliska explained as best she could.

But though the girl knew nothing about the game, she was eager to go to the Club, so that she could display her new clothing. Mary Eliska arranged for an early dinner, and they all decided to drive over in Mary Eliska's roadster.

Green Falls was a small resort, and Mary Eliska and her aunt knew practically everyone there. As they seated themselves on the wide veranda which overlooked the tournament court, they nodded and smiled to the other spectators on all sides. Jax Gray y came out of the Clubhouse, and stopped to ask Mary Eliska to wish her luck, for she was playing against Sarah Wheeler in the girls' finals.

As she left them to take her place on the court, Lt. Hulbert came over to the Carltons, bringing a stranger with him. The visitor was an exceedingly attractive man of perhaps thirty-five, perfectly dressed, obviously a person of wealth and distinction. Mary Eliska thought he might be an ambassador, or perhaps a doctor or lawyer.

"Mary Eliska," said Tom Hulbert, "I want to present a gentleman who is very anxious to meet you, who has heard of your wonderful exploits, and who is something of a flyer himself. Mary Eliska, let me introduce Lord Dudley, of England."

Mary Eliska blushingly held out her hand, and Tom proceeded to introduce the titled foreigner to Mary Eliska. Not knowing Amy, he did not include her, but he noticed that the man was looking at her.

"I hear your praises sung wherever I go, Mary Eliska," Lord Dudley said, with an engaging smile. "Not only in your own country, but in England, France,—even Germany. You are a very famous person."

"It is very kind of you to say that," replied Mary Eliska, embarrassed as usual at the praise. "But tell me about your own flying. Have you your plane here?"

"No, it's being repaired—I left it in England. I drove up here in a hired motor."

"It's too bad you haven't your plane," said Mary Eliska. "For we are to have a treasure hunt by airplane on Saturday." She glanced shyly at her aunt, who was frowning. "But you can use one of Mr. Clavering's——"

The tennis matches were to begin immediately, for Jax Gray and Sarah were shaking hands with formality, and the umpire was mounting his stand. So Tom drew his friend away to the seats which Kitty was saving for them.

"I've seen that man before!" cried Amy, excitedly.

"Where? When?" demanded Mary Eliska, hopefully. Was another memory coming back?

"I don't know."

"But if he had known you, he would have said something," remarked Mary Eliska. "I was going to introduce you, dear, but I didn't get a chance."

"Oh, that's all right!"

"He looks like Ronald Colman," remarked Mary Eliska, after some thought. "Yes, that's it. You've seen him in the movies, Amy."

"What are movies?" asked the girl, to Mary Eliska's and Mary Eliska's amazement.

There was no time to explain, for the tennis match had begun, and Mary Eliska was anxious not to miss a single play. But all the while she was thinking of the titled Englishman whom she had just met; later in the evening, when the dancing began, she unconsciously searched the room for him. But he had evidently left early, for she did not see him again.

Chapter 17.5
A Flying Engagement

At seven o'clock the following morning, just as the cook was putting on her apron, the doorbell of the Carltons' bungalow rang sharply.

"Beggar probably wants his breakfast," the woman muttered, as she slowly went to the door. But there were few beggars at Green Falls, and they always came to the back door.

A blond, freckle-faced young man, without any hat, stood on the porch, grinning shyly. At the gate was the most dilapidated-looking Ford she had ever seen.

"Good morning," he said, briskly, and the cook would never have suspected from his bright, cheery tone that he had been driving all night. "I'm a reporter from the Grand Rapids *Star*, and I want to see Miss Mary Eliska just as soon as possible."

"Miss Mary Eliska ain't seein' no more reporters," replied the woman, flatly. "She seen enough a couple of weeks ago to last her the rest of her life."

"But I want to help her," insisted the young man. "Help her find the lost child's parents."

"Oh! That's different. Come along in, and give me your card."

Smiling happily at his success, the young man entered the living room.

"Had your breakfast?"

"Why—er—I had some coffee in a thermos bottle."

"You could eat some?"

"I'll say I could!"

"All right. Set down there and read the paper while I fix some. I don't want to wake Miss Mary Eliska jest yet."

The cook kept him waiting an hour, but she rewarded him with such a breakfast as he could not have bought at the best hotel. The choicest honeydew melon, griddle cakes, home-cooked ham, coffee, and even fried potatoes. It made the young man think of the meals his mother cooked on the farm.

Just as he was finishing his second cup of coffee, Mary Eliska appeared, followed immediately by Mary Eliska and Amy.

The boy stood up and flushed a vivid red in a vain effort to murmur apologies and explanations. It was plain to be seen that he was from the country, and that this was his first newspaper job.

"My name's Michael O'Malley," he finally said, producing a card from his pocket. "And the paper is going to give me a tryout on this story; I can stay as long as I like, provided I get something interesting." He was talking very fast now, almost as if he were afraid to stop, lest Mary Eliska put him out. "You see, I'm crazy about detective stories, and this seems like a chance to do some real sleuthin'. If we can only find the young lady's family, and run down that guy that ran her down!"

Mary Eliska smiled. She couldn't help liking the boy; he was so sincere, so earnest, so eager to please.

"Sit down again, Mr. O'Malley," she said; "while we eat our breakfast, we'll talk it over."

"Thank you, Mary Eliska," he breathed, reverently. He treated Mary Eliska as if she were some sort of goddess.

"And have some more griddle cakes," urged Mary Eliska, hospitably. She, too, liked the boy.

He grinned.

"You know, they taste exactly like my mother's!" he exclaimed. "I never found anybody who could make 'em like this except her. We lived on a farm, you see—and there were five boys. And maybe my mother couldn't cook!"

"Now," continued Mary Eliska, after her aunt had seen to the boy's wants, "there really isn't a whole lot to do. I'm sure we'll get a phone call from Amy's parents today, for they'll be crazy to get her back, and must be watching the papers. The only 'detective' part of the story is to find that man. After all, it probably was only an accident, but still, he ought to be punished."

"What did he look like?"

"Well, you see we were up in the air, and couldn't get a very good look at him. But he wore no hat, and he had an immense amount of gray hair—and, I think, whiskers. I know it seems funny that a man his age should be driving so fast."

"What kind of car was it?" demanded the reporter.

"Gray—and open. But I couldn't tell you the make, or anything more in description. It all happened so quickly, and it shot away before we could really see it."

"You didn't even get the state or the license number?"

"No, of course not."

Mr. O'Malley sighed.

"Looks pretty hopeless. But do you mind if I stick around here today 'til Miss Amy's parents show up? I'd like to be on tap with that much of the story."

"We'll be glad to have you," replied Mary Eliska, hospitably. "Stay until tomorrow if you like, Mr. O'Malley, as our guest."

"Oh, thank you, Mary Eliska!" he answered gratefully. "It—you—make me feel so at home, and I've been kinda homesick in Grand Rapids. And—would you call me 'Mike,' please?"

"Certainly, Mike," agreed his hostess.

"And I'll see that you get the story of our treasure hunt for your paper," added Mary Eliska, generously. "A treasure hunt by airplane."

"Gee Whitakers!" cried the boy, enthusiastically. "That is something new!"

Mary Eliska frowned, but said nothing. Amy, too, was silent. She could not be hopeful like the others of hearing from her parents, for she felt sure that there were no parents to hear from.

The telephone rang, and Mary Eliska jumped up eagerly, hoping that it meant good news for Amy. To her amazement she heard the fascinating voice of Lord Dudley at the other end of the wire.

"Good morning, Great Aviatrix!" he said. "This is one of your many admirers—Claude Dudley."

Mary Eliska flushed; this was going to be more exciting than news of Amy's family.

"Good morning, Lord Dudley," she replied.

"I am going to ask you a big favor, Mary Eliska," he said. "I have to get back to Chicago today, and I was wondering whether you would take me across Lake Michigan in your autogiro. We could lunch at the Lakeside Inn—a place that I know to be particularly charming."

Mary Eliska's heart beat rapidly; no young man had ever been able to thrill her like this before. How flattered she was to have him call upon her!

"I'd love to, Lord Dudley," she replied, slowly. "But you must wait until I ask my aunt's permission."

"Well! Well!" he exclaimed, in amazement. "I didn't know modern girls did that anymore!"

Mary Eliska laughed.

"This girl does. Will you hold the wire, Lord Dudley?"

"Certainly, Mary Eliska. Your favor is well worth waiting for."

Mary Eliska put down the telephone and turned to her aunt, repeating the conversation.

"We don't know anything about him," remarked the older woman. "But he seemed like a gentleman. And Tom Hulbert introduced him, so I guess he is all right. If your autogiro is in perfect condition, I suppose I am willing."

Mary Eliska turned to her young guest.

"Do you mind if I go off, Amy?" she inquired.

"Not a bit, Mary Eliska. I want you to have a good time."

So Mary Eliska returned to the telephone and promised to be ready at half-past eleven.

She would not admit to herself how thrilled she was, but she selected her prettiest dress, and was ready for Lord Dudley some minutes before his taxi arrived. She ran out on the porch to meet him.

"We must keep the cab," she said, as she shook hands with him, and noticed that he was even better looking than she had thought, "in order to get to the airport."

"Right," he agreed, giving the necessary directions to the driver.

"Now you must tell me all about yourself, Mary Eliska," he said, as he seated himself beside her in the cab. "I mean the things that haven't been in the papers."

"There really isn't anything to tell," replied Mary Eliska, modestly. "I'm just an ordinary girl, with a high-school education and a year at a ground school, where I earned my transport pilot's license. The only thrilling thing about me is my 'Ladybug'—that's the name of my autogiro."

"I know something more thrilling than any of those things," he said, with his engaging smile. "Something the newspapers have never been able to describe— Your flawless beauty!"

Mary Eliska flushed to the lobes of her ears at the compliment; it didn't seem possible that a young man like this, who had been everywhere and met thousands of beautiful girls, could find her so attractive. Yet there was a note of sincerity in his low, deep voice that prevented any doubt.

"I wish you would tell me about yourself, instead," she urged, anxious to change the subject. "About your family in England, and how you happened to come to America."

"There isn't much to tell about that, either," he replied. "There is an old castle at home, but I'm afraid it wouldn't interest you. It's so run down. It needs lots of money spent on it. My father is an old man, and it has been the dream of his life to see the castle in good order again, with the gardens well kept, as they were in years gone by. So I have come

The smile which was usually on Lord Dudley's lips had vanished, and his eyes grew wistful. What a wonderful man he was, Mary Eliska thought, to put his father's wishes above everything else!

"Here is the airport, Lord Dudley," she announced. "We'll have to postpone our conversation until we get to the tea room. You can't talk in an autogiro."

"No; I realize that. But how interesting it will be. I have heard of Cierva, the inventor, in England, and I even saw him once on one of my trips to Spain, but I have never flown in an autogiro."

"You'll get the thrill of your life!" Mary Eliska promised.

"I got the thrill of my life last night," he said, and Mary Eliska could not help knowing that he was referring to his meeting her.

She gave the "Ladybug" a hasty inspection, although the head mechanic at the airport assured her that it was in perfect condition. Lord Dudley shouted his admiration of its quick take-off into the air, and settled himself comfortably for the beautiful flight over the lake. Mary Eliska, too, found the trip delightful; in the dreamy mood that she was experiencing, she was almost glad that they could not talk. Was it possible, she wondered, that at last she had fallen in love?

As Lord Dudley had promised, the Inn was charming, and the luncheon excellent. Mary Eliska was sorry when it was over, for it meant parting from her fascinating companion.

"I can never thank you enough, Mary Eliska," he said in a low tone, as he took her hand into both of his for a moment. "And—may I come back again?"

"Oh, yes, indeed!" she answered, with eagerness.

"When I do come back, I—I—will just have to ask you something—Mary Eliska, my dear. I know I shouldn't—I am a poor man—but—" He hesitated, and leaning over, pressed a kiss on her hand. Then, without another word, he put her into her autogiro.

Her heart in a turmoil, Mary Eliska mechanically started her motor and flew away. Lord Dudley's meaning was clear, but what was the answer? Could she possibly decide so quickly whether she loved him or not, whether she was ready to give up everyone else for his sake, even her own country, to cast her lot with his? It was too much to think about; she was thankful when she reached home to be able to put the question aside in favor of Amy's problems.

She ran up the steps hopefully, wondering whether there was any news, and she found Amy and Mike in their bathing suits and rain coats, all ready for a swim.

"Haven't you heard anything?" she demanded eagerly. "No phone calls?"

"Only from other reporters," sighed Mike, and Amy suddenly burst out crying.

"I must be an orphan," she sobbed. "That is why you and Miss Polly seem so wonderful to me, Mary Eliska. I am sure that I never knew anybody like you in my past life."

"Don't give up yet, dear. If you had been in an orphan asylum, the authorities would have claimed you long ago. Maybe your family is poor, and can't get the money immediately. Please don't cry—you don't have to make a pool of tears like Alice in Wonderland to swim in. There's a marvelous lake this side of the falls!"

"Alice in Wonderland!" repeated Amy, slowly. "I've heard of her."

"Of course you have. I'll hunt up a copy of the book, and see what it recalls to you. Now if you wait five minutes for me, I'll get into my bathing suit and go along with you!"

Fifteen minutes later the three young people parked the roadster at the shore of the lake, and joined the others in bathing. Mary Eliska introduced both Mike and Amy to everybody, so that the strangers felt quite at home.

Ralph Clavering immediately took possession of Mary Eliska.

"Where were you today?" he demanded. "I expected you to play tennis with me."

"I thought you were angry at me, Ralph," she returned, demurely.

"I was, but the worst part of it all is, I can never stay angry. Are you going to enter the treasure hunt?"

"I sort of hope so. Aunt Sally hasn't said anything against it lately, and I was flying today."

"Flying! Where?"

"Across Lake Michigan."

"Alone?" This jealous young man always felt that he had a right to know of all Mary Eliska's engagements.

"No; I took Lord Dudley across." She tried to keep her tone matter-of-fact.

"How you girls fall for titles!" he almost sneered. "I don't like the man."

"Men never do admire handsome men," Mary Eliska answered, slyly.

"If you call him handsome!— Well, you have to give us tomorrow. Kit's expecting you to lunch."

"O.K.," agreed the girl, disappearing with a swan dive into the lake.

Chapter 17.6
The Telegram

"I hear you have made a new conquest, Mary Eliska!"

Tiny Kitty Hulbert, Ralph Clavering's married sister, sat on the edge of the diving board the following morning and talked to Mary Eliska, who was watching the newspaper reporter, Mike O'Malley, trying to teach Amy to swim. But the young girl was terribly frightened, and was not making progress.

Mary Eliska blushed and smiled.

"I wouldn't say that, exactly———"

"But it's true," said Kitty. "I never saw anybody more thrilled than Lord Dudley. He thinks you're just about perfect."

"When did you see him?" asked Mary Eliska, trying to keep her voice calm. This was Wednesday, the day after her flight across the lake, and incidentally the last day for the contestants to register for the treasure hunt.

"Oh, we haven't seen him since you did yesterday," returned Kitty. "But I heard about the flight before he left, and he seemed awfully excited. Just like a kid of sixteen, in love for the first time."

Mary Eliska blushed; so other people had noticed it, too! She wondered if it would be the talk of Green Falls.

"Have you known him long, Kit?" she inquired.

"No. One of Tom's friends—John Kuhns—met him in a railroad station, just after he had landed from England, and he seemed so sort of lost and lonely that he entertained him. His family liked him so much that they invited him to their summer place, and then suddenly changed their plans and went abroad instead. So John asked Tom to look out for him, and that is how we happen to be entertaining him at Green Falls. I was kind of scared at the idea of royalty, but he seems just like anybody else."

"I wonder how old he is," mused Mary Eliska, more to herself than to Kitty.

"Too old for you, dear," replied Kitty. She knew how much Ralph cared for Mary Eliska, and she hated to see him suddenly cut out by a foreigner with a title, charming as Lord Dudley was. "You're not serious about him are you, Mary Eliska?"

"Oh, I like him," replied the other. "I guess all the girls do— By the way, Ralph invited me to your house to lunch today. Is that right?"

"Yes indeed, I'm expecting you. And you know it's the last chance to register for the hunt. You're entering, aren't you?"

"I hope to. I'm going to pin Aunt Sally to a definite answer before I come over today. I must go in now, Kitty, for I see that Amy is tired of swimming. She'll want to go home in a minute."

"Haven't her parents turned up yet?"

"No, they hadn't when we left."

"It seems queer."

"Yes, it does. I'm really worried about her now. If she could only remember!"

"Well, as long as your Aunt Sally is taking care of her, she'll be all right. Now go along— get your swim, and I'll see you at one o'clock."

Mary Eliska dived into the water, but she did not swim long. Amy was standing still, up to her neck, clinging nervously to Mike's hands. Though the sun and the air were warm, she seemed to be shaking all over.

"Miss Amy's scared to death," announced Mike. "She acts like a person who has never gotten over a drowning scare." He turned to the girl. "Have you ever been drowned, Miss Amy?"

The girl burst out laughing at the absurdity of the question, and seemed her normal self again. But she was glad that Mary Eliska suggested that they all go home.

They entered the house with the usual hope, a hope which was gradually dying now, of hearing from Amy's family. But Mary Eliska had to tell them again that no one except her own friends had telephoned. Mary Eliska hurried off to dress for the luncheon at Kit's.

"Where are you going, dear?" Mary Eliska asked her, half an hour later, when her niece appeared in a new dress, a flowered chiffon, which she would hardly have worn for lunch at home by themselves.

"I'm going to Kitty's, Aunt Sally. To help plan for the treasure hunt. You—you don't mind if I take part in it, do you? I have to let them know today."

Mary Eliska sighed.

"I suppose it would be unreasonable to try to keep you out," she admitted. "But I am so afraid of crashes with other planes. It is just like driving a car—much safer where there is no other traffic, for you never can tell what the other people will do."

"I know. But I'll be careful, Aunt Sally. And Ralph and Kitty are so anxious for me to go into it."

Mary Eliska weakened; as usual the mention of the Claverings had a softening effect upon her. She liked Mary Eliska to be with them, to take part in the social affairs of her young friends.

"All right, dear. I agree, though I really don't approve."

Mary Eliska kissed her.

"But you never do approve, even if I only go up in the air for half an hour," she teased.

"I thought I was growing used to it, 'til those awful things happened to you in the Okefenokee Swamp."

"But it was thieves, not airplanes, that caused all the trouble. It might have happened if I had been riding horseback."

"True. Have your own way, dear." But Mary Eliska could tell by her voice that she wasn't angry.

Ten minutes later Mary Eliska parked her roadster in front of Kit's bungalow and ran up the porch with the good news. Kit and Jax Gray, Ralph and Mr. Clavering were all sitting on the big couch hammock, poring over a map.

"We have to fly over Lake Michigan!" announced Jax Gray, proudly. "Isn't that marvelous?"

"Perfect," agreed Mary Eliska, glad that this hunt was not to be a "play" flight of a few miles or so. A hundred miles as a beginning—that ought to be thrilling.

"The first landing is to be the Milwaukee airport," said Mr. Clavering. "That is all I am going to tell you. The seven planes are to leave Green Falls at ten o'clock Saturday morning."

"Seven?" repeated Mary Eliska. "Who are the seven?"

Fumbling in his pocket, Ralph produced a typewritten list. He read it aloud.

"1. Tom and Kitty Hulbert.

2. Jax Gray y and Jim Valier——"

"So you're taking Jim after all!" interrupted Kit. "I thought you said he was too lazy."

Dot smiled.

"I guess I was only teasing," she admitted.

"To continue," said Ralph.

"3. Bert and Madge Keen.

4. Frank Lawlor and Sue Emery.

5. Joe Elliston and Sarah Wheeler——"

"Joe Elliston!" cried Mary Eliska. "Since when has he become a flyer?"

"He just received his private pilot's license last week," explained Ralph. "He hasn't a plane of his own, but Dad's renting one for him."

"I guess I'm taking a chance," remarked Mr. Clavering. "But the plane's insured."

"And you and I are the sixth and seventh, Mary Eliska," concluded Ralph. "May I ask who your passenger is to be?"

"If you tell me who yours is," she countered.

"I am going alone."

"Oh, I see. Well, I'm taking Harry."

"Not Lord Dudley?" inquired the young man, with a gleam of jealousy.

"Oh, no. I promised Harry."

"Lord Dudley thinks he's going with you," remarked Kitty. "He expects to be back."

"Then why doesn't he take a plane and enter," sneered Ralph. "I'll bet he's not so much of a flyer as he makes out to be."

"How you love him!" remarked Kitty, rising to greet Madge Keen, who was the last of her guests to arrive.

"Now come to luncheon," added the young hostess, with a nod to the maid who was waiting for the signal. "You must all be starved after your swims."

A simple affair like this was always a party at Kitty Hulbert's, for the young matron had such beautiful things, such lovely flowers, such trained servants that she enjoyed displaying them. The table was arranged as elaborately as if a banquet were being served.

As usual, Mary Eliska found herself seated next to Ralph, and she began to talk to him immediately, to take his mind away from the subject of Lord Dudley.

"Has your autogiro come yet?" she inquired.

"No, but it'll be here tomorrow. Want to go up on a test flight with me, Mary Eliska?"

"Of course I do!" she replied eagerly. "I think it's wonderful that you're getting it, before you even graduated from college."

"Now Mary Eliska, don't rub it in," replied the young man. Although he should have completed his course at Harvard the preceding June, there had been a condition in mathematics, which kept him from getting his degree. His father had wanted him to go to summer school, but with his usual lazy attitude towards life, Ralph had refused. He was just as well satisfied that he did have to return in the fall; it would be more fun to hang around college than to buckle down to his father's business.

"I didn't want to be mean," apologized Mary Eliska. "Only you know you weren't supposed to get a plane of your own 'til you graduated."

She stopped talking; Kitty was taking a telegram from the maid, and glancing at Mary Eliska. What was it? For her? News of Amy—or a message from her father?

"This is for you, Mary Eliska," said her hostess. "I do hope it isn't bad news."

"Maybe it's something about Amy," she said expectantly, and all eyes were on her as she slit open the envelope.

But as she read the message, a vivid blush spread over her face, and she felt as if the others about the table must know what it contained.

"Am returning tonight with Tom for my answer. Love. Claude."

"Why Mary Eliska! What's happened?" demanded Jax Gray, in surprise.

"Nothing, nothing," she murmured, in confusion. "Nothing's wrong. It's—just a personal message."

"Not about Amy?"

"No."

There was an embarrassed silence, and Kitty came to the rescue by leading the conversation back to the subject of the treasure hunt.

"I'm allowed to tell you this much about it," she added. "Everybody flies to Lake Winnebago after the hunt for a big celebration. Dad's rented an entire Inn for the week-end, and all our parents are invited to be chaperons."

"And will the prize be awarded then?" asked Jax Gray, more to keep the conversation away from Mary Eliska than because she wanted to know.

"No. The lucky pilot finds the prize for himself—after following the directions he receives."

"You better say 'she,'" remarked Ralph, "for I think it's a great deal more likely that Mary Eliska or Jax Gray will get it, than any of us fellows."

Mary Eliska forced a smile, but her mind was not on the conversation. Even the treasure hunt had lost its interest; she longed to get home, where she could be alone to think things out.

The party broke up at last, and she managed to get away without even an explanation to Jax Gray of the mysterious contents of the telegram.

She paused in the living room of her own bungalow only long enough to give Mike O'Malley the facts and the names of the contestants in the hunt, for the young man was returning to Grand Rapids. With a sigh of relief, she rushed up to her own room, and locked the door, there to try to come to some decision.

But the conclusion she came to was not at all to Lord Dudley's liking, as he learned to his dismay after supper, when he came over to take her canoeing.

"My plan is this, Mary Eliska dear," he said, as they pushed off from the shore: "Take me as your passenger in the hunt on Saturday—win the prize, as, of course, you will—and instead of returning, simply elope in the autogiro. We can wire your aunt from the nearest city, wherever that happens to be, when we are married. Doesn't the romance of that appeal to you?" he asked, rapturously.

Mary Eliska slowly shook her head.

"I couldn't, Lord Dudley——" she began.

"Please call me 'Claude!'" he pleaded.

She smiled.

"Well, then—Claude—I couldn't. First of all, I've promised to take Harriman Smith on the flight——"

"Shucks!" he interrupted, abandoning his usual dignity.

"And besides, I couldn't be so mean to Aunt Sally. She would hate it—and she'd have a right to. No, Claude, I'm not willing to marry you on so short an acquaintance. A year from now—or possibly six months—I don't know."

The man stopped paddling and regarded her helplessly.

"It's because I've told you I'm only a poor man," he said, thinking immediately that money had something to do with her refusal. "And you're an heiress!"

Mary Eliska opened her eyes wide in amazement.

"What makes you think I'm an heiress, Lord Dudley?" she asked, forgetting to use his first name. "Really—we're not rich."

"But the newspapers said you were. And that big prize you won, flying the Atlantic alone——"

The man's surprise was evidently as great as Mary Eliska's.

"Yes, I have that—invested in bonds. But $25,000 isn't a fortune. And I haven't anything else, except the money I sold my Bellanca for, which Daddy put into a trust fund for me, in case his business fails. No, Lord Dudley, I really expect to earn my own living."

"I see," he replied, and he could not keep the bitter disappointment out of his tone. "That is why we had better not risk it?"

He seemed content to leave it at that, and Mary Eliska was silent. As a matter of fact, money had never entered into her consideration of the marriage. The idea of leaving her aunt, her friends—especially Harry and Jax Gray, and even Ralph—to go to a strange country had been a much more vital drawback. Charming as he was, Lord Dudley was only a stranger.

"Let's forget it, and talk about something else," she suggested, quietly. "Tell me why you don't go into the treasure hunt yourself. It's going to be lots of fun."

"I'm too busy," he replied irritably, as one might speak to a child. "I have to get back to Chicago early tomorrow morning."

"In that case," concluded Mary Eliska, "hadn't we better paddle back home now?"

Without any reply the Englishman turned the canoe about and silently made for the shore. It was only half-past nine when he left her at the steps of her bungalow, refusing her invitation to come in to see her Aunt Sally.

"And that is the end of him," Mary Eliska thought as she went quickly to bed, little imagining that she would ever see him again.

Chapter 17.7
The Widow in Black

"Mary Eliska, it's come! My autogiro!" shrieked Ralph Clavering, bursting into the Carltons' bungalow, without even waiting to knock. "And I've had her up already! The man gave me a lesson!"

Mary Eliska almost fell down the steps in her wild excitement at this piece of news. Another autogiro in Green Falls! Her "Ladybug's" twin!

"Wonderful! Great!" she cried, seizing both his hands and executing a dance. "In plenty of time for the treasure hunt."

"Yes. Don't forget that you promised to go up with me this afternoon!"

"Try and keep me out!" she replied. "I just can't wait. I don't even care about lunch, if you'll just give me time to get into my flying suit———"

"What's this? What's this?" demanded Miss Polly Carlton, entering the living room with Amy at her heels. "You're not going to go without your lunch, Mary Eliska!"

"Then may we have ours right away?" pleaded her niece. "Ralph and I, I mean?"

"Yes, I suppose so. Only do be careful, Mary Eliska, with a new plane. Are you quite sure all the parts are there?"

Ralph smiled.

"The autogiro couldn't have arrived safely, Mary Eliska, if it hadn't been perfect. You see they don't deliver planes in trucks—they fly 'em!"

"All right, then," agreed the older woman, grudgingly. "Then I'll go and see about lunch."

It was a thrilling afternoon for Mary Eliska, and even more pleasant for Ralph, in the possession of his first flying machine. Together they went over to the airport and took the new autogiro into the skies, first with Mary Eliska, then with Ralph at the controls. In the joy of flying Mary Eliska forgot for the time being all about the queer experience of the preceding day with Lord Dudley. She was Mary Eliska the aviatrix today, interested in nothing but aviation.

She even forgot about Amy until she returned to the bungalow at supper-time, and found the little girl waiting wistfully on the porch all alone. Mary Eliska knew from her expression that no one had telephoned.

"Nobody cares about me except the newspaper reporters," she remarked the following day—the Friday before the treasure hunt—when s'til nothing had happened, and no one had come to claim her. "And even they are beginning to lose interest."

"Not Mike O'Malley!" replied Mary Eliska, cheerfully. "I had a letter from him today—he's arriving this morning. He expects to drive that battered Ford of his over to Lake Winnebago, to be in at the finish of the hunt."

Amy sighed; she had not been included in the plans for the event, although Mary Eliska had been invited for the week-end at the Inn. The girl would have to be left in care of Anna, Mary Eliska's competent cook.

"I wish Mike would stay here with me," said the girl. She didn't add that she would be lonely; it wouldn't be grateful to these wonderful people who were doing so much for her.

"Mike has work to do for his paper," replied Mary Eliska.

Scarcely had she finished the sentence when the Ford stopped at the gate, and the young man, sunburned and grinning, jumped out. He felt almost as if he were coming home, to be back again at the Carltons'.

"Hello, everybody!" he cried merrily. "Here I am—all ready for the big hunt!"

"It's more than I am," replied Mary Eliska. "I've got to spend the whole day going over the 'Ladybug.' But come on in, Mike—I'll get you something to eat. Of course, you're hungry?"

"You said it!"

"And as soon as you finish eating, you better take Amy swimming. Aunt Sally went shopping, and I have to go to the airport, so I'll be glad if you can keep Amy from being lonely."

"O.K. with me," he agreed, following Mary Eliska into the dining room. "By the way, Mary Eliska, any change in plans, or contestants, for the treasure hunt?"

"Not that I know of," she replied, as she hunted some buns and milk for the boy, who ate hungrily, as usual.

Suddenly he stopped eating, and peering towards the living room, listened intently.

"Do my ears deceive me, or is somebody snitching my Lizzie?" He jumped up and ran to the living-room window.

"No, I think that's the station taxicab," replied Mary Eliska. "Its engine sounds like a boiler factory."

"Almost as loud as an airplane's!" teased Mike.

"Who is it, Mary Eliska? Who is that getting out of the cab?" demanded Amy holding the other girl's arm tensely. "Do you know her?"

"No," replied Mary Eliska, as she watched a woman in black who was coming up the porch steps. "She's a stranger to me—oh—maybe—Amy, do you remember her?" She peered anxiously into the younger girl's face.

The latter shook her head sorrowfully.

"No, I don't. Not a glimmer—not even a vague memory, like I had when I saw that man at the tennis matches."

"What man?"

"Lord Somebody——"

"Oh! Lord Dudley. But you saw him afterwards. He was here——"

"No, I never happened to be around. And I couldn't remember anything about him anyway. But I feel positive I never saw this woman."

The girls were standing close together, Amy still clinging to Mary Eliska's arm, when Mike opened the screen door to the stranger's knock.

The woman hesitated a moment, and stepped inside, looking quickly about the room. With a bright smile of recognition, she came over to Amy.

"Helen darling!" she exclaimed, pushing Mary Eliska aside and kissing Amy gushingly. "Oh, I'm so thankful to have you safe!"

Tears came to Amy's eyes, but she could not pretend that she remembered the woman.

"Who—are you?" she stammered.

The woman looked shocked.

"Helen! Can't you remember me? I am your Aunt Elsie—I've cared for you ever since your mother died. Oh, surely, dear—" She looked helplessly at Mary Eliska.

"Helen—we call her 'Amy'—has lost her memory," explained the latter. "You see she was hit on the back of the head by a car. But surely you read about it in the papers?"

"Yes, yes. But I thought that she would recognize me," wailed the woman hysterically, wiping tears from her eyes. "She disappeared about two weeks ago—we live in a little town in Montana—and I was almost crazy with fear. Then I read about this girl being hit by something—it was an airplane, wasn't it?—and I came on to Grand Rapids, and a newspaper man there showed me the picture."

Mike swelled with pride. That must have been his newspaper!

"It was a car she was hit by," corrected Mary Eliska. "An airplane rescued her."

"You don't say!" exclaimed the woman. "I heard it the other way about. Well, we'll prove that later. Now, come along, Helen."

But anxious as the girl had been for people of her own to claim her, now that this stranger had done so, she was afraid to go. She did not like the woman.

"What is my other name?" she questioned, without making any move to obey her.

"Tower—Helen Tower. I am Mrs. Fishberry. Can't you possibly remember, dear?"

The girl shook her head.

"Couldn't I stay here a little longer—Mrs. Fishberry?" she asked.

"Certainly not." The woman looked annoyed.

Amy clung to Mary Eliska, her whole frame shaking violently.

"She must have been unkind to me before," she sobbed. "You know I felt that there was something to be afraid of in my past life. Oh, Mary Eliska, please keep me 'til that doctor who is treating me can make me well! I'll work and repay all you do for me!"

"Of course, we'll be glad to, Amy, dear," replied Mary Eliska, reassuringly. "Just so long as you're content to stay!"

"That is impossible," interrupted Mrs. Fishberry. "I cannot allow it for a minute, and will bring legal proceedings if you try to steal this child! Come, Helen—the taxi's waited long enough!"

Reluctantly Amy started to obey, when Mike O'Malley stepped forward and held up his hand like a traffic cop.

"Just a minute! Just a minute!" he said.

All eyes turned towards him instantly.

"You spoke of legal proceedings, Mrs. Fishmarket, or whatever your name is—what legal proofs have you that the girl belongs to you?"

The woman winced in surprise, and Amy and Mary Eliska looked at Mike with admiration. How clever of him to think of that!

The stranger drew herself up haughtily.

"I confess I did not bring legal proofs," she said. "I thought that after sacrificing the best years of my life to bringing up Helen, that she would know me, and want to come to me. But it seems that I cannot expect love or gratitude."

"Well, you can't expect us to turn her over to a person she dislikes, unless that person has a right to her," returned Mary Eliska.

"Very well," concluded the other. "I'll go. But I'll be back with the proofs. And you are going to be sorry for your insolence, Miss Mary Eliska!"

With this final remark, she turned and left the house.

"Whew!" exclaimed Mike, wiping his forehead. "She's a hot one. But I think there's something fishy about her, besides her name. I don't believe she's your aunt at all, Helen."

"Don't call me that!" pleaded the girl. "That name means nothing to me, and I am used to being called 'Amy' now."

"All right, dear," agreed Mary Eliska. "Now don't think any more about it. You'll be my adopted sister, for as long as you like—" She turned to the boy, "Mike, you are a bright man—I certainly am thankful we had you here!"

The young man blushed vividly over his freckles, and suggested that they go on with their swim as they had planned.

Drying her eyes, Amy ran off to get into her suit, but Mary Eliska remained some minutes where she was, thinking. It was queer—terribly queer. The woman was so unlike Amy, so different a type, so common—so really vulgar. Yet Amy was one of the sweetest, most refined little girls Mary Eliska had ever met; she might almost have been brought up by her own Aunt Sally, from the training she showed. Yet if the woman weren't a relation what could she possibly want with Amy? The child was obviously poor; what could be the reason, unless it were love?

Mary Eliska sighed; the problem was too much for her. So, as she often did with other difficulties, she put it aside while she flung herself wholeheartedly into the inspection of her autogiro.

Dressed in overalls, and covered with grease, but satisfied that her afternoon's work had been worthwhile, she returned to the house just in time for supper. She parked her roadster in the garage and dashed into the house, hoping to be able to get to her own room to dress before anyone saw her. But she was unsuccessful; Harriman Smith was waiting for her in the living room.

"Hello, Harry!" she exclaimed, laughing. "Don't look at me! I'm a sight. But if you'll just give me fifteen minutes——"

"You look fine, Mary Eliska!" protested the boy, thinking that her blue overalls were becoming and that her hair was all the more attractive when it blew around her face. "You see," he continued, talking rapidly, "I'm in a hurry. I'm here because I have bad news—at least bad for me, though it will be good news for some other lucky fellow. I have to go back to work tonight, and that means I can't go in the treasure hunt with you tomorrow."

"Oh, I'm so sorry, Harry!" she exclaimed, with genuine regret.

"Another fellow in the company got sick, and so they just had to recall me," he explained. "I shouldn't have cared so much if it had happened Monday, but I was looking forward to this affair a great deal."

"I'm awfully disappointed, too," said Mary Eliska, wondering whether she would go alone or ask somebody else.

"Thanks, Mary Eliska—I really appreciate that. When there is a whole stag line just dying for the honor— But Mary Eliska, may I ask a favor?"

"Why, yes, certainly, Harry."

"Don't take Lord What's-his-name in my place. Anybody but him!"

"Why?" asked Mary Eliska in surprise, not that she had the slightest idea of doing any such thing, but because she wanted to know Harry's reason. Unlike Ralph Clavering, Harriman Smith never stooped to petty jealousy.

"Well—I want to be fair, but—there's something slimy about that man."

"What do you mean?"

"Oh, he's too smooth. None of us fellows like him. It's not because he's an Englishman— I've known several of them, and thought them O.K., but—well—he just doesn't click with me. So will you take somebody else?"

Mary Eliska smiled.

"I wouldn't take Lord Dudley anyway, Harry, because he has gone away," she replied. "But I really think you're unfair about him. It's because he's a lot older than all you boys that he seems so different. He's halfway between us and our parents. That sort of makes him a different generation."

"You do like him, don't you, Mary Eliska?" persisted the young man, keeping his eyes fastened on her, fearing her answer.

Mary Eliska shrugged her shoulders.

"You needn't worry, Harry," she said. She was silent a moment, thinking of something different. "I know what I'll do!" she cried. "I'll take Amy with me!"

"Amy!"

"Yes. The kid is crazy about planes. She's afraid of a lot of things, like the water, and the dark, and a strange woman who came here today, but she adores flying. And she hates to be left alone."

"Well, that's O.K. with me!" exclaimed Harry, with a sigh of relief. It was better than he had expected. "Now I must say good-by, Mary Eliska. I just have time to get supper and catch my train."

Mary Eliska hurried into her bath as soon as the young man left, and in half an hour she was ready for supper, when she told Amy her good fortune about being included in the hunt. The girl was so delighted that she almost forgot the unpleasant experience of the morning.

But Mary Eliska, who had listened gravely to the story when she returned from her shopping trip, was worried.

Chapter 17.8
Amy's Relatives

The day after Mrs. Fishberry's visit to the Carlton bungalow, the woman stepped off the train at Chicago and took a taxicab to an apartment house in the center of that city. Ringing the bell three times, she was finally admitted by a man about her own age.

"Hello, Ed," was her greeting.

"Well, Elsie," he said, questioningly, as she drew off her gloves and seated herself in a large leather chair. The apartment was obviously that of a bachelor, furnished by the hotel, in a style that one would expect to appeal to a man.

"Did you see the kid?" he asked, as he lighted a cigarette.

"Yeah. But she didn't like me. Claimed she never saw me before, and that I'm not her real aunt."

"Well, of course, you aren't," he observed, in a matter-of-fact tone.

"No, but I will be soon—when you and I are married. You're surely her uncle, aren't you?"

"Yeah. No doubt about that."

"Well, then——"

"We won't be married 'til we make sure we get the money!" he announced, firmly.

The woman looked sulky.

"You've got the money, haven't you?" she demanded. "The girl's father is dead, isn't he?"

"Listen, Elsie," he said, irritably. "I've told you about this before, but you can't seem to get it through your thick head. There were two of us boys, and the old man. My mother died young. Well, I was supposed to be a 'bad egg,' but my brother was everything my father admired. That's the kid's father, you see. He married early, but soon after the child was born he and his wife were killed in an automobile accident. So, of course, Dad—the kid's grandfather—took her to raise."

"But I've heard all that!" interrupted Mrs. Fishberry.

"Sure you have. But you don't understand about the old man's money. It seems he left a will hidden in the house, and nobody could find it. And I happen to know that he meant all his money to go to the kid, and not a cent to me."

He smiled, in a way that was always fascinating to women, and Elsie Fishberry smiled, too. How clever he was!

"Lucky thing for me," he continued, "that the will was lost! I might have had to work all these years!"

"Well, you got the money!" she concluded, happily. "So it beats me why you want more, when the old man left a hundred thousand dollars!"

Ed frowned impatiently.

"I tell you I haven't got it, Elsie! Why can't you believe me?"

"Then how is it that you live in luxury while that kid and her nurse almost starved in that old house?"

"Because a Trust Company still keeps charge of the bonds. They won't hand 'em over to me 'til the girl dies, or 'til the old man's will is found. But they give me the income, and I'm supposed to let the nurse have some of it to take care of the kid."

The woman laughed harshly.

"Did you ever give her a cent?"

"Yes. You'd be surprised. I visited the old place two or three times and gave the woman five dollars. Once the kid almost drowned in the Fox River, when I was there."

"I guess you didn't do anything to save her!" laughed Mrs. Fishberry.

"No, I can't say that I did. It would have been easier for me if she had died. But a couple of boys happened along and fished her out."

"Didn't she yell for help?"

"Sure. But I pretended I was deaf. And that nurse really is deaf—she's so old. About eighty, I figured. She took care of me and my brother—the kid's father—when we were children."

"And where is that nurse now?"

The man shrugged his shoulders.

"Maybe at home—maybe out looking for the kid."

"That reminds me what I specially wanted to tell you," remarked Mrs. Fishberry. "So long as they won't believe I'm the child's aunt—they call her 'Amy,' you know—we've got to dig up some pictures and records to prove it."

"You mean *you've* got to dig them up—at the old house," corrected Ed. "I'm not going near the place 'til Monday, and then I'm going to set it on fire."

"Set it on fire!" exclaimed the other, in horror.

"Sure. If the Trust Company knows that the place is burned, they will give up all hope of finding the will, and hand out the old man's bonds to me. After all, I'm the real heir. I'm the son, and this kid is only a granddaughter, even if Dad did like her better than me."

"You're a wise one," remarked Mrs. Fishberry, with admiration. "But suppose that old nurse happens to be inside—and catches you?"

"I've thought of that. I'm going disguised as an old man, and I expect to work at night, anyway. Don't worry, Elsie—I'm not going to bungle this— But you get those pictures before Monday—they ought to be in the family Bible and the album on the parlor table. I'll map out the directions how to get to the house."

"Suppose the nurse is there?"

"If she is, don't say anything about the kid. Just tell her that I sent you for the stuff. After all, I've got a right to 'em."

"And if she isn't there, how'll I get in?"

"I'll give you my key."

The woman was silent for a moment, thinking rapidly.

"Listen, Ed," she said, finally, "if you're going to get all that money in bonds from your father's estate, let's give up this other scheme. It's not worth it."

The man jumped up angrily.

"Not worth it!" he snarled, and his face was far from attractive now. "Not worth it for twenty-five thousand dollars!"

"We may not get it," she whimpered.

"Oh, yeah? Well, if we don't, it'll be your fault! Because you balled up the works. Listen, Elsie, did you do what I asked when you were at the Carltons'? Suggest that you believed it was Mary Eliska hit the kid with her autogiro, and not a car?"

"Yeah. I did. But I don't believe they hardly took it in."

"Mary Eliska'll take it in when we sue her for damages. I think maybe we better ask fifty thousand, and then we'll be sure to get twenty-five."

"Are you sure Mary Eliska has twenty-five thousand?"

"Positive. Didn't she get that for her ocean flight?"

"Sure. But maybe she blew it in on clothes," suggested the woman.

"Somehow I don't believe she did," replied Ed, with a knowing smile. Then, abruptly he frowned. "Elsie, you've got to get hold of that kid and take her away somewheres—pretend it's her old home. It's a lucky break for us that she lost her memory."

"I'll say so."

Suddenly Mrs. Fishberry jumped up and darted over to her host's chair, seating herself on the arm.

"Listen, Ed," she said, coyly taking his hand, "have you thought that we've got to be married before this suit comes into court, if you don't want to appear in it? If I sue for damages, I've got to be the child's real aunt."

The man laughed.

"You win, Elsie! O.K. with me. You get those pictures by Sunday, and the kid too, and I'll get the license. We'll get married Monday morning."

Mrs. Fishberry stood up, satisfied. She had won everything she wanted. The plan was simple; she would go out in the country to that old house on the Fox River on Saturday, and get her pictures and records. On Sunday she would take them to the Carltons', and demand that the young girl come away with her. She would return to Chicago and put the child into an insane asylum, from which there would be no hope of escape. On Monday, Mrs. Fishberry would be married to Ed Tower, and after the old house was burned to the ground, they would go on their honeymoon. When they returned, they would collect the small fortune from the Trust Company and proceed to sue Miss Mary Eliska for the sum of fifty thousand dollars!

She did not see a single flaw in the plan, for if the young girl was in an asylum, there would be no one to protest.

Chapter 17.9
The Take-Off

"I think Mr. Clavering is too optimistic," remarked Mary Eliska at the breakfast table Saturday morning. "It doesn't seem possible to me that all seven planes will come through that treasure hunt without any mishaps. And if someone is injured, nobody would feel like having a week-end party at that Inn."

"Nothing's going to happen, Aunt Sally," Mary Eliska replied, her eyes sparkling with excitement. She and Amy were both dressed for the flight, and anxious to get off.

Mary Eliska rose from the table and kissed her niece good-by. She and half a dozen of the older folks were going by boat across Lake Michigan, and then on by automobile to Lake Winnebago, where the party was to be held.

"I hope you win, dear," she said. "And don't forget to take the lunch Anna has packed for you."

"We'll see you tonight, Auntie," returned Mary Eliska. "At the Inn."

"I sincerely hope so," answered the other, a little doubtfully.

In fairness to the contestants, Mr. Clavering had arranged that the planes start from different places, so that they would not have to wait long in turn for their take-offs. Mary Eliska and Ralph were to go early to the Green Falls airport to fly their autogiros up the shore, to wait until ten o'clock, the appointed time. Tom Hulbert and Frank Lawlor were to motor to a town a short distance from Green Falls, where their planes were in readiness, while Joe Elliston, Jax Gray y, and Bert Keen were all to leave from the Green Falls airport.

These last three pilots, with their passengers, were waiting at the airport when Mary Eliska, Ralph, and Amy drove over about half-past nine.

"Hurry up and get those windmills out of the way!" ordered Joe Elliston. "They clutter up the place."

"And be sure you don't cheat!" remarked Sarah Wheeler. "Wait 'til ten o'clock before you start."

"As if five or ten minutes would make any difference," replied Ralph. "The victor will probably win by hours, not minutes."

"I hope there won't be a thunderstorm," observed Madge Keen, who was flying with her husband. "It certainly is hot."

"I'm dropping out if anything like that happens," said Sarah flatly. "I'm not taking chances."

Joe looked a little doubtfully at the sky, although the sun was shining brightly. But, being an amateur, he was nervous, although he had been lucky enough to secure a Fleet, which was the kind of plane he had used for his lessons.

Mary Eliska put Amy into the autogiro, and started her motor. How smoothly it was running! Yesterday's work was worthwhile.

"Good-by, everybody! See you all in Milwaukee!" she called. They had been given instructions to fly to the airport in that city, and there to ask for directions.

Ralph took off a few minutes later, not quite so gracefully as Mary Eliska, but nevertheless without any mishaps.

Fifteen minutes later they waved to each other as they came down along the shore of the lake, a short distance from each other, to wait for ten o'clock to arrive.

"Are you going straight across the lake?" Ralph asked Mary Eliska.

"No," she replied. "If I fly southwest, I can reach Milwaukee a lot faster. If we went directly across the lake from here, we'd have over thirty miles to fly down the western shore of Lake Michigan."

The young man looked dubious.

"I guess I'm a fool, but I believe I'll take the longer route. I'm kind of afraid of that lake. I'd hate to have to swim it."

Mary Eliska smiled, but not in contempt. She admired him all the more for his cautiousness in handling his new autogiro.

They waited together until two minutes of ten, then, with a handclasp and a mutual expression of hope for good luck, they walked back to their machines and gave them the gun.

Like Mary Eliska, Amy was in high spirits, and she thoroughly enjoyed the beautiful flight over the water. It was lovely and cool in the sky, so different from the hot atmosphere below. Mary Eliska watched her compass carefully and reached Milwaukee without any deviation.

Looking about cautiously, to make sure that none of the other planes was making a landing at the same time, she brought her "Ladybug" down on the runway and climbed out.

A smiling mechanic came towards her, congratulating her upon her success thus far, and handing her a typewritten message.

"Fly to Columbus airport," she read. "And there receive further directions."

"How far is Columbus?" she asked the mechanic. "Fifty miles?"

"A little over, perhaps. Want an inspection, or some gas?"

Mary Eliska glanced at the indicator. "I don't believe so," she answered. Then, turning to her companion, she asked, "Are you hungry, Amy?"

"No! No!" cried the girl. "Let's not take the time to eat. Let's have a drink of water, and get on our way. We just have to win!"

Mary Eliska smiled and nodded in agreement, and the mechanic brought them some water.

"Have you any news of the other flyers in our race?" she asked him. "How many have been here so far?"

"Two—Lt. Hulbert and a Mr. Lawlor, I believe. About fifteen minutes ago—the lieutenant was the first. And I heard that one fellow couldn't get his plane into the air at all, and that he had to drop out before he even started."

"That must have been Joe Elliston!" exclaimed Mary Eliska, immediately. "He was scared, anyway."

"Yes, I believe that was the name, though the message wasn't very clear. His plane is a Fleet?"

"Yes. Poor kid!" remarked Mary Eliska, sympathetically. "I wish we could help him."

"Come on, Mary Eliska, we must go!" urged Amy, impatiently.

"Now you're going to taste some speed, Amy," Mary Eliska said, as they climbed into the cockpits. "I'm going to let her out to the limit. I want to reach Columbus in half an hour—I'm very hungry!"

Scarcely had they made their ascent when they spotted another plane approaching the airport. Though they could not see the pilot, Mary Eliska identified it as an Avian, the plane which Jax Gray y had selected for the hunt.

"Step on it! Step on it!" cried Amy, clapping her hands. "Go on, Mary Eliska!"

Thrilled with the excitement of the race, Mary Eliska urged her "Ladybug" to her greatest speed. What fun it was to know that you were safe, and yet to fly along at more than a hundred miles an hour! And how glad she was that she had brought Amy! The child was having the time of her life.

Clouds, deep piles of heavy white clouds were gathering above them when Mary Eliska brought her autogiro down at the Columbus airport. Again a mechanic came out with a typewritten message, but this time a warning was also issued.

"We are advising all pilots in the hunt to wait until the storm is over," he said. "The sky looks bad, and the weather report is unfavorable."

Mary Eliska frowned and opened the lunch box which Anna had packed.

"You really think it is dangerous?" she asked, looking up at the clouds.

"We certainly do. Those clouds mean a thunderstorm."

"Oh, what do we care?" demanded Amy, as she hastily ate a sandwich. "It didn't stop the others, did it?"

"No. But they were here a little earlier, before the skies were so black."

"How many?" inquired Mary Eliska.

"Three. Two Moths and an Avian."

"Tom Hulbert and Frank Lawlor—and—and Dot!" cried Mary Eliska. So Jax Gray y had caught up to them and had beaten them! Funny, they hadn't seen her plane go past. But perhaps she was flying higher.

"Then we'll have to go, too," Mary Eliska decided, rather recklessly for her. "We'll eat while you put in some gas."

She opened the paper and read the directions. This time they were more difficult. This was to be the finish!

"Fly northwest, past Beaver Dam to Fox River. Follow the river, west, then north, to Lake Waupin. Continue about ten miles, looking for a large old house of gray plaster, with a flat roof and a tower. Land in a field behind this, and search the barn. Treasure is hidden in the barn. It is in bright red wrapping."

Reading the words over her shoulder, Amy gasped in excitement.

"Those words are familiar, Mary Eliska. I—I know the Fox River! I'm sure I do."

Mary Eliska, who had completely forgotten the mystery about the girl in the excitement of the morning, gazed at her in surprise.

"But you are supposed to come from Montana," she said. "You couldn't have come this far."

"I don't know," replied the perplexed girl. "But I do know these names are familiar."

All the while the skies grew darker than before, the thunder sounded nearer and nearer, and Mary Eliska became more fearful. Was she acting foolishly, in defiance of her aunt's dearest wishes? But how she hated to give up, now that she had come this far!

Suddenly another plane swooped down from the skies with an awful speed that sent a shiver through Mary Eliska's body. It was going to crash, she felt sure; the pilot could not control it. She pulled Amy back into the hangar, and watched her autogiro nervously. Would it be hit by that speeding plane, hit and dashed to pieces, too?

But miraculously the descending plane passed over the "Ladybug" and hit the ground with a thump, bouncing high into the air—seeming to hover a breathless second—then turning a pancake. It was all Mary Eliska could do to restrain a scream, and Amy cried out in fright.

But a second later a woman crept smilingly from the upturned plane, and dragged a man after her. It was Madge Keen and her husband.

"Thank Heaven!" cried Mary Eliska, dashing breathlessly to their side. "You're not hurt?"

"No, only bruised a lot," replied Madge. "It was a wonderful escape. I guess Bert was in too much of a hurry—we were frightened of the storm. Doesn't it look black?"

"It certainly does," Mary Eliska admitted. "But I guess I'll try it."

Madge seized the other girl's hand and pleaded with her to wait.

"It's certain death!" she said. "You'll never make it, Mary Eliska!"

"I thought maybe I could get above the clouds," replied the other. "And my autogiro's so safe, compared to ordinary planes."

"Nothing's safe in a storm like this," remarked Madge. "We're going to wait here for Ralph, and take a taxi to a hotel. We saw him in Milwaukee, and we agreed to do that if the storm came on—that all three of us would drop out of the race. We'd have to now, anyhow," she added, pointing to the wrecked plane.

"Well, so long, then," answered Mary Eliska, hurrying Amy into the autogiro.

They had scarcely left the ground when the rain came in torrents and the thunder and lightning grew sharper and sharper, until the terrific claps seemed to be breaking right about them, almost into their ears. With stoic courage Mary Eliska made for the heights. But she could not get out of the storm by climbing, so wisely she directed her plane as best she could away from its direction, going almost exactly west.

Though well protected with their slickers and helmets, the rain poured into the girls' faces, making it impossible for Mary Eliska to see anything. With the clouds and the rain all about her, the earth was entirely invisible, and she had to depend solely upon her instruments.

"We're getting away from it!" cried Amy, who had been pretty well frightened for a while. Indeed, they did seem to be making progress, for the thunder seemed a little more distant.

The pilot could not take time to bother with the speaking tube, so she made no reply. She was afraid that she would come upon another plane in this semi-darkness, and that there would ensue one of those crashes which her Aunt Sally so dreaded.

But it was over soon—they had evidently passed through it, and the skies were lighter, with blue patches appearing here and there. With a deep sigh of thankfulness, Mary Eliska dipped her autogiro lower, that they might study the landscape, for she felt sure that they were now off their course.

It was ten minutes later, and the sun was shining, when they came to a river, a broad, beautiful stream that seemed almost too wide to be the Fox River, as Mary Eliska had pictured it.

"I don't think this is it!" she shouted to Amy. "But look for a gray stone house with a tower."

"There are too many houses," replied Amy. "The one we want is supposed to be all alone."

Mary Eliska flew still lower, along the bank of the river. Suddenly Amy spied a tower.

"That must be it!" cried Mary Eliska, in excited joy. "And there's a good big field—" Abruptly all her delight died. For there were already three planes standing in that field! She must have lost the treasure hunt!

"We're too late!" she wailed.

"Don't land!" shouted Amy, with intense excitement. "There isn't any barn around here. Besides, I know—I'm sure—this isn't the Fox River! It's the Wisconsin."

"Then those pilots are wrong?"

"They must be."

"Amy, are you sure?"

"Yes, positive. Go on, Mary Eliska! We'll beat 'em yet. Fly north! This is somehow familiar ground to me!"

Chapter 17.10
The Treasure

Mary Eliska directed her plane upward and consulted her map. If Amy was right, and this was the Wisconsin River, there was still a chance of getting that prize. If the girl was wrong, it would be too late anyhow, for one of those three pilots would certainly have found the treasure by this time. In which case it would be better for Mary Eliska to fly directly to Lake Winnebago.

Assuming that Amy was right, and this was the Wisconsin and not the Fox River, she turned her plane to the northeast. Unfortunately, however, this act headed her right back into the storm.

Fresh clouds seemed to be gathering everywhere; it was impossible to climb above them, or to pass through them. The wind was blowing fiercely, sending the rotor blades about at a terrific speed. The autogiro seemed to sway; she felt herself suddenly in the grip of a whirlwind. Amy, frightened at last, held on to the sides of the cockpit with a deadly grip. Neither girl wore a safety belt; it seemed any moment as if they would both be dashed over the sides of the plane.

"Be ready to jump, Amy, if I give a signal!" Mary Eliska shouted through the speaking tube to her companion. Her face was white and her lips tense with fear; the autogiro was out of her control entirely. She could only wait, and trust grimly to the rotors.

Had it been any other plane than an autogiro, Mary Eliska realized that it would long ago have been hurled mercilessly through space, probably upside down. But the little "Ladybug" was gallantly battling the winds, and Mary Eliska prayed fervently that she might get it under control.

Again it rocked violently, and with a shiver of agony, she turned to the tube to tell Amy to step off. Perhaps, she thought, she could stay with it herself a little longer. Just as she was about to speak, the autogiro righted itself again and the rain began to fall in torrents, wetting them thoroughly, but dispelling the worst of the cloud. A moment later the joy stick responded to Mary Eliska's touch; the plane made headway out of the grip of the wind. The young aviatrix breathed a prayer of thanksgiving.

They continued to fly onward amid the driving rain for some distance until the storm was spent at last, and Mary Eliska came low to take a look at the landscape. It was Amy who first spotted the river.

"There it is, Mary Eliska!" she cried joyously, as one who sees a familiar sight after a long sojourn in a foreign country. "The Fox River! I know it! I'm positive of it! Keep right on— past Lake—Lake—I forget the name."

"Lake Waupin?" shouted Mary Eliska, consulting her map.

"Yes! Yes! How did you know?"

"By my map. How did you?"

"It's where I lived. I'm sure."

"Of course!" cried Mary Eliska. "This is somewhere near the spot where you met with your accident. I remember Jax Gray and I flew over Lake Waupin, though we didn't know its name then. But where is there any house around here? It looks so desolate."

"Keep on going—follow the river. I'll watch for a tower."

Mary Eliska's excitement was intense; even if she didn't succeed in finding the treasure, she must be on the way to clearing up the mystery of Amy's past life. She pressed forward eagerly, watching the river, and looking for signs of a house.

A few miles farther on Amy spotted it, and almost rose in her seat.

"There it is, Mary Eliska!" she called. "And it's sort of familiar to me. Oh, can it be my home?"

"It seems reasonable," replied Mary Eliska, although it certainly did not fit in with Mrs. Fishberry's theory that Amy lived in Montana.

Just as Mr. Clavering had said, there was a field beyond, large enough for any kind of plane to land. Mary Eliska, however, did not bother with this; she selected a small spot behind the barn and brought the "Ladybug" to earth.

Wild with excitement the two girls jumped out and ran hand in hand to the barn. The big doors stood partially open; the place was empty and deserted. Amy peered inside.

Almost immediately Mary Eliska spotted the treasure. A soap box conspicuously painted red was reposing in the corner of the barn, where it could easily be seen at a glance. With a scream of delight she darted forward and made a motion to drag it out to the light to examine its contents. But it was no effort at all; the box was evidently empty.

"Don't you s'pose there's anything in it?" she gasped, as she set it down at the door, and began to pull out the newspaper packing. "Or is the box itself supposed to be the prize?"

Amy laughed.

"I don't know what you could use it for, except as an ash box," she replied. "It wouldn't make a very good parlor ornament."

Mary Eliska continued to pull out the papers, thrusting them aside in haste, until at last her hands touched a candy box. But as she lifted that out, she realized that it, too, was empty!

She held it over to Amy, and the girl's eyes grew angry, as she took hold of the box.

"If it's a trick—after all we went through—" she began.

"Well, we'll have to be good sports," replied Mary Eliska, taking the box back and untying the red ribbon. "But before I open it, Amy, I want to say that if there is anything valuable in it, it's to be half yours. I'd never have found it if it hadn't been for you."

"That's sweet of you, Mary Eliska dear," replied the younger girl. "And I'll agree—provided it's something that can be divided. But if it should be a watch or a bracelet, or something like that, you have to consent to keep it."

"O.K.," answered Mary Eliska, and the girls clasped hands solemnly on the agreement; then laughed at themselves for taking so seriously what might prove to be only a joke.

Mary Eliska opened it at last, and found an envelope inside addressed to "The Winner of the Treasure Hunt."

She guessed now what the prize must be: money, of course! That would be something which either a man or a girl could use, no matter which one won it. But she was not prepared for the amount which greeted her, as she slit the envelope, and drew out the long green paper inside. A check of one thousand dollars, payable to the winner of the hunt, with a space left for the proper name to be filled in, and with the signature of R. W. Clavering at the bottom!

"What is it?" inquired Amy gazing at the odd piece of paper, without any understanding. "Does it mean you will get a thousand dollars?"

"It is a thousand dollars!" replied Mary Eliska. "Surely, Amy, you have seen checks before?"

The girl solemnly shook her head.

"Never," she asserted.

"Well, it's all right! And you have to take five hundred!" cried Mary Eliska, in delight. "That will pay your way at a business college, Amy—so that you never have to go back to that horrid Mrs. Fishberry! Oh, isn't it just too good to be true!" She gave the girl a joyous hug. "Now let's start back, Amy."

Her companion hesitated.

"I'd love to see that house," she said. "It—it is somehow familiar to me."

Mary Eliska consulted her watch.

"We might as well," she agreed. "It's early. And we can easily make Lake Winnebago in an hour. All right, come on."

"But suppose somebody lives there——"

"Then we'll just make up an excuse and go away. Or—Amy—suppose it were your real family!"

"Oh, Mary Eliska, suppose!" The tears came to Amy's eyes, and she added, wistfully, "Isn't it strange that I can't remember a thing about Mrs. Fishberry, or anybody else?"

"You will soon," Mary Eliska insisted optimistically. "Things are coming back gradually. Come on, let's knock at the back door."

Hand in hand, the girls ran across the field of tall grass and weeds which separated the house from the barn and came to the kitchen, which was built out from the house as a separate wing, two stories in height. But the door was closed and barred, and all the windows apparently were locked up. There seemed to be little doubt that the place was deserted.

"Do you remember it, Amy?" asked Mary Eliska, anxiously.

"Yes—but only like something that happened in a dream," she replied. "It seems to me that I ran barefoot through the fields—and—and—I can sort of remember drowning in the Fox River, and nobody helping me— Yes, it must have been here."

"Let's go around front," suggested Mary Eliska, watching Amy's face all the while.

"Yes, let's. It's an ugly house, isn't it, Mary Eliska? So big and gloomy—and—ugh!" A shiver ran through the girl's body, and she clung to Mary Eliska wretchedly. Another memory flashed into her brain.

"Mary Eliska," she sobbed, "there's a ghost in that tower."

Mary Eliska stepped back and looked up at the roof of the house. As Mr. Clavering had said, there was a tower by which the pilots could identify the house. It rose straight from the flat mansard roof, about two stories in height. It was square, with a small window on each side, but from the ground where the girls stood, it was impossible to see within.

"How do you know?" asked Mary Eliska.

"I know it because I could see it at night from my bed-room window. I slept over the kitchen, in that wing, and I could see the tower. Oh, Mary Eliska, I'm afraid! We're here all alone!"

"Don't, don't, dear!" pleaded Mary Eliska. "But we'll go back to the autogiro unless you want to go around front. There can't be anybody at home now——"

She stopped suddenly, for she heard a queer noise inside, as if someone were moving about.

"Do you hear that?" whispered Amy, as if she were afraid to speak aloud.

"Yes. Let's go see if we can get in!"

Amy held back, but Mary Eliska went over to the nearest window and peered in. She saw only a dreary room, with dark, ugly furniture—a room which looked as if no one had recently lived in it.

"That wasn't anybody real, Mary Eliska," protested Amy. "It was the ghost. It often made queer noises at night. Oh, please let's get away before anything happens!"

"All right. But I would love to investigate. I'm going to make Jax Gray come over with me on Monday, if we have to climb in a window. I don't believe in ghosts, Amy!"

"Oh, you mustn't do that, Mary Eliska! The house is evil—I know now that I'm lucky never to have to go back to it. I don't ever want to see it again!"

Anxious to get the girl away from her morbid thoughts, Mary Eliska challenged her to a race back to the autogiro, and they reached it together in a couple of minutes.

They climbed into the cockpits and Mary Eliska went through the usual motions of starting the engine. But, though the self-starter responded to her efforts, the motor refused to take hold. There would be a little spurt, then silence again. Patiently Mary Eliska tried over and over; each time the engine failed to respond.

With a greater sense of fear than Amy had experienced even in that terrific whirlwind, she clung desperately to the sides of the cockpit.

"Mary Eliska, what's the matter?" she gasped, hoarsely.

"Only a faulty spark plug, I think," responded the other, cheerfully. "I can easily fix it."

"No, no," said the other girl, with assurance. "I know what it is—it's that evil spirit—that ghost in the tower!"

"Now Amy, be sensible," returned Mary Eliska, lightly. But when she glanced at the girl's white, drawn face, she realized how intensely she was suffering, and a real fear took possession of her, too—a deadly fear that the child would lose her reason as well as her memory.

"Mary Eliska, you don't know! You can't know!" Amy leaned over and gripped her companion's hand. "If we stay here after dark, something dreadful will happen to us!"

"Well, we're not going to stay here that long," Mary Eliska assured her, with a great effort to keep her voice calm and natural. "Now jump out and help me."

As fast as she could, Mary Eliska went to work to locate and replace the missing spark plug, and all the while she tried to keep Amy occupied with little jobs to help her. But it was pitiful to watch the young girl's trembling hands, her white face, her shaking body. She was more of a hindrance than a help, yet Mary Eliska worked on as fast as she could, desperately hoping that nothing else would prove to be wrong.

The tests and the work took longer than any job Mary Eliska had done since she had taken her course at the ground school, and it was after six o'clock when the engine finally responded. Mary Eliska heaved a deep sigh of relief, as she turned to announce the good news to Amy.

But the girl was not listening; her eyes were fixed upon the figure of a woman hurrying towards them.

"Who is it?" demanded Mary Eliska, excitedly, hopefully. Oh, if this should only prove to be the girl's mother! "Do you recognize her?"

"Yes," replied Amy, stepping back and clutching Mary Eliska's arm. "It's the Fish!"

At the same moment Mary Eliska too identified the woman who had come to her house that week to claim the young girl as her niece.

Mrs. Fishberry advanced triumphantly.

"I'm glad to find you here, Helen," she said. "Though why you trust yourself with a person who almost killed you, is beyond me."

"What do you mean?" demanded the girl, angrily.

"You know what I mean. And I have a witness, Mary Eliska, to prove that you—and not a car—knocked Helen down— But never mind that now. I have a picture of you, Helen, and here is your baptism certificate, and your mother's Bible. Now will you come with me?"

"No! No!" cried the girl. "I don't ever want to see you again."

Mrs. Fishberry held out the Bible and the family album for Mary Eliska to examine. At the same time she grasped Amy firmly by the arm.

"Do I have to go?" implored the girl. "I'll die if I ever have to live in that house again."

Mrs. Fishberry's eyes narrowed.

"So you remember it, do you?" she demanded.

"Only faintly—it—seems to me that I did live there. Was there a ghost?"

"Of course not," replied Mrs. Fishberry. "You lived here with your old grandfather and when he died, maybe you imagined you saw his ghost— But come along. I'm taking you to Chicago with me. I promise you won't have to live there again."

Amy looked reassured.

"All right," she agreed. "I'll go. But please give Mary Eliska our address, so that she can write to me, and can send me my pretty clothes."

"Mary Eliska will hear from me soon," replied the woman with a knowing smile. "Just now I can't give any address, for we'll go to a hotel in Chicago. Now come. I have a taxi down the road."

Tearfully Amy kissed Mary Eliska good-by, as if she were her only real friend in the world, and the aviatrix returned to her autogiro. But she was despondent; all the joy of finding the treasure was lost in the grief of the parting with Amy.

She climbed into the cockpit and started her engine. As the "Ladybug" rose into the air, and reached the height of the tower, Mary Eliska remembered the ghost and could not restrain her impulse to circle back around the house, to take a glimpse for herself through the windows. Luckily there were no large trees close to the walls; she believed that she could pass the place on the side, and with the use of her field glasses, peer into the very window which had been visible to Amy if she had really slept in that wing over the kitchen, as she believed.

Turning the autogiro about, Mary Eliska dipped it to the proper height, and directed it back towards the tower. She decreased her speed to the lowest that she dared, and passed slowly by the tower, her glasses at her eyes.

The sight which Mary Eliska saw through the dusty window almost brought a scream of horror to her lips. It was unreal! Uncanny! Unbelievable! There, as clear as the tower itself, was a horrible dark figure, crouching against the pane of glass, with a face so thin that it seemed nothing but bones. Yet it was not a dead skeleton, for two evil, gleaming eyes stared vacantly at Mary Eliska. And, as the plane passed by, a deadly white hand was raised from the figure's dark cloak, and seemed to point with menace at the young pilot.

Dumb with horror, Mary Eliska continued to stare at the apparition, forgetful of the autogiro she was piloting. Then abruptly she realized that she was dropping to the ground, and with a jerk she pulled back the joy stick.

Wiping the cold beads of sweat from her forehead, she put on all possible speed, and made a record flight to Lake Winnebago. Yet the ghastly vision haunted her all the way to her destination; never in her life was she more thankful for a safe landing than when she finally brought the "Ladybug" to earth on the field near the Inn, where Mr. Clavering's party had already gathered.

Chapter 17.11
The Return of the Flyers

The older people who had gone by boat and taxicab to the Inn at Lake Winnebago arrived early on Saturday afternoon. What was their surprise to be met at the door by Joe Elliston and Sarah Wheeler!

"How did you get here so soon?" demanded Mr. Clavering in amazement. "And did you find the prize?"

The young man flushed.

"No, sir, we never even got started. One of my wheels dug into a sand bank at the take-off, and was slightly damaged. There didn't seem to be much use waiting to have it fixed, while the others got all that start. So I went back and got my car, and Sarah and I drove."

Mary Eliska nodded approvingly.

"You certainly showed good sense, Joe," she remarked. "I have been terribly nervous and worried all afternoon, on account of that frightful storm."

"Oh, you can be sure that Mary Eliska is equal to any kind of weather," put in Sarah, reassuringly. "If there's one aviatrix in the world who knows what she's doing, it's your niece!"

"I hope so," commented the older woman. "But it isn't only Mary Eliska I'm worried about—it's everybody. I shan't have a happy minute until all seven planes arrive."

"Then you'll never have a happy moment, Mary Eliska," remarked Joe, teasingly. "Because our plane can't arrive!"

"Well then, six planes," corrected the other, smiling.

"It's possible," observed Mrs. Crowley, "that they may all have been forced down on account of that storm. So they may not get here 'til morning. I don't intend to worry until I hear bad news."

"That's the idea!" approved Mr. Clavering. "Now how about some iced drinks, and some sandwiches. What'll it be?"

The whole group, composed of half a dozen older people and the young couple, seated themselves on the beautiful porch overlooking the lake and sipped the cooling drinks with which the maids supplied them at Mr. Clavering's orders. They had scarcely finished when a taxicab drew up to the Inn and Ralph and the two Keens got out.

"What luck?" demanded everybody at once.

Madge Keen laughingly told the story.

"The only prize we got was a lot of bruises at Columbus, trying to make a landing in too great a hurry, to get out of the storm. Bert smashed the plane, Mr. Clavering."

"Don't worry about that," replied the latter, reassuringly. "The insurance will take care of any damage. Are you sure you're not hurt?"

"Positive."

"And you, Ralph?"

"I left my autogiro at the Columbus airport," replied the young man; "because I didn't want to risk the storm. I knew if I waited it would be too late, for the other four planes had already gone when I arrived."

"Then Mary Eliska and Jax Gray were both flying through that dreadful thunderstorm!" cried Mary Eliska, woefully.

"And Kit and Sue!" added Mr. Clavering.

The party separated to go to their respective rooms to unpack, and half an hour later the young people gathered at the lake in their bathing suits. The storm had completely passed and the sun was shining brightly. Several of the older people joined the group, but both Mr. Clavering and Mary Eliska preferred to wait at the Inn for news of the missing flyers.

It was still early, however—too early to worry about their arrival—and Mr. Clavering was rewarded about five o'clock by the sight of two planes flying one behind the other. Both passed over the Inn, and the passengers leaned out and waved. Although neither Mr. Clavering nor Mary Eliska could make out who they were, the latter knew that neither was Mary Eliska. She did not know much about airplanes, but at least she could identify an autogiro when she saw it.

Both planes landed some distance from the Inn, and Mr. Clavering decided to go after the flyers in his car.

"I was afraid there weren't going to be any planes here at all," he remarked to Mary Eliska as he left the porch. "It would have been humiliating to have all the pilots come over in cars."

"Humiliating, perhaps, but very sensible," returned the other. She watched the sky all the while he was gone and kept looking at her watch. Why, oh, why, must her precious child be the last to arrive?

Kit and Tom Hulbert, Sue Emery and Frank Lawlor returned with Mr. Clavering in a few minutes. They were all in high spirits, obviously unharmed by the storm, but they announced immediately that they had not found the treasure.

"Mary Eliska got it, of course," said Kit. "But she deserves it, and I'm glad."

Mary Eliska's face lighted up with joy, not because her niece had won the prize, but because she believed she was safe.

"You have seen Mary Eliska?" she asked, eagerly.

Kit shook her head.

"No, Mary Eliska, we haven't. Nobody has seen her since the storm. But we four got on the wrong track, and got lost, and Jax Gray y did the same thing. We all landed beside a river, where there was a house with the tower, but it wasn't the right house."

"Where is Dot?" inquired Mary Eliska.

"Coming. And you see that accounts for everybody except Mary Eliska, because Dad told me that the others have already arrived. So Mary Eliska must have the prize."

Mary Eliska groaned.

"I don't agree with you, Kitty dear," she said. "It's more likely that Mary Eliska has crashed during that storm, and is stranded—possibly hurt—in some lonely place."

"Now please don't worry, Mary Eliska," urged Kitty, sympathetically. "It's only six o'clock, and you know Mary Eliska is the best flyer of all. Besides, the 'Ladybug' is safer than an ordinary plane."

Mr. Clavering had given orders that the dinner be moved on to seven-thirty, in the hope that Mary Eliska might arrive in time. At exactly five minutes after the hour the "Ladybug" came roaring through the skies, and to the amusement of everyone, landed right on the front lawn of the Inn. Trying to smile gayly in spite of her encounter with Mrs. Fishberry and her vision of the strange ghost in the tower, Mary Eliska stepped out.

Everybody ran down the steps to greet her, and her aunt kissed her as if she had never expected to see her again.

"You're safe!" she cried, with intense relief.

"Get the treasure?" demanded Jax Gray, excitedly.

"Yes," replied Mary Eliska, smiling. "And it's wonderful, Mr. Clavering!" She dug into her pocket and displayed the thousand-dollar check to everyone's view.

"Whew!" exclaimed Jim Valier. "Congratulations, Mary Eliska! And can I go with you next time?"

At his joking words everybody all at once remembered Amy. "What has happened to the child?" demanded several of them at the same time.

Mary Eliska looked serious.

"She's all right," she hastened to inform them. "But the queerest thing happened. That house must have been her old home, and Mrs. Fishberry was there. She took her away with her."

Mr. Clavering nodded.

"That isn't so strange as you might think," he said. "When I picked out the spot to hide the treasure, I was flying over the country where Jax Gray y said the accident must have occurred. And I selected that house because the tower was so easily visible from the skies."

"And did you meet Mrs. Fishberry when you hid the treasure?" inquired Mary Eliska.

"No. The house was locked up and deserted. So I went to the barn. I thought if anyone should happen along to steal it, that a check like that wouldn't be of any use to them. I gave my bank a list of the people who might be entitled to cash it, with strict orders to refuse anyone else."

The banquet and the dance that followed were a huge success; even Mary Eliska had to admit that the treasure hunt had ended wonderfully, without a single real mishap. Moreover, there was no jealousy regarding Mary Eliska's triumph; they all thought that she deserved her good fortune and rejoiced with her. Strangely enough, she herself was the only member of the party who was not entirely happy. She was worried about Amy, and still haunted by the dreadful apparition which she had seen.

She could not bring herself to confide her experiences and her fears to her aunt, who was so timid about everything, but the following day, when the party had scattered for swimming and for golf, she sought Jax Gray y, and took her down to a bench beside the lake, where they could be alone.

She told the other girl of her mistrust of Mrs. Fishberry, and of her dread of what might happen to Amy, in the keeping of that woman. Then she concluded by describing the ghost in the tower.

Dot's eyes opened wide in amazement.

"It must be a fake, Mary Eliska," she said.

"It can't be," replied the other. "Because it *moved*. I saw the hands move, and I'm almost positive the eyes followed me!"

"No wonder the poor girl was so terrified. Remember that first night in the hospital?"

"Yes. The thing frightened me, I can assure you, Jax Gray. And yet I feel that I've got to get to the bottom of it all. It fascinates, too, but it terrifies me."

"What terrifies you, Mary Eliska?" asked a voice behind them.

"You do!" replied Mary Eliska, laughingly, as she turned about to see Mike O'Malley grinning at her.

"Well, I didn't mean to," he apologized. "But will you forgive me and tell me all about the hunt, and winning that marvelous prize?"

"Of course," agreed Mary Eliska, and she proceeded to relate the story, even including Mrs. Fishberry's reappearance.

"Did you get her address, when she took Amy away?" he asked.

"No, I tried, but Mrs. Fishberry wouldn't give it—said she hadn't a permanent one, only a hotel in Chicago."

"Shucks!" cried Mike, in dismay. "There's something queer about this business! That fish is crooked, if I know what I'm talking about. How about that home in Montana she talked about the first time? And why didn't she mention this place before, if she had a key, and could get in?— Mary Eliska, if you care for Amy, I think you'd better go after her— I'd—like to help you."

"Yes, I believe you're right, Mike," agreed Mary Eliska. "Only I don't know just what to do."

"Let's fly over to the place tomorrow," suggested Jax Gray. "We could go right from here, instead of going home to Green Falls first."

"It suits me," agreed Mary Eliska. It was just what she was wanting, yet dreading to do.

"May I trail along after you in my Ford?" asked Mike.

"Yes, indeed," replied Mary Eliska. "I'd love to have you. And will you bring some tools, so that we can force our way into that tower, if it is necessary? I suspect trouble there."

"You're really going to dare that?" demanded Jax Gray.

"Dare what?" demanded Mike.

Mary Eliska and Jax Gray exchanged whimsical glances. "You wait and see," said Mary Eliska. "If we get into that tower, I'll show you the strangest sight you ever laid your eyes on!"

"Then," asserted the boy, "we'll get in, if we have to scale the walls! I'm always out for strange stories for the *Star*."

"Well, you'll get one there," Mary Eliska promised, "if you help us get in."

Chapter 17.12
Trickery

When Mary Eliska left Amy with Mrs. Fishberry at the old house, the latter slowly led the way towards the road. But as soon as the autogiro vanished from sight she stood still, and gazed straight at the girl.

"You still don't remember me, Helen?" she asked.

The girl shook her head.

"No, I don't, Mrs. Fishberry."

"Call me Aunt Elsie, please— But you claim to remember the house?"

"Yes—sort of. But you said I lived in Montana," she replied, in confusion.

"You lived here with your grandfather for a while," Mrs. Fishberry explained, "after your father and mother died. They were killed in an automobile accident when you were a baby—" So far this was the truth. But what the woman went on to add was a lie which she told at Ed Tower's request.—"After your grandfather died, I took you to Montana to live with me. Your uncle Ed is your only living relative. He and your father were brothers."

"And their name was Tower?" asked Helen.

"Yes. I think that's why your grandfather built that high tower on his house—because of his name. The idea pleased him."

"But if my uncle Ed is my only living relative, what are you? I thought you said you were my aunt!"

"I'm not really your aunt yet—but I will be on Monday, for I'm going to marry your uncle Ed," admitted Mrs. Fishberry. "No, I am a widow now—an old friend of the family. But I offered to bring you up when your grandfather died, and you have always called me 'Aunt Elsie.' Your uncle was traveling so much on business that he couldn't take care of you."

Mrs. Fishberry smiled to herself with satisfaction as she told this story. Not a bad story, she thought, for one that had to be made up so quickly. And the girl actually seemed to believe it!

Both were silent for a moment, while another idea leaped into the woman's mind. Why not leave the girl here, locked in this empty house, while she returned to Chicago? They could get her again on Monday, when Ed came over to set fire to the place. Surely there must be food in the kitchen. But she mustn't let Helen suspect that she was going to be left alone!

"I don't see the car," she remarked, casually. "The driver must have gone away. I told him if I didn't come back in half an hour that he needn't wait— We'll spend the night here, dear, and your uncle will drive over for us tomorrow."

The girl stared at the speaker in horror. She simply couldn't spend another night in this awful house! All too vividly she remembered the ghost in the tower.

"We can't, Aunt Elsie!" she protested. "It's too—awful!" Her voice had sunk to a hoarse whisper.

"What's too awful?" asked Mrs. Fishberry, lightly.

"That house. The ghost in the tower." "What ghost?"

"There is a terrible ghost in that tower at night. I can see it from my old bed-room window. His—hands—move!"

"Now dear, you're being silly," reproved the woman. "How can you remember anything like that, that happened so long ago! It must have been some foolish dream you had when you were not much more than a baby."

"But I can even picture it now!" she persisted.

"Oh, come on," urged the other, grasping her by the arm. "You're too old for such ridiculous fancies now. Besides, I'm right here. Nothing can harm you." She almost dragged her back by force to the house.

"I—I—know I'll die, Aunt Elsie," sobbed Helen, her voice shaking with fear. "Or go crazy."

Mrs. Fishberry drew down the corners of her mouth.

"I think that you're crazy now," she remarked, with biting scorn.

The girl started to cry piteously. She was weak and helpless; now that Mary Eliska and her dear Aunt Sally had been taken from her, there was no one in the world to protect her. For she had no faith in this strange uncle, who apparently cared as little for her as did this harsh woman.

"I want Mary Eliska!" she cried. "Oh, Mary Eliska, why did you leave me?"

"You little fool!" exclaimed Mrs. Fishberry in exasperation. "You're acting like an idiot. That girl was no friend to you."

"She was the best friend I ever had!" cried Helen, vehemently.

"Oh, yeah?" snarled her companion. She was so irritated that she gave up her pretense of being the kind aunt. "And you were too dumb to see through those scheming Carltons!"

"What do you mean?" demanded Helen, up in arms at the slur to her new friends.

"They were trying to pull the wool over your eyes, of course! So that you wouldn't remember anything."

"What do you mean by 'pull the wool over my eyes?'"

"It's just an expression, Miss Dumb-bell. I see that I have to explain everything to you, as if you were a child six years old. I'll have to tell you in words of one syllable:

"Mary Eliska was doing stunts with that plane of hers near to the ground. Somebody, never mind who, but somebody we know, saw her. And she crashed and *hit you!* There wasn't any car driving along the road at all. So she made up the story and got her friend to swear that it was true!"

Helen's dark eyes were blazing with righteous anger.

"Don't you dare to say Mary Eliska would lie!" she exclaimed. "She's the soul of honor, and so is Jax Gray y!"

"You don't say so," observed Mrs. Fishberry, sarcastically. "Well, I happen to know she did lie, and we've got proof of it. Why do you suppose she and her aunt were so nice to you? Because they thought you were beautiful, or interesting, or rich?"

"No, I guess not," admitted Helen, choking over the words. "I guess I was a sight in those dreadful clothes—" She turned to her companion accusingly. "If you took care of me, why didn't you dress me better?"

"Because we're poor. I had to sacrifice everything to provide food for you."

"But your clothes are pretty nice," observed the girl, shrewdly.

"Well, what of it?" snapped the other. "You haven't answered my question yet. Why did the Carltons make so much of you, if it wasn't to stop your mouth? They thought that if they entertained you for a week in their house, afterwards, if your memory came back, you wouldn't sue them."

"What do you mean by 'sue them?'" asked Helen, with that amazing ignorance that she showed every once in a while regarding ordinary words. "There was a girl in Mary Eliska's crowd named Sue Emery——"

"You get dumber by the minute!" returned Mrs. Fishberry. "We're going to make Miss Mary Eliska pay fifty thousand dollars damages because she smashed into you with her plane. Now, do you get that?"

"You wouldn't!" cried Helen, in horror. "You just couldn't!"

"Sure we could. The law is on our side." The woman's manner suddenly changed, and she remembered to play the part of the fond aunt. "Now don't you worry, Helen," she added. "It's for you we're doing it. We'll spend the money on you. First, for a good doctor—a specialist to restore your memory—and then for education and pretty clothes. You'll be a fine lady someday, if you don't act silly about Mary Eliska."

"But I love her, and I don't believe anything against her."

"You love her more than you do me, because she took care of you for a week, while I gave the best years of my life to you!"

"I'm sorry, Aunt Elsie, but you can't expect me to be grateful for something I can't remember."

While they had been talking they had reached the front door of the house and stopped at the steps of the porch. The wooden boards had rotted and the heavy door was sadly in need of paint. Everything about the place suggested neglect, ruin, and decay.

Helen shuddered.

"Let's not stay here!" she begged. "I'd rather walk all the way to town than sleep in this haunted house overnight."

"Nonsense," replied the other. "I'm tired and hungry. Come on in."

She pulled the girl up the steps, and, selecting a large key from her hand bag, inserted it into the lock and turned the knob. The heavy door creaked and opened.

Inside, the house was gloomy and forbidding. All the old-fashioned shutters were closed so that the appearance within was almost of night. Helen stopped at the doorway and shivered with fear.

"Come along back to the kitchen and we'll see if we can find something to eat," said Mrs. Fishberry in a cheerful tone.

"I don't want to!" objected Helen.

"Don't be a coward!" returned the other. "I'm ashamed of you!"

Plucking up her courage the girl led the way through the large dim hall, with its great dark staircase in the center, to the wing where the kitchen had been built. The door of this room was locked on the outside with another huge key.

"Here we are!" exclaimed Mrs. Fishberry, as she opened the door. "Now can't we get some light into this room?"

She walked over to the windows and tried to raise them. But they were evidently nailed and barred on the outside.

"I wonder whether there is any food," she remarked. "And what kind of stove this is."

"It's an oil stove," answered Helen, in a flash. "And there's a supply of oil under that table. And here's where the food is kept," she added, pointing to a large cupboard.

Mrs. Fishberry eyed her narrowly.

"You remember pretty well, Helen," she said.

"Yes, I do. Look, here's tea and sugar and oatmeal. Well, we won't starve."

"That's good. Now can you remember where to get the water?"

"Yes, there's a pump out back. But this door won't open. It must be barred up—yes, I remember it was when Mary Eliska and I looked at it."

"That's all right. You go out the front door with these two buckets and bring in some water. I'll be looking about for a place to sleep."

While the girl was gone, Mrs. Fishberry made an inspection. A small, winding staircase led from the kitchen to a room above, a bedroom, and in this she decided that Helen could sleep. It would be a simple matter to slip out of the kitchen and lock the girl in, leaving her here until Monday morning. With food and water at hand, no court could hold Mrs. Fishberry responsible if anything happened. And what was the use of taking her to Chicago and paying unnecessary board for her in the meanwhile?

It was all accomplished without the slightest difficulty. When Helen returned, Mrs. Fishberry waited only long enough to light the oil stove and to put some oatmeal on to cook. Then she asked the girl to run up the staircase and see whether she had dropped her handkerchief when she was up in the bedroom. By the time Helen had returned the kitchen door to the hall was locked and Mrs. Fishberry was turning the key in the outer door of the house.

Five minutes later she stepped into her taxicab and bade the driver return to the railroad station.

Chapter 17.13
The Haunted House

When Helen came down the crooked staircase from the bedroom into the kitchen, she did not perceive at once that she was alone. Though not so dark as the rest of the house—for there were no shutters at the kitchen windows—this room was far from bright. Two small windows afforded the only means of admitting the light, and each of these had several boards nailed across the outside.

"Aunt Elsie, where are you?" she called, trying to keep her voice calm.

There was no answer.

"Aunt Elsie!" she cried, in a louder tone, as she rushed over to the door. To her horror she found it locked.

Darting to the nearest window, she peered outside. But as there was no view of the front from the kitchen, she did not see her.

In a panic she started to scream.

"Mrs. Fishberry! Aunt Elsie! Where are you?"

Wildly she looked about the dimly-lighted room, as if in some corner she expected to see the ghost of the tower, working its evil upon them, because they had dared to return to this old house.

But she saw nothing, and overcome with terror, she sank to the floor in a bitter abandon of weeping.

The room grew darker; the silence became ominous. Any moment she expected that weird apparition with its skinny hands to enter through the closed windows, and torture her. Now and again she heard queer moans and creaks, but whether they were caused by the wind in the trees outside, or mice in the ancient boards, she did not know.

She must have fallen asleep, crouched in that position on the floor, for when she regained consciousness it was entirely dark in the kitchen. Hardly realizing where she was, she stumbled to her feet and went right to the drawer in the cupboard where the candles were kept. She lighted one, and shivered anew at the weird, gloomy shadows it cast upon the walls. If the house seemed forbidding before, it was actually ghostly now. Strange shapes seemed to rise out of the darkness, to leer at her in her loneliness. She groped her way to the stove and sat down upon the hard kitchen chair beside it to think.

It was the thought of Mary Eliska that kept her from losing her reason. Mary Eliska, who had flown over the Atlantic Ocean alone in the darkness, Mary Eliska who had assured Helen that her fears were groundless. She must live through this experience, she told herself, live to be a credit to the girl who had saved her life! Live to stand up for Mary Eliska when she should be accused by false witnesses! With a grim determination to control herself at any cost, she walked back to the cupboard for a saucer and a spoon, and forced herself to eat the oatmeal which had all the while been cooking on the oil stove.

The food revived her, and the water tasted good. Somehow she felt better.

Remembering that her bedroom was lighter than the kitchen, because she could open the shutters, Helen took a candle and ascended the stairs. But here a new terror took possession of her. She recalled the fact that she could see the ghost in the tower from the window!

Trembling at the very thought, she placed her candle on the old-fashioned wash stand and sat down on the big wooden bed to try to get command of herself. What would Mary Eliska do in a case like this, she steadfastly asked herself?

"Forget it, of course," she replied aloud in a natural tone, and the sound of her own voice, without even a tremble, gave her courage.

"I won't even open that shutter," she decided, "and then I shan't have to see it!"

With this resolve, she set herself to the task of opening the other window and of making her preparations for bed. How familiar it all was! She remembered even the contents of the bureau drawers: an old doll which she had kept since her childhood, some other toys, and a few clothes. Very few indeed, for she must have been exceedingly poor.

As she wandered about the old-fashioned room, so different from the bedrooms of Mary Eliska's friends, her eyes lighted upon the book case. Filled with strange volumes of adventure, which must have belonged to her grandfather. And then, on a bedside table, she came upon her own little Bible.

As she opened this worn black book, a picture fell out. An old-fashioned picture of an old woman—a kindly person, with a sweet smile. Helen's heart beat fast; she seized the picture with trembling fingers. Memories flooded back to her in wild confusion, but at the center of them all was this dear woman—her old nurse—Mrs. Smalley!

"Oh, darling Nana!" she cried, ecstatically kissing the photograph, and calling the woman by the old familiar name. "Nana, you have brought back my memory to me!"

But a start of dismay followed closely upon her joy. Where was Nana now?

"Why, she's out looking for me, of course!" she answered herself. "And she is so poor that she probably had to walk all the way to the city, and never even saw a newspaper until she got there! Oh, my poor dear Nana! She can't walk fast! Those wretched feet of hers! And her deafness, and her failing eyesight!"

The thought of the beloved nurse's plight took Helen's worries away from herself entirely. She forgot how lonely, how fearful, how forsaken she was. If only she could get out of this house, and hunt the dear soul! Do something for Nana, who would gladly lay down her life for her child!

But escape was impossible now; she must wait until tomorrow when Mrs. Fishberry had promised that her uncle would return.

"My uncle?" thought Helen, trying vainly to remember such a man. Surely he had not lived here, for she could recall her life perfectly with Mrs. Smalley. They had lived alone after the death of her old grandfather, whom she could still vaguely recall. They had slept together in this bed, and cooked on that little oil stove, and tended a garden on the side of the house. Oh, there had been precious little money—she remembered how her nurse had sometimes sold books and pieces of furniture, and how she had often sent her to the post office to see whether there was a letter. Probably it was there she was walking on the day of that accident. But what letter could she have expected? From whom? From her uncle, of course! Who once in a while sent Mrs. Smalley a five-dollar bill.

But Helen could not remember what he was like. Perhaps he had visited them when she was a very small child, but she did not know what he looked like. And from what Mrs. Smalley had said, he was not a good man, or a kind one.

But who was Mrs. Fishberry? Try as she might, she could not recall ever having seen her before. And why did her uncle want her now, after neglecting her all these years? Oh, if she had only known all this when she was with Mary Eliska, she need not have gone away with that woman! And now she would be free to hunt for Mrs. Smalley! Mary Eliska would have been glad to help, would have flown all over the country, if need be, in her autogiro, to find her.

Helen sighed, but she did not despair. With the return of her memory a great weight was lifted from her heart. That ghost would not come into her room, she assured herself, with the shutters tightly closed, and the morning would bring freedom. Freedom to find Mrs. Smalley, to share with her that wonderful prize of five hundred dollars which Mary Eliska had so generously insisted that she take.

So she read her Bible for a while, as her nurse had trained her to do every evening before she went to bed, and at last, tired out by her exciting day in the skies, she fell fast asleep.

When she awoke, without even once experiencing any bad dream, she was in high spirits. How good it was to see the sunshine pouring in through the one open window and to hear the birds singing in the trees. Surely today her uncle would come for her.

She dressed and cooked herself some oatmeal and made tea for her breakfast. A search in the cupboard rewarded her with the discovery of some dried beans and a few home-made cookies. Made for her, of course, by dear Mrs. Smalley—in the hope that her child would return! How unhappy the good woman must have been when day after day brought only disappointment!

All day long Helen watched at her bed-room window for some signs of arrival; all day long she listened for the sound of a motor car. But hour after hour passed quietly, until the sun began to sink in the sky, and she at last gave up hope of being rescued.

With the horror of approaching night a new fear took possession of her. Suppose they never came at all! Suppose Mrs. Fishberry meant to abandon her entirely in this gruesome house, until she starved to death, or lost her mind? How long could she hope to keep alive on those dried beans? And the limited supply of water! How dreadful it must be to die of thirst—far more horrible she believed, than of hunger.

But she must not give up so easily. There were knives in that kitchen cupboard; if she worked patiently enough she could cut the woodwork. By cutting the wood and breaking the glass she need not be a prisoner long.

But she would not begin that night, she hastily decided. Such an act of destruction might enrage that ghost in the tower, if it were the spirit of her grandfather, as she had always believed it to be. No, she would wait for daylight. How sorry she was that she had wasted this whole day!

It was more difficult for her to go to sleep that night than upon the previous one, for she was not tired. But she resolutely read her Bible and kept her thoughts upon Mary Eliska and Nana until her eyelids began to droop.

Then, with a contented sigh, she fell back on her pillow asleep.

Chapter 17.14
Two Surprises for Mary Eliska

Mike O'Malley, the young reporter who had volunteered his help in making an investigation of the empty house, departed immediately after his conversation with Mary Eliska and Jax Gray on Sunday morning at Lake Winnebago.

"I'll be over at the place tomorrow, late in the afternoon," he promised, as he put the map of directions into his pocket. "And I'll bring tools with me. Maybe I'll even commandeer a ladder from the nearest farmhouse, so we can climb in a window if it is necessary. Like regular robbers!"

"That's an idea!" approved Mary Eliska, thinking how useful such a thing might be in getting into the tower. "Make it a good high one!"

The two girls left their secluded spot and strolled back to the Inn to join the other guests. Here a surprise of an exceedingly unpleasant nature awaited Mary Eliska. Her Aunt Sally handed her a telegram which was far from being a message of congratulation upon winning the race, as the older woman suggested that it might be.

Opening it hastily, she read these threatening words:

"Miss Mary Eliska,

Green Falls, Mich.

"You are hereby informed that my client, Mrs. Edward Tower (formerly Mrs. Elsie Fishberry), of Chicago, will sue you for $50,000 damages for striking her niece, Helen Tower, with your autogiro. We have a witness.

Leo Epstein,

Attorney at Law."

Mary Eliska read the message through twice before she could really believe it. With a blank stare she handed it silently to her aunt.

"Why, that's absurd!" cried the older woman, unusually angry for her. "Fifty thousand dollars! Why, you haven't got that much money!"

"I know. But I suppose Mrs. Fishberry thought we were enormously rich. Mike O'Malley said there was something crooked about this woman, and I believe him. I bet this is the only reason she bothered to get Amy back."

"It's a frame-up, of course," said Mary Eliska. "The witness is someone who is being bribed to lie. And a dishonest lawyer, who is willing to take the case for what he can get out of it. You have a witness too, however, in Jax Gray."

"Yes, but the judge may say that since she's my friend that of course she would testify for me. Oh, Aunt Sally, what shall we do? Wire for Daddy to come to Green Falls?"

"I'm afraid we can't do that, my dear. I had a telegram from him yesterday just before we left home—I forgot to tell you in the excitement over the treasure hunt—informing me that he was sailing for Paris today. He is going to wander about France, in some of the smaller towns, partly on business and partly for pleasure. We simply can't wire him."

"Then what shall we do?" repeated Mary Eliska, desperately.

"I don't know. We'll have to think about it. Write to Mr. Irwin, I suppose. He is a wonderful lawyer, you know."

"Will you do that for me right away, Aunt Sally?"

"Yes, dear, if you'll promise to cheer up and forget it for the time being. After all you have done nothing wrong, and there is nothing to worry about— Now, will you go get ready for lunch? It ought to be announced any minute now."

Leaving the disagreeable telegram with her aunt, Mary Eliska went to her room to dress. When she returned, another surprise awaited her, which she did not know whether to regard as pleasant or not. She had tried to put the thought of Lord Dudley out of her mind, and here he was again—as fascinating and as handsome as ever.

He was standing in the corner of the reception room talking with Tom Hulbert and another man, a stranger to Mary Eliska, when the girl came down the stairs.

"Mary Eliska!" he exclaimed, with his charming smile, and in another moment he was shaking hands with her and introducing the stranger, John Kuhns, a friend of Tom Hulbert, to her.

"But how did you know about this party?" demanded Mary Eliska. "We all told you about the treasure hunt, but I didn't think you knew about the house-party here at the lake."

"Oh, Mr. Clavering invited me to join you all here, before I left Green Falls. But I've been very busy, in Chicago, and I couldn't get away last night. If it hadn't been for Mr. Kuhns, I shouldn't be here now."

At this moment Ralph Clavering and his father joined the little group, the younger man as usual looking annoyed at the reappearance of another admirer of Mary Eliska.

"I hope that you and Mr. Kuhns can arrange to stay until tomorrow, Lord Dudley," said the older man cordially. "The party isn't breaking up 'til the afternoon."

"That's awfully kind," replied the Englishman, "but I'm afraid I can't. I have some rather important business on for tomorrow. So Kuhns and I are flying back this afternoon." He turned to Mary Eliska. "In which case," he said, "since my time is so short, may I have a stroll with you after luncheon, Mary Eliska?"

Mary Eliska hesitated.

"We were all going to take our planes up this afternoon—" she began.

"That can be postponed until four o'clock," suggested Mr. Clavering, graciously. Ralph, however, frowned moodily, and walked away.

Mary Eliska herself was not so sure that she wanted a tête-à-tête with this man. It would be easier to forget him if she did not see much of him. But there was no real reason to refuse, so she met him again at half-past two on the porch.

"I certainly want to congratulate you, Mary Eliska," he said, as they strolled towards the lake. "And I hear that the prize is money."

"Yes," she replied, smiling. "A thousand dollars. But I am sharing it with Amy, because she really found the place."

"Amy?" he repeated. "That girl—your protégée?"

"Yes."

"And where is she now?" he asked casually. Mary Eliska wondered whether he were merely talking to keep the conversation impersonal. Well, he needn't worry about her; fascinating as he was, she didn't want to marry him!

"Her aunt took her away from me," she replied. "It seems that where the treasure was hidden, was really her old home."

"Indeed!" he remarked. "And you say you met her aunt? Then you found out who she was, and everything is all right?"

"Yes. Her real name is Helen Tower. The woman had pictures, and a key to the house. But she was a very disagreeable person."

"Too bad for the child," he muttered. "Did the girl know her?"

"No, she didn't. And she didn't want to go. But Mrs. Fishberry insisted. And now she is making things very unpleasant for me."

"How's that?"

"She claims that I smashed into Amy with my autogiro—that there wasn't any car at all. And she's going to sue me for fifty thousand dollars!"

"How can she?" demanded her companion, angrily. Then his eyes twinkled, and he asked suddenly, "Was there really a car, Mary Eliska?"

Mary Eliska's eyes blazed. Did this man actually think she would lie? Of course, he hadn't known her long, but she thought he knew her well enough for that.

"Of course, there was a car," she replied, haughtily. "A gray car, driven by an elderly man, at eighty miles an hour—or something like that. I have Jax Gray as a witness, but they say they have one, too, and I suppose I shall have to go to court."

"Always in the newspapers," he remarked, teasingly.

"Yes, and not only that, but I expect to take a job in the fall that may take me far away from Chicago. It's going to be awfully inconvenient, even if I don't have to pay any money."

They strolled along in silence for a little while, and Mary Eliska had a sudden desire to be back with her other friends. This Englishman was not so fascinating upon further acquaintance, and she longed for Jax Gray. If she had a chance to talk to her about the telegram, she would feel better. Jax Gray always had such wonderful suggestions.

Lord Dudley, however, had one to offer.

"Why don't you try to buy the woman off, Mary Eliska?" he asked.

"What for?" she demanded, angrily.

"Oh, say for about twenty-five thousand—maybe less, if she'd take it. It would save you a lot of time and worry, and maybe money in the end. You may be telling the truth, but how's a judge to know that, if the other people have a witness?"

Mary Eliska drew herself up proudly. She was actually beginning to dislike the man.

"I wouldn't think of it!" she exclaimed. "That would be the same as admitting that I was guilty. No, thank you—I'd rather fight."

Looking ahead of her, she suddenly spied Ralph sitting alone on a bench beside the lake. He was probably furious with her for going off with this stranger, and all of a sudden she saw his point of view. Who was Lord Dudley anyhow, to step in between them like this?

"I'll race you to that bench!" she challenged, abruptly. "Ralph looks lonely."

"I'm too old to run," he replied, smiling. "But you go along. I really must be getting back to the Inn. We're leaving soon—" He hesitated, and held out his hand. "It's good-by, now, Mary Eliska. I'm sailing for England early next week. I don't suppose I'll see you again 'til you come there on one of your flights."

"Good-by, Lord Dudley," she replied. "But don't expect me soon! I've been across the Atlantic you know, and next time I'll be flying the Pacific."

Chapter 17.15
The Ghost in the Tower

Mary Eliska spent Monday morning inspecting her autogiro and making some minor repairs in preparation for her flight back to Green Falls. She did not tell her aunt that she and Jax Gray were planning to stop at the empty house, for she did not want to worry the good woman. If everything went well, she ought to be home before supper.

Dot had persuaded Bert Keen to return the airplane which she had flown in the race, and she took the precaution of packing some sandwiches and some fruit in the autogiro. On an adventure like this, you never could tell what would happen.

"I hope that Mike O'Malley is there when we arrive," she remarked, as, early in the afternoon, she and Mary Eliska climbed into the "Ladybug."

"So do I," agreed Mary Eliska. "But I am not counting on him. I have my own tools, and—guess what?"

"What?" demanded her companion.

"I've been practicing picking locks! We won't need a ladder, after all! I'm quite good at it. I think I'd make a first-class burglar."

"That's some accomplishment!"

"It really is. And you never can tell when it will come in handy. If some child were locked in a burning house, or some old woman with heart disease had a spell in the bath tub———"

"Now, Mary Eliska!" protested her companion. "So you really think that you can get into that house?"

"Without a doubt. And it's going to be lots of fun."

"Yes—maybe. Suppose there really is a ghost in the tower, Mary Eliska! You know you do read of such things———"

In spite of her gayety, Mary Eliska shivered. The memory of that ghastly face at the window was still vivid to her.

"It won't be so bad if we go together," she replied. "And there must be some explanation of that queer apparition."

The day was beautiful and clear, and the sun shining; amidst all this loveliness the girls could not believe in ghosts. Dismissing the gruesome subject from their minds, they gave their attention to the country over which they were passing. Mary Eliska was flying low in the hope that she might identify the spot where the accident had occurred. She wanted to see how far it really was from the house which Helen Tower believed to have been her home.

It was Jax Gray who spied it first—the big oak in the field, where they had landed to offer help to the injured girl. A moment later they saw the road, winding as it did over the hill, from whence that gray car had so suddenly and so disastrously appeared.

Dot marked the spot on the map which she held in her lap and Mary Eliska flew on towards the house with the tower. About three miles beyond they caught a glimpse of it through the trees.

They flew across in front of the house, over a big field which had evidently once been a lawn, but which was now overgrown with weeds and tall grass, but Mary Eliska decided not to land there. It was too conspicuous a place to leave the "Ladybug," in case anyone came along. Instead she came down behind the barn as before, the girls walked around to the front of the house, by the side away from the kitchen. Mary Eliska carried her tool kit—"just like an ordinary robber," she remarked—and they climbed the wooden porch steps to the front door.

"Wait!" whispered Jax Gray, in awe. "I hear an awfully queer sound!"

Both girls stood motionless and listened. A dull, rasping noise reached their ears, which continued with monotonous regularity, now and then changing to a squeak.

"The ghost!" breathed Jax Gray.

"No," replied Mary Eliska. "It's some animal—or possibly a human being. We better knock on the door before I start to pick the lock. If Mrs. Fishberry is here, she'd jump at the chance to have us arrested."

Raising her hand, Jax Gray thumped loudly on the door. A reply instantly came to them.

"Mary Eliska! Oh, Mary Eliska!" a girl's voice screamed.

"It's Amy—I mean Helen!" exclaimed Mary Eliska, breathlessly. "Just what I was afraid of! That woman locked her in!"

"But what could be the point of torturing the child?" demanded Jax Gray.

"I don't know. That's for us to find out." She lifted her voice. "Amy!" she cried, at the top of her lungs.

"Here I am—around the back!" yelled the girl.

In excited haste Mary Eliska and Jax Gray ran down the steps and around the side of the house. There at the kitchen window, from whose panes the glass had been broken, stood the girl, patiently cutting away at the woodwork with a dull carving knife.

Both girls ran up and kissed her through the broken window.

"I heard the plane, and I was hoping it was you!" said Helen.

"Are you all right?" demanded Mary Eliska, almost afraid to ask. She dreaded to think what confinement in this ghastly house might have done to the nervous girl.

"I'm fine," replied the other. "Only I'm a prisoner. But I was going to work my way out."

"Are you alone?"

"Yes. Mrs. Fishberry locked me in and ran away on Saturday."

"Oh, you poor girl!" cried Mary Eliska. "And are you starved to death?"

"No. I had oatmeal and water and dried lima beans. Really, I'm all right. And Mary Eliska—I remember everything!"

"Honestly?"

"Yes. You can call me Helen now—that really is my right name. I'll tell you all about it when I get out of here."

"I'll get you out," replied Mary Eliska. "I'll pick the lock on the front door, and on your inside door."

"Can you really? Is there anything you can't do, Miss Mary Eliska?"

Mary Eliska laughed; it was wonderful to find the girl in such good spirits.

"You stay here, Jax Gray," she said, "and keep Amy—I mean Helen—company. I won't be long."

She was right in her surmise; the job did not take long, and she was extremely proud of her new accomplishment. In less than half an hour she opened the heavy door and stepped into the dimly-lighted house. The huge square hall, with its great staircase, the closed shutters, the sparsely furnished rooms cast a gloomy atmosphere. It was just the sort of house a ghost might be expected to haunt.

By means of her flashlight she made her way through the hall to the door where she supposed the kitchen to be. She knocked loudly, calling,

"Yo-ho, girls!"

"Yo, Mary Eliska!" was the reassuring reply.

But here it was not necessary to pick the lock, for Mrs. Fishberry had left the key in the door. So Mary Eliska merely turned it and walked into the room.

The two girls rushed at each other in joy, and Jax Gray bounded around the house to join in the happy reunion.

"First I'm going to get some fresh air and some fresh water," announced Helen. "Then let's go."

"Go?" repeated Mary Eliska. "Why, we just came."

Helen looked puzzled.

"But didn't you come for me?" she asked. "And now that you've set me free——"

"We weren't sure that you'd be here," explained Mary Eliska. "In fact, we didn't expect to find you—we thought you were with Mrs. Fishberry. We really came to explore."

"Explore?"

"Yes. The tower—the ghost you were so frightened of." Mary Eliska did not add that she had seen it herself.

"Oh, maybe that was my imagination," returned Helen, lightly. "I don't care about it now that everything has come back. All I want is to find my old nurse—Mrs. Smalley."

"Mrs. Smalley?" repeated Jax Gray. "You don't mean Mrs. Fishberry?"

"No, I don't. I'll tell you all about it, while we explore the house, if you insist on doing that."

So, as the girls walked about from room to room, examining everything, peeping into closets, inspecting Helen's bedroom, the girl told them the story of her life. They listened breathlessly, sharing with her the intense desire to find the dear old nurse who had been all the mother Helen had ever known.

Both Jax Gray and Mary Eliska agreed that it was necessary to set to work at once, but Mary Eliska was not willing to leave until she had visited that tower. Though Helen had been able to put the vision of the ghost out of her mind, Mary Eliska could not do it so easily. She had seen for herself—in daylight.

"We'll go as soon as we have a look at the tower," she agreed. "But I've just got to go up there, Helen. Please show us the way."

The girl shuddered.

"I'm afraid something may happen, Mary Eliska. I—I don't want to go."

"Well, just show us the staircase, and you can stay at the bottom of it and wait for us."

"But I'm as much afraid for you as I am for myself," she insisted.

"Nevertheless, I've got to go. It may have something to do with Mrs. Fishberry—it may help clear things up. By the way, Helen, do you remember her now?"

"No, I don't."

"Do you remember your uncle?"

"Only that there was one, and neither Mrs. Smalley nor my grandfather liked him. They both said he was wicked."

"He may be up in this tower, ready to spring at us with a gun," suggested Jax Gray. "That would be worse than a ghost."

Helen led the way to the third floor of the big old house, and thence to a room which was scarcely more than a closet, with a spiral staircase which ascended to the tower. Mary Eliska went up first, followed by Jax Gray, while Helen slowly mounted after them.

It was so dark that had it not been for the flashlight, Mary Eliska would never have noticed the door at the top. This opened inward, and she stepped into the tower room. But it, too, was pitch black—a fact which she could not explain when she recalled seeing at least two windows in the tower from the autogiro.

"What a horrible place!" exclaimed Jax Gray, as she too reached the top. "Such a musty smell! And dust!"

"Are you still alive?" came a faint voice from below, and a moment later Helen joined them.

"Better close that door," advised Mary Eliska. "We don't want to fall down the steps."

"Where are the windows?" demanded Jax Gray.

"Behind those curtains," cried Mary Eliska, making the discovery as she turned her flashlight upon a heavy drapery which hung over the wall.

"Let's pull them down and get some daylight," she suggested. Grasping them with both hands, she gave a tremendous pull, and the heavy curtains fell to the floor in a heap.

The sight which she disclosed made all three girls cry out in horror. The ghost which both Mary Eliska and Helen had seen was revealed to them now!

Helen hid her head on Dot's shoulder, but Mary Eliska was no longer afraid. Seen from behind, for the figure was facing the window, it was by no means so gruesome. A human skeleton had been draped with a black cloak, and the hollows in the bones of its face had been filled with some preparation like wax. When she examined it closely, Mary Eliska saw that the eyes were glass, probably covered with some phosphorous compound, to make them gleam. And the hands, which had especially confounded her on that previous occasion, were actually moving now. But there was a reason: a light string attached them to each other, and a small weight slid along the string, pulling first one hand down and then the other. It was clever and ingenious—and horrible.

But Mary Eliska could not help laughing at herself for being fooled so.

"It looks like a college boy's prank," she said, as Helen was finally induced to examine it for herself. "I suppose your father or your uncle did it in their youth—to frighten the other boys. And they must have forgotten all about it, and left it here."

"Maybe my uncle did it on purpose to frighten me," remarked Helen. "I think he had some reason for wanting Mrs. Smalley and me to move—perhaps so that he could get the house for himself."

"Possibly," admitted Mary Eliska.

"Well, let's pull the old thing down, anyway," suggested Jax Gray. "No use frightening the countryside. And hadn't we better take down the other curtains and see whether there are any more?"

Mary Eliska turned about and pulled at another drapery. This, however, disclosed only a bare window. A third showed a blank wall behind. Then she and Jax Gray proceeded to dismantle the ghost and to pile it into the corner. It was while they were doing this that a panel fell out of the wall.

"More mysteries!" exclaimed Jax Gray, excitedly. "Here's a hidden closet. Maybe we'll find some money!"

"Or a lost will," added Mary Eliska, jokingly, never thinking that she had guessed the very thing.

"How did you know, Mary Eliska?" demanded Jax Gray, picking up the yellowed packet. "That's exactly what it is! What was your grandfather's name, Helen?"

"Henry Adolph Tower," replied the girl. "I never knew that he left a will. Is it his?"

"Yes. Oh, come on over here, Mary Eliska—give me your flashlight. It's getting dark in here again. Let's read it!"

So busy had the girls been that they had hardly noticed the fading light until they tried to read the words on the written and printed pages. But they had not started from Lake Winnebago until three o'clock, and the flight had been a considerable distance.

Breathlessly, Jax Gray read out the formal, legal words of the will, picking her way slowly among the unfamiliar terms. But there could be no doubt about the contents. Henry Adolph Tower had left the house and grounds and the sum of one hundred thousand dollars in bonds and cash to his granddaughter Helen, and a bequest of five thousand dollars to Mrs. Smalley. A Trust Company in Chicago had these in keeping until the will should be probated.

Helen's eyes were gleaming and her cheeks were flaming. She simply could not believe her good fortune. Oh, if she could only tell dear old Nana about it, this very minute!

"Now aren't you glad we came up here?" demanded Jax Gray.

"I should say I am," she replied. "Oh, Mary Eliska—and Dot—you have done so much for me!"

"What's that queer smell?" asked Mary Eliska abruptly changing the subject.

"Something's burning," said Jax Gray.

"I wonder if I left any beans on cooking," remarked Helen. "I was so excited when I heard you girls come in that plane, that I don't remember whether I left the oil stove burning or not."

"Could the kitchen be on fire?" demanded Jax Gray, holding the will tightly in her hands. "Girls, we've got to get out of here!"

Taking the flashlight Mary Eliska led the way down the staircase and opened the door of the small room that led to the hall. An overpowering cloud of smoke rushed against her, stifling her so that she closed the door immediately again.

"Stay here!" she commanded to the others, who had just come down the spiral staircase. "Keep the door closed, while I see whether I can force my way through. The house is on fire!"

Closing the door again, she crept out on her hands and knees through the smoke-filled passageway. The atmosphere was dense with the smoke, so overpowering that Mary Eliska gasped helplessly for breath. But she pushed onward to the main staircase, only to see that great wooden structure already in flames.

With a cry of terror she crept back to the door of the room that led to the tower, and fell with a dull thud against it. Jax Gray rushed forward and opened the door, and knew from one look at her chum's face that escape through the house was impossible.

"Come back to the tower!" she cried, "where we can get some air through the windows!"

But Mary Eliska only leaned weakly against the steps. She could not answer.

"We'll have to carry her, Helen!" Jax Gray said. "Take hold of her feet. I'd rather jump from the tower if I have to die than be burned alive!"

Together the two girls managed to get Mary Eliska up the steps and once there they shattered the glass of the tower windows, for they could not raise them. The fresh air was reviving; Mary Eliska was able to stand up and lean out of the window while the others cried for help.

At that very moment, Mike O'Malley drove up to the house in his car, followed by a huge telephone repair truck!

Chapter 17.16
While the House Burned ...

When Mrs. Fishberry left Helen Tower locked in the empty house on Saturday evening, to take a train back to Chicago, she was exceedingly pleased with herself. Everything had turned out wonderfully, she believed, and she would soon be married to a rich man. When the law suit was over she would go abroad with Ed—or perhaps join him abroad, for he seemed to think it was necessary to get out of the country immediately. Well, perhaps he was a little bit crooked——

But Mrs. Fishberry did not believe him to be as wicked as he really was. She thought that perhaps Mary Eliska had hit Helen with her autogiro, and though there was no real witness to the accident except Jax Gray, Mrs. Fishberry did not consider it wrong to bribe someone to make up the testimony. After all, Mary Eliska must be rich; there was no reason why she shouldn't part with some of her money. The girl was always winning prizes—probably without much effort on her part, Mrs. Fishberry believed.

She was so late getting into Chicago that night that she waited until Sunday noon to call Ed. She was anxious to tell him of her success, not only in obtaining the pictures and the records about his niece, but of securing the girl herself under lock and key. Ed would rejoice at the news, for he had not expected her to accomplish this feat before Sunday.

To her dismay, however, a strange voice answered the telephone in Ed's apartment. When Mrs. Fishberry gave him her name, he explained that he was Leo Epstein, the lawyer whom Tower had employed to take charge of the damage suit against Mary Eliska.

"And I have sent a telegram to Mary Eliska, informing her of our intentions," he said.

"In my name?" demanded Mrs. Fishberry.

"Yes, of course."

"But I'm not married to Mr. Tower yet," she protested. "It won't be legal for me to sue Mary Eliska unless I'm the girl's real aunt."

"It'll be legal by the time the case comes up. Those things take a long time—unless Mary Eliska is willing to settle out of court. Maybe she will pay us twenty-five thousand dollars to keep us from suing her."

"She'll never do that!" asserted Mrs. Fishberry.

"Why do you say that?" asked the lawyer. "Mr. Tower seemed to think that there might be some chance of it."

"Because I know Mary Eliska. She isn't the sort of person to run away from trouble. And Mr. Tower doesn't know Mary Eliska, or he wouldn't think she would."

"Hm," remarked Mr. Epstein.

"Well, when will Mr. Tower be back?" the woman inquired impatiently. "I would like to be married before we get the girl."

"That isn't possible, Mrs. Fishberry," he said. "And it really doesn't make a bit of difference. Mr. Tower is out of town now and may not be back for several days. He left word for me to tell you to call him up at the Central Hotel in Milwaukee tomorrow morning, if you had anything to say to him that was important. I suppose if you wanted to see him, you could go there. That is the only message I have, Mrs. Fishberry."

"I see," replied the other, as she hung up the receiver. She was so angry at the way Ed Tower did things, the way he never seemed to consider what she wanted to do, that she thought of going home to Montana, and dropping her part in the affair. After all, was it worth it? What was she going to get out of it? And she certainly didn't want to have to look after Helen Tower for the rest of her life.

Ed was certainly a selfish man. Oh, he was attractive, and nice if he wanted to be, but wasn't he just using her now to help him get this money? How was she to be sure that he would ever share it with her if he did get it?

She would have dropped the whole thing then and there—for Mrs. Fishberry had never been a dishonest woman before—had it not been for the thought of poor Helen Tower locked alone in that empty house. Although she had no love for the girl, and believed her to be feeble-minded, she could not bear the thought of her being burned alive, as she might be if Ed went alone to the house without knowing that Helen was there. No; Mrs. Fishberry couldn't back out now. She'd have to take the sleeper to Milwaukee in time to be there in the morning, to go with Ed and rescue the girl.

A little after eight o'clock the following morning she arrived at the Central Hotel and was informed that Mr. Tower was at breakfast. She joined him, for she had eaten nothing on the train.

"Hello, there, Elsie!" he cried, cheerily, as she seated herself at the table with him. "Have you found my niece?"

"Yes," she replied, briefly.

"Where is she now?"

"Locked in the empty house."

"But we don't want her there!" he stormed. "Of all the fool places to leave her—" He stopped, remembering that he was in a public place, and refused to discuss the subject until they were both seated in his gray open roadster, speeding away from Milwaukee somewhat later in the day.

It was then that Mrs. Fishberry insisted upon an explanation of his disapproval of what she had done with Helen.

"I don't see why I should have been bothered with her over Sunday," she said resentfully, "when you were off having a good time!"

"Oh, is that so?" he retorted, in irritation. "Well, I told you to get hold of her—and keep her. Now if she sees me set fire to the house, how's that going to fix me with the police?"

"I never thought of that," admitted Mrs. Fishberry.

"That's the trouble with you! You never think! Well, we'll have to think of something now."

They drove along at a rapid rate after leaving the city, stopping only once to have an early dinner at a wayside inn. It was then that the man decided upon a plan.

"I think the best idea is for you to drive when we get in sight of the house, and I'll get out and hide somewhere while I put on a disguise. You take the key and go into the house and get the kid. But when you get outside again, you'll have to pretend that there's something the matter with the car, because I want it left for me. So you and the kid can walk to the station. I won't sneak up to the house 'til after you're well out of sight, so as Helen won't see it burning."

"That's all very well for you," objected the woman, "but not so good for me. You know it's at least five miles to the station!"

"Can't help that! It's your fault for not thinking what would happen if you left the kid in that house."

"Oh, all right," she agreed, sullenly. There seemed to be nothing else to do.

But this plan was naturally never carried out, for the simple reason that when Mrs. Fishberry arrived a little after seven o'clock, the girl was nowhere to be found. A hasty glance at the broken lock on the front door, the open kitchen door, and the smashed windows assured her that Helen had made her escape. It never occurred to her to suspect that the latter might be somewhere else in the house—or in the tower. She felt relieved that she was gone; she was tired of the whole affair.

She ran back to her companion with the news. He fairly snorted with anger.

"Balled everything up, didn't you?" he cried.

Mrs. Fishberry stood still and laughed. He was such a funny-looking object in that disguise—a gray wig and a false beard, and a long linen duster. Though the sun had set, it was not yet dark, and she could plainly see him, crouched under some bushes.

"You're a sight!" she sneered. "And I bet they catch you!"

"What's the matter with you, Elsie?" he demanded.

"Nothing—oh, nothing," she replied hastily, but already she had decided that she was through with Ed Tower.

The man came out of his hiding place and lifted a suitcase from the rear of his car. But he did not think to ask Elsie Fishberry for the key, and here he made a mistake which he was to regret bitterly later on.

He trudged along up the path to the house, afraid to hurry lest someone see him and suspect him. If he walked along like an ordinary old peddler, nobody would think anything about him.

But once inside the house, he did not loiter a minute. Opening up his suitcase, he took out great wads of cotton waste which had been previously soaked in oil. These he piled under the huge wooden staircase, and applied a match. As the rags burst into flames he hurriedly left the house, carefully closing the door behind him.

Before he had reached the road he could see the smoke pouring through the chimney of the fireplace, and out of the broken kitchen window. There was no doubt that he had succeeded in setting the house on fire, no doubt that it would burn to the ground. By tomorrow the news would have reached the papers. On Wednesday he ought to be able to go to the Trust Company in Chicago and collect that money which was his father's small fortune. For now at last the officials would be assured that Henry Adolph Tower's will could never be found.

He chuckled to himself with satisfaction as he reached the road and looked about for his car. But that chuckle abruptly changed to an oath as he failed to see it. It was gone! Elsie Fishberry had double-crossed him, and had run away!

For a few minutes he stood there in the road, hoping that she was only playing a practical joke upon him, and that she would suddenly drive into sight. But as the time passed he gave up hoping, and snatching off his wig and his beard, he flung them, with his linen coat, into the bushes, and started on his five-mile hike to the station.

Chapter 17.17
The Rescue

The very cause of Mike O'Malley's delay in arriving at the empty house on Monday evening proved to be the thing that saved the three girls in the tower. It was the huge ladder on the telephone repair truck.

When Mike left the girls on Sunday with his promise to help them, he drove straight back to Milwaukee to give the story of the treasure hunt to his newspaper. At the same time he asked for Monday afternoon off, in order to follow the "Mary Eliska Mystery," as he called the accident to Helen Tower. When this leave was granted he sat down in his boarding-house bedroom to contemplate what he had better take with him.

"There's something in that tower that mystifies Miss Mary Eliska," he said to himself. "And she seems to think it is closed off from the rest of the house. I wonder how we could get in."

He had all sorts of ideas—of going up in the autogiro and coming down in a parachute, of jumping from the "Ladybug" to the window—but, of course, these things wouldn't do, because most likely the windows would be closed and locked. No; a ladder was the only solution; but how could he carry a ladder on his little Ford?

It was one of his brothers who solved the problem for him. As he had told Mary Eliska on the occasion of his first visit to the bungalow at Green Falls, Mike O'Malley was one of a large family. Two of his brothers had left the farm for jobs in Milwaukee, and one of these was with the telephone company. Pat—for that was his name—would be the very person to help!

It was easily arranged, the only difficulty being that his brother could not leave until four o'clock. However, the boys planned to meet outside of the city, thereby avoiding the worst of the traffic, and they made good speed along the country road. A little before eight, supperless but happy, they drove up to the empty house.

"We're too late!" shouted Pat, leaning out of his truck. "She's on fire!"

Mike had been pretty sure of this fact several minutes earlier, when he had noticed some smoke in the sky, but he had said nothing. They must go on, he had decided, for Mary Eliska and Jax Gray might be trapped inside.

"We better get out of here," called Pat, above the noise of the two engines. "Don't forget we've got gas, and both our cars may explode."

"Pull over there in the field," directed Mike, briefly. "I've got to make sure that the girls are safe."

And then they heard the cries, the wild terrified screams of those three girls trapped in the tower of the burning house.

There wasn't a moment to be lost. Pat took down his extension ladder, and directed Mike how to help him get it up. They worked as fast as they could, but the task appeared to be endless to the tortured girls, watching them in breathless silence from the high windows. It seemed to them as if the ladder would never reach to their height.

"Wish I was a real fireman," was the only remark which Mike made during the whole tense proceeding.

The flames were reaching the roof of the house now, and smoke was streaming from the tower windows. Forcing his hands not to shake, Mike held the ladder while Pat pulled it to its full height. There was one terrible moment, while they all waited to see whether it would reach to the edge of the window— It did! The boys let out a cry of, "Ready now! Come down, girls!" and held tightly—and prayed.

Dot leaned out of the window to make sure that the ladder was firmly gripping the ledge, and to Mike's surprise, neither she nor Mary Eliska climbed out, but little Helen instead. Holding on to Dot's hand, the young girl stepped over, and made her perilous way down the ladder, to the ground.

There was a slight delay, while more smoke poured from the windows. Evidently Jax Gray and Mary Eliska were arguing about who should come next, but Jax Gray had to give in, for she knew it was of no use to try to withstand Mary Eliska. So she climbed over the ledge and started downward, only to see the window ledge itself catch fire when she was halfway down!

If Mary Eliska had been wearing a dress instead of knickers, there would have been little hope for her now. But as it was she managed to straddle the flame and to step on the ladder, just as it, too, caught fire at the top. It swayed for one dreadful second, but the boys held tightly, and pushed it farther against the wall. No one ever came down a ladder faster than Mary Eliska at that moment; it seemed as if her feet scarcely touched the rungs. When she was finally only six feet above the ground she jumped. It was none too soon; the ladder gave way, and the young people all ran to safety.

"Mike!" cried Mary Eliska joyously grasping his hands in an ecstasy of relief: "You're a wonder! How did you ever know to bring a ladder?"

The young man was too excited to talk. He couldn't say a word.

"We must get these cars out of the way," ordered Pat, who had not even been introduced. "Let's all meet down by the road."

"O.K.," agreed Mike, signaling to Helen to get into his Ford.

"My 'Ladybug!'" exclaimed Mary Eliska abruptly. She had all but forgotten it. Suppose it were burned!

"Want any help?" asked Mike, as Pat started to drive his truck down to the road.

"No, thanks. But take Jax Gray and Helen with you. I'll meet you there—I hope!"

Running as fast as she could, keeping her face turned from the intense heat of the fire, she passed the barn and saw that it too was beginning to burn. Oh, if the "Ladybug" were only safe! Next to their lives she valued her trusted autogiro. Insurance would mean little to her; it was this particular plane that she loved, almost as if it were a horse or a dog.

But, miraculously, it was all right, though she realized that she was just in time, for now that the barn was burning, a spark might fly any moment that would set it into flames. Never before had she been so quick in starting its engine. Thank goodness it was in perfect condition, after her work of the morning!

As soon as she had left the ground she circled down to the road, and saw the lights of the truck and the Ford, for it was almost dark now. Selecting a field opposite, she landed her autogiro again and ran across to join the group around the cars.

All the young people had by this time regained their spirits and were talking excitedly and happily, asking each other questions, hardly waiting for explanations, and all shouting at once. Though Pat O'Malley had been a stranger to the girls fifteen minutes before, he now seemed like one of their best friends.

"If we only had something to eat!" sighed Mike, "my joy would be complete."

"Didn't you boys have any supper?" demanded Jax Gray. It was quite dark now, it must be after eight o'clock, she thought.

"No. Did you?"

"No."

"Did you, Helen?" inquired Mike, who still had only a hazy idea how the young girl had happened to be there.

"No. And I only had dried lima beans for lunch."

"The nearest village is about five miles," volunteered Pat. "I've worked along this road before. Shall we all pile into my truck and hunt it?"

"I couldn't leave my autogiro—" began Mary Eliska, when Jax Gray interrupted with a suggestion. She had just remembered the food she had brought from the inn at Lake Winnebago.

"Wait!" she cried, joyfully. "I've got chicken sandwiches and peaches in the plane! Does that sound good?"

"Does it sound good!" repeated Mike. "Oh, boy!"

Mary Eliska and the two young men ran over to the field immediately, and returned in a few minutes, their arms piled with boxes and the thermos bottles of water which Mary Eliska always carried in the "Ladybug." Going over to the bank beside the road, they all sat down while Jax Gray untied the bundles.

"I'll have to count the sandwiches and divide them evenly," she said, laughingly. "Just as if we were all starving Armenians."

"I think Helen should get the most," suggested Mike. "She really has almost starved."

"Oh, this is great!" exclaimed Jax Gray, as she examined the boxes. "There are ten sandwiches—and six peaches—and—and——"

"And what?" demanded Pat, hungrily.

"And two apple pies!"

Both boys let out a whistle, and Helen clapped her hands.

"But how did you two girls ever expect to eat all that for your supper?" asked Pat.

Dot giggled.

"I told the cook to put in a lot," she replied, "because when Mary Eliska and I go off on trips we never know how long we'll be stranded."

"But there aren't any desert islands around here," remarked Mike, who had heard the story of the girls' adventures in the Okefenokee Swamp.

"No, but you never can tell," returned Jax Gray. "Now—fall to! Here are two sandwiches and a peach for each one of you, and Helen gets the extra peach."

They ate silently for several minutes, everybody too hungry to talk. Suddenly Helen stopped in the act of breaking her second peach in two, and cried in dismay,

"Dot! We forgot the will!"

"What will?" demanded Mike.

Mary Eliska explained briefly, while Jax Gray reached down into her blouse. Even in the darkness they could all see the yellowed packet which she triumphantly held up to their view.

"I wasn't going to let that get away!" she announced, proudly.

She handed it to Mike who, with the aid of his flashlight, examined it with the greatest satisfaction.

"That's bully, Helen!" he cried, when he had seen enough of it to make sure that it was legal. "And don't let the Fish get any of the money!"

"You're not planning to go back to her, are you?" asked Mary Eliska. She was thinking of the law suit, and wondering how Mrs. Fishberry could sue her if Helen denied ever having known her.

"I certainly am not!" replied the girl, emphatically.

Dot proceeded to cut the pies, which they ate perhaps less ravenously, but at least with as great enjoyment as the sandwiches, while they discussed what they would do next.

"I've got to get back to Milwaukee tonight," announced Pat, as he began to collect the sandwich papers into a pile.

"So do I," agreed Mike. "Anybody want to come with me?"

"No, thank you," replied Mary Eliska, rising from the ground. "I'll take both the girls back to Green Falls with me in the 'Ladybug.'"

"You aren't afraid to fly at night?" inquired Pat.

"Mercy no! The only thing I'm worried about is Aunt Sally. She expected us for supper."

"Perhaps she didn't get there herself," suggested Mike. "They had a motor trip and a boat trip both you know."

"But Mr. Clavering's cars and boats are always reliable," returned Mary Eliska. "Oh, well, so long as we arrive before midnight, I don't suppose that she'll be terribly worried."

"We'll wait here 'til we see you safely up in the air," concluded Mike. "Then Pat and I will be going."

"Wait a minute!" exclaimed his brother, who had just finished his task of picking up the papers. "Look what I've found over here in the bushes!"

To the amazement of everyone, he held up a gray wig and beard, and a linen coat to their view.

"What are they?" demanded Mary Eliska, as Pat turned the flashlight upon his discovery.

"Looks like a Hallowe'en suit," volunteered Mike. "But what is it doing here?"

"Helen," asked Jax Gray, turning to the young girl, "can you remember having any masquerade parties at your house?"

"We never had *any* parties," she replied. "We were too poor. On my birthdays Nana—I mean Mrs. Smalley—would make cookies, and she and I and my doll would play it was a party. That was all."

Mary Eliska was silent. There had been something familiar about the beard in particular, for it was bigger and longer than most real ones. Now she remembered what it reminded her of.

"Remember that old man who knocked Helen down, Dot?" she inquired.

A smile broke over Dot's face.

"Of course! A disguise! I never could understand why a man apparently so aged would be driving at that reckless rate of speed. He wasn't old at all, I guess!"

"By George, that's the answer!" cried Mike, positively elated by the discovery. "Now all we've got to do is to catch the man. Helen, have you any idea who he could be?"

"I'm afraid," answered the girl reluctantly, "that he's my uncle. And if he is, you won't catch him. He's wicked—and clever."

"Anyhow, we'll try," Mike assured her. "Shall I take charge of this stuff, while I see what can be done?"

Helen nodded, and he walked with the girls over the field to the "Ladybug," and stood watching Mary Eliska take off into the sky. Fascinated, he continued to gaze at the autogiro until its light was all that he could see—a little spark of flame in the heavens—and then he turned about and joined his brother across the road.

Chapter 17.18
In Quest of the Money

It was a strange and wonderful experience to Helen Tower to fly at night—for on that other occasion she had been only semi-conscious—and she was more thrilled than she had ever been in her life. No longer did the darkness frighten her; the immensity of the heavens, the brightness of the stars, the exhilaration of the swift motion through the air all held her entranced. She did not try to say a word to Jax Gray who was sitting so close to her; she only watched the sky with wide-open eyes.

It was cold, up there in the skies, in the night, but all the girls were dressed warmly, for even Helen wore the flyer's suit which she had put on Saturday morning for the treasure hunt. How many things had happened in the meanwhile; yet here she was riding back to Green Falls in the autogiro, just as she had expected to do!

The night was calm and pleasant, and Mary Eliska felt sure of her way. She made the journey in record time, crossing Lake Michigan, and arriving at the airport long before midnight. Before summoning a taxicab, she hastened to telephone to her aunt.

"Hello, Aunt Sally," she said. "I'm so sorry we had to be late——"

"Are you speaking from long distance, Mary Eliska?" asked the older woman, immediately. "Where are you? And are you all right—you and Jax Gray both?"

Mary Eliska laughed. It was exactly what Mary Eliska always asked, every time her niece took the autogiro up in the air.

"Of course we are!" she replied. "And we're right here at Green Falls airport."

"Oh, that's a relief, dear! I was so worried. Ralph is here with me, waiting for news. I'll send him right over in his car."

"That's fine, Aunt Sally. And by the way, we have Helen—Amy, you know—with us."

"That's good news! And tell her that I have some news to tell her, too. I hope that she will find it good this time—not like Mrs. Fishberry's surprise visit."

"What is it?"

"Better wait and see," replied Mary Eliska. "Ralph's leaving now—see you in ten minutes—good-by dear."

Mary Eliska turned to Jax Gray, who had just finished calling her mother.

"Ralph's coming for us," she told her. "So he can take you home first——"

Dot giggled.

"Jim's on the way, too," she explained to Mary Eliska. "Isn't it funny, though, the way our boyfriends go and sit with our families when we are out on our adventures?"

"They really didn't know what an adventure this was," said Mary Eliska. "How much shall we tell them?"

"Oh, everything, of course. It'll be all in the papers tomorrow—trust Mike O'Malley for that! But it can't worry our folks now, because it's all over."

Ralph and Jim arrived at the same time, and almost fell over each other in their wild rush to the girls.

"Where have you been, Mary Eliska?" Ralph demanded, as if he were a father speaking to a disobedient child. "Bert Keen's and Tom Hulbert's planes both came back ages ago. What made the 'Ladybug' so slow?"

"We were rescuing Helen," she replied, with a nod towards the girl beside her. "And being rescued ourselves!"

"Rescued! Mary Eliska, why don't you let me go with you when you're planning something dangerous, instead of always taking another girl?"

"I didn't know it was going to be dangerous, Ralph," she apologized. "But I'll tell you all about it when we get home, because Aunt Sally will want to hear it, too."

And recount it she did to every last detail, even including the improvised ghost in the tower, to the consternation of Ralph and her Aunt Sally, when, fifteen minutes later, they were seated on the porch of the Carltons' summer home.

"It's a miracle that you came out alive!" exclaimed Mary Eliska, incredulously, when Mary Eliska had finished the story. "If Mike O'Malley and that brother of his hadn't just happened along——"

"They didn't *happen* along, Aunt Sally," Mary Eliska insisted. "Mike had promised to help us!"

"Why is it that some outsider like O'Malley or Ted Mackay always has to be the one to protect you," muttered Ralph, "when I'd be only too glad——"

"Well, you can next time," agreed Mary Eliska, smiling. "Now, Aunt Sally, how about something to eat?"

"Certainly, dear," agreed the latter. "And we ought not to sit out here on the porch, for you girls must be cold. Come into the dining room, and I'll make some hot cocoa."

It was while they were drinking this, and eating their cookies, that Mary Eliska suddenly remembered the surprise which her aunt had mentioned.

"What is the news you have for Helen?" she inquired.

"Oh, I almost forgot!" exclaimed Mary Eliska. Then, turning to the girl, she asked, "You say that you have recovered your memory, dear? Can you recall a woman named Mrs. Smalley?"

Helen's eyes lighted up with affection and joy.

"Indeed I can! She's the very dearest memory I have!" she replied, eagerly.

"Well, dear, she's here. Up in bed. She arrived yesterday, while we were away—absolutely worn out. It seems that she had trudged miles and miles in search of you. So Anna very wisely put her to bed. She was somewhat rested today, but decided not to get up."

"Can I see her?" demanded Helen.

"I think that she's asleep."

"Oh, I won't awaken her! I just want to look at her."

"All right, dear," agreed Mary Eliska, and, as soon as Ralph had left, she led the girls up to the old lady's room.

Helen tiptoed over to the bedside and, kneeling down, looked eagerly at the worn face on the pillow. Her voice choked with emotion, as she sobbed in thanksgiving.

"Nana darling!" she whispered.

The old lady opened her eyes, and put out her wrinkled arms to embrace the girl.

"My precious child!" she cried. "You do remember me, Helen?" she asked hastily, for Mary Eliska had told her of the girl's loss of memory.

"Yes, yes! I am all right, Nana dearest! And so happy!"

The reunion of the two devoted friends—the child and the nurse—was touching to see. Mary Eliska and her aunt crept noiselessly away, and Helen slept that night with her dear old nurse.

The morning newspapers carried the story of the fire, as Mary Eliska had expected. But she was surprised to see no mention of her own name, or of the terrifying rescue. Mike O'Malley had actually sacrificed that thrilling piece of news because he was too modest to mention his own part in the affair!

But a question which had not occurred to Mary Eliska before had been played up in the headlines. "Who," the newspaper demanded, "was responsible for setting this house on fire?"—A man in disguise was suspected, it said, because a gray wig and beard had been found near the road. And these must have been left there recently, for otherwise they would have been wet from Saturday's storm!

"Clever Mike!" thought Mary Eliska, as she read this deduction. "Now why didn't we think of that before?"

She and Helen and Mrs. Smalley discussed the question from every angle that morning and decided that the criminal who ran Helen down on purpose was the same man that had set fire to the house. And both Helen and Mrs. Smalley agreed that this must be Ed Tower.

"But do you remember a Mrs. Fishberry, who claims that she took care of Helen, ever since her grandfather died?" Mary Eliska asked Mrs. Smalley.

The old lady shook her head.

"It is a lie," she answered, quietly. "I have always taken care of Helen. And I never heard of any person by that name."

"She claims to be Mrs. Edward Tower now," added Mary Eliska, telling about the threatened law suit.

But none of these things worried Helen now; she was too much excited over the joy of finding her old nurse and of discovering her grandfather's will in her favor, to worry much about her uncle, or this new aunt. She wanted to talk about the happiness the future held for her and Mrs. Smalley.

"We'll get the money," she said, "and then we'll buy a house in Spring City, shan't we, Nana—to be near to the Carltons!"

"Near to Aunt Sally—yes," agreed Mary Eliska. "But I shan't be in Spring City next winter. I am going to take a job as soon as we get back."

"A job?" demanded Helen. "Where? What?"

"Flying, of course. Relief work with a lumber company perhaps. I may go to Alaska. But don't tell Aunt Sally yet, for it isn't settled."

"Oh, poor Mary Eliska!" sighed Mrs. Smalley, and added, turning to her charge, "Helen dear, I hope that you don't ever decide to go in for flying!"

"I only want to go to school," returned the girl, simply. "With girls of my own age."

"And thank Heaven that you can now!" exclaimed Mrs. Smalley, happily.

"Which reminds me," put in Mary Eliska, "that we must go to Chicago to collect that money, Helen. Suppose we rest today, while I give the 'Ladybug' an inspection, and fly tomorrow? Does that suit you?"

It suited the girl perfectly, and accordingly, the following day, Mary Eliska and Helen flew across Lake Michigan to Chicago, the aviatrix as usual promising her aunt that she would return before dark. But once again that promise was not to be fulfilled.

Leaving the "Ladybug" at the Chicago airport, the girls took a taxi to the Trust Company which had been mentioned in Henry Adolph Tower's will. When Mary Eliska sent in her card, the Vice-president, a Mr. Hudson, came out himself to meet her.

"How do you do, Mary Eliska?" he said, cordially. "I have read a great deal about you in the newspapers. I am very much honored to meet you."

Mary Eliska blushed; she was always embarrassed when older people showed her such deference. So she hastily told the part of the story that concerned the finding of the will, and produced that document to prove it.

The man examined it gravely.

"You are too late, I am afraid, Mary Eliska," he said. "We waited all these years, and refused to give Mr. Edward Tower the money because we believed that his father must have left a will. But when we learned that the old house had burned to the ground, we felt sure that there was no longer any hope of finding one. Yesterday morning we handed over all the bonds and money to Mr. Tower."

"Oh!" gasped Mary Eliska in dismay. What a dreadful thing to happen to Helen, after she had built such high hopes! Was she really penniless after all?

"But when Mr. Tower hears of this, perhaps he will give it all back," said Mr. Hudson, soothingly.

"No, no—he won't!" cried Helen, miserably. "You don't know my uncle, Mr. Hudson, or you couldn't suggest such a thing! He never gave us anything in our lives!" The bank officer looked surprised.

"But he was supposed to be taking care of you out of the income from the estate," he protested. "That was the understanding we had, when we gave him the interest every six months."

"Well, he wasn't! We almost starved—my nurse and I! If it hadn't been for a little garden we had—and now and then selling some of grandfather's books, I don't know how we should have lived!— Oh, he was cruel—my uncle, I mean! It was he who set fire to the house!" She was speaking rapidly, in jerks, so that it was difficult to understand her.

"You mean you think he actually burned that house down on purpose, so that this will would be destroyed?" inquired Mr. Hudson.

"Yes. Disguised as an old man! Didn't you see that in the papers?"

"Yes, I do recall it, now that you mention it. If you really think that is the case, you girls must take out a warrant for his arrest, and try to catch him—before he sails for England."

"England?" repeated Mary Eliska. "He is going abroad?"

"Of course," put in Helen. "He's running away with the money as fast as he can."

Mr. Hudson nodded.

"Yes, you may be right, Miss Tower," he said. "For when I asked him his address—whether it was still the same one we have on our records—he said he couldn't give me any, because he was going to England, and probably going into air service there."

Mary Eliska stood up.

"There isn't a moment to be lost!" she cried. "Mr. Hudson, do you happen to know how he was traveling to New York, or wherever it is he is sailing from?"

"Yes, I do. He mentioned the fact that he was flying—going by the first scheduled plane this morning. He said he never used trains."

"So he's air minded," muttered Mary Eliska, thinking how much harder that would make things for them.

"I'm afraid you can't catch him," said Mr. Hudson. "If I only knew what boat he was taking we could wire——"

"We're going to catch him!" announced Mary Eliska, with that firmness which she so often displayed in a crisis. "We're flying, too! In my own autogiro! And though Mr. Tower has a start on us, we shan't have to stop for stations, and passengers!"

"Wait a minute," urged the officer, seeing that she was determined to carry out her plan. "Let me help you! While you girls get some lunch, I'll see about obtaining a warrant for Tower's arrest. And you can telephone your folks at the same time."

Mary Eliska nodded, and pressed the elderly man's hand gratefully. People were always so good to her—so kind! And, handing him the will for safekeeping, she and Helen rushed off to follow his instructions.

Chapter 17.19
A Clue to Follow

After Helen Tower's outburst of rage and disappointment over losing the money which she had been counting on receiving, she became absolutely silent. Without a word she followed Mary Eliska out of the office to a telephone booth, then to a restaurant across the street from the Trust Company's building. It was an automat, and Mary Eliska thought that the novelty of putting nickels into a slot machine to obtain food might divert Helen's thoughts from her own troubles. Surely a girl who had lived in the country all her life had never seen anything so unusual as this; surely she would be interested. But Helen showed no enthusiasm at all.

"What do you want for your lunch, Helen?" Mary Eliska asked.

"I'm not hungry," replied her companion, listlessly.

"But you must eat, while we have the chance!"

Tears came up into Helen's eyes.

"I'm a pauper again," she said, in a melancholy tone. "I can't even pay for what I eat."

"Don't be silly, dear!" urged Mary Eliska, with an effort at cheerfulness. "Don't forget you have five hundred dollars of that prize money—which you earned yourself! And besides, I think we're going to catch that man."

Helen, however, refused to be encouraged.

"Even if we do, he'll have spent it," she objected.

"Then he'll have to pay it back! Or go to prison— But come along, we must get into line with our trays. We'll choose a regular hot dinner now, and then I'll buy some sandwiches to tuck into the autogiro for our supper, so we shan't have to stop on our way, and lose any time."

In spite of her indifference, the attractive food did make its appeal to Helen, and once she began to eat she found that she was hungry. She even smiled when Mary Eliska went back to the slot machines for ice cream and chocolate cake.

It was while the girls were eating their dessert that a familiar figure entered the restaurant. A woman, whom both Mary Eliska and Helen had been hoping they would never see again in their lives. It was none other than Mrs. Fishberry!

Helen's eyes met Mary Eliska's in annoyance.

"I sincerely hope she doesn't see us," remarked the latter, giving all her attention to her ice cream.

But this wish was not fulfilled, for the woman noticed them and recognized them immediately. And, glad of a chance to clear herself of her part in the unpleasant affair, she hurried over to their very table and sat down with her tray.

"How do you do?" she said, brightly. "I am so glad that you are with Mary Eliska again, Helen. When I came back to the old house for you on Monday, I wondered where you had gone."

The old sense of fear came back to Helen, and she reached for Mary Eliska's hand. What was this woman planning to do to her now?

Noticing this gesture, Mrs. Fishberry smiled.

"You needn't be afraid of me," she said, reassuringly. "I'm not after you now—in fact, I don't want you! I've broken with Ed Tower."

"You mean you aren't married to him?" demanded Mary Eliska, thinking at once of the threatening telegram, and of the law suit that was planned.

"No, I'm not—and I'm not going to be!" returned the other, emphatically. "He's too crooked for me." She did not add that Tower himself had tired of her, and tried to escape from her first.

"I ran away from him in his own car," she continued, "while he was setting that house on fire. A crime like that was too much for me."

"He did set the house on fire?" Mary Eliska repeated, excitedly. "We thought so."

"Mary Eliska and I and another girl were in it," remarked Helen, grimly.

"Oh, my heavens!" exclaimed the woman, aghast at these words. "But you got out?"

"Yes," replied Mary Eliska briefly, as she rose from her seat. "We must go now, Mrs. Fishberry— Oh, I might ask you—I suppose that law suit is off, then, if you are not Mrs. Tower?"

"Yes, of course."

"And one thing more—just to clear things up in my own mind—did you ever see Helen in your life before your visit to Green Falls?"

"No, I didn't," admitted the woman. "That was all Ed's lie—to get money out of you. Oh, I am innocent—I've never done anything bad 'til I got in his clutches. But he looks like a prince, and smiles like an angel, and he wound me right around his little finger!"

An inspiration came to Mary Eliska: perhaps Mrs. Fishberry knew something of Ed Tower's plans. Perhaps she would be willing to tell, now that she was so angry with him.

"You don't know where he is now, do you?" she asked, trying to speak casually, as if she were not much concerned.

"No, I don't!" replied the other, flatly. "And I don't care! I'm going to clear out of here, and go back to Montana."

"Mr. Tower didn't say anything to you about going abroad?"

"Oh, yes, he did. He's clearing out of the country, the minute he collects that money from his father's estate. He got some kind of job with an air-transport company at Newport News."

"Air-transport company!" repeated Mary Eliska, in amazement. "But why should he want to get a job, when he had all that money? Does he like work so much?"

"No, but he was afraid to go to England by an ordinary passenger boat, for fear he'd be caught. You know—passports, and all that sort of thing. Nobody but me and the man who got him this job know that he's going."

"So if the police look for him, they won't be able to find him?" concluded Mary Eliska, with a twinkle in her eye. What luck it was, to get the very information she wanted—and from a person she had actually tried to avoid!

She held out her hand.

"Shall we part good friends, Mrs. Fishberry?" she asked, pleasantly.

"O.K. with me," replied the woman, accepting the hand shake with a smile.

The girls were hardly out of the door when Mary Eliska grasped her companion's arm and whistled for joy.

"We're going to get him now, Helen!" she cried, exultantly. "Think of the time we'll save by flying straight to Virginia, instead of going around by New York!"

"You believe Mrs. Fishberry was telling the truth?" inquired Helen, doubtfully.

"Oh, yes! Your uncle has let her down—decided that he didn't want to marry her and share the money with her after all—and she's sore. She was glad to tell all she knew about him!"

They were walking rapidly, approaching the Trust Company's building, when Mary Eliska suddenly stopped, and frowned.

"Why didn't I ask Mrs. Fishberry to describe Mr. Tower?" she demanded. "We may not know him if we do see him!"

"I might recognize him," remarked the other girl. "Though at the present minute, I haven't the slightest idea what he looks like. But that really doesn't matter, Mary Eliska. If Mr. Hudson gets that warrant for his arrest, all we have to do is ask for him."

"Maybe," agreed Mary Eliska, trying to be hopeful. "Only I'm afraid that once he got that money, he'd travel under a different name."

Helen looked dismayed at the idea.

"He would if he could, I suppose," she said. "But let's hope that he got this job under his own name—and had to keep it."

Returning to the office where Mary Eliska was to meet Mr. Hudson again, she sat down at a desk to plot out her flight to Virginia. She had expected to follow the regular air line from Chicago to New York, but, of course, this plan was changed now.

"It's going to be fun, Helen!" she cried, as she bent over the map. As usual the anticipation of a long flight gave her a joyous thrill.

"We'll fly southeast," she announced, "and I think I can pass right over Spring City. The only difficult part is the Allegheny Mountains—but I've flown over mountains before. You aren't afraid, are you, Helen?" she asked. "You wouldn't rather go back to Green Falls, and wait for me there?"

"I should say not!" protested the girl, eagerly. "I love flying, you know that, Mary Eliska! And I never get a bit sick."

"There's not much danger of that in an autogiro," replied the capable young aviatrix. "You see we don't feel air pockets, as people do in other planes—now, let me see—I think we can make Spring City before dark tonight! Wouldn't it be fun to stay in our own house?"

"I should say it would!" exclaimed Helen, in delight. "But could we get in?"

"Surely. I always carry a key with me—with my other keys, you know. Oh, Helen, that will be fun! And we'll start early tomorrow morning for Newport News, Virginia."

"Do you suppose we'll catch him?"

"I hope so. If he left here this morning, he'd hardly be planning to sail before Friday morning. And I think we'll arrive some time Thursday afternoon."

"If everything goes right," amended the other.

"Yes," agreed Mary Eliska. "If everything goes right. If we don't run into a storm over the mountains!"

Chapter 17.20
Flying Over the Mountains

Everything went well with Mary Eliska and Helen Tower on that first lap of their flight in the autogiro from Chicago to Spring City, in Ohio. The weather continued fine all afternoon and the "Ladybug's" motor droned on in perfect rhythm. It was not yet dark when Mary Eliska made her landing in the field behind her own house.

Helen was wildly excited at the idea of seeing the Carlton home; for the time being she had forgotten her terrible disappointment at the loss of her money. In the calm happy hours of the flight her faith in the goodness of the world had been restored. She believed that somehow, some way, Mary Eliska would succeed in the end.

"Why, your place is as big as our old house!" she exclaimed. "All except that extra wing— and the tower. But so different! So beautiful!"

Mary Eliska smiled; she too had always admired her charming home.

She unlocked the door, and after they had both washed and eaten some supper which Mary Eliska ordered sent in from a delicatessen store, the aviatrix spent the rest of the daylight going over her engine. She wanted everything in perfect shape to start again on their journey at six o'clock the next morning.

She took the opportunity, however, to call her aunt on the telephone, and enjoyed surprising her with the news that she and Helen were sleeping in her own home that night.

When the alarm clock rang at five-thirty the following morning, Mary Eliska could not believe that day had really come. Then, as she sleepily crept out of bed, she glanced out of the windows, and saw the reason for the total lack of light. The skies were cloudy!

"Just our luck!" she muttered. "The day we have to fly over the mountains!"

"Hadn't we better wait awhile?" suggested Helen, sleepily; "to see if it clears up?"

"We daren't," replied Mary Eliska, gravely. "If we don't get to Virginia today, there won't be any use of going at all. Mr. Tower will surely be off for England tomorrow."

At these words Helen became wide awake, and recalled the importance of their flight to her, and she dressed quickly, even insisting upon getting the breakfast, while Mary Eliska filled her autogiro with gas and oil from a supply which she kept at home.

While Helen packed sandwiches and filled the thermos bottles with water for their lunch, Mary Eliska hunted an old rain coat and some extra clothing from the closets. Her own slicker was packed in the "Ladybug," but Helen would need something if they ran into the storm.

They made their start about half-past six, before it was actually raining. Mary Eliska made good time across Ohio and West Virginia, keeping steadily onward, bearing to the southeast, in spite of the light rain that was falling. Neither girl wanted to land for lunch, so Helen fed Mary Eliska sandwiches and water from the passenger's cockpit. The aviatrix's one idea was to cross the Allegheny Mountains before the storm grew too intense.

But it was not to be, for as she came to the hills, Mary Eliska saw that she was running right into the storm area. All about her was grayness; she could not see land anywhere, and in this mountainous region, her altimeter was not an infallible guide. In the effort to play safe she directed the "Ladybug's" nose upward, to keep clear of the mountains, but here the wind was intense, sending the rain into their faces, delaying their progress.

Never, she thought impatiently, had she been flying so slowly. It was impossible to make headway in the face of this wind. At this rate, they would be too late; they could not hope to reach the coast before nightfall!

Desperately deciding that she must take a chance for once, she dropped her autogiro several hundred feet. The relief was immediate; the winds were far less intense, and her progress became more rapid. But she must watch carefully, she warned herself; in this obscurity she could not tell how near to the ground she was.

At that moment she was far from the earth, just as her altimeter intimated, for she was flying over a valley. But she could not know that it was a valley—at least not until it was too late! Even to Mary Eliska's watchful eyes the disaster came suddenly. In an instant the mountain seemed to be rushing at her, with the same inevitable force that Ed Tower's car had run into Helen. With a gasp of horror she shut off her power, praying that the rotors would break the fall. The plane hovered a moment, for it had not been going fast, and began to descend on the side of that mountain. But it was too close to it; a moment later it crashed against the hill, with an impact that threw both girls from their cockpits.

Mary Eliska jumped to her feet immediately, unharmed except for some bruises, and dashed over to her companion who was lying in the bushes, still unable to understand what had happened.

"Are you hurt, Helen?" Mary Eliska cried, fearfully. How dreadful it was that everything seemed to happen to this poor child! Now, if some bones were broken, in this lonely place far away from doctors and hospitals, there would be little chance for the girl's recovery. Mary Eliska shivered with fear as she knelt down beside her.

But Helen sat up and smiled reassuringly.

"No, I'm all right, Mary Eliska," she said. "But what happened?"

"We bumped into a mountain," returned Mary Eliska, laughing in sheer relief. "It's this awful weather—I couldn't see where I was going."

"Is the 'Ladybug' wrecked?"

"I don't know yet. I haven't examined her. I was too much scared about you."

Helen stood up.

"Well, come on, let's look and know the worst. I guess it's good-by to my money now."

Mary Eliska did not reply, but dashed back to the autogiro to examine it for damages. The propeller was all right, and the rotor blades—thank goodness—for evidently the "Ladybug" had struck on her side. But one wheel and one wing were damaged.

"It doesn't look so bad," remarked Helen, as she watched Mary Eliska anxiously. "Can you make it fly again, or shall we have to stay here the rest of our lives?"

Mary Eliska laughed good-naturedly.

"Oh, somebody'd rescue us before that. Ralph Clavering, probably—Aunt Sally told him just where we were going. But that isn't going to be necessary, because I can fix it."

"Can you really, Mary Eliska? Even that broken wheel?" demanded the girl, in awe.

"Yes. I carry an extra wheel and material to mend the wings. But it's going to take time."

Helen's smile faded; she knew what this meant. They would be too late to catch her uncle!

"Well, it can't be helped," she remarked, with a sigh of resignation. "We're lucky that we got out alive."

Mary Eliska looked about her, surveying the landscape. It was a lonely place, with no house anywhere in sight. Trees and bushes covered the mountainside sparsely, and below in the valley a stream was running. But there was no shelter anywhere from the storm.

"I'm going to get right to work," she announced to Helen, "and you better see what you can do about making a fire. If you go up the mountain farther, under those thick trees, you may be able to find some dry wood. And then we can get warm and make some hot tea for our supper."

"Supper?" repeated Helen. "It isn't time for that yet, is it?"

"No, not yet. But I'm afraid I'll be a good while fixing the 'Ladybug.' We'll have to make the best of it."

Helen nodded, determined to be a good sport and not to make things any harder than was necessary for Mary Eliska. After all, it was for Helen's sake that the brave young pilot had risked this flight over the mountains in the storm. She would do her part to make the older girl as comfortable as possible.

She spent the rest of the afternoon collecting wood and clearing a dry spot under the trees for their camp fire, and she managed to cook supper from a can of baked beans which Mary Eliska had in the autogiro. What light there was—for it was still drizzling a little and the skies were gray—was fading when Mary Eliska, tired and dirty, announced that she had completed her task.

"That supper certainly smells good," she said, as she used a little of their water to wash her hands. "And I'm starved!"

"So am I," agreed Helen. "Are you really finished, Mary Eliska? Do you think the 'Ladybug' will fly again?"

"I hope so," replied the aviatrix, seating herself beside the fire and taking the plate of beans which Helen offered. "My only difficulty will be to get her started. There's no place for a take-off."

"I never thought of that. I believed that an autogiro could start anywhere."

"Well, not quite anywhere. There must be a little runway," explained Mary Eliska. "But I think the two of us together can push her over to that road—at least it's supposed to be a road, I guess—if we go carefully. Will you help me after supper?"

"Of course," agreed Helen. "It isn't much of a road—I was looking at it this afternoon—but at least it's clear of bushes. But do you really think we can make it?"

"I hope so. There aren't any trees in the way. If there had been any in the spot where we hit," she added, "I don't suppose we should be alive to tell the tale."

Helen shuddered.

"You do have the most marvelous escapes, Mary Eliska!" she remarked. Then she looked grave. "But all on account of me. What a peaceful summer you would have had, if you hadn't happened to see my accident."

"My summer has been fine!" Mary Eliska assured her. "And I should have been flying somewhere, anyhow—and probably would have met with other adventures. I don't like things to be slow, you know."

The girls finished their supper, and as soon as they had cleared up and put out the fire, they started upon their dangerous task of getting the "Ladybug" out of the underbrush. For a time it seemed as if it were going to be impossible, but by digging up some bushes, and removing some rocks in its path, they finally got her started. The difficulty then was to stop her, but Mary Eliska carefully applied her brakes, and finally they managed to reach the road.

It had grown dark by the time they had finished, but the rain had ceased and they felt well pleased with their success. Hot and tired and damp with perspiration and the recent rain, Mary Eliska sat down on the wet grass for a rest.

"Let's take a swim, Helen," she suggested. "I see a stream down in the valley. Then we ought to be able to get some sleep, so long as it's stopped raining. We can spread our slickers on the ground."

"Sleep!" repeated the other girl in dismay. "Aren't we going to fly?"

Mary Eliska shook her head.

"I'm sorry, dear," she replied, gently. "But I'm not going to risk it. I don't know where we are, and these mountains are too unfamiliar for me to try it on a night like this, particularly when I'm so tired, and I haven't even tested the 'Ladybug.'"

Helen nodded; she saw the wisdom of Mary Eliska's decision. They were probably too late now, anyway. This was Thursday night; they must have lost all chance of catching her uncle before he sailed.

The mountain stream was shallow and cold, but it felt good to Mary Eliska after her hard afternoon's work. She waded about until she found a place deep enough to lie down, and here she relaxed with content.

But it was too cold to stay in the water long, and fifteen minutes later, with renewed energy she began to build a new fire, down by the stream, away from the autogiro. By this time her young companion was exhausted; when she made a feeble effort to help Mary Eliska with the fire, the latter commanded her to spread out her slicker and go to sleep.

An hour or so later, when Mary Eliska's fire was burning brightly, the clouds dispersed and the stars shone out in the sky. With a contented sigh Mary Eliska sat there for a long time, until the fire had burned out, and the mountains looked black and forbidding. She could not help wondering about them; they were so deep and silent in the night. What strange creatures might live there? Were there any dangerous animals prowling about, to molest these two lonely girls? The thought made Mary Eliska shiver for a moment, and she rose abruptly to her feet, determined to get her revolver out of the autogiro.

Her sudden movement brought a quick response from the woods. A black, shadowy creature appeared from behind a tree only a dozen feet beyond her, and she involuntarily cried out in terror. Oh, why hadn't she thought of that revolver sooner? She hadn't even a stick to protect her if this was a bear or a wolf, sneaking up in a nightly attack in search of food.

Her cry wakened Helen, who shot up from the ground as if she had been hit.

"What is it, Mary Eliska?" she demanded, her voice hoarse with terror. "A bear, or a ghost?"

"Neither—" returned the other, vexed with herself for her fear: "It's—it's—a deer! And look—Helen—he's running for his life! He's much more afraid of us than we are of him!"

Helen sighed in relief, but she still clung to Mary Eliska's arm.

"Come and sleep beside me," she urged. "The next visitor may be a lot worse!"

"I'll be prepared for the next one," asserted Mary Eliska. "With my revolver, my knife— and a stout stick!"

But though she put all these weapons beside her, Mary Eliska had no use for them that night, and both girls slept soundly until the sun wakened them the next morning.

Chapter 17.21
A Strange Landing

Flying over the mountains in the bright, calm sunlight was a very different proposition from clearing them in the face of wind and rain, and Mary Eliska encountered no difficulty at all as she set out the next morning. Neither she nor Helen had much hope of catching the man who had stolen the bonds and the money, but both girls decided it was worth taking a chance. So long as they had come this far, it would be foolish to turn back without finishing the flight.

They arrived at the Newport News airport a little before ten o'clock, and Mary Eliska set herself immediately to the task of finding out where the air-transport company was located. When she had secured this information she stepped back into her autogiro, prepared to fly to the spot. She was not wasting any time now with taxicabs, for wherever she went, she felt sure there would be a landing place large enough for the "Ladybug."

She had been directed to the shore on the Chesapeake Bay, and here she found hangars and planes and officers. A smiling young man came to greet her immediately.

"Good morning," said Mary Eliska, quickly. "We have come from Chicago to find a man named Edward Tower. I understand that he was sailing to England on an air transport—leaving today, perhaps?"

Her heart beat rapidly while she waited for his answer.

The young man nodded.

"There was a transport that left at nine o'clock this morning," he replied, to both girls' utter dismay. Only an hour ago! They had lost the race by sixty short minutes!

"Oh!" gasped Mary Eliska, sadly, and tears of disappointment came into Helen's eyes.

The young man seemed to be thinking.

"I can't recall anyone by the name of Tower," he said. "And I myself went over the lists."

Mary Eliska's eyes narrowed.

"Then Mr. Tower must be using another name—just as he used the disguise of an old man—" she added, to Helen. Then, turning to the officer, she explained that she had a warrant for Tower's arrest.

"There couldn't be another boat going to England?" she asked.

"No. Air transports aren't like passenger boats," he replied, "sailing every few days. There are only a limited number in existence."

Mary Eliska was silent, trying to think of something that she could do. It was the young man who finally made the suggestion which she followed.

"Look here, Miss," he said, "why don't you go after the boat? You have an autogiro, haven't you?"

"Yes—" replied Mary Eliska, not knowing what he meant.

"Well, fly out over the ocean 'til you find them. I'll show you a picture of the transport, so you can spot it. But you couldn't miss it anyhow. Then hover over it, and I'll give you a mail bag to drop down. That'll be a signal—the Captain'll clear the deck for you to land."

"Land on a ship's deck?" repeated Mary Eliska, in amazement.

"Sure. With a 'giro it's easy—if you know how to manage her. Lt. Melville Pride did it a while ago—maybe you read about it in the papers?"

"No, I must have missed that," answered Mary Eliska. "But did he take off again? I wouldn't want to go all the way to England."

"Sure he took off. The crew helped, I believe— But, of course, Lt. Pride is an expert. If you're a beginner, I wouldn't advise you to try it."

Mary Eliska looked grave, but Helen burst out laughing.

"I guess you don't know that this is Miss Mary Eliska!" she announced proudly. "The girl who flew the Atlantic Ocean alone!"

The young man gasped, and held out his hand, which Mary Eliska shook cordially.

"I'm honored to meet you, Mary Eliska," he said. "And, of course, you can land on that ship. Go ahead and do it!"

"I will," replied Mary Eliska, who always made her decisions quickly. "Just let me look at my gas——"

Ten minutes later she took off from the shore, pointing her autogiro out towards the ocean. Her spirits were high; she had never been so excited before. This, she thought to herself, must be the way the pirates of old felt, when they went after a ship!

It was not long before she spotted the ship, for the "Ladybug" made much better time than the transport. Circling about, she gradually descended until she was almost over the ship. Then she leaned out of the cockpit and dropped the mail bag, with a message pinned on it to the effect that she wanted to make a landing.

Confusion immediately arose on the ship's deck, as Mary Eliska could easily see, without even the aid of her glasses. Men and officers hurried to and fro, clearing a large space. They had no way of knowing that their visitor was not some high government official, but only a girl of eighteen!

At last the man who was probably the captain gave her the signal, and Mary Eliska descended cautiously, thankful that she had had plenty of practice in coming down on exact spots. Her experience in the Okefenokee Swamp had not been in vain, for she landed with confidence now. It was as pretty a demonstration as the crew had ever seen.

"Pretty neat!" exclaimed the Captain, rushing over to her side. Then, in consternation, he exclaimed, "By George! It's a girl!"

"Two girls!" corrected Mary Eliska, climbing out of the cockpit, and trying not to look embarrassed. How she wished her companion were Jax Gray y, instead of modest little Helen Tower! For Jax Gray would do all the talking, and take charge of everything.

She looked about in confusion at the men who gathered so quickly around her, and she could not distinguish the Captain. Then, all of a sudden, she spied a familiar face. Lord Dudley, amongst all those strangers!

"Mary Eliska!" he exclaimed, in surprise. "Am I the reason we are being honored with this visit?"

Mary Eliska laughed and shook her head.

"I'm afraid not, Lord Dudley," she said, holding out her hand. "But it's good to see somebody that I know. Now will you please introduce me to the Captain?"

"Certainly," agreed the man, and he hastened to do the honors.

Cautiously, however, Mary Eliska asked to speak with the Captain alone, and he took her into a cabin while she stated her business, asking for a man named Edward Tower, and showing her warrant and a note from Mr. Hudson, stating the facts concerning the will, and the taking of the money and bonds.

The Captain, however, gazed at the papers gravely.

"We haven't any man by that name," he stated.

"Then he must be using another name," Mary Eliska replied, desperately. "Oh, he must be here! He just must!"

The Captain looked exceedingly sorry for her, but he explained that he did not see how he could possibly find out. "We haven't a detective on board," he added, helplessly.

Mary Eliska stood up. She had forgotten Helen, had left her sitting alone in the autogiro. Their only hope now lay in the girl's recognizing her uncle.

She went back to the deck, where Lord Dudley met her and claimed her as his guest. That he was proud of her, in front of all those officers and men, could not be disputed. He had almost decided to ask her again to marry him.

Together they walked towards the "Ladybug," from which Helen Tower suddenly leaped.

"Uncle Ed!" she cried, in wildest excitement.

Mary Eliska and Lord Dudley looked about them, questioningly.

"You've found him, haven't you, Mary Eliska?" demanded the girl, rushing over and grabbing Lord Dudley by the arm. "Hand over my money!" she commanded, dramatically.

Lord Dudley pretended to look puzzled, but beneath it all Mary Eliska could see a hidden tinge of fear in his eyes.

"But this is Lord Dudley, Helen—" Mary Eliska insisted.

"It's my uncle Ed Tower!" repeated the girl, emphatically. "I know it. Don't you remember, Mary Eliska—when I saw him before on the Country Club porch, at that tennis match, I said he looked familiar?"

"Why, this is nonsense," objected the man, trying to keep his voice calm. "I will appeal to the Captain if you think it is necessary, Mary Eliska."

But the Captain, it seemed, was only too ready to help the girls. Immediately he demanded a search of the man's belongings; if Lord Dudley was in reality Edward Tower, the money and the bonds must be hidden somewhere in his quarters. The Captain sent three trusted officers to find out.

Mary Eliska and Helen remained on deck with the Captain and the man posing as Lord Dudley, and the girls told the story of the finding of the will and the confession of Mrs. Fishberry. Ten minutes later the searchers returned, bringing fifty thousand dollars in bonds, and fifty thousand in cash! There could be no doubt now of the man's identity.

"You want to arrest Tower, don't you, Mary Eliska?" asked the Captain, as he put the valuables into her hands. "Even though you got the money?"

Mary Eliska looked questioningly at Helen.

"We had better," answered the younger girl. "He might try to run over me again. Or burn more houses, with people in them!"

Mary Eliska nodded; it was not safe for a man like Ed Tower, who could even pose successfully as an English lord, to be at large. There was no telling what wickedness he might accomplish in the future.

"Then suppose I send a pilot back with him in your autogiro—with the warrant for his arrest. You girls can wait here until the autogiro returns."

Mary Eliska agreed, and it was all accomplished in an incredibly short time. An hour later, with their small fortune carefully stored in the "Ladybug," they set out for home.

Their first stop was Baltimore, for they flew north this time, and here they were met by an old friend of Mary Eliska's father, a banker who took charge of their money and bonds, and who insisted upon taking them to his home to spend the week end with his daughters.

It was Monday afternoon when the girls finally reached Green Falls, having flown the whole journey—through Pennsylvania, over the Allegheny Mountains, north through Ohio and Michigan—without a single mishap. The entire summer colony was out to greet them, it seemed, but little Helen Tower saw only Mrs. Smalley, her dear old nurse.

The look of happiness and gratitude on the faces of these two devoted friends—happiness that they could live comfortably together, gratitude to Mary Eliska for what she had done for them—was enough to repay the brave aviatrix for her perilous summer.

Readers who have enjoyed this story will be interested in reading the next and final chapter– *On Adventure Island.*

CHAPTER 18

On Adventure Island

CHAPTER 18.1
Hazardous Flight

Flying a mile high above the rolling hills of the countryside, Mary Eliska suddenly put *Skybird*, her little blue-and-gold monoplane, into a series of loops. She was feeling good, her blue eyes were keenly alive and her slight boyish figure sat erect as she handled the controls of her plane. And being a young and lively girl, she wanted to turn somersaults in the sky to express her joy.

Her older sister, Martha, strapped in the rear cockpit, spoke to her through the earphones, "Quit your circus stunts, Mary Eliska, and keep going! We've got a long trip ahead of us."

"You guessed it, Martha. That's why I'm feeling so full of pep!" answered Mary Eliska and her voice died away as she put *Skybird* into another loop among the clouds.

The next minute her plane was on an even keel and Martha repeated: "Mary Eliska, *will* you stop clowning? Save that pep! You'll need it before we get to South America."

"Don't I know it! I'll be good and tired before I reach Peru, but right now I feel like a million dollars. I wouldn't change places with the President of the United States or the Prince of Wales," said Mary Eliska with a laugh. "I'm perfectly satisfied to be Mary Eliska, airplane pilot on a secret errand to the wilds of South America."

"And I," interrupted Martha, settling back for a comfortable trip, "would rather be just Martha, the sister of the cleverest girl flyer who had ever done a barrel roll.—But I wish she'd cut out the stunts for the present!"

Albert Stricklin, the father of the girls was an former airmail pilot. He had taught both girls to fly. The home-loving Martha had become a good pilot but she was not as fond of the sport as her younger sister. Mary Eliska was a pretty blonde, brilliant as a girl detective and easy-going as a companion, while Martha tended to be more serious, high strung and nervous. Mary Eliska loved to fly and now that her father was crippled from a recent airplane crash and still unable to leave his wheel chair, she was trusted with many important air jobs.

To Mary Eliska it was not half so venturesome to cut up antics in the air as it would have been to race in a motor boat or automobile. She always felt perfectly safe and perfectly happy when she could put a thousand feet of air between her plane and the earth.

Martha, in spite of her protests, had perfect confidence in her younger sister's ability to handle her plane and whether she was stunting or flying straight. Martha could feel sure of a happy landing and enjoy herself.

At last Mary Eliska had worked off her excitement. She leveled out her plane and throttled the engine down to a steady cruising speed. Mary Eliska's success as a flyer was due to the fact that the girl understood her airplane thoroughly and treated it with respect. Apart from an occasional burst of speed to work off her excess energy and a few stunts to keep her in practice, Mary Eliska kept her plane on a level keel and never overtaxed it.

Mile after mile sped by below them and Mary Eliska's mind was racing ahead to the work she had to do, a mission which might be full of perils and thrilling hazards.

Since the day when her father had started out with such high hopes of success in the venture of The Albert Stricklin Flying Field, things had gone all wrong with him. He had obtained an option on a large tract of land at Elmwood from the owner, Sean Hall who lived at a small gold mine in the wilds of Peru, and it was this field that had aroused the envy of his business rival, Thatcher Allen.

Most of Albert's misfortunes had come through the jealousy of this unscrupulous flyer. Thatcher Allen was anxious to get control of Albert Stricklin' field, as it was situated near his own and was at a safe point for carrying on his illegal business. If he could once get this field he would be isolated and not run the risk of being seen when loading and unloading his planes.

Thatcher Allen was a dangerous rival. He would stop at nothing to carry out his schemes. And for the last two years he had kept Albert Stricklin and his helpers in a state of anxiety. At first there had only been slight inconveniences, mishaps that were annoying, but through his agent, Culley May, who worked as mechanic for Albert Stricklin, Thatcher Allen was able to learn all the plans of the field. He grew bolder and with Culley May to carry out his orders, the field was the scene of frequent accidents.

Suspicion pointed to Culley May after the crash in which Albert Stricklin was injured. Albert was a careful pilot and always checked up on his plane before starting out on a trip. Yet as soon as he was in the air that day, he found that someone had been tampering with his plane. It was too late to save himself. The plane crashed from a height of five hundred feet. It was a miracle that saved Albert from death.

Liam McAdams, his young partner, declared that he had seen Culley May near the plane just before Albert took off. But no one could say for sure that Culley May was guilty, although most of the people on the field believed he was. Albert was too tender-hearted to discharge the boy without a reason and it was only after Culley May had proven beyond doubt that he was working against the field that Albert let him go.

One thing after another had happened to discredit Albert and for a time it looked as if he might have to give up the field entirely.

And as a final blow word had come from Sean Hall saying that he did not care to extend the option, after he had let it be understood that he would do so. Albert felt as if the struggle were too much for him. Sean Hall had gone on to say that he'd received reports that Albert was using his field for smuggling purposes, and he did not care to be mixed up with business of that sort.

Albert knew, without being told, who had been the slanderer. His enemy, Thatcher Allen was still trying to injure him.

Bennett McAdams, his backer, came to the rescue once more and gave Albert the money, but the time limit was almost up. There were only about ten days left. And with Sean Hall believing Albert to be a crook, there was little hope of taking up the option without a personal interview.

Albert Stricklin in his wheel chair, fretted and fumed at the problem facing him. Liam McAdams, the son of his backer, and Syd Ames had been his first student-flyers and were now working at the field. They had been gone a week on a trip to Chicago. No one was left to take the long trip to Peru.

Of course he had Mary Eliska and Martha! Albert could trust Mary Eliska anywhere with a plane, but it was a long flight to Peru and there might be storms and dangers. Albert grew restless and impatient under the misfortune that kept him tied to his wheel chair.

"If I were only well enough to fly!" he fumed.

"But what's the idea, Dad! Don't you think I can *fly* well enough?" Mary Eliska faced her father with flaming cheeks, her large blue eyes were flashing. "Why not send me?"

"Send you? To South America? Alone?"

"Not alone! Martha can go."

"But Mary Eliska, don't you realize that Peru is a long way off? You may have to face grave dangers, storms, fevers, savages! And while Sean Hall and his wife Amanda may be all right, you never can tell ahead of time what rough characters you may meet there!"

"What of it? I'm not afraid. You wouldn't think twice about sending Liam McAdams and Syd," said the girl with a frown.

Albert Stricklin shook his head. "That's different," he said. "They are boys!"

"Which means that you don't trust me. You think I'm not a good flyer!"

Albert laughed. "Mary Eliska, don't be silly! I'd trust you to fly anything you could get off the ground. That isn't it. But I don't feel as if it would be right for me to let you risk your life."

Mary Eliska sat down beside her father's wheel chair and took his hand. "Listen Dad, while I talk. Haven't I proven over and over again that I'm a capable flyer. I'm pretty good at getting out of a jam in the air."

"I've said it often, Mary Eliska. I've never seen a better stunt flyer. You're clever and you *think* when you're in the air! And that's what half the flyers don't do. That's why they crash."

"All right, so far, so good! We've been in lots of jams and got out of them by using our brains. Weren't Martha and I *The Gypsies Of The Air*, and didn't we go after the boys in Newfoundland and get them away from the kidnappers? Nothing terrible happened to us. Of course old Jim Heron kept us locked up and we had to think hard to find a way out of that old fortress, but we escaped without any harm." Mary Eliska's eyes were snapping as she recalled their imprisonment in the old fort. "Oh, I know, Mary Eliska. You and Martha can look out for yourselves. But I don't like to send you into a jam deliberately."

"But Dad, you don't know that there *will* be a jam, this time, and if there is, we can get out of it."

Albert did not answer as Mary Eliska hesitated and gave him a chance. The girl went on:

"Now we're in one of the biggest jams we've ever had yet. We're almost sure to lose our flying field, though we have the money to take up the option, because our enemy Thatcher Allen has written mean letters to Sean Hall and set him against us. Now you can see for yourself, if I could get down there before the option expires he would think differently."

"I know he would, Mary Eliska. But it's too dangerous. No."

"But it's the only way out. Liam McAdams and Syd are not here and may not be for a week. And we are apt to lose our flying field because you still have this one old-fashioned idea. You're up to date in every other way, Dad. What makes you think that girls can't look out for themselves?"

"Mary Eliska, you should have been a lawyer. You're wasted in aviation," her father said with a laugh. "You can make a fellow believe that black is white.—All right, if your mother consents, I will."

"That's passing the buck! You've got to answer 'yes' or 'no.' You know it will be a deadlock for mother always says, 'If you can get your father's consent, I suppose I'll have to agree!' and if that argument keeps up, the day for taking up the option will be long past and we'll have to give up the field."

Mary Eliska loved a struggle, her eyes were shining as she noted that she had almost reached success.

Albert Stricklin slapped her hand playfully. "All right. When do you start?"

"At daybreak tomorrow," answered Mary Eliska in a business-like manner. "The plane needs a few repairs, small ones, then we're all set to go!" The girl wasted no time. The next minute she was running to the hangar, and drawing on an overall suit was getting ready to look over her airplane.

Her mother, agreed without a struggle. "In fact I don't feel half as frightened as I did when you went north to find the boys. You'll have a wonderful trip to the south. Your father and I trust you perfectly, we know you'll look over your airplane at every stop and never take a chance with it."

"There you see, Dad!" said Mary Eliska with a happy laugh. "When mother agrees, it's bound to be all right."

Martha was already busy at their flying togs. There were a few repairs to make and this was left to Martha, who liked to sew and cook and do other domestic jobs while Mary Eliska was a good mechanic and kept the plane running without a hitch.

"A born flyer!" said Albert Stricklin and he followed his daughter's figure as she tested her plane, listening intently to the hum of the motor, going over every part, making adjustments here and there to bring her plane to the highest pitch of efficiency. And when Mary Eliska was satisfied that *Skybird* was in perfect running order, Albert Stricklin could never find a flaw. Mary Eliska knew her job.

Bennett McAdams had all the necessary legal papers ready and a certified check to close the deal, so there would be no hitch at the last minute. These papers were carried in a small brown leather case and sewn into the lining of Mary Eliska's flying coat.

Martha loved stylish clothes and her white flying suit was smartly cut. Mary Eliska turned to admire her pretty blonde sister just before they were ready to hop off.

"What's the idea of that necklace?" said Mary Eliska with a laugh. "Girl flyers don't wear necklaces with bright red jewels."

"Don't they? Well, this one does! It just suits my fancy, Mary Eliska. I think it looks smart, it adds a bit of color to my white costume."

"All right, Martha, just as you say. Now, is everything set? How about your sweet tooth. Got plenty of cake chocolate?" teased Mary Eliska, for Martha was always nibbling at something sweet. "Sure, my pockets are full. Here put this little package of crackers in your coat. We may get hungry as we fly along. And I've put up a big lunch in case we need it."

At the last minute, Martha adjusted the harness of the parachutes about Mary Eliska and herself not minding her sister's impatient shrugs of disdain.

For some reason Mary Eliska was always impatient of parachutes. She felt like an amateur even though she knew that many of the big flyers never went up without putting one on, as a safeguard in case of accident.

Mary Eliska looked with satisfaction at Sally Wyn, the little waif they had brought with them from the far north. The girl was fluttering about the field like a butterfly. She seemed to be in half a dozen different places at the same time, running errands and making herself useful. With Sally there, her father and mother would not be so lonely. The little orphan had found a place in the hearts of Albert and his wife, and they would not hear of her leaving them to go to work. With her happy disposition she kept the household filled with laughter. Mrs. Stricklin often wondered how she had ever been happy without this fun-loving girl. And she had a way of making Albert forget that he was a cripple. She amused him.

As the girls said goodbye to her, Sally called out: "Next year Mary Eliska, I'll race you to Peru!"

It was a glorious morning, the sun was just rising as Mary Eliska sent her plane into the air and headed south. There were no last-minute delays.

Now it remained for Mary Eliska and Martha to reach Peru, find Sean Hall and convince him he was mistaken and make him want to sell Albert the property. And in Mary Eliska's mind there was no doubt that she could accomplish it.

Below them was a vast stretch of fertile country with streams, lakes and broad green valleys. And high in the air, Mary Eliska's hand at the controls felt the spring of her little plane and was certain that *Skybird* was thrilling at the adventure.

Mary Eliska held the plane down to a steady speed, hour after hour, only changing the monotony by diving to a lower level or rising to greater heights. They were following along the general line of the airway. They could pick out the landing fields and see the position of the great beacons that would flash at night to guide the flyer to the hangars on the ground.

Mary Eliska and Martha had decided to stay all night at the Waverly Field, far to the south. That meant steady flying all day, only coming down to refuel at long jumps.

They saw the lights of the Waverly Field a full half hour before they expected to be there. "Shall we go on?" asked Mary Eliska through the earphones. "We can easily reach the next landing field before dark."

"No, let's stay here. You look tired and besides I like the looks of this pleasure beach," replied Martha.

Mary Eliska put *Skybird* into a steep spiral, leveled and circled the field and then put the plane neatly down on the ground.

Little did the girls think as they were greeted by the manager of the flying field that this was where their troubles would begin. That before they reached Sean Hall's mine they were to face an enemy who was desperate with greed and hate. And that at times the girls would despair of escaping with their lives!

CHAPTER 18.2
Pursued by a Flying Foe

Waverly was a popular beach resort and Martha was delighted to see that there was a pleasure pier which was gaily lighted up.

She cried, "Oh, Mary Eliska, it looks as if there might be dancing down there. Let's hurry to the hotel and change to our party clothes."

"Martha, you promised me that you wouldn't take any party dresses this time. You said we'd be just girl flyers with no excess baggage," retorted her sister.

Martha laughed. "I tried to Mary Eliska, but I couldn't leave out our new frocks. I was certain we'd run into some sort of entertainment where we'd want some pretty dresses."

Mary Eliska looked her disgust. "But Martha, I don't even want to dance. What am I going to do with these documents while I'm dancing?"

"You could leave them at the hotel in the safe," Martha said.

"Just forget that, Martha. Wherever I go, these papers go with me. If you insist on dancing I'll have to go along, but I'll have the papers on me."

As the girls talked over their plans they arranged for the care of their plane for the night and for refueling, as they intended to have an early start the next morning. Then they went to the hotel where many summer guests were staying.

Martha made friends easily and by the time Mary Eliska had registered for them at the desk and made arrangements for getting away early the next morning, Martha had a group of girls around her and was laughing and joking with them as if she had always known them. Mary Eliska envied her sister this ability to get acquainted with people at a moment's notice. It would have taken her a week, at least, without Martha to break the ice, to become friends with these strangers. When the two girls came down to the dining room half an hour later, their new acquaintances hardly recognized them. Martha was dressed in a fluffy gown which made her look like a lovely bit of Dresden china. Mary Eliska was very boyish and trim in her sports dress. She had an aristocratic manner, attracting notice by her very aloofness.

The dancing pavilion was built out over the water and they could hear the surf breaking about the pier. Martha danced to her heart's content, for partners flocked about her. But Mary Eliska was uneasy for pinned to her slip were the valuable papers she must deliver in Peru. She was relieved when Martha finally consented to go back to the hotel, exchanging addresses and promising life-long friendship with her new friends as she went along.

At the first flush of dawn, Mary Eliska and Martha were at the hangars preparing to take off. Mary Eliska made a careful check-up on her plane to see that everything was in order and as they were about ready to climb into the cockpits, they heard a shout and their new friends came hurrying to the field to bid them goodbye.

Martha was glad they had come. She wanted to show off her quiet sister who always got her plane into the air so gracefully, and her face glowed with pride as Mary Eliska taxied across the field, swung around and headed into the wind for a good take-off. *Skybird* took to the air like a great bird and under Mary Eliska's guidance circled the field several times for the benefit of their friends, then headed out over the Atlantic, flying south.

They did not know that a plane had been set down on the field half an hour before. The pilot had recognized *Skybird* and kept well out of sight. As he watched the girls from the shelter of the hangar, his face expressed the hatred and treachery that he felt.

It was Thatcher Allen, their father's business rival and dangerous enemy! "What are those girls doing here? Do they imagine they can fly to Peru and see Sean Hall?" thought Thatcher Allen to himself. He made up his mind that the girls would never reach Peru. He would stop them, somehow. He *must* do it.

Thatcher Allen frowned. As his plane was more powerful than *Skybird*, he could easily outfly them and reach the mine a day before the two girls could do so. But, first, he had some mysterious business to attend to before he would have the money for the option. Meanwhile he must do something to prevent the girls from continuing their trip until he was ready.

Before *Skybird* had disappeared into the clouds, Thatcher Allen had left the field and was following after that tiny speck in the sky, trailing it relentlessly.

The next stop was Miami, and here again the girls made a thorough inspection of their plane. From now on their way would be over the Caribbean, where storms might spring up without warning. *Skybird* must be in perfect form. And when Mary Eliska finished her inspection, the little plane was ready for the hop to Havana. The girls congratulated themselves that everything was going along well. They were even a few hours ahead of their schedule and Mary Eliska's face was glowing with happiness and excitement. Ahead of them was the Caribbean. She had often dreamed of making this flight over tropical waters and now she was really here.

Below her were the keys and reefs of the Florida coast spread out flat on the blue water. They were like a painting in delicate pastel shades. Crossing the line of the reefs, *Skybird* headed boldly out to sea. Martha watched the smooth water, fascinated by the patterns made by steamers as they cut through the water, leaving an ever-widening wake behind them. She felt safe, knowing that their amphibian plane could land on the water and float.

Mary Eliska sighted the coast of Cuba first, a delicate outline seen through a haze that dimmed the view and gave it a fairy-like appearance. Soon they sighted the grim old Morro Castle, the Spanish fort, and as they came nearer and flew above it, they could see the broad avenues of the lovely city of Havana. The marble capitol was dazzlingly white in the sunshine and the colored roofs of the houses, as seen from the air, arranged themselves in a fantastic design. It was a city of gay pleasure.

Mary Eliska brought her airplane down at the Havana airport with a sense of relief. The first lap of that journey was over now.

A few minutes later she was handed a telegram which read: "Liam McAdams and Syd will join you at Havana. Wait. Dad."

Mary Eliska's eyes blazed for a moment. "What do you think of that, Martha? Liam McAdams and Syd are coming here. We're to *wait* for them! I'll say that's nerve! Dad thinks we can't make the trip without the help of the boys."

"That's nonsense, Mary Eliska! Dad knows we're equal to it. The boys probably want a holiday and are coming just for the fun of it. I'm going to be really glad to see them. The more the merrier, I say," replied Martha.

"I'd be glad to see them if I thought that their trip was not just because they think that we have to be looked after," declared Mary Eliska. "I want to make this flight without help from anybody."

"Don't get too independent, Mary Eliska. It doesn't pay," her sister cautioned her. "But right now let's go and get some breakfast. I'm starved."

After they had finished with the customs and entry regulations the girls started toward the restaurant. A plane was circling about their heads looking for a landing.

Suddenly Mary Eliska grabbed her sister's arm. "Oh Martha, look there! It's Thatcher Allen!"

"Where did he come from? What's he doing down here?" demanded Martha, as if her sister knew all about Thatcher Allen's affairs.

Mary Eliska laughed nervously. "Ask me something easy! But of one thing we can be sure. Whatever it is that has brought Thatcher Allen down here, it's bound to be crooked, whether he is on business of his own or just trailing us. That man *couldn't* be decent!" Mary Eliska said with indignation.

"What are we going to do, Mary Eliska?" asked Martha.

"We are going to do nothing at all, except keep our eyes open," answered Mary Eliska as she slipped back to the hangar and spoke to the mechanic who was looking over her plane. She gave him her sweetest smile as she spoke to him. "Keep your eye on my plane. Don't let any stranger near it." And she gave him a five-dollar bill.

The young man promised and as Mary Eliska turned away he smiled to himself. "Guess she's new to the game," he thought. "Afraid someone will want parts of her plane for souvenirs."

"Come on Mary Eliska, hurry. If you only knew how hungry I am!" cried Martha. But now another plane had approached and made a neat landing.

Martha stopped short and grabbed her sister's arm. "Oh Mary Eliska," she cried, "I'm almost sure that's Liam McAdams in his new plane."

"You're right. That's Liam McAdams! And Syd is with him!"

A few minutes later Liam McAdams and Syd leaped from the cockpits and were waving to the girls with whoops of delight. Mary Eliska and Martha hastened back across the field to welcome them.

"Hurry up!" cried Mary Eliska. "Martha is starving!"

"She's got nothing on us," Sid answered. "We could eat our shoe strings,—almost!"

When they were all seated at breakfast, Mary Eliska suddenly turned to ask Liam McAdams, "What's the idea of trailing us down here? Are you taking a vacation?"

"A sort of vacation," answered Liam McAdams. "About an hour after you left the other day, Syd and I got home. We finished up our business in half the time we expected. Then we heard some reports. Thatcher Allen had been back at the field and was bragging around that he was starting out to make the final deal with Sean Hall for your father's flying field. He sent notice to your father to vacate the field."

"Why the nerve of that man!" cried Mary Eliska. "He'll do no such thing! I won't stand for it!"

"Anyway," went on Liam McAdams. "We found out that Thatcher Allen had started south and your father wanted to warn you, so he sent us. And here we are."

"Yes," Mary Eliska broke in. "And Thatcher Allen set down his plane at the Havana airport just a little while ago. I'm sure he saw us. Even if he didn't he'd recognize *Skybird*. That man is up to mischief."

"Do you think he's going to try to make trouble for us?" asked Martha anxiously. "I'm afraid of that man, after what he did to you boys in Newfoundland."

"We are not going to worry about it," Mary Eliska announced with decision. "We are going to keep right on at the job we set out to do, and trust to luck to get us through safely."

The four friends had an excellent breakfast with tropical fruits and delicious Cuban dishes. At times they forgot all about Thatcher Allen and his threats to take away their father's flying field. It was good to be together in this romantic city of Havana, and hard to realize that danger threatened them.

All about them were smartly dressed care-free people, spending money lavishly on the pleasures of the gay city. People came here from all over the world just to enjoy themselves.

But Mary Eliska would not allow them to forget that a difficult job lay ahead of them. It was necessary to push on. Consulting their maps, they laid out their route. The next hop would be across the open waters of the Caribbean to the landing field at Gracias a Dios in Honduras. That would be their next meeting place in case they became separated. Liam McAdams and Syd had planned to see them safely through the treacherous tropical weather of the Caribbean, before returning to Elmwood. Now that they were tipped off to the fact that Thatcher Allen might make trouble, Mary Eliska could be depended on to keep her eyes open and avoid him. But the boys decided they would watch Thatcher Allen and find out what he was up to.

The weather reports were favorable. There was always the warning to watch out for sudden storms that were common over the Caribbean.

Their take-off was delayed by Mary Eliska insisting that her engine was not working properly. Liam McAdams came alongside to listen as she warmed up the motor. "Why it sounds all right, Mary Eliska. I don't hear anything wrong," he said.

"But listen!" shouted Mary Eliska. "Listen to that rough hum."

"You're right, Mary Eliska," said Liam McAdams as the girl shut off her engine and got out. Slipping into her overall suit, she started to work.

"Has anyone been near my plane?" asked Mary Eliska of the young mechanic whom she had warned.

"No. That is nobody touched it. There was another flyer who stood around admiring it and asking who you were. He even wanted to know where you were going. Then he said he'd like to take a look at your engine to see what kind you had. But I didn't let him stick around," replied the youth. "I told him to clear out!"

Liam McAdams and Mary Eliska got to work without waiting for further explanation. A full hour went by before they had the engine humming smoothly enough to suit the trained and sensitive ear of Mary Eliska.

Once more they were ready to take off. Mary Eliska taxied over the long field, making sure that the engine was working properly before she pulled back on the stick and sent *Skybird* nosing into the brilliant blue sky.

Mary Eliska's heart was beating with happy excitement. The take-off never became a commonplace occurrence to her. She thrilled as she felt the ship lifting from the ground and in the face of the wind, rising to dizzy heights above the earth.

Liam McAdams and Syd followed and for half an hour they flew at about the same altitude. Then Liam McAdams lagged behind and rose above them to a height of five thousand feet. Both flyers were watching the sky behind them to make sure that their enemy was not in pursuit.

Thatcher Allen had put in a busy morning in Havana. Here was where he had some shady business that would give him the ready money for taking up the option on the Albert Stricklin Flying Field. And when he started out half an hour after the other planes, he flew high and well out of sight.

Mary Eliska and Martha were content to fly at about two thousand feet. They were enjoying the view of the southern sea dotted with islands and failed to see the pursuing plane, high above them in the distance.

But Thatcher Allen was watching intently every move of the two planes, and the cold, menacing light in his eyes was a threat against these young flyers who dared to upset his plans, and keep him from realizing his ambition.

His mind was working fast. At the next flying field, he would have a show-down with them. His business deal in Havana had not been successful. It would be necessary to return to that city once more before he got the money. Thatcher Allen did not know just what kind of a show-down he would have with these girl flyers. He would leave it to chance and his usual good luck unless he could think of some plan as he flew through the blue sky. Up in the clean air of the heavens this man was planning to destroy them.

But Mary Eliska and Martha, unconscious of his plans, were watching the changing colors of the islands, then faced once more the open sea toward Honduras.

CHAPTER 18.3
Tropic Storm

High above the sapphire mirror of the Caribbean, Mary Eliska kept her airplane in a southwesterly course. The sun was a pitiless ball of flame that sent out long fingers of fire. It was tropic weather.

Above them Liam McAdams's plane was soaring ahead now. The sight of Thatcher Allen at Havana had made them fear an attack, and the four flyers were watching to see whether a third plane was following them.

Leaving the islands behind they flew out over the sea, a great expanse of deep blue and purple water.

Suddenly Martha called to her sister. "Look Mary Eliska, there's land over there, away to the left."

"Yes, I see," answered Mary Eliska. But she was watching the horizon with anxious eyes. That dark purplish mass looked to her like a low-lying cloud. There was something unnatural about it. Its color was changing rapidly to a reddish hue.

"I don't like the looks of it, Martha," called Mary Eliska. "See how the light is changing."

A reddish haze had spread over the whole sky, the sun appeared like a great disc of hot metal. The sight was weird and menacing.

"What's the matter, Mary Eliska? Is it a storm?" Martha asked.

"Yes, a tropic storm. We've got to race it. Where are the boys?" Martha leaned over the cowling and strained her eyes to the sky, but that strange and terrifying haze had blotted out the other plane. Mary Eliska circled and banked in an effort to find their friends. Then, opening the throttle wide, the girl sent her plane straight before the storm. It was her only chance. If she could out-race that storm, she would be saved.

Sending her plane ahead and in a gradual rise, the girl aviatrix tried to get above the haze. These tropical storms often covered only a small area, but very soon she realized that the cloud was coming on and rising faster than her plane.

Below them the sea was still visible, a dull lead color now with greenish tipped white-caps. The wind had not reached the plane yet and the girls hoped that they might be able to keep ahead of the tempest.

Then it came, first with a gust that made the little ship bob and dance about. Mary Eliska knew this was only the beginning. The storm was upon them! The next deep breath of the hurricane would threaten their lives with its fury. Mary Eliska held her plane to the only course she dared to take. She was racing for dear life!

The throb of the motor told that the engine was being strained to the limit of its power. There was no time to lose. If the girls were to escape destruction, they must take that chance.

When the full force of the tempest struck the plane, it was tossed about like a straw in the wind. Under less experienced hands than Mary Eliska's the plane would have crashed. Mary Eliska could feel the craft being shaken as if a mighty hand had taken it in its grip, as the gusts of wind struck vicious blows at the wings.

Mary Eliska's grim face was set with determination. But her hand on the stick showed no sign of her fear, it did not tremble or lose its power to control. She was glad now that her father had insisted on training her in all the stunts of the air, for there was no possible position that her plane would take that Mary Eliska had not put it into deliberately above her own flying field, and brought it out safely.

But this was altogether different. There she had *put* the plane into those dangerous positions, now she was being *forced* into them and she never knew what was coming next.

Mary Eliska knew the danger she was in but she felt no panic. Every nerve was tingling, every sense alert. She knew she was doing her best. Her head was clear, her hand was steady and she kept the little plane, climbing, ever climbing.

The girl pilot felt that *Skybird* was fighting for life, with what seemed like human intelligence. It shuddered and shook and it seemed to try to right itself after a gust of angry wind.

Martha clung to the cowling, terrified yet fascinated as she watched her younger sister. At times it seemed as if the plane had turned clear over, as if it were going down in a tail spin, but the next moment Mary Eliska would bring it up for a second. It was a big fight.

"She'll win," thought Martha. "She's wonderful!"

Only for a second did Mary Eliska lose hope of victory. There was a sputtering of the engine that her trained ear heard. It sent a chill to her heart. Her hand shook. She gave a frantic glance back to see if Martha had heard that menacing sound. And that one look showed her a clear space in the dark masses.

The storm was passing. Mary Eliska held to the controls, praying that the engine would hold out until the wind ceased.

Suddenly Mary Eliska was able to put her plane into a steep climb that brought her above the storm. Coming out of that black cloud Mary Eliska saw Liam McAdams' plane ahead of her. She followed it, her heart singing for joy. A mist came to her eyes as she realized that it was only by a miracle that both planes had gone through the storm and survived.

Mary Eliska signaled with the wings of her plane and was answered in the same manner. She followed Liam McAdams' lead, hoping that her engine would not go back on her. At intervals she heard a sputter that terrified her, but now the sky was clearing. She felt hopeful.

Liam McAdams finally headed east. This was strange. Mary Eliska looked at her compass and a frown came to her face. What was Liam McAdams doing? He was going far out of his way. At last she understood. Away in the distance was an island. He was going to land. She wondered if he were having engine trouble.

Mary Eliska did not dare to open her throttle wide. Any extra strain might be her undoing. But, as she neared the small island the plane ahead banked, circled and signaled, then went into a dive for landing on the far side of the island.

Mary Eliska tried to follow but her engine was sputtering once more. She made a long dive which brought her amphibian into the water at the near side of the island. There was a broad strip of sand and Mary Eliska sent her plane cutting through the spray on to the beach.

"We're safe!" cried Martha as she nimbly stepped from the cockpit, followed by her sister. "Wasn't that an awful storm?"

"It's just luck that we're alive. Now let's go over and see the boys. It looks as if they might be having engine trouble, too," replied Mary Eliska.

After making fast their plane by a rope to a palm tree at the water's edge, the two girls scrambled up over the rocky ridge to the low summit. The island was narrow at this end and soon they were looking straight down upon a sheltered cove where the boys had landed and saw the amphibian floating on the water. A launch shot out from the shore and when it reached the plane, several bundles were dropped into the boat by the aviator, who then got out of the plane and was taken ashore. The girls looked at each other, distress on their faces.

"We've followed a plane, but it's the wrong one!" cried Mary Eliska. "What a stupid thing to do! Martha, how can you ever trust me again?"

"But *I* thought it was Liam McAdams and Syd, too," replied Martha. "Never mind, these men will help us fix our plane and we'll be off in an hour or two."

With a wave of his hand the aviator started upward toward the summit where the girls stood.

"He seems to be friendly," commented Mary Eliska. "But let's wait here to greet him. How he'll laugh when I tell him that I thought I was following another plane." The girls waited at the summit until the stranger came up the winding trail. As they heard his footsteps Mary Eliska moved forward to speak, then grabbed Martha's arm with a nervous grip. The man had come out on the summit and was staring at them with a triumphant grin. His eyes were glittering with a fierce and cruel light that made the cast in his eye more pronounced. It added to the sinister look in his face. The man facing them was Thatcher Allen!

A moment later the girls gasped with dismay for their enemy, Culley May, came shambling up the trail.

"Well, look who's here!" said Culley May and added sarcastically, "this *is* a pleasant surprise!"

But Thatcher Allen silenced his rough-neck follower with a scowl and a low snarl. "Don't get funny. Shut up!"

Thatcher Allen, with menace in his voice, addressed the girls, "Why did you come here?" he demanded. "What do you want?"

Mary Eliska stammered for a second then answered: "I was having trouble with my engine after that storm and I knew I'd have to come down, so I followed you here."

Thatcher Allen stared at the girl and shrugged his shoulders. "That sounds fishy to me. I think you're trying to spy on me. What brought you away down here?"

"We're on a vacation," answered Mary Eliska. "We are on our way to the Canal Zone."

Thatcher Allen watched the girls contemptuously. "I don't believe you!" he said. "I think you came here to watch me." Suddenly he turned to Culley May. "Go on down there and see what's the matter with Mary Eliska's plane."

"But I'd rather fix my own plane. I'm used to it and can fix it in a minute. I know exactly what's the matter."

"No! Let Culley May go as I told him! You stay here!" There was a note of command that frightened the girls. Martha touched Mary Eliska's arm and said softly. "Careful, Mary Eliska, don't make him angry."

Mary Eliska gave her sister a grateful smile. She turned to Thatcher Allen and asked pleasantly. "Did you get into that storm?"

"No, I knew too much to let that happen. I saw your plane go into it and thought you were done for," he answered.

"How did you avoid it?" asked Mary Eliska.

"I was flying high, fifteen thousand feet. It never touched me. The storm was all below me. I'm used to these hurricanes and I can usually guess about how far the storm extends."

"I tried to get above it, but I didn't go far enough." Mary Eliska was watching Thatcher Allen's face while she was talking. Would he guess that she was carrying an important paper for Sean Hall? Would she be able to keep it hidden where he could not find it?

Now it was safely sewn once more in the lining of her flying coat but that was not a good hiding place if he thought to search her.

A sudden shout from the harbor sent Thatcher Allen hurrying down the trail. Then he turned back. "Stay right where you are," he ordered the girls. On second thought he said. "No, go on down the trail ahead of me."

"But I don't want to go!" flared Mary Eliska.

"If you're wise you'll do as I say!" Without another word he thrust the girls ahead of him toward the beach.

Mary Eliska went without any further argument. For suddenly it had occurred to her that she might learn something of Thatcher Allen's schemes if she pretended, to be friendly with him and didn't make him angry.

At the harbor a gang of men were loading a boat, preparing to take it to the plane. Pedro, the chief was over six feet tall, wore only a loin cloth and looked mean. This giant was watching his men, who were working for Thatcher Allen. Pedro seemed to have a few words of English but he spoke to his men in creole.

"What terrible looking people!" whispered Martha. "They look as if they might be cannibals."

Mary Eliska laughed to conceal her fear. "I could even stand having a cannibal around if I were sure that Liam McAdams and Syd had come through the storm. They were flying higher than we were but I'm afraid they weren't high enough, even then."

Mary Eliska was looking about her taking stock of the camp, which was composed of mud huts, and several shacks that had evidently been built recently. On the trail loomed a tall, weathered rock. Mary Eliska was pointing out to her sister a great crevice in this stone and explaining the formation of that wide fissure when Thatcher Allen turned and saw her. His face flushed angrily. He gave a final order to the leader of the workers and then signaled the girls to precede him up the trail.

"This is no place for you, after all. I shouldn't have brought you down here where those men could see you. They belong to a fierce tribe living in the clearings in the jungle. Pedro, the chief, that big fellow, lives in one of my mud huts down there, so you'd better keep away." Thatcher Allen was nervous and stammered as he talked. As they reached the summit once more Mary Eliska took a good look at him, and saw that he was agitated.

"Evidently there is something down there that he doesn't want us to see," whispered Mary Eliska to Martha as soon as she could do so without Thatcher Allen hearing her. "When I was interested in that big fissure in the rock, he was scared stiff. I'd like to find out what he's got down there that he doesn't want me to see. I'm going to find out! Just watch me!"

"Please don't! What do you care about his affairs? We've got troubles enough as it is. How are we ever going to get away from here? How will we fly to Peru with Dad's papers? My head is whirling with problems and all I want to do is to get out of this jam as quickly as possible." Martha ceased whispering as Thatcher Allen came closer.

Mary Eliska was looking toward her plane. Culley May was busily testing the motor. The girl could not bear the idea that Culley May should touch *Skybird*.

"If you don't mind, I think I'd like to do my own repair work," said Mary Eliska with as polite a smile as she could muster. "I've always done my own overhauling and somehow, I'd rather attend to it myself. It's very kind of you to want to be so helpful, but please tell Culley May to leave my plane alone."

As she started toward the beach where *Skybird* was standing, Thatcher Allen stepped ahead of her. "Now don't bother yelling and carrying on for there is no one around to hear you except my men. I'm boss here, and I tell you to keep quiet. I'm giving that plane to Culley May. It's his from now on."

"You're giving him *my* plane!" stormed Mary Eliska. "You have no right to do that!"

"Is that *so*? Well, I'm taking the right!"

"But what about us? How can we get away?" cried Martha, almost in tears. "If you take our plane, we've got to stay here."

"That's it exactly!" Thatcher Allen sneered. "Here you stay until I get ready to let you go."

He stared at them coldly then turned and walked away.

CHAPTER 18.4
Island Prisoners

Prisoners on a desert island!

Dazed by Thatcher Allen's brutality, Mary Eliska and Martha looked about for a way of escape, but there seemed no way out. Apart from the few huts in the cove where Thatcher Allen had his camp, there was no sign of life. They were alone and at the mercy of these unscrupulous men who had every reason to destroy them.

Martha clung to her sister with a grip that hurt. "Whatever will we do now?" she asked in a hoarse whisper. "We're up against it for sure."

But Mary Eliska did not hear her. She was watching with flashing eyes as Culley May worked over the plane. The next instant she was running down the slope in frantic haste with Martha at her heels.

"You let that plane alone, Culley May! Take your hands off!" Mary Eliska picked up a large stone, raised it above her head and with a wide sweep of the arm, she started to throw the missile, but at that moment her hand was seized from behind and a low, mocking voice said, "Not so fast, young lady!"

Mary Eliska turned to face Thatcher Allen.

"Let me go!" she demanded.

Thatcher Allen released his grip with a vigorous shove that sent the girl spinning across the sands. Martha caught her as she staggered.

"Mary Eliska, listen to me," said Martha with decision in her voice. "I don't know what we are going to do, but one thing sure is that you mustn't make that man angry. He's capable of anything. He'd think nothing of leaving us here to starve. He'd even kill us if it suited his purpose." Martha shook her sister's arm. "Don't talk to him at all if you can't do it without getting angry."

Mary Eliska was deathly white, not from fear but anger. "But look, Martha! You don't seem to realize that Culley May is going to take our plane away from us. Now we'll be real castaways!"

Martha searched the sky. "Oh, if Liam and Syd would only come! I'm afraid something terrible has happened to them. I didn't see them after the storm struck our plane. Where did they go?"

"Don't talk about it, Martha. Let's get busy and do something so we won't have time to think. I don't dare!" Mary Eliska said with trembling lips.

The girls stood watching as Culley May and Thatcher Allen wheeled *Skybird* around to head away from the beach and over the water. They started the engine. It coughed, it wheezed, it sputtered but at the same time the amphibian taxied over the smooth blue waters and took to the air. *Skybird* was flying away without them.

Thatcher Allen waved his hand toward the departing plane, then turned and climbed the hill, looking back at the girls with a triumphant grin, far more menacing than an angry scowl would have been. Mary Eliska knew that he had never forgiven her for her part in the rescue of Liam McAdams and Syd when he had kidnapped them in the far north.

Now was his great opportunity to settle matters once and for all. This was his chance. He had them at his mercy.

Everything had worked out to Thatcher Allen's advantage. Culley May's plane had been wrecked some weeks before and on that account they had worked under a handicap, waiting to replace it. Now a fine little plane had miraculously dropped from the sky at their feet.

Thatcher Allen smiled. "Luck comes that way to me," he said to himself. "I have a few bad breaks, but often they work out for my good. If I had succeeded in getting the Albert Stricklin Flying Field six months ago as I planned. I'd never have started this island base. At least not so soon.—And this has turned out to be the best graft I've ever struck."

Culley May had flown *Skybird* around the tip of the island to the quiet waters of the little harbor. The engine was sputtering and protesting but Culley May was able to bring the plane down safely on the shore. As he turned to Thatcher Allen, he saluted and exclaimed, "That was some trick you played! How did you do it. Chief?"

Thatcher Allen laughed heartily as he answered: "They thought they were following Liam McAdams's plane. I'm almost sure that the girls were starting out to go to Peru to see Sean Hall. When I was up there Liam McAdams and Syd were away. Probably when they got back they learned that I was heading south and decided to catch up with the girls and go with them as a protection against *me*."

"What happened to the boys?" asked Culley May.

"That's the joke. Liam McAdams's and Mary Eliska's planes both got into a storm. I didn't see Liam McAdams's plane when it was over, so I hope he went to the bottom of the

Caribbean. Mary Eliska didn't see it either. But she saw mine and followed me, thinking it was Liam McAdams."

"That was a neat dodge. How did you ever happen to think about it?" Culley May not only thought his boss was smart, but took pains to tell him so.

Thatcher Allen might have told Culley May that he had not planned the ruse and that it had been entirely an accident. But instead of that he looked wise and said. "I think fast! That's how I always win!"

Meanwhile his two captives had taken shelter from the sun under a spreading tree.

"How I'd like to down that man!" exclaimed Mary Eliska with blazing eyes as she watched Thatcher Allen's figure disappear. "This is the worst jam we've ever been in."

"And Mary Eliska, this time there's no way out that I can see," said Martha, her body trembling with fear and nervousness.

But Mary Eliska was in a fighting mood. "There *is* a way out, I'm sure of it, and what's more I'm sure we can find it! I had to bite my tongue to keep from telling Thatcher Allen what I thought of him. He looked so smug and self-satisfied because he put something over on us."

"You did well, Mary Eliska, not to talk to him. I was scared stiff you'd fly out at him."

"I probably would have if you hadn't gripped my arm the way you did. Sometimes you spoil a good scrap that way. It might have done Thatcher Allen good to know what people think about him."

Suddenly a loud shriek broke the silence of the island. Mary Eliska and Martha clung together but the next minute Mary Eliska pointed with a smile to two brightly colored macaws above her head.

"Did you ever see anything as gay as those birds? Aren't they beautiful!" exclaimed Mary Eliska.

"I'd like them better if they wouldn't squawk so loudly," said Martha. "I do believe they have scared me out of a year's growth."

The macaws shrieked again as if protesting at the intrusion of the girls. Other strange birds took up the challenge and answered until the air was filled with their noise.

"Let's go!" said Mary Eliska with the faintest glimmer of a smile. "They don't seem to appreciate the honor of our company."

Hand in hand the girls climbed the ridge but kept out of sight of Thatcher Allen's camp. Below them and around a sharp point of rocky shore, they looked down over a forest of tropical trees, tall, slender stems and around the lower part of their trunks wound a thick tangle of vines.

"I wonder if we will ever get out of here alive?" whispered Martha in a strained voice. "You've read stories of people who were stranded on desert islands and lived there until they were old and ready to die."

"Well, this wouldn't be such a bad place to live," answered Mary Eliska. "If we had the family here and a nice house and books and things."

"But I don't like the idea of starving to death and that's what we would do here."

"We couldn't starve to death! Look down there, I've been waiting for you to say something. Those trees to the right are bananas, your favorite fruit!"

"I'll say so! Let's go get them. I'm starved!" Suddenly Martha stopped short. "Mary Eliska," she said hopefully, "could two girls live on bananas all their lives?"

"Possibly, but we wouldn't need to go on a full banana diet. There are coconut palms!" replied Mary Eliska.

Martha brightened up. "And if it comes to the worst, we will catch some fish."

"Fish!" cried Mary Eliska. "You know I *hate* fish!"

"Well, clams, oysters! We might find them here!"

"They're even worse," Martha declared. "*You* can have my share. I'll stick to bananas."

The girls were clambering down the rocky ridge to the clearing. As they found their way around a thick mat of low-growing bushes, they came suddenly upon a collection of mud huts. They were among them before they knew it.

The girls drew back to the shelter of the vines, half expecting to be surrounded by a howling mob. But not a sound came from the huts. Everything was quiet. No sign of life!

"Here's where we've got to watch our step, Martha! These men may have a way of hiding in ambush and shooting poison arrows at their enemies," whispered Mary Eliska.

"But we're not their enemies. We'd—why Mary Eliska, we'd try to *like* them if they'd give us a chance," Martha was looking anxiously around the shrub as she spoke.

Mary Eliska started to tiptoe toward the mud huts, although it was not necessary to guard her footfalls, for the soft green floor of the jungle gave back no sound. Martha tried to pull her sister back but Mary Eliska jerked away.

"Come on. We haven't any need to worry yet. This place is deserted. Look at those old mud huts, they are half destroyed by the rains." Mary Eliska drew her sister with her as she peered into every hut as she passed.

"Look at those huts ahead. They're altogether different. See how they've twined roots and vines and twigs together. They're like great birds' nests. I think that is a *clever* idea! I wonder if these houses belonged to the chief and his family?"

"Come on in and make an afternoon call." Mary Eliska laughed as she ran toward the doorway, then sprang back in terror.

"What's the matter, Mary Eliska? What did you see?" cried Martha, clinging to her sister's arm.

"Somebody was in that hut. I saw a child! It was a little one!" said Mary Eliska, then suddenly she broke loose from her sister and went once more toward the hut.

"Watch out, Mary Eliska," cried Martha. "Children are apt to scream and that will bring the whole tribe down upon us."

At that moment Mary Eliska burst into a happy laugh, a little face was peering around the side of the opening. A curious, wise little face that was wrinkled and hairy.

"It's a monkey!" exclaimed Mary Eliska with relief. "Only a cute little monkey!"

"Isn't he funny?" Martha was choking with laughter which she tried to hide, for the little creature looking up at them seemed so human that the girl felt she was being rude to laugh in its face.

Mary Eliska had a happy thought. She felt in her pockets and brought forth a little package. There were half a dozen crackers left from the supply Martha had provided.

"Say Mary Eliska, what's the idea! Don't feed him crackers. Are you crazy?" pleaded Martha.

But Mary Eliska was approaching the little animal and offering a bit of the cracker. The monkey shrank back, but only for a second. His curiosity was too great. As Mary Eliska dropped the morsel beside him, he grabbed it quickly and with a sudden leap slipped by them to the refuge of a tall tree. Then he devoured it greedily.

"Don't be too generous, Mary Eliska. We may need every bite we can get before this jam is over."

"All right, but I thought I'd better start by making friends with everything on the island. He's a nice little fellow. I wouldn't be surprised if he'd get quite friendly."

The monkey stared down at them with interest and when they moved away he scrambled to another tree nearer to them.

"Just watch him," laughed Martha. "Mary Eliska, you've made a big hit with that fellow."

"It's pleasant to find one friendly creature on the island. Come on and let's see what the inside of these woven houses are like. I'm not anxious to sleep out in the open. I think I've heard something about the moon in the tropics making people crazy." Mary Eliska led the way into the hut as she spoke, "Why, it's not so bad, we might manage to sleep in here."

"There's nothing else to do. I wouldn't want to take any chances with the moon," said Martha. "We have troubles enough now without losing our minds."

Mary Eliska laughed. "I guess you're right. We'll need all our wits to get ourselves out of this jam, and we'd better not get them addled."

Mary Eliska's laugh had relieved their taut nerves.

"If I could only be sure that Liam McAdams and Syd were safe, I could even take this disappointment and get some fun out of the situation. I'm really not frightened of Thatcher Allen,—very much!" she exclaimed.

If Mary Eliska could have heard the conversation between Thatcher Allen and Culley May at that moment she might have feared them, for Culley May had just asked, "What are you going to do with those girls? One thing sure they'll never leave this island alive, if I have my way."

Thatcher Allen turned on him with an angry snarl. "You haven't a word to say here! What's more you never will have. Just wait until you get your orders from me. I'll see that they don't get back to civilization for a long time, perhaps never, but I'll settle with them in my own way and when I get ready. I want no suggestions from you or anybody. You understand? I'm boss here on this island!"

"Yes, that's what I meant," replied Culley May.

"And if they come into this camp just keep your eye on them. Especially Mary Eliska! She was here about two minutes and was nosing about the big rock as if she knew I had things hidden there," snarled Thatcher Allen.

"Did she see anything?" asked Culley May.

"No, I got her away in time, but if she comes back she is apt to go right there. And if she'd ever get hold of those papers, we wouldn't be safe anywhere."

"Do you think Mary Eliska suspects and will try to get hold of them before they get away from the island?" inquired Culley May once more.

"They're not going to get away. At least not until I'm safe."

But Mary Eliska and Martha knew nothing of this threat against their lives. They went about the preparation for the night and their greatest fear was from animals and insects that were strange and terrifying to them.

"I'm awfully hungry, Mary Eliska. Come with me to get some bananas," said Martha as she started toward the clearing.

"They look green to me, you're apt to get good and sick if you eat them. Martha. I don't think I would," cautioned Mary Eliska.

"I'm sick now, I'm so hungry, so it won't hurt to be a little sicker," answered Martha as she reached up for one of the green bananas. "Anyway I think they're ripe." She passed one to Mary Eliska, who stripped back the skin and bit into it.

Mary Eliska rolled her eyes ecstatically. "Martha, we're in luck! I've never tasted anything so good in all my life. I'm sure I could live on bananas like these. Now, I *know* we won't starve to death."

Suddenly Martha caught her sister by the arm. From the clearing they could see a strip of the sea and across their line of vision came a small tramp steamer. It was headed from the south and was making straight toward the island.

"Now's our chance! We'll signal them and they will come to the rescue." Martha was trembling with excitement. Together they ran to the top of the ridge. The heat was intense but the girls carried their flying coats with them, hoping that they would have a chance to escape.

The girls waved their hands toward the steamer, but their hearts sank as it steamed past the headland and turned toward the harbor. On the shore of the cove great preparations had begun. A launch was put out from the beach and made toward the ship. Bales were dropped into the boat and taken ashore. A dozen trips were made with loads of food in cases, gasoline in metal drums and bale after bale of goods.

"Whatever does it all mean?" asked Martha in her sister's ear.

"It's my opinion," declared Mary Eliska, "that every word we've heard against that man is true. Someone said he was a smuggler. Now I believe it."

Thatcher Allen was busy directing the workers as they stowed away the bales in the old mud huts in the camp.

"What kind of smuggled goods would come in bales?" asked Martha. "I can't imagine what it can be."

"It might be lots of things, but probably it's silk. There's big money in that," explained Mary Eliska.

Mary Eliska did not voice all her thoughts. She was thinking that they had very little chance of getting back to their homes with the secret of Thatcher Allen's smuggling base known to them. She realized that the situation was far more serious than she imagined. He was not merely attempting to get the flying field away from her father. Thatcher Allen was mixed up in a crooked business. He would take desperate means to keep them from getting back to tell where his smuggling hang-out was situated.

Mary Eliska started back down the slope, dragging Martha with her. "Come away, I hate that man! I don't want to know what he's doing."

Night was fast approaching and the girls watched with dread the shadows creeping down over the jungle. They put their heavy flying coats on the ground, gathered large banana leaves for pillows and decided to sleep out in the open.

But no sooner had darkness come than weird sounds filled the jungle behind them. Crickets shrilled in the trees. Wild animals howled and slinking forms scurried by at the edge of the forest. Frogs kept up a continual, deafening chorus, and there were shrill cries of night birds. Mary Eliska and Martha held each other closely and stared into the darkness toward the jungle, trembling with fear.

"Look at the sky, Martha," said Mary Eliska trying to keep her mind from the strange and terrifying sounds of the tropical night. "You can see millions more stars down here than we can at home."

But even the brilliance of the moon could not hold their attention for long at a time. The rustling sounds all around them made their hearts thump.

"I can't stand it out here! Let's go into the hut," Martha pleaded in an anxious voice.

Although the noises continued, the girls felt a certain protection when inside the four walls, even though the opening in the front was no protection at all.

"Now Martha, I want you to go to sleep and get some rest, and I'll watch. In an hour and a half I'll waken you and you can take your turn." Mary Eliska took Martha in her arms as if she were a small child.

Martha burst into tears and threw herself on the floor of the hut, burying her head in her sister's lap. Mary Eliska stroked her head soothingly. And Martha was soon fast asleep.

When the hour and half was up, Mary Eliska did not have the heart to waken Martha. She looked pale and tired. Moving her head to the pillow of banana leaves, Mary Eliska lay down beside her. She had no desire to sleep.

Once she thought that some small animal had come into the hut. She sat up and strained her eyes into the dark corners, but could see nothing. The moon had set and the black night seemed a protection after the bright moonlight. Mary Eliska grew very drowsy. She had no energy with which to waken Martha.

The next thing Mary Eliska knew it was broad daylight. The sun was already sending its fiery blasts toward the earth. Martha was still sleeping; she had never stirred. Mary Eliska sat up suddenly. In the doorway was a woman. The girl's heart stopped beating for a moment. The woman stared at her and then giving forth a loud, weird, throaty call, she clapped her hands to beckon to her followers, who answered with yells and howls.

Martha awoke with a cry of terror. The two girls, pale and terrified, stood waiting their doom. They were trapped in a hut and outside was a band of people. What terrible fate was in store for the trembling victims?

CHAPTER 18.5
The Cave of Wonder

The woman stepped back and was talking excitedly with the others. Mary Eliska grabbed Martha by the arm. "Let's get outside," she said. "There may be some way of escape even yet. Don't give up!"

The two girls stepped out of the hut to be met by the grinning faces of a dozen or more women, who rolled their eyes and jabbered shrilly. Martha clutched at Mary Eliska.

"They're cannibals! They'll eat us! Look at their sharp teeth. Let's run!"

But the woman who had fiercely stared at them in the hut now stepped forward and offered a gift. It was a big package, something wrapped in leaves.

Mary Eliska accepted it, trying to force a smile and while she opened the leaves she said in an undertone to Martha, "We'll have to make them a gift in return. What have we got? Think fast, Martha."

For answer Martha unfastened the silver necklace with its bright pendant and Mary Eliska passed it to the woman. There were grunts of approval, smiles and nods as the others pressed close to examine the royal gift. They all seemed satisfied.

Mary Eliska had opened the package now and disclosed a big fish baked to a turn and garnished with leaves. "Horrid stuff!" she thought. "How I *hate* fish! But I'd better pretend to like it!"

Mary Eliska broke a bit from the fish, tasted it and tried to look pleased. Then she passed some to Martha and offered to share her gift with the women.

"Me Pedro's wife. Me Rosa. Come!" said the leader.

The woman repeated the words as if they meant nothing to her. Perhaps Pedro had spent hours teaching her those few phrases.

"Don't go," begged Martha. "They'll get us to their village, then eat us!"

But Mary Eliska laughed. "Why no, Martha, we've exchanged gifts. We're friends, like sisters."

Martha grumbled as Mary Eliska nodded her willingness to go and followed after the chief's wife who led the way straight toward the jungle. At first the girls could not see an opening in that wall of tangled leaves, but when they reached the trees, Rosa led them into a dark green tunnel and Mary Eliska and Martha followed, wondering what was coming next. They must have walked for half a mile through that passageway cut from the creepers, when the girls saw light ahead and soon emerged on a clearing, among mud huts, a swarm of men, women and naked children.

When the girls appeared, a cry went up from everyone that sent a chill to the heart. It was a sharp, penetrating cry that made shivers run up and down the spine.

But only for a moment were the girls afraid. The people were friendly, there was no doubt about that. The children stared at them with wonder in their big eyes. The girls lost no time in giving the little ones the few pieces of chocolate they had in the deep pockets of their flying coats.

"I'll take back everything I ever said, Martha, about you wearing a necklace with flying togs and making me, as well as yourself, carry a supply of chocolate. They have served us in good stead today," said Mary Eliska, her eyes glowing as she watched the children devour the sweets.

Martha was smiling triumphantly at Mary Eliska. "Your apology is accepted, my dear sister! Only don't let it happen again! And if they are going to spread a feast for us, I wish they'd hurry up, for my stomach is crying for food. Those bananas I ate last night weren't so very filling after all. And I don't care whether I ever see another one."

"No wonder, Martha! I was counting how many you ate and after the twelfth I stopped," answered her sister with a laugh.

The girls tried by gestures and smiles to indicate their pleasure at everything around them. They complimented Rosa, the chief's wife, for her fine hut. They admired the babies and by different signs expressed their delight. That they were understood was shown in the shining face of their hostess.

Martha gave a sigh of relief as a young girl, walking like a princess, was seen approaching with a huge bowl of steaming food. Plaited mats were spread for the guests and food was offered them while the whole village made a circle around them to watch them eat. Mary Eliska, never a big eater, was inclined to be a bit fussy about her food, but today she ate a portion of everything offered, whether it tasted good or not. Martha watched her in surprise and chuckled at the joke on her sister as she pretended to enjoy the fish.

"I don't care, Martha, go on and make fun of me! I'd rather eat than be eaten!" she retorted. "It's not too late for them to change their minds, even yet!"

Half an hour went by and Mary Eliska and Martha had succeeded in making friends with the shy little children. Suddenly Pedro walked into the clearing. He was scowling angrily. Once more the girls started in fear.

Pedro explained in the few words of English that he knew, how Thatcher Allen was very angry and had hit him.

"Thatcher Allen much bad man! Culley May, much, much bad, too! He kill you, maybe!"

"That's what I expected!" whispered Mary Eliska to her sister.

"No can do!" the chief dramatically cried, waving an arm around his little settlement. "No! My people, they watch, they hide you far away! Thatcher Allen no find!"

Mary Eliska explained to the chief what she wanted to do. They must put up some sort of signal so that Liam McAdams and Syd, their friends, would see it if they flew over the island.

"If only we had some white cloth," said Martha. "We could put out one of those signals we talked about once, a big letter T, on the top of a ridge. I'm sure the boys would understand that."

"They might if we had cloth to do it with, but we haven't. So that's out!" answered Mary Eliska.

Pedro had risen suddenly. He understood. He called to his wife and spoke to her in their own language. Rosa bobbed into her hut as fast as she could and in a few minutes returned bringing a roll of white goods which she presented to the girls.

At that moment a sharp whistle broke the quiet of the jungle village with a discordant note. Pedro jumped to his feet and the next moment Rosa was shoving the girls before her into the hut. Someone was coming! The whistle was a warning from one of the boys who was guarding the village.

When Thatcher Allen strode into the settlement a few minutes later, Rosa was busily plaiting a mat. All the women were at work and scarcely looked up as the man faced Pedro. "You lazy good-for-nothing! Get back to work! This is my busiest day and you lay off! The men won't work unless you're there!"

Pedro knew that this was no time to show fight. "Yes sir! I come by-em-by," he answered.

"Now!" shouted Thatcher Allen. Then he turned with a menacing glare at Rosa. "Did those girls sleep here last night?" He shook his fist at the woman.

Rosa jabbered in reply and looked bewildered, so Thatcher Allen turned to Pedro and repeated the question.

Pedro shook his head.

"Then what's happened to them? Not that I care much!" stormed Thatcher Allen as he stared about him.

"We no see 'em!" repeated Pedro.

Thatcher Allen went from one hut to another, peering inside. As he neared the chief's large house, he was met by Rosa's broad grin. She was sitting in the doorway and her large body completely filled the opening. She refused to get up, pretending not to understand what he wanted.

Suddenly Thatcher Allen turned and faced Pedro. "Now let me tell you one thing, Pedro. Listen to what I've got to say! If you or your people shelter those girls, you'll be sorry. I'll clean you out!" And with that threat Thatcher Allen strode back through the jungle track.

When he got far enough away, Rosa began to laugh in a low rumble which gradually increased in volume, until it reached a high, full roar. The other women joined in and the clearing was filled with their raucous shouts.

That was their answer to Thatcher Allen's threat.

It was very evident that the girls were being treated as honored guests. Mary Eliska found it hard to sample all the food that was brought her, but Martha was in her glory. She liked to eat. She liked strange dishes, and she ate enough for two. Mary Eliska had to pretend to be ill in order not to offend her hostess. And then as suddenly she had to pretend to get well again, for the kind-hearted woman insisted that she must give her medicine.—And it was made of fish oil!

That night when Pedro returned from the shore, the news he brought was not good. Thatcher Allen was planning on taking the girls in the launch over to a small island to the eastward where they would be absolutely alone. There were still wild beasts on that island. It meant certain death.

That night the girls slept in the hut belonging to Pedro. They stretched out on mats and the women stood guard. Not a breath of air was stirring in that close interior. Mary Eliska and Martha felt as if someone were clutching at their throats it was so hard to get a breath. They were not troubled with fears of capture, for Pedro had stationed sentinels beyond the clearing to give warning if anyone approached. But in spite of this the girls slept fitfully. The air was stifling.

At the first glow of dawn Rosa appeared at the door of the hut. She said, "Come!" And there was an excited light in her eyes as she rolled them.

The girls lost no time in obeying her command. A guard of young men went ahead, then came Pedro and his wife, followed by Mary Eliska and Martha with two tall and powerful guards. The young women of the tribe came next, and the procession ended with more guards.

"We don't know where we're going," said Martha in a whisper to her sister as they walked along. "But we're going in style!"

It was a long walk through the jungle passage, a mile perhaps, but it was hard for the girls to tell how far they had come. The damp heat of the tunnel was oppressive. Perspiration streamed from their bodies. Their thick clothes were unbearably hot, although one of the guards carried their heavy coats.

Mary Eliska and Martha arrived at the next clearing, pale, hollow-eyed and ready to drop. But the end of their journey was not yet. They had reached the edge of the jungle and now had to climb up a steep ridge to a broad plateau. But the hot air was a relief after the humid atmosphere of the passage through the vines and creepers of the jungle. Suddenly they stopped, looking toward the sky, Thatcher Allen might be watching from the air.

Mary Eliska and Martha scanned the horizon for signs of an approaching plane. It was hopeless. They both knew that it would never occur to the boys, if they were saved from the storm, to hunt for them to the eastward.

Finally as they reached the ridge, everyone stopped and prepared to camp. "What's the matter with these people?" whispered Martha. "Do they imagine they can hide us on the very top of the ridge? What are they going to do?"

"I haven't the least idea, Martha, but I'm going to trust Pedro. I believe he is honest and really wants to help us," answered Mary Eliska as she watched.

Suddenly Pedro dropped to the ground. Mary Eliska looked just in time to see the earth swallow him up. She rubbed her eyes and looked again. Pedro had disappeared. Then Mary Eliska saw what was going on. Evidently these people had a subterranean hiding place, the opening of which was at the summit of the ridge. The entrance was narrow and Rosa had some difficulty in getting her large body through. She squeezed and struggled, and Pedro pulled from below until she finally slid through. Mary Eliska was invited to follow.

What were they up to? How could she explain to them that she must be above ground to watch for her friends?

"Come!" The girls heard Rosa's voice coming from the cavern. Mary Eliska sat down and putting her feet through the opening, found that they rested on a slippery rock. Getting a foothold she put up a hand for Martha. Slipping and sliding down the slope the two girls found themselves in a strange purple glow. When they reached the first level place, Pedro and Rosa were waiting for them.

Mary Eliska stood gazing about her. They were in an enormous cave, lined with crystals, and the sunlight which shone through the opening, caught the facets of the crystals and shot out in flashes of color: red, orange, yellow, blue, indigo, violet, and all the thousands of shades between. It was a gorgeous spectacle. The girls were breathless. They had often read of the crystal caves and wished that they could see one.

Finally Mary Eliska turned to her sister. "Would you believe it, Martha? For a few seconds I thought something had happened to us, that we had fallen down and been killed."

"Killed! What are you talking about, Mary Eliska? Have you gone crazy from all this excitement?" cried Martha anxiously.

"I thought—well you see I wondered if this was heaven. It's so beautiful, it might easily be. Even yet I can hardly believe it's real," said Mary Eliska with a little catch in her voice. "I want to cry!"

"You cry! That's a joke! Let me see you do it once!" teased Martha. "It's not often you feel that way, so go ahead. Don't let me stop you."

But Mary Eliska did not cry. She turned to Pedro and Rosa and thanked them for bringing her to this wonderful cave.

Sea water rose in the cave and made a lake. Finally as their eyes got used to the darkness below they could see a boat. It was built of woven twigs and covered with skin. A small boy who had followed them into the cave, dived into the dark water and swam to the boat. Others followed and the small craft was soon full of little figures. With whoops of delight they paddled the boat wildly about the lake.

"Even these boys have to show off," said Martha with a laugh.

"Don't laugh, Martha. They are doing their best to entertain us," Mary Eliska answered as she clapped her hands, which sent the boys into still wilder stunts.

The girls were now in a worse jam than ever. Here they were perfectly safe, they felt sure. But how could they watch for Liam and Syd? How could they signal for help? When Mary Eliska explained this to Pedro, he produced the white cloth that Rosa had given them. Mary

Eliska tore it to the proper size and shape to make an enormous letter T. Much against his wishes Pedro allowed the girls to climb out of the cave and direct the spreading of the cloth on the ground, where it could be seen from the sky.

"It's only a long chance, Martha, but it's the only thing I can think of. If we made a smoke signal or anything like that, Thatcher Allen would suspect at once," explained Mary Eliska.

"I know, but don't you think he'll suspect if he sees this white cloth spread out on the ground?" asked Martha.

Mary Eliska expressed her fears to Pedro, who was arranging the work of some men nearby. The big chief assured her that he would attend to that. His people would camp on the hill, then Thatcher Allen would think that the cloth had something to do with the work of the tribe.

In less than an hour one or two huts were ready, a crude cooking place had been built and the women were preparing breakfast.

Mary Eliska and Martha wanted to stay above ground, but Pedro shook his head vigorously and explained that Thatcher Allen was "very much bad," and was planning to take them away where they would surely be killed. Mary Eliska and Martha slid down the opening and reached the level in safety.

"After all, Martha, we have nothing to complain of. It's a gorgeous place to be imprisoned. Let's make the best of it and enjoy it, for we're not apt to see anything like it again," comforted Mary Eliska as she saw Martha's frowning face.

"It's all right here, but I'd rather stay in the open. Besides I'm beginning to like that tribe. I'll say that Pedro is a prince."

"Oh no, he isn't," laughed Mary Eliska. "He's the whole show! He's the Big Chief. He's king! And Rosa is a queen, a very big queen!"

The queen herself brought them their breakfast, more strange food, more fish, more bananas. Pedro had already eaten and was on his way with his men to the beach to help Thatcher Allen and Culley May.

The morning seemed long. There was nothing to do but watch the flashes of color in the dome. And even Mary Eliska lost some of her enthusiasm at the monotony of the playing light. Finally it got on her nerves. Suddenly a face appeared at the opening. A hissing sound came from his lips, then the face disappeared.

"What do you make of that?" asked Martha. "Do you suppose that hiss can be translated to mean the same as in our language? Are they hissing us, and why?"

Mary Eliska was already making her way up the steep wall of the cave. "I don't know what it's all about, but I'm going to find out," she called back.

As Mary Eliska reached the opening, she heard the hum of a motor overhead. Then she ducked back quickly, for there was only one man in the plane. He had banked and circled low, and Mary Eliska had seen that mocking face.

It was Thatcher Allen!

CHAPTER V18.6
Trapped!

For a moment Mary Eliska withdrew her face from the opening, then like a flash she had scrambled through the hole at the surface and was standing in plain view of the flyer. What's more, she was sobbing and shaking her fist toward Thatcher Allen.

"It's *Skybird*! He's taking our plane!" she cried.

As if mocking her, *Skybird* flipped its tail gracefully and zoomed into the blue.

As Mary Eliska stepped on to the plateau, the women surrounded her, trying to hide her from the man watching them from above. Mary Eliska could not be sure that he had seen her, but Martha had no doubt in the matter.

"Now you've done it, Mary Eliska!" she cried. "Why don't you think before you do such a thing? You're apt to get these people into trouble! Thatcher Allen said he'd clean them out!"

"Oh, I know, Martha. I'm sorry I did it, but just then I couldn't help it. I was crazy! I can't bear to have *Skybird* used by a smuggler. I'll feel as if my little plane were dirty after he's had his hands on her. Martha, what are we going to do?"

But Martha had no suggestions to offer. They were prisoners without question. How long they would have to remain here, she had no idea. They knew only too well what their father and mother were thinking. If Liam and Syd had escaped destruction in the storm, their report would leave no doubt in Albert's mind, at least, that the girls had been lost in the hurricane. Mary Eliska knew that the suspense would mean torture for her parents. How thankful she was that Sally Wyn was with them to comfort them and, with her cheerful ways, keep them hoping that all was well.

If Albert and his wife could only have seen them surrounded by these friendly people, they would not have been any more hopeful of their final escape.

Thatcher Allen had flown off into the blue with *Skybird*, and Mary Eliska's heart was sore and bitter with anxiety and anger against her father's enemy.

If she could have known Thatcher Allen's thoughts at that moment, she would have realized that she was in grave danger. Thatcher Allen had planned to search for the girls as soon as the important matter of the smuggled silk had been attended to. He guessed that Mary Eliska was on her way to Sean Hall's mine to plead with him to renew the contract and extend the option on the flying field. He had an idea that she was carrying some money.

Thatcher Allen was not in a hurry. He had the girls safely on the island. They were his prisoners. He could take his time in getting the papers from them and not run any risk by rushing it. So when the captain of the tramp steamer decided not to leave the harbor that night, Thatcher Allen and Culley May were only too glad to go on board for a good meal, and it was well on toward morning when they reached their huts and prepared to sleep.

In the morning when Thatcher Allen went to find the girls, they had disappeared. Pedro seemed truthful when he declared that his people knew nothing about them.

"If we see 'em, we catch 'em for you!" he said.

Pedro's grin assured Thatcher Allen that he would be only too glad to do it and was eager to earn the reward which Thatcher Allen offered to any of the tribe who would bring the girls to him.

But it did not take Thatcher Allen long to suspect that they protecting the girls. He threatened Pedro with destruction of his village, he swore that no one would be left alive on the island, but the chief merely nodded and promised that he would find the girls and bring them to the camp.

Thatcher Allen knew that he did not dare to molest anyone. He could rage and threaten, but he dared not carry out his threats. Once angered, these people were ugly and he and Culley May might be caught and tortured.

So Thatcher Allen and Culley May decided to wait their chance. Whenever the work at the beach let up for a moment, Culley May set out in search of Mary Eliska and Martha. He was anxious to curry favor with Thatcher Allen by finding the girls himself and bringing them into camp.

So as soon as Thatcher Allen flew off in *Skybird* with a load of smuggled silk to be turned into the much-needed cash, Culley May took this chance to look about the island.

He left Pedro in charge at the beach and began wandering around the jungle, skirting the island. With the Big Chief out of the way he thought he could terrify the other members of the tribe and learn where the girls were hidden.

But Pedro had suspected his plan and, taking a short cut through the jungle, he hurried to the cave and talked to the girls.

"Let him come!" cried Mary Eliska. "I'm not afraid of Culley May. He's a big braggart, but it's all a bluff. He's just a coward!"

"I'd like to get Culley May down in this cave and keep him here," said Martha angrily. "I'd like to keep him here forever."

"I can't see how that would help any," answered Mary Eliska. "What we want to do is to get away from the island and down to Peru with this paper. And we'll not get away by making a prisoner of Culley May. That won't help in the least."

Pedro was shaking his head. He frowned and his face looked fierce and cruel. The girls felt shudders go through their bodies and realized that the tribe might be dangerous if roused to anger.

Suddenly Pedro spoke, and in his halting, broken sentences he expressed his ideas. Culley May was on the way to the new village, and when he came, if he made trouble, it would be good to put him down in the cave. Besides they might make him talk so that they would know what Thatcher Allen was planning to do.

"And where will *we* stay?" asked Mary Eliska.

"My house!" replied the chief with a wave of his hand toward the hut. "Pedro's house, your house!" And Rosa led the girls inside the hut.

Pedro covered the opening to the cave with straw mats and giving orders for his followers to guard the girls well, he left to go back to the beach.

But Mary Eliska and Martha were far less comfortable here than they had been in the cave. Here there was not a breath of wind, for Pedro's wife seated herself in the opening and kept out what little air there was.

Finally Mary Eliska could stand it no longer. She jumped up and shoved Rosa aside. The big woman laughed as she watched Mary Eliska and Martha mopping the perspiration from their faces.

At that moment one of the half-grown girls ran with a cry of fear to Rosa. She pointed back toward the far side of the ridge, where a man was scrambling up to the settlement.

There was no time to hide away. Mary Eliska and Martha stood face to face with Culley May.

Culley May laughed as he had seen Thatcher Allen do, a sarcastic, triumphant laugh. He moved toward the girls aggressively, but Rosa was by their side and was shoving them gently but firmly backward.

"You're to come with me, girls!" exclaimed Culley May. "Hurry up and get going! I've got you now!"

Rosa pulled them back with a vigorous hand as Culley May rushed at them. But his foot slipped, he stumbled and sprawled headlong for a second then went sliding down through the earth. For Rosa had cleverly moved around the straw mats in a straight line from Culley May, and when he charged at them, the force of his stride sent him slipping and sliding down the slippery walls of the cave. He did not stop until he had bumped all the way down and splashed into the dark waters below.

"Help, help!" he cried. "You rascals, get me out of here!"

A young boy hauled him out to safety. Culley May was half stunned and glad enough to stay in the cave for a little while until he could think what to do. He finally called Mary Eliska, but she refused to go down into the cave to talk to him.

Hour after hour slipped by. Culley May saw none of the brilliant colors of the crystals. He was sore and disgusted, his plans had all gone wrong, and instead of being praised by Thatcher Allen, he would be despised and blamed and ridiculed.

A strong guard was placed at the opening of the cave and Mary Eliska and Martha could enjoy the air. Muggy and oppressive though it was, it was better than the stifling closeness of the hut.

Rosa glowed with triumph, taking all the credit to herself for trapping Culley May, and for the rest of the day she was in high spirits, commanding the young people around her. It seemed to Mary Eliska and Martha that these people were eating half their time. Huge amounts of fish and fruit were consumed. They started at sunrise and only ended at bedtime.

Mary Eliska and Martha slept that night in the chief's hut, with the faithful Rosa sleeping on a mat before the door. They rose at dawn when the others began to stir.

It was still early in the morning when they heard the drone of a motor in the sky and hurried into the hut. For now the real trouble was beginning. Thatcher Allen had returned.

Skybird soared, banked and circled about the island. Thatcher Allen headed her low over the plateau, so low that Mary Eliska, peering through the matted vines, saw Thatcher Allen's face distinctly. His grin of triumph was always unpleasant, now it was threatening as well.

Mary Eliska's face went white with anger as she saw *Skybird*.

"How dare he use our little plane for his shady business! The crook!" she exclaimed.

If Mary Eliska and Martha could have heard the Big Chief when Thatcher Allen returned to the beach, they would not have been so trusting. For Pedro told Thatcher Allen that his men had captured the girls and had them safely in the cave. Culley May was there now to guard them.

Thatcher Allen nodded approvingly. Things seemed to be working out just as he planned. His trip to the mainland had been successful and now he was free to fly to South America where he would attend to that little matter of taking up the option on the Albert Stricklin Flying Field. But in the meantime he would search the girls and see if they were carrying the money.

"Guess I'll go on up and take a look at them," said Thatcher Allen carelessly. "You might fill up the plane with gasoline. I may need to go out on another trip soon."

As Thatcher Allen followed the path through the jungle he thought to himself. "You have to handle these folks rough! If I hadn't threatened to kill them all, they'd have turned against me. Someday I'll have a big base here and they'll all be working for me." But Thatcher Allen had come by the jungle path and the girls were fully warned of his approach. Rosa went to meet Thatcher Allen with a broad grin on her face.

Mary Eliska's heart sank as she watched from the shelter of the hut. She gripped Martha nervously. They clung together in terror. Why had they been so easily fooled? There was Rosa telling Thatcher Allen that she had the girls safely trapped, waiting for him. The girls shrank back in the hut afraid to come out to face the man who had them in his power. With the whole tribe on Thatcher Allen's side, there was little chance of escape. This was the end.

"I'd have sworn they were real friends," whispered Martha in a frightened voice. "It would be lots better to be on that island with wild beasts than here with these treacherous people." But just then they heard Rosa directing Thatcher Allen to the cave. With the few words of English she knew she was telling him that the girls were prisoners in the big cave. "You go down!" she said.

"Sure!" replied Thatcher Allen with a broad smile. "I'll kill two birds with one stone. I've always wanted to see the inside of one of those big caves. And when I find those girls, I have a few things to say to them." Thatcher Allen put his leg down the opening and felt for the rock. Then his other leg found a foothold. As his head disappeared. Culley May's voice called to him.

"Watch out, Thatcher Allen, they're tricky! The girls are not here!"

But it was too late. When Thatcher Allen started to scramble out of the cave, shouting his threats, he was thrust back by a huge man, who held a long knife in his hand. Down he tumbled, bruised and shaken.

At that moment Mary Eliska and Martha rushed out of the hut and saw Thatcher Allen disappear. "Now is our chance to get away, Martha!" cried Mary Eliska. "Let's get to the beach!" Mary Eliska grabbed up her flying coat and helmet.

"Hurry, hurry, Mary Eliska, he may get out!" cried Martha. Her face was white with the strain.

Mary Eliska was saying goodbye to Rosa and the other women of the village. She was trying to express her thanks. It seemed ungrateful to hurry away without a farewell. But Rosa shook her head and shoved Mary Eliska ahead of her toward the jungle path, calling back in a shrill voice to the women.

Suddenly Mary Eliska started and looked upward. "Listen Martha. It's a plane!" She had heard the distant hum of an airplane motor and was searching the sky anxiously. Then through the trees she saw the plane driving toward them.

"Who is it, Mary Eliska?" asked Martha.

"I wish I knew. Maybe it is a friend of Thatcher Allen's," replied Mary Eliska as she gazed with dread toward the plane that was coming nearer and nearer to the island. Now the plane was circling above them. The girls watched with anxiety as the pilot put it into a long, fast dive toward the near-by clearing.

CHAPTER 18.7
Crashed!

The girl flyers watched with thumping hearts as the plane, diving with wide open throttle, headed straight toward the plateau.

Martha gripped her sister's arm. She felt giddy and faint. A cry escaped her.

Mary Eliska turned to her with a frown. "Snap out of it, Martha! This is no time to get hysterical. That plane may be piloted by a friend of Thatcher Allen. If it is, we'll need to do some quick thinking. Don't lose courage now!"

Martha was gazing toward the plane. "It looks to me as if there were two men. And someone is waving! Do you think it's a rescue plane?" cried Martha.

Mary Eliska did not answer. Every nerve was tense as she watched the plane banking and circling for a landing. She dared not tell Martha that she believed it was Liam and Syd. It would be too great a disappointment, if she were mistaken.

Then suddenly Martha screamed with delight. "Look Mary Eliska, look! It's Syd and Liam McAdams! We're saved! We're saved!"

Rosa stood beside the girls until she realized that they did not need further help, then as the plane circled low for a landing, she scurried into the hut, calling on the women and children to follow. In a moment the place was deserted. Mary Eliska smiled at the idea of Rosa finding protection in those flimsy huts of twigs and leaves.

A few minutes later Liam McAdams set down his plane before the huts. Before the boys could step from the plane, the girls were beside them, shaking their hands and almost crying with relief.

"We thought you were lost in the storm, Liam McAdams!" cried Mary Eliska.

"And we had almost given you up for lost!" answered Liam McAdams, his voice husky.

"How did you find us?" Martha asked excitedly. Her cheeks were flushed, all her fear was gone.

"We recognized *Skybird* and followed her," replied Liam McAdams, looking around anxiously. "Thatcher Allen flew her to Honduras and then back here."

"Don't I know it!" exclaimed Mary Eliska. "What a good thing it was that I didn't have a chance to stop him. I was angry enough to smash the plane rather than have him use it for smuggling."

"Let's be going!" said Syd. "We can tell you how we found you when we're out of danger. Are you sure these folks are friendly?"

"I'll say they are. They're wonderful people!"

Mary Eliska burst out. "They've kept us out of Thatcher Allen's clutches. He and Culley May were trying to put us on an uninhabited island. And Pedro, the Big Chief, hid us away and fooled him. These people saved our lives!"

"Someday," said Martha with a laugh, "I'm going to send a whole barrel of presents down for them, beads and candy and brightly colored calico. They'd love it!"

"But when do we go and how?" asked Syd. "I won't feel safe until we get away from this island. Do you think there is any chance of getting *Skybird*? Thatcher Allen won't give that plane up without a fight."

"He isn't going to put up a fight for that plane," answered Mary Eliska. "When we heard you coming, we were just on our way to get her."

"Thatcher Allen is down there!" cried Martha triumphantly, pointing at the opening to the cave, near which a huge guard was sitting, fingering a knife menacingly. "And as you see, he's under a strong guard! He and Culley May are both prisoners down there."

"Prisoners! Where?" asked Syd.

"It's the most wonderful prison in the world! It's a crystal cave! The roof is of sparkling emeralds, rubies and sapphires. It's beautiful!" Mary Eliska explained with sparkling eyes.

"Yes, you ought to see it, boys!" interrupted Martha.

"We'll save that for the next trip. Much as I'd like to see a crystal cave, I think my pleasure would be all spoiled if I had to share the view with Thatcher Allen," answered Liam McAdams.

At that moment Pedro came running up the trail. He had seen another plane arriving and feared that Thatcher Allen and Culley May might be rescued by some friends. His white teeth showed in a broad smile when he saw the girls happy.

"My plane? Is it ready?" asked Mary Eliska.

"All ready!" Pedro started to lead them back to the harbor, but Rosa stood in his way, frowning and talking in a high pitched voice. The chief explained to the young people that the tribe wished to give the flyers a farewell feast.

"Guess we'll have to wait long enough to eat something," said Mary Eliska under her breath to Liam McAdams.

"But we really ought to be going when luck is with us. You can't tell what may happen!"

"It's impossible, boys. It's the only way we have to repay these people for their kindness to us," Mary Eliska begged.

"That's a brand-new idea, repaying people by eating some more of their food. I don't know as I'd want that kind of pay for a debt."

"You would if you were in the place of these people. It's the greatest honor we can show them."

After assuring Liam McAdams and Syd that Thatcher Allen and Culley May were well guarded in the cave, Mary Eliska led the way to the fiber-mats before the huts where the meal was about to be served.

"How did they guess that we hadn't had a thing to eat today?" asked Syd. "We were too busy watching *Skybird*. We didn't dare leave the field for fear Thatcher Allen would take off and we'd lose him."

"I'm glad you're hungry," said Mary Eliska in a whisper to the boys. "I wish *I* were, then I might be able to eat their fish. And unless you eat a lot, Rosa is offended." As the bowl was brought in, strange spicy odors filled the air. They had several courses. The feast began with fish, continued with fish and ended with fish.

Mary Eliska bravely faced the ordeal, trying to smile and enthuse over each dish as it was brought. But it was hard work. However, the boys made up for her lack of appetite. They declared that they had never tasted anything so good and when they accepted a second helping, Rosa's face was beaming with happiness.

Liam McAdams was thoughtful for a time, then his face brightened. He had been racking his brains to think of some gift to present to Pedro. At last he had it. From his pocket he took a wrist watch. Liam McAdams usually carried an extra watch.

Mary Eliska saw the idea and smiled. "He'll love it, Liam McAdams! But make a lot of fuss when you present it," she whispered. "They like that even better than the gift."

The four friends rose and bowed low before Pedro. Then Liam McAdams stepped forward to fasten the watch on Pedro's wrist.

Pedro did not know what to say. He tried to speak but his few words of English were forgotten in his excitement. Like a king, he strode among his people with extended hand to show them the honor that had been given him. Rosa beamed her pleasure. It was a great day on the island.

Liam McAdams and Syd were restless. "I think we'd better go!" said Liam McAdams suddenly. "I won't be happy until I get you girls a thousand miles away from Thatcher Allen and Culley May."

"O.K.," replied Mary Eliska. "Come Martha," she said, and her sister followed as Mary Eliska went among the helpful, friendly people and bade them goodbye.

Liam McAdams and Syd started their plane and flew above the forest toward the beach, while the girls hurried through the jungle by a short cut that Pedro took and Rosa followed as fast as she could.

The boys were putting their plane down on the smooth water beside *Skybird* when the girls arrived. Pedro leaped into the launch and beckoned the girls to follow.

Suddenly they heard wild, piercing cries coming from the direction of the jungle, savage cries that sounded more like the night call of some jungle beast.

"Hurry!" exclaimed Pedro, looking back. "It's Thatcher Allen. He escape!"

Thatcher Allen and Culley May were racing madly toward the beach. In a moment the reason for their panic was seen. Behind the two men came a stream of howling people chasing them.

"Will Thatcher Allen hurt you, after we are gone?" asked Mary Eliska anxiously.

"Me no afraid!" Pedro answered. "My people, they fight him!"

Culley May made for a boat, but one of the natives came up and shoved him aside violently. Thatcher Allen was struggling, and all he could do was to shout furiously to Mary Eliska. But *Skybird* was free from her moorings and the girl started the engine ready for the take-off. She could not hear what Thatcher Allen was saying, but it was abusive and threatening.

Sending a spurt of water before her, *Skybird* taxied in a wide sweep to head into the wind. Pedro stood up in his boat and waved his big friendly hand. There were shouts of farewell from the shore, mingled with threats from Culley May and Thatcher Allen.

As the airplane soared over the island, Martha said through the earphones, "I'll count these people among my very best friends. What's more, I'm coming back some day to see them."

Liam McAdams took the lead, straight westward. The deep blue water spread beneath them to the horizon. There was hardly a ripple on the mirror-like surface of the sea. The sky was clear and like birds the two planes soared alone in the great blue dome.

Only occasionally Mary Eliska looked back in the direction of the island to be sure that Thatcher Allen was not in pursuit. She had confidence in Pedro.

It was still early in the day. Mary Eliska and Liam McAdams had consulted their maps and decided to head for Tela on the Gulf of Honduras. If possible they wanted to get over to the Pacific side by night. There they would feel safe.

Flying in a northwesterly course, they left the high rocky coast of Honduras that lay exposed to the Caribbean storms, and made a landing at Tela. But they did not stay long, a heavy mist had come in from the sea. Within an hour they had made a check-up on their aircraft, refueled and were taking off for Salvador on the Pacific where fair weather was reported.

A low-lying cloud made Mary Eliska nose her plane up to a height of ten thousand feet. There was a brilliant sky and sunlight overhead. Below it looked as if they were still flying over the ocean. The broad sheet of fog spread beneath them like a blanket. But when they neared the Pacific late that afternoon, the mist began to thin and they could see the ranch houses with their cultivated fields. Leaving the cloud behind, they flew over Salvador. From that height they could see far north to the towering Guatemalan plateau, with here and there a cone-shaped volcanic peak. Plumes of blue smoke shot from the craters.

Martha gave an exclamation of astonishment, then was still. Both girls felt the overpowering majesty of the outlook over that vast panorama. Soon they saw the red and green roofs of Salvador City and a lofty Gothic spire. Mary Eliska circled over the town and came down on the flying field.

Here they intended to spend the night and have their planes thoroughly overhauled for the trip down the Pacific. The air was clear and dry, perfect flying weather.

But Mary Eliska was restless. While she enjoyed seeing the foreign city, she was fearful that Thatcher Allen might still be pursuing them. Now he had a still greater reason for finding them. In the plane Mary Eliska had discovered a large legal envelope with several important looking papers marked "Confidential." Looking at them hurriedly, Mary Eliska gasped. Among them was the will of Colonel Roger Fairfax, a document that disposed of millions of dollars-worth of property.

At the hotel when she showed them to the boys they agreed that they were extremely valuable. Yet they saw that the possession of these papers would add to the peril of the girls. Thatcher Allen would not rest easy until he had caught up with *Skybird* and recovered the documents which he had stolen, no doubt, and expected to sell for a huge sum.

Mary Eliska did not sleep well. She wanted morning to come so that she could be on her way, and long before daybreak she was up and ready to go. After a hasty breakfast, the four flyers took off and were under way by the time the sun was rising.

It was a long day. The flight down the Nicaraguan coast was jumpy, for the cool air from the high mountains poured down to meet the warm air from the plains. They passed near to some of the volcanoes and once they could see into the crater with its boiling lava and clouds of steam and smoke.

"We've been lucky!" said Martha through the earphones. "From now on it's clear sailing!"

"Touch wood, Martha! We're not there yet," answered Mary Eliska.

But Martha had not touched wood quick enough. A few hours later when they stepped from their plane on the field in Panama, they noticed at once that there was trouble. Men were running about excitedly, looking into the sky and the ambulance was being started ready for an emergency. In the sky a plane was out of control and diving wildly.

"Oh Martha!" cried Mary Eliska. "It's Liam McAdams! He's falling!"

The plane above had gone into a tailspin and the girls knew that Liam McAdams was not the kind to show off his skill or attempt a stunt over a strange flying field.

Martha clung to her sister with cries of fright but Mary Eliska's face was grim. Her lips moved with a prayer, but no words came.

Liam McAdams's plane was falling! Nothing could save it now. It was too near the ground to be righted and landed safely.

But the next minute the plane straightened out. By some miracle of luck Liam McAdams had it under control again, but it was too late. The plane landed on one wheel and with a bound it turned clear over. Even before it touched the ground, the ambulance was speeding across the field.

Martha ran screaming toward the plane but Mary Eliska stood as if turned to stone.

Liam McAdams and Syd had crashed! Their bodies must be crushed and bleeding under that crumpled wreck. Liam McAdams and Syd were dead! Mary Eliska saw no hope.

But strong hands had dragged Syd from the rear cockpit. He was dazed from the shock of landing but Mary Eliska saw that he was alive.

Frantically she ran toward the plane. Where was Liam McAdams?

Liam McAdams, strangely white, was taken from the wreck and placed in the ambulance. His limp form was covered with blood. Next minute the clanging ambulance was racing the injured boy to the hospital. Syd was given first aid on the field and was able to ride with the girls to the hospital in the automobile of the field manager. The boy was shaken up, bruised and sick from the shock, but he had no serious injuries. The girls watched him anxiously as he trembled and twitched, but the doctor at the hospital assured them that it was entirely nerves and after a night's rest he would be himself again.

But with Liam McAdams it was far more dangerous. Behind the closed doors of the operating room, strange white-clad figures were working over Liam McAdams. Mary Eliska caught glimpses of hurrying nurses, but dared not speak to any of them. A moment's delay in carrying out an order might be a risk to Liam McAdams's life.

Suddenly Syd seemed to come out of his stupor. He tried to get up, looked wildly around and cried: "Where's Liam? Tell me, is Liam McAdams dead?"

"No, Syd, lie down and keep quiet. Liam McAdams is alive! He has a fighting chance. That's all we know now."

An hour went by and dragged slowly into two hours before they brought Liam McAdams from that operating room. His long body was motionless under the sheet. Mary Eliska had slipped into the corridor and was watching. She held her breath with dread. Would they bring that still form toward a room, or was it all over? Was Liam McAdams dead? Would they take him away?

No one had time to answer her questions if she could have spoken. But her heart leaped with hope as she saw them turning into the room next to Syd. Liam McAdams was alive!

Then came the thought, as it had come when her father was injured: "Would this happy, care-free boy be left a cripple?" She thought of her father, spending his best years in a wheel chair and her eyes filled with tears. It was agony to think of that alert and active Liam McAdams doomed to the same fate. If only someone could relieve this terrible suspense!

CHAPTER 18.8
Jump!

Mary Eliska turned to the doctor who had just come in. She tried to speak, but words would not come.

The doctor approached with a smile of sympathy. "I guess this fellow was born under a lucky star," he said. "He's pretty well shaken up, but there is nothing serious that we can find. A few broken bones! The shock of a fall like that is always bad. He'll be flying again in a few months!"

Mary Eliska did not wait to ask questions. She flew to Syd and Martha to tell them the good news.

Liam McAdams is alive! He would fly again!

Mary Eliska set out for South America two days later with a heart full of gratitude that Liam McAdams was not seriously hurt. The morning after the accident he was able to talk to her and while he looked worried to think of the girls flying alone into the dangers of a strange country, he did not try to keep them from going on.

Mary Eliska was getting nervous. The day set for taking up the option was almost there. The work she set out to do must be done quickly.

From his bed in the hospital Liam McAdams watched the airplane soaring away from the field. It remained a tiny speck in the sky for a long time in that clear air.

"I feel as if we should have stayed to look after Liam," said Martha through the earphones. "Do you think Syd can do everything that's needed?"

"Liam McAdams is in a good hospital," replied Mary Eliska. "He's well cared for and there's nothing we can do right now. We'll get this job through as quickly as we can and get back."

Following the airway down the coast, Mary Eliska had no difficulty in reaching the town of Trujillo in the northern part of Peru, at which point she was to turn inland to Majora, a settlement of adobe houses and stores, the center of supply for a number of mines in the mountains.

Over an early breakfast at Trujillo, their spirits rose once more. The trip inland was not far and they should reach the foothills in an hour.

"South America is different from what I expected," remarked Mary Eliska, as she drank her breakfast coffee. "I thought that most of this country was jungles and tropical vegetation. Did you see that strip of brown sand, along the coast? It's like a desert."

"Which shows you didn't study your geography very well or you'd have remembered that all along the coast, especially from here down, there's a strip of desert, and in places it never has been known to rain," replied Martha. "I always remember that, for it was one place I never had any desire to go. But here I am!"

"We'll just give it a good look and fly high! I don't like desert country either. But we'll soon get to the foothills."

"Let's hurry, Mary Eliska! I'm anxious to get to the mine. I wonder what Sean Hall and his wife will be like? I hope they won't turn out to be friends of Thatcher Allen." Martha picked up her belongings and hastened toward the door of the restaurant.

A few moments brought them to the flying field, where their plane had been refueled and stood ready for the take-off. There was no wind and Mary Eliska taxied across the field to get plenty of speed for the rise. As usual Martha had insisted on the parachutes. The harness always annoyed Mary Eliska, but she did not voice any objection. Anything that would make Martha feel satisfied was worth doing.

The rising ground beneath them told that they were getting into the foothills. They saw the jagged peaks far ahead. Mary Eliska was glad that she would not have to cross the Andes on this trip. She had had enough excitement for a while; that could wait for another flight.

Seeing a small settlement ahead, Mary Eliska recognized it by the description given her of Majora. She flew straight toward the town, circled and came down on a wide, smooth field. Although it was not intended as a flying field, Mary Eliska had seen worse places to alight, and brought *Skybird* to a neat three-point landing.

But here the girls met disappointment. Ed Jenkins, an American storekeeper in the settlement, told them that it would be impossible to land a plane in the mountains near Sean Hall's mine.

"There isn't a square foot of level space anywhere in these hills. That pair of fools who went up there in a plane this morning will meet sudden death. They're bound to!" exclaimed Jenkins.

"Two men went up there in a plane this morning!" cried Mary Eliska excitedly. "Who were they?"

"I can't say, Miss," replied Jenkins. "One had red hair and the other's eyes were funny! A queer looking pair of crooks!" Ed Jenkins was fumbling in his pocket. "Here's a message. I guess it must be for you. The man with the squint said to give it to two girls in a plane. I reckon that's you!"

Mary Eliska ripped open the envelope and read these words scrawled on a scrap of paper: "He laughs best who laughs last!"

"Come on. Martha, let's go!" Mary Eliska's face flushed, then set in determination. "That's a challenge! If Thatcher Allen thinks I'm through, he's mistaken!"

But Ed Jenkins was pointing to the mountain, where a few stone huts were visible. "That's Sean Hall's mine up there! You can see for yourself there's no place to land among those peaks!"

But Mary Eliska had already started the engine. The propeller was spinning. And with a wave of her hand to the storekeeper, she sent her plane across the field and into the air. Circling for altitude, she pointed straight toward Sean Hall's mine.

"I believe that man is right," said Martha a few minutes later, as the hills became more rugged and menacing with their sharp peaks.

Mary Eliska flew slowly over the hills, watching for a spot to put her plane down. If Thatcher Allen and Culley May could find a place, surely she could. She brought her plane as low as she dared above the mountains but there was no sign of level ground, and soon she saw little figures running about and waving at her excitedly.

"They're warning us not to try a landing," Martha called to her sister. "i'm afraid it's no use."

"Then I'll have to use the parachute! Come over here and take the controls. I'll have to jump," cried Mary Eliska.

"Don't, Mary Eliska. It's a terrible chance to take!" pleaded Martha.

"Nonsense! I've made lots of parachute jumps!" Mary Eliska snapped impatiently. "Don't waste time! We have less than ten minutes to get there. Sean Hall can't close a deal with Thatcher Allen until twelve o'clock. Our contract holds until then."

Martha's face was white as she climbed into the pilot's seat, protesting nervously. "Don't jump, Mary Eliska! Don't take such a big chance!"

But Mary Eliska was studying the ground below her and she answered, "I'll jump when we are directly over the mine. You take the plane down to Jenkins' store and wait for me there. I'll be down after a while. Bye!"

Then at sight of Martha's tragic face, she laughed and began crawling out on the wing. Mary Eliska watched the ground beneath her, then with a catch in her breath, stepped out into space.

No matter how many times Mary Eliska jumped, she never could get used to that long drop. Her mind was clear, every sense alert to what she had to do.

In a few seconds she pulled the rip cord but there was no response from the parachute.

Had something gone wrong? Mary Eliska was falling with terrific speed toward those jagged rocks. "This is the end," she thought. But suddenly she came up with a tremendous jerk as the parachute opened above her head and she began sailing gently downward. Working with the shrouds, the girl steered the parachute toward a safe landing.

At the sight of a figure hurtling through the air, Amanda Hall had screamed, "Oh Sean, Sean! A man has fallen from the plane! Help! Help!"

Horror-struck, Sean Hall watched the falling figure, then gave a lusty cheer as the white parachute opened, the little figure in the sky was righted and came sailing down gracefully.

"I was hoping she'd break her neck!" muttered Thatcher Allen to Culley May. "Just as I was getting the did man interested, she had to spoil everything! But I'm not through! He's got to take my word against hers!"

"Sure!" answered Culley May. "Mary Eliska is no good at a business deal. She'll not convince Sean Hall!"

While Culley May and Thatcher Allen looked on sullenly, Mary Eliska landed on the mountain at some distance from the astonished Sean and Amanda Hall, who hurried along the trail to reach her.

"He's a brave man whoever he is," said Amanda Hall. "Jumping from the sky like that! It scares me to think of it!"

"I wonder why he's coming here?" asked Sean Hall.

Mary Eliska was just picking herself up and rubbing a bruise on her arm, as Sean and Amanda Hall scrambled up the rocky ledge.

"Bless me, if it isn't a girl, and a pretty one! Did you *have* to jump out of that plane?"

"Yes," replied Mary Eliska with a laugh. "I *had* to jump! I had to get here before twelve o'clock and that was the only way I could do it. I'm Mary Eliska and I've come to take up the option on the flying field."

Sean Hall stared at the girl in astonishment. "You did that? You brave, brave girl!"

Amanda Hall was brushing Mary Eliska off and helping her to get out of her parachute harness. "Come along to the house," she said. "I'll make you a cup of good strong coffee to brace you up, though goodness knows it would take more than that to bring me to, if I'd jumped from a plane! What are girls coming to! When I was young I'd never have dreamed that girls could do a thing like that!"

"Times are different!" agreed Sean with a shake of his tousled head. "And you made it without an accident, which is more than my other two visitors did."

"Were they hurt?" asked Mary Eliska.

"Not much! They landed their plane somewhere down the slope and broke the propeller. Thatcher Allen has a sprained ankle and a bruised shoulder," replied Sean. "He isn't feeling very good."

Mary Eliska looked at the man anxiously. "You haven't signed any papers, have you, Mr. Hall?" She looked at her watch. "It's just one minute before twelve. I still have time to take up that option. Here's your check!"

Sean shouted with laughter. "What a girl!" he exclaimed. "No, I haven't signed any of his papers!"

"And what's more you *won't* sign any of them!" Amanda Hall cried. "I don't like the looks of those two men!"

"No more do I!" agreed Sean.

As they reached the ledge of rock where their cabin stood, Sean was confronted by Culley May. "Don't have anything to do with that girl!" he stormed. "She's been in more crooked deals than you can count. You'll be making a great mistake."

Sean gave a quiet laugh that was more provoking than if he had stormed at the men and accused them of fraud. He turned to Mary Eliska. "Come right in, Mary Eliska," he said with a deep old-fashioned bow, "I'll just sign that paper and close the deal!"

Thatcher Allen bit his lips in rage. His face was deathly white. Mary Eliska had never seen the man so angry before. Thatcher Allen had staked everything on this trip to get the flying field, and he had lost. Even his plane was a wreck and he was miles from a railroad.

Thatcher Allen's brain was working hard on a new plot. How could he get *Skybird*? And how could he get those stolen papers back? Perhaps they were still in the plane, maybe the girls had overlooked them! But that was not likely. Mary Eliska and Martha were too clever to miss a chance like that!

Thatcher Allen studied the sky. Far down in the valley he could see the airplane, with Martha at the controls, just making the landing by the store. Mary Eliska noted the look of hatred and villainous hope; and her eyes followed his.

Suddenly she understood. Already Thatcher Allen was talking to Culley May. They were preparing to leave.

"Stop them, somehow!" said Mary Eliska to Sean Hall. "He's going to try to reach Majora and get our plane. My sister Martha is down there! Don't let them go!" Sean stood in the path in front of Thatcher Allen. "You have a few things to clear up before you leave, Thatcher Allen," said Sean Hall. "I'll not let you go until you explain some of the stories you've told me about Albert Stricklin and his family."

"Get back!" shouted Thatcher Allen furiously. "Out of my way!" His voice cracked in rage. Suddenly his fist shot out. Culley May landed a second blow and Sean Hall reeled and staggered back, shouting for help.

There was a sound of running feet and the next moment a gang of miners rushed at the two men and tied their hands. After their struggles had quieted the pair were thrown into a corner and ordered to behave or take the consequences.

Mary Eliska looked anxiously toward the valley where she could see a small figure on horseback. It looked like Martha coming to her rescue.

"What shall we do with these crooks?" asked Sean Hall.

"Lock them up until Martha and I have time to get away," Mary Eliska begged.

At Sean Hall's command, the miners dragged the two rascals to a stone shed. The heavy door had a strong lock.

"There they'll stay until I'm sure you girls are safely home," said Sean Hall. "I've a notion to have them jailed!"

When Martha arrived in camp she was greeted as if she belonged to the family. She and Amanda Hall were soon like old friends. They had many interests in common. And while Martha was being shown over the house, Mary Eliska and Sean Hall were exchanging stories of their adventures.

"Wait 'til I show you this!" said Sean going to a shelf in the corner. "Here's a map I made on one of my trips. I went through the Land of the Incas with a local guide. We were looking for a lost temple. It is said that there's a sacred emerald in the altar. Now the temple is lost, no one knows where it is. If I were young and had an airplane, I'd go and find that temple. Besides there's treasure there."

"I'd like to find it myself," said Mary Eliska eagerly.

"Why don't you? It's a wonderful country down there. You'd see new sights and have new adventures and maybe you'd find the treasure." Mary Eliska's eyes were dreamy as she studied the map. "Would you be game to go with me?" asked the girl. "This map is like a challenge. I'm going to do it!"

"Going to do what?" asked Martha.

"First I'm going to Panama and after that we'll go on a treasure hunt in the Land of the Incas."

Amanda Hall laughed. "Sean has been showing her his map! I do believe he'd start out himself to find that treasure, if I'd let him."

"Maybe I will," replied Sean. "Mary Eliska says she'll take me along. And I'll trust myself to her any time. After seeing her jump from a plane I know she'll get what she goes for, so I've given her my map."

Mary Eliska rose to go. "We've got to get started! I wish I had more time to look around, but some day I'm coming back."

Amanda Hall threw both arms around the girl. "Promise me that you will. And next time don't be in such a hurry to arrive. Come up the mountain on horseback. I was scared to death, almost, when I saw you falling."

Sean saddled his own horse for Mary Eliska with instructions to leave it with Ed Jenkins, who would see that it got back. The girls waved at the couple as long as they could see them and when they reached the store in Majora, Martha ran to the airplane and got the binoculars. Looking back to the mine she saw the two still standing on the rocky ledge and waving their hands.

As they took off. Martha suggested that Mary Eliska fly once more over the mountain, but Mary Eliska shook her head.

"Not this time, Martha. We must get back to Panama. But if Liam McAdams is all right and doesn't need us, I would like to take that trip to Peru on a treasure hunt," replied Mary Eliska.

From Trujillo, where they stopped for fuel, she sent a cable to her father and also one to Liam McAdams and Syd, who would be anxiously awaiting word.

Then as they headed up the Pacific it seemed to Mary Eliska that *Skybird* knew that she was facing homeward, the engine hummed and the country unrolled beneath them, like a great moving picture.

They found Liam McAdams recovering rapidly, although it would be many weeks before he could be moved. Mary Eliska and Martha were making their plans for the trip to Peru.

But Liam McAdams seemed troubled, and after much questioning Mary Eliska learned the cause of his worry. Someone was needed to follow up on that business deal. Albert could not attend to it all from his wheelchair and the other men about the field were not dependable.

"So you want me to go back?" asked Mary Eliska. "Is that it?"

"No, I don't *want* you to go back! I *want* you here!" replied the boy.

Mary Eliska was quiet for a long time, she was thinking hard. Again she stood where duty called. She had to choose between her own pleasure and her duty to those she loved. There was a fierce struggle in the girl's soul. Why did she always have to give up her own desires?

Suddenly she rose and held out her hand to Liam McAdams. "I'm starting home in the morning," she said simply.

Liam McAdams looked troubled. "But Mary Eliska, your trip to the Land of the Incas! Your hunt for treasure!"

"Oh, that's nothing. That can wait!" she said with a laugh.

Even Liam McAdams did not realize how great had been that inward fight. Mary Eliska wanted to get away from all the problems of the flying field, the conflict and jealousy of Thatcher Allen and Culley May.

She wanted a month of freedom, just flying around and enjoying herself without any thought of duty or business details. She wanted to fly for her own pleasure.

The next morning she was on her way north. She circled her plane high up into the clear air. Ten thousand feet above the earth she could forget the problems of life. She could dream undisturbed for Martha always knew when to keep quiet.

But little did Mary Eliska dream that in the Land of the Incas, the Girl Aviatrixes would endure many hardships, face grave dangers and many times would escape with their lives only by a hair's breadth.

Hawai'ian Bedtime Stories -The Legends and Myths of Hawai'i

Anthology of Bedtime Stories by William A. Stricklin

Table of Contents

Writer's Note:

Early after my arrival in Hawai'i I made the time to join a Hawaiian language class at the University of Hawai'i Manoa campus taught by a woman from Ni'ihau. Among my classmates was Beatrice Burns, wife of then-Governor John Burns. My teacher was a child living on Ni'ihau at the time of the Imperial Japanese attack on Pearl Harbor and her recollections inspired and are part of my 2020 nonfiction book ***Day of Infamy - The Ni'ihau Incident*** *© 2020* TXu 2-222-380 Case No. 1-9381160911 ISBN 978-1-09834-126-8 **Published and Copyrighted by William A. Stricklin 02/2023**

Twelve Books of Christmas © **2022 TXu 2-296-788 Case No. 1-11000033441** *Hawai'ian Bedtime Stories - The Legends and Myths of Hawai'i* © **2022 TXu 2-330-801 Case No. 1-11467523541** by William A. Stricklin 840 pages

Athenaeum of Jack London's Best 52 Books (Twelve Volumes 9000 pages) © 2022 TXu 2-323-131 Anthology Case No. 1-11437933441 by William A. Stricklin All Rights Reserved

The Saga of MTA Charlie -Fiction – Parody Lyrics - © 2014 PAu 3-733-895

Book Club - Nonfiction - © 2017 Case 1-5999900821

I Left My Wife in San Francisco - Parody Lyrics- Copyright © 2021

They Try to Sell Us Egg Foo Young - Parody Lyrics- © **Case** 1-7262926821 - © **2018** - © **Case** 1-6288304641 © **2018 PAu 3-967-588**

Family Secrets - Nonfiction - Copyright © 2018 Case 1-6475069411 ©2018 TX 8-813-325 TXu 2-093-545 ISBN 978-1-48098-155-3

Family Secrets – Wednesday's Child - Nonfiction - Copyright © 2017 Case 1-5782187081

Family Secrets – Thursday's Child - Nonfiction - © 2017 Copyright Case 1-5805231561

Aethelflaed's Secret – First Feminist of England – Nonfiction – Copyright © 2017 TXu 2-064-267

Catherine's Secret – The Banned Books of Queen Catherine Hidden at Strickland Manor Secret Library – 6th and *Final Wife of King Henry VIII* married July 1543 Catherine Parr (1512-1548) Peacemaker Outlived Henry- Nonfiction - Copyright © 2017 Case 1-5607493201 – TXu 2-060-893

King Eadgar's Secret - Oblate Expectations - Nonfiction - Copyright © 2017 Case 1-5600182531

Nun of My Dreams © 2018 TXu 2-093-545 ISBN 978-1-48098-155-3

Dollie's Secret – Survivor of the DeKalb, Texas, Indian Raid - Nonfiction – © Case 1-5564559089 © **2017 TXu 2-067-664**

A Pregnant Nun a historical novel - Nonfiction – Copyright © Case 1-8558966897 © 2019 Pau 3-833-744 - ISBN 978-1-09830-437-9

A Hundred Secrets Volume 1 Books 1-20 nonfiction Copyright © Case 1-7072486931 © **2018 TXu 2-105-513 - ISBN 978-1-64530- 435-7 - &**

A Hundred Secrets Vol 2 Books 21-100 nonfiction 100 secrets © Case 1-6749127961 © 2018 TXu 2-105-513 - ISBN 978-1-64530-435-7

Why Weren't the Kurds at Normandy? **Parody Lyrics © 2019 Pau 3-998-562**

S'more Secrets - Sleepover Stories to be Told in Darkness Volume 1 Bedtime stories for kids ©2019 - TXu 2-129-150 - ISBN 978-1-64426-708-0

S'more Secrets - Sleepover Stories to be Told in Darkness Volume 2 for tweens and teens - Fiction -© 2018 Case 1-7262889391 © **2018 TXu 2-129-150 - ISBN 798-1-64530-433-3**

S'more Secrets - Sleepover Stories to be Told in Darkness Volume 3 scary stories to be told in darkness to grownups – Fiction - © 2018 TXu 2-189-150 - ISBN 798-1-64530-454-0

The Nurse's Secret - Kjellfrid's Secret - Nonfiction - ©2019 Case 1-5985073311 © **2019 TXu 2-074-508 –**

Emily's Secret – Emily's Cargo Cult of 40 Mates in Irian Jaya - Nonfiction - © Case 1-5985016941 © **2019 TXu 2-074-514**

Katie's Secret – The Arsenic Murder Trials of Katie Browder Stricklin - Nonfiction - © 1-5714428421 © 2019 TXu 2-065-209

Bad Breakup at 430 Lafayette Street - Nonfiction - Copyright © 2017 Case 1-5592907361 - © **2017 TXu 2-060-686**

Aesop Fables and The Candy Rabbit bedtime stories for kids - © 2019 - ISBN 978-1-54399-921-1

The Prince and I - Miss Olive - historic novel - Unsolved murder of my nanny's former charge © 2019 TXu 2-139-737 - ISBN 978-1-64530-432-6

One Corinthians nonfiction sermon delivered at Saint Clements' Church, Berkeley, at 11AM December 11, 1949 © 2020 - ISBN 978-1-54389-951-8

Senatorial Courtesy – nonfiction life-saving senatorial courtesy Senator John William Warner III - Nonfiction - Copyright © 2020 1-837259272592781 ©2020 - ISBN 978-1-54399-891-7

Ladies Day – nonfiction account of misogyny at Harvard Law School professors during 1960s © 2020 ISBN 978-1-5499-920-4

A Perfect Crime a historical novel © 2020 - ISBN 978-1-09830-140-8

Four Score and More – nonfiction autobiography of a long life Case © 2019 TXu 2-167-560 ISBN 978-1-54399-922-8

Easter Parade nonfiction COVID-19 © 2020 - ISBN 978-1-09830-945-9

Ambrose Bierce anthology of Ambrose Bierce's 70 best of his 249 short stories © Case 1-8725184511 Copyright © 2020 - ISBN 978-1-09831-080-6

George Sterling A Wine of Wizardry anthology of George Sterling's 20 best poems 1-8731197451 © 2020 - ISBN 978-1-09831-102-5

The Boss – nonfiction my 18-months service to Vice President Richard M. Nixon Copyright © 2020 - ISBN 978-1-09830-750-9

Epilogue – nonfiction account of crimes of President Richard M. Nixon and Presidential staff 1-8592617481 © **2020 - ISBN 978-1-54399-891-7**

White Fox and **White Buffalo** – Comanche abduction my maternal grandmother's maternal grandmother:

White Fox – Book 1 Prequel to White Buffalo -Nonfiction Copyright © 2020 – Case 1-8842056821 and *White Buffalo – Book 2 Sequel to White Fox* -Nonfiction © 2020 – Case 1-8862149151 TXu2-093-545 ISBN 978-1-09831-836-9

Roses among the Thorns -The Founders of the Bohemian Club ©**2020** TXu 2-195-987 ISBN 978-1-09831-738-6

© 2020 Case No. **1-8791258541**

Crazy – Nonfiction plus five short stories that are fiction historical novels © 2020 Case No. 1-8946543741 – first edition ISBN 978-1-09832-149-9 and second edition ISBN 978-1-0983-2399-8

Thistlewood Non©2020 TXu 2-206-871 ISBN 978-1-09832-390-5

Twice Upon A Time – ©**2020 Case 1-9245623151 ISBN 978-1-09833-861-9**

Alice Blue Gown –©**2020 Nonfiction Case 1-9105640341 - ISBN 978-1-09833-191-7**

Day of Infamy – Pearl Harbor Day – The Ni'ihau Incident - **Nonfiction - © Case No. 1-9381160911** © *2020* TXu 2-222-380 ISBN 978-1-09834-126-8

The Plumbers Introduction – **© 2020 TXu 2-217-462 Case No. 1-9185174771 ISBN 978-1-09833-500-7**

The Plumbers Volume 1 – United Airlines Flight No. 553 - Unsolved Mystery of Missing $2,000,000 – Watergate Burglars - Nonfiction Copyright © 2020 TXu 2-217-462 Case No. 1-9185174771 - ISBN 978-1-09833-400-0

The Plumbers Volume 2 – Nonfiction Copyright © 2020 TXu 2-217-462 No. 1-9185174771 - ISBN 978-1-09833-401-7

Ted historical novel ©2020 Case 1-9620202411 TXu 2-225-762 - ISBN 978-1-09834-717-8

Trump Plague – What did he know and when did he know it? Nonfiction - © 2020 TXu 2-219-947 Case No. 1-9264731081 ISBN 978-1-09833-825-1

Reverse Santa Nonfiction Case 1-9990314981 © 2020 TXu 2-234-240 ISBN 978-1-09835-902-7

Pardon Me Nonfiction Case 1-10029277321 © 2021 TXu 2-237-084 ISBN 978-1-09836-275-9

Tiny Hands Loser Non© 2021 TXu 2-237-155 Case No. 1-10029325830 ISBN 978-1-09836-204-1

Widow of Friedrich Christian Anton "Fritz" Lang Non©2021 TXu 2-251-784 Hardcover ISBN 978-1-09837-577-5 ISBN 978-1-09837-157-9

The Man in the Brown Suit by Agatha Christie - Fiction Republished 2021

Poirot Investigates by Agatha Christie - Fiction 2021

The Mysterious Affair at Styles by Agatha Christie - Fiction Republished 2021

Ghost Stories –The Speluncean Explorers © **202**2 **TXu 2**-295-124 **Case No. 1**-10977740461

125 Bedtime Stories Still Untold to My Most Beloved Daughter Sarai Stricklin (09.28.1959 – 06.19.2021) - *Book 1* – Stories 1-52 - Fiction by original authors Republished 2021- © **2021 ISBN 978-1-09837-566-9**

125 Bedtime Stories Still Untold to My Most Beloved Daughter Sarai Stricklin (09.28.1959-06.19.2021) *Book 1* **Stories 1-52 - Fiction Anthology Republished in June 2021- © 2021 ISBN 978-1-09837-566-9**

Mary Eliska's Untold Stories - Bedtime Stories Still Untold to my Daughter Mary Eliska Books 1-26 © **2021**-

Mary Eliska's Untold Bedtime Stories of Japan, China, India, Israel, Europe and America - © 2021 TXu 2-254-154

Mary Eliska's Untold Stories - Book 1 The Yellow Fairy Tales Book - © **2021** ISBN 978-1-09838-368-8

Mary Eliska's Untold Stories - Book 2 The Red Fairy Tales Book - Tales of India by Rudyard Kipling - © **2021** ISBN 978-1-09838-424-1 *Mary Eliska's Untold Stories - Book 3 The Blue Fairy Tales Book - Jungle Books by Rudyard Kipling* - © **2021** ISBN 978-1-09838-425-8 *Mary Eliska's Untold Stories - Book 4 The Orange Fairy Tales Book - Kim by Rudyard Kipling* © **2021 ISBN 979-1-09838-438-4** *Mary Eliska's Untold Stories - Book 5 The Purple Fairy Tales Book – The Wind in the Willows by Kenneth Grahame; The Tale of Jimmy Rabbit by Albert Scott Bailey; The Velveteen Rabbit by Margery Williams; The Adventures of Danny the Meadow Mouse and The Adventures of Reddy Fox by Thornton W. Burgess; and, by Beatrix Potter: an anthology of Bedtime Stories; The Tale of Peter Rabbit; The Tale of Benjamin Bunny; The Tale of Johnny Town-Mouse; The Tale of Squirrel Nutkins; The Tale of Ginger and Pickles; and The Story of a Fierce Bad Rabbit. Mary Eliska's Untold Stories - Book 5 The Purple Fairy Tales Book –* © **2021** Case 1-10518564131 *Mary Eliska Girl Detective – Vol 1 Books 1-13 Mildred Augustine Wirt Benson's Penny Parker Stories -*© **2021** ISBN 978-1-09837-244-6

Mary Eliska Girl Detective - Book 16 - The Mystery of the Sundial - [Republished as Book 4 Stave Three]

Mary Eliska Girl Detective - The Mystery of a Hansom Cab– Book 20 © 2022 TXu 2-307-367 Case No. © 2022 1-11231552371 318pp

Mary Eliska Girl Detective – The Mystery of Madame Midas– Book 21 © 2022 TXu 2-314-023 Case No. 1-11299310531 327pp

Mary Eliska Girl Detective - Book 28 – Behind the Green Door - [Republished as Book 1 Stave Two]

Mary Eliska Girl Detective - Book 29 - The Missing Formula - [Republished as Book 2 Stave Two]

Mary Eliska Girl Detective - Book 30 – Danger at the Drawbridge - [Republished as Book 1 Stave Two]

Mary Eliska Girl Detective - Book 31 - The Mystery of 31 New Inn - © 2021 ISBN 978-1-09837-694-9

Mary Eliska Girl Detective - Book 32 – Mary Eliska Finds A Clue - [Republished as Book 6 Stave Three]

Mary Eliska Girl Detective - Book 36 - The Eye of Osiris - © 2021 ISBN 978-1-09837-705-2

Mary Eliska Girl Detective - Book 37 - The Mystery of the Lost Key - [Republished as Book 6 Stave Two]

Mary Eliska Girl Detective - Book 38 - The Mystery of the Red Thumb Mark -

Mary Eliska Girl Detective - Book 39 - The Uttermost Farthing - © 2021 ISBN 978-1-09837-695-6

Mary Eliska Girl Detective - Books 40-48 - Doctor Thorndyke's Cases - © 2021 ISBN 978-1-09837-706-9

Mary Eliska Girl Detective - The Mystery of the Rainbow Feather – Book 41 © 2022 TXu 2-307370 Case No. 1-11231594691 234pp

Mary Eliska Girl Detective - The Mystery of The Silent House– Book 45 © 2022

Mary Eliska Girl Detective - Book 50 – The Orinda Mystery - ©2021 TXu 2-264-787 - [Book 12 Stave 2] *The Orinda Mystery Book 50 -* © 2021 Case 1-10130208421 © 2021 TXu 2-264-787

Mary Eliska Girl Detective - The Millionaire Mystery – Book 54 © 2022

Mary Eliska Girl Detective - The Mystery Whom God Hath Joined– Book 58 © 2022

Mary Eliska Girl Detective - Book 59 – Mary Eliska Girl Detective and the Lorelei Rupert Mystery – © 2021 - Case 1-10582290111©2021 TXu 2-265-775 -* [Republished as Book 8 Stave Two]

Mary Eliska Girl Detective - The Mystery of a Coin of Edward VII - Book 63 © 2022 TXu 2-309-496 Case No. 1-11243958179 269pp

Mary Eliska Girl Detective - The Mystery of the Yellow Holly – Book 64 © 2022 TXu 2-309-497 Case No. 1-11243958228 366pp

Mary Eliska Girl Detective - The Mystery of The Girl From Malta– Book 65 –© 2022

Mary Eliska Girl Detective - The Mystery of the Mandarin's Fan - Book 68 © 2022 TXu 2-309-498 Case No. 1-11243958130 282pp

Mary Eliska Girl Detective - The Mystery of the Red Window – Book 69 © 2022 TXu 2-309-502 Case No. 1-11243958070 399pp

Mary Eliska Girl Detective - The Mystery of Lady Jim of Curzon Street – Book 73 © 2022 TXu 2-315-157 No. 1-11337674021 526pp

Mary Eliska Girl Detective - The Mystery of the Opal Serpent - Book 74 © 2022 TXu 2-313-114 Case No. 1-11277466081 298pp

Mademoiselle Mary Eliska and The Phantom of the Opera - Book 76 © 2022 TXu 2-298-864 Case1-11110548251 326pp

Mary Eliska Girl Detective - The Mystery of The Red-Headed Man - Book 81 © 2022 TXu 2-301-967 No. 1-11152531130

Mary Eliska Girl Detective – The Mystery of the Sacred Herb – Book 84 © 2022 TXu 2-313-113 Case No. 1-11277515711 344pp

Mary Eliska Girl Detective – The Mystery of the Sealed Message –Book 85 © 2022 TXu 2-313-112 Case No. 1-11277515950 296pp

Mary Eliska Girl Detective – The Mystery of the Green Mummy – Book 88 © 2022 TXu 2-310-325 Case No. 1-11277549430 282pp

Mary Eliska Girl Detective – The Mystery of the Disappearing Eye – Book 91 (1909) © 2022 329pp

Mary Eliska Girl Detective – The Mystery of the Solitary Farm - Book 92 © 2022 112pp

Mary Eliska Girl Detective – The Mystery of the Crowned Skull – Book 99 ©2022 TXu 2-309-552 Case No. 1-11263042361

Mary Eliska Girl Detective - The Mystery of Monsieur Judas– Book 104 © 2022

Mary Eliska Girl Detective – The Mystery Queen – Book 106 (1912) © 2022 294pp

Mary Eliska Girl Detective – The Mystery of Red Money – Book 107 © 2022 268pp

Mary Eliska Girl Detective – The Mystery of the Lost Parchment - Book 115 © 2022

Mary Eliska Girl Detective – The Mystery of Streets of Fear © 2022

Mary Eliska Girl Detective - Fantômas Captured - Book 176 - © 2022

Mary Eliska Girl Detective and the Mystery of the Harlequin Opal – Books 91, 92 and 93 © 2022 Case 1-11299311170

Mary Eliska Girl Detective - Professor Brankel's Secret © 2021 1-11299173361 98pp

Mary Eliska Girl Detective - The Mystery of The Yellow Room – Book 70 © 2021 TXu 2-274-3701-10740460241 266pp

Mary Eliska Girl Detective – *The Mystery of the White Room* – Book 71 © 2022 TXu 2-301-956 Case No. 1-11152531001 *Mademoiselle Rouletabille Mary Eliska Girl Detective - The Secret of the Night* – Book 72 © 2021 TXu 2-295-430 Case No. 1-11064158121 294pp

Mary Eliska Girl Detective – *The Guarded Heights* – Book 73 © 2022 TXu 2-201-503 Case No. 1-11144498241

Mary Eliska Girl Detective – *The Mystery of The Spider* – Book 74 © 2022 TXu 2-301-934 Case No. 1-11152531030

Mary Eliska Girl Detective - The Temple of Death – *The Bride of the Sun King* – Book 75 © 2021 TXu 2-296-617 Case No. 1-11077748851

Mademoiselle Mary Eliska Girl Detective - The Phantom of the Opera – Book 76 © 2022 TXu 2-298-864 Case1-11110548251 326pp

Mary Eliska Girl Detective - The Mystery of The Abandoned Room – Book 77 © 2022 TXu 2-299-769 **ISBN:** 978-1-64314-738-3 Case No. 1-1119216531 559pp

Mary Eliska Girl Detective - The Mystery of The Gray Mask – Book 78 © 2022 TXu 2-300-373 Case No. 1-11125258241 261pp

Mary Eliska Girl Detective – *The Mystery of the Scarlet Bat* – Book 79 © 2022 TXu 2-301-961 Case No. 1-11152531059

Mary Eliska Girl Detective – *The Mystery of The Secret Passage* – Book 80 © 2022 TXu 2-301-964 Case No. 1-11152498331 278pages

Mary Eliska Girl Detective – *The Mystery of the Red-Headed Man* – Book 81 © 2022 TXu 2-301-967 Case No. 1-11152531130

Mary Eliska Girl Detective - Book 82 – *The Pagan's Cup and Silver Bullet* - © **2021** TXu 2-307-868 Case No. 1-11237102261 - ISBN 978-1-09837-420-4 and 978-1-09837-717-5

Mary Eliska Girl Detective - The Mystery of the Pagan's Cup - Book 82 © 2022 TXu 2-307-868 Case No. 1-11237102261 218pp

Mary Eliska Girl Detective - Book 86 - The Mystery of the Disappearing Eye © **2021** -

Mary Eliska Girl Detective - Book 88 - The Mystery of the Opal Serpent - © 2021 -TXu 2-313-114 Case No. 1-11277466081

Mary Eliska Girl Detective - Book 90 - The Mystery of the Yellow Holly - © 2021 - ISBN 978-1-09837-713-7

Mary Eliska Girl Detective - Books 91, 92, 93 Mystery of the Harlequin Opal © **2021**

Mary Eliska Girl Detective - Book 97 - The Mystery of the Sealed Message - © 2021 TXu 2-313-112

Mary Eliska Girl Detective – The Mystery of the Society of Flies - Book 106 © 2022 TXu 2-314-501 Case No. 1- 11326931241 299pp

Mary Eliska Girl Detective - The Mystery of The Peacock of Jewels– Book 107 © 2022 No. 1-10336308231 452pp

Mary Eliska Girl Detective - Book 108 - The Mystery of a Hansom Cab - © 2021 TXu 2-307-367 Case No. 1-11231552371

Mary Eliska Girl Detective - Book 134 – The Mystery of the Whispering Lane - © 2022 TXu 2-317-000 Case No. 1- 11354442141

Mary Eliska Girl Detective - Book 135 – The Mystery of the Caravan Crime - © 2022 TXu 2-316-997 Case No 1-11354441431

Mary Eliska Girl Detective - Book 423 - Vanishing Man © **2021** -

Mary Eliska Girl Detective - Book 543 - The Gentleman Who Vanished © **2021**

Mary Eliska Girl Detective - Book 546 - The Lady From Nowhere - © 2021 – 1-10759399892

Mary Eliska Girl Detective - The Mystery of the Purple Fern Book 553 ©2021 TXu 2-315-921 Case No. 1-11338176181

Mary Eliska Girl Detective - Book 564 – The Mystery of the Wooden Hand - © 2022 TXu 2-316-088 Case No. 1- 11344674401

Mary Eliska Girl Detective - Book 566 - The Mystery of the Sycamore - ©2021 - [Republished as Book 8 Stave 2]

Mary Eliska Girl Detective - Book 567 - The Mystery of the Red House 1-10547943101 ©2021 TXu 2-264-820 ISBN 968-1-09838-972-7

Mary Eliska Girl Detective - Book 568 - The Little French Girl – by Anne Douglas Sedgwick - Fiction - [Published Book 3 Stave 2]

Mary Eliska Girl Detective - Book 569 - The Clue of the Gold Coin - ©2021 TXu 2-265-659- [Republished Book 7 Stave 2]

Mary Eliska Girl Detective - Book 570 - The Silver Ring Mystery - © 2021 TXu 2-265-652 [Published Book 7 Stave 3]

Mary Eliska Girl Detective - Book 571 - The Stowmarket Mystery - © **2021** Case 1-10595752961 ©2021 TXu 2-2662-430 - [Republished as Book 9 Stave 2]

Mary Eliska Girl Detective –The Mystery at Dark Cedars Book 572 © 2021 TXu 2-308-721 Case 1-10602161171

Mary Eliska Girl Detective - Book 572 – The Mystery at Dark Cedars - © 2021 TXu 2-308-721 Case No. 1- 10602161171 and Case No. 1-10595752961 - © **2021** [Book 10 Stave 2]

Mary Eliska Girl Detective - The Mystery of the Secret Band Book 573 ©2021 TXu 2-270-007 Case 1-10676090161

Mary Eliska Girl Detective - Book 573 – The Mystery of the Secret Band - © Case 1- 10595752961 – [Republished Book 10 Stave 4]

Mary Eliska Girl Detective and the Mystery of the Fires - Book 574 © 2021 TXu 2-269-991 Case 1-10676148519

Mary Eliska Girl Detective - Book 574 – The Mystery of the Fires - © 2021 - Case 1-10595752961 - [Published Book10 Stave 3]

Mary Eliska Girl Detective - Book 575 - The Uttermost Parts of the Sea –- © 2021 - Case 1-10692479811 - ISBN 978-1-09839-778-4

Mary Eliska Girl Detective - Book 576 - The Polly Page Yacht Club – Fiction by Izola Louise Forrester - [Published Book 1 Stave 2]

Mary Eliska Girl Detective - Book 577 - The Vanishing Comrade - © 2021 - [Republished as Book 2 Stave 3]

Mary Eliska Girl Detective - Book 578 - The Mystery Girl - Fiction - [Republished as Book 4 Stave Two]

*Mary Eliska Girl Detective - Book 579 – The Phantom Friend - © **2021**-* [Published Book 11 Stave 2]

*Mary Eliska Girl Detective - Book 580 - The Puzzle in the Pond - **©2021*** [Published Book11 Stave3]

Mary Eliska Girl Detective - Book 584 - The Last Stroke - © 2021 – Case No. 1-10759399851

*Bedtime Stories for Bad Children – Ghost Stories - Vol 1 © **2022** TXu 2-333 - 189 No. 1-11616027741*

*Bedtime Stories for Bad Children – Grimm Stories – Vol 2 © **2022** TXu 2-333-962 - No. 1-11626445221*

Disconcerting Stories for Grownups - Not To Tell to Children in Darkness at Bedtime - ©2022 No. 1-11701275891

Liam McAdams Boy Aviator Stories Series

Volume 1 Liam McAdams Boy Aviator Stories
Book 1: Liam McAdams In the Clouds for Uncle Sam; Liam McAdams of the Signal Corps
Book 2: Liam McAdams and the Stolen Airplane; how Liam McAdams made good.
Book 3: Liam McAdams and the Airplane Express; the Boy Aeronaut's Grit.
Book 4: Liam McAdams and the Boy Aeronauts Club; Flying for Fun.
Book 5: Liam McAdams' Cruise in the sky; the Legend of the Great Pink Pearl.
Bonus Book 10: Liam McAdams The Quest of the Aztec Treasure

Volume 2 Liam McAdams Boy Aviator Stories
Book 6: Liam McAdams Battling the Bighorn; the Airplane in the Rockies.
Book 7: Liam McAdams When Scout Meets Scout; The Airplane Spy.
Book 8: Liam McAdams On the Edge of the Arctic: An Airplane in Snow Land.
Book 9: Liam McAdams' Ocean Flyer – New York to London in Twelve Hours
Book 10: Liam McAdams The Quest of the Aztec Treasure

Marlow Ray Girl Detective Mystery Stories for Grownups Volume 1: Books 1 - 4 --
Book 1: The Female Detective; Book 2: Secret Service – Recollections of a City Detective; Book 3: A Woman of Mystery; Book 4: The Adventures of Arsène Lupin

Mary Eliska Girl Aviatrix
Mary Eliska Girl Detective Girl Aviatrix Air Mystery Stories
18 Chapters Girl Detective Girl Aviatrix Air Mystery and Romance

Chapters 1 - 6 © 2022 Case No. 1-11371703511 and Chapters 7 - 18 © 2022 Case No. 1-11376521721

1. **Chapter 1 Girl Aviatrix Series - Mary Eliska Girl Detective Wins Her Wings © 2022 Case No. 1-11371703511**

2. **Chapter 2 Girl Aviatrix Series - Mary Eliska Girl Detective - The Mystery Plane © 2022 Case No. 1-11371703511**

3. **Chapter 3 Girl Aviatrix Series - Mary Eliska Girl Detective Solves the Conway Case © 2022 No. 1-11371703511**

4. **Chapter 4 Girl Aviatrix Series- Mary Eliska Girl Detective – The Double Cousins © 2022 Case No. 1-11371703511**

5. **Chapter 5 Girl Aviatrix Series- Mary Eliska Girl Detective - The Air Pilot Mystery © 2022 Case No 1-11371703511**

6. **Chapter 6 Girl Aviatrix Series- Mary Eliska Girl Detective - The Ocean Flight Mystery © 2022 Case 1-1137170351**

7. **Chapter 7 Girl Aviatrix Series- Mary Eliska Girl Detective – Flying Girl © 2022 Case No. 1-11376521721**

8. **Chapter 8 Girl Aviatrix Series- Mary Eliska Girl Detective - Flying Girl and Her Chum © 2022 No. 1-11376521721**

9. **Chapter 9 Girl Aviatrix Series - Mary Eliska Girl Detective - The Hollywood Flight © 2022 No. 1-11376521721**

10. **Chapter 10 Girl Aviatrix Series - Mary Eliska Girl Detective – Gypsies of the Air © 2022 Case No. 1-11376521721**

Epigraph for Mary Eliska Girl Aviatrix

Mary Eliska Stricklin
March 10, 1963
September 12, 1963